"LOVE AND SEDUCTION . . .

ONE LONG SEXY CHASE THROUGH CALIFORNIA, ACROSS THE TEXAS BADLANDS, EUROPE, AND RUSSIA . . .

HEADY STUFF!"

Publishers Weekly

The fiery passion that sustained Virginia Brandon and Stephen Morgan through the tumultuous events of SWEET SAVAGE LOVE lives on, blazing anew,

in

DARK FIRES

Avon Books by
Rosemary Rogers

DARK FIRES	23523	1.95
SWEET SAVAGE LOVE	17988	1.75
THE WILDEST HEART	20529	1.75

DARK FIRES

ROSEMARY ROGERS

 AVON
PUBLISHERS OF BARD, CAMELOT, DISCUS, EQUINOX AND FLARE BOOKS

To my patient family . . . and to Dean

DARK FIRES is an original publication of Avon Books. This work has never before appeared in book form.

AVON BOOKS
A division of
The Hearst Corporation
959 Eighth Avenue
New York, New York 10019

ISBN: 0-380-00425-9

First Avon Printing, August, 1975
Tenth Printing

AVON TRADEMARK REG. U.S. PAT. OFF. AND
FOREIGN COUNTRIES, REGISTERED TRADEMARK—
MARCA REGISTRADA, HECHO EN CHICAGO, U.S.A.

Printed in the U.S.A.

BOOK ONE

Ginny

Part One
THE PRINCE

Chapter One

The vast army of Porfirio Díaz sprawled outside the very walls of the ancient city of Puebla, and, in spite of the vicious fighting that had been going on, almost every man was in good humor. It would be a matter of a day or two only, now. Puebla would be theirs, and then—on to Mexico. *Viva Díaz! Viva la revolución!*

While the sentries paced and watched, the majority of the great army slept or reveled; but if it were the latter they did it quietly, for General Díaz was a strict disciplinarian.

At the rear of the place that the General had chosen for his own headquarters, the carretas and wagons of the camp followers were huddled together as if for protection from the coldness of the night. In the improvised enclosures, chickens squawked; an occasional cow or goat moved clumsily on hobbled legs; here and there a baby cried, and was quickly hushed.

The women talked among themselves as they prepared for the night, letting their small cookfires burn down into crimson embers.

"They say that General Marquez is on his way from Mexico City to relieve the garrison."

"Pah! That old coward! He would have stayed in Mexico if they hadn't thrown him out! And before he reaches Puebla, *our* General will be in possession!"

Seated on the ground, with her back propped up against a wagon wheel, Ginny listened idly with a part of her mind to what she called "campfire talk." The other part strained to hear a certain footfall; her eyes watched for the distant shape of a certain man to come walking toward her with that lithe, pantherish grace that was so much a part of him. *Her* man. Her husband. Why was the conference with General Díaz taking so long?

The dim light of the fiery coals at her feet threw the young woman's features into sharp relief, although her hair was discreetly covered by a black shawl, known as a rebozo. She was dressed like the other women, in a full, red-patterned, ankle-length skirt and a low-necked white blouse that barely covered her shoulders, but her skin, tanned a tawny-gold, was several shades lighter than theirs, even in the firelight; and if one looked closely enough at her eyes, which slanted upwards very slightly at the corners, they revealed themselves to be a deep, mysterious shade of green. She had rather high cheekbones, a barely clefted small chin that could have a stubbornly determined tilt to it, and a mouth that always tempted men to kiss it. "The mouth of a demi-monde," her cousin Pierre had once described it, when Ginny was only sixteen and still a child, her body maturing into womanhood, her mind full of the thought of her first ball, when she would be presented to the Emperor and Empress of France. What a lot had happened since then! How could she have dreamed, even with her vividly romantic adolescent imagination, that she— who had wanted nothing else but to dance, and flirt, and wear beautiful clothes—would be sitting here, dressed like a Mexican peasant, her bare feet tucked under her as she waited for her man?

Ginny leaned her head back against the wagon wheel a trifle wearily, and the rebozo slipped, allowing tendrils of copper-gold hair to escape, curling softly around her face. If only Steve would come! Was it significant that General Díaz was keeping his officers longer than usual at their nightly meeting? So far, they had been biding their time, starving out the garrison that still held Puebla, but now, with news of Marquez' advance from the west, perhaps the General would decide it was time to stop playing cat and mouse, and his army would pounce at last. It was high time, too! An army was for fighting, and not for sitting in one place too long. They would go on from here to Mexico City, and from there—"Yes," Ginny thought suddenly, "it's strange to think that after that it will all be over." Where would they go then? What would they do? She was certain only of one thing—that whatever Steve decided to do, he would not leave her behind again. They had both suffered too much—for each other and because of each other—to stand another separation.

"You green-eyed witch, you've managed to make me completely besotted with you. You're the only woman I've ever needed," he'd told her the night he had come to Vera Cruz to bring her back here with him—the night before the ship she had booked passage on had been due to sail. She still shuddered at the thought that it might have sailed a day earlier.

"What would you have done, if you'd found me gone?"

"Do you think I'd have let you escape so easily? I'd have turned pirate, probably, and intercepted your ship just off Monterey—and I'd have made you walk the plank, you little vixen, for having tried to run away!"

The thought that he loved her after all gave Ginny a pleasurable thrill. They had loved each other all the time, from the very first, but neither of them would admit it. What a lot of time they had wasted!

She had closed her eyes, her lips curved in a slight smile, but now her husband's voice made them fly open to gaze up at him.

"What a witchy look you can wear, even when you're asleep, *querida mia!*" He dropped down beside her, lips brushing her temple. "God—I could use a drink! The General insists on a hot fire, even on a night like this. *And* we have to wear our tunics buttoned up to the neck, not one button undone." Even as he spoke, he was ripping impatiently at the offending buttons.

"If you'll hold still I'll do that for you—that way I won't have to sew the buttons back on! And I'll get you a drink, too—you're lucky I'm such a well-trained soldadera!"

Ginny leaned against him, her hair brushing his face as his arm went round her.

"You're a tease—and far too beautiful to remain a soldadera. Even the General said so."

"The General! Oh, Steve. . . ." Ginny's green eyes

widened before her lashes dropped, covering the mixture of shock and guilt.

"Yes—the General! And don't you look away from me that way, or I'll begin to think you're guilty of something more than flirting with him."

"But I—I didn't flirt! It was just that the wind blew the rebozo off just as he was riding by, and he stared so hard! What was I supposed to do? He smiled at me, and I smiled back; I thought he knew who I was."

Still trapped by the pressure of Steve's arm, which held her against him, Ginny found him surveying her with that half-mocking, half-tender smile she had come to know so well.

"You really are a baggage, green-eyes," he murmured softly. "I was hoping you'd be able to stay out of Don Porfirio's way. As it is—" he paused, teasingly, shrugging the tunic off his shoulders with a sigh of relief.

"For heaven's sake, Steve! What did he say?"

"You created quite a difficult situation, you know. He didn't know who you were—do you think I went to the trouble of describing you to him? But he did ask Felix to find you and invite you to join him for a short while this evening. It appears he was quite struck by you."

"Oh—oh, no!"

"Oh, yes! And then poor Colonel Díaz had the difficult task of explaining, very tactfully, that you were *not* a little French whore one of the soldiers had picked up. Of course, I didn't know anything about it until after the meeting, although I did wonder why he kept shooting those dark looks at me."

"He—he wasn't *angry*? Steve, I think you're teasing me."

"By no means, sweetheart. I'm late because he asked me to stay after he'd dismissed the others. And he told me, in no uncertain terms, that he did not approve of my wife following the army like a common soldadera. After all, as he reminded me sternly, I am a gachupine, and you're the daughter of a United States Senator. How will it look, when we march triumphantly into Puebla and then into Mexico City itself? What if the foreign newspapers were to get hold of the story?" His drawling, sarcastic voice made her shiver with apprehension. Was he really angry with her? Had the General really been very angry?

She had taken his jacket and was folding it automatically, smoothing it between her hands. It was all she could do to force herself to look up unflinchingly into his hard blue eyes.

"Well? And if they do?"

"The General does not want the world to think of Mexico as a country of barbarians. And in other countries, the wives of army officers do *not* usually follow the camp!"

"You're not going to send me away! He's not—"

The sarcastic inflection left Steve's voice as he put his long, brown fingers under her chin, tilting it slightly.

"I'm not sending you anywhere, love. But I'm afraid that after we take Puebla, you'll have a new job."

"I don't—"

"If you'll shut up, I can finish explaining. The General needs a secretary, he says. Someone who can keep his papers in order, write a passable hand, and translate. In other words, you will officially join his staff—and your pretty presence will grace General Díaz' headquarters from now on. You know we're taking prisoners who can't speak a word of Spanish—well, you can speak some German and Italian, can't you? And your French, chérie, has always been excellent. Perhaps Don Porfirio thinks a pretty woman will have a softening effect, and certainly, the newspapermen will be impressed."

"But—but when will we ever be together, then?"

This time he laughed, leaning over to kiss her lightly.

"I've been ordered to make sure of requisitioning suitable quarters for you wherever we go, madame. And fortunately, since I'm your husband, I'll be permitted to share these quarters with you—at least at night! So, you'll have no excuse to avoid your duties towards *me*."

"You're not angry?"

"What would you do if I were?"

Her eyes flashed. "Fight you tooth and nail! Especially since it was really not my fault."

He twisted her hair like a rope around his wrist, pulling her to him.

"You're a little spitting hellcat. God knows why I put up with you. But please try to control your temper, *and* your language, around the General. He's a very conventional man, underneath the steel and the swagger. He expects a lady."

"I can act like a lady when I must!" Ginny pulled a face, wriggling her body closer to his, her arms going around his neck.

"But not tonight—and not with you," she whispered in the instant before his lips took hers.

There was a strange bond between them, a bond of passion, and of something that went even deeper than passion—something that had been forged during the year and a half when they had fought each other, and mistrusted each other, and yet had been powerless to resist each other.

Steve Morgan had been Ginny's first lover, taking her with a tenderness and consideration that was all the more surprising considering his usually off-handedly selfish relationships with women. And she had been more than half in love with him, until his harshness and cruelty had turned her first girlish affection into hate. And then he had kidnapped her, and she had learned to fear him—his unyielding, arrogant temper, his cruelty when she would not give in to him. And yet, even then, he had been not just her master but her lover as well, and her body had responded to his lovemaking even while her mind rebelled at the callous way in which he had used her. It was only much later—after the shock of learning that Steve Morgan was known in Mexico as Esteban Alvarado, of the wealthy and respected Alvarado family, and after their marriage had been precipitated by his grandfather—that Ginny had realized she loved him.

Now, lying drowsily content in her husband's arms on their makeshift bed in the wagon, Ginny turned her face against his shoulder. She loved him. There had been other men, during the long, ghastly months when she'd thought him dead—executed by a French firing squad. She had loved none of them, although her body had occasionally responded to sheer physical want. But then she had found Steve again, and Steve, in spite of himself and the unreasonable jealousy he had displayed at first when he learned of her other lovers, had discovered that he loved her too.

"Nothing will keep us apart again—nothing," Ginny told herself suddenly. She didn't know what made her think this, or what formless fear had crept into her mind when she had been almost on the verge of sleep. Under the blankets that covered them, Ginny moved her body closer to Steve's and felt his arms tighten instinctively around her. They were together again at last, and even though tomorrow there would be fighting outside Puebla, she could carry with her the knowledge that, because of her, Steve's natural recklessness in battle would be tempered with caution.

Puebla, many-towered city of cathedrals, lay waiting to be taken, like a woman about to be raped and too weary to fight any longer. For over a month now, Porfirio Díaz had held his army in check, surrounding the Imperialist outpost, merely waiting. The several fierce skirmishes that had already taken place could not really be called battles, but now, at last, Díaz' patience was exhausted. General Marquez, at the head of a hand-picked company of cavalry, had cut his way through the "steel ring" that Escobedo had thrown around the besieged city of Queretaro; and in Mexico City, Marquez had tried to drum up more men and money for the lost cause of the Emperor Maximilian. Failing in Mexico, Marquez was now rumored to be leading his men towards Puebla.

To Ginny, waiting with General Díaz' staff officers in the small adobe building he had commandeered as his headquarters, the cool, clear day had a feeling of hazy unreality. In spite of the tension, the men found time to joke with her and tease her, nicknaming her "la teniente" when the General was out of earshot. "Suitably" attired in a very plain white muslin gown, her hair severely pulled back from her face and knotted at the nape of her neck, Ginny found herself either pacing from door to window in the small anteroom, or trying to arrange papers in black japanned boxes. The General expected to move out very soon—that much was obvious. But would the taking of Puebla really be as easy as he expected?

All morning, messengers arrived on lathered horses with personal reports to the General on the progress of the battle. And at midday, Colonel Felix Díaz entered the headquarters for further orders, with a reassuring smile for Ginny.

"We'll be there by nightfall," he whispered to her before he disappeared into the General's office, and his confident words and friendly smile made her sigh with relief.

A little later the General himself called her into his office, and with a faint smile on his face dictated a letter to El Presidente Juarez, informing him that terms of the surrender of Puebla were even now being negotiated with General Noriega, and that they would take the city in the name of the Presidente this same day—April 4th, 1867.

Once the letter, carefully sealed and pouched, had been handed to a young officer for dispatch, General Díaz leaned back in his chair, lighting a cigar while he studied, with the unabashed curiosity of the Latin male, the young woman who sat across from him.

Now in his thirties, General Porfirio Díaz was a strong looking, ruggedly handsome man with the straight nose and light coloring of the Criollas, in spite of his Mixtec Indian blood.

"So—you are the wife of Esteban Alvarado. I must confess, señora, that I had expected someone—different! And especially since that rascal Felix told me you were the bride chosen for Esteban by Don Francisco Alvarado himself!" He gave a full-throated laugh when Ginny blushed uncontrollably. "Ah, but I should have guessed you would be a beauty when Capitan Alvarado was so anxious to get the leave to fly all the way to Vera Cruz and back—a lovers' quarrel, eh? And now you two cannot bear to be parted again, I suppose. Well, I can understand that myself, now that I have seen you."

His brown eyes held unabashed admiration, and Ginny was not sure how she should react.

"You're too kind, General," she said demurely, and his teeth flashed whitely under the drooping mustache he affected.

"You will have to teach me something of the manners and graces of polite society, señora. I have spent most of my life being a soldier, you see, but I have a mind to be more—perhaps later, eh? Esteban tells me you were brought up in France and have travelled in Europe— later, when we have more time, you must tell me of Europe; but with your husband's permission, of course," he added with a teasing twinkle in his eyes.

Ginny had started to smile at him irrrepressibly. So the "Tiger of the South," Díaz the warrior, could also be Díaz the gallant when he chose! She thought he could be a charming man when he put his mind to it, and since he seemed quite unconcerned about the outcome of the battle that was still being fought at the gates of Puebla, she was able to relax, and they passed at least an hour chatting in a friendly fashion, with the General himself full of curiosity about European ladies and European customs.

Much later that night, while they sat over a cold supper in the small upper room of one of the best posadas in Puebla, Ginny told Steve all about her pleasant afternoon with the General.

Through the partly-opened windows, the sounds of revelry and shouting drifted to them. Díaz' soldiers were celebrating their victory in the usual fashion of triumphant armies all over the world.

"Are you sure you'd rather not be down there with them?" Ginny questioned teasingly as she sipped another glass of the excellent French champagne that Steve had produced as his share of the plunder. She was standing by the fireplace.

"I'm afraid that the General has other ideas where his officers are concerned," he drawled, cocking an eyebrow at her. "And besides, querida, rape has lost its savor for me of late." She watched him drain his glass and put it on the table. She stood there in her shift and watched the way his eyes seemed to darken as they travelled very slowly over her body, outlined in the firelight.

Here in this small room they seemed isolated from everything, and yet some instinct made Ginny stop posing for him and run quickly across the room on bare feet, to suddenly fling herself against her husband and hold him tight, her arms twining around his neck.

"Steve—" but she could not put her nebulous fear into words; how could she, when she did not know what she feared, or why? She felt a strange presentiment, like a fluttering wingbrush against her cheek . . . . She only sensed, with some deeply-rooted, primitive femaleness, that she wanted to be near him, to have his arms hold her this way for always.

"Baby, what's the matter? You're not worried about anything, are you?" Next he would be telling her that perhaps she shouldn't come with the army to Mexico after all, and she wouldn't be able to stand that!

"Nothing . . . it's nothing," she whispered against his lips. And then, forcing herself to slant her eyes teasingly up to meet his probing gaze, "Perhaps I only wanted to reassure myself that you still want to rape *me*!"

He carried her to the bed, and the fire burned itself out into faintly glowing ashes before they fell asleep.

By the time morning came, Ginny's barely-sensed fears of the night before had vanished before the reality of the day that lay ahead. Steve had had to leave early, after a hurried breakfast, in order to round up the troopers of his own company, who were still celebrating; but Ginny had time to make a more relaxed toilette before she went downstairs to join the General and the rest of his staff.

It was on to Mexico City, that very day, she discovered. General Marquez was said to be lurking near San Lorenzo, still undecided as to what he would do now that Puebla had fallen. Steve would be fighting again, but this morning even that thought had lost the power to frighten her. How ridiculous she had been! It was just the waiting outside Puebla that had unnerved her—the feeling of snatched moments together when they should have had time and leisure.

But now, at last, they would be moving forward; it was inevitable that Mexico City should fall eventually, just as Puebla had, and then. . . .

They had not talked very much about the future yet, she and Steve, but there would be one. Whatever he wanted to do, whatever he decided to do. Ginny remembered his casual mention of a ranch near Monterey and hoped he'd take her there. "I'm a married woman," she thought suddenly, "but I feel more like his mistress." And yet, that was the way she wanted it to be with them. She had always thought of marriage as something stale and boring, a kind of prison and drudgery for a woman. Married couples took each other for granted. You wondered, after a few years had passed, if these two people had ever been in love, or why they had sworn to adore each other forever. It would be different with them—Ginny would never be bored with Steve because he was so unpredictable! And she would make sure he was never bored with her.

Ginny's thoughts kept her mind occupied while her fingers worked nimbly at sorting out the General's precious papers. Teniente, the previous clerk, had handed everything over to Señora Alvarado with obvious relief. And as the morning progressed, Ginny was to find out that General Díaz' headquarters was a hive of activity, especially after a battle. A shrewd leader, he allowed his men their hours of celebration after a victory—and then a few more hours in which to recover afterwards. And in the meantime, any prisoners that were important enough to be taken could pace their cells, listening to the sounds of jubilation outside and wondering what their fate would be. By the time they were brought before the General or one of his aides, they were usually in a chastened and quite fearful mood.

At ten o'clock, the little anteroom leading into the General's office was crowded. Messengers came and went. A guerrillero leader, coming in person to inform the General of the Imperialist troops' whereabouts, leaned insinuatingly over the small desk that Ginny had chosen to hide herself behind, until she told him, in no uncertain terms, that he should be sure to take a bath the next time he leaned so close to a woman. Since she addressed him in his own dialect, he moved away shaking his head and grinning with unabashed good humor.

The hardest part for Ginny, on that first day, was the translating she was required to do. There had been a few Frenchmen among the defenders of Puebla, men who had married Mexican ladies and had elected to stay in Mexico to fight for the Emperor. Naturally, when confronted by her fluent French they considered her a traitor, and it was an effort for her to keep her features coldly composed during the interrogations that were conducted by Colonel Felix Díaz himself.

"You'll get used to it," she adjured herself, and it was true. She felt sorry for some of these Frenchmen, and for the dashing young Austrian officers too, but at least Díaz had decided to be merciful and they would not be executed—merely imprisoned for a time until it was decided what to do with them.

She remained in Puebla, with the General's staff, while the rest of his army took the road to San Lorenzo late that afternoon—determined to chase Marquez out of his rathole. And Steve went with them.

Chapter Two

It seemed to Ginny as if time had never passed so
slowly. It was the middle of May, and General Díaz had
established headquarters in the little town that had sprung
up around the Shrine of the Virgin of Guadalupe; the
spires of the massive cathedral were dwarfed by the hill of
Tepeyac in the background. Between the little town of
Guadalupe and the beautiful city of Mexico itself, Díaz'
restless soldiers made their camp and waited.

Don Porfirio approached everything he did with caution. He kept his soldiers busy routing out scattered Im-
peralists from small villages and townships, and he waited
while the leading citizens of Mexico City quarreled with
General Marquez and the other generals of the now-
shrunken Imperial armies who had found their way back
to the comparative safety of Mexico City itself.

"Mexico City is our capital. Why destroy it? Sooner or
later, when they realize it is inevitable, they will surrender.
And in the meantime, Señora, we wait—and you teach me
French and better English, sí?"

The General possessed some of the fatalism of his Indian forebears, as well as the gallantry of the Spaniards. It
was clear that he enjoyed the presence of a pretty woman
in his otherwise rather austere headquarters; and he was
proud of Ginny's adaptable manners and her knowledge of
languages. Yes, decidedly, she was an asset—and what
was more, she was strong and courageous as well, quite
unlike the so-called grand ladies that Don Porfirio had met
before. He could even discuss political matters and military strategy with her, and found her surprisingly intelligent and knowledgeable in both subjects. A lucky man, to
have found such an admirable woman, and a beautiful one
at that, for a wife! Don Porfirio had on many occasions
told Steve so himself.

"I've an idea the General wishes he had discovered you first, my love," Steve commented lazily one evening. "I've never heard him be so complimentary towards any woman before. And now he's promoted me to Major and made me a courier, which will take me away from you quite often. It makes me wonder!"

"Steve! You're not serious?"

She propped herself up on an elbow to gaze inquiringly down into his face and was relieved to see that he was smiling.

"I'm serious about the promotion, and being made a courier—but what the hell, I have to admit it was partly my doing. I get too damned restless just sitting around with the rest of the army, wondering what to do next, especially since you, my sweet, are always so busy during the daytime."

"But—but it will mean that you'll be gone for *days!*" she wailed. "I—I'll die of boredom."

"You can turn the hearts and heads of all the young officers—and Don Porfirio himself, not to mention the American legionnaires who have just been quartered at Texcoco."

"You said you'd beat me if you caught me looking at another man!"

"And so I will, if I catch you. So you'd better be discreet."

She bit her lip, unable to decide whether he was teasing her or not. Was he, perhaps, merely warning her indirectly that if *he* encountered a pretty face on his travels, he'd take whatever was offered? "I really don't know him well enough yet to be *sure*," Ginny thought, as she continued to gaze inquiringly into his eyes.

How beautiful she was! Steve reflected. Her green eyes with their mysterious gypsy slant; her peach-gold body, all rosy in the firelight; the magnificent copper-gold cloud of her hair, falling like a curtain on either side of her face as she gazed down at him so seriously. The thought that he had crept subtly, unknowingly under his guard, until it had the power to come close to frightening him.

To think that this particular woman, of all the women he had known, had the power to make him feel a primitive, savage jealousy for the first time in his life—to make him confess, even to himself, that he couldn't live without her! It was true; from the time of their first meeting, she had crept subtly, unknowingly, under his guard, until it had finally come to him with all the force of a thunder-clap that he actually loved her.

Innately selfish in his dealings with women in the past, Steve Morgan had found himself trying to understand this one; to be sensitive to her moods. Something was worry-ing her. What? Very gently, he drew her body close against his, and began to caress her, without a word, feel-ing the slight quivering of her flesh under his fingers be-fore she suddenly lowered her head and leaned it against his shoulder, with a small sigh of surrender. What was she thinking of?

She was thinking of the strong, irresistible bond between them; a bond not only of the flesh, but of the mind as well. When they lay so closely together, as they did now, naked flesh pressed against naked flesh, desire was always present; but there was something more, too, something more subtle—a need for each other, and a contentment they both felt at being close again. If only she understood him better! She had withstood the worst of his moods be-fore—his sarcastic accusations about her past life and her lovers, and even his cruelty—because she had realized that she loved him. Now, he was almost invariably gentle and tender with her, even though an occasional caustic inflec-tion could creep into his voice when he was in one of his withdrawn moods. But she loved him. No matter what had happened between them, and how much he had hurt her at one time, she loved him, and her only fear was of losing him—of having him turn back into the harsh, rather frightening stranger who could reduce her to trem-bling by a mere quirk of his eyebrows or the hardening of his eyes.

Ever since he had admitted that he loved her, one of the barriers between them had crumbled. Now, all they needed was time. Time to adjust to each other, to under-stand each other better; time to break down all the barri-ers.

With the new tenderness he had begun to show her, Steve was smoothing her hair back from her forehead, turning his head to plant light kisses along her neck and cheek.

She knew suddenly, with a flash of intuition, that he had

sensed her unease, but he wouldn't press her. He was beginning to respect her privacy as an individual.

"I love you, Steve. Only you."

"I know, sweetheart. And I love you."

No other words were necessary. At moments such as this, even though the words they used to each other were the banal words of lovers everywhere, she could hardly believe that she had really succeeded in making this man love her. He had always seemed to be able to detach himself from her so easily, to regard her with a mocking, caustic half-smile on his face, as though she interested him only slightly and he was only amusing himself with her. And how many times had he told her, in the old days, how highly he valued his freedom and his independence from all ties. Hadn't he told her once: "Women like to make marriage a trap for men with their clinging arms and their tears. . . ." But she wouldn't be like that; she wasn't that kind of woman. Hadn't he already sensed this for himself?

Held in her husband's arms, with his voice murmuring soft love-words in her ear, Ginny let her unnamed fears slip away from her as she gave herself up completely and wholly to the passion that even his slightest touch could arouse in her. No matter how often or how far he had to travel, Steve would always come back to her, and Ginny would always wait for him. Fate had brought them together, and love would keep them together.

Steve left very early in the morning, and when the dusty messenger arrived from Queretaro, Ginny was already ensconced behind the plain deal table that served as her desk in the anteroom that led to General Díaz' office. Queretaro had fallen, and the Emperor had surrendered his sword to General Escobedo. They had been betrayed, it was whispered, by none other than Colonel Miguel Lopez, one of the ex-Emperor's most trusted "friends"—Miguel, who had always boasted of being an opportunist; the man with a foot in both camps. Miguel, who in his own way had been her friend, and who had been instrumental in re-uniting her with Steve. Was it possible that he had always been a double agent, working secretly for the revolution?

Ginny had been lost in thought, depressed in spite of herself when she'd heard the news, although she knew that it meant a quicker end to the war.

Suddenly, an unmistakably American voice wrenched her back to the present with a jerk.

"I beg your pardon, ma'am, but one of the soldiers out there said you could speak French."

The bearded man who stood before her was tall, and wore a familiar blue uniform with a Captain's insignia on the shoulders and on the cap he had removed and now carried in one hand.

Ginny had been staring down unseeingly at the papers that already littered her desk, but now, as she looked up, her green eyes widened, and she felt the blood drain from her face.

Before she could speak a word, the blond-bearded Captain gave an exclamation of astonishment.

"Ginny! Ginny Brandon!"

She felt the room sway around her, and it was only with a monumental effort of will that she was able to compose herself into some semblance of her normally unruffled manner.

"It *is* Carl Hoskins, isn't it? I—I can hardly deny that it's a surprise to see you here! Why, when I last saw you. . . ."

He had put both his hands on the edge of her desk, leaning close, his eyes devouring every inch of her face and figure as if he could not quite believe that it was really she.

"I quit your father's employ after we got to California. Joined up with a posse for a while, as a US Marshal, when we heard. . . that is. . . ." He stumbled over the words, embarrassment flushing his face, and she noticed with detachment that the beard did nothing to detract from his Nordic good looks. Had it only been about two years ago when she had felt herself quite attracted to Carl Hoskins? His sudden presence here was inexplicable. . . . Of all the coincidences!

By now the color had begun to seep back into her cheeks, flushing them quite becomingly, although she was still too astounded to be aware of it.

"What on earth are you doing *here*? And in uniform?"

"Good God!" His manners forgotten, Carl continued to stare at her, oblivious of the looks he was getting from some of the Mexican officers in the room, all of whom had appointed themselves as "la teniente's" unofficial protectors. "Ginny Brandon—I can't believe—"

"You had better stop staring at me, Captain," she reminded him tartly, something of her old impatience creeping into her manner. "And you still have not explained what you are doing here, and in that uniform! Have you come on business?"

He straightened up, obviously trying to pull himself together, but his eyes did not seem capable of removing themselves from her face.

"I—I'm a part of the American Legion of Honor, under the Command of Colonel Green, come to help President Juarez. We've just been moved up to Texcoco. But to find *you* here, of all places—why, your father thought, when he heard that you'd disappeared from Mexico City, that you might have been taken prisoner, or gone back to France. . . . Dear Lord, Ginny," he burst out suddenly, "don't you have any idea how worried everyone was about you? After Mrs. Brandon came back, quite hysterical with worry and grief, to tell your father you'd been abducted, he had me sworn in as a marshal, and I joined some Texas Rangers who'd volunteered to try and find you. We almost caught up, a couple of times, at that, but. . . ."

Ginny had begun to blush again, in spite of herself, remembering only too well that long, miserable journey, racing across deserts and through the mountains—a journey on which she had been Steve's prisoner, and had thought she hated him; had longed only for escape, or rescue. It was obvious that Carl had been one of the few persons her father had taken into his confidence, and now she suddenly began to wonder if his arrival here were really as coincidental as she'd thought at first. He had been a lawman! But surely, now that he was in the army, he had no jurisdiction here. . . . She was suddenly glad that Steve was away; that here, in Mexico, he was known as Esteban Alvarado.

Her green eyes had begun to narrow slightly as she tilted her head back to regard Carl.

"Why talk about the past when it's all been over so long ago? As you can see, I'm quite safe now. And—and I enjoy what I'm doing; I feel I'm being useful at last."

Carl had begun to frown. Ginny Brandon! Ginny of the laughing green eyes, the teasing, seductive mouth, who had been both a lady and a bold coquette. He had been half-mad with jealous frustration when she'd left the wagon train in El Paso with that Frenchman; and later, when he'd heard that she had been forcibly abducted by the man he had always hated and mistrusted, his jealousy and rage had known no bounds. He had been determined to find Steve Morgan and kill him—to hunt him down like the criminal he was, and rescue the Senator's lovely daughter. What had happened to her during the past two years? What kind of experiences had she undergone? And secretly, even while he stared down into her face—she looked as beautiful and as coolly composed as ever!—the thought nagged at him: How many men had she given herself to?

"I can't imagine it's really you," he muttered now. "And you must be the female lieutenant one of my troopers was talking about. He said that the latest addition to General Díaz' staff was a golden-haired woman who looked European, but was really a Spaniard, a creole—how could anyone mistake you for a Mexican?"

The barely veiled contempt he put into the last word made Ginny's lips tighten with anger. Carl had always had the knack of annoying her—he hadn't changed one bit, except for the beard! And now she remembered that she had hardly been able to endure his kisses.

"Did you come here merely out of curiosity, then? In that case, Captain Hoskins, let me satisfy it, so you may set your men clear about my position here. I am attached to the General's staff, but *not* in a military capacity. And you might as well know this—" her green eyes veiled themselves for an instant, and then met his levelly. "I am married to Major Esteban Alvarado, who is one of the General's officers."

Carl threw her a look of stunned disbelief mixed with anger.

"You can't be serious! Your father, when I spoke to him only a few months ago, did not mention—"

"He did not mention my marriage because he did not know of it yet! There's a war going on here—I only recently had the time to write a letter of my own, I'm afraid. But did you join the Legion of Honor in order to find *me*, or from a sense of patriotic duty?"

He had the grace to flush.

"I had already enlisted in the army when I had this opportunity offered me," he said stiffly. "But I must admit that your father expressed his worry and his concern for your safety, when I talked to him before I left California. Can you blame him? He's heard nothing from you for months! And now you inform me that you are *married*, and that your father doesn't know it. For God's sake, Ginny, what's got into you?"

Anger crept into her voice as she stared back at him, her eyes hardening.

"I'm afraid that is hardly your concern, is it? I'm married—and a Mexican by adoption." She saw a strangely inflexible, stubborn look creep into Carl's face, as though he refused to believe her, and her anger grew, although she took pains to keep her voice calm and unruffled. "Really, Carl, you seem to forget that I'm hardly the green girl you knew over two years ago! I'm here by choice, and I'm happy."

Her voice had softened almost imperceptibly when she said those last words, and the green of her eyes seemed to become darker. Carl Hoskins felt his jaws tighten as he looked down at her. God, how beautiful she was, in spite of the severe way in which she had arranged her hair, her simple clothes! And the expression that had crept into her face when she said she was happy—how could she possibly be? How could she possibly have brought herself to marry a Mexican? It was with a determined effort that Carl Hoskins managed to pull himself together and force a smile.

"Well—I guess I owe you an apology, and my congratulations. I'm sorry, Ginny. It was just that seeing you here was something of a shock."

She gave him a faint smile, at last.

"And you're turning up here was rather surprising to me, as well! But what are you really doing here, Carl? Surely you didn't ride all this way just to get a look at the woman your men have been gossiping about?"

He flushed under his faint tan.

"I shouldn't have blurted that out, I'm afraid. I did come here on business. Colonel Green sent me with a message for General Díaz. You see, none of us speaks French very well, and it appears we're to expect a rather distinguished visitor here soon—a Russian prince."

"A Russian Prince?" This time her eyebrows arched in surprise. "But why on earth would a Russian prince be coming here, of all places, and at a time like this?"

"Prince Sahrkanov has been in Washington for the past few months, negotiating the sale of the territory of Alaska to the United States. It's been a secret all this time, but I believe Secretary Seward has already released the news to the press, so I'm not divulging anything I shouldn't."

"Alaska! I've always thought there was nothing but snow and ice there."

"So a lot of people think, but Mr. Seward seems to feel that, because of its close proximity to the United States, it would be better to have the territory in our hands rather than that of a foreign power."

"But why is the Prince coming here?"

"Oh—" Carl Hoskins gave a careless shrug, although he was secretly pleased at having engaged Ginny's full attention at last. "He's a man who enjoys wars, I believe. So, with the full permission of President Juarez, he's here to observe. In fact, I've a feeling Colonel Green is rather alarmed in case the Prince decides he'd like to volunteer his services for some fighting—he's got quite a reputation as a marksman, I believe."

"I'm sure he'll find that fighting a real war is a lot different from dueling" Ginny retorted with some annoyance. Then, recalling herself and her duties, she said thoughtfully, "I suppose I'd better let the General know you're here! I'm afraid he's been very busy this morning—you've heard that Queretaro has fallen at last? But in view of what you've just told me. . . ."

Carl Hoskins helped Ginny out of her chair and watched her go over to talk to one of the Mexican officers who lounged around the room, watching him narrowly. He wondered, with a certain degree of sourness, whether one of them was her husband. What on earth could have possessed her? She could have been a French Countess, and instead she'd chosen to marry some Mexican peasant—it did not make sense!

Ginny had now disappeared within the General's office, and Carl was forced to cool his heels until she emerged. The young Mexican Capitan Ginny had spoken to walked over and offered him a chair, his white teeth showing in a smile.

"So you are an old friend of the Señora Alvarado, eh? I suppose it was a surprise to find her here? General Díaz swears he does not know how he would manage without her. She is lucky to know so many languages."

"I'm sure her husband considers himself a lucky man, too," Carl ventured, and the Mexican's smile broadened.

"Ah, Esteban Alvarado is one of the most envied officers under the General's command! Especially to have a wife who is not afraid to follow him to war. It's unfortunate he's not here right now."

So her husband was away somewhere, was he? Carl found himself more curious than ever; without appearing too obvious, he managed to glean from the amiable young officer that Ginny's husband was off on courier duty, and that he was a particular friend of the General's brother, Colonel Felix Díaz.

Captain Hoskins looked much more pleased with himself when he emerged from General Díaz' office a half hour later, after having been granted his interview. Since Ginny was official translator to General Díaz, courtesy alone decreed that he could not refuse her services to Colonel Green, who was an ally. And the fact that El Presidente himself had agreed to the Russian's visit here was sufficient indication of the man's importance. Whatever General Díaz himself felt at his President's rather highhanded action in authorizing a foreigner's presence here without first consulting the Commanding General, Diaz kept to himself, although Ginny had not missed the annoyed tightening of his lips. She had problems of her own, now, it seemed, for Carl Hoskins was determined to spend time with her, and there was no polite way in which she could refuse to talk to him, at least.

She was glad that Steve was away, and yet unreasonably annoyed and upset, too. Carl Hoskins, of all people! Why did he have to turn up here? All the feelings of uneasiness that she had thought swept away seemed to have returned to plague her, and now she did not even have the comfort of Steve's presence and his arms about her at night. It was awkward—especially since she would be thrown so much into Carl's company, and Steve had always been jealous of Carl, had accused her of having him as a lover at one time. Would Steve still think the same thing when he returned? She could not help thinking again, almost frightened by the thought, how new and how tenuously fragile their marriage still was. They loved each other, yes, but they had not been close to each other long enough to trust each other completely yet. To love left one open to hurt. . . .

Chapter Three

Love! Before a week had ended, Ginny was heartily sick of the word. Ever since she had gone with Carl to have dinner with Colonel Green and his officers, she had been plagued with declarations of love. Half the men in the regiment were in love with her, or so it would appear from the flowers and the notes that were constantly brought or sent to the little posada where she lodged.

She complained to Colonel Díaz, who laughed teasingly and quite unsympathetically.

"Ah, but I understand that you are quite able to take care of yourself should one of your admirers forget himself, is that not true, chica? And in the meantime, let us not be inhospitable to our brave American allies. No doubt you remind them of the girls they left at home, eh?"

"And what do you think my husband will say when he comes back and—and finds all this going on? I might as well tell you, he has always had his suspicions about that Captain Hoskins, and now, when he comes back and finds Carl constantly underfoot—"

"Then Esteban will find out all over again what an attractive woman he's had the good fortune to marry!" Colonel Díaz winked at Ginny. "Which one of them are you worried for the most, little one?"

"How could you ask such a thing!" She shot him an angrily reproachful look, but he merely laughed and patted her shoulder.

"Come, now—surely you can see the humor of all this? Those poor Americano's need a lovely woman to flirt with and admire. And when the Russian arrives here, we'll be proud to show him that we have women as beautiful and accomplished as you are in Mexico."

"I'm beginning to dread his arrival, believe me," Ginny retorted grimly.

It was partly because Carl Hoskins was becoming far too familiar and too bold in his manner towards her, and partly the fact that she was tired of the open adoration of half the men in his command that Ginny had taken to spending more and more time with the soldaderas again. She felt more at home in the company of these earthy, friendly women than she did with her fellow Americans, whose polite manners barely covered the fact that they wanted her and considered her marriage to a Mexican officer as bringing her down, in some way, to their own level.

The small room she had shared with Steve seemed unbearably lonely to Ginny, especially since some of the Americans had taken to frequenting the small cantina below, mostly for the opportunity it gave them of catching a glimpse of her. And she was so tired of coping with Carl's questions; his continuing incredulity at her assertions that she was, indeed, quite happily married, and of her own choice.

"But for God's sake, Ginny, have you considered what you will do afterwards? How, and in what manner will you live? Your father will hardly be happy to know—"

"That I'm married to a Mexican? Well, I am, and there's nothing he, nor anyone else, can do about it. For heaven's sake, Carl, if you insist on discussing my personal affairs, then I'd rather we terminated all discussion between us!"

When he realized that she had truly become angry with him, he apologized, and swore he had only her interests at heart.

"I am still in love with you, Ginny! I can't help it. You've haunted me right from the beginning, and there was a time, I'm sure of it, when you had begun to grow fond of me!"

She had to admit to herself that she *had*, in fact, led Carl on, and it was only her own feelings of guilt that made her continue seeing him. She had to admit, too, that it was pleasant and rather reassuring to have an escort sometimes. And if she were nice to Carl, perhaps he'd tell her father that she was content here—perhaps he'd forget about the outlaw Steve Morgan whom he had hated and continued to hate so bitterly. She had to make sure that Carl never found out that Steve and her husband were one and the same person, although there were times when she wondered nervously whether Steve would appreciate her concern for him.

The only person she had confided her problem to was the General himself, and he had grinned with amusement.

"So you're afraid that this hot-headed husband of yours will have a fight with the persistent Captain Hoskins and endanger our good relations with the Colonel Green? Don't worry, señora, I'll explain it all to him myself—and in the meantime, perhaps I'll find some other places to send him."

She blushed.

"Oh, no! I—I didn't mean that you should keep him out of the way! He'd be furious if he knew that I—"

"But we don't want trouble, eh? No—once this Russian has left, señora, perhaps we'll find ways of keeping Esteban and this Captain Hoskins apart, sí?"

But would even the General be able to make Steve understand? And would he believe that she hadn't encouraged Carl at all?

Ginny had taken to escaping from her room and going down to the wagons and the cookfires. Here, dressed once more in her oldest, most comfortable clothes, her hair concealed by a rebozo, she would sit with the other women and talk about the war, and about men, and even, on some occasions, about children. The women teased her about the time when she, too, would have a child. After all, she was married—it was high time!

"You should visit the Church of the Virgin of Guadalupe," one of the women told Ginny seriously. "Look at Consuelo here—see how big she is? Manuel had begun to wonder if she was barren, so she made a novena, and now we can all see the results!"

"But I don't want a child just yet—Esteban is such a restless man, he likes to travel, and I want to go with him."

"Ah, but you do want to settle down somewhere after the war is over, don't you? There's nothing like the responsibility of a child to make a man settle down—just ask me!"

Carmencita had eight children already, and had just been married to her fourth husband, so that her remarks brought forth some robust laughter, which she took with a toss of her head.

But the conversation had made Ginny thoughtful. Suppose she did become pregnant? Would it change things? It was rather a frightening thought—to be tied down by a child, never to be able to call herself really free again. And what about Steve? How would he react?

Well, she wouldn't think about it until it actually happened, Ginny told herself firmly, and put the thought away from her.

She went the next evening, though, with some of the women, to the enormous Cathedral of the Dark Virgin that stood at the foot of Tepeyac, where a poor peasant had seen the Lady on the mountaintop.

It was the name-day fiesta of Dolores Bautista, who was one of Ginny's particular friends among the women, being the common-law wife of none other than the villainous-looking ex-guerilla Manolo, now a sergeant in the army.

"After we have been to church, you will join in the fiesta, will you not, Doña Genia?"

Ginny shook her head in exasperation that Dolores still insisted on tacking the "doña" in front of her name.

"Only if you forget, for heaven's sake, that I am anyone else but the soldadera I used to be before Don Porfirio became so—so stuffy about it!" Ginny said tartly. But she smiled the next minute and hugged the small, brown-skinned Dolores as she slipped into the girl's hand the present she had found for her—a thin gold necklace with a tiny, seed-pearl encrusted medallion of Our Lady of Guadalupe herself. She had bought it in Vera Cruz, meaning to give it to Sonya, her step-mother, when she returned to California; but fortunately, Steve had come to fetch her back with him.

"Just for tonight I'm not going to worry about anything—I'm going to be content," Ginny whispered to herself as she started out with some of the other women—a barefooted, giggling crowd she could lose herself in.

She could not repress a smile at the thought of what Carl would say if he could see her now! Poor Carl, he could be so terribly overpowering sometimes! She had seen him for a short while earlier on in the evening, and had finally escaped to her room, pleading a headache. He would be horrified if he'd known that she had changed clothing and slipped out of the back door without anyone giving her a second glance. No doubt the General himself wouldn't exactly approve, but none of the soldiers or their women would give her away. In fact, the cool, starry night was so beautiful, and their walk so invigorating, that Ginny found herself looking forward to the celebration later on. She hadn't been able to dance or let herself go for such a long time now!

They walked up the hill to the cathedral, good-naturedly calling out replies to the bold banter from the soldiers they passed. A small patrol of Americans paused to ask if the señoritas needed an escort, and Ginny, feeling herself indistinguishable from the others, joined in the taunting cries: "Get lost, gringos, we can fight as well as you can!"

The church was full of worshippers this evening, as it always was, and like the others Ginny crossed herself as she gazed up at the altar, a blaze of candles illuminating the miraculous cloak of the Mother of all Mexico. In spite of the fact that Ginny had never been particularly religious during her girlhood—going to church, even while she lived in France, being merely an observance of custom—it was impossible not to feel *something* here in this high-vaulted church with its crowd of devout worshippers who believed without question.

There was a late evening mass in progress, and the women became silent as they slipped inside the church, pulling their rebozos even more tightly around their heads.

It was only when they were about halfway through the mass that the strangest sensation took hold of Ginny—the feeling that she was being stared at. She lowered her head, allowing her eyes to slant through her clasped hands, even while she told herself firmly that she was being silly and foolish. No doubt some man had recognized the women who sat huddled together as soldaderas, and was staring boldly. Why should she suddenly feel as if a cold wind had swept through the church, making her shiver?

It was impossible to distinguish faces or individuals here, for the chuch was quite dark, except for the lighted altar. Still, the feeling of being watched made her so uncomfortable that she began to long for the mass to be over. And the next moment Manuela, who knelt beside Ginny, bent her head closer to whisper,

"I think one of us has an admirer! Look—those two hidalgos who are standing there by the pillar to the right—I swear that one of them, at least, has not taken his eyes off us all evening!"

Manuela, who had a luxuriantly abundant head of black hair she was inordinately proud of, wore only a white lace mantilla over it, instead of the warm rebozos that Ginny and the others had worn, and now she tossed her head a trifle proudly.

"Better get rid of them before we get back to the camp, or your man will start a fight!" Carmencita warned the girl, who only smiled.

"Trust her to notice the men, even in church!" Carmencita sniffed shortly. Ginny said nothing, although she had indeed noticed the two men that Manuela had pointed out, and they *were* staring.

At least it was no one she knew. Deliberately, Ginny refused to look in their direction, keeping her eyes down and her face obscured by her hands.

It was with a feeling of relief that she left the church with the others. They paused outside to cross themselves again with holy water, and then Dolores decided suddenly that she must light a candle and sped back inside the church, leaving them to wait for her.

"Look, they're coming out—they're looking this way again."

The irrepressible Manuela touched Ginny's arm with her elbow, and sure enough, the two well-dressed men, their dark suits making them stand out in the crowd composed mostly of peasants or soldados, had emerged from the church to stand watching the women, the men's faces shaded by broad-brimmed hats.

"Huh!" Carmencita grumbled, "They're probably Norteamericanos, or some hacendados who slipped up here from the City to take a look around! I've a mind to have one of our boys take a good look at their faces and question them!"

"Oh, leave them alone, they're not doing any harm, they're only staring!"

Manuela pulled the mantilla from her hair and carelessly draped it around her shoulders with an affected shiver.

"Next thing they'll be taking us for a bunch of putas," Maria Torres grumbled. "Come on, let's start walking."

Ginny pretended to be tracing patterns in the dirt with her bare toes, but she hadn't escaped the fact that the men were very obviously staring at them.

She wished, suddenly, that Dolores would hurry. Who were those two men? She could almost have sworn she caught a glimpse of pale eyes under one hat brim, and the thought made her shiver uncontrollably, although she scolded herself for having an over-active imagination. Whoever the men were, it was no concern of hers, and she refused to let their rude stares further disturb her evening or her nerves.

One of the men detached himself from his friend and began to walk towards them, causing the women to giggle nervously. Instinctively, Ginny took a step back toward the rear of the small group of women, deliberately keeping her head lowered.

"Excuse me, señoritas."

There were more giggles from the women, but Carmencita, older and bolder than the rest, put her hands on her hips and faced the gentleman.

"And what makes you think we are not all married women, visiting the church for a little peace and quiet, eh?"

"If you are, then I beg your pardon—but believe me, I meant no disrespect, ladies, in approaching you. My friend and I—"

"Ah, yes, your friend! Why is he so shy? Does he always send you to do his dirty work for him?"

"Believe me, señoritas," the man suddenly swept his hat from his head and bowed deeply with a kind of old-fashioned courtesy that impressed even Carmencita in spite of herself, "my friend would be with me now, joining his compliments to mine, if he knew our language. But unfortunately, he does not. He is a visitor here, and very desirous to make the acquaintance of some of our beautiful Mexican señoritas."

"Indeed! What you are trying to say, in your politely roundabout way, is that you and your friend thought we were a bunch of putas on our night off, isn't that so?"

Carmencita's voice was belligerent, but Manuela, full red lips pouting slightly, shouldered her aside.

"Give the señor a chance to explain himself before you jump to conclusions, Carmen! I'm sure he could not have mistaken us honest soldaderas for common putas!"

"What Manuela is dying to find out is which of us the two señors picked out for themselves," one of the women whispered to Ginny with a laugh. "I have never seen a vainer female than that one!"

The señor, his hat still in his hand, was now revealed, in the faint light, to be a well dressed, rather slim man of below middle age—his light brown hair, parted in the center, gave him a slightly dandified air. His manner of speaking, in spite of the women's ribald comments, remained almost incongruously grave and dignified.

"Ladies, let me repeat that neither my friend nor I meant any offense! We merely wondered if a couple of you might consider joining two lonely men for a friendly drink, perhaps—a meal, if that would please you. We are looking only for company, of course, nothing else!"

"Oh yes, of course! That's all you fine gentlemen could ever want from the likes of us!" Carmencita said coarsely and gave her raucous laugh.

"Well, it's obvious the gentlemen didn't want *you*," Manuela said sharply. She added in a softer voice, "Really, señor, your kindness flatters us, but I don't know—which of us did you have in mind when you extended your kind invitation?"

"Señorita, with hair as magnificent and night-black as yours, who could resist? But my friend—he seemed to find the shyness of your friend over there most intriguing."

Ginny glanced up with a gasp of anger to find them all looking at her, the women's eyes full of mischief, the man's strangely piercing, as if he tried to penetrate the disguise that her tightly-wound rebozo provided her with.

Speaking in the Mestizo dialect, she said coldly, "I can't speak for the others, of course, but your friend's interest fails to flatter me. I am a married woman, señor, and it is only my husband's attentions that interest me!"

"Yes, yes, Genia and her man are still like lovebirds, always off somewhere together!"

And at that moment, to Ginny's intense relief, Dolores came running back to join them, slightly breathless, glanc-

ing curiously at the gentleman who now stood rather un-
certainly before them.

"Let's go back to the camp, eh? Manuela can stay if she
wants to. And I wish you a good night, señor, and better
luck elsewhere!"

Carmencita gave a mocking inclination of her head and
started off down the hill, while Ginny, with a last cool
glance at the gentleman, linked arms with Dolores and
followed her. Even Manuela went with them, pouting
slightly.

"We could have stayed, even for a little while," she
grumbled. "I would have liked to see what that strange
'friend' looked like!"

"Well, believe me, you'll have more fun down at the
camp tonight—me, I didn't trust the looks of those two,
or the way they stared, even while mass was being said!"

Ginny did not join in the lively discussion for once, although mentally she agreed with Maria's comments. There
had been something almost ominous about those two,
something that made her uneasy. And why pick on her? It
was only when they reached the camp—its flickering
cookfires looking like fireflies at a distance—that she managed to throw off her sudden mood of depression. She was
safe here, and she intended to have fun this evening.

They had quite a feast, in the end—the chili-spiced food
washed down with tequila that had been purloined when
the Army took Puebla. And by the time the guitars and
the fiddles struck up and the dancing began, Ginny's earlier mood had been replaced by one of gaiety.

The dances of Mexico seemed to be in her blood, and
when she danced she could forget everything else, giving
herself up with passionate abandon to the wildly rhythmic
music. Tonight, as usual, Ginny had no lack of partners,
and in spite of the coolness of the night she was soon
forced to discard her rebozo, letting her hair hang loose
around her shoulders like the other women. Lost in the
dance, she had no idea what a provocative picture she
presented, her hair like a red-gold flame, her skirt whirling
up around her legs to display her slim calves and ankles.

The spontaneous, frenetic enjoyment of the dance—the
sounds of music and revelry—had brought other watchers
as well. Soldiers who were not on sentry duty came from
all over the camp to watch and join in if they could.

A few American soldiers, just come off patrol, stood and watched rather wistfully, although their eyes widened with shock when the crowd of dancers parted and they recognized the copper-haired woman who stood out from the others, both by reason of her hair and the way she threw herself into the dance.

There were others who recognized her, too—Carl Hoskins, accompanying Colonel Green, was hardly able to contain his rage and disgust; General Díaz himself, hid a half smile under his full mustaches, which he stroked thoughtfully; his brother, the Colonel, merely raised his eyebrows in mock-dismay.

"She cannot resist the dance, our little Genia. Wouldn't you say she's a true Mexican?"

"She's a gypsy—I'd guess Russian or Hungarian. And by God, the most beautiful woman I've ever seen, on this or any other continent!"

The man who had spoken with such fiery conviction spoke French, his head slightly inclined towards his companion, his eyes never leaving the dancers. Now he added, "What do you think, Señor? Did I not make the right choice at the beginning? We Russians can always recognize true grace and beauty, even if it's carefully hidden!"

"As the lady so coldly reminded me outside the church, she is a married woman, your Highness! And Mexican husbands are notoriously jealous."

"Ah—but her husband is not here, is he? And she *is* a lady—that is what makes her so much more intriguing. You say she is to be my interpreter when you leave? I have the devil's own luck, have I not?"

"Be careful, Prince. Mexican women are said to carry little daggers with them, to defend their honor."

The Prince merely threw his head back and laughed, his strange, blue-green eyes reflecting the firelight.

"So do our Russian gypsies! However you don't need to worry, Señor Lerdo. In this case, I have my reasons for discretion. Believe me, the lady will meet with nothing but respect from me."

Chapter Four

Ginny's first meeting with Prince Nikolai Ivan Vassilyvitch Sahrkanov could hardly have taken place under less auspicious circumstances, as General Díaz himself was to remind her, with a somewhat assumed manner of sternness the next morning.

"But why did he have to turn up earlier than he'd been expected? And how was I to know the gentleman with him was Señor Sebastian Lerdo de Tejada himself?"

"The fact that El Presidente sent his most trusted cabinet member to greet the Prince should give you some idea of the man's importance! Really, señora, you could hardly have chosen a worse moment to participate in a fiesta with the soldaderas! You're lucky that the Prince did not get the wrong idea about you."

"I suppose so," she muttered a trifle rebelliously, and the General gave her one of his sudden, winning smiles.

"Comt, come, señora! I'm not really angry with you, although I must admit I was a trifle annoyed last night! It's unfortunate our Prince had to turn up with so many others in tow, including that persistent Capitan Hoskins of yours!"

"I'd be just as happy if Carl Hoskins decided he never wants to talk to me again!" Ginny said a trifle waspishly.

Still, later on, she had to admit, with a sigh, that she had been a trifle indiscreet. The Prince had been politeness itself, but she had recognized the look in his pale eyes—eyes whose hardness belied the look of respect on his admittedly handsome face.

It had been bad enough having her wrist grasped by Colonel Felix Díaz himself, and practically dragged away from her friends, while he whispered in her ear with a tremor of unfeeling laughter that she was really in disgrace this time. Far worse was the realization that the man who had accosted her outside the church had been one of President Juarez' cabinet members, and that his mysterious "friend" was none other than the Russian Prince whose arrival they'd all been waiting for!

Willy-nilly—with bare feet, her hair hanging down her back, and suddenly acutely conscious of her peasant dress—Ginny found herself presented to the Prince, and meeting his searching eyes for the first time. Colonel Green had been obviously embarrassed, Carl Hoskins had been furious, and Señor Lerdo amused.

But they were the least of her problems now. Señor Lerdo had already begun his journey back to San Luis, and from now on Ginny's main duty would be to act as the Prince's guide and interpreter. And to make matters worse, she had decided that she did not like him. In spite of his excellent manners, and his almost over-done politeness, there was something vaguely menacing about him.

A tall and handsome man with dark brown hair, clean-shaven except for his fashionable sideburns, the Prince was no doubt used to turning women's hearts with his flattery and his somewhat arrogant air of mastery. He also was obviously used to getting his own way, and it was he who decided that first afternoon that she must ride with him.

"I think that you will ride as magnificently as you dance, madame," he said, his eyes flickering over her in a way that somehow belied the polite flattery of his tone. She noticed uncomfortably that his eyes never left her, even when she pointed out this place of interest or that, making her voice as cool as she dared.

In spite of her coolness and the severity of style she had deliberately chosen for her dress and hair, the Princess pretended not to notice. His tone, when he addressed her, was lazily polite and gentlemanly with only occasional undertones of mockery, as though he wanted her to know that he saw through her little game.

"The wretch!" Ginny thought fiercely to herself that night. "He probably thinks I am playing hard to get on purpose, so as to catch his interest." She was glad that he had not persisted when she refused his invitation to dine with him that night. And, in spite of Carl Hoskins' presence so close by, she wished that Steve would return. Why did he have to stay away so long? It was hard to be patient, when she missed him so terribly. And especially now, when she was alone, and the feelings of fear and reasonless presentiment seemed to crowd round her, making her head throb.

Ginny was, indeed, seized with the almost irresistible impulse to run away; to go somewhere, to escape from the web of intrigue she felt closing around her. No, she was being ridiculous! The Prince was merely a man, after all, and there was nothing he could do to harm her, surrounded as she was by friends. All she had to do was find out exactly why he was here, and why the President himself had shown him so much preference. That was all—and soon the Prince would be gone, back to Russia, and Mexico City would be taken, and the Americans would leave; and above all, Steve would be back and she would feel safe again.

It was, unfortunately, not quite as easy and uncomplicated as she tried to persuade herself it would be that first night. For the Prince Sahrkanov was a subtle and rather disturbing man, not at all easy to handle or outthink. Carl Hoskins was another problem.

Carl was too angry with her and too infatuated to stay away long. When Ginny was not with the Prince she could be sure of encountering Carl somewhere, even if it was leaning against the door to the General's headquarters, his gaze on her both somber and frustrated.

"God, Ginny, what kind of woman have you become? How could you associate yourself with women of that kind and dance the way you were dancing that night? And now you've got a Prince dancing attendance on you!"

"Quite the contrary, it is I who am forced to dance attendance on the Prince," Ginny answered him sharply, her face flushed with annoyance. Carl was too trying! Since she had refused to accept him as a lover he had tried, heavy-handedly, to play the part of her brother, but the unconcealed lust in his eyes when he looked at her gave him away.

"What kind of a man are you married to, anyhow?" he demanded now. "How is it he stays away so long?"

"Carl, he's a soldier! He has to follow orders. And please, *don't* start on that topic again. How many times have I told you that I happen to love my husband? I intend to stay married, and I will probably live in Mexico."

"You're talking crazy! Your father—for heaven's sake, don't you owe him something? How can you bury yourself away in an uncivilized country with a man—"

"That's enough, Carl! And until you've mended your manners I don't care to converse with you further."

On this occasion it was the Prince who came to her rescue, striding into the General's headquarters without his usual escort, his eyes suddenly becoming steely as they fell on Carl Hoskins.

"Has the Captain been annoying you again? Shall I ask Colonel Green to have him transferred elsewhere?"

"Are you sure the Colonel will go so far just to be obliging, sir?"

She could not refrain from showing him her claws, and he gave her a smile of mocking appreciation.

"Perhaps I have more influence than you might think, madame! Come—" he seized her wrist in the imperious manner he had and began to walk her outside—"I think it is time I surprised you a little," he said mysteriously. He handed her politely into the small, open carriage that Colonel Green had provided for his distinguished visitor's use.

Part of Prince Sahrkanov's surprise was a visit to Cuernevaca, which Ginny had visited before, when the Emperor was in residence. La Borda, his summer "palace," was now the headquarters of Colonel Luis Adiego, who had been informed ahead of time of the Prince's visit.

"Your baggage has arrived from Acapulco." Translating, Ginny shot a small look of surprise and irritation at her companion. Was he really planning on a long stay in Mexico? What was he up to?

She had been more than a little annoyed to learn that they were journeying so far, and thankful for the small escort that General Díaz had provided. She felt safer with the familiar uniforms and faces. More than ever, she had begun to distrust the Prince.

It was already late afternoon, and he was planning to dine here, as the guest of Colonel Adiego. *Her* wishes in the matter had not been consulted at all—in fact, Ginny found to her growing fury, they were all treating her as if she were, indeed, a soldier under orders herself.

The Prince seemed determined to show her that he had genuine need of her services as an interpreter, for he kept her busy, as they were conducted on a tour of the former

Emperor's home. It was as if he had to understand every
word the obsequious Colonel Adiego poured out.

Her feet were aching by the time they were invited to
rest in the comfortable patio, while the Colonel's personal
staff brought cool drinks.

"Oh, by the way, would you ask the Colonel if any
compatriots of mine also arrived here this afternoon?"

Gritting her teeth, she relayed the question, and the Colonel, in a burst of eloquence, informed her that indeed
four Russian sailors had brought the Prince's belongings,
and that his personal physician, the Count Chernikoff, was
also here and resting in his room.

"You don't seem very happy today, little one," the
Prince commented with a lift of his eyebrow. "Perhaps
your meeting with the Count will cheer you up—you'll
find him an exceptionally interesting man, and very well
travelled. Perhaps you'll discover acquaintances in common!"

She felt as if his words had some hidden meaning that
seemed to amuse him inwardly, but whatever it was, she
refused to rise to the bait.

He was determined then, that she should meet this other
Russian. She considered it unlikely, though, that they
might have any friends in common, for to her recollection
the Prince Sahrkanov was the first Russian that Ginny had
met.

"My friend the Count has begun to feel his years, I'm
afraid," the Prince said in his drawling, half-amused voice.
"However, you'll find him charming and an excellent con-
versationalist. He'll be here soon, no doubt."

Ginny had almost expected a stooped, old-fashioned
man—an *old* man. But in spite of the Prince's words, the
Count was tall, well-built and had a curiously unlined face
in spite of his iron-grey hair and mustache. He emerged
from the house with a quick and almost jaunty step, and
his eyes, a peculiar steely grey, seemed to bore into
Ginny's face for so long that she could feel herself redden.

Count Chernikoff apologized for his rudeness immediately and quite charmingly as he bowed over her hand.

"You must forgive me, mademoiselle! But for a moment, I could hardly believe . . . yes, indeed, the resemblance is remarkable!"

Ginny was thoroughly puzzled, her eyes widening as she

looked from the Count's smiling face to Ivan Sahrkanov's ironical one.

"But—you say I resemble someone, monsieur le comte? Someone you knew?"

"But of course! Did not the Prince tell you? It was merely to look at your fresh young face that I rode so many miles on such terrible roads, mademoiselle! However, it was worth it—much more than I can say, eh, Ivan? My dear, you are the image of your mother, as she was at your age."

"My—my mother?" Ginny breathed the words, finding that her eyes kept clinging to the older man's face. And, indeed, he in his turn seemed reluctant to move far from her, for he deliberately pulled up a chair and seated himself beside her, with a word of apology to the Prince.

"Your mother—yes, indeed, my child! You'll forgive me if I call you that? I knew your mother. And your dear Tante Celine—a remarkably kind and sensible woman. I had the honor to visit with her shortly before I accompanied the Prince to America."

"Perhaps, Colonel, you will do me the honor of showing me the collection of guns you spoke of earlier? I think we should let these two indulge in some—shall we say, reminiscing?"

Prince Sahrkanov's English was heavily accented, but nevertheless quite adequate to make himself understood by the Colonel, who also knew some English, and Ginny flashed him a coldly angry look, which he returned with a smile and a slight narrowing of his eyes. Why had he pretended not to speak English? Why had he insisted on the services of an interpreter? Before Ginny could collect her thoughts, the Prince had given her a bow, and walked back into the estancia with the Colonel.

"You must not be angry with Ivan. It was I, mademoiselle, who insisted upon this meeting."

Count Chernikoff's soft voice made Ginny swing her face around to his again, with a frown puckering her forehead.

"You must forgive me if I confess that—that I don't understand! In fact, I must confess that I'm completely confused! Do you mean to say that you and the Prince—that my being here today was all *arranged*?" A note of anger had begun to creep into her voice, and the Count put his hand out, touching hers understandingly.

"My dear, be patient with my ramblings, and I'll explain everything. I understand your shock; yes, and even your anger. But if I can make one request of you—please hear me out before you ask questions. Humor an old man, and one who knew and admired your mother. In fact, although you cannot remember me, I saw you once, when you were only a baby."

Again, his eyes gazed searchingly at her, and she shrank instinctively. His voice was gentle, and yet there was something about his eyes, something that alarmed her. Why did he look at her in that strange way? What was he going to tell her?

"You must try to trust me—you must listen carefully and believe, my child, that as wild as it may sound, as incredible, every word of the story I am about to tell you is the absolute truth. I had waited only until your majority to reveal it to you, and then, when I went to Paris, your aunt informed me that you had left for America. A kind and well-meaning woman, your tante, but she should not have—well, never mind, what was done is done, but my duty remains."

Her cold hands pressed against her strangely burning face, Ginny listened, at first with growing amazement, and then with incredulity. If not for the stern face of the old man, his unfaltering words, she almost might have believed that none of this was real, or that she was hearing a story concocted by some novelist. Time and time again she wanted to interrupt, to cry out that it was all impossible— he could not be speaking of her mother, of *her*—but there was a steely, inflexible quality to the Count's eyes and his voice that kept her silent, listening almost against her will.

"Your mother was Genevieve La Croix. . . ."

That was the way he started. And quite suddenly, as the old Count continued to speak slowly, choosing his words, Ginny found her mother—whom she remembered only vaguely as a sickly shadow of a woman, lying in bed with her face turned from the light—become alive and young, as young and vivacious and full of life as she herself was now.

The lovely Genevieve—so young, so headstrong; she

had been determined to follow the dictates of her heart and her young body, even as Ginny, her daughter, was doing now, so many years later.

"They met quite by accident, you see, in the Cathedral of Notre Dame—and he could not take his eyes from her face . . . . She was very young, of course, only sixteen, and still under the care of the good nuns in the convent school; but still, when one is young and in love and determined. . . . They found ways to meet, of course. There was a friend of hers, a young married woman with a romantic heart, who arranged a place for them to meet. And so it began. I had been chosen to be his companion, but I'm afraid that in those days I was young and reckless myself, and although I knew it was quite unsuitable and that it could never last, I'm ashamed to say that there was nothing I could do to prevent what happened."

He was going to tell her something startling, something that was going to frighten her—or had she already guessed, with her heart, what the old man was leading up to? Quite involuntarily, Ginny had leaned forward, her hands tightly clasped in her lap, her eyes looking wider and more mysteriously slanted than ever. Why wouldn't he get to the point?

In his own way, however, the Count Chernikoff was striving to do just that, but in the most tactful way possible. After all, he realized what a shock it was going to be for this young woman to learn such facts about her mother, and worst of all, to learn that the man whom she had looked on all these years as her father was not her real father at all. . . .

"My child, since you're young yourself, I'm sure you can understand what happened between those two young people, so madly in love! And don't forget, all this happened so many years ago—it was more difficult for the young to follow the dictates of their own hearts then! What I am trying to say is—it was all discovered in the end, as, inevitably, I had always known and always feared it would be. Your mother's family found out, and she was hastily given in marriage to the young American who had adored her so, but who would have been considered quite unsuitable under any other circumstances. She went back to America with him, of course, and you were born there, in New Orleans."

Almost compulsively, Ginny said, through lips that were suddenly stiff,

"And—and he—my—"

"Your father, your *real* father, my dearest child, was the Tsarevitch at that time. He is now the Tsar of Russia."

Something in the pedantic, almost satisfied, way in which the Count made this pronouncement made Ginny sit up straighter, seized with a sense of unreality, of disbelief.

"Oh, no! No! I've listened to you—I've tried not to interrupt—but that is really too much for me, for anyone to grasp! You cannot just appear in my life after all these years and inform me calmly that my father is not my father, that I—that I'm illegitimate, and my real father is. . . . No, it's quite impossible! And whatever your motives are in telling me this wild fairy tale, Count Chernikoff, I can only imagine that—"

"My child, hush!"

With a strength that was quite surprising in an elderly man who had complained of the rigors of his long journey here from the coast, the Count now leaned forward and grasped both of Ginny's shaking hands in his own, holding her firmly when she would have torn them from his grasp and leaped to her feet. Now he continued in a sterner, more resonant voice.

"You must listen—hear me out! Your father could not possibly have followed the dictates of his own heart and married Genevieve, although that was exactly what he wanted to do, he was so madly in love! *His* father would not permit it—and neither would her family. What a scandal it would have caused, what a disaster to Russia! No—Alexander went back to Russia when he was practically forced to do so, and eventually he married the Princess to whom he had even then been betrothed. But he never forgot his first love. Do you know that he still has a miniature of her that he carries with him at all times? He was made to think that Genevieve had found contentment in America, if not happiness—all attempts to find out about her, through your Aunt Celine, were met with the same words: 'Genevieve's happy—leave her alone, for her own sake!' What could we do? It was only by accident that I happened to learn, myself, of your mother's flight to France, with you—and that she had died so young."

"But—oh, God . . . even as a child, I wondered why

Maman was always so pale, so unhappy! I used to—to make up stories about some mystery in her life and wonder why she left papa, but they told me I had a romantic imagination."

The Count sighed heavily, and his grasp of Ginny's hands became more gentle, even comforting.

"They did what they thought was best for *your* interests, child! As I did what I thought was best for my friend, who is now my Emperor. You see, I did not tell him until much later what I, as a physician, had discovered at once—that Genevieve was pregnant. With you. It was your Tante Celine I told—for I had already been ordered to bring the Tsarovitch back to Russia, or face exile to Siberia forever. *She* knew what had to be done, and it *was* done. It was only much later that I confessed to Alexander that Genevieve had given him a daughter. And let me tell you, child," he added with a smile, "it has been quite a job to find you! The Secret Police of two countries—even your Pinkerton men in America—and at last, we heard rumors that you were, or had been, a member of the unfortunate Maximilian's court here. So you see. . . ."

This time she did manage to withdraw her hands from his grasp, and now Ginny was staring at him with the eyes of a hunted animal.

"No—no, I don't see! It has been a shock—yes, I'm still not quite recovered from all that you have told me; I can't comprehend any of it—but after all, what is it to me *now*? You could have let me be in peace. Why have you come here at all? What do you expect me to do?"

As if he hadn't heard her breathless speech, the Count continued to gaze piercingly at Ginny, just as he had earlier.

"But you are so much like her! It's almost uncanny, the resemblance! And yet—yes, I can see something of your father in you as well! Your mother's chin was small and pointed—you have determination in yours, and a tiny cleft. And your cheekbones are Russian, yes, even the slanting of your eyes."

"But I still do not see what my looks have to do with this! I am like my mother, everyone has told me so, but what is the point of it all? Why did you have to tell me all this?"

She was almost sobbing with shock, and with a creeping, insidious kind of fear. She didn't want to hear any more; she wouldn't, she mustn't listen!

"Surely you must realize why?" The old Count's voice was inexorable, his eyes had grown harder, and he frowned at her now. "Why do you think I am here? Why do you think I was ordered to accompany the Prince Sahrkanov on his mission to America? Your father wants to see you."

Chapter Five

"Your father wants to see you. . . ."

The words continued to beat in Ginny's ears, repeating themselves over and over during the course of that strange, strained evening.

"My dear child" the Count insisted on calling her, and in spite of her heated protests, in spite of her vehement and sometimes angry repudiation of the strange facts he had insisted upon relating to her, he continued to smile at her benignly and a trifle paternally, and to call her "child."

He wanted her to go back to Russia with him—he was insane, obviously! He spoke to her of duty and obligations, of her descent from royalty; and worse still, he brushed aside with a lift of his eyebrow, her heated reminders that she was married.

"But my child—how could you get yourself married without your father's consent? Your *legal* guardian is, of course, the Senator William Brandon. Didn't you know that he was so full of rage when he learned from a certain French Colonel of your marriage to a—if I may be frank, a completely unsuitable person, a *Mexican*, that he had the marriage annulled of course!"

"But—" she felt as if she were drowning in a sea of soft cotton wool, and her voice rose desperately—"but I wrote to him, I told him—"

"Ah, yes, you told him this Señor Alvarado is from a

good family. Nevertheless, he has had the marriage annulled."

"He can't do it! I'm twenty-one years of age!"

"But obviously, child, you were not twenty-one yet when you contracted your present alliance. Come, don't you realize what you're being offered? You're a Princess. Even if your father cannot acknowledge you openly as his daughter, there are other arrangements that can be made. He desires to provide for you, to see you have everything. By his own decree, you are now entitled to call yourself the Princess Xenia Alexandrovna Romanov, and wait until you see the magnificent estate which is yours! It's not very far from the Tsar's summer palace. And, of course, you'll have a magnificent income of your own. Needless to say," he added, preventing Ginny from protesting again by the quickness of his words, "Senator Brandon does not need to know the *real* facts. We decided that it was better for him not to know. He only knows that the Prince Sahrkanov has expressed his desire to make you his wife, and he has already given his consent."

"Oh, no!" This time she did spring to her feet, before he could prevent her. "Count Chernikoff, I meant every word I said earlier. I'm no silly, spiritless European miss who will let herself be ordered around, and have her life nicely arranged for her; it's too late for that! I don't care what anyone has to say—either of my fathers, for that matter! I am married, and I intend to stay married. I don't believe any high-handed annulment will stand up in a court *here*! And even if I am *not* legally married according to your laws, then I'd rather be the mistress of the man I love than be a princess and be married off to a man I loathe already!"

"Think about it, my child. You'll change your mind, I'm sure. And no one, I promise you, will attempt to force you into a marriage you dislike! But suppose your—er—husband decides that you ought to go? Suppose *he* can be persuaded to release you from your marriage?"

"My husband is not very easily persuaded into doing something he does not want to do!"

"Ah? Well, as I've said—think about it, Princess."

She refused to think about it, and said so, but the Count merely smiled and said she was naturally suffering from shock. It must not spoil their dinner, and the rest of the evening.

"And as for the rest of it, we'll see—we'll see," he said soothingly, still talking to her as if she had been behaving like a sullen, ungrateful child.

"But I must go home tonight. I don't intend to spend the night here," she said sharply, and he gave her a rather reproachful look.

"My dear Princess, did you for a moment imagine I had some wild scheme cooked up to have you abducted? Please—do not think it! The Tsar, in spite of our long friendship, would have me dispatched directly to Siberia if you were to be harmed in any way!"

Count Chernikoff came somewhat stiffly to his feet, holding out his hand to her.

"Come, won't you forgive me for sounding a trifle autocratic? As you say, I'm not used to customs and manners in this new world—nor the independence of its young ladies! Still, you are a Russian princess, whether you'll have it or not, and, as such, won't you accept an old man's arm? We'll talk at dinner, and I'll tell you more about Russia. Perhaps you'll decide on your own that you might like to visit us."

Because she did not know what else to do, and because she *was* after all still shocked and dumbfounded at what he had told her, Ginny accepted his arm at last, and went into the house with him.

True to his word, Count Chernikoff kept his conversation to trivialities and descriptions of life in Russia, but Ginny would have felt less on edge if she had not been seated next to the Prince, and had not been conscious of his speculative gaze upon her all through the meal. For him, she felt nothing but contempt and anger. What kind of a man was he? First, thinking her a soldadera, he had tried to pick her up outside the church at Guadalupe. And all the time, he had come here to meet the illegitimate daughter of his Tsar—he had actually had the effrontery to ask Senator Brandon for her hand in marriage, without even having met her!

After dinner was over, to keep from hurting Colonel Adiego's feelings, Ginny consented to join the men on the patio for a few short moments; but soon after they had done so, she was sorry, for Count Chernikoff made a point of monopolizing the Colonel's conversation, giving the Prince a chance to lean close to Ginny, his strange eyes smiling into hers.

"So—he told you, and now you are angry with me!"

"Of course I am, what else did you expect? How could you possibly be so deceitful? I don't believe you really need a translator at all, you just wanted—"

"But I *do* need a translator. Few of these people speak English. And then, you see, I fell in love with your portrait, before I had even seen you. I even recognized you without recognizing you, as paradoxical as it sounds—in the church. Do you remember?"

Her eyes flashed at him angrily.

"I remember too well! And then you had to bring me here to listen to—to this story I would much rather *not* have ever heard!" She went on, in a low, angry voice, "Why can I not be left in peace? Why won't anyone believe that I'm happy here, and that I love my husband?"

"But if you do, ma petite, then how will it hurt your marriage if you were to visit Russia? I won't force myself on you—but perhaps, some day, in surroundings that better suit your beauty and your breeding, you might come to realize—"

"To realize what?"

He gave her a grin that was somehow both mocking and promising.

"Who knows? But in all the fairy tales, does not the princess always meet her prince? Commoners, my lovely princess, are not the only men with strong backs and thighs."

The true impact of his statement took some time to penetrate, and then Ginny felt her cheeks burning.

"Why you—you are insufferable!"

"Why do you call me so? Because I am honest with you, and speak to you without insinuations, but directly? Don't disappoint me, I had taken you for a femme de monde! Will you deny that your husband has not been the only man in your life? They called you the loveliest courtesan in Mexico City, did they not? And with reason—ah yes, with reason!"

His eyes seemed to burn into her flesh, and she remembered the eyes of other men who had looked at her in the same way, as if they wanted to devour her. He had dropped his mask at last, this Russian prince; and although his words seemed designed to insult and annoy her, his eyes gave him away. He desired her—and his desire for her made him a man, like any other man. Why should she let his words have their intended effect? She had coped with men and their lusts before.

Ginny's eyes had grown cold and hard as she returned Prince Ivan's look. They narrowed slightly, and the annoyed tightening of her lips reminded him, for an instant, of a panther, ready to spring.

Because the Prince was a man who liked a challenge above all things, he exulted, and a smile twisted his lips for an instant. What a lovely creature she was! And especially when she was furious. . . . No, the picture he had seen in her aunt's house, one her cousin had painted of her when she was only sixteen, did not do her justice at all. She should have been painted as a gypsy, with her hair flowing wild and untrammelled down her back, as it had been the night he watched her dancing.

The first flush of rage had begun to fade from Ginny's cheeks, and now, without dropping her eyes from those of the Prince, she slowly took a sip of the sweet liqueur that the Count had produced from his baggage.

"You seem to know a great deal about me! Why did you go to all the trouble? And after all, considering the life I've led, I'm sure my—your Emperor can be persuaded that his bastard daughter is really not at all fit to be a princess, or to be presented to him! Why disappoint so many people?"

He gave a short, almost delighted laugh.

"So! You are now carrying the battle into my territory, are you? No, indeed, I haven't been wrong about you! You're a real woman, and you're not ashamed to admit it, are you? I like that—in fact I am beginning to like everything about you, more and more."

She gave him a cool, almost derisive look.

"That's of no consequence to me, I'm afraid—and since you prefer honesty, dear sir, I'm sorry to say, but there is nothing I like about *you*."

She could see the almost imperceptible hardening of his eyes, although his lips continued to smile.

"Perhaps you will change your mind some day! But to

me, your—indifference, shall we say, only makes you more delightful! An ivory tower to be conquered."

"There is no need for conquest, Prince Sahrkanov, since I've already surrendered willingly to the man I happen to love."

"Pah! Women and their talk of love! And what is this love except lust in disguise? Women must rationalize, I suppose, but men, at least, are more direct." Suddenly, he was leaning forward, his eyes burning into hers. "I desire you more than I have ever desired any woman in my life. If that is what you like to call 'love,' then I am in love with you. And I will have you."

Although she had risen to her feet and swept away from the Prince in icy disdain following his last words, which had sounded ominously like a threat—Ginny could not help the fear that began to creep over her afterwards.

"I will have you!" Why? Why did he want her? Was it because he had expected her to be overjoyed at the thought of being a princess, and would therefore fall into his arms with gratitude because he had, in a way, been responsible for the stunning revelation? Or was it only because he wanted her and was the kind of man who could not stand being thwarted? The frightening thing was that she sensed something about the man—something threatening, almost evil. Or was she only imagining things?

Ginny had walked over to join the Count and Colonel Adiego, and the respect that both men showed her made her feel somehow stronger, and almost ashamed of her earlier feeling of blind fear. She was being nonsensical! What could Prince Sahrkanov do, after all? She would simply tell General Díaz that she did not choose to be the Prince's interpreter any longer—because he had indicated in no uncertain terms that his intentions toward her were hardly honorable. . . . That was all she had to do.

"Please excuse me for interrupting, gentlemen," she said charmingly, "but, it *is* getting rather late, is it not?"

"Too late for you to travel back to Guadalupe *now*, señora!" The Colonel looked genuinely concerned. "Please, surely you will be comfortable spending the night as my guest. I have rooms set aside for you, and there is a woman to attend the señora."

"And, of course, we will leave extremely early in the

morning, I promise you that!" The Prince had sauntered
up behind Ginny. "You're surely not afraid I'll do anything as crude as attempt to rape you?" he added softly in
French, although Count Chernikoff frowned at him re-
provingly.

"I do not care for being deceived!" Ginny snapped
sharply in the same language. It was only out of consideration for Colonel Adiego's worried expression that she
forced a smile soon afterwards.

"You are very kind, Colonel. As it happens, I am rather
fatigued. So, if you gentlemen will excuse me. . . ."

"And while our kind host is seeing to your accommodations, you will take a turn about these beautiful gardens
with me?" Prince Sahrkanov's voice was suave, polite.
"There are some inscriptions in Spanish on the sundial that
intrigue me, and the moonlight is bright enough so that
you should have no trouble deciphering them. Please?"

The Colonel and Count Chernikoff had already risen to
their feet, and before Ginny realized what was happening,
the Prince's hand had closed over her elbow. Short of
making a scene, there was nothing she could do but allow
herself to be lead by him; but the rage she tried to contain
within herself made her almost breathless, so that she did
not feel herself capable of uttering a single word until they
were already out of earshot of the others.

"How the moonlight changes and softens everything! It's
difficult to imagine that there's a war going on not so
many miles away from here, don't you agree, mademoiselle?"

But Ginny was in no mood for pleasantries, especially
those uttered in a wheedling tone, overlaid with the false
politeness that she had learned to distrust coming from
this man.

"I am not a mademoiselle, and you had no right to drag
me out here with you in such an autocratic fashion! Must
I remind you, sir, that I—"

She felt his grip on her elbow tighten.

"You are going to repeat again that you are a married
woman, and then I would have to remind you that you
must no longer think of yourself as such. But don't worry,
the fact that you have been the mistress, not wife, of this
man you declare yourself so much in love with is of no
consequence to me. Rather, I admire you for your—loy-

alty. In fact, I find you admirable in many ways, *mademoiselle*."

His slight, mocking emphasis on the last word made Ginny suck in her breath, almost speechless with fury. And yet, some warning voice in her brain cautioned her to be calm. This man was deliberately trying to provoke her, to force her into some display of emotion that would put her at a disadvantage.

The orange torchlight that had illuminated the patio had faded from sight now, and the moon seemed to cast an opalescent, milky-white glow everywhere, deadening all the bright flower colors of the daytime and creating instead illusions of shadow and lightness. The white stones of the crazy-paved path gleamed under their feet, and the perfume of jasmine and gardenia seemed to hang heavily in the still air. A romantic night, under any other circumstances, but Ginny was in no mood for romance. Reason told her that the Prince would not dare harm her in any way, but all the same, without reason, she was afraid— and she would not, on any account, show it!

"You said you wanted me to translate an inscription on a sundial," she said in a cold voice. "Hadn't you better show me where it is? It's getting rather chilly out here."

"Would you like me to keep you warm?" His words held an undercurrent of laughter. "Or can it be that you are a little bit afraid of me?" he added cunningly.

Her lips tightening, Ginny faced him on the narrow path, pulling her elbows from his grasp.

"Do I have reason to fear you?"

The moon was behind him, and his face seemed shadowed, almost sinister, as he bent his head, putting one finger under her chin to tilt her face up to his.

"No reason at all. Did I not make that clear to you earlier? I mean to make you my wife."

Angrily, Ginny struck at his hand and found her wrist imprisoned.

"Whatever it is you're playing at, you go too far! Why pick on me? There must be plenty of other women who would be only too willing to oblige you, if a wife is what you're looking for! And now, will you please take me back inside?"

Her eyes looked angrily into his, and had she but known it, the moonlight, falling on her face, seemed to emphasize

their gypsy slant, and the faint hollows beneath her
cheekbones. Her hair seemed to reflect the light with a life
of its own, and Prince Ivan Sahrkanov, a man of wide experience and somewhat jaded appetites, felt his pulse
quicken in spite of all the cold detachment he prided himself upon. She was quite lovely! And more than that, a
challenge. He had not expected such resistance from her.
From conversations with her aunt in Paris, and the Senator and his wife, he had expected a biddable girl—a trifle
headstrong perhaps, or even, after all the sordid experiences she had been through, slightly hardened. A woman
who had been a courtesan. But he had expected her, after
some token resistance, to jump at the opportunity that was
being offered her. Instead she continued to resist, and to
pretend a coldness that he was sure was only a surface
veneer. Ivan Sahrkanov prided himself on being an excellent judge of both horseflesh and women, and he had begun to think that this particular woman would only yield
to a man who proved himself her master.

His fingers tightened around her wrist almost cruelly, as
if he meant to test her strength. Good! He could see her
wince almost imperceptibly, but she did not cry out. Instead she became very stiff, her voice contemptuous.

"Will you let me go?"

He smiled, beginning to enjoy himself.

"In a moment. And with regret. But I think we ought
to get to know each other a little better, you and I. It is
such a beautiful night—made for lovers, and for delicious
intrigues. Come, surely you are not as cold and unmoved
as you pretend to be." He was drawing her toward him as
he spoke, his voice a silky murmur. "How hard you try to
pull away from me! Can it be that it is your own
passionate nature you are afraid of? A kiss in the moonlight, what harm can there be in that—especially since we
are an engaged couple?"

"You're insane!"

Still holding her wrist, he had put his arm about her waist,
and now, as he began to kiss her, Ginny's first impulse was
to struggle wildly. But some sixth sense told her that this
was what he hoped for, so that he could force her into
submission and thus prove his own superior strength. And
so, her body remaining stiff and unyielding in his embrace,
she merely endured the pressure of his lips on hers, keep-

ing her eyes wide open and staring contemptuously into his until, at last, he released her.

Deliberately, she wiped the back of her hand across her lips, sensing his anger, and suddenly unafraid of it.

"Now that you've had your stolen kiss in the moonlight, will you excuse me, Your Highness? It's been a tedious day, and I would like to retire."

Chapter Six

In spite of the luxurious appointments of the large room she had been shown to, and the big, soft bed, Ginny passed a restless and uneasy night. She could not forget the look on Ivan Sahrkanov's face when she had left him, and in spite of all her rationalizing she could not prevent the feeling of apprehension that stayed with her afterwards.

In retrospect, the evening that had just passed seemed unreal. Her being here, Count Chernikoff's ominous, shocking disclosure, and worst of all, that detestable Prince's air of self-assurance when he had spoken with such certainty of making her his wife. How could this be happening to her? She was married to Steve—to Steve! They loved each other. . . . But Count Chernikoff had told her that the marriage had been annulled, and she had learned already that the Prince was not only influential but forceful and used to getting his own way as well. And where *was* Steve? Why did he stay away so long?

There were dark smudges beneath Ginny's eyes the next morning, and she was relieved that the journey back to Guadalupe was accomplished in virtual silence, with Count Chernikoff sharing the small carriage with her, and the Prince riding beside it.

Tactfully, the Count indulged only in occasional small talk, resting with his head back and his eyes closed for the most part, having apologized to Ginny for being such bad company.

"I'm getting to be an old man, I suppose! I find that travelling tires me. You'll excuse me, child?"

Today the Prince's face was inscrutable, his manner towards her unchanged. But Ginny was far too conscious of his eyes upon her to be comfortable. If only the journey would be over quickly! She could not wait to get back to her own small room—to find General Díaz as quickly as she could afterwards and tell him what an impossible situation she now found herself in. He would understand—she would make him understand! And she would beg him to send for Steve. . . .

However, by the time that Ginny had finally gained the haven of her own room, it seemed as if everything, even fate itself, had turned against her.

Disdaining the hand that the Prince offered her, she had almost fallen out of the small carriage in her haste to be alone again. To Count Chernikoff she had bid a hurried, polite farewell, promising that she would visit him soon— yes, the very next day, if the General would give her leave. She had already determined that she would put an end to all the nonsense about her "duty" and "obligations" as the Tsar of Russia's daughter. It wasn't true—it was all a fairy tale, and she refused to be taken in by it. She would make it clear that she had no intention of leaving Mexico, no matter what they said, and as soon as they saw that she was adamant they would have to leave her alone.

Not wanting to face the usual crowd that frequented the cantina below, Ginny made her way up the back stairs to her room, sighing with relief as she pushed open the rough wooden door and walked inside.

And then, as she looked around her, a stunned, numbing feeling made her gasp out loud, leaning against the door for support. Steve's clothes, his saddlebags, everything that had belonged to him was gone, leaving the room empty-looking and bleak. "But it can't be—it can't!" she muttered feverishly. "Not last night, of all nights—and he wouldn't have gone without waiting for me, without leaving some word for me!"

Her eyes traveled about the room, looking for something, for some sign, while she began to tell herself that some thief must have broken in—it had to be that, of course!

But *her* belongings were all still in place, and the only other sign that someone had been here in her absence was a crumpled piece of paper, lying on her pillow.

Slowly, like a woman in a dream, Ginny walked over to pick it up, smoothing the closely written sheet between her fingers. Oh God! Of all things, it was a letter from Carl Hoskins, addressed to her—it was full of recriminations, of jealousy; he accused her of throwing him over for the Prince.

"He makes it sound as if I'd deliberately led him on," Ginny thought sickly. "As if we'd been lovers." And Steve—Steve had read it, and left it here for her to find. Oh no! She wanted to scream aloud, and found herself pressing her clenched fists against her lips like a child stifling sobs.

Like a pendulum, her mind went from shock to desperation, from determination to despair. For some time, she could hardly believe it was true. Steve loved her. They had found a new confidence in each other. He had sworn he could not live without her. It wasn't possible that he could have left her stranded and alone so callously! And yet, as days passed, and Ginny could find no comfort anywhere, it seemed as if that was exactly what he had done.

Even those whom she had considered her friends seemed to have become aloof, with no help to offer her. Carl Hoskins was in the hospital, as a result of a fight he had had with Steve, and suddenly, it seemed, everyone was agreed that she should leave Mexico and return to her father.

Colonel Felix Díaz, the General's brother, came closest to being frank with the distraught young woman.

"Listen, niña, why don't you play a waiting game? Thank God I'm not married—I don't think I could stand the strain! How am I to tell you in what ways a jealous man's mind can work? All I know is that Esteban was here, and against orders at that. By the time I spoke to him, he was too angry to reason with. And that was after he had gone recklessly to visit Colonel Green. I tried to explain, but he did not seem ready to listen. 'I understand that we are not legally married,' he said. 'You can wish her better luck with her latest fiancé.' And believe me, little one, if I did not think that you are not only strong enough but intelligent enough not to fly into hysterics, I would not repeat his words." He added, consolingly, "Of course, he said so in a jealous rage. Sooner or later, when he's had time to cool down, I'm sure he'll regret his impetuosity. But in the meantime. . . ." Colonel Díaz stroked his chin thoughtfully. "I must admit that we are all very anxious to get rid of this Russian Prince. He's been a troublemaker ever since he arrived here."

What even Colonel Díaz was trying to tell her, of course, in the nicest way possible, was that she should go back to the United States, like the prodigal daughter. Prince Sahrkanov had told Colonel Green that Senator Brandon had had her marriage annulled—he had even written to President Juarez himself. And, like one of Shakespeare's smiling villains, Ivan waited for Ginny to succumb to circumstances and give in.

To make matters even worse, it appeared that Carl Hoskins had seen and recognized Steve that night. They had actually had a run-in, at one of the local cantinas.

It was Dolores Bautista who whispered it to Ginny, her great, dark eyes full of pity and concern.

"Please—you will not tell anyone? Manolo would beat me if he knew I had come to talk to you. When he told me what happened—he was there, you see—he made me promise to keep it to myself. But Doña Genia, I know how much you love Esteban! I think that there are certain persons who are trying to make trouble for you, and would like to see you kept apart."

Ginny herself had already reached this conclusion, but she kept silent, merely biting her lip and nodding. And after a while, with another pitying look, Dolores took up the story she had begun.

"Well—Esteban was very angry, of course, when he came here and found you gone. He came down to the camp, and his face was like a thundercloud! I think he had just come from seeing the American Colonel, and ... I should not have listened, I suppose, but I heard him tell my man that he had learned he was no longer a married man, and that he had been ordered to make sure you were returned safely to your father. What else he said I do not know, for just then Manolo shouted for me to fetch the jug, and then Esteban suggested that they should both have a few drinks at the cantina."

The cantina that Dolores referred to was, of course, the

same one over which Ginny had her room—a place much frequented by the American Legionnaires of late, Ginny recalled bitterly. And Carl, no doubt, had been waiting and watching for her return; or had he already learned what she herself had been the last to find out—that it had been planned, all along, that she and the Prince were to spend the night at Cuernevaca?

During the past few days, Ginny had found herself growing almost numb with misery, but now Dolores' stumbling, hesitant voice brought back all the pain she had been trying to push away from her consciousness. Yes—unfortunately, she could just imagine how it must have happened, although Dolores was reluctant to put into words the exact nature of Carl Hoskins' ugly comments.

He had already been angry when he had written her that long and garbled letter, and by the time that Steve walked in, he'd had several drinks. To see the one man, of all men, that he hated most, and to realize that he had been deliberately misled by Ginny must have been the last straw as far as Carl was concerned.

Words had been exchanged, Dolores said. The American Capitan had turned red in the face, and had immediately begun making loud and provocative remarks to some of his friends. And—yes, Dolores had to admit miserably—those ugly comments had to do with Ginny. The man had actually hinted that he had been one of her lovers, and that the Russian Prince was her latest "friend."

"Are you sure he stopped at that?" Ginny could not help interjecting bitterly. "I think I've learned enough about Captain Hoskins' temperament to guess that he would have gone much further! Please don't try to spare my feelings, Dolores. Don't you see that I must know exactly what he said to make Esteban so furious that he—he would leave without so much as a message for me?"

It was all she could do to try and remain calm. Why did Steve have to pick that particular night on which to return? And why did he have to run into Carl, of all people?

Dolores Bautista dropped her head, picking at a corner of her torn skirt. It was clear she didn't want to go on, but at last she admitted, in a low voice, that the American had been insulting. Not only had he said many unpleasant and defamatory things about Doña Genia, but Carl had grown bolder when Steve had ignored his loud-voiced comments, and had started to taunt him, while Carl's friends laughed loudly and added ribald remarks of their own.

"And then? What happened?"

"Esteban hit him. Manolo told me it was all he could do to keep him from killing the gringo with his hands. He said that a little war between the gringos and our own men might have started up right then if one of the other American officers, who was not as drunk as the rest, had not intervened." Dolores raised her eyes to Ginny's, and they were filled with tears. "Oh, Doña Genia! Whatever will you do now?"

It was a question that Ginny had already asked herself, over and over. What was she to do? What *could* she do? She had never felt so completely alone and cut off from friends and support as she did now. When she lay alone in the bed that she had shared with Steve, she stared at the ceiling, feeling unreality smother her. How could it be possible that within the space of a few hours her whole life could be changed so drastically, that she could find herself torn from the heights of happiness and dreamy contentment and thrown to the depths of pain and despair? But it was in vain that she tried to tell herself she was merely having some kind of nightmare from which she would soon awaken to find things exactly as they had been before. And she had almost given up hoping that even now Steve might relent enough to get in touch with her.

"He loved me! Yes, I am sure of it. How can he cut himself off from feeling so suddenly? Isn't he human?"

Most hurtful of all was the realization that Steve did not trust her. Perhaps he never had.

Feeling like a sleepwalker, Ginny forced herself to move through the days. There were no more duties for her in General Díaz' busy headquarters, although she learned that more and more prisoners were being taken daily, most of them deserters from the Imperial army. She no longer went down to the camp. What right did she have to be there *now*? And beside, Dolores had told her that Manuela, always jealous, had been whispering to the other women, tossing her head, saying that she had always known Genia was a slut, for all her surface virtue.

Ginny found herself spending the majority of the time that now hung so heavily on her hands in the company of

Count Chernikoff. Listening to him talk about her mother made Ginny wonder wryly if they were both cursed—finding love only to lose it. Poor Genevieve, they had always said. And now it was poor Ginny.

For the day or two that followed her return from Cuernevaca, Ginny had been almost beside herself, her grief and hysteria making her storm violently at the Prince, who had been the cause of it all.

He had merely listened to her tirade with raised eyebrows, and the knowing, rather supercilious smile she had come to recognize too well.

"My dear mademoiselle! Although you are exceptionally lovely when you are in a rage, I must ask you to be reasonable. How was I to know that your—er—lover would choose to return so clandestinely on the very night I chose for your meeting with Count Chernikoff? You might as well blame President Juarez himself!" And he added, with a purring undertone to his words that immediately started her heart beating faster, "Shall I tell the President how annoyed you are? I shall be leaving for San Luis the day after tomorrow, on an errand for my Emperor. You know there's talk that the unfortunate Prince Maximilian will be executed? I understand that at least half the crowned heads of Europe are vastly concerned."

"I—I don't want you to say anything to the President!" Ginny burst out. Had he been threatening her in an oblique way? "Why should you mention my name to him at all?"

"But he's sure to ask me if I found you. I understand your estimable father and my good friend has been sending cables to everyone in his efforts to locate you. President Juarez will, I am sure, be glad to know that you are safe." He paused calculatedly and said softly, "Shall I make some effort to locate this hot-headed man who's caused you so much unhappiness, lovely one? I'm sure it won't be too difficult. Colonel Green had it from General Díaz—who was quite annoyed, by the way; it appears he sets some store by Major Alvarado—that the good Major is now attached to the President's staff, and has been sent to help patrol the border. A dangerous assignment. Those Yaqui Indians are fierce, I'm told, and if it's true he's actually an American outlaw with a price on his head, he might have trouble with bounty hunters as well. It's too bad—but then, you won't want to be bothered by him any longer, will you? Not with a man who would believe the vile aspersions cast on a loyal and faithful woman—such as you've shown yourself to be."

Whirling on her heels, unable to bear any more veiled insinuations, Ginny had run from the room, hearing his soft, mocking laughter follow her.

"I'll never marry him!" she stormed to Count Chernikoff later. "Even if I am forced to go back to my father, Prince Sahrkanov is the last man on earth I would consider. I wish with all my heart that you had both left me alone!"

But the Count insisted on treating her like a recalcitrant child who did not know her own mind. *His* mission was to persuade her to go to Russia, and the Prince could do his own courting.

When they met again, Ivan Sahrkanov's manner was as inscrutable as if nothing had passed between them; and Ginny, ashamed of her lack of control, pretended that she was completely unconcerned by his threats.

Now, with the days slipping by far too slowly, and the prospect of an outright attack on Mexico City becoming more and more imminent, Ginny began to wish, feverishly, that something would happen to save her. Strange that "save" was the word that sprang into her mind. They were all taking it for granted that she meant to leave Mexico as soon as the Prince returned—even the General, who shook his head with something like regret showing for an instant in his eyes.

"I shall be sorry to see you go, and I apologize for being, inadvertantly, the cause of the—um—trouble with Esteban. But I'm sure he'll find you as soon as the fighting's over; he would be crazy if he did not. However, I'll not be sorry to see the Russian leave. The man's a born intriguer!" A note of annoyance hardened the General's voice. "I understand he's hinted to el Presidente that I treat our European prisoners too leniently."

Carl Hoskins and this wretched Prince have ruined my life, Ginny thought dully. Suddenly like an echo out of the past she thought she had put behind her forever came the thought: "It doesn't matter . . . I've withstood much worse and survived. The pain will go away after a while."

But could she forget? She had too much time in which

to think, and to torture herself with suppositions. This was one of the reasons why Ginny had taken to spending so much time with the old Count, who, in his way, was a charming and interesting man, with old-fashioned manners and fascinating tales of his extensive travels. He told her a great deal about the Tsar Alexander—Ginny could not, somehow, manage to think of such a remote personage as her father! And yet, she did not know quite what her feelings were towards William Brandon. She hardly knew him, of course, and all her girlish admiration for him as a strong and intelligent man had somehow been dissipated over the months that had passed since she had seen him last. What was his connection with Ivan Sahrkanov? Why had he given his consent to her marriage with a man she had not even met at the time? It seemed as if he were only too anxious to get her off his hands, in spite of his apparent concern for her well-being.

"Come with me to Russia!" Count Chernikoff said constantly. "We'll visit San Francisco first, and you shall spend as much time as you wish there. I believe Prince Sahrkanov has some business there; and he desires to remain in the United States until your Senate has ratified the purchase of Alaska. But after that is all taken care of— surely a change of atmosphere will do you good? Visit Europe again—your uncle and aunt in Paris. And afterwards, once you have seen Russia, who knows? You might wish to make your home there after all."

He made it clear to her, in a subtle way, that he'd been astounded to see in what fashion she had chosen to live. Following a Mexican army! Living like a peasant, among peasants! Unthinkable! She belonged in a glittering, sophisticated society with the finest of jewels and gowns. And, he hinted, a husband who would do justice to her exalted position—a man of rich and impeccable background.

She supposed he was right. Once her first, acute feelings of misery and frustration had lessened, leaving only a dull ache, she became determined to cling to her pride, at least. What else did she have left to console her? Since Steve had managed to turn his back on her without a qualm, she would force herself to forget him. Jealousy was no excuse for the way in which he'd acted, and if he'd felt his pride at stake—why couldn't he have considered *her* feelings for a change?

So Ginny found herself waiting with what was almost resignation for the Prince's return from San Luis. Once he arrived, they could leave. Yes, she had made up her mind to make everyone happy by getting herself obligingly out of the way.

She had dinner with Count Chernikoff one evening early in June, and discovered that the Prince was expected at any time.

"I had almost hoped he would arrive in time to join us for dinner," the old man told her. "Perhaps the rain has delayed him."

Ginny followed the direction of his eyes and saw the dark clouds that seemed to pile up over each other and darken even while she watched through the open window. She shivered slightly, and made some comment about how comfortable and attractive the Count had made what had been a bare room in the small house that had once belonged to a Mexico City merchant.

"Ah, yes—when one is used to a certain degree of comfort, and is as used to travelling as I am, it's not difficult to know exactly what to pack. My valet is a wonder." Then he gave her a piercing look from beneath his bushy eyebrows and added, "He's already started to pack up again. We should be ready to depart in a day or so, and I must admit I will be relieved."

She forced herself to ask, "Is there any news about the—the Emperor?"

"You mean Maximilian Von Hapsburg? Ah—a sad affair! The poor, misguided man, he should have known when that upstart Louis Napoleon revoked the Treaty of Miramar what would happen in the end." Seeing her expression, he added in a kindly voice, "I'm sorry, my child—you knew him, did you not? Well—who knows what the President of this barbarous country will decide to do in the end. Perhaps he'll let him off. At any rate, we'll hear when Ivan gets back. And now, please enjoy your dinner. It's not much—but my chef has received compliments from the Emperor himself. He'll be desolated if you don't do justice to the meal he has produced."

Chapter Seven

Ginny had made herself eat, and even to respond to the Count's banter. But in spite of all her efforts, her mood of depression remained, made deeper by the black rain clouds that had by now gathered ominously overhead.

Rain. She had seen the violent rain showers in this part of the world—had felt their slashing fury. The rain would come pouring down, turning the dusty earth to mud, and then the sun would shine again and bake it dry. This was Mexico, and she would be leaving it soon, putting a whole segment of her life behind her.

Count Chernikoff had not pressed her to stay longer because of the impending storm, and had sent her back in his own hired carriage to the room that she hated by now, because of its impersonal loneliness.

A wind had sprung up, and Ginny pulled her shawl more closely around her shoulders. Distant shafts of lightning laced through the dark clouds, followed by a soft rumbling of thunder. So they were to have a storm—in June. How unpredictable the weather was here! Just as unpredictable as the turn her own circumstances had taken.

Ginny directed the driver of the carriage to the back door of the cantina where she insisted upon staying, in spite of Count Chernikoff's protests. She sprang down as soon as the rather shaky vehicle had been drawn to a halt.

"It's all right, there's no need to get down. At least we've missed the rain so far. Gracias," she added quickly, pulling the shawl over her head as she tugged open the door.

Sounds of music and raucous laughter drifted to her ears. The cantina was doing a roaring business as usual, and the noise would keep her awake for half the night. Ginny did not quite know why she had insisted upon remaining here—unless it was the feeling that she was, in some way, preserving some sort of independence. Suddenly she felt very tired. Why did she bother? She would be returning to America in a few days, in the company of two men she hardly knew—one of whom she completely distrusted. By now, she had given up hope that Steve would have second thoughts and return. Hadn't Ivan Sahrkanov taken pleasure in informing her that he had a new assignment? A dangerous one. . . .Well, she mustn't let it matter to her. Steve was used to danger, he could look after himself. And she must stop thinking about him!

"Señorita . . . psst! Señorita!"

A ragged urchin, not more than ten years old, had sprung up from where he had sat crouched against the wall, to tug at her skirts.

"Señorita, please, you will not cry out? I am not supposed to be here, but I have a message for you. Look for a señorita with the color of fire in her hair, this man said to me. And he gave me two whole pesos. Señorita? You will listen?"

Ginny tried to still the sudden beating of her heart. A message? Perhaps this was what she had unconsciously been waiting for. Perhaps. . . .

"You had better come up to my room with me, muchacho," she said softly. "Come along. And perhaps I will give you another peso for your trouble."

His name, he informed her, was Bernado. And since his father had been killed in the fighting, he was the supporter of his mother and two sisters.

"I do all right," he boasted, staring curiously around the room. "I am big for my age, sí? The señor told me you would speak Mexican—as good as I do, he said. And the message was very urgent. Why else would he stop me on my way out of the church?" Bernado puffed out his chest importantly, proud that the lovely señorita hung on his words, her strange-colored eyes wide, and filled with some emotion he could not read. "He said—well, first he described you, and where I would find you. He said I was to wait, no matter how late you were getting back. And I was to tell you that you must come to the church. Alone, he said. And walking, with a rebozo over your hair, so that you could mix with the crowds. 'Tell her it is very important,' he said. 'I have news of Esteban. Tell her that.' "

Outside, the thunder rattled even more loudly than it had

done before, finding an echo in the sudden thudding of Ginny's pulse—the veins in her temples.

"This señor—what did he look like? Did he say nothing else?"

The boy frowned, shaking his head as if he tried to think.

"I could not see his face very well. It was dark, you see, and he wore a big hat and a serape. But I thought, maybe, that he might be an Americano. He was very tall, and he spoke with an accent. But he sounded very anxious, señorita. He said it was a matter of life or death—that you would understand. You must come to the church, he said—to the small door on the east side. It was dangerous for him to attempt to come here." The large, bright eyes that had been studying her face suddenly seemed to gleam. "Is this news worth another peso, do you think? We are very poor people, señorita. My mother, my sisters—"

She cut off his practiced beggar's whine with an abrupt gesture, handing him a peso from the reticule she wore looped over her wrist.

"Yes, it's worth it. Gracias, muchacho. And now, you had better run back home before the storm catches you. Hurry!"

But he hesitated, still watching her curiously.

"For another peso, Señorita, I will guide you to the church. You should not go out alone. There are many soldiers on the streets here, and these Americanos—pah! I do not trust them. They make me offers for my sister, and Rosita is only thirteen years old. You do not speak like a gringa, and you are kind. Shall I go with you? It's on my way."

In spite of her confused, feverish thoughts, Ginny rumpled his hair.

"You're very kind. But I know my way to the church, and it's getting so late."

But the look of offended pride she suddenly discerned in his dark eyes made her change her mind. The pride of the Spaniards! In spite of his tender years, this boy considered himself a man, and he was treating her with the inborn gallantry of the Latin male. And perhaps she could do with some company after all!

As if she had merely paused to think it over, Ginny

gave him a smile, and said consideringly, "But it *is* quite a distance to walk alone, after all, and if you're sure you won't mind, I shall be most grateful for your escort. If you'll be gallant enough to turn your head while I put on some clothes that would be more suitable for walking and will not draw too much attention, I'll try not to be too long!"

Leaving the gown she had just discarded tossed carelessly across her bed, Ginny found herself out on the street again, with Bernardo, his shoulders thrown back, staying close to her side.

She wore her oldest skirt and blouse, and a black rebozo wrapped tightly about her head and shoulders, making her indistinguishable from the few other women they encountered on the streets.

"Stay close to me," Bernardo advised in a whisper. "They will not bother you when they see you are with *me*. And if anyone stops us, we will say that you are my sister. You do not mind?"

"No. I'm glad you're with me," Ginny said, and she *was* glad of his company. It was black and windy, with the smell and the feel of rain in the air.

And they were, indeed, stopped several times by drunken, rowdy men who wanted a woman to keep them warm on a cold night such as this.

Bernardo took charge, eyeing them belligerently.

"No, no! Not tonight, señors. My sister is sick, and the doctor said it might be infectious. I am taking her home to our madre."

Grumbling, or cursing, they let them by, and Ginny made sure she kept her head lowered and her arms crossed modestly under her rebozo, as if she were actually ill, or unusually modest.

"You see?" Bernardo whispered triumphantly, "You did well not to come out alone."

She agreed. She must be mad, to venture out like this on the off chance that she might hear some news of Steve. It was quite a distance, and all uphill, to the church, and all the way she had to stop herself from running, in spite of the breathless pounding of her heart.

She prayed there was nothing wrong! That Steve had sent a message to her because he had had time to think about it, and see how ridiculously he had acted. How could she have ever imagined she could cut Steve out of her thoughts? No matter what she told herself, she could not stop loving him.

When the dark outline of the church loomed up before them at last, it had started to rain. Big, slow spatters of water, warning of the slashing downpour that was to follow. Not a soul was in sight; and although candlelight was shining through its narrow windows, the church seemed almost deserted.

"Are you *sure*?" Ginny whispered. "He said he would wait?"

"Sí, señorita! He said he'd be here, no matter how late it became." And then, with a slight hesitancy in his voice, Bernardo said, "Perhaps I should wait here, in the shadow of these trees. He said you were to come alone—perhaps he might not want to show himself if he saw us together. But I will wait here and make sure you are all right before I go back."

"Bernardo, you are a true gallant!" Ginny murmured, her voice almost breaking with the strain she was under. "Here—you deserve more than two pesos for your kindness, but it's all I brought with me. Have a good dinner— you and your family. And tell your madre from me that she has a son to be proud of."

For all her outward show of boldness, she was ridiculously comforted, knowing that the boy would remain watching. An Americano, he had said. A friend of Steve's? Or—Steve himself?

Unmindful of the rain that was now beating against her face and wetting her skirt and her shawl, Ginny walked quickly towards the church. How dark and deserted looking it was here! There were many trees growing thickly together on this side of the building, and beyond, as she knew, there lay nothing but an open stretch of land, bounded on the far side by a few deserted cottages. A good place for a clandestine meeting. No one used this entrance, which was once used by the nuns whose nearby convent was crumbling and almost in ruins now. It was the war, and the crisscrossing of opposing armies, that had given this side of the church its air of lonely desolation. The nuns had long ago removed themselves to a safer convent, and only rats and a few stray felines were left to sing their "aves" here.

Ginny had almost come abreast of the building when a tall, shadowy figure moved forward from the recessed doorway. Strong fingers seized her by the wrist.

"I must say you took your time getting here!"

"Steve!" She had opened her mouth to say his name, but now shock and a sudden feeling of terror made her gasp instead.

"Surprised?" His voice was a snarl, for all its deceptive softness. "Well, you shouldn't be. You and I have unfinished business to take care of, Ginny Brandon. Did you think I'd let you off so easily after all the dirty tricks you've pulled on me?"

"Carl," her voice cracked before she could force some strength into it, "Carl, what's the meaning of this? Haven't you done enough to ruin things for me? Let me go this instant!"

"Oh, no!" His hold tightened, and as she brought her other hand up instinctively, to strike at him, he caught it with a harsh laugh.

"Thought it was *him*, didn't you? Steve Morgan! How you must have laughed, thinking you'd pulled the wool over my eyes with all your talk of being married to a Mex officer—being happy and in love. Well, Morgan wasn't laughing when I got through telling him exactly what kind of a cheating, conniving little bitch you are!"

Panting, Ginny tried to break free, but with a vicious movement Carl tugged her off balance, pushing her into the doorway, and against the heavy wooden door.

"This time, you're not talking your way out as easy and slick as you did before. Do you hear me?" He shook her roughly for emphasis, making her teeth rattle. "You see, I know exactly what you are now—and what you've been. A whore! Yes, that's right! Did you think you could hide it forever? After Morgan and I had our little set-to, I talked with some prisoners we took—men who deserted from Tomas Mejia's army. That mean anything to you, you slut?"

Somehow, she managed to find words.

"Carl—stop this! I don't know why you enticed me up here, or what you were thinking of when you did, but it's not going to do you any good. You—you must be crazy! What do you think to achieve?"

He shook her again, slamming her back against the

door until she felt her head would come loose from her body; her back and shoulders felt bruised.

"You really want to know? Well, I had lots of time to think about it, to plan all this while I was lying in that hospital bed where your goddamn half-breed lover put me, you hear that? You owe me plenty, Ginny Brandon, for all the times you led me on and teased, and played the innocent lady, while all the while you were sleeping with *him*, and that Frenchy, and God knows who all else—every stinking Mex soldier who could spare a peso—isn't that so? Isn't it? You bitch, you're going to pay up now, and you're going to keep paying until I've had my fill. I'm going to use you like I should have before—the way you deserve to be used—like a cheap, stinking whore!"

All the time he was talking, his words muttered between clenched teeth, he kept shaking her, still gripping her cruelly and painfully about the wrists. The rebozo slipped from her head, and her hair spilled loose as she tried to fight him, her soaking wet skirt impeding her.

"No, Carl, no!"

"Oh, but it'll be 'yes, please, Carl, do anything you want with me,' by the time I'm through with you, do you hear me? You're not going to make a fool of me again. Didn't I tell you I had plans for you? No one's going to know where you are, or what's happened to you—they'll think you ran off to Morgan. And *he*—yes, I'll have the last laugh on him, too, before I collect that bounty money your pa's offering for his hide. I'll let him know I have you—I'll offer to trade. What do you think of that?"

With a movement too quick for her to anticipate, he suddenly gave her wrists a vicious twist, bringing her to her knees.

"Now, you just hold still a moment," Ginny heard him mutter, and suddenly she found the strength to scream.

If only Bernardo hadn't run away already! If only he were still hiding among the trees and could hear her!

"Help—bring help, quickly!" She screamed the words in Spanish before Carl cut her off with a vicious blow across the mouth.

"Goddamn bitch! You listen to that thunder—and the rain! Think anyone is going to hear you?"

He struck her again and again, across the face and across her breasts, until everything began to go dark and waver before her eyes. Dazed, her head throbbing with pain, only half-conscious, Ginny felt him tug her arms behind her back and tie her wrists together. Pushing her down on the wet, muddy earth, he hobbled her ankles, seeming to take pleasure in pulling the rope as tightly as he could, until even in her semi-stupor Ginny felt as if her circulation had been cut off. The last and worst humiliation was the gag he thrust between her lips to stifle her cries.

Moaning, fighting for breath, Ginny felt herself picked up roughly in his arms and carried, with the rain beating down on them both, and almost drowning her.

Afterwards, she could not remember how long he walked with her, or which direction he took. The noise of the storm assailed her eardrums, and the rain was cold—and then, suddenly, the noises seemed to fade away, and in a sudden flash of lightning she thought she caught a glimpse of walls, open to the sky in places, and she heard the sound of crumbling masonry under his boots. And then it was dark again, and close-smelling, and she was being carried down a flight of steps, hearing Carl's panting rasping breathing in her ears, still hardly able to believe what was happening.

Suddenly, Ginny found herself lowered to the ground, and although the floor under her was dry, it was cold and hard, and she could hear Carl muttering.

"Now you're just going to lie there quietly until I find that candle I left here—and then you'll get to see the nice little hidey-hole I've fixed up for you. Some of the boys and I came over here exploring once. Sure is an interesting place, as you're going to find out!"

She heard him strike a match, and the yellow light flared, hurting her eyes. Pain shot through her whole body when she attempted to move. And the next moment she was picked up again, clung over his shoulder, and carried down a narrow flight of stone steps into what appeared to be a black, gaping hole—revealed when he had lifted a heavy wooden trap door set in the floor.

"Used to be a wine cellar. Nuns used to make the wine themselves, someone told me. But I guess they took it all with them when they left. Nothing down here but rats and a few spiders and roaches now. But you must be used to that, as long as you've lived in Mexico, and considering the kind of company you like to keep!"

Ginny could feel herself shudder uncontrollably, and he laughed as he put her down again, none too gently—this time on what appeared to be a pile of sacking in one corner of the small, cold chamber.

As Carl turned away to stick the candle in the neck of an empty wine bottle, he was aware of the sound of his own breathing, rasping in his throat. Part of it, he knew, was from the exertion of having had to carry her, and part of it a mixture of rage and excitement. He'd done it! His patience, his careful preparations had worked after all, and she was here, just as he had planned to have her.

He made his movements deliberately slow, knowing that she was watching him fearfully through those slanting green eyes he had alternately hated and loved. Yes, there was a time when he'd been foolishly infatuated by her, taken in by her cold, unapproachable airs. But he despised her now, even while he lusted for her. He meant to punish her for everything—and most of all for having kept him at arms length while she gave herself to everyone else. Well, everything would be changed now, and he was going to enjoy watching her squirm while she begged him to show her some mercy. And it would be a pleasant thought to carry with him when he went back to the headquarters, that she'd be here whenever he wanted her. Waiting. . . .

He was wet, all the way through. Carl ran his fingers through his hair, raking out some of the excess water that dripped down the back of his collar. Deliberately, he avoided looking at Ginny as he put his improvised candlestick down on the wooden box he'd carried in here earlier. From behind the box he took a bottle of wine—only a few sips gone from *this* one—and tilted it to his mouth, letting the slightly sour, warmish liquid trickle down his throat. And then, still dragging out each movement as long as he could, he took off his wet jacket before he turned, at last, to look at her.

Most of the lower part of her face was obscured by the neckerchief he'd used as an improvised gag, but her eyes, no longer glazed looking, were staring at him. And he felt a cruel sense of satisfaction at seeing that his slaps had left ugly bruises which marred the classic perfection of her features.

Her blouse was ripped at one shoulder, baring it, and part of her breast, and her sodden skirt had ridden up to expose her legs. She looked like a whore, with mud all over her; and as he stood there, letting his eyes move over her with exaggerated slowness, Carl could feel himself stiffen with uncontrollable desire.

Ginny's eyes, like green, shiny glass in the leaping candlelight, never left his face. She was afraid—by God, he wanted her to be afraid, to wonder exactly what he was going to do with her. And he'd meant to take more time over it, making her suffer, but his own desire and the shortness of time before they'd expect him back drove him to walk over to her.

The look on his face, with the livid, ugly gash from his fight with Steve across his forehead, was unmistakable, and Ginny felt a tremor go through her cold body. As he bent over her, she bit down on the damp cloth that seemed to fill her mouth, tasting blood. Now, she was just as glad he'd gagged her. She would not be able to add to her humiliation by screaming, and begging him not to . . . not to. . . .

And then she felt his hands on her body and closed her eyes, hearing the ripping of wet cloth as he began, with calculated deliberation, to tear every stitch of clothing she wore from her body.

Chapter Eight

Ginny had never experienced such stark, unreasoning terror in her life before, nor such impenetrable blackness; she felt as if she were being slowly suffocated.

When Carl had finally left, taking the candle with him, Ginny had felt too numb and degraded to care that he was leaving her here alone, her wrists and ankles tied a trifle more loosely than before. Then the trap door thudded shut behind him, leaving her encased in a shroud of sooty darkness, and she had been capable of feeling a faint glimmer of relief. He had left the gag off, and thrown a blanket carelessly over her aching, nude body. For a long time after he had gone, Ginny lay there sobbing drily, conscious, at the moment, only of physical pain that was coupled with a worse agony of mind.

It was only later, when the blackness seemed to push in at her from all sides, and she became aware of soft, rustling noises, that the real agony began. She didn't dare move, but was forced to lie on her side, beginning to feel the pain of her bound wrists and ankles shoot through every nerve before they became numb. And worst of all was the thought that she was alone in this filthy hole and completely helpless. Rats and spiders, Carl had told her earlier, laughing. Then, she had paid hardly any attention, her mind too busy with wondering what he intended to do. Now, her body broke into a cold sweat, the perspiration stinging each cut and bruise he had left on her naked, abused flesh. It had been worse than anything that had happened to her since Tom Beal.

"He cannot really mean to leave me here," Ginny thought feverishly, trying to fight back the nausea that threatened to overwhelm her. It was the wine he had forced her to drink, forcing the neck of the bottle between her bruised and swollen lips.

"Here, drink some of this! Might put some life into you—" and he had chuckled when she gagged on the cheap, wretched-tasting stuff.

A sudden thought made Ginny go rigid with fear. Perhaps he meant to leave her here, buried alive, and the rats would eat her. Something ran over one bare foot and she screamed. And as if her scream had unleashed all the terror she had tried to hold leashed inside her, she found she could not stop screaming.

She was overcome by a sheer, primitive terror that left her mindless. For a few minutes, until her throat became too raw and dry for her screams to have any sound, she felt that she had actually gone mad. She felt herself being strangled, stifled by the darkness that pressed against her face like a black velvet pillow. And now that she was silent, she could hear distinctly those soft, scuttling noises again. Rats? Or—oh, God, suppose there were snakes down here as well? She began to moan, and wondered why her own voice—if it could be called that any longer—sounded so strange. She felt as if millions of creatures scurrying on tiny feet were crawling over her body, and her thrashing movements only pulled the blanket half off her, leaving bare flesh exposed.

She was gasping for breath, hearing the sound of her own breathing over the dull pounding in her temples. And then, with a final, smothering plunge, the blackness seized her by the throat, blotting out everything.

When Carl returned sometime during the next morning he was whistling softly, smiling and looking fresh. He had trimmed his beard and his hair, emphasizing his blond good looks; and indeed, on his way up the hill, clad in a freshly-laundered, immaculate blue uniform, he had drawn several sly feminine glances.

He was enormously pleased with himself this morning, although, last night, he had hardly been able to sleep from reaction, and from thinking of her—of the way his scheme had worked without a hitch. Ginny—was it possible that after all the months he'd spent dreaming of her, desiring her, wondering what had become of her, she was actually his at last? And he could do whatever he wanted with her. A series of images came flooding back into his mind. Her body—long-limbed and smooth-fleshed. The frightened, tortured look in her green eyes, the whimpering noises that had come from behind the gag as he began to caress her. He had never raped a woman before, but it had been a pleasure. More than that, he had derived a kind of sick excitement, such as he had never experienced before, from the thought that her body belonged to him; he could do whatever he wanted with it, anything at all! And with a latent sadism he hadn't known he possessed, he had proved that to her, over and over, until she had stopped her struggling and lay acquiescent beneath him, the only clue to her inner agitation being the long shudders that seemed to ripple under her skin at intervals.

This morning, after he'd allowed her all night in which to think and to fully realize the position she was in, he had a feeling she'd be more malleable. Strange—he wanted her willing and cooperative, wanted her to play the whore for him. And at the same time, he almost hoped there was still some fight left in her—so that he could show her all over again that he was her master.

He was a handsome young American officer, taking an off-duty stroll before the sun got too hot. Except for a few women who looked again, hoping to catch his eye, Carl Hoskins attracted no undue attention as he skirted the hill of Tepeyac in order to avoid the crowds that thronged towards the church, even at this time in the morning.

The old convent, its adobe walls giving the crumbling building a decrepit and almost mysterious appearance, was supposed to be haunted—a notion that kept away the Mexican urchins who were everywhere else. Partially roofless, the walls showing gaping holes, filled with crumbling masonry, the place was as deserted as usual this morning.

Without haste, picking his way carefully, Carl Hoskins gave a quick backward glance to make sure no one saw him before he picked his way over rubble and entered what had once been the sala of the convent. Puddles of water from last night's storm lay everywhere, and it was noticeably cooler in the shade cast by the thick old walls. Now, at last, he began to hurry. Down one flight of shallow stone steps—and here a portion of the tiled roof still remained. He had hidden the trap door under an untidy pile of loose bricks, and now he kicked these aside impatiently and picked up the candle he had left. It was gloomy in here, and in the cellar it would still be dark. He grinned to himself. Maybe she would be glad to see him, and be ready to show it.

But Ginny lay motionless, even when Carl let the trap door fall shut with a deliberate thud. The candlelight flickered, casting a tiny yellow glow, illuminating her bare, white-gleaming body.

Sometime during the night she'd lost the blanket and hadn't been able to pull it up around her again, and now she lay with her knees pulled up for warmth, her hair covering her shoulder and most of her face, which was turned away from him and pressed against the dirty sacks.

"Hope you had a good long rest," Carl said with heavy sarcasm, as he walked towards her, and still she neither moved nor spoke, although he could discern the slight motion of her breathing. Frowning, he stood looking down at her. Her white body was marred by the marks he'd left on it. In a way that was too bad, but she'd had to be taught a lesson.

"Damn you!" He put the light down and shook her

roughly by the shoulder. "No use trying to play possum, I
can see you're breathing. And if you don't feel like talking, maybe I'll put that gag back."

He could see her head shake slightly as he turned her
over, having to exert all his strength because she was so
limp. For a moment, when he saw her face, he was almost
startled. Bruised, swollen, it was no longer pretty. And
even her eyes seemed to have lost their luster. They stared
at him dully and almost uncomprehendingly.

Sitting back on his heels, he cursed. Maybe he'd been
too rough with her. What was the matter with her, anyhow? She was pretending—trying to lead him on into feeling sorry for her, that was it.

He shook her again, and her skin felt like ice. Unable to
help himself, he ran one hand over her curving flesh,
watching for some reaction from her, even if it was a
movement of revulsion. But her face showed nothing, and
she didn't try to twist and squirm away as she had last
night. Damn it, why didn't she say something? Still testing,
he slapped her, and her head moved limply sideways. He
thought he heard her make a faint protesting sound in her
throat, but that was all. Damn the bitch, what was the
matter with her? There was something strange about her
sudden immobility. Could it be that she'd caught a chill,
lying here without the blanket to cover her? But that was
her own fault, for not lying still.

Cursing under his breath again, Carl picked up the blanket and began to chafe her cold flesh with it, being purposely rougher than he had to. Damn her, damn her! She
deserved to suffer, and she hadn't suffered enough. He
wasn't going to let her escape him yet. It occurred to him
suddenly that he might have tied her too tightly, and her
circulation might be cut off. Well—it was plain that she
was in no shape to try to wrestle with him, and if she tried
it wouldn't take much to subdue her.

So, still swearing, Carl cut her free, and immediately, as
the blood began to flow back into her numb, cramped
limbs, Ginny started to moan with agony.

"Here, for God's sake, let's put some fire into you—"
He propped her up and held a bottle of wine to her lips.
She drank obediently, grimacing with pain when the liquor
stung her cut lips. It was bad wine, but it was strong

enough to hit the pit of her stomach like a jolt. And Carl forced her to drink far too much.

Suddenly, he was pushing her backwards, and already weak and dizzy, her limbs sprawled laxly under him.

"What the hell is the matter with you? Bet you didn't lie like this when some man was paying for it, did you? Look—" he grasped a handful of her hair, tugging it viciously—"why do you think you're here? It's not as if I'm asking for something you haven't sold or given away for free before. You lie like this when that bastard Morgan was taking you? Listen"—he brought his face close to hers—"if you can't show me you're pleased to see me, I'll just tie you up again, and tighter, this time. Leave you down here for another day or so!"

At last, he obtained some reaction from her. Shaking her head, her eyes squeezed shut, she was trying to speak; her voice emerged as a hoarse whisper.

"No! No—don't—"

"Don't what, you slut? Say it. Say, 'Don't leave me Carl, I want you—I want you to—' "

"Don't . . . leave . . ." Her breathing was shallow, fast; her eyes still closed. He laughed, leaning the weight of his body above hers, his hands everywhere, as if he couldn't get enough of the feel of her flesh—all the hidden shadowy places she'd never let him touch before.

"Say it! I want you to use the words, and don't pretend you don't know what I'm talking about. Whore!" His breath, with the fumes of wine, was sour in her face. He was beginning to pant, not able to hold back his own lust.

All this time, ever since the horror of the night, Ginny had been in a kind of stupor—a state of shock, with neither her mind nor her body capable of functioning. Even when she had heard Carl come in, she had felt literally incapable of either sound or motion.

But now, with the life starting to flow back into her arms and legs and the wine burning her stomach, she came back to the full realization of what was happening to her, the pain and degradation he was determined to inflict on her once more. Her body stirred under his, and her eyes opened, seeing his face, suffused with red. He was hurting her, violating her. Tom Beal, come back to take his revenge. . . .

Hearing her begin to gasp and thrash under him, Carl

thought he had actually begun to reach her. The little bitch, he was making her hot for him, and against her will! The thought put him beyond control. Breathing heavily, he fumbled at his clothing, wanting to take her now, needing to. She was arching up against him, whispering something in Spanish, her voice husky and the words unintelligible. And then the world exploded with a splintering sound. There was a cry—his own? Sharp, blinding pain, and then—nothing.

Ginny had hit him across the side of the head with the only object she could reach—the bottle of wine—swinging it with all the strength and desperation left in her. She was still a little bit crazy; she kept thinking her attacker was Tom. But she had killed Tom Beal, hadn't she? With a knife in his throat. Who was this man?

Somehow, she managed to wriggle free of Carl's heavy body, watching the blood that flowed from his scalp and his temple almost objectively. What a lot he had bled in such a short time! There was even blood on her, and bits of glass had cut her breasts and her fingers; but the cuts hadn't started to hurt yet. It was strange, how little she felt. Her mind was as numb as her body.

The next thing that Ginny remembered clearly was crawling up a flight of seemingly endless steps—and then the warmth of sunshine. After that, there was another blank place in her memory, and then, suddenly, she was lying in a bed, with someone bending over her, talking in a quiet, persuasive voice.

"Come, little one. It is all right to wake up now. You have had a long sleep; yes, a good, long rest. Wake up now, you are safe." Her eyelids felt so heavy! She heard the same voice say softly, "I think she's coming out of it at last—she's been in a state of shock."

"Will she be strong enough to talk yet?" A different voice. Stronger, harder, and with an odd accent.

"I cannot say. It depends—on how bad the memory is. Be patient with her, Ivan."

Ivan?

Ginny's eyes forced themselves open, blinking as she tried to focus them. She felt so ridiculously weak. What was the matter with her? And why was Prince Ivan Sahrkanov, of all people, bending over her?

"Virginie!" He had seen her eyes open, and now he

leaned even closer, holding both her hands in his own. His voice was urgent. "Tell me—what happened? Who was it? You must tell me. Surely you remember?"

"Ivan!" That stern, warning voice belonged to Count Chernikoff. Ginny's eyes, wide-open now, flew to his face, found it worried and tired looking.

"What . . . ?" Her voice was husky, hardly above a whisper. And then, against her will, memory came flooding back, making her wince. She was suddenly aware of bandages everywhere. Even her hands were bandaged.

"Ginny—" Count Chernikoff's voice was soft, yet resonant. "Do not try to force your memory. If you don't feel like talking, then you must rest longer. You have been under a terrible strain. It's clear that you have undergone some terrible experience."

"Virginie—you must tell me." Why did Ivan Sahrkanov insist on calling her by the French version of her name? She realized, belatedly, that he was still holding her hands, and that his eyes looked almost transparent in the sunlight that streamed in through an open window. "Who was it?" he repeated again. "What happened? We were out of our heads with worry, all of us. And then, some little boy I saw hanging around outside that vile cantina asked me if I was a friend of yours."

She tried to sit up, and fell back against the plumped-up pillows. "You didn't hurt him? Bernardo was trying to help me."

"Let me talk to her, Ivan."

Count Chernikoff bent over her now, his dry, old man's hand touching her forehead lightly. "Good. You have no fever. But when we found you, you were so dazed I had begun to worry for your reason, my child."

Gradually, it all became clear to her. She had gone, by instinct perhaps, to the house of the padre who usually officiated at mass at the Church of Our Lady of Guadalupe. The good padre's housekeeper had taken her in. She had been clad only in a blanket, and had babbled almost incoherently in Spanish and English. Not knowing what to do, the woman had told the padre, who had sent a discreet message to General Díaz, thinking that perhaps some of his soldados had attacked one of the women they'd taken prisoner.

"And that is where we finally found you," Count Cher-

nikoff said, his voice gentle. "As I've said before, you were
in shock. You hardly realized where you were, or who we
were. You kept talking of a man—a man who had mis-
treated and misused you—a man you had killed."

She whispered, "It wasn't Tom Beal after all. I
thought—I thought he'd come back! But it was—it was
Carl. He—"

"Are you sure? Are you positive it was not that man
you called your husband? Jealousy—some idea of revenge,
perhaps! Virginie, I insist that you tell me."

Count Chernikoff's voice murmured warningly in Russian, but anger made Ginny sit upright, in spite of all the
aches and pains in her body; her eyes clashed with those
of the Prince.

"It wasn't Steve! How could you dare suggest it? It was
Carl Hoskins. He was so jealous. I think—" with a sigh,
she lay back again—"I think he had begun to hate me,
you know? He accused me of—of leading him on. Making
a fool of him. He tricked me into going to the church to
meet him, and then he. . . ." Remembering the terrifying
experience of that night she had spent alone, bound hand
and foot in the cellar, while the rats ran over her, she
paled. "I—I think I killed him," she said finally, in a
small, stony voice. "I hit him over the head with the wine
bottle, and then I—I think I crawled outside, to the fresh
air. All I wanted to do was get outside, don't you understand that? To breathe again. It was so dark in that cellar,
and there were rats. . . ."

Supporting her shoulders with an arm that was surprisingly strong, the Count made her drink some sweetish tasting stuff that made her grimace.

"It's a mild draught that will help you rest. We cannot
have you going back into shock again, you know!"

Over his soothing voice came Ivan Sahrkanov's harsh
tones.

"And this cellar, where is it? You must tell me, Virginie. I will go myself and see. You must be protected.
Your good name. . . ." And then, after she had told him,
her speech already stumbling with renewed tiredness, she
heard him say softly, "Don't worry, my princess. No one
will know."

After that she had fallen into a deep, dreamless sleep

again. And when she woke up, she was in a carriage or a wagon of some sort, with the Count beside her.

"We are on our way to the coast. Lie still. It's a good thing you are a strong young woman with a healthy constitution. You are healing already, and the next time you look into a mirror, you will not notice any difference in your appearance."

A strange feeling of lethargy made her shake her head wearily. What did it matter, after all, how she looked? The lassitude that seemed to have taken hold of her persisted, even when they stopped to rest the horses and Ivan came to sit by her.

"You are looking better already," he said softly. And then, his voice dropping, "I found him. You had killed him, all right! I'm proud of you, chérie. Vermin like that—someone who dared do what he did to you—deserve an even worse death. He would not have gotten off so lightly if I had been fortunate enough to rescue you. Don't worry," he went on. "There will be no investigation, no inquiry. I left him there—they will think he was murdered for his money or his uniform. And you must have made quite an impression on General Porfirio Díaz, for in spite of all the preparations he was making for a final assault on the City, he took the time to assure me that there will be no more questions asked on *his* side. So you see, there is no scandal to be feared. And soon you will be on our ship, and feeling completely recovered."

It was his rather alarming kindness and gentle consideration that disarmed her. Or perhaps it was her own feeling of listlessness, of weakness; perhaps it was the "healing draughts" that the good Doctor insisted she must continue to swallow.

In any event, Ginny's leave-taking of Mexico was a fact she hardly realized had taken place until they were well out to sea, with the ship rocking beneath her. And even then, she continued to be apathetic.

"So, you leave one part of your life behind you," the Count said to her, "but only to begin another. It is always so, my child. And from now on you must only look forward, to the magnificent future which will be yours. Destiny," he sighed, "is sometimes a hard thing to accept. Especially when one is young and headstrong. But its responsibilities are inescapable, as is the blood that flows through your veins. It's fate, my child. And if you set your mind to it, and will it to be so, you can be happy."

But what was her fate? On their third day out at sea, Ginny caught herself gazing into the mirror in her luxuriously appointed cabin, watching her reflection as she might have watched some strange woman. Tentatively, her fingers came up to touch her face; it was just as smooth and unmarred as it had always been.

What was the fate she was meant for after all? She thought she had found it once, with Steve. She tried to conjure up his image, but saw instead Ivan Sahrkanov's enigmatic smile and chiseled, clean-shaven countenance.

Steve—had he been part of a dream, too? Oh, but she had felt far too happy and far too confident of the future for it to have lasted. And now that Steve had deliberately turned his back on her—put her out of his life—she must try to do the same.

"It *was* a dream," Ginny thought, and her eyes seemed to darken. Steve wasn't meant to settle down—perhaps he was only too glad of an excuse to be rid of a burdensome responsibility. If he had really loved her, he would have believed in her. And then, almost frantically, Ginny realized that she mustn't continue to think of him! That Count Chernikoff was right. She must try to put the past behind her and start afresh.

"It seems to me that this—this villain you say you loved was responsible for all your troubles and misery, my child," the Count had said. "Please—try to forget him! I think you have the Romanov pride, as well as the courage the Royal House of Russia is noted for."

And, of course, the Count was trying to hint, indirectly, that she must not be like her mother, who let her life fall into ruins and finally end because she could never get over her first love.

"Poor Genevieve!" The long-ago echo of some friend's pitying voice seemed to float across the stillness. And how often, how impatiently she used to think of her poor mama—and feel angry that Genevieve would take no notice of her.

Some of her old spirit came back to stiffen her spine, and Ginny found her chin tilting defiantly. "Well, they'll never be able to call me poor Ginny—or pity me! I won't have it. I'll make myself forget—I'm going to make a new life for myself!" she thought with a sudden determination.

Everyone on board the Russian ship was enormously polite. Ostensibly, this was a naval vessel, but it had been fitted up to carry distinguished passengers. There were stewards and cabin boys. The captain, a bearded, handsome man who did not speak too much English, always stood up, clicking his heels together and bowing deeply, when Ginny appeared. She even picked up a few words of Russian.

"Princess Romanov" they all called her, although in San Francisco it would have to be kept a secret.

"But you were born to be a Princess. You have that air about you, chérie." Ivan Sahrkanov invariably spoke to her in French, which he said was a language far more civilized than English.

Listlessly, Ginny shrugged. "I don't care. What does it matter what they call me? I've been called worse."

Unbidden came the thought of Carl Hoskins' desire-suffused face, bending close to hers. His bloody head. And before that, Tom Beal, his life escaping through the gaping wound in his throat.

"I've killed two men, and it doesn't seem to matter one bit. Perhaps I don't have a conscience any longer," she thought.

Count Chernikoff was in the habit of resting for the greater part of each day, but whenever Ginny left her cabin Ivan Sahrkanov would suddenly appear at her side. He had commanded a naval ship at one time. He told her small anecdotes, pointed out this feature or that.

Her mood of indifference persisting, Ginny had begun to accept his presence. Leaning on the ship's rail, she watched the ocean change colors; saw the coastline of Mexico fall away as they sailed out of the Sea of Cortez.

The weather, too, seemed changeable. One day was cloudless and still, and the next, they were scudding before a strong wind, watching the fog banks that shrouded the distant coastline.

"That's California, at last—hidden behind that nasty damp fog. Within a day or two we ought to be in San Francisco."

Again, it didn't seem to matter one way or another. Not

even when the Prince leaned so close to her that their shoulders brushed.

"Yes—San Francisco. And we shall be remaining there for a while. It's a very cosmopolitan city. People are actually civilized there; the European influence, of course. I think you will enjoy it."

Since they had been at sea, Ivan had not attempted to press her in any way, or to persist in the earlier, blunt declarations that had once made her so angry. But he had said "we." What, exactly, had he meant?

Ginny gave him a slanted, inquiring look, and he smiled urbanely. As if he could read her mind he said:

"The Count and I will be remaining in San Francisco for some months—until the Alaskan Purchase is settled. Of course, there are some who are much opposed to such a thing, but it is up to your American Senate now, of course. In the meantime, since I am only a minor diplomat, not a politician, I think I am going to enjoy presenting San Francisco to you—and vice versa."

"What pretty speeches you can make," she responded mechanically. Her head had begun to ache, as it invariably did on a glare-filled afternoon, and she felt tired. Was it possible that only a few weeks ago she had been capable of walking for miles at a time behind a wagon, or riding bareback, with the sun beating down on her head? But then, a few weeks ago she had everything to look forward to, especially the nights. . . .

Abruptly, Ginny turned away from the rail, her brow wrinkled.

"I—I think that I must go and rest for a while, it's so hot! Please excuse me."

"I shall see you again at dinner time, then. And don't forget to take one of the powders our good doctor made up for you. It will help you rest better."

She had begun to feel like an invalid—but all the same, making a wry face, Ginny took his advice, and sleep came easily, as it always did when she took her magic powders. Instant forgetfulness—and there was so much she needed to forget!

Chapter Nine

"I'm afraid Count Chernikoff will not be joining us tonight. He is slightly indisposed. Nothing serious—a case of too much sun, I believe. You will not mind dining alone with me?"

Her mind still slightly clouded from her long sleep and the effects of the drug she had taken, Ginny did not particularly care. Even when she discovered that covers had only been laid for two.

So—it was to be an intimate supper *à deux*. Perhaps, at last, she would find out what Ivan really wanted of her.

Except for the swaying, gently rocking motion of the ship, they might have been dining in the private room of some expensive and discreet little restaurant. Everything was just right, from the rose-shaded lamps to the exquisitely laid table with its array of gold cutlery and diamond-studded napkin holders.

As the soft-footed stewards moved discreetly back and forth, disappearing from the small cabin until it was time for the next course to be served, the Prince set himself out to be charming. Ginny listened to stories of the different parts of the world he had visited, the adventures he had encountered. For some time, he had even governed the Russian province of Alaska, and this was one reason why he had been named to the Tsar's delegation when the matter of the Purchase came up.

So far he had not attempted to take advantage of their dining alone and in such intimate circumstances, but in spite of his excessively polite manners, Ginny still did not trust Prince Sahrkanov. There was a certain look in his eyes when they rested on her at times that even the soft, rosy light that bathed the cabin could not disguise. While she responded to his idle conversation, Ginny could not help thinking: I wonder when he's going to drop the mask?

He waited until the steward had brought in a steaming samovar filled with the strong tea that the Russians so delighted in, and had left, closing the door behind him. And then, leaning forward, Ivan extended the little gold-encrusted cup to her and said softly, "I have added some of my friend Chernikoff's special liqueur to it. Shall we drink to the future—Russian style?"

She sipped slowly, trying to hide her involuntary grimace at the excessive sweetness of the beverage.

"But what is 'Russian style?' "

He smiled, showing strong white teeth.

"Why, we Russians toast everything in tea or vodka. But it takes time to become accustomed to the latter." He leaned back in his chair, his eyes openly studying her now. "I noticed that you did not join me in my toast. Does not the thought of what lies ahead hold any excitement for you?"

Ginny could sense that he was challenging her, but the same mood of indifference that allowed her to dine all alone with him, made her shrug.

"Not particularly. Why should it? I think I've had quite enough excitement, as you call it, in my life already to look forward to more."

"So? And yet, you are the kind of woman who is an excitement in herself. Whether you seek it or not, I think your life could never be dull and ordinary. Why don't you accept your destiny? Go forward to meet it. Surely, after all you have survived and surmounted, you will not run away?"

Her eyes widened at the sudden fierceness in his voice. He was leaning forward now, those strange, blue-green eyes of his seeming to pierce into hers.

"Run away? But—what is this destiny I should not try to escape?"

"Don't you know? I think I made my intentions clear one evening, not very long ago, when we walked in a moonlit garden and you—fenced with me."

"I think I made it perfectly clear to you then—"

"You made excuses, Princess. That was all. But all the reasons you gave me then are no longer valid. And instead of remaining in Mexico, as you vowed to do, here you are, on your way to the United States. Listen to me!"

He suddenly leaned over the table, grasping her wrist with strong fingers.

"Will you go back with your head high, as a princess should? Or scuttle around like a little timid field mouse, like someone's disgraced governess? Perhaps you've forgotten how cruel society can be—and particularly to one of its own. There are rumors. There has been quite a bit of gossip regarding your—er—various activities ever since people who had once hung around Maximilian's court began to drift back home. And—" his eyes narrowed—"just before I left for Mexico I was introduced to a fat and talkative American lady, the widow of a man named Baxter. Ah, I see you remember! She said she met you in Vera Cruz. . . ."

Ginny had gone pale at first, but now she could feel her face burn. Vera Cruz. *That* particular memory still had the power to twist like a knife-thrust in her heart.

"I've been gossiped about before! Do you think I have any desire to take my place in this so-called society of yours?"

"You could take your place anywhere, in any society, I tell you. And look down upon them all if you choose. As my wife, my Princess."

The sweetish taste of the tea she had gulped down far too fast in order to be rid of it stayed on Ginny's lips as she moistened them nervously.

"I thought—and especially after what has happened—I thought you'd given up that nonsense!"

Sahrkanov was drawing Ginny to her feet, and the room was all rose-colored light, reflecting off the magnificent rubied decoration he wore on his chest.

"Why do you call it nonsense? Did you not sense from the very beginning that I am a man accustomed to having my own way? Be sensible, Virginie—beautiful green-eyed Russian gypsy! Think of your pride. Would you have them think you are eating your heart out for this man who abducted you, ravished you, and then deserted you as if you'd been no more than a common camp follower?" He was drawing her against him as he spoke, and she seemed powerless against his strength. "I am no brutish, unsophisticated American, who would take you against your will. I think that in time you will want my embraces. I think that at this moment you want me to kiss you. . . ."

Had she really expected, when she had come here to dine with him tonight, that this would happen? Was it possible that, against the outraged screaming of her mind, she was actually responding to the lips that were covering hers, forcing her mouth open? Kisses to wipe out the memory of other kisses. Warm, strong arms holding her close to shut out the recollection of other arms. Yes, what was it he had said earlier? She must be sensible.

Ginny surrendered herself, sighing, her eyes closed. She felt his hand begin to caress her back, very gently; and it was the strangest thing, but her skin seemed suddenly to have become very sensitive. She pressed herself closer to him, gasping, and made no protesting movement when his hand slid around, across her shoulders, and his fingers brushed against her breasts, tautening her nipples. Her breath came faster and faster as his hands continued to excite her. Even his demanding kisses, which had once aroused only anger in her, now brought out an answering passion she was no longer able to fight.

"I really don't know what's happening to me," she thought dazedly. "Perhaps I am really just a slut at heart!" She remembered yielding willingly to Michel, and after that to Miguel Lopez. And now, she seemed unable to stop this Russian prince, whom she had detested from the first moment they'd met, from taking all kinds of liberties with her. Worse, she could not deny her own body's reaction to his caresses. "It's true—I'm nothing but a whore. . . ." But no matter what names she called herself in her mind, Ginny could not prevent the tingling sensitivity of her skin that actually made her crave rough hands on her flesh.

Ivan had slipped her gown free of her shoulders, and was bending his head, kissing her breasts. Ginny clung to his shoulders as if she were drowning, her head thrown back. She was filled with a languorous, purely sensuous feeling that drove everything from her mind except pleasure.

How beautiful this little room was! There were rich velvet hangings on the walls, and the dim, rosy lights made everything glow. It was just like standing in the center of a glass full of the palest pink wine, and watching the slippery translucent colors undulate around her.

Suddenly, Ivan had his arm around her waist, his lips buried in her hair.

"Look through the open porthole, chérie," he whispered. Do you see how beautiful the ocean is in the fading light?"

And he was right. She had never seen such colors before. Against a glowing sky that was streaked with crimson, the ocean was dark blue—but then this color seemed to fade into turquoise, then aquamarine or a pale, opalescent green when a great wave tipped with white foam flung itself back from the side of the ship.

"You—you are like the ocean. Beautiful, changeable—a creature of moods. And your woman's body has its own tides, has it not?" His hands stroked her, and her flesh responded, quivering under his fingers. "Ah, yes! I was not mistaken, that first night, when I saw you dancing. You have a gypsy soul—all passion and fire—yielding only when *you* are ready. And you are ready now, are you not?"

Her breath caught in her throat. Laughing softly, Ivan picked her up in his arms.

She was at the heart of a crimson rose, watching the petals unfold around her. There was a poem, written by William Blake, an Englishman, that had always fascinated her. She heard herself reciting it out loud, leaning against Ivan.

"Oh Rose, thou art sick!
The Invisible worm
That flies in the night,
In the howling storm,
Has found out thy bed
Of crimson joy;
And his dark secret love
Does thy life destroy."

Ivan was laughing, squeezing her waist.

"Ah, Virginie! I didn't know you were a poetess. So you are the rose, eh? And who is this secret lover who would destroy you? I would not love you in secret, lovely one.

You are going to be my wife, my princess, for all the
world to see!"

She began to laugh, too.

"But this is not a fairy tale, where the princess always
meets her prince. Didn't you say that to me once?"

"Your memory is as wonderful as the rest of you. But a
prince can be human, too."

Later, there was a bearded man, she remembered. The
captain. And he was reciting, in Russian. Every now and
then someone would tell her what she had to say, and she
mimicked the Russian words, only too conscious of Ivan's
blue-green eyes that seemed to hold her transfixed, and the
feel of his arm around her. And then, after all the silly
talk was done, Ivan was kissing her again, lifting her up in
his arms.

"And now, I have the right to hold you this way. To
take you."

Somehow, they were in her cabin, and his fingers were
like fire against her skin as he undressed her.

"Tonight I am maid and valet rolled into one. Tonight
you belong only to me."

He held a glass to her lips, containing some wonderfully
cool liquid, and obediently, she drank. And then his touch
sated the strange hunger in her blood, the tingling aching
of her loins. It was as if she had been on fire, every inch
of skin aching to be touched. Deep, crimson petals
opened, and then she was swallowed in their depths as
they closed around her.

She imagined, for a short moment after she woke up,
that she had been lying with Steve. Her "dark secret
love"—how closely he always held her, even in sleep!

And yet, when she opened her eyes, the rocking motion
beneath her reminded her where she was, and her memories of the night before must have been dreams, for she
was alone in her bed, soft sheets feeling like silk against
her skin.

"I hate to wake you out of such a sound sleep, my
dearest, but we are almost in San Francisco. In fact, we
have just sailed past the Farallones Islands. Shouldn't you
be dressed to meet the good Senator and his wife?"

With an instinctive movement, Ginny snatched the sheet
up around her neck. "What are you doing here?"

Fully dressed, freshly shaven, Prince Sahrkanov lifted one eyebrow in mock dismay.

"My love! I made sure you did not drink too much wine last night. If you mean to tell me that you have forgotten we were married last night, I shall be desolate."

"M . . . Married?"

Following the direction of his eyes, she looked downward and saw the heavy rings she wore: A pigeon's blood ruby, set in gold; and beneath it, a wide gold band, intricately engraved.

"They are both a trifle loose, I'm afraid, but we will get them altered to fit your finger better. There will be many more jewels for you to wear, later."

He came closer, and she stared up at him.

"Virginie. My crimson rose, who opened for me. You make me forget that a man is not supposed to be in love with his wife. I wish we were still at sea, and quite alone. I would sail you around the world and back, and not notice that any time had passed."

"Do you mean that we are really married? I don't . . . yes, I do remember something, but I didn't realize. . . ."

He sat on the bed beside her, stroking the hair back from her temples.

"You gave your responses without hesitation, in perfect Russian. You won't have any difficulty in learning the language properly, I'm sure. But you needed no prompting in the language of love. Virginie," he said, his voice deepening, "I would very much like to remind you all over again how we passed most of the night, you and I. Unfortunately, there is not even a fog bank to delay our sailing into the harbor. Shall I help you dress?"

Later, as she walked down the swaying gangplank on the Prince's arm, with Count Chernikoff following closely behind them, Ginny felt as if she were caught up in a strange dream. She remembered. And yet, even memory seemed dreamlike. She had let Ivan kiss her . . . she had recited poetry to him. And then, the Captain had married them, while Ivan translated his words, and she had given her responses in an undertone.

Two of the ship's officers had witnessed the ceremony, and afterwards . . . afterwards Ivan had carried her across the threshold of her cabin and she had responded ardently, shamelessly to his caresses.

"You young people! Why did you have to be so impetuous?" Count Chernikoff's voice had sounded testy. "You
could have waited to be married properly, in the Church.
Why pick an evening when I was unwell?"

"Ah, but there are some things that cannot wait."

Ivan's arm pressed intimately about her waist, just under her breasts, and Ginny, who had swallowed a "soothing powder" without protest, did not say a word, feeling
the familiar, delicious feeling of lassitude creep over her.
She was married to Ivan. What difference did it make?
There was a part of her mind that was dead anyway.

"Princess," they all called her.

"Ah, Senator! May I present the Princess Sahrkanov?
They were married on board ship, only yesterday."

Sonya, tears slipping down her cheeks, did not look
changed at all. And her father—but he was not her father
after all; how should she think of him?—The Senator had
lost none of his charm. The slight greying at his temples
only made him look more distinguished.

"Ginny! Daughter!"

He was embracing her, smelling faintly of tobacco and
cologne. And then there was Sonya's perfumed cheek lying
against hers for an instant, still damp from tears.

"Oh, Ginny! If you only knew . . . but dearest, we are
all so happy for you!"

At least Ivan protected her from the reporters who
thronged around them, staring, questioning.

"Princess! It *is* Princess, isn't it? How does it feel to be
back in the United States?"

"Do you have any comments about the revolution in
Mexico?"

"You know that the Emperor Maximilian was executed. What was your impression of him?"

"Gentlemen, gentlemen! My wife is overtired. And she
is meeting her parents after a long separation. Won't you
allow us some privacy? She'll answer your questions later,
I assure you. Yes, we shall be living here for some time,
you'll have plenty of opportunities."

"Later—later! Please, my friends. I shall be happy to is-
sue a statement later, after I've taken my daughter home."

The Senator's town house was situated on fashionable
Rincon Hill. But Ginny felt too tired to exclaim over its

magnificance, nor the drive through the winding, upward leaning streets of San Francisco. She was almost relieved by Ivan's presence at her side, and the way he had answered the questions for her.

"I hope you like your room," Sonya babbled, her blue eyes resting on Ginny's face with a strangely worried, unfamiliar look in their depths. "It's really a suite, of course. You'll have all the privacy you want. . . ." Her words trailed off, and impulsively, she caught one of Ginny's cold hands in hers. "Ginny! What's the matter with you? You —are you happy? You *are* married . . . oh, dear!"

Turning away from the window, Ginny frowned slightly. "Why do you say it in that tone? I thought this what you and . . . my father wanted."

Sonya spoke almost too quickly, biting her lip. "Yes, of course! We wanted so much for you to—to be happy! But Ginny, so soon? So suddenly? Are you sure. That is—"

"There was no need to wait, was there?" Ginny's voice was cold. "And Ivan thought this would be the best way—to introduce me to people as his wife. After all," her voice turned brittle, "I would not have wanted to embarrass you with a *scandal*. Do you think my being married will shut the gossips up?"

"Ginny!" She could not mistake the note of shock. "You've changed so!"

"Of course I've changed! Goodness, Sonya, are we going to pretend that nothing has happened since the last time we saw each other? Shall I detail all the events that caused the change you discover in me?"

Ginny broke off abruptly, seeing the expression on Sonya's face.

"I'm sorry! As Ivan explained, I'm just overtired. I really ought to rest, I suppose."

Sonya's large, china-blue eyes were fixed on hers. "I—I'll send Tilly to you. You remember Tilly? She's been so anxious to see you again. And later—well, I suppose you'll want to engage your own personal maid. But we can talk about all that afterwards, can't we?" If the lightness of Sonya's voice sounded forced, they both pretended to ignore it.

Ginny accepted her stepmother's light kiss, and made herself smile. "Yes, once I've rested, I'm sure things will

seem different. Thank you for everything, and especially
for being so patient with me."

The room had a distant view of the curving bay, with
the city seeming to be spread out beneath her for inspection. Although she berated herself for seeming ungrateful,
Ginny was glad, nevertheless, to have a few moments
alone.

Why did everything, including her recent marriage, still
seem so unreal? And yet, the unaccustomed heaviness of
the rings on her finger reminded her all over again that
she was now the Princess Sahrkanov. Ivan's wife, not
Steve's. At least, this was one marriage her "father" would
not try to have annulled!

"Miss Ginny, Miss Ginny!"

She had hardly noticed the sound of the door opening,
but suddenly Tilly was there, staring at her with rounded
eyes.

"Oh, miss! That is, ma'am—I *still* can't believe it! You
being here, after all this time, and married, too. Oh, but
he's such a handsome gentleman! So aristocratic, too. You
don't know how happy for you we all are, ma'am."

Their eyes met, across the room, and suddenly, intui-
tively, Ginny knew that at this moment they were both
thinking the same thing. Not of Ivan, but of another man.
A dark-haired, blue-eyed bandit, with crossed bandoliers
across his chest, dragging Ginny onto his horse to carry
her off. The same man she had fought and hated and
loved—halfway across a continent.

Oh, Steve! Where was he now? What would he think
when he found out?

Chapter Ten

❦

He was furious. And in spite of his rage, he felt as if he
had been delivered a mortal blow.

She hadn't wasted a moment, had she? Ginny, actually

married to another man. Why was the thought harder to take than that of Ginny lying with Carl Hoskins, reliving their old love affair? And why couldn't he dismiss her as easily from his mind as he had a hundred other women?

Because he had loved her. God damn her treacherous, hypocritical little soul to hell—he had actually loved her! And it was in vain that Steve Morgan told himself that it was only hurt pride that made him pace the floor like a crazed animal when he should have been sleeping; he was unable to shut out the images that rushed across his mind whenever he as much as thought her name.

Ginny. Soft, loving, lying lips. "I love you, Steve. Only you."

What had made her say that? Why had he been fool enough to have left her alone? The biggest mistake he'd made in his whole life had been to go tearing down to Vera Cruz to bring her back with him. But once he had done so, he should have made sure she was kept out of temptation's way. He should have sent her back to the little hacienda—or brought her here, to his grandfather's house. And in fact, that was exactly what he had intended to do that night he had arrived in Guadalupe, expecting to find his warm-blooded, passionate little wife waiting for him in her bed, where she belonged.

Instead, there was a note from another man lying on her pillow. And Ginny herself had been spending the night in another bed, in Cuernevaca. Coupled with the fact that he'd ridden for almost eighteen hours without sleep or rest, and in direct defiance of orders at that, it had been the last straw. His temper, already touchy, had exploded into violence, and, had he come across Ginny herself, he might very easily have strangled her with his bare hands.

Three months had passed since then—the war was over, and so was his stint with the army; the last few weeks of the war he had spent dodging the bullets of the bounty hunters who had somehow got wind of his presence near the border. *That* was another thing that had made him angry and crystallized his determination to put his *ex*-wife out of his mind completely. He had no desire to get himself killed merely because her father was still out for blood. It had even occurred to him to wonder if Ginny herself hadn't had something to do with it. Had his rejection of her made her angry enough to want him killed,

or—now that she was married again, and to a Russian no-
bleman—was the fact that he was still alive, and just
across the border, too much of a reminder of her sordid
past?

Damn Bishop for sending him the news in such an enigmatic manner! Stopping his angry pacing, Steve walked
over to the desk that stood against the window, its surface
a cluttered mass of papers. Irritably, he swept some of
these aside, looking for the long yellowish manila envelope
that had been handed to him this morning, along with a
verbal message that a Mr. James, a cattle buyer from the
United States, would be calling on him within a day or so
to discuss business. There was only one kind of business
Bishop would want to discuss with him, of course, and it
didn't concern cattle. Steve found himself staring with a
kind of distaste at the envelope he'd been looking for. He
should have torn it up right away. Sometimes, Bishop had
a macabre sense of humor! Well, he was through with
Bishop *and* the Service. He'd made his grandfather a
promise, and sent in his letter of resignation. From now
on, his life was going to belong to himself, and any traveling he did would be to suit himself, and for his own pleasure.

"I ought to tear the damn thing up right now," Steve
thought angrily. He dropped into the chair that had been
pushed away from the desk, stretching his long legs before
him as he continued to stare moodily at the yellow oblong.
But even while he was thinking that, he had opened the
envelope, and was drawing out the newspaper cutting
which it enclosed.

The lamp, turned up high, threw the black lettering under the rather blurred photograph into sharp relief: *The
Prince and Princess Sahrkanov at the Opera. Accompanying the Newlyweds are Senator and Mrs. William Brandon, parents of the Bride.*

They were all posed rather stiffly for the photographer,
but even that fact, and the stark black and white of the
print, could not disguise the supple, graceful way Ginny
held herself—nor the sensual look her face wore in repose.
Her hair was piled high on her head, with a single, thick
curl falling over her bare shoulder; and she wore a tiara,
as well as a necklace of some enormous stones. Square
cut. Emeralds, probably, Steve reflected dryly, still staring

down at the picture. She had no right to look so lovely. So—unchanged. She was unsmiling, her gloved hand resting lightly on her husband's arm. *"Bitch!"* Steve thought, suddenly and violently.

Crumpling the cutting in his fingers as if it had been her throat he was crushing, he stood up, and walking over to the fireplace, threw it into the flames. The tiny piece of paper flared up brightly for an instant before it dissolved into ashes. Like the passion that had existed between them. How was it possible for a woman to be so two-faced? She had had every opportunity to be free of him, yet she had followed him, fought for him, clung to him persistently and tenaciously, wept copious tears; and then, like any experienced coquette, she had run away. What a fool he had been to follow her, to actually break down and declare he loved her!

"Christ!" Steve swore softly and savagely under his breath. He should have known better than to let her become too sure of him; to let her under his guard. If he had continued to treat her in an off-handed, harsh manner, he might have continued to hold her.

So occupied was he with his bitter thoughts that Steve had not heard the door open. He swung around from his angry contemplation of the fire when he heard his grandfather's voice behind him.

"I am not sure, Esteban, that such single-minded devotion to duty does not perturb me more than it pleases me. Don't you find the young women in this part of the world attractive any longer?"

Don Francisco leaned on a cane, one leg dragging slightly. Since the stroke he had suffered some months ago, he had begun to show his age, although he still refused to give into it. It had been a shock to Steve, seeing him like this for the first time, but he had managed to hide his reactions well enough, seeing the irascible spark in the blue eyes that glared into his.

Now, meeting his grandfather's eyes again, seeing the lined face, with one side of his mouth drooping slightly under the full white mustache, Steve forced himself to shrug unconcernedly.

"The women here are as beautiful as ever, grandfather. But I confess I find myself more intrigued by this." He swept an arm out towards the desk, and grinned. "How

many irons do you have in the fire? I get the impression
you have been amusing yourself with all these stocks and
shares you happen to own, and when you translate these
many pieces of paper into money, which manipulates people—"

"Ah!" The old man nodded, almost imperceptibly. "So
you've discovered the challenge, have you? It can be quite
fascinating, as long as one keeps it in perspective, and this
manipulation you speak of remains a game in your mind."

He limped further into the room, sinking stiffly into the
chair Steve offered him.

"Since it seems that neither of us is in the mood for
sleep tonight, perhaps we can talk."

Beyond making some sarcastic comments when his
grandson had first turned up so unexpectedly, Don Francisco, hiding his pleasure under his usual fierce look, had
asked very few questions, waiting for the time when Esteban would see fit to confide in him. Whatever he had
learned for himself during the past few months, and that
mostly from his nephew, Renaldo Ortega, the old man
kept to himself. But he had noticed the change in his reckless, restless grandson, and knew some of the reasons for
it. It was for that reason that he had not brought up the
subject of Steve's wife—or ex-wife, if what he had been
told was correct.

Steve eyed his grandfather a trifle warily, and without
asking, he walked to a wall cabinet and came back with
two glasses of wine.

"What did you wish to discuss with me, sir?"

The ebony cane banged down on the floor, although with
less force than the old man used to pound on the rug with
his riding crop. How well Steve remembered that riding
crop, and the way his grandfather had been quick to use
it when he was in a rage.

"Damn it, there's no need to put on that blank, polite
look for *me*! All this shutting yourself up in here with
books and papers—there will be plenty of time for that
later! How is it you're not careening around the countryside with Diego Sandoval as you used to do, or visiting
that gypsy wench more often?" Don Francisco's voice became heavy with sarcasm. "I would not want to feel responsible for turning you into a hermit, merely because
I've thrust a few responsibilities on you that have become

too burdensome for an old man. Well? What do you have to say for yourself?"

In essence, it was the same question that Concepción flung at Steve the next day, when he visited her.

"Perdition take you, Esteban! So—at last you have decided to come and see me, eh? What have you been doing with your time? Who is she?" Stamping a bare foot in the dust Concepción raised one hand to claw at his face, spitting with rage when he moved aside quickly, grabbing her by the wrist so that she fell off balance.

He let her fall, and stood looking down at her, grinning.

"You—you animal! You. . . ." She reeled off a string of invectives until he yanked her up by the hair.

"I thought Renaldo was trying to turn you into a lady. Instead you're more of a gutter-bitch than ever. Is this a way to greet a man who's ridden a long way to see you?"

"You come only when it pleases *you*. I should never have come back here—I should have gone to Texas with my padre and found myself a real man there. I think she's softened you, that milk-faced ramera, that unmentionable puta who boasted of the fact that you were forced to marry her."

"Shut up, 'Cepción!" There was an angry, warning note in Steve's voice that warned her, and she subsided, glaring at him.

"Well then," she said in a sullen voice. "What have you been doing? Where have you been?" She had learned not to talk about that gringa female who had called herself his wife. They weren't really married at all, and Esteban was free again. But he had changed, and although she sensed that the change had something to do with Ginny, she was afraid enough of his black rages not to press him too far.

"I've been busy," he'd snap at her when she questioned him. "Damn it, woman, why must you start pestering me the minute I turn up to visit you?"

Now, before he could say the same thing, she suddenly flung herself against him, her body pressing greedily against his until she felt him relax, putting an arm around her waist.

"You should learn to stop asking so damn many questions," he said harshly, and began to kiss her. Wild, warm Concepción. The kind of woman with whom a man would always know where he stood. He wiped away Ginny's

memory and the bad taste seeing that newspaper picture
had left with him—letting the pure, uncomplicated flame
of desire take over. His grandfather was right. He should
come down here more often, to the house he had given
Concepción. In fact, although he hadn't told her so yet, he
planned to spend the night with her. Although—a sudden
thought struck him, making him smile ironically to himself. It was just possible that *she* had other plans. For all
the show of violent jealousy she might put on, Concepción
was enough like him so that if her current lover made a
habit of not showing up when she expected him, she was
capable of getting what she needed elsewhere.

Later, when they lay together with the hot sun falling
through the windows and across their sweating bodies, he
said casually, "Are you expecting a friend tonight? Maybe
I should leave before it gets too late."

She gave the deep, throaty chuckle of a sated woman,
squirming her body over his.

"Would you be jealous?"

Dark blue eyes squinted at her lazily.

"What do you think?" he said.

"I think you would not care—either way. But I tell you,
Esteban, a woman has to look out for herself, sí?"

"Sí," he agreed solemnly. And then, "Who is he?"

"Ah!" She gave an angry shrug, her hair brushing his
face as she leaned over him. "What does it matter? Maybe
it is Diego Sandoval. Maybe even your cousin—for all
that he has his nose stuck in his books for most of the
time, Renaldo is a man, too. But why do you pretend that
you care? You and I, we have known each other for a
long time, and while *this* is always good—" she wriggled in
such a way that his breathing quickened, even while he returned her impudent grin—"I am the kind of woman who
does not like being alone. I am not a whore, Esteban. But
I will not sit here night after night, wondering when you
might come or *if* you might come. Although, now that
you are here, I can think of many, many things to keep
you." She added softly, "Don't worry, tonight there is no
one. And I do not intend that you should leave me."

There came a time, though, in the early hours of the
morning, with dawn barely streaking the sky, that they began to talk like friends who had known each other a long
time.

"I hate her," Concepción said softly. "But I think you truly loved her. And it has changed you. Why aren't you honest with me? Do you think it makes a difference? The funny thing is," she added thoughtfully, turning her head against his shoulder, "I could have sworn that she loved you too." And in the face of his silence, she continued defiantly, "Why is it that you were so jealous of *her* and you are not of me?"

Steve was sleepy; and, at this point, irritable enough to be frank.

"Oh, damn! How do I know? I thought she was my wife, and there's nothing more ridiculous than a cuckolded man! I got angry when I found her gone off with that damn Russian who, I heard, had been dancing attendance on her constantly. And there was Captain Hoskins, and his sentimental, loverlike letter. Not to mention the way he kept throwing out those comments about his relationship with her. What was I supposed to do, hang around until she got back—*if* she got back—and risk a court-martial?"

"Perhaps you should have done so, and listened to what she had to say. And in any case, if she were as lonely as I have been sometimes, why should she not have consoled herself? Look at me—married or not, do you think I could stand it? And you—what of you? If you desire a woman, and she's willing, would you hesitate?"

"I thought you hated her," Steve murmured caustically.

"Yes, I do! If I ever meet up with her again, I have a score to settle with that gringa bitch, make no mistake about that! But after all, what makes her so different from any other woman?"

"Nothing," he said, his voice hard.

But it was not quite as easy to convince Bishop—the "Mr. James" from Texas, who was "looking for cattle to buy" while the market was good.

As usual, Bishop looked ill-at-ease on horseback, his short-brimmed derby hat hardly an adequate protection against the sun that beat down on them both. But in spite of the heat, Bishop's arguments were as coldly logical as they had always been.

"You've been thinking with your gut, Morgan, instead of with your mind. It's a pity. You used to be a good man. I think that what I admired most about you was that you did not possess a conscience, like some of the others. But ever since that marriage of yours—"

"Jim, it's not going to work. I'm through. I sent you a formal letter of resignation. If you want to know the truth of it, I've had my bellyful of intrigue and being shot at and spending half my days in hiding and the other half chasing. Damn it, I quit! So just forget whatever it is you had in mind when you took the trip out here."

Bishop sighed. "As I thought. You've not been listening very well. Nor, it would appear, have you been thinking." He shot out a question, taking Steve off-guard for an instant. "Did you happen to kill Carl Hoskins?"

"Goddamnit! Now look . . . "

"When they found him lying at the bottom of a cellar in a deserted convent, he had been hit over the head with a bottle of wine. But the actual cause of his death was a stab wound. Carefully placed through the jugular vein." Bishop shrugged, in the face of Steve's sudden stillness.

"He had been searched for, of course. And I'm afraid you were the prime suspect, especially since your—er— Miss Brandon had mysteriously disappeared a day earlier. But then she reappeared. In a state of shock, so I am told. But Hoskins did not. "So—" Bishop's voice softened—"the jealous Captain Hoskins, with whom you were foolhardy enough to engage in fisticuffs a few days before, is found dead. The small boy who seemed to know most about the whole sorry affair related to Colonel Díaz that he met a man—a gringo—in the Chruch at Guadalupe, and this man sent him with a message to Miss Brandon. The message contained *your* name. "For news of Esteban, meet me at the east door of the church," or words to that effect. She rushes out, escorted by the boy. He hides in a grove of trees, waiting to make sure she is safe. He sees an encounter, with a man. A tall man, his face covered by a hat. There is a struggle—he does not see very clearly, for by now it is raining hard. But he does hear her scream for help. And then—then, being a small boy, and frightened, he runs away, meaning to get help. But who shall he go to? They would laugh at him, or else cuff him out of the way. . . ."

"You sure tell a good story," Steve said between clenched teeth.

"Certainly." Bishop's voice was unperturbed; the cigar

he had just lit stuck out at an incongruously jaunty angle
from between his teeth. "And as you may remember, I always make sure of my facts first. Having vanished overnight, Miss Brandon is mysteriously returned to her concerned friends by the local padre. His housekeeper was remarkably close-mouthed, unfortunately. All she would admit was that a young lady—in a state of undress—had
wandered to the door, having been attacked by American
mercenaries. Perhaps you begin to see?"

"It seems I've lost the capacity to think straight," Steve
muttered harshly. "Why don't you save us both a lot of
trouble and tell me the rest of it?"

"Well—" Bishop shrugged deprecatingly. "I think you
know the rest. Prince Sahrkanov, strangely enough, appears to have a great deal of influence in high places. Ever
since he arrived in Mexico, in fact, things began to happen—or hadn't you noticed? You get transferred to a remote and extremely dangerous assignment. Your—Ginny is
appointed official translator to the Prince, courtesy of
the Señor Lerdo de Tejada himself. And after everything
has happened, the Prince himself comes to the rescue. It
seems he is a good friend of Senator Brandon's. They are
partners in certain business ventures, in fact. Senator
Brandon gives his consent to the Prince paying court to
his daughter—he informs the Prince that he has had her
marriage to you annulled. The Prince passes *this* piece of
information on to various persons—yes, Colonel Green
told you, did he not?—and, in the end, the Prince, and his
physician, Count Chernikoff, leave Mexico satisfied. I
think they took with them what they had come to find.
And when they land in San Francisco, Miss Brandon has
been married to the Prince, and is now the Princess
Sahrkanov."

There was a silence between them. Bishop, glancing
sideways under his hat brim, saw that Steve Morgan's face
had gone wooden, without expression.

"So Ginny's a princess. And I bet that makes the Senator happy, too. She doesn't seem to be miserable by any
means. Where in hell do I come into it?"

Imperceptibly, Jim Bishop's stiff shoulders relaxed.

"Well, there are a lot of puzzling things we've been
asking ourselves questions about," he said smoothly. "This

Prince Sahrkanov's connections with the Russian-American Company, for instance. The company, after having brought in fabulous profits for so many years, has suddenly started operating at a loss. And they say the Prince is a gambler. He left Russia to recoup his fortunes—met up with Count Chernikoff in Turkestan. From there, the Prince went to Alaska—and quite suddenly, he turns up in the United States, part of a diplomatic mission whose purpose is to negotiate the sale of Alaska to us. But I ask you, why is there suddenly so much opposition in the Senate? In April, they refused to ratify the Treaty. They're still arguing about it, with our mutual friend Brandon being one of the key men *against* ratification. And Sahrkanov, the man who went to Alaska to make money, is suddenly a wealthy man. He has married the Senator's daughter, and can afford to buy her expensive jewelry. He is an extremely close friend of the Tsar's personal physician—who also happens to be a close intimate of the Tsar. Would you call all this mere coincidence?"

"You always were pretty smart at fitting pieces in a puzzle together, Jim. And at playing poker, as I recall." Steve Morgan's voice was cold. "But this time—Goddamnit, this time I'm not buying in. Ginny's no longer my wife, nor any concern of mine. And you're not going to convince me she was forced into marrying Sahrkanov. You forget—I know her too well for that; and there's that newspaper clipping you sent me. . . . Sorry, Jim. If Sahrkanov and Brandon are mixed up in some kind of dishonest business deal, then Ginny's probably in on it, too. I remember the time she thought the whole idea of smuggling gold into Mexico was exciting. My God, she actually thought her father was a clever and resourceful man! No—you can count me out. I've no intention of interfering with Ginny's life again—nor spending any more of mine dodging her father's bounty hunters."

"Yes." Bishop's voice was colorless. "I'd heard about that. And I suppose I can't blame you for growing tired of running great risks for very little pay. In fact, your friend Diego Sandoval gave me to understand you'd taken over the running of the hacienda now that you're back and your grandfather's stroke has left him a semi-invalid. Ah, well. I suppose you'll be settling down now."

Steve shot him a suspicious glance.

"As a matter of fact," he said carefully, "my grandfather isn't exactly an invalid. And I'd been planning a trip to Europe, in a few months."

"Oh?" Bishop's face seemed to brighten slightly. "Well, if you'll be visiting Paris and London, there are a few small favors that you might do for me. Or for the Department, I should say. No need to worry about your ex-wife, or the Prince. I suppose I can put one of my other men on that assignment. Do you think Parker might be a good man?"

"Dammit, Parker's trigger happy! You told me so yourself. If you set him on Ginny. . . ."

On the verge of exploding with suppressed anger, Steve caught Bishop's bland, grey-eyed gaze and swore feelingly.

"Goddamn you to hell and back, you cold, calculating son of a bitch!"

Bishop smiled.

Part Two
THE MILLIONAIRE

Chapter Eleven

In San Francisco, half-grown, lusty child of the gold rush, everyone was money hungry. Men made—and lost—vast fortunes with amazing rapidity; and social distinctions here were based not on who you were, but how rich you were.

Ostentation, Ginny discovered, was everything. If you were wealthy you showed it, and took pride in what, in Europe, would have been deplored as vulgar exhibitionism.

"Here, my love, great ladies dress like whores, while the high-class whores imitate ladies," Ivan Sahrkanov announced lazily to his wife one evening, while she was dressing to go out. Arrogantly waving aside her maid, he picked up the magnificent emerald necklace he had presented her with, and bent to fasten it around her neck. Their eyes met in the mirror before which she sat—hers wide and slightly inquiring, his burning with a strange kind of anticipation.

"If my luck holds this evening, you shall have diamonds to wear soon." He stepped back and studied her rather pale face, his head to one side. "You wear jewels exceptionally well, Virginie. When we return to Russia, you will be all the rage."

"Because of my jewels or because everyone will be curious to get a glimpse of the Tsar's bastard daughter?"

Despite the very slight narrowing of his eyes, Ivan Sahrkanov continued to smile.

"One of the things I admire most about you, my dear, is your outspokenness. Come—you are ready?"

Tonight, before Ivan departed for one of the elegant gaming houses he frequented, they would be dining downstairs, with the Senator and guests. As Ginny descended the curving staircase, one gloved hand holding up her trailing skirts and the other resting on Ivan's arm, she was cynically aware of what a charming picture they must present to all those upturned, smiling faces. "A handsome couple"—she had heard the remark so often she was heartily sick of it. Wherever they went, heads turned to watch them. Women whispered enviously that she was lucky to have made such a catch; men clapped the Prince on the back and told him he was a lucky fellow to have captured such a prize. They were still referred to as "newlyweds" by the newspapers, although they had resided in San Francisco for almost three months now.

"Ginny, my dear . . . Ivan. . . ." Her father—it was easier to think of him that way—came hurrying forward to meet them. In spite of his smile, Ginny was aware of the fine tension lines in his face, the slight frown that now seemed permanently etched in his high forehead. She had not missed, either, the quick look he had exchanged with Ivan over her head. Business again, she supposed, smiling mechanically. And as soon as dinner was over they'd retire quickly into the library to "have a cigar or two" before Ivan left. . . .

But for the moment William Brandon was playing the part of polite host, and he introduced his daughter and son-in-law to the small circle of distinguished business aquaintances and their wives.

"Mrs. William Ralston. You've met Mr. Ralston before, of course."

Ginny smiled, putting out her hand. "Of course. At the bank. Mrs. Ralston, I'm so happy to meet you."

"Mr. and Mrs. Crocker—my daughter Virginia, and her husband, Prince Ivan Sahrkanov. And Virginia, may I present Sir Eric Fotheringay, our Consul from England."

"Such a pleasure, my dear Princess. Prince Sahrkanov. . . ."

Behind the artificial brilliance of her smile, and the slanting green eyes that matched the emeralds at her throat, Ginny's thoughts would have startled them all:

"Oh, God! Another interminably long, boring evening. I wonder how long I shall be expected to wear this polite simper on my face? And if someone suggests that the ladies might enjoy a game of piquet I shall—I shall immediately develop a splitting headache. Why must he feel that he has to entertain on such a large scale when Sonya tells me he is having business reverses?"

Of course all the men here were rich and influential. Sir Eric, the only bachelor present, was supposed to be possessed of an enormous fortune, amassed in India. And at the moment, as she had already gathered from snatches of conversation as she passed through the room, they were all interested in railroads.

When they sat down to dinner, with hired musicians providing soft music from a hidden alcove, Ginny found herself seated next to Sir Eric—a dull and pompous man of just past middle age, with a bristling mustache and a habit of speaking in short, staccato sentences.

It took her some time to realize that in a bluff, almost off-handed way, he was actually flirting with her.

"Always did like sitting beside a pretty gal. Hem! Pretty necklace you're wearing—nice stones." While he spoke, his slightly protuberant eyes devoured her bosom.

"Thank you," she said demurely, and he leaned closer to her.

"Half French, aren't you? Thought I heard someone say. Always did like French women. Know how to wear clothes. And they're not as prissy and stiff as the ladies in my own country—or Germany, for that matter. Hmph! Never did care much for German women."

"But what do you think of American women, Sir Eric?"

Ginny made her voice sound deliberately naive, while at the same time she slanted a provocative look at him from under her long lashes. Predictably, Sir Eric's face reddened.

"Why—ahem! They're lovely, of course. But you don't call yourself American, do you, my dear?" His pop eyes travelled from her face to her bare shoulders. "I—well, I understand I'm to be your escort to the theater this evening. Pity the Prince can't accompany us, of course, but . . . you won't mind an old man's company, I hope."

As she lowered her eyelashes with pretended shyness and then gave him a smile, Ginny thought: I have missed my real calling after all. What a good courtesan I would have made.

Aloud she said the obvious. "But how can you call yourself *old*? You're a man in the prime of his life—a *mature* man."

She caught Sonya's eye for a fleeting moment. Appraising—could it actually be pleading? This small "informal" dinner was important then. Sonya had hinted at it earlier, while Ivan had urged her to be charming to the important guests. And how far was her charm supposed to extend?

Fortunately for her, the men were talking railroads again, and Ginny made herself listen, if only to avoid Sir Eric's eyes. Central Pacific ... Union Pacific—Charles Crocker was boasting about cheap and efficient Chinese labor. And there was talk about federal land grants to the railroads, the importance of help in Washington.

From railroads, the conversation turned to mining, and Mr. Ralston praised the acumen of his bank's manager in Virigina City, a Mr. Sharon. The women present, obviously used to business being discussed over dinner, either listened without interest, or talked among themselves in low voices.

"Money!" Ginny thought bitterly. "That's all they can think about—or care about for that matter. Making more money, and then finding new ways to spend it."

As the dinner dragged on, through its interminable courses, each preceded by a fine imported wine, Ginny heard for the first time a name that she was to hear many times again, over and over.

". . . Murdock," the Senator was saying. "Does anyone know anything about him but his name?"

"The name's all *I've* heard. But it's backed by a pretty sizeable bank account." William Ralston cleared his throat. "Seems to be a very cagey man, though. Diversified interests."

Ginny was too occupied in trying to move her foot far enough and tactfully enough under her chair to avoid the sly pressure of Sir Eric's shiny leather shoe to pay too much attention to the conversation.

"I feel sure that I can trust you to keep the man at a distance, of course," Ivan whispered to her later, before he departed for Colonel Gamble's Gaming House, some fourteen miles out of San Francisco. "But be nice to him, Virginie. It is important—both to me and to your father. Sir Eric has money to invest in the right kind of venture, you see."

"I have done my best to be charming, as you put it. And now I must be nice. Just how far would you have me go, Ivan?"

His eyes hardened until they looked like glass, but he smiled, running one finger along the side of her face.

"How lovely you are! Just the kind of wife I have always looked for. I'm sure you'll know just how to cope with any situation that might arise, won't you, my dearest?" Bending down, he kissed her cold, unresponsive lips. "Don't wait up for me. I'll try not to disturb you when I come in. And have a pleasant evening."

Ginny left for the theater with the others in a thoughtful mood. "Have a pleasant evening." His invariable words when he left her. Words that had come to have a double-edged significance. He always said so, and especially when she was going out without him—usually escorted by another man. Never alone with the man, of course. There must be no sly gossip about the Princess Sahrkanov. But the last time . . . yes, the last time he had made his pleasant, smiling speech was on the occasion when Frank Julius had been her escort.

The handsome, charming Southerner she had first met in Vera Cruz had made part of the fortune he had then promised her he was going to win. Well-dressed, suave, it was Ivan himself who, not knowing they had met before, had introduced him to her at a reception they had both attended.

And from that time on, it seemed as if Mr. Julius was constantly underfoot; he turned up at every function she attended. She had been grateful to him, at first, for pretending that they had not met before. But later. . . .

"You are just as lovely as ever," he had whispered to her while they were dancing. But—forgive my curiosity— what happened to your last husband? When you left Vera Cruz so abruptly, we all missed you."

Her temper flared, making her green eyes turn brilliant.

"I'm married to Prince Sahrkanov now. I . . ." she hesitated and then said abruptly, "I lost my last husband. Does that satisfy your curiosity?"

It did not, of course. As he had done before, he began to pursue her, ever so subtly. He sent her flowers; he seemed to know exactly what nights Ivan would be busy elsewhere. And apparently, he studied her movements during the day, for one afternoon, when she had been visiting Mr. R. B. Woodward's famous Art Gallery on Mission Street, he appeared to intercept her.

"Take a stroll through the gardens with me. What would be wrong with that? I recall a time when you enjoyed being unconventional."

"You remember a great deal, Mr. Julius!"

"Frank, please. We've been acquaintances for a long time, haven't we?"

His dark, smiling face looked down into hers, the expression in his eyes unmistakeable. "Surely you're not afraid of me, Princess? Your husband and I have business interests in common, didn't he tell you? I'm sure he would have no objection to our taking a harmless and quite innocuous stroll together."

Or to whatever else might follow, his eyes told her; and although she did not walk with him, he continued to be persistent, so that she finally confronted Ivan with the matter.

"You've been throwing Frank Julius at my head. Urging me to be polite to him. Am I to allow him to become my lover?"

A week later, the Police Gazette had a highly-colored story of a vicious attack by Barbary Coast hoodlums on a certain Mr. Julius, who, it was hinted, owned several houses of ill-repute, and was involved in the smuggling of young women from all over the world into San Francisco. Mr. Julius did not die, but his handsome face had been beaten and slashed so terribly that he would be scarred and ugly for life.

And before that, Ginny found herself thinking with a sudden uneasiness, there had been that poor young man from Boston, who swore he'd kill himself if she would not elope with him. The scion of a wealthy and socially prominent family, *he* had been the victim of bandits, when he was traveling to visit friends on the Peninsula one evening.

And now there was Sir Eric Fotheringay, whose manner grew bolder every moment. Ivan's "friends" all acted as if they had a right to subject her to their unwelcome attentions. And Ivan cared more for the gaming tables than sharing her bed. But *that* fact she did not mind in the least, and she had even told Sonya so, quite bluntly, when her stepmother, a rather worried frown puckering her forehead, had hinted delicately that perhaps the Senator could drop a word in the Prince's ear about his evenings out.

"Good heavens! I do hope you won't do so, Sonya. Like most Europeans, Ivan is used to going his own way, and *I* do not in the least object to the nights he spends with his friends."

"It's some of his so-called friends themselves that I object to," Ginny thought now, as she allowed Sir Eric to hand her politely out of the carriage before the theater, where they were to see a performance of that shocking play, *Camille*.

With the Englishman sitting far too close to her in their box, Ginny found herself unable to enjoy the drama being unfolded on stage. As soon as the house lights were lowered, he placed one arm across the back of her chair, so that his pudgy fingers touched her bare shoulders; and every now and then he would pat her knee with his other hand, whispering that French women were certainly far more worldly than their counterparts in other countries, and he had always admired them.

During the intermission he insisted on bringing her champagne, and before the play was ended he had asked her to join him for supper in his sumptuous bachelor apartment at the Baldwin Hotel.

"How kind! I shall ask my husband when he will be free," she answered him lightly, and he looked taken-aback and rather puzzled. What had he expected her to say?

"Sir Eric certainly appears to have taken quite a liking to you," Sonya mentioned casually after they had returned to the house on Rincon Hill. "He asked so many questions about you, it was quite embarrassing! Ginny—" catching her step-daughter's uncompromising and suddenly hard look, Sonya hesitated, biting her lip. "Ginny, why is it that I find it so hard to—to talk to you any more? It's as if we've become strangers to each other, and I used to think—well, there was a time when I thought we had become *friends*. Ginny, you're happy, aren't you? Your father and I . . ."

". . . were anxious to see me respectably married off; and now that I am, that should make you both happy. Doesn't it?"

Tired, her head aching from the combined effects of a late night and too much champagne, Ginny felt herself goaded beyond endurance. All evening, she had been asking herself what she was doing here, playing a part, pretending that the life she was leading was all that she had ever wanted her life to be. It was the happy ending to a fairy tale.

"Ginny!" Her blue eyes open wide, Sonya's face mirrored both shock and hurt. "I find I don't understand you any longer! Surely you can't think we wanted anything but your happiness? I thought it so romantic that Ivan should have fallen in love with your portrait, and when you came here already married to him, after such a whirlwind courtship, why, we all thought—"

"Then why do you begin to have doubts now?"

"I . . ." Sonya began to twist her fingers together helplessly. "I don't know! It's just that . . . well, Ivan leaves you alone so much, and you—you're just not the same girl I remember! Sometimes I feel as if you have deliberately erected a fence between us, and yet I seem to sense. . . ."

With an effort, Ginny forced herself to smile.

"It's late, and we're both so tired that I'm afraid we might start quarreling in a moment. Champagne always makes me impatient and irritable, you see, and I—I am not used to being asked questions."

Sonya's face flushed, but she did not say another word as she stood back and watched Ginny walk along the carpeted passageway that led to her own suite of rooms. The door closed firmly behind the young woman; with a sigh, shoulders drooping, Sonya made her way back to her own room, where her husband waited for her.

"Well?" William Brandon said, although one look at his wife's face had told him already that her efforts to wring some kind of confidence from Ginny had met with failure.

"It was just as you had supposed, I'm afraid. She won't talk to me. In fact she—she snubbed me, William!"

Brandon frowned. "Damned if I know what to make of the girl any longer!" he said gruffly. "Instead of being grateful to us for rescuing her from that unpleasant situation in Mexico, she seems to have turned into an iceberg. And Sahrkanov—" he sighed, and Sonya saw the lines around his mouth deepen. "I tell you, I don't know what to make of him either. He's all charm on the surface, but underneath—I don't mind confessing that he's begun to worry me."

Chapter Twelve

Senator Brandon was not the only person who had begun to worry about those hidden facets of Prince Sahrkanov's character which were just beginning to reveal themselves. The Count Chernikoff, who had returned only two days before from visiting New York and Washington, was even more concerned, for he knew the Prince better than most people did.

The Count had been away for a little over two months, and no sooner had he taken up his temporary residence at the Baldwin Hotel than he began to hear whispers—they were hardly rumors yet, for Sahrkanov, known as a dangerous enemy, also exercised a certain amount of caution. Still, the Count pondered heavily, there was the gambling—for how long could that be hidden? It had been Ivan's downfall once before; that, and certain other habits. And now, in spite of all his careful discretion, it was inevitable that rumors would begin to leak out—these things always did. But what could *he* do about it?

There was only one solution, of course, the old man knew. He must persuade the Prince to return to Russia. With the girl beside him, as his wife, and her remarkable resemblance to Genevieve, the Emperor could not help but soften. Besides, Ivan had been away a long time, and he was older, and a little more in control of his—moods.

The Count made up his mind to call at Senator Brandon's house that same afternoon, to see for himself how things were. Strange that Ivan, who no doubt knew of his arrival in the city, had not come to see him. The thought made the old man slightly uneasy, although his manner, when he bowed with old-fashioned gallantry over his hostess' hand showed no traces of it.

"I hope you will forgive me for this unannounced visit, madame."

His sharp grey eyes had noticed that Mrs. Brandon wore a slightly distrait look, and that her normally placid face looked paler than usual, and a trifle tired. Merely a late night? Or perhaps she, like her husband, was worried at the latest news from the once-booming Comstock region? Even in New York, there had been whispers, and the value of shares that were once sky-high were dropping. It was said that the veins of gold and silver that had seemed inexhaustible were petering out, and the new millionaires were beginning to worry. Those who had been far-sighted in the beginning had invested in the railroads that were connecting the vast continent of America, in the river steamers, shipping lines, and real estate. But was Brandon one of these?

Even while the thoughts flashed through Count Chernikoff's mind, Sonya Brandon was protesting that his visit was welcome, and they had all been wondering when he would return.

"Ah, but you seem to be dressed for going out. I must not inconvenience you."

"Yes. I had planned to visit some friends, but Ginny is here; she slept late this morning, for we were all at the theater last night. I'm sure she'll be happy to see you. Please, won't you sit down? I've already sent one of the servants to tell her that you're here."

While the Count waited, occupied by his own thoughts, Ginny was frowning at her reflection in the mirror while her mulatto maid worked with deft fingers at arranging her hair.

So Count Chernikoff was back. She wondered if he had already spoken to Ivan. And when she thought about Ivan, her head began to ache slightly, although not half as badly as it had last night, when she had left Sonya.

Perhaps she should ask the Count to give her some

more of his magical powders, which seemed to soothe her and make the headaches go away. Ivan had brought her some, but already the supply was running low, and she needed something to help her sleep, to help her go through the days that stretched endlessly and emptily in front of her. Yes, she would take one before she went downstairs, Ginny thought. It would help her face those sharp eyes of his, and the questions he was bound to ask.

He would ask where Ivan was, of course, and she couldn't tell him. Not that she cared! She was happier and more comfortable when Ivan was away.

This morning, awaking from a night filled with strange dreams, full of colors and writhing figures, she had found him standing at the foot of her bed, staring down at her. He was fully dressed, his clothes as immaculate as usual, and she had found herself wondering dully if he had just returned.

"Good morning, my love! Shall I have them bring your breakfast up to you?" He studied her critically. "You're looking a trifle tired. Were you very late returning from the theater?"

"Yes. It was a wonderfully boring evening, as usual. And you? Was your night successful?" She remembered thinking how blasé she sounded, and then Ivan decided to sit down beside her on the bed, solicitously propping the pillows behind her so that she could sit up. The covers fell away, revealing her bare, white shoulders, and his eyes took on a new look, which made her say quickly:

"I believe I would like a cup of coffee. Would you mind ringing, please?"

"In a moment. Do you know how adorable you look in the mornings?" His fingers caressed her shoulders, and she had to force herself not to shrink from their touch. "You look like a frightened gazelle," he said softly. "Were you afraid I might force myself upon you?" His eyes seemed to laugh at her, but there was that strange glow in their depths that she had begun to recognize, and she waited for his next words, which came abruptly.

"Did you find Sir Eric good company? He admires you. In fact, he has asked me if I have any objections to your acting as his hostess at a small supper he is giving for some business acquaintances—very important men, among them this mysterious Mr. Murdock everyone is talking about. And all you would have to do is to look beautiful—and to listen." In the face of her sudden, taut silence he leaned forward, pressing his lips against her throat, where a pulse beat agitatedly. "Your father's quite worried about the way the Comstock shares have been falling off recently. And these men are the manipulators, the big ones. Who knows what interesting bits of information an intelligent woman might pick up? I'm sure that like most men, they believe a lovely woman has no brains to speak of. Wouldn't you like to prove them wrong, ma petite?"

"And you? Will you be there, too?"

Ginny made herself ask the question, her voice even. Her body stiff, she felt the covers slide downward, his fingers brushing against her half-exposed breasts.

"Have you been missing me? But you were brought up in Europe, you are understanding, I know. The business that takes me away so many nights is—merely business, my dear! This is the country, and the city, where a clever man, backed by an intelligent and understanding woman, may make a fortune. When we return to Russia, I don't wish them to say that the Prince Sahrkanov is content to live off his wife's money and estates." His voice hardened. "I come of a very old and proud family, Virginie. You understand? No—I had not planned to be present at this supper. Perhaps my presence would—inhibit the conversation which would otherwise flow quite freely, I'm sure. But I trust you completely, of course. And your discretion. Did I not promise you that I would prove an understanding husband? So—you will consent to this small request from our good friend, will you not? I assure you it will all be quite proper. Sir Eric Fotheringay is no crude American captain—"

"No!" she said it violently, sitting up quite straight. "No, Ivan, I will not be used like this. It just happens that I find Sir Eric an obnoxious bore, who cannot seem to keep his hands off me. But as much as I dislike him, I would not want to hear that he, too, has met with an unfortunate and violent 'accident' a few weeks from now! Do you understand me?"

She refused to shrink from the sudden violence that flared momentarily in Ivan's light, greenish-blue eyes. Their eyes met, hung together in silent combat, and then he stood up; the only sign of anger in his face was the slight flush that came up under his fair skin.

Without another word, as if he could not trust himself in her presence any longer, he turned on his heel and left. And shortly afterward, she had rung for her own breakfast.

Delia, her personal maid, had brought her a flat jewelry box along with the coffee and rolls she had ordered.

"The Prince said I was to give you this, ma'am . . . Your Highness." Delia was still learning; her big, dark eyes could not hide her curiosity. "Said he was going to the Bankers Exchange for luncheon, but he'd be back later on, in the evening. And you're to wear them tonight with your new gown. . . . Oh, ma'am, I'm sure they must be beautiful, although I didn't look."

Emerald eardrops, shining against a white velvet background. So he had been lucky last night. But the sparkling stones could not arouse any pleasure in her. More baubles, to help the Princess play her role better.

Delia was finished at last, and patting at Ginny's shining coils of hair with a satisfied exclamation, she went to pull the heavy draperies aside, letting in the sunshine.

"You sure look beautiful, ma'am . . . Princess." She giggled. "It'll be wasted on that old gentleman waiting downstairs, though." And then, remembering herself, "Will you be needing anything else now?"

"No—nothing else. Thank you, Delia."

This afternoon, she wore pearls, to go with a biscuit-colored gown trimmed with brown. Outside, through her window, the sky looked very blue since the morning fog had been driven away by the sharp breezes that blew in from the bay. Suddenly, unwillingly, she was reminded of Vera Cruz, the seemingly endless waiting; and at its end— Steve. Names she had forbidden herself to think. Emotions she had forced herself to forget.

"He wanted me because he thought he had lost me . . . by now, he's forgotten." And by some odd quirk of fate, she was married to Ivan Sahrkanov now; and remembering the past was far too painful, as well as useless. It was over. She wouldn't think about it! She took a powder and left her room.

"My dearest child!" Why did he insist on calling her so? As spry-looking as ever, Count Chernikoff had sprung to his feet, bending over Ginny's outstretched hand. She made herself smile as his piercing eyes studied her face.

"It's good to see you again." Banalities; politely exchanged.

Ginny felt herself on guard, tautly drawn up inside. But soon, when the powder had taken effect, she would feel ready to cope with anything.

The Count's eyes seemed to see behind her carefully erected defenses.

"But you are far too thin!" His voice was disapproving. "Haven't you been eating well?" She saw the way his eyes travelled over her slim figure, and wanted to giggle hysterically. Perhaps he imagined she was pregnant! How would he react if she hinted as much?

"Come, sit down. And tell me how you have been. You're happy?" Again, another sharp glance from his piercing eyes. "And Ivan, how is he? I have not had an opportunity of meeting him since I've been back, and so, you see, I am here, to find out at first hand, as you say in America."

So he hadn't spoken to Ivan at all. What did it matter? Ginny had mixed feelings about the Count, in spite of his kindness towards her. Was it only a coincidence that he had been feeling ill that night when she had drunk far too much, and found herself maneuvered into marriage with Ivan? No, she didn't trust him, any more than she trusted Ivan himself. They were all using her, in some way or another.

But what did that matter either? Ever since she had left Mexico, nothing seemed to matter, except finding forgetfulness.

She heard herself say: "I've been fine. And Ivan's been busy. He has so many business friends! Haven't you noticed that everyone who comes to San Francisco wants to acquire a fortune? The city is full of millionaires, falling over each other to find new ways to spend their money."

She had not meant to say that, but no matter. Let the Count draw his own conclusions. A delicious, soothing feeling of strength crept over her as she felt the powder take effect, and her eyes brightened.

"Tell me about New York. I was only there for a short time, you know, and that was shortly after the war. Is it very gay?"

"Not as gay as San Francisco, I'm sure, although there, too, the streets are lit with the new gaslights. So—" the Count's voice sounded thoughtful. "You are happy here?" he asked then.

Why did everyone keep asking her that? Happiness was not feeling, not thinking, and especially not remembering. Ginny shrugged.

"Why shouldn't I be? I find San Francisco interesting."

They fenced with each other—the Count asking questions and she parrying them. And finally, when he rose to take his leave, there had been no advantage gained on either side, or so Ginny thought.

Very casually, as she walked with him to the front door, she asked: "I wonder if you'd be kind enough to make me up some more powders? I find it difficult to get to sleep sometimes, and occasionally I have a headache that nothing else will help."

"Certainly." Did she imagine the sudden sharpening of his gaze? "I'll call again, if you'll let me—or perhaps you can persuade your husband to visit an old friend?"

"I'll tell him. I'm sure he'll want to hear all the news." Her voice was suddenly light, and she felt filled with energy, ready to face anything. Why was the Count gazing at her so steadily.

"My child, you're sure you feel—well? There's nothing wrong?"

She laughed.

"Of course I feel well! I feel wonderful. Can't you smell the sea on the breeze that comes up off the bay? San Francisco is such an exciting city, don't you think so?"

"Perhaps," he said. "Perhaps." But when he entered his carriage and was driving away, Count Chernikoff's look was still thoughtful. It was cold, and a trifle stern when he faced Ivan Sahrkanov later on.

"So—you have decided to visit me after all. Can it be that you went back home long enough to learn that I had called?"

"As a matter of fact, I have been busy. But yes, I was told of your visit. Had I known earlier that you had returned to San Francisco, I would have come before."

"I am sure that your informants are as efficient as mine," the Count said drily. "Well, Ivan?"

"Well? Do you want a report of my activities? I am

sure you are aware how things have been going. Comstock shares are dropping. It's an open secret that the veins of precious ore are thinning out. Unfortunately, my father-in-law is an overly-cautious man. Those land deals in the southern part of the state are not going too successfully. Therefore, I have had to find my own methods to protect our investments."

"And these include spending your nights in gaming houses? Mixing with persons of dubious repute? Have you forgotten that you are now a married man?" The Count began to pace about his room, hands clasped behind his back. "If I had known that it would come to this when you tricked that poor child into marriage by giving her some of the liquid I had distilled from those cactus buttons the natives call peyote. . . . But, God forgive me, I thought that after all it might be for the best. She seemed calm enough afterwards, and I thought—yes, I thought that perhaps *you* had decided to change, too. I have never seen you as intrigued and attracted by a woman before. But if you have injured her in any way—"

"My dear Dimitri! Or should I call you uncle? What do you think I am? A brutish creature with no intelligence? The lovely Virginie is everything I had hoped a wife would be. And even if she were not, do you think I would dare lay a finger on our Tsar's daughter? No—indeed, you misjudge me!"

Ivan Sahrkahov continued to wear a slightly mocking smile when he left the Count's apartments. But by the time he had taken up the reins of the matched horses that drew his phaeton, the smile had vanished.

This interference in his life, just as if he had still been a child, was intolerable! As was the command, phrased as a suggestion, that their return journey to Russia should not be put off for too much longer.

The old man had talked, pacing up and down, and Ivan had listened, with the slight, scornful smile tugging at his lips. Well, old men enjoyed the sounds of their own voices. And for all his hectoring tone, Count Chernikoff was his uncle, the ties of blood still strong.

Prince Sahrkanov drove to a house on Washington Street, and tossing the reins to a shaggy-haired boy who seemed to appear from nowhere, let himself in with his key, and strode upstairs.

Gaslights already flared garishly on the streets outside; no doubt, at the Senator's house on Rincon Hill, dinner was already in progress. He was supposed to be dining with the Count tonight—there would be no questions asked afterwards. Not that his charming wife ever asked questions. Tonight, no doubt, she would be wearing the emeralds dangling from her small ears as she made conversation with the Senator's usual guests, including Sir Eric Fotheringay.

Ivan Sahrkanov's face darkened when he remembered the little scene that had taken place that morning. "No!" she had flung at him, her green eyes gleaming defiantly—and she had dared face him with her accusations. But she would change her tune. His mind pictured her as he had seen her dancing, that first time, all gypsy fire, and then later, with bruises on that pale, gleaming body that had belonged to so many men before; it belonged only to him now. This morning—this morning it had taken all the willpower he possessed to turn on his heel and walk away from her. Just in time, he had remembered who she was and where he was.

Upstairs, in the crimson-hung room where the woman he owned waited for him, Ivan Sahrkanov could be himself again. She was half-Chinese, and undesirable to her own people because her father had been a foreign devil like himself, and had left her feet unbound. She was beautiful. Dark brown hair slipping long and straight like silk, past her shoulders, below her waist. He made her knot it up, high atop her small, bowed head, before he took his particular pleasure of her body.

A flush had arisen beneath his fair skin, and his breath came sharply, raspingly. A lock of brown hair, bleached on top by the sun, fell across his forehead as he looked down at her silent, writhing body; marks of his attentions marred the ivory flesh from her shoulders to her thighs. In places, tiny drops of blood oozed freely, spotting the sheets.

She was his—his slave, his thing. And she adored him; worshipped him because he had saved her from a Chinatown crib and a life of servicing one man after another until, in a few years time, they would have thrown her body in the bay, to the sharks. He had bought her, only three weeks ago, and she had been a virgin. Naked, taller than most Chinese women, she was like an exquisite porcelian statuette except for the livid, striated marks across her naked flesh. Marks that proved his ownership of her—his need for her.

"Get up!" He dropped the whip, and she picked it up, crouching at his feet now, in the age-old attitude of submission. She was woman conquered; woman mastered and put in her proper place.

His breath still coming fast, the monster inside him still unsated, Ivan looked down at her bent head, the trembling body.

"Bitch! Get up, I said. No," he snarled as she made an abortive move to reach for the thin silk robe she had tossed aside at his orders. "Did I tell you you could get dressed again? Go now, and bring your brother to me. And the perfumed oil. . . ."

Smiling, ignoring the tears that slipped silently down her face, he began to undress.

Chapter Thirteen

&\o

For the first time in weeks, the Prince Sahrkanov returned to his bedroom at an hour shortly before midnight. He had shared a glass of port with his father-in-law in the library downstairs, briefly discussed a few business matters, and noticed with some amusement that while Brandon obviously wanted to broach the subject of his many late nights, he could not quite bring himself to do so.

Ginny, the Prince was told, had retired early, pleading a headache. "Perhaps she needs a little change of scenery," the Prince announced easily, biting off the end of his cigar. "Sir Eric was speaking of inviting us down to his country cottage on the Peninsula—not too far from Ralston's place at Belmont. I must see what she thinks of the idea."

And with that he strolled casually up the stairs, leaving

the Senator staring after him; a slight frown was etched between the Senator's brows.

The Sahrkanovs had been allotted separate bedrooms, connected by a dressing room, and now, without knocking, the Prince walked swiftly through the dressing room, tying the belt of his brocaded dressing gown around his waist. Ginny's door was unlocked—of course it would be! She had no reason to close it against him.

Very gently, Ivan lifted the covers from her sleeping body, which was almost as slim as a boy's, except for the curving roundness of her hips and small, perfectly shaped breasts. She lay with one arm cuddling the pillow, her face partly buried in it, as if she were embracing a lover. And indeed, she slept so deeply, her coppery hair lying in tangles about her face and shoulders, he guessed she had taken another powder before she had retired. So she was still trying to forget—but in the process, she would be binding herself, closer and more and more irrevocably to him.

After a moment, Ivan discarded his dressing gown, tossing it carelessly aside, and lay beside her. He drew the covers up over them both, and although Ginny stirred and sighed in her sleep, she did not wake. Making no attempt to touch her, he lay on his back, with his arms crossed beneath his head, staring up at the ceiling. And his thoughts made him smile slightly to himself.

His face, smiling down at her, was the first thing Ginny saw when she opened her eyes in the morning.

"When—"

"Last night, my love. I made it a point to be home especially early, but alas, you had already gone to bed with one of your headaches. So—I decided to join you here."

Her eyes had begun to blink at him stormily, but when she would have moved, she found her hair trapped beneath his shoulder.

"You should not have—"

"Should not have? Should not have joined my sleeping wife in her bed, you mean? But why not? We're married—and I've been reminded that I've been neglecting you most shamefully. And indeed, seeing you in such delicious dishabille, I began to feel that I have, indeed, been missing something."

Ginny stared up into his bland, smiling face with its

cold eyes that reminded her of windowpanes with rain
streaming down their surface. It was impossible to know
what he really thought by looking into those strangely
opaque eyes. And, she thought despairingly, if she tried to
fight him off now she would only make herself look ridiculous. But why did she have the impression that he was actually punishing her for something, in some subtle way?

"My darling, what a perfect body you have. So slim—
your flesh so firm and warm. What man could fail to desire you?"

There was something mechanical about Ivan's lovemaking, in spite of the flattering ardency of his words, that always repelled Ginny slightly. She had the feeling that he
was in the habit of detaching a part of his mind so that he
could study her reactions; and although he was a consider-
ate lover, taking pains to arouse her with caresses, she
could not help holding back—or, shamefully, feigning the
response he seemed determined to wrest from her unwilling body so he would be satisfied quickly and leave her
alone.

This particular morning was a repetition of other occasions, and after the first involuntary stiffening of her body
as Ivan drew the sheer lawn nightdress over her head, she
closed her eyes and let his hands and his lips have their
way.

At least, thank God, Ivan was not overly imaginative.
She could not have borne it if he had been. And then,
even as she thought this, he suddenly caught her by the
shoulders, turning her body over.

"Ivan, no!" Ginny tried to wriggle free, but his weight
pinned her down against crumpled sheets; his hands slipped
under her body to cup her breasts.

"Yes, why not? I'm sure you've made love this way before; you're no innocent, easily shocked child, are you?
Come Virginie, I will not hurt you—don't resist me."

There was a strange new note in his voice that she had
not heard before, a rasping breathlessness. She could hear
him panting, his breath hot against the back of her neck.
And although she tried to struggle, his strength was inexorable; she felt as if the weight of his body would break
her back as he held her pinned to the bed. He held her
that way, caressing her roughly, until her muffled, angry

protests were stilled, and, half-sobbing, she became acquiescent.

"You see, I mean to make up for my neglect of your lovely body," he whispered as he took her perversely, painfully, so that she had to bury her face in the pillows to keep from screaming out loud at the agony and degradation he was inflicting on her.

Afterwards, Ivan was all tender consideration, as he sat stroking her body.

"There is no reason why a man should not be—inventive in his lovemaking, is there my love? You know, I was beginning to feel that you were becoming bored! All these headaches—what is a husband to think? I know I'm partly to blame for staying away at night, but it's for you—for us—that I pursue this business. I thought, being half-American, that you would understand; but if you'd rather have me home with you every night, so that I may perform the—uh—pleasant duties of husband and lover, then of course I shall be happy to oblige you."

Knowing by now what was expected of her, Ginny said stiffly:

"There's no need for you to put yourself out. Please—you must do as you feel is best where your business matters are concerned. I—I have been so busy that I truly haven't had too much time in which to feel neglected."

"Ah!" His hand paused, resting lightly on her thigh for an instant. "So you do understand. I thought you would! From now on we'll live our lives as *we* see fit, shall we? And let the busybodies manage their own affairs. What do you say?"

"I agree with you, of course."

Their eyes met, and with a small, sardonic smile, Ivan leaned over her, dropping a light kiss on her forehead.

"Thank you, my love. And now, I'll leave you to rest awhile, if you'd like. You don't have another one of those headaches, I hope?"

Ginny shook her head silently, waiting only until he had left the room to spring from the bed, crossing to the mahogany washstand that was discreetly screened off in one corner of the room.

She began to scrub at her body almost viciously, until her skin looked chafed and reddened.

How she despised herself! And how she had grown to

dislike and mistrust the man who was her husband! The thoughts beat against her mind until Ginny wanted to press both hands against her temples to still their throbbing. How unreal everything seemed! It just wasn't possible that her life could have changed so drastically within the space of a few months—that she was married to a strange man she hardly knew, who had the right to use her body in any way he pleased, and did so. And yet, she suspected that if she had never met Steve—if none of it had happened—she might actually have been content with the kind of life she had now. . . .

Freshly bathed and dressed, her hair tied back with a wide green ribbon that matched her eyes, Ginny joined her stepmother for breakfast in the small morning room. The Senator had already left the house, to go down to Montgomery Street.

"He's worried, you know," Sonya said abruptly. And then, as if the words had been forced from her, "Or aren't you aware of what is happening around you any longer?"

Startled out of her lethargy, Ginny looked up, meeting barely veiled hostility in Sonya's blue eyes; there was a slight knitting of her brows.

"What is the point of worrying about anything? If something's going to happen it will happen in any case. And sometimes it is far more pleasant to avoid reality." Her voice was calm and uninflected, and the air of indifference she wore habitually now annoyed Sonya almost beyond endurance.

"Escaping from reality! Is that why you so constantly have headaches? And why you do not seem to care for anyone or anything? Oh—oh, for God's sake! Ginny, I could—could shake you. Why do you insist on keeping such a distance between us?"

Sonya's normally unruffled voice was sharp, her face flushed with the force of her emotions.

"But you *shall* hear me out this time, unpleasant or not! I have not asked you any questions about those months you spent in Mexico, after you—after that terrible, horrifying afternoon that I shall never forget, for as long as I live! And your father and I have never reproached you for not writing. We had nothing from you but that cold, emotionless note, when we were frantic with grief and worry. And even then you had to lie to us! Do you realize how much time and money your father has spent in trying to find you? In trying to ensure that you were returned here safely? And now you are married to a Prince, a man who obviously adores you, and gives you everything you want, and yet you. . . . Have you ever asked yourself why Ivan spends so many nights away? Do you care?"

Ginny had remained silent all this time, her lips pressed tightly together, but now, as her stepmother paused for breath, she looked up, and her eyes were bright with anger.

"Do I care? No! In fact, I prefer it that way, if you must have the truth. And I would much rather have been allowed to stay in Mexico, where I was happy—for a time at least—until other people began meddling in my life. And now, as you've reminded me, I'm married to a Prince! But this is no fairy tale, Sonya dear, and you must forgive me if I choose my own ways of trying to escape from inescapable boredom."

Sonya leaned across the table, two bright spots of color in her cheeks.

"For all that you talk like a woman of the world, you are still a child, Ginny. You're barely twenty-one years of age, and you've been exposed, unfortunately, to certain ugly and undesirable aspects of life. Do you think your father has ever forgiven himself? But it was *your* fault, too—I warned you against flirting so boldly, and especially with a man of that detestable, treacherous type. It's too bad he wasn't killed, after all, but you may be sure that if he ever dares show his face close to the border he'll be shot down mercilessly, as he deserves, or caught and hanged. Oh, Ginny, how *could* you have made yourself so —so cheap? How could you have thought—well, Ivan has told us how quick Steve was to desert you. Do you think a man of his kind, who is nothing more than an animal, would not tire of a woman after a while? And for *this*—for rescuing you from further humiliation, from even worse, perhaps—you would turn your back on those people who really care for you? Your father—"

"Oh, stop it!" Ginny sprang to her feet, eyes narrow and glittering with exasperation. "Neither you nor my father has known me long enough to know what I am really like, or what kind of a woman I am. If I had turned out to be plain and dowdy I'm sure I would have been packed back to France or married off soon after I arrived here. And as it is—you *did* succeed in getting me *suitably* married, did you not? The Prince Sahrkanov—what a great catch! But I married Ivan only because I was—because I had had a shock, and I was frightened and unhappy and.... Oh, God! Even *I* do not know why I married him, except that I was either drunk or drugged at the time. And what does it matter now? It's done. But if my father had let me stay married to Steve. . . ."

Her breath caught over his name, and she was panting now, as Sonya, too, rose to her feet.

"After all he subjected you to, after everything he's done—oh, I hope they find him and kill him! And they will—for almost fifty thousand dollars in bounty money there are men just as vicious and as dangerous as *he* is, who will do anything!"

Ginny had gone so pale that her eyes seemed enormous and unusually bright in her white face.

She had forgotten, for a moment, that she had been so angry with Sonya a minute ago.

"But, why?" she whispered. "Why do you want him dead? Is it for revenge? Because of me? Do they imagine. . . ." She began to laugh, softly and hysterically. "Oh, no! Are they afraid he'll come after me and—and spoil things for everyone? Because if I thought he wanted me, I'd run away to him myself—even if I had to lie or cheat or kill to get there! Why do you look frightened? Haven't you been told that I've killed two men already?"

Sonya stared at her with horrified fascination. Already, she was sorry that she had let her temper run away with her tongue and her usual caution; but Ginny—the change in the girl was unbelievable. She had grown so hard, so cold and callous, that it was almost a relief to find she retained some human emotions after all.

"Oh, Ginny! How can you. . . ."

It was at that moment that a discreet tap at the door, followed by the entrance of the Senator's recently-hired English butler, drove both women to a temporary, silent truce.

"Excuse me, Madam. But it's Sir Eric Fotheringay, to call on the Princess. May I tell him you are at home?"

Because of the turmoil that raged inside her, tearing her nerves to shreds, Ginny's manner was quieter than usual, leading Sir Eric to think that she was a quiet, shy little creature after all, and not as sophisticated and flippant as he'd begun to think earlier. Perhaps the sly gossip he had heard about her rather flamboyant past was exaggerated after all. He'd still like to find out for himself—and that husband of hers, the Prince, didn't seem to mind in the least if other fellows, finding his wife attractive, paid her attention. Strange chap, Sahrkanov! But then, some of these Europeans were not nearly as straitlaced in their way of looking at things as people were in England. Perhaps they had a comfortable arrangement, these two.

It was all that Ginny could do to sit still, and to try and keep half her mind on Sir Eric's flow of polite banalities. All the memories, the sheer agony of hurt and rejection that she had tried to keep caged in the deepest recesses of her mind seemed to have been set free during that brief, ugly scene with Sonya. She felt as if they were ripping her apart. Oh God! She needed another of those powders. Sweet dream medicine. Anything to stop her thinking, feeling. She wondered if he noticed that her hands were shaking, and she hid them in the folds of her skirt, clasping them so tightly together that her rings bruised her knuckles.

"Had to come myself to tell you how grateful I am! Difficult for a confirmed old bachelor like myself to organize things just right, y'know? Nothing like a woman's touch—always makes any kind of social function go smoothly. And there'll be two or three other ladies present. I must say it *is* kind of the Prince to say it would be all right. You'll tell him he must come, too, if he can break away from that journey he has to take to Sacramento? Be glad to have him."

What on earth was he talking about? Ginny's nails bit into her palms. She smiled. "That's very kind of you. I'll tell him, of course," she said mechanically.

Why did they want Steve dead? Why couldn't her feelings for him be dead? She had to stop them. She must make her father see how pointless it was. Because if Steve had really loved her, even if he only *wanted* her, nothing would have stopped him. . . .

"Fine, fine!" Sir Eric seemed to have noticed nothing of her agitation. He was rubbing his pudgy hands together, with an expression of satisfaction. "You don't know how

happy it makes me, how much I appreciate your—um—
kindness. We'll make a weekend of it, eh? After all, with
Mrs. Brandon coming along later, and your father—who
knows, your husband might be able to join us, too; those
river steamers make good time, I'm told." He chuckled,
mistaking her suddenly blank look for consternation.
"High time you saw something of the Peninsula, m'dear.
And if it's the proprieties you're thinking of, why, I already told your husband. And it's all perfectly aboveboard
and proper. My housekeeper will be there—good, respectable woman, good family, fallen on bad times, you know?
Well. . . ."

He stood up, taking her cold hands in both of his and
squeezing them just an instant longer than was necessary.

"I can see you're looking rather peaked today—not
enough sunshine, eh? Won't keep you now—I know
women, and shopping! But I'll call again, if I may. The
Senator's been kind enough to invite me for supper next
Thursday. We'll discuss wines and a menu then—be glad to
have your advice."

How he talked! She had hardly said a word, and her
inattention had trapped her into the very thing she had refused to do earlier. That, and Ivan's subtle, unpleasant
brand of blackmail.

So she was to play his hostess at a weekend houseparty
in the country somewhere. The thought was suddenly almost hysterically funny. "I wonder what my *other* duties
will consist of?" Ginny thought dully—and she didn't care.

Chapter Fourteen

Later, when she looked back, Ginny could remember
hardly anything of the week that followed her encounter
with Sonya in the morning room—and Sir Eric's visit. It
seemed as though she watched the world from a distance,
through a gold-speckled veil of gauze.

Suddenly, they were all so very kind to her! Even Sonya, who apologized prettily for her outburst of temper. And Ivan bought her an emerald ring of such size that it seemed to weigh down her finger, and a bottle of some tonic he said the Count had prescribed for her nerves.

"He says you have grown far too thin, my darling. And these headaches of yours—"

"But they go away as soon as I take one of those powders!"

"Well, you can continue taking those, of course, but only when you really need them. The tonic is to help you sleep better, and to put some color back in your face."

His solicitude might have touched her if she hadn't realized, even in her somnambulistic state, that he had his reasons for it. Hadn't she decided to be a good, helpful girl after all?

They were all happy—and grateful. Even her father— *was* he her father? Had Ivan and the Count between them made up the whole fairy story she had been told?—oh yes, the Senator was proud of her, too. Hadn't he told her so himself? Things were looking bad for shareholders in the Comstock; the information she could pick up during her visit to Sir Eric's country house could prove invaluable.

"Ivan and I are—well, you might say we are partners, of a sort, in a few business ventures. He had some money to invest when he first arrived here, and I was able to give him some advice. But now. . . ." For the first time the Senator had looked a trifle distracted, and Ginny noticed how his fingers began to drum absent-mindedly on his desk top. He said abruptly, "It's become very important to me, Ginny, to find out exactly what is happening with the mining industry; which shares the men in the know are investing in right now. Being a politician, I can't afford to get officially involved, or show too much interest. And that's why I'm not attending that dinner party. The men who have been invited all know each other, and are likely to talk far more freely of business matters in *your* presence than in mine."

"Oh, yes, I remember what Ivan said. I'm supposed to be a pretty ornament, with nothing but frivolous thoughts in my head!"

But for all the sting in her words, Ginny's tone was almost apathetic. Much easier *not* to have to think at all. Or to remember.

Her father had been exaggeratedly patient when she had spoken to him of Steve—forcing herself to bring the subject out into the open between them for the first time.

She mustn't start worrying herself on that rascal's account, he told her soothingly. He didn't deserve her concern. And as for the fifty thousand dollar reward, well—perhaps Sonya had exaggerated slightly! It was only meant as a *warning*, after all. A hint that Steve Morgan should stay in Mexico, where he belonged.

To protest any further, to fight against them all, was just like struggling against the enveloping folds of a silken cocoon—the struggle was too much effort.

Once or twice, and especially when she had not had one of her powders and every nerve end in her body seemed to be screaming, Ginny had thought: I could run away; I'm not a prisoner. But where would she run to? And the most humiliating thought of all, she had no money of her own; or not enough, at any rate, to take her very far. So she *was* a prisoner of a sort, after all—imprisoned by the luxury and comfort that surrounded her, and by all the kind people who said they wanted only her happiness. When she looked back at herself as she had been a year ago, or even months ago, it was like looking at a different person. A stranger so completely at variance with the woman she was *now* that it was hardly possible to recognize herself.

She was—detached. Yes, that was the word. How pleasant to be able to detach herself from all that was unpleasant to contemplate—to hide herself away in her mind while her body went on quite mechanically, moving and smiling and saying all the right, trite things at the right times.

"The Princess Sahrkanov?" Sir Eric's friends all said. "A lovely young creature, of course, but rather dull. Doesn't have much to say for herself. Surprising, in view of all the stories. . . ."

"All exaggerations, obviously!" Sir Eric winked heavily. "And as for brains—who needs brains in a woman, eh? Give me a pretty woman with a good figure who knows how to wear the right clothes and doesn't try to think for herself. Now *that's* what I expect a woman to be!"

Sir Eric, a rapacious and remarkably shrewd businessman, for all his dull, rather ponderous-seeming manner, was known to have boasted that he always got in the end whatever it was he set out to get. Among the few friends in his intimate circle, it soon became understood that the Englishman had marked the Princess Sahrkanov as his next quarry. And, was it not also common knowledge that the Prince, a sophisticated European, was a remarkably tolerant and understanding husband? He was also the kind of man who liked to travel about a lot—they said he was looking for land to buy in California; they whispered also that he loved the gaming tables. But at least he wasn't the selfish kind of man who would expect a young and pretty wife to stay home and mope during his absences. Sir Eric said the Prince was a "fine chap," and the democratic Americans, impressed in spite of themselves by his title, called him a "splendid fellow."

Very few people knew anything about the real man who lurked beneath the Prince's suave, smiling exterior—and of them, Ginny knew the least.

She tried not to think of Ivan when he was away from her, and was immeasurably relieved when, following her capitulation, he kept his side of their rather unsavory bargain and stayed away from her bed.

Locked away in her own ivory tower, Ginny found she could regard the preparations that were already being made for their journey down to the Peninsula with something approaching equanimity. She had a new supply of powders for her headaches and occasional moods of tension, and the tonic that Ivan had brought her had actually seemed to help. She slept better, and felt better in general; not even Sir Eric's clumsy attempts at flirting with her, or the sly pressure of his knee against hers as he sat beside her on the night he came for dinner, had the power to make her angry.

While she felt incapable of any strong emotion, Ginny felt herself filled with a sense of well-being and strength. She was no longer constantly tired, as she used to be, and even Sonya remarked on it.

"Why, Ginny, I do believe you are beginning to enjoy San Francisco after all! Admit it—aren't you looking forward just a little bit to the weekend?"

They were leaving San Francisco very early on Friday morning, accompanied by Sir Eric, himself. Ivan had departed for Sacramento the day before, and the house would be closed up and left in charge of the servants until the following Wednesday.

Ginny was reminded of a stately cavalcade as their journey commenced. It was as if they were embarking on a voyage that was going to take them months. So many trunks full of gowns! And jewel boxes. And their own personal maids, riding in a separate carriage with the Senator's valet—not to mention Sir Eric's own entourage.

It was hard to believe that she and Sonya had once embarked on a long and arduous journey with nothing but a few cotton gowns and two evening dresses, forced to handle the reins of their own wagon. There had even been an attack by Indians... but *that* was one of the things she had schooled herself not to remember.

Senator and Mrs. Brandon had been invited to spend a day and a night at the palatial estate of Mr. William Ralston, at Belmont. And after a light meal, and a short rest, Ginny would go on with Sir Eric to his country home, which he referred to modestly as a "cottage." However, since the cottage and the acres surrounding it adjoined Governor Leland Stanford's 1,700 acre "farm," Ginny had been warned what she might expect.

She remained silent for most of the journey that was to take them as far as Belmont, pretending to sleep in order to avoid Sir Eric's flow of conversation. Every now and then she would hear Sonya exclaim how beautiful the scenery was, and how countrified, in contrast with the city itself.

"I'm sure you will enjoy yourself, Ginny, if you will only decide to do so," Sonya whispered before they parted. "And remember that your father and I will be joining you soon. And perhaps Ivan as well, if he can manage to get away."

"I'll expect you to tell me all about your impressions of Sam Murdock," the Senator said with somewhat forced heartiness. "Don't forget, daughter, that I will be counting on what you have to tell me."

And indeed, even during their short stay at Mr. Ralston's palatial house, it seemed as if everyone were talking of California's newest and most eccentric millionaire. "Murdock!" they whispered, and men like Sir Eric—who had actually met the man—merely smiled and kept silent.

"He was one of the few men far-sighted enough to buy shares in both the Union Pacific *and* Central Pacific Railroads, when they were nothing more than a dream. . . . They say he owns the controlling interest in the Lady Line. . . . He's bought up half the old Spanish land grants in Southern California. . . . He discovered one of the richest silver mines in the Territory of New Mexico. . . . He's dumping his shares in the Comstock. . . ."

Ginny paid hardly any attention to the flow of conversation that eddied around her. She had already taken a small dose of her new tonic, and the feeling of euphoria it invariably brought made her smile, even in reply to Sir Eric's heavy-handed banter.

On the last leg of their journey, she rode beside the Baronet in his London-style brougham, dutifully fixing a look of interest on her face as he pointed out various landmarks.

"Everyone's buying land on the Peninsula now. The Mexicans who used to own most of it are selling out. Not able to adjust to the new, faster way of living, y'know, my dear. Murdock, now—no one knows exactly how much land he owns, but it's said he's bought half of the Portola Valley. Beautiful country—unspoiled. Just finished building a mansion I've heard is a show place. And he's bought that half-finished lot on Nob Hill that poor Griffith started to build on before he lost all his money gambling and investing unwisely and killed himself."

Idly, because she was tired of hearing him talk, Ginny said, "Why does everyone talk of this Mr. Murdock as if he is a man of mystery? Have you actually met him?"

Pleased at having caught her interest, Sir Eric chuckled.

"Of course I've met him! In Virginia City, the first time. He's what you American's call an old-timer. Came up the hard way. Always surrounded by bodyguards, too—they say he doesn't trust anyone. But he's a shrewd investor, and a clever man, for all his rough manners. Well—you'll see for yourself, soon enough! Can't tell you how glad and happy I am you've decided to help me out." He patted her hand and shot her a sly look. "He's got an eye for a pretty female, too. A bachelor, like myself, but I've heard of a little Spanish girl he calls his ward. . . ." He broke off, as if he had allowed himself to say too much; and Ginny, already bored, asked no more questions.

Soon, she would see for herself. For the moment. . . .
She leaned back with a sigh, closing her eyes. Hadn't she
learned to take each moment as it came? There were no
surprises left, and if there were, she didn't care.

Once again, as she had fallen into the habit of doing,
Ginny was able to wrap herself in her gold-sprinkled veil
of indifference. Quite often, as she gazed out at other people, she wanted to laugh out loud as she wondered what
they would do if they really knew what she was thinking.
If only thinking were not such an effort! And so she was
able to look at Sir Eric's "cottage"—which was a grandiose
version of an English manor house—through expressionless
green eyes; she assured him in her cold, polite voice, that
it was beautiful, and, of course, she could hardly wait to
see the inside, with its imported, antique furniture and fit-
tings.

"You must be tired, of course," Sir Eric murmured solicitously, squeezing her fingers. "My housekeeper will show
you to your rooms, and you're to rest as long as you feel
like it, mind. She'll send two of the maids to help yours
unpack."

The brougham finished the drive up the circular, gravel-
led driveway, and drew up with a flourish before the imposing entrance, with its brick pillars.

"I've had guest cottages built around back too, you've
noticed? And when you're rested, you must see the stables.
I have two Indian grooms—great with horses, those natives
over there. Brought them with me. Perhaps tomorrow
you'd care to take a ride—you ride, I'm sure? Good! Got
a spirited little Arabian mare you might care to try out.
Now come and meet the housekeeper."

The black-clad housekeeper, a thin, sallow-faced woman
with lips that seemed always to be pursed, had been very
polite as she led Ginny to her rooms.

"You have the Roman Suite, Your Highness," she said,
and pointed out the heavy, gold-encrusted bellcords, and
the small adjoining room where Delia would sleep, and the
remarkably opulent bathing room with the bath already
drawn.

Soaking her body in a marble tub that was a replica of
a sunken Roman bath, Ginny found herself wishing that
her visit was over with already.

Why was she here? What exactly was she supposed to

do? Forbidden thoughts. So she concentrated instead on the appointments of the bathing room—the steps that led down into the tub; its size; the beauty of the marble.

Delia stood waiting with an enormous fluffy towel as Ginny emerged from the scented bath, her hair dripping wet.

"Oh ma'am! It's all so grand! And you should see the courtyard outside. They told me Sir Eric had every stone carried by ship from some old castle they was tearing down in England. Listen, ma'am—do you hear that music they're playing? One of the gentlemen brought some Spanish cowboys with him. It sure sounds pretty, don't it?"

"Please close the window, Delia! The music is—very pretty, but I'm tired, and I don't want to be kept awake all night."

Useless trying to explain to the girl that the distant music was not Spanish at all, but Mexican, and brought back too many memories. How many months had it been since she had last danced to the music of a mariachi band, with her skirts whirling up over bare ankles and her hair flying loose? But the woman who had danced so light-heartedly had been someone else, and in her place now was the Princess Sahrkanov, so bored and unhappy she needed her tonic and her headache powders to help her survive from one day to the next. When had she stopped fighting?

Delia brought her medicine to her in a tiny, exquisite liqueur glass. It glowed a rich red, like wine, as she held it to the light in a silent, cynical toast to herself. "My elixir of life. Special juice, to help me forget."

And in a little while, when the sweet, familiar feeling of drowsiness crept over her, making every muscle, every limb relax, she was flying, floating—delicious languor making her whole body seem weightless. Ginny's last conscious thought before she slept was of a pair of very dark blue eyes, half-shadowed by long, dark lashes, looking down at her with a gleam of mocking devilry in their depths—in exactly the same way Steve had looked at her the first time they had met. Thought dissolved into dreams in which all her carefully built-up defenses melted away, leaving her at the mercy of all the memories she tried to hide from.

Chapter Fifteen

The old, reckless Ginny would have indulged in some wild and probably irresponsible escapade as an outlet for her confused and bitter feelings, to escape the pain she still felt when she thought about Steve. But the Princess Sahrkanov woke up with a headache, took one of her powders with a glass of iced lemonade, and went riding with Sir Eric Fotheringay, who found himself more and more intrigued by the strange paradox she represented. Was it possible that a woman with a reputation of having led rather a fast life in Mexico for the past year or so could actually be as quiet and demure as this one seemed to be? Or was her shy and reserved manner designed to lead him on? Certainly she could not be so innocent as to think that his interest in her was purely platonic, and the fact that her husband had so readily acceded to her visit here, virtually unchaperoned, should serve to remove any silly scruples she might have.

Sir Eric allowed his rather cold blue eyes to linger on the figure of the young woman who rode easily and gracefully beside him. She rode sidesaddle, the folds of her elegant and formfitting riding habit exposing high-buttoned kid boots made of bronze-colored leather. Her habit was of a slightly darker shade of bronze that set off her copper-sheened hair to perfection; the severity of its cut only served to enhance the delightfully feminine curves of her breasts and hips. As for her mouth—it was all Sir Eric could do to tell himself to be patient. It hinted of hidden smoldering passions, waiting for the right man to fan into blazing heat. Yes, he could almost imagine how her lips would feel under his—softly parting. And her mysterious, slanted green eyes would close with ecstasy; lashes lying like fans against her flushed cheeks. Once he had overcome her initial reserve, he would possess her. And after that, there would be other times, of course. He'd make her understand that he would be discreet. It would be amusing, at that, to hint to his cronies later that he'd once had a Princess as his mistress. And the marvelous thing about married women was that they couldn't very well complain or make scenes later, when things began to cool off.

While Sir Eric laid his plans for her seduction, Ginny enjoyed the fresh woodland scents of the breeze that fanned her face. What beautiful, unspoiled country this was! And over there to the west, behind that mountain range that loomed against the horizon, was the ocean.

It was going to be a clear, warm day. No creeping, chilly fog to spoil the crystal clarity of the vista that stretched on all sides. If only Sir Eric had not been riding beside her, his little piggy eyes never leaving her body, Ginny might actually have felt slightly exhilarated. As it was, although her green eyes held a sparkle they usually lacked, she made an effort to curb her pleasure in the morning—the green, lush countryside with its wooded slopes that were splashed with patches of brightly colored wild flowers; the endless stretches of blue sky, only lightly flecked with milky, translucent clouds that arched above.

"Reminds me of parts of England, this section of country," Sir Eric said, his pompous voice breaking unpleasantly into her transient feeling of well-being.

"Yes, it is quite beautiful," she responded dutifully, in a deliberately colorless voice.

And that was the role Ginny had decided upon playing this evening. Colorless. Unobtrusive. Let the men feel free to talk—and perhaps Sir Eric would not make such a point of *noticing* her; or stripping her with his eyes.

Ginny stood quite still before the mirror while Delia, making small, admiring noises, adjusted the diamond tiara in her hair. She wore no other jewels. Her gown, a dark, dull green brocade, was subtly interwoven with silver thread, the color so dark it almost looked black until the light caught it. Almost stark in its simplicity, it lacked the plunging décolletage that characterized most evening gowns of the period, while leaving her shoulders bare except for thin silver straps. Her gloves were silver lamé, and the tiny evening slippers that showed when she walked

were also of silver, with tiny diamante buttons that
reached all the way up to her ankles.

"Oh, ma'am!" Delia sighed. "You look—you look like
something out of the *Lady's Book*! Or a picture of a princess." And then, more practically, "Shall I get you one of
them powders now? It'll make you feel better, I'm sure.
Mrs. Crawford said I wasn't to sit up, because you'd be
late—and they're having a party for the servants, too. If
you're sure it's all right. . . ."

"I want you to enjoy yourself, Delia. And it's nonsense
for you to wait for me. I'm sure I can manage to undress
myself!"

How many times had she done so? Or had her clothes
ripped from her back? But tonight was not the time for
memories. Tonight her role was not only that of the Princess Sahrkanov, but Sir Eric Fotheringay's hostess—the
charming wife of his distinguished friend, her presence
gracing his otherwise austere table.

The Tudor mansion Sir Eric had designed boasted an
enormous dining hall, lit by chandeliers of crystal, and wall
sconces. This was hardly the quiet, intimate dinner for a
few close friends that he had spoken of earlier. There were
gold plate and flat silver at each table setting, and Vene-
tian goblets, their rich colors catching the light, for the
fine, vintage wines that were served with each course.

Ginny had not had the opportunity to meet the late-
comers among Sir Eric's guests; she was especially curious
about the Sam Murdock that so many people were talking
about.

Having slept heavily for most of the afternoon, she
walked in late, seemingly unaware of the hush in the conversation—the eyes that were turned upon her. The
women weren't important, as she had guessed from the
beginning. None of the men here had brought their wives,
and their elegantly dressed partners were, no doubt, their
current mistresses.

Ginny tried to remember names, as she was introduced
to the guests.

Dr. Thomas Durant, of the Union Pacific, founder of
the famous Credit Mobilier. Congressman Oakes Ames,
and his brother Oliver. Grenville Dodge; Silas Seymour.
They were all from the East Coast. From California itself
there were the loud-voiced Charlie Crocker; Collis Hunt-

ington, whom she had met before; and Mark Sharon, President of the Bank of California's branch in Virginia City. And the bonanza kings, as they were just beginning to be called—Mackay, Flood, Fair and O'Brien. It was impossible to remember them all. The vice-president of the mighty Wells Fargo Company, Alvina Hayward, had journied here from his country home in San Mateo, and Mr. Reese had come all the way from southern California.

But it was Sam Murdock, coincidentally placed next to her, that Ginny noticed most. He was the quietest of them all, but when he spoke, the most knowledgeable on every subject. And yet, Mr. Murdock was not half as richly tailored as the other men, all millionaires like himself, and he sported neither diamond cuff links nor a golden nugget on his watch chain. And he was a bachelor, although Ginny remembered sly comments about his beautiful Spanish ward, whom everyone said was his mistress.

The strange thing was that Murdock appeared to be quite taken with her; and she actually found herself liking him. He paid her no extravagant compliments, nor did he talk down patronizingly to her. He was friendly, but not overly so, and on a few occasions, he actually asked her opinion. There was the slightest trace of a pleasant Scottish burr in his soft, almost diffident voice.

Ginny found herself studying Sam Murdock when he wasn't aware of her scrutiny. He was tall, and had broad shoulders. In his middle fifties at least, he had not run to fat as most men of his age did. And his hair had once been red, although now its color had faded and it was liberally sprinkled with grey. Clean-shaven, he sported heavy sideburns, and his eyebrows almost met in the center of his square, strong face.

The men talked freely, and the women had started to giggle rather shrilly by the time the fifth course had been cleared away. Only Murdock, who sipped sparingly of his wine, remained laconically noncommittal. But he was aware of her, all the same. Ginny had had enough experience with the ways of men to sense this, and it puzzled her. Indeed, she had the feeling that he studied her as covertly as she had begun to study him, even while his manner remained completely irreproachable.

But why did he watch her? And keep her occupied with polite small talk when she was supposed to be listening to

the rest of the conversation—mainly concerned with business matters—that flowed around her?

Murdock was the only one of Sir Eric's guests who was
honest enough to ask her directly whether she had enjoyed
her stay in Mexico. Without surprise, she heard him mention that he had interests there as well.

"Of course, I'm more fortunate than mose men, Princess. I have an old friend there—a partner of sorts. There
was a time—more years ago than I care to remember,
that would be—when we were on opposite sides. But I
won't bore you with stories of wars I've fought in. Tell
me, do you like California?"

"Of course I like California, although I must confess
I've not seen much of it yet. But oh," and unconsciously
her voice had grown wistful, "I did love Mexico! I—" and
then she caught herself up, sipping far too fast at the
goblet of champagne by her plate.

In his dry voice, Mr. Murdock said, as if he had not no-
ticed her sudden hesitation, "Then you must see more of
California. I hope your husband will not take you off to
Russia with him too soon."

If the powder she had swallowed had contrived to put
her in an almost light-hearted mood, all the wine she had
consumed made Ginny feel light-headed as well.

With a distant kind of horror she heard herself giggle.

"Oh, but I believe that Ivan has fallen in love with California, too. He's gone to Sacramento looking for land to
buy."

"Ah? Well I'm sure he's had good advice. Land values
are booming right now."

Ginny had almost forgotten about Sir Eric, who was
glowering at her from the other end of the table. Pooh!
What did it matter? She was supposed to be his gracious
hostess, and Sam Murdock was one of his most important
guests. Sam Murdock was also the only one who wasn't a
dead bore, and he was treating her like a person, instead
of an ornament.

His presence at her elbow and his quiet voice, encour-
aging her into conversation, helped the evening to go faster. And Ginny found herself almost regretful when she
was obliged, as hostess, to shepherd the other women onto
the covered terrace, while the men sat over their cigars
and port.

"I feel like a madame, marshalling her girls for the fray," Ginny thought wryly. And then one of the Chinese waiters brought out several magnums of champagne for the ladies, "compliments of the gentlemen," and she almost ceased to think as she recklessly drained her goblet and allowed it to be refilled.

The chattering of the slightly intoxicated "ladies," and their shrill laughter, reminded Ginny of her own rather untenable position here. When the night was over, and the guests scattered to their various rooms, did Sir Eric expect to accompany her? And had Ivan known all along what kind of house party this was to be?

"Drink more champagne . . . don't think about it," she admonished herself sternly; she wished that she could steal away to her suite to swallow some of her ruby-red tonic.

But in spite of her silent wishes, the evening dragged on. There was to be dancing in the English-style conservatory that opened onto the terrace and from there into the carefully terraced lawns and ornamental gardens that surrounded the house. Business was forgotten for the time being, as the men clasped laughing, flushed-faced girls in their arms. Still more champagne—this time Crug's Private Cuvee, meant only for connoisseurs—was brought out, and drunk and wasted. Couples whispered, heads close together, at small tables placed discreetly in dark corners that were concealed by potted plants. Others drifted out onto the terrace, or disappeared into the gardens as the musicians continued to play their slow and sentimental tunes.

Ginny was forced to dance with Sir Eric, who held her far too closely, his hot breath fanning her cheek. She felt breathless. The pressure of his groin against her thighs gave all too clear evidence of his intentions towards her.

Almost without realizing what she was doing, Ginny found herself looking for Sam Murdock. Where had he disappeared to? With whom was he dancing? Sir Eric had sharper eyes than she imagined. His diamond-studded shirt front pressing against her breast, he gave a sudden, coarse laugh.

"You little baggage! You're sharper than I thought, after all. I saw the way you were making eyes at old Sam. But then, he's a sharp one, too. Not to be caught as easily as I am, and you know you've got me hooked, don't you?

I've had my eye on you from the start, and I think you knew it. No need to play hard to get *now*."

His pudgy fingers squeezed hers significantly, and his hand, moving down her stiff spine, encountered her bustle and moved upward again to press firmly against the small of her back, pushing her hips against his.

Trying to pull away from his embrace, Ginny stumbled, and heard gruff laughter as her body leaned involuntarily into his.

"That's right! I knew you'd be sensible enough not to waste time pretending to be shy. And I haven't made any bones about the way I feel about *you*, have I? Time we took a walk—and no one's going to miss us. No one's going to know, either, if that's what's bothering you."

The smell of ripe cheese on his breath was overpowering, and Ginny found herself thinking wildly: In another minute I shall be sick! There was a dull pain in her temples, and she felt herself go cold all over.

She said the first thing that came into her mind, which happened to be the truth.

"I—I have a terrible headache! I keep getting them—the kind the doctor calls migraines. Please! I would like to go back to my room and lie down."

She almost tore herself out of his arms, feeling the hot, humid air in the conservatory make the perspiration break out on her body. Oh, if only she could reach the safety of her room before she disgraced herself! Even her vision seemed blurred, and she had to hold up her long skirts in both hands, to keep from tripping over them.

Purely by instinct, she seemed to find her way down carpeted corridors where the lamps had been dimmed. But then, oh God, Sir Eric was there before her, barring the entrance to her rooms.

"In a hurry to lie down, eh? Well, that's all right. That's what I had in mind too, matter of fact!"

He caught her in his arms, pressing his wet, thick lips over her mouth, while waves of nausea choked her, making her head whirl dizzily.

She was leaning back against the door, his body pressing heavily against hers.

"No need to worry about your maid tonight! Had Mrs. Crawford take care of her. No doubt she'll be sleeping sounder than a top, and we won't wake her up, will we?

Undress you myself . . . always wanted to do that, ever since I first looked at you. Pretty little thing. . . !"

Ginny heard herself moan like a trapped animal, and then—thankfully, almost unbelievably—felt herself released, while her hands went up to press against her mouth to keep back the choking, sick feeling that still threatened to engulf her.

As if it came from a distance, she heard Sam Murdock's dry, emotionless voice.

"There you are, Sir Eric! I was looking for you, to tell you I'd decided to turn in." And then, a slight hardness creeping into his tone, "Seems to me the Princess doesn't look too well. You feeling all right, ma'am?"

Silently, not daring to speak, Ginny shook her head, even that slight movement sending pain lancing through her temples and down the back of her neck.

"I was making sure she found her room and got to bed safely." Sir Eric's voice was full of suppressed rage, making it hoarse. "All the servants are out enjoying themselves too, you know. Wouldn't want anyone blundering in here, disturbing the Princess by mistake."

"Ah—well, if that's all that's worrying you, I can post one of my bodyguards outside her door. They haven't been drinking with the rest."

"That won't be necessary! Darn it all, Sam—"

"Well—as a matter of fact, there were a few small matters I wanted to talk to you about. Didn't get a chance earlier. If you're free?"

His bright blue eyes fixed on Ginny's pale face with a peculiarly intent stare, Sam Murdock made a courtly bow in her direction.

"May I wish you a pleasant night, ma'am? You look like you need your rest. You're sure you're all right now?"

Somehow she found the strength to nod; and under Sir Eric's baleful gaze, she fumbled with the handle of the door, barely managing to lock it behind her before she raced across the room and was miserably, violently sick into the scrolled copper washbasin.

Ginny thought there was no feeling more wretched in all the world. "I'll never touch another drop of champagne again—never, never!" Her skin felt icy and clammy, and every time she closed her eyes, the whole room seemed to start whirling about. She thought she would never stop being sick; that she was being turned inside out. Weakly, she clung to the edge of the marble-topped washstand and wished that she might die, rather than go on feeling so miserable.

After a while—she had no idea how long it took her—Ginny managed to make her way to her bed. She was weak and trembling from the spasms of nausea that seemed to have left all of her muscles sore, and to attempt to undress *now*, feeling as she did, was unthinkable. But the moment she let herself drop across the bed, the dizziness returned, and she felt as if she were on a gigantic swing.

Moaning, Ginny pushed herself erect again. Perhaps, if she had some fresh air, she would feel better. The air within the room smelled sour and stale.

With an effort she forced herself back onto her feet, and kicking off her shoes, went barefoot and weaving slightly to the large French windows that opened onto a terrace. Somehow, fumbling with the catches, she managed to get them open, and the night air, with its slight chill, was like a glass of cold water thrown in her face. Ginny found herself leaning thankfully against a wide brick balustrade, close to where a shallow flight of steps led downward to another terrace.

She felt better already—she actually felt a little better! And now she shivered, partly from cold and partly with revulsion at herself.

What was she letting herself turn into? She remembered Sam Murdock's sharp, blue eyes that seemed to take everything in—the ugly little scene with Sir Eric, her own drunken, helpless state. Disgusting. Sordid. How could he not have thought so? What must he think of her? But Sam Murdock, for all that they said he was ruthless in his business dealings, was also a gentleman. He had rescued her, and the old-fashioned politeness of his manner had remained unchanged. But how could he not have seen her as she must have appeared, as she *was*? Why had she allowed herself to drink so much? To make it easier for Sir Eric to seduce her? And he certainly would have done so if Mr. Murdock had not turned up so providentially.

Closing her eyes, Ginny breathed deeply. "Try not to think about it," she told herself. There were too many unpleasant thoughts that she was not ready to face yet—

among them the prospect of facing Sir Eric in the morning. Think, instead, of how clean and sweet the night smelled. There was the faint, spicy tang of pine and sagebrush, and the cloyingly sweet odors of jasmine and honeysuckle from the terrace below. Even—she could almost have sworn it—the faint but unmistakable aroma of a cigar. Some other guest who needed fresh air? Perhaps it was time she went back inside again.

A faint, scraping sound behind her made Ginny turn, and her eyes widened with shock and repulsion.

Sir Eric Fotheringay stood there, swaying slightly, framed in the open windows that led out from her bedroom. He took a step forward, and she saw that he had changed into a military-style dressing robe. He was grinning at her.

"Waited up for me, didn't you? Think you knew I'd come—unfinished business, eh? But you should have undressed—or were you saving that task for me?"

She would have backed away, if the brick wall hadn't pressed against the small of her back, trapping her.

Looking about her wildly, Ginny could find no means of escape, unless she tried the steps—and she was not sure that her legs were strong enough to carry her.

"What's the matter, little lady? Not shy are you? Too late in the game to play at *that*—and why pretend? We both know why you're here. Come along now—" he advanced on her, speaking coaxingly, but keeping his small, gleaming eyes fixed on her. And for all his lumbering, unsteady walk, he looked enormously strong. "Come along," he repeated. "Don't want to catch cold, do you? We'll be nice and warm in bed."

"Stop it!" Ginny burst out, suddenly and violently. "If you only knew how ridiculous you look—and how aggravating you're being. I have no intention of going to bed with you, and I do not enjoy being raped. Now will you please go away?"

His small, protuberant eyes squinted at her angrily as he thrust his head forward between his shoulders.

"Hoity-toity all of a sudden, aren't you? After the way you were leading me on—and don't pretend you didn't, my dear! Didn't struggle too hard when I kissed you, did you? You're a hot little piece, for all your sullen looks, and don't think I didn't sense it from the beginning. You

come along now, and forget about playing games. We'll
have time for that later."

Without warning, he made a grab for her. Although
she attempted to avoid his grasp, she heard the ripping of
material as her gown tore, baring one shoulder.

He chuckled—an avid, greedy sound. And his hands
reached for her again, pulling roughly at her gown,
pawing at her breasts. He was a man-beast—he was all
the other rutting animals like himself who had forced her
and used her body without consideration for her feelings.

Filled with a passion of rage and loathing, Ginny cried
out. Pushing both hands against his thick body, she gave
him a violent shove, using all the strength she could muster. And with a grunt of surprise, Sir Eric, taken una-
wares, went staggering backwards.

His arms flailed wildly, and his mouth opened—and
then he fell with a crash that sounded like thunder in
Ginny's ears. He lay half in and half out of the bedroom,
with great, jagged shards of glass all about him, for the
momentum of her violent push had sent him crashing
through one of the open French doors.

"Oh God! I've killed him," Ginny thought sickly. And,
driven by blind panic, she whirled and began to run. The
steps . . . she had to escape. . . . She had started down
them recklessly when she ran into someone coming up,
and a pair of strong arms grasped her. Shock and terror
almost made her scream out loud, until she recognized
Sam Murdock's voice—calm and soothingly matter of
fact.

"I've learned that running away from trouble is always
worse than staying to face it. Sir Eric?"

She could see the faint, white glimmer of his shirt front;
she nodded wordlessly. And the way he continued to hold
her, comfortingly, without passion, helped her to start
thinking again.

"That noise is going to bring all of them running—those
who haven't already passed out, or are too busy to bother
themselves," Sam Murdock said. He released her then,
patting her shoulder almost absent-mindedly as he did.
Ginny felt comforted by the calm, sure sound of his slow
voice.

"You come with me—and leave me to do the talking.

No need to worry—none of the gentlemen here are going to want any scandal, and least of all Sir Eric."

But I . . . I think I've killed him! He looked so—he looked *dead!"*

Murdock gave a short, mirthless chuckle.

"I doubt that! And if he is, it was his own fault, wasn't it? Now remember—you let me handle this. You're upset, and no one's going to blame you. Cry, if you feel like it. I've heard it helps a female. But you keep remembering that there's nothing to worry about."

The strangest thing was that she trusted this man, who was a stranger to her. And there was something about his quiet strength and air of self assurance that made her obey him without another word.

Cool, completely sober, and self-possessed, Sam Murdock took charge, as he had promised. His opportune appearance had saved her from going to pieces; and while she listened with one part of her mind to his laconic, unemotional explanations, Ginny tried to control the shaking of her hands. Delia appeared from somewhere, her eyes swollen with sleep. And again it was Sam Murdock, his voice sharpening commandingly, who cut across the girl's incipient hysteria and ordered her to fetch her mistress something to drink.

"Water will do. And something to soothe her nerves."

Fortified by one of her headache powders, Ginny was able to endure the rest of it—the whispers and sidelong glances, the small, alarmed shrieks of the women. As Murdock had assured her in a cynical undertone, the men present were more concerned with protecting their own reputations than with their host's "accident." For that was what it was to be called. An unfortunate accident.

Thomas Durant, who had been a medical doctor before he had turned financier, examined the unfortunate Sir Eric and pronounced his condition as not serious, although he was badly cut in several places by splinters of glass. Luckily, as he fell, his head had struck the carpeted floor of the bedroom.

Still unconscious, but breathing heavily, Sir Eric was carried to his own bedroom; his gashes were disinfected and bandaged.

"I'll talk to him myself," Collis Huntington promised.

"There'll be no more heard about this unfortunate little episode."

"But I cannot stay here!" Ginny said, her voice agitated in spite of the transient calmness that the powder had brought her. "Surely you can see that? I don't want to face him again. It would be intolerable."

She was alone with Sam Murdock again, and although dawn was already streaking the sky to the east with pale patterns of light, she no longer felt sleepy.

"There's no need to." He was still in command; and of her, too, it seemed. "I've already told my men that we'll be leaving in an hour. And your maid is packing for you."

"But. . . ."

In the faint light she caught the slight smile that tugged at one corner of his lips.

"I've already gained the impression that you're an independent young woman. So I'm not carrying you off to my own place, although it's less than twenty miles away. I thought you might prefer to join your father and stepmother at Belmont first. Tell them there's been a change in your plans. I'll make the invitation formal when I meet them, of course. I'd be flattered if you'd all be my guests this evening—call it a housewarming if you like. My house was completed only a few weeks ago, and I'd already invited some friends and acquaintances over. You'll come?" His bright blue eyes held nothing but kindness. "There'll be a few familiar faces from last night, of course, but you've no need to worry about them. And perhaps, if your husband returns early enough, he'll join us, too."

Ivan—she had almost forgotten about him. And the sudden remembrance was not pleasant. He had known . . . of course he had known! Perhaps Sir Eric might have met with an unpleasant accident later; but first, she had been supposed to let the man seduce her, as she might have done if Sam Murdock had not stepped in.

Ginny became aware that the man was watching her without seeming to—and that, in spite of everything, she still continued to trust him.

"Well then," Murdock said briskly, as if she had already given her consent, "do you think you can be dressed within an hour, Princess?"

Chapter Sixteen

Right up until the time that their carriage drove around a circled, tree-shaded drive, to stop before the house, Ginny had been able to keep her thoughts in check. She had almost been able to convince herself that nothing unpleasant had happened during the past twenty-four hours. Leave a blank where Sir Eric had been. Substitute the man of mystery, Sam Murdock, who was still a man of mystery, or so she had been given to understand. She had done well, apparently. Her father was pleased with her; Sonya was excited at the prospect of meeting Mr. Murdock at last. Sir Eric was no longer important. . . . It was strange, how few questions she had been asked about her hasty departure from Redbrick Grange, and the circumstances surrounding it. Sam Murdock's name, and his personal escort when they arrived at Belmont, had provided a magical passport. She was a good daughter, a good child. And Count Chernikoff's prescriptions kept her outwardly composed.

It was dark, except for a lopsided moon which had kept them company on the long drive, silvering the surface of the narrow stream the road had followed for the past few miles. Corte Madera Creek, Ginny had heard someone call it. This was land that had belonged to the Spanish, long ago, and they had given names to every creek and mountain and valley.

The darkness of the night was suddenly broken, invaded by the lights glowing from every window of the rambling, two-story house that suddenly appeared around a curve in the driveway. It was built in the familiar style of Spain, and of Mexico, but of brick and stone, rather than adobe. Sam Murdock had disdained the fashionable, imported styles of architecture that were so much loved by his contemporaries, and gone back to the roots of the country he had chosen to build in.

Instead of uniformed footmen, mustached vaqueros came running to hold the horses and help the señor's latest guests alight.

Ginny walked up wide steps, and through an enormous, arched doorway; its massive wooden doors stood hospitably open, and led into a room that was filled with lights, music, and laughing conversation.

Most of the guests were Mexican or Spanish, although, as Sam Murdock had promised, there were many familiar faces to be seen and recognized as well. Some of the gentlemen who had been Sir Eric Fotheringay's house guests earlier were present here, along with more plainly dressed men who, Ginny discovered later, were miners from Nevada. And intermingled with the crowd, clad in somber black and white, were Mr. Murdock's famous bodyguards; the bulges of their guns were conspicuous under long jackets.

Sam Murdock himself, quietly dressed as usual, had come forward to greet them, his manner just as Ginny had remembered it. Polite, kind, underlaid by unselfconscious assurance.

"Senator—Mrs. Brandon? I'm glad you were able to come. And I apologize for the lateness of my invitation. But this housewarming was a kind of afterthought, I'm afraid. My ward's idea, really. There's a young Englishman she wanted an excuse to see again."

Ginny remembered the speculation concerning Mr. Murdock's lovely ward and found herself curious. His mistress? No, surely not, for the manner in which he'd spoken of her had been affectionate, almost paternal. What kind of a man *was* he? And did he have any weaknesses? He was clever, without being obvious, and also a good host.

The Senator and Sonya were left chatting with Mark Hopkins and his young wife, and Ginny found herself being drawn along to be introduced to some of the other people present.

The Azevedos and the Serranos—the Señor and Señora Rivera, who spoke only Spanish. Lonnie O'Hara, unabashedly Irish, who was a mine foreman, and Angus McLeish, who owned a cattle ranch. "Why," Ginny found

herself thinking, "these are the first *real* people I have met
since I arrived in California." Except for Mr. Murdock
himself, of course, and he remained a puzzle. Why had he
chosen to single her out? Why, for that matter, had he
been so exceptionally kind?

He introduced her to the young and handsome Viscount
Marwood, a blond and elegantly dressed young man who
kept watching the double stairways that descended on either side of a long gallery, overlooking the enormous reception hall.

"He's waiting for my ward," Sam Murdock chuckled
softly as he continued to lead her along with him. "I've
never seen a more infatuated young man—and, of course,
she leads him a dance. I've had trouble taming her; but
then you'll see for yourself, when she decides to make her
entrance."

Ginny could not help but be aware of the curious,
speculative glances that followed them, and she asked herself again: Why was Sam Murdock paying her such
marked attention?

The gown she had worn this evening was cut defiantly
low at the bosom; folds of pale-patterned, blue-green silk
draped tightly across her stomach and hips to fall into
flounces of silk and lace at the bustle, which ended in a
small train. For some reason, she had wanted to look her
best tonight, and the masculine eyes that lingered on her
told her she had succeeded.

So did Sam Murdock, when he asked her to dance.
They were in a room that was half ballroom and half covered terrace, supported by stone pillars that led out into a
softly lighted garden.

"If I may say so, you look exceptionally lovely tonight,
Princess." In spite of the conventional flattery of his
words, the dry, slightly drawling voice remained the same,
and the pressure of his hand at her waist did not increase.
An unusual man, this—and a difficult one to know.

He danced rather stiffly, but well enough for a man his
age; and he did not attempt to keep up a polite flow of
banalities as they circled the floor—allowing her the freedom to let her thoughts wander.

The hauntingly beautiful Strauss waltz ended, dispelling
Ginny's thoughtful mood. Her partner bowed to her politely, and in the small pause before the musicians struck

up the next tune, Ginny became aware of a sudden buzz
of talk in the salon they had just left.

"Ah! I think that my ward has finally decided to join
our guests. She has a sense of the dramatic, I'm afraid.
Will you come with me? I'd like you to meet her."

They paused in the arched doorway, and thunderstruck,
Ginny stared at the young woman who had just descended
the stairs, and now stood surrounded by a small knot of
admiring young men.

So great was her shock that she actually swayed, feeling
the light pressure of Mr. Murdock's fingers on her elbow
grow firmer. It was impossible—she was seeing things! That
laughing, vivid creature with her head thrown back flirta-
tiously, throat encircled by rubies matching those that
dangled from her ears—that could never be Concepción.
In a gown of wine-red velvet, every bit as smart and as
fashionable as Ginny's own evening dress, her black hair
piled regally on her head with curls escaping down her
back—surely it was not the same gypsy wench she had
fought with one hot, dusty afternoon? It was too much of
a coincidence to be possible. How could *that* Concepción
end up as a millionaire's ward?

And yet, seemingly unaware of her inner turmoil, Sam
Murdock was drawing Ginny forward with him as the
crowd parted to give them room.

"Ah, here you are at last, my dear." Effortlessly, he
switched to Spanish, for the benefit of the girl whose English was still rather stilted. "Princess, I would like to
present my ward, the Señorita Concepción Sanchez. She's
the daughter of an old friend. Concepción, you remember
the manners you've been taught? The Princess Sahrkanov."

For all her newly acquired veneer of elegance and so-
phistication, there was no mistaking the tigress under the
smoothly polished surface of velvet and rubies. Tawny
eyes and green eyes clashed, and Concepción drew herself
up haughtily, reddened lips curving slightly in a smile that
wasn't a smile at all, but a grimace of rage. She spoke in
the Mexican dialect that Ginny was all too familiar with.

"We have met, unfortunately. Do you still carry a knife
around with you?"

"Since I no longer have a reason to fight you, I don't,
as a matter of fact. Do you still have the scar I gave you?"

The involuntary narrowing of Ginny's eyes made them

appear more slanted than ever, and she was unaware of the puzzled looks that traveled from her to the flamboyant Concepción and back again.

The gypsy girl had given a hiss of pure rage at Ginny's taunting words, fingers curving into claws at her sides. But smoothly, quickly, Sam Murdock intervened; his soft voice carried a touch of steel.

"Why don't you go and see if all our other guests are comfortable, my dear? Perhaps, now that you've decided to come down, we can have supper."

The dangerous moment passed, although Concepción's venomous look promised another confrontation later. Taking a deep breath, she managed a flashing, insincere smile.

"May I not dance first? I have already promised Eddie—is that not so?"

Thus appealed to, the Viscount, who had been standing by rather glumly, brightened up. It was clear he thought the girl's heavily accented English quite charming.

"Ah—oh yes, of course! As if I could forget. May I, sir?"

"Well—go ahead then." Murdock shrugged, looking benevolent. He glanced down at Ginny, who stood as stiffly as a statue by his side. "I apologize. Concepción's manners still leave much to be desired, but she's learning."

"Did you understand what was said?" She could not help it if her words sounded blunt. She was far too distraught—still wondering what strange quirk of fate had brought Concepción *here*, of all places.

"I—understood that you two had met before," Sam Murdock said drily. And then, for the benefit of the people around them, he added in a slightly louder voice, "Would you care to see the gallery? This house is built around a large central courtyard, or patio, as they call it in Spain. The windows on the west side of the gallery overlook it."

"But your guests. . . ." Ginny knew that she still sounded distracted, and she could not help it. Her heart was thudding, and it was not just because of Concepción's startling appearance. Seeing Concepción had reminded her suddenly and painfully of Steve.

"My guests will think I am very much taken with the Princess Sahrkanov. And there will be all kinds of whispers and speculations. But I've grown used to that. Do *you* mind?"

They were climbing the stairway, Ginny holding up her trailing skirts with one hand. She sent her companion a questioning look, in spite of her own confused state of mind.

"I am quite used to having people gossip about me, but I find you a difficult man to understand, Mr. Murdock. You have been extremely kind to me—but I find myself wondering . . . why?"

They had reached the gallery; the sound of music and animated talk and laughter reached up to them.

Without answering her, Sam Murdock led the way to where rich tapestries seemed to cover one complete wall. He pulled a concealed cord and the embroidered hangings seemed to draw apart magically, revealing windows that were shielded by a tracery of delicate wrought-iron bars.

"There—what do you think of it? Forgive me for sounding so inordinately proud, but I helped with the design of this house myself. I like the practical, yet comfortable style of Spanish living. Have you visited the Alhambra in Spain? This was patterned after one of the inner courtyards there."

"It's beautiful," Ginny murmured sincerely. In the moonlight, the patio—with its tiled flooring and tinkling fountains flowing into an oval-shaped pool—looked half-asleep, like an illustration from an old book. A peaceful place. But there were too many unanswered questions in her mind, and it seemed as if Sam Murdock had read her thoughts, for Ginny heard his quiet chuckle behind her.

"You're still wondering about my motives, aren't you? And about my ward. But the fact is, I'm a man who prides himself on being a judge of character. I don't go on gossip and hearsay—I like to make up my own mind. And I admire a woman with intelligence and spirit, who is honest as well. I think you have all those qualities. Just as I had the feeling, the first time I met you, that you need a friend."

"A—friend?" She could not help repeating his words, more puzzled than ever.

"A man who has no other designs on you, Princess, if you'll forgive my bluntness. You wear a look of disillusion, a look that says you have learned to trust nobody. Well—I've learned the same thing, in all the years I've lived. By you remind me of a woman I once knew. Of the daughter I might have had. Will that do for a start, Princess?"

She hardly dared believe him. How many men had asked her to trust them, and afterwards. . . . And yet, what did she have to lose? In spite of everything, there was something about Sam Murdock's quiet strength that made Ginny *want* to trust him. In spite of Concepción. . . .

"I used to know her father," Sam was saying. "A very fierce man—a Comanchero. And the girl herself is willful and headstrong, but she is lovely, and she deserves better than a wandering life. I promised a friend of mine that I would take her under my wing and introduce her to society. And I must say, she's been a success. She dances— I've heard her compared to Lola Montez. And she's quite bowled over young Marwood."

Somehow, not quite realizing how or why, Ginny had found herself wandering through the rest of the house with her host, quite alone and unchaperoned. No doubt they'd all be wondering downstairs—but what did it matter? She pushed the thought of Ivan far back into the recesses of her mind. Ivan wasn't here, and if he was, he'd probably encourage her. And Sam Murdock had his bodyguards to protect him from unpleasant and unforeseen "accidents."

The house was much larger than it had looked at first. Almost as big as a castle. There was an upstairs reception room; suites for important guests; and, in another wing, the rooms that were alloted to members of Murdock's "family," which included, so it seemed, his unobtrusive bodyguards.

Concepción's room was large and untidy, with brightly colored gowns strewn across the foot of her bed. Next to it was the master suite, rather austere-looking in comparison to some of the guest rooms. The furniture was of heavy, carved mahogany and teak, with rosewood inlays. The big bed, dominating the room, made Ginny draw in her breath. Somehow, she could not imagine Sam Murdock occupying a room like this. There were big windows, opening onto a small terrace, with steps leading down into a small, private patio that was enclosed by high walls. And the adjoining dressing room, with a mirrored wall, was half as big as the bedroom itself.

It was a room where a woman could see herself reflected

from every angle; and the built-in dressing table held silver and tortoise-shell toilet articles that any female would have delighted in; brushes and combs and jewelry boxes that played tinkling tunes when they were opened.

Who was the woman? All the jewels, so carelessly displayed, were meant for some cherished female, as were the toilet articles. And the bathroom, with aquamarine tiles, and mirrors on the walls and ceiling. . . .

Why was he showing her all this? What did it mean? The jewels, so carelessly displayed—shimmering sparks of color. And the mirrors. Especially the mirrors. It struck Ginny, with a sense of shock, that there had even been a large mirror affixed to the ceiling above the bed. What kind of man was Sam Murdock?

He seemed to sense her unease, for he didn't try to delay her in his rooms, but led her out and back downstairs instead; his manner remained unaltered.

And for most of the evening, after he had taken her back to her father and Sonya, Sam Murdock played the perfect host, mingling with his other guests.

"You certainly seemed to have made an impression!" Sonya whispered—and had there been the slightest trace of malice in her voice? The Senator, on the other hand, was pleased, and nodded with a slight smile whenever some guest asked Ginny to dance.

She was aware of the comments that her long absence had caused, and in one way she didn't care. After all, she was used to being the subject of gossip and speculation—hadn't she answered as much to Mr. Murdock's subtle challenge? But in some strange way she continued to feel uneasy. Perhaps it was the knowledge of Concepción's glowing presence, and her secure position as Murdock's ward. Perhaps it had something to do with the sly, malicious glances that the girl cast her way from time to time. Above all, it was Sam Murdock himself. He had offered her friendship, had shown her nothing but respect in spite of the rather invidious circumstances under which they had first met. But why had he shown her such marked attention? Why had he flouted convention by showing her around his own private rooms?

To calm herself, Ginny swallowed another powder just before dinner, thankful that she had been placed between her father and an elderly Spanish gentleman who had been born and brought up in California and also owned a ranch in the Portola Valley.

Ginny ate and drank sparingly, and endured the short period when the ladies retired, leaving the men to their cigars and wine. Concepción made a point of avoiding her, leading Sonya to whisper:

"I don't think that girl likes you, my love! Do you imagine she's jealous?"

"She has no reason to be," Ginny responded shortly. She had no desire to be quizzed by Sonya, nor to enter into idle conversation with any of the other ladies who were obviously curious to know more about her. She was tired of aly questions about herself, her absent husband the Prince, her plans for the future. Why couldn't they leave her alone? She wanted to hide herself behind her familiar veil of euphoria, through which she could watch everything that went on around her as if from a distance. It was growing late, and she wished that they might retire.

Concepción, however, had other ideas. After a while, in her heavily accented English, she asked the ladies if they wished to go out onto the patio, where there would be Spanish music and dancing for their further entertainment.

"And I think that when the men hear the music and the clapping, they will not be long in joining us ... you will come?"

No, Ginny thought. That, of all things, she could not bear. Perhaps she could say her head ached. . . .

But then she caught Concepción's flashing glance, and the contempt in those tawny eyes made her shoulders stiffened. If there were some kind of drama being acted tonight, she would see it through to the end. She'd find out what it all meant!

Chapter Seventeen

The beautiful tile and mosaic courtyard was now lit by torches that were thrust into wall sconces. Their orange light made the oval-shaped pool look like endlessly shimmering liquid gold, as water from the fountains trickled into it. The high walls were almost completely covered by flowering vines, and the whole courtyard had the appearance of a very old garden.

Ginny heard many exclamations of delight and admiration from the ladies as Concepción led them outside, to the carved Spanish-style chairs that had been arranged under the overhanging gallery on one side.

"What a beautiful, still night," Sonya remarked as they sat down. "One would almost think that our host had ordered it, especially for us."

At the far end of the courtyard the musicians had already begun to play, with the plaintive sounds of a guitar dominating. A woman's voice, with a sob in it, began singing a plaintive flamenco—an age-old song of passion and heartbreak.

If she closed her eyes, she might almost imagine that she were back in Mexico. Ginny felt her throat become constricted. Where had she first heard the music of the flamenco? Yes, it had been on the night of Don Juan Sandoval's fiesta—the night when she had been hastily and surreptitiously married to Steve, and he had gone off with Concepción. Why was it that everything that happened this evening brought back memories? Was she never to escape reminders of the past?

Ginny sat silently, her hands clasped tightly together in her lap. The night was warm, not hot; all the same she felt perspiration trickle down between her breasts, and along her thighs.

The music of Spain gave way to the music of Mexico,

and by the time the men had joined them, the courtyard swirled with life and gaiety as dancers, wearing the traditional dress of Mexico, entertained the guests. With an effort, Ginny held herself stiffly erect. No, she would not let the music move her! Perhaps that was what Concepción wanted to do—to remind her of that night, of other nights. Concepción herself was leaning back in her chair, laughing in a way that made her vivid, bright beauty seem even more flamboyant. Standing a little behind her, the young English viscount bent his fair head, whispering to her. And if Concepción was really Sam Murdock's ward, who was the woman who shared his private suite? The woman for whom he had provided all those precious, flashing jewels and exquisite toilet articles—the mirrored walls to reflect her body? It seemed quite out of character. until Ginny reminded herself that she really knew nothing at all of Mr. Murdock's real character.

She became aware that her father had belatedly strolled outside, with their host. In the flickering torchlight his face suddenly looked old—and worried. She continued to watch them, mainly to keep herself from watching the dancers. Sam Murdock was smiling, imperturbable. Her father had begun to rub absent-mindedly at his clean-shaven jaw, a gesture that showed he was upset by something. The two men continued to talk for a while until Mr. Rosario, one of the wealthy Spanish ranchers, called out some question.

"Will the lovely Señorita Sanchez honor us by dancing tonight?"

Sam Murdock cast an inquiring look at Concepción, who shook her head slightly.

"I think she's tired tonight. But tomorrow, perhaps. In the meantime, would any of you ladies and gentlemen care to join in the dancing?"

Promptly, several of the Mexican and Spanish couples present rose; and, caught up in the spirit of the dance, several other guests began clapping in time with the music.

"I really can't stand much more of this," Ginny thought wildly. Her fingers ached from the way she had been twisting them together, and her hands felt clammy. She had the strange feeling that Concepción planned to humiliate her in some way. And even though Ginny had Sam

Murdock's professed friendship, she did not want to test it
by tangling with Concepción.

Ginny rose to her feet as unobtrusively as possible,
whispering to Sonya that she had one of her migraines
again and meant to go up to her room and lie down.

"Oh, Ginny, that's too bad. Are you sure you would not
like me to come with you?" But Sonya's voice sounded
mechanical, and she was watching her husband, a worried
frown puckering her brows.

"No, no, that would seem very rude, and Mr. Murdock
might believe we do not care for the entertainment he's
provided. Really, Sonya, I can find my way to my room
quite safely."

Threading her way between the people who now crowded this part of the courtyard, Ginny looked for Mr.
Murdock, but he seemed to have disappeared. She saw
her father standing, cigar in hand, with a small group of
men she recognized as being some of the major stockholders in the newly reopened Con Virginia mine. They
were deep in earnest conversation, and paying no attention
whatsoever to the music.

Well, it didn't matter. The fewer people who noticed
her departure the better. And Sonya could make her apologies to Mr. Murdock.

Thankfully, Ginny had just reached the massive folding
doors that had been thrown open to provide easy access to
the patio, when Concepción's honey-sweet voice stopped
her.

"Ah, Princesa—you are not leaving us yet, are you?
And here I have a gentleman who has said he's waited all
evening to dance with you."

Ginny swung around, and saw a tall, rather dark-
visaged man with a very white smile—a man she had
noticed staring at her several times during the evening.

Now he said quickly, "Forgive me if I bother you, but
you see—I am a friend of poor Frank Julius'; Armand Petrucchio is the name, perhaps he's spoken of me? Frank
told me what a marvelous dancer you are, and that you
have even danced for the late Archduke Maximilian himself."

Concepción stood by, smiling her curved, triumphant
smile, and Ginny noticed that several heads had turned to
listen.

"But I forget my manners, do I not?" Concepción said with sweet insincerity. "This lady is now the Princess Sahrkanov—I pronounce the name right? We used to have friends in common in Mexico—is that not so?"

Drawing in her breath to keep her voice steady, Ginny said politely that she had been on the point of retiring to her room. "I have a slight headache ... the long journey here. ..."

"Ah, yes, and this same morning, very early you journeyed from near San Mateo to Belmont, did you not?" And again Concepción's smile flashed. "But I had *so* hoped that you would join in our dancing, as an encouragement to the other ladies who might be persuaded that if *you* could learn the folk dances of Mexico they, too, will not find them hard to learn."

"Princess, I hope you will not disappoint us all!" Another gentleman now added his pleas. "Señorita Sanchez has agreed to change her mind about dancing if you will also join."

"Can you really dance to this wild and beautiful music?"

"Surely you'll oblige us all—Senator, can't you persuade your daughter to remain with us for a little while longer?"

More voices had joined in, and Mr. Petrucchio added his entreaties, his dark eyes lingering on Ginny's face.

"I beg of you—my friend told me that he could never forget the way you danced."

And now even her father had left his friends, and was adding his persuasions to those of the others, although the worried frown she had noticed earlier still creased his forehead.

"Surely you're not going to disappoint our charming young hostess and so many of our fellow guests, daughter? I, myself, had no idea you were such an accomplished dancer."

"Ah!" Still smiling, Concepción let her yellow-gold eyes flash at Ginny with a look of venom. "Even *I* heard that your daughter has danced many times for the ex-Emperor Maximilano and his guests. And of how well and how feelingly she dances to the music of Mexico." She made her voice deliberately full of meaning. "Perhaps you do not remember, but I saw you dance once."

Senator Brandon looked surprised.

"Is that right? Ginny, you didn't mention—"

"No, I didn't. I *had* almost forgotten. It was such a crowded affair."

Ginny felt cornered, as if she had suddenly become the center of everyone's attention. Which was precisely what Concepción had planned, she supposed.

"Yes," the girl was saying, her red lips still smiling. "It was a wedding celebration of sorts, a—how do you call it here? A marriage of convenience? And there was a big scandal because the groom left soon after the ceremony. You remember?"

Again their eyes clashed, the tawny and the green, and Ginny felt an angry buzzing in her head as her spine stiffened. Whatever Concepción was attempting to do, she would not let her succeed. If she had nothing else left, she would cling to her pride.

"Oh, I'm sure my memory is as long as yours, for those things which I consider important," Ginny said carelessly. But her lips felt stiff and numb, and her temples throbbed. Even the music seemed to have receded into the background, and all she could see was Armand Petrucchio's flashing white teeth and Concepción's smile. The buzz of interested conversation seemed to pin her like a butterfly against a wall.

"Good. Then you *will* dance! I cannot say how honored I am." The Italian with a French first name bowed deeply, holding out his hand.

Smiling mechanically, Ginny took it.

She was hardly aware that he was leading her out into the center of the courtyard, the other dancers making room for them with curious looks. "Oh God!" she thought suddenly, panic-stricken, "I cannot! How can I dance when I feel nothing inside and my head hurts and I feel my hands shaking? She wants me to make a fool of myself—" And, somehow, it was *that* thought that strengthened Ginny. No, and no! And how many times in the past had she lost herself in the dances of Mexico? Once they had been her only escape from a reality too painful and degrading to bear.

Concepción snapped her fingers at the musicians, tossing her head back.

"El Jarabe Tapatio, muchachos!" And then to her partner, "Come, Señor—you are ready?"

The music was suddenly very loud—the guitars almost silent now as the more noisy instruments of the traditional mariachi band took over. It was perhaps the most popular regional dance of Mexico, this particular one, with its changing tempo.

Ginny lifted her head, looking at her partner. His teeth flashed again.

"I have lived in New Mexico for several years. This is familiar to me."

Strange, how without conscious thought on her part her feet took up the rhythm and kept it. And her arms, so stiff a moment ago, felt loose and supple as her fingers began to snap in time to the beat.

Spontaneously, the musicians and the other dancers began either to clap or give the traditional cries of exultation and enjoyment. And this, too, was part of Mexico, and the fiesta—the dancing for enjoyment, to forget the dreary, miserable life that was otherwise the lot of the peasant.

The movements, the slightly flirtatious gestures and the lifting of swirling skirts—all these came back to Ginny as she danced. And she forgot herself, as she used to before. She ignored Concepción, and even her partner belonging only to the music.

And in spite of the lateness of the hour, there were others that wanted to join. The courtyard was full of laughing, exhilarated couples. Ginny hardly noticed any longer as she went from one partner to the next, and the tunes and the tempo changed. Some were slow, and some were fast. Sometimes a man clasped her in his arms, and at other times she danced apart from him, teasing, challenging. And when Concepción kicked off her shoes, Ginny did, too. She no longer cared who watched, or what they thought.

"I didn't know that Ginny could dance like that! William—she looks so ... so abandoned!" Sonya exclaimed.

The Senator had come to stand beside his wife, and although his face still wore a frown he whispered comfortingly that she mustn't object.

"I notice that our host's little friend is just as abandoned to the dance. Don't worry, my love. After tonight, the Mexican dances will become all the rage."

"But. . . ." Sonya swallowed the rest of her objections as

she saw more and more people she had considered staid and conservative jump to their feet, as if unable to resist joining in the festivities. And indeed, it seemed as if everyone was having a great deal of fun. There was clapping; cries of "ole!"; the laughter of the dancers themselves. Waiters, moving unobtrusively among the guests, provided wine and other light refreshments. Surprising herself, Sonya almost wished that *she* might have joined in.

And there was Ginny, who had complained of a headache and feeling tired, in the middle of the crowd of dancers, her face flushed; her hair had escaped from its tidy coils and fell over her shoulders. She seemed tireless, and she had actually begun to smile.

But where, Sonya thought querulously, was Mr. Murdock? The perfect host at the beginning, he seemed to have disappeared, ever since one of his menservants had come outside to whisper something in his ear.

"William," she began, and her husband, not taking his eyes off the dancers, whispered back that he would tell her all about it later; this was hardly the time or the place.

"I had a talk with Murdock, of course. A strange man—and I think he can be dangerous. Seemed to know far too much. But, at least, I think he's a fair man. And he's taken a liking to Ginny. I hope she won't spoil everything with a fit of the megrims, or those headaches she's constantly complaining of. . . ."

"William!"

He said rather irritably, "Well, you know what I mean! There are times when I wish. . . . Sahrkanov should have waited. He's become . . . but let's talk about it later, shall we? The dancing's getting rather wild. We'd better keep an eye on things."

The dancing was indeed becoming wild, and Concepción and Ginny were rivals. Sam Murdock, watching from the gallery, still flanked by his inevitable bodyguards, had begun to frown.

"Damn it! I should have known that Concepción would start something like this the minute my back was turned."

"Seems to me like the Princess is holding her own." His companion's tone was dry, but Murdock continued to frown.

"To tell you the truth, I've begun to worry about that little girl. There are times when she seems—well, far too detached from everything. And I happen to know she lives from one headache powder to another. Or dose of tonic. But even her father seems to take that for granted. He told me she was highly strung."

"Perhaps you'd better ask her for a dance. There's a gate, isn't there, into the small patio?"

"I think you keep forgetting I'm an old man. Hardly up to that kind of intrigue!"

"But you're the host."

Sam Murdock swore softly under his breath as he went downstairs. Maybe they'd play something a trifle slower by the time he emerged into the courtyard. It took him some time to move through the crowd, making his apologies, smiling. He paused deliberately by Senator William Brandon and his wife.

"My apologies for neglecting my guests. A business acquaintance of mine chose this strange hour to turn up. Would you mind if I asked the Princess to dance? I'm not too agile, at my age, but some of my bodyguards who are going off-duty would like to join in."

"We were thinking of retiring," Sonya Brandon said impulsively.

"In that case, I'll see that Concepción—my ward—sees the Princess to her room. Now, if I may. . . ."

Sam Murdock's face showed nothing but its usual imperturbability as he moved through the crowd of dancers.

But Concepción bit her lip, and almost imperceptibly, the music seemed to become slower. Looking up, Ginny suddenly found Sam Murdock before her.

"It's been a long time since I've tried to dance to *this*. And it seems as if apologies are in order again. I'll speak to Concepción later."

"No!" Ginny's voice sounded breathless. "No—that won't be necessary. I don't need to be—protected, you know. I can look after myself."

"Well, I'm certainly glad to hear it. But I am not too certain of myself, I'm afraid. I get out of breath easily, and I'm not used to this rather energetic style of dancing."

"But you're here." She sounded almost flirtatious. "Why, Mr. Murdock? Are you really such a mystery as you seem to be?"

She caught his faint smile—an upward tug of his lips.

"I'm really no mystery at all. Just a man who is getting old. A successful gambler, if you prefer. And you—but I don't need to tell you that you dance magnificently. Or that I've noticed a certain aliveness and awareness in you that seemed to be missing before. Again—you'll forgive me for being blunt? You see, I have a favor to ask of you."

Somehow, they were at the far end of the courtyard, somewhat removed from the other dancers. After she had heard his rather puzzling request, Ginny glanced involuntarily in the direction of the place where her father and Sonya had been sitting, watching her, and found that they had risen and were making what seemed like their polite good-nights to the other people present.

"I asked your father's permission to dance with you. And promised that I would have my ward see you safely to your room afterwards."

How was it he seemed to have the uncanny knack of reading her mind? Ginny's feet stumbled slightly, and Sam Murdock's strong hands held hers for a moment. She said quickly, "No! That is, I'm sure I can find my way back to my room by myself."

"You see that everyone is very much occupied with enjoying themselves. I'll arrange to have you escorted back to your room myself. There are always my silent, tactful bodyguards. Well? Would you indulge an old man's whim, or would you prefer to continue dancing with those of my guests who are younger and more—er—active?"

"I'll come with you," Ginny said abruptly. She did not quite know why she did so—was it to see the disgruntled, angry look on Concepción's face, or to prove to herself and her critics how little convention mattered to her?

No matter—with an agility surprising in a man his age, Sam Murdock had danced her past the musicians, and into the shadows. And she thought that very few people noticed they had vanished.

Here was the gate he had mentioned; forbiddingly closed. Iron-barred, set into the thick wall, it was hardly noticeable.

"Just a minute." Murdock rapped sharply on it, and it opened soundlessly from the inside. Aladdin's cave, Ginny thought light-headedly.

She heard the gate close behind them softly, locks clicking into place, and here, in this miniature, private courtyard, it was almost dark; the music drifted faintly over the high wall.

A fountain tinkled in a corner, falling into another pool. Trees grew against the wall; blossomed vines trailed over it.

As if on cue, the music had changed from a fast, frenetic tempo to a softer, more melancholy tune. Almost a waltz. Almost. A tune that spoke of yearning, of unfulfilled dreams.

"Will you dance?"

"Aren't you going to dance with me?"

She made her voice sound light, to fight off the sudden heaviness in her heart. Perhaps Mr. Murdock, too, was like all the others—only a little more subtle. Why had she come here with him?

And then she noticed the bodyguards, two black-clad men who stood against the wall with their arms folded. Watching, while seeming not to. Didn't he trust anyone? Or was their strange presence here meant to ensure that she would not repeat her violent reaction to Sir Eric's unwanted embraces?

Sam Murdock's voice sounded regretful, as he poured her a glass of wine from a decanter that stood on a stone table.

"I wish I were a good dancer—or that I were younger. But this music was not meant for clumsy feet like mine."

Over the rim of her glass, automatically raised in reply to his silent toast, Ginny gave him a puzzled glance.

"But you said—"

"I said I would be honored if you would dance for me. Here, away from the crowd. And I meant that. Will you drink?"

Still confused, watching his face in the dimness, Ginny raised her glass and drank from it. Dry white wine. A delicate Reisling.

"Do you want me to dance alone, then?"

"No. I hardly think that would be fair. You are not a hired performer. But if I may offer a substitute. . . ."

She thought he murmured, "Forgive me," before he moved away, and one of the bearded men who leaned negligently against the wall came forward. Or perhaps it was "Excuse me." Afterwards, she could not remember.

Because the man who had suddenly taken her in his arms was Steve.

Chapter Eighteen

The stars, silver-dusted against the dark purple of the night sky, seemed to have begun whirling dizzily around her.

"I think I am imagining all this," Ginny thought wildly. There must have been something in the wine. She closed her eyes while disjointed, confused thoughts seemed to scramble around in her brain. It just didn't seem possible! And Steve's arms held her in such a stiffly formal manner, as if they'd only just been introduced. It wasn't possible. . . .

Almost fearfully, Ginny opened her eyes again, and this time she felt his arms tighten as she stumbled, her feet suddenly refusing to move any longer. In fact, her breathing was so uneven and she felt so dizzy that she could not even speak as she stared up into his eyes.

"Are you feeling all right—Princess?" Except for the slight, mocking intonation he gave the last word, his voice sounded coldly dispassionate. "Would you prefer to sit down?"

"Steve!" Her lips formed his name, but no sound emerged.

Except for the brightness of her hair and eyes, she seemed suddenly without color—as pale as marble, and just as cold. In fact the very act of breathing seemed to grow more and more difficult, even while she could not tear her glazed, dilating green eyes away from his face.

He wore a closely-cropped beard that could not disguise the hard, rather reckless slant of his lips. And those pitiless, narrowed blue eyes, so dark they looked almost black in the dim light—one eyebrow lifted slightly as he repeated his question with exaggerated patience.

"Would you like to sit down? I'm sorry if my turning up

here like this has upset you, but I'm afraid I couldn't very well mingle with the others in case your father got the idea of saving himself all that reward money he's offered for my—extermination."

Ginny kept staring at him, barely aware of the import of his words. All she noticed was that they were suddenly quite alone, and that Steve's voice held the old, sarcastic inflection she had once hated. Why couldn't she speak—or move?

Instead, "He's here, he's here!" drummed in her mind, shutting out everything else; and as she swayed on her feet, Steve caught her, one arm going around her waist. She was suddenly leaning against him, wondering vaguely why he wasn't holding her more closely, why he hadn't begun to kiss her yet.

But it seemed he didn't intend to at all—and that he hadn't taken her in his arms because he wanted to, but because he was afraid she might faint.

Still dizzy, Ginny felt herself being helped, quite impersonally, to a seat on an extremely hard stone bench. And Steve was holding a glass of something cold to her shaking lips.

"Here—I'm afraid it's all I can find, so it'll have to do. Christ, is seeing me alive really such a shock?"

She choked over the wine, but swallowed it before he spilled it down her throat. Yes, he was capable of that, as she remembered only too clearly. And now she was finally gaining enough control over her treacherous senses to become ashamed of her own, too-obvious reactions.

The thought had begun to be borne in on her that she was no longer married to Steve—she was married to Ivan, Prince Sahrkanov, to whom she represented a profitable investment. But what did she mean to Steve, if anything? Why had he come here?

Unconsciously, as she pushed the empty glass away from her lips, Ginny's soft mouth had taken on a hardness that was unfamiliar. A rather cynical droop. Her eyes, when they met Steve's again, had lost some of their glazed look, although they were still unusually large and brilliant.

He could sense her withdrawal from him, where only seconds ago she had been softly yielding, her body trembling helplessly against his. And it had taken all his self-control not to take advantage of her weakness, to crush

her body against his and hear her whimper as her head
fell back, her lips parted, waiting for his kisses. Instead he
had made her sit down, and in giving her the wine had
given himself an excuse to toss down a glassful as well.
And now, as he looked back at her cold, defiant face,
Steve's black brows drew together in an involuntary frown
as he felt the anger and bitterness he thought he'd learned
to hold in check come up to ride him.

It made his voice sound harsh, although she wasn't to
know why; she brought her chin up in that stubborn gesture he remembered far too well.

"Feel better now?" And then, before she could answer,
"Mind if I sit down beside you for a while?" He dropped
down beside her, stretching long legs before him, and it
was all Ginny could do not to reach out to him, touch
him. How could he act as if they were strangers? How
could *she?*

"What are you doing here? Why did you come? And
Mr. Murdock—"

"That's a hell of a way to treat an old acquaintance,
isn't it, Princess?" he drawled, one eyebrow going up hatefully as his cold eyes rested on her.

"Oh!" At the outrage in her voice, *his* turned placating,
and somehow, this only served to infuriate her more.

"Look—I didn't come here to start quarreling with you.
What's the point? And I apologize for my rudeness. Believe it or not, I didn't come here to ruin things for you,
nor to interfere with your new life." He looked straight at
her and shrugged, his expression unreadable, and at his
even, indifferent words Ginny felt a creeping coldness
spread from her mind to her chest.

"I admit I was angry, and even jealous—at first, that is.
But later, when I'd had time to think things over—what
the hell, Ginny, I guess we were both fooling each other,
thinking it could last. Wars and fighting have a way of
putting things out of perspective, especially when all you
do is live from day to day. And what was I offering you,
anyhow? A bed under a wagon, a lot of moving around—
I really can't blame you for seizing your opportunity to
better yourself. I guess I'd have done the same myself.
And seeing you now, in the right clothes, against the right
background, I realize how crazy I was to try to take you
away from what you've been used to." She was silent,

wanting to weep, wanting to scream out in repudiation of the flat, unemotional sound of his voice as he continued. "What I'm really trying to say is—I blame myself for ruining your whole damn life, and for all the bad times you've had. And I feel a kind of responsibility to make sure everything's all right with you, as crazy as that may sound."

She could not bear to listen to any more. She could hardly believe that this quiet stranger who spoke of blaming himself and feeling—yes, actually feeling *responsible* for her was Steve. Not the Steve she had known—reckless, arrogant, selfish, even cruel. And yet, damn it, in spite of it, her man. Loving her, and finally admitting it. Angry-tender, harsh-gentle. But above all, never, ever indifferent!

He could never have loved her—hadn't he just admitted as much? And now, all he could talk of was a sense of responsibility, as if he wanted to salve his own conscience, nothing else. But since when had Steve ever possessed a conscience?

Her voice had become breathless again, as she cried out angrily: "Oh, stop! Don't go on any further. As you just said, it isn't necessary. And as for—for—well, you can see for yourself how I am, can't you? You gave me such a shock. . . ." And then, seizing on the first excuse that came to mind, "When did you become one of Mr. Murdock's bodyguards? How did you. . . ."

He laughed shortly.

"I'm glad to see you can recover so quickly from a state of shock, Princess. And as for my being here—I must admit it was partly curiosity on my part, and partly because, to put it plainly, I needed occupation of some kind, since the war's over. I've known Sam Murdock for a long time, and he pays well. It's the kind of work I'm best at, as even you must admit!"

"Hiring your gun out when you don't *need* to—you just enjoy risking your neck, don't you, Steve Morgan? Or haven't you heard that half the bounty hunters in the country are hunting you?" And now her eyes were flashing angrily, and a slight flush had come into her cheeks. "I wish I knew what you are *really* up to! What is it about you that makes you deliberately look for trouble?"

Quite suddenly, as the music on the other side of the wall became louder, and there were shouts and delighted "ole's" of encouragement, the vision of Concepción sprang into Ginny's mind, and she gasped out loud.

"Concepción! Why didn't I guess it before? She's your mistress, isn't she? You're here to be with her—that ... that...."

"My dear Princess, you surely weren't going to use some of the unladylike language you were so fond of at one time, were you?"

He had the effrontery to grin mockingly at her, crossing his long legs comfortably.

They were back in time for an instant, as pure rage shot through Ginny's veins, making her long to claw at his dark, rakehell's face with her nails. She had actually raised her hand, fingers curved, when he caught her wrist.

"Be careful, Princess. Or have you forgotten you've another husband now?"

His words, sarcastically uttered, acted like a slap. Ginny could feel all the fire, all the anger ooze out of her and she stared at him, almost disbelievingly. How could she have forgotten? All the months between them, all the misunderstandings—and now, he actually acted as if he was relieved to have her off his hands.

Her hand had gone limp, and, shrugging, he let her wrist drop.

"Why don't we leave Concepción out of this? As you just reminded me, we've been friends for a long time, she and I. But unfortunately, I haven't been around here long enough to renew too many old acquaintances yet. I've been traveling. In fact, I just arrived a short while ago, from Virginia City, and I'm damned tired. But when I heard that *you* were here, by some coincidence...."

He let his words trail off deliberately, continuing to watch her face from under those lashes she had always accused him of being far too long for any man to possess. They could give his eyes a shadowed, almost menacing effect sometimes, and in this instance Ginny wanted to shiver—both from misery and apprehension. He didn't want *her*. He'd taken pains to make that clear right from the start. But what *did* he want?

Whether she hated the thought or not, she knew Steve. *Had* known him. The way his mind could work—how completely unscrupulous he could be when he was after something. And she didn't believe his being here was sheer coincidence either.

But by now, Ginny found herself almost too tired to think. She had been keyed up all evening, and during the past two hours only anger and shock had kept her going. Now, suddenly, she felt drained of everything. Emotion—feeling—even grief.

"Whatever you're really here for, Steve, I expect I shall find out, sooner or later. And now, if you'll excuse me, I really am very tired. My head hurts so."

She felt as if her bones were dissolving; as if she were a cloth doll. Almost unconsciously, as she spoke she put both hands up, fingers pressing against her temples. It was all she could do to keep her teeth from chattering, although it wasn't cold. Nothing mattered now except getting her to her room, and swallowing some of the tonic that would soon bring its soothing relief—calming her taut nerves, relaxing every muscle in her body, bringing her escape from painful reality in dreams that sparkled with color and pretty patterns. Oh, God, how tired, how sick she felt! But she had to try to stand up, to make some effort at normalcy. . . . Without knowing she had done so, Ginny closed her eyes. A moment later she felt rough, impatient hands on her shoulders.

"Ginny! For God's sake, what's the matter with you?"

In spite of the bitter, frustrated anger inside him, Steve could not help feeling alarmed at her sudden pallor, the contrast in her now from the way she had looked and acted only a moment ago. He shook her slightly, wanting to bring her back to life, still fighting the urge to take her into his arms instead, to hurt her, curse at her, punish her for the fickle, shallow-minded bitch she had become.

"Ginny. Damn it. . . ."

Why was he shouting at her? Why was his voice so hard and hateful?

She tried to pull away from the roughness of his grasp.

"Don't! Why won't you leave me alone? Why did you have to come back? I'm not your responsibility any longer, I'm not your—not anything to you. I want to go to bed. If I could only have some of my medicine for this headache. . . ."

She heard him swear softly and violently under his breath, and wondered why he was so angry with her. And the next moment, she felt herself lifted, carried up in his arms, with her head resting willy-nilly against his shoulder.

"No! I don't want—"

"You don't even have the strength left to struggle, do you? But you don't have to worry, Princess. I've no intentions of raping you, if that's what you're afraid of."

She wanted to retort that she wasn't afraid—that she didn't care any longer what happened to her—but her tongue felt too heavy, just like her eyes. And somehow, in the strangest, most contradictory fashion, it was comfortable to be held in strong, familiar arms again, even if Steve *were* angry with her. She remembered how he had carried her up the carpeted stairway of Lila's fancy house in El Paso, and how she had fought against him and hated him then. But now she was too tired for anything—for fear, for unhappiness, even for hate.

Delia gave a small shriek of alarm when the door was unceremoniously kicked open and a tall, bearded man dressed in black, with a gun that was barely concealed by the jacket he wore, carried her mistress into her room.

She swallowed back a second, louder scream when he fixed her with a pair of hard, uncompromising blue eyes.

"Get those covers off that bed. And stop acting like you've been snake-bit. She—the Princess isn't feeling too well. Are you sure you know what to do?"

"But. . . ." The blue eyes seemed to darken, and Delia swallowed. "Yes, sir. She'll be needing some of her tonic. Always makes her feel a whole heap better, and it's been quite a while since she took one of them headache powders. I can take care of her now, sir."

He lowered her onto the bed surprisingly gently, and Ginny opened her eyes, blinking them against the lamplight.

"Steve—?" she started to say, but her voice sounded slurred and almost incoherent. And he was still looking at Delia.

"I guess you'd better get her some of that medicine you were talking about. And if there are any questions asked—I work for Mr. Murdock. He sent me up here."

"Oh, no, sir! I ain't going to say a word to a soul. Miss Ginny wouldn't like that. And I wouldn't anyhow."

"Sleep well, Princess."

His voice sounded flat and unemotional—Sam Murdock's hired bodyguard, performing his duty towards one of the guests.

Delia had already turned away, to measure out some of the tonic, when the door closed gently and somehow finally behind him. And Ginny felt the silent, tired tears slipping down her cheeks and was powerless to prevent them.

Chapter Nineteen

Ginny woke late, with the memories of the previous night to contend with. In some ways, it all seemed too unreal to be true, and she tried to tell herself that she had dreamed it all. Of course she had! Any other possibility was unthinkable. And yet. . . .

"They all gone out riding, ma'am," Delia said, as she helped Ginny to dress. "Left 'bout an hour ago, but they said I was to let you sleep, long as you wanted to. And you're to have breakfast right here in bed, too, if you like."

"*Who* said?" Ginny questioned sharply, and the girl looked surprised.

"Why—the Senator did. And Mr. Murdock, himself. They all wanted you to get your rest. Mr. Murdock said if you did get up, you was to feel like this was your home. Do anything you feel like doing."

Without being told, Delia was bringing her a headache powder, neatly wrapped in its twist of rice paper, along with a tall glass of lemon juice, which was actually iced. As Ginny reached out automatically, she thought the girl's face took on what was almost a sly expression that reminded her of Tilly.

"Mr. Murdock—he's a grand, rich man, ain't he? I could tell, just from hearing the way people talk about him. An' he thinks a lot of you. Anyone could tell that, from the worried look he had when he was askin' about you."

Down went the powder. And the iced lemon juice felt so cool, so cool in her throat.

"Have they all gone riding then?"

Sound casual, she was telling herself. Sound unconcerned. If it really were Steve last night, he's gone by now. He wouldn't dare stay around. And how much did Sam Murdock know? What kind of a game was *he* playing?

"All of them's gone." Delia sounded pleased with herself. "Even that Spanish young lady. You have the whole place to yourself, ma'am. Anything you want to do—that's what Mr. Murdock said. An' that's what he told the other servants, too."

Dressed in her favorite bronze-colored riding habit, Ginny was served a breakfast of coffee and rolls on the small, private patio. Without comment or explanation, that was where she had been led. In her splendid isolation, she was being made to feel like a *real* princess ... but why had she thought that?

"No, I won't think," Ginny told herself. She forced herself to drink her coffee and eat half a roll, although she wasn't in the least hungry. How quiet it was here. The stone bench and table, the miniature fountains and pool. And the weathered-looking stone steps that led to Sam Murdock's bedroom. Did he come down here often to be by himself? Or was this house merely the passing whim of a man who was far too rich?

She had dismissed Delia, and the silent, smiling servants who had waited on her had disappeared. The blood flowed in her veins, and the sun was warm on her. She felt alive and well and ready to face anything; even the past. She had meant to go riding—perhaps to catch up with the others. But did she really want to have other people around her?

It was only when she saw him, coming down the steps, that Ginny realized she had been waiting.

He was wearing a white linen shirt, open at the throat, and black pants. And he looked unkempt and angry and tired, as if he hadn't slept very well. Her heart had already begun to leap, but Ginny told herself sternly that, no doubt, having salved his conscience where *she* was concerned, he had spent the night with Concepción. Why did that thought make her angry?

"What are you doing here?"

He rubbed at his jaw reflectively, the beard rasping against his fingers; the sound grating against her nerves.

"I'm not sure. Except that I happen to live here, for the moment. And Sam asked me to keep an eye on you. See you had everything you wanted. Do you mind if I join you? I'd hate to let all that good breakfast go to waste."

Without waiting for her reply, Steve dropped into the chair opposite hers, reaching for a roll. Stiffening, Ginny was almost too much aware of the way his eyes rested on her critically.

"You've grown thinner. And you've lost that peachy-gold tan that used to suit you so well. Too many late nights, I guess. Have you forgotten how to pour coffee? Or is that one of the things you leave to the servants?"

"Since you're almost in that position yourself, aren't you being too familiar?"

Her voice was cold, but he met it with a lifted eyebrow.

"I can tell you're feeling more your old self this morning. Well, I guess I can get my own coffee. Sorry I presumed, Princess."

He had begun to reach for the silver coffee pot, but she almost snatched it away from him.

"I'll do it—just this once. And I'd like to know exactly what you're doing here, Steve Morgan. What are you up to? You're forgetting that I know you—almost too well!"

"I haven't forgotten. Thank you."

His words sounded curt as he accepted the cup from her shaking fingers, but she wished all the same that his eyes wouldn't dwell on her in precisely the old manner— bright blue in the sunlight; taunting and questioning. So she persisted sharply:

"Why are you here? Are you going to tell me the truth for a change, or do I have to ask Mr. Murdock?"

"Sam doesn't know too much. Except that we once knew each other rather well. He's got old-fashioned notions about women. And he was worried about you last night. Perhaps you ought to tell him I kept my distance. I wouldn't want to lose my job."

The sarcastic note in his voice mocked her as he leaned back in his chair, regarding her over the silver-rimmed cup.

"I think you know each other better than you admit. You—you came down from his bedroom just now, didn't you?"

Again, he cocked an eyebrow at her, the grooves in his face deepening.

"I'll be damned. I wouldn't have thought it of Sam. So you've been up in his bedroom already? For shame, Princess. Or is your husband understanding enough not to mind?" Color flamed in Ginny's face.

"You haven't changed at all, have you?" she said bitingly. "You'd even impugn the man who has helped you—"

"What makes you think I was being insulting? I think Sam's a lucky man. And so's your husband, of course. Sure is a pity he's not here."

Her mouth half-opened to retort, Ginny closed it, her lips tightening. It had suddenly struck her, with the force of a blow, that Steve was drunk. Ugly-drunk. And she'd never seen Steve drunk before. He hardly showed it; but she *knew*.

"I think I'd better leave you now," she said with freezing politeness. "You've reminded me I have a husband and accused me of taking a lover—all in the same breath. And in your present condition, I'm sure it's hardly worthwhile reminding you that it isn't any of your business any longer. You made that clear last night, didn't you?"

She rose to her feet, the sunlight blurring before her eyes. She had to get away—he was here to torment her, to punish her. And even the headache powder she had taken wasn't sufficient to arm her against this kind of hurt.

"Seems to me that we both made our positions clear," he drawled. "So there's no need to run away as if you're afraid I'll rape you. *Those* days are past and done with, Princess."

But then, why had his hand shot out to catch her wrist? Ginny stood immobilized and angry, her one attempt to tug herself free having reminded her how steely-strong his fingers could be. More than ever she felt as if he had come here determined to play some cruel game with her.

Biting her lip, Ginny managed to make her voice sound cool.

"Very well, Steve. Perhaps, once you've told me what you want, you'll let me leave."

Steve Morgan knew, with a detached kind of clarity, that he was drunk. And he also knew that he should have let her walk away. Ever since he'd left her last night, the desperate, angry words she'd flung in his face had haunted him.

"Why won't you leave me alone? Why did you have to come back?"

And at that point he'd been just about ready to turn his back on the whole damn mess—tell Bishop to find himself another man. Even now, damn her, in spite of his talk with Sam Murdock last night, she had a way of making him want to either shake or strangle her. Was it possible that she'd actually fallen in love with Sahrkanov? How much dared he tell her?

They eyed each other warily, thoughts carefully hidden.

"You're dressed for riding," Steve said abruptly. "Sam wouldn't want you to be disappointed. If you'll sit down long enough to let me finish this cup of coffee, I'll go with you. He wouldn't want you to get lost."

Ginny still wanted to run away. But she would never let him see that. Let him think she was just as unmoved by his nearness as he was by hers.

"I suppose I have no choice. But I'm surprised that you dare to show yourself here so boldly. If my father sees you, or Sonya. . . ." She was rubbing at the wrist he had just released as she spoke, and to her surprise he rose politely to pull her chair back for her.

"My goodness!" she could not resist saying sweetly, "you've actually learned some manners, haven't you?"

"And your tongue's lost none of the sharpness I remember! But in case you're worried, Princess, let me relieve your mind—I plan to leave here tonight. There's no telling if we'll meet again or not. So why don't we try to have a pleasant ride. No more recriminations. I'll try to curb my tongue if you will."

He was watching her as he spoke, through lazy-lidded eyes, and his sudden change of mood and tactics confused

her. Hadn't he always had the power to do so? Thank
God she had learned to make a mask of her face.

Ginny nodded her head slightly, without answering; her
thoughts were bitter. Now that he had fulfilled this sense
of responsibility he had spoken of, he was going to leave—
why should she care if he did? Not only did he not love
her any longer, he had also stopped wanting her. Only a
few months ago he would most likely have torn the
clothes from her body if she didn't undress fast enough.
And now, in spite of the fact that they were all alone out
here, all he'd done was watch her, in that new, half-contemptuous manner he'd developed towards her, while he
spoke as if she were some strange woman he didn't particularly like.

"If you don't mind," Steve said politely, "we'll ride in
the opposite direction to that which the others have taken.
And I'll have you back at the house before they return, in
case you feel nervous. They took a picnic meal with them,
so they're not likely to be back before afternoon."

Was it really possible that she was riding beside Steve
again? And that they were actually conversing like distant
strangers, ill at ease with each other? What was there to
say?

Steve seemed familiar with the wooded, gently sloping
country they were riding through, and Ginny no longer
cared in what direction they rode, or where he was taking
her. As he'd reminded her earlier, she was quite safe with
him. How he had changed! He seemed barely aware of
her presence at his side.

A breeze had come up, fluttering coppery strands of
hair against Ginny's face, which remained pale and pensive. Was she happy? Steve wondered. Did she enjoy the
kind of life she had chosen for herself? A husband who
had given her a title and a position of respectability in society, and who, it was whispered, didn't particularly mind
if his young and beautiful wife took other lovers on the
side. But what in hell had she been doing with that old
roué, Eric Fotheringay? Even if she had changed her
mind about him in the end—Christ, what had she expected? She had turned into a rotten, promiscuous little bitch,
all right, but he'd contributed to turning her into one. And

with it all, she still managed to retain that rather innocent air. How did she do it?

Steve had deliberately chosen a path that was hardly a path at all—a barely defined trail he had followed before, leading to a small clearing by the creek. But it was densely wooded here, and he had to pick his way with care, mentally cursing the liquor fumes that still seemed to obscure clear thinking. He must have been crazy to allow Bishop to talk him into coming. If Ginny had been unhappy, or even if she had been tricked in some way by the machinations of Sahrkanov and her father, she would have said so. What a fool!

They had reached the clearing at last. And now what? Ginny was sitting on her horse, staring at the water. She had suddenly realized how still and silent it was, except for the incessant chirping sounds of birds and the cool splash of running water. A fallen tree, with grass growing high around it, lay half in and half out of the stream, causing the current to eddy around it. There was no sign that anyone had been here before.

She turned her head slightly. Steve was staring at the water, a morose expression on his face, as if already he regretted having brought her here. The sun beat down fiercely, now that they had ridden out of the shelter of the trees; it reminded Ginny that it must be almost noon already. Almost time to turn back and return to the house.

"Would you like to rest for a while? The horses could use it."

With a touch of his old arrogance, Steve had already slid off his horse, letting the reins trail to the ground. And without waiting for her answer, he put his hands on her waist, lifting her from the saddle.

Automatically, she had put her hands on his shoulders to steady herself. And when he put her down it seemed just as natural that his hands should slide from her waist and up her back. Why not? He wanted her. Why had he been holding back?

Ginny made a small, gasping sound. Shock? Apprehension? Too late, then. Steve was the only man who made her feel as if he were possessing her, invading her with just his kisses. Her fingers clung to his shoulders, touched his hair; and then she closed her eyes, letting the old feelings

of languor, of rapture, of desire fill her, making her lean
against him weakly. He kissed her mouth, lingering over
it, and then her cheeks, her closed eyelids, her hair—impatiently ripping away the hat she had pinned on so carefully, together with a quantity of hairpins. And as her hair
came down he crushed it in his hands before he twisted his
fingers in its silky mass, pulling her head back while his
lips burned against her throat, and then her breasts, as the
buttons holding her bodice together gave way to his impatient fingers. She was on fire, and he was flame. She felt
herself consumed, dissolving, falling; and then there was
heat—the sun hot overhead, the smell of crushed grass
and sage under her body as still, without words, without a
single wasted motion, he undressed her and took her.

Ginny felt as if she had died, and were slowly coming
back to life. *Le petit mort.* Little death. The whirling, kaleidoscope world slowly settled back on its axis as her
breathing slowed. How long had she lain here? And where
was Steve? It was an effort, lifting her arm to shield her
eyes from the sun. Almost too much effort, like turning
her head.

He emerged, naked and dripping from the stream, raking his fingers through his hair. She saw him glance at her,
eyes a hard, dark blue like sapphires, and then, still without speaking, he began to dress.

Ginny felt her heart begin to pound heavily—felt as if
the pulse in her throat was choking her. Surely, after what
had just happened, he was going to *say* something?

She raised herself up on one elbow, wondering why she
still felt so weak, and saw her ruined riding habit lying
crumpled where he had let it drop. How was she going to
return to the house dressed like that? The others might be
back by now—the servants would all know ... but since
when had Steve cared what people might think?

He sauntered over to her, buckling on his belt, shirt
slung across his shoulders like a cape.

"You look uncommonly enticing lying there like that,
my sweet. But hadn't you better start getting dressed? You
don't want your husband to be greeted with any unpleasant gossip when he turns up, do you?"

His casual words and the offhand manner in which he'd
referred to her *husband* made Ginny feel as if he'd struck

her. At first, she was so shocked that she could do nothing but stare up at him—at that hard, beard-shadowed face that showed no feeling at all.

"Well? Come on, Ginny—if you want to take a bath in that stream, you'd better hurry."

Reaching down, he pulled her easily to her feet. For just an instant, as they stood close again, she thought she saw a flicker of feeling in his eyes. Contempt? Regret? Whatever it had been, it was gone. And he was propelling her forward impatiently, as if his only thought now was to make a quick end to a pleasant but quite unimportant episode. A romp in the woods with a married woman, whose husband must be kept in the dark.

Humiliation and a growing anger made Ginny pull herself from his grasp. "Do you think I cannot manage by myself? If you're in such a hurry, why don't you go on without me?"

Knotting her hair on top of her head with fingers that shook treacherously, she turned her back on him and stepped gingerly into the stream—the coldness of the water made her gasp.

Steve straddled the log that sloped down into the water, watching her. And the knowledge that his eyes were on her, scrutinizing her openly, made her nervous. Oh, God, after everything, after the casual way in which he'd possessed her and then walked away from her, how was it that just the way he looked her over in that assessing, critical manner still had such an effect on her?

Pretending to ignore him, Ginny moved further into the center of the creek, feeling the increased pull of the current that fought to take her off her feet.

"Be careful!" he called out to her in the same slightly caustic voice he'd used before. "Or were you thinking of turning yourself into an Ophelia?"

Her teeth were chattering as she lowered herself into the water, and then splashed it over herself, letting icy-cold rivulets run down her shoulders and back.

"I—I'm surprised that you've read Shakespeare! And, you—do you think of yourself as Hamlet, unable to make up his mind?"

He ignored her sarcasm.

"You're turning blue with cold, Ginny. Why don't you

come on out now?" The impatient note in his voice had the effect of stiffening her spine and making her angrier than ever.

Oh yes, how could she have forgotten? There was a time when she had hated Steve Morgan quite fiercely, and he was making it too easy for her to start feeling that way again.

Continuing to ignore him, she cupped her hands, burying her burning face in cold water.

"Ginny!" How dare he use that bullying, peremptory tone with her?

"Oh—go away, if you're in such a hurry!"

Half-blinded by water, she had turned her head to call back at him, and her sudden, careless movement made her lose her balance. When she surfaced again, gasping for breath, her arms flailing wildly, the first thing she heard was his laughter.

"Oh you, you unfeeling brute—you bastard! You. . . ." She swore at him in Mexican, using all the worst epithets she could recall, pushing heavy tangles of hair off her face.

"You sound more like a *puta* than a princess, Ginny. And, by God, I've a good mind to push you back under and let you drown!"

"Try it! You just try it, Steve Morgan!"

Childishly, hating him almost beyond endurance, she waded clumsily towards him; and when she was close enough, she showered him with water. And when he instinctively ducked, turning his face away, she made a grab for his leg, tugging with all her frenzied strength. This time, she almost drowned them both in her angry efforts to drown *him*, and he was angry enough, by the time he had dragged her back onto the bank, to have thrown her back in.

They were both dripping wet, but at least she had dry clothes to put on her back. And, invigorated by their struggle in the water and his fury, it was her turn to laugh. Steve looked down at himself in disgust. At least he hadn't worn his gun. But when he rode back, that would be about the only dry thing he had on.

Ginny, escaping from him as if she'd sensed his anger,

had begun to dry her hair and body with her torn chemise.

"Why don't you just wrap a blanket around yourself? Like a Roman toga. I'd offer you my pantalettes to wear, but I hardly think they'd fit. Shall I go back and send one of the servants out with some dry clothes for you? If Concepción's back I'm sure she'd be glad to come."

"Get your clothes on. And climb on that horse. Or you're going to have some black and blue marks on that pretty body of yours to explain to your husband—or your latest lover!"

He spoke through gritted teeth, and Ginny made an involuntary grab for her dress.

"Don't you dare! You've no right. . . ."

He gave her a long, considering look that made her quail.

"I wouldn't be too sure of that. And I'm out of patience. I think you're the kind of woman who needs to be beaten regularly. And I'm of a mind to do just that, if you don't hustle."

Shivering, she put her clothes back on; she was angry at herself for giving in, but far more angry at Steve for threatening her. She had half a mind to tell her father, to tell Sam Murdock just what kind of man he'd hired as a bodyguard.

In the end, they rode back in silence, Steve bare chested, with his shirt slung over the pommel of his saddle. And by now, Ginny was only too conscious of her own disheveled state. Her hair was still dripping wet, and she was miserably conscious of the water that trickled down soaking the shoulders of her riding gown and her back. She could not help shivering as they rode through densely wooded sections where the heat of the sun seemed suddenly cut off. Why didn't Steve say something? He had deserved it—he'd had no right to use her as if she had been a whore, a woman he'd picked up the night before to have a few moments of pleasure with. She began to think longingly of a hot bath first and then warm clothes. And one of her powders to drive away the headache she felt threatening her.

Angry or not, Steve was cautious enough to approach the house from the rear. He had ridden slightly ahead of her, and Ginny reined in when she heard him swear feelingly.

"Damnation! I ought to let you go on ahead and explain your state. Perhaps your husband has decided to honor everyone with his presence. I hope you've got some plausible excuse cooked up."

"Why should *I* find excuses? I'll leave that to you—you're such an expert liar!"

His head turned, cold blue eyes sweeping over her.

"You'd better get ready with your lies, baby. I don't have a reputation to lose. And *I'm* not married, thank God!"

The stables were a hive of activity. Horses were being unsaddled, wagonettes unloaded. Grooms and vaqueros were everywhere.

In spite of her brave words, earlier, Ginny flinched.

"Oh!" Her voice sounded small and alarmed.

His look damned her, but he was already sawing on the reins of his horse, swinging its head around.

"Looks like they've only just got back. And they'll be in their rooms, by now, freshening up."

She was vividly reminded of other times. Steve's angry, drawling voice: "You're my ace in the hole, baby. Maybe, when that posse isn't as close as they are, and I've no more use for you, I'll let you go. But don't get your hopes up. . . ." "Paco's in that jail, and I aim to get him out. . . ." "I'm taking you to a house this time, Ginny. Friend of mine. . . ."

Why did she have to remember?

She followed him, though. Unquestioningly. There was no point in worrying now.

They walked in through the front door, and the elderly butler's face was impassive.

"No need to say anything." Steve's voice was curt.

"No, sir."

His fingers closed painfully over her arm.

"Where do you think you're going? This way."

Avoiding the vast emptiness of the entrance hall, Steve led the way up a concealed side staircase. Ginny was out of breath, stumbling over her trailing skirts, by the time they reached the landing.

Down a carpeted passageway they heard faint voices, and laughter.

"Hell!" Steve swore softly. And then he rapped on a door, turning the knob almost simultaneously.

It resisted for a moment and then gave way, and Ginny found herself dragged inside, the door kicked shut behind them.

She was looking into Concepción's astonished, angry face.

"*Por Dios!* Are you crazy? What are you doing with *her*? I tell you, Esteban—"

"Don't, I'm in no mood to hear it. Not even from you, querida."

Dropping Ginny's arm as if she had suddenly turned into a leper, he kissed Concepción's open mouth, silencing her. And Ginny stood their frozen, watching the way the girl's arms went up around his neck after a moment, so that he had to pull himself free in the end.

"There was a slight accident. . . ."

"You fell into the water. I can see that. Both of you?"

"Well—"

"*I* was in the water first. And then—he decided to join me. Do you really have to make excuses to her, Steve? Why don't you tell her—"

"Ginny, shut up!"

"No! Why do you stop her? Assuredly, I would like to hear the rest of this story!"

"You both disgust me!" Ginny said wildly, and turned to run.

He caught her, scooping an arm around her waist so that she was forced to fall against him.

"Do you think I went to all this trouble for nothing? Hold still, Princess, until I figure out a way to get you back to your room without having half of San Francisco know what you've been up to."

"What *I've* been up to? Why, you. . . ."

Concepción laughed shortly.

"It's plain to see what you both have been doing. And at least, Princessa, *I* am not married to another man. Do you want them all to know what you really are? An adulteress! Why do you waste your time with her, Esteban? She'll lie with any man who offers her the chance."

If Steve's arm had not been clamped around her waist, Ginny would have clawed at the other woman's face. He said harshly:

"You two can fight over who's the worse bitch later. Right now, I'm not in the mood for a fight. Where's Sam?"

And Ginny noticed for the first time that Concepción, entirely at her ease, her shoes kicked off, had been waiting in Sam Murdock's bedroom.

Chapter Twenty

Disgust—disillusion. These were the feelings that remained uppermost in Ginny's mind later.

She had gained the comparative safety of her room and managed to soothe a frantic Delia with some story of having gone riding in the woods and being thrown from her horse.

"Oh, ma'am—Princess! I just didn't dare tell them 'case they was mad at me. I kept hoping you'd get back; that you wasn't hurt or met up with an accident—you ain't hurt?"

Not on the outside, Ginny thought bitterly, but she merely shook her head at the girl, who kept on chattering from sheer relief.

"Oh, what a terrible, terrible shame!" she said as Ginny tossed aside what had been her favorite riding habit. "It's all ripped—see, right here at the shoulder, and where the skirt buttons at the side. But maybe I can fix it."

"Please—don't try!" Ginny said sharply. "I—I don't want to see that garment again. Throw it away."

She lay down on her bed after Delia had drawn the curtains, darkening the room, and deliberately closed her eyes, trying to make her mind a blank as she waited for the delicious sense of drowsiness which would soon claim her. One small dose of her tonic ... and soon, forgetfulness.

"I'll tell them you was out in the sun too long and got a headache—they'd only been back about ten minutes when *you* came in, ma'am." Delia's whisper came from far away, as images chased each other across Ginny's mind.

Steve—who judged her with the new, cold look in his eyes. And the way he had taken her this afternoon, without a word, without tenderness ... and she had let him!

And Concepción, red lips curved with mockery, fingers clutching Steve's arm possessively, saying:

"You are shocked that I am here? But why not? Sam lets me use his room whenever I want to, and I like all the mirrors—don't you, *querido*?" And her eyes had looked meaningfully into Steve's—for a moment it seemed as if they had forgotten Ginny's presence! It was no coincidence, then, *her* being here, and Steve's sudden arrival. Too many coincidences that weren't coincidences at all.

But worst of all was Sam Murdock—oh, she should have been more careful, she should have believed everything she had heard about the man. How ruthless he was, how he had clawed and fought his way to the top. And why should a man who had led a blameless monastic life need bodyguards? She should have suspected what kind of man Murdock really was when she saw his bedroom—a room he hardly ever slept in himself, if she understood Concepción correctly. A room for seduction. Was Sam Murdock stalking *her*? But if he was, why had he turned her over to Steve, who was, after all only his bodyguard—or so Steve *said*?

"Oh, I don't know what they're all up to! And I don't care any longer. I'm not going to let myself be involved in any more intrigue, I don't want to think. ..."

And then, for a while, she did stop thinking, and went drifting off on a pink-tinted cloud sea that was softer and yet more buoyant than anything she had known before, and she wanted to stay there, floating gently, forever.

Someone was shaking her by the shoulder—she was falling off the edge of the world.

Ginny woke very suddenly, with her heart pounding and her own voice ringing in her ears.

"No! No, I don't want. ..."

"Virginie! What is it you do not want, chérie? Was it a bad dream?"

Her eyes blinked, and for a moment she imagined that she was still dreaming. Ivan, of all people—*here? Now?* Mechanically, while she tried to collect her senses, she murmured:

"I—I dreamed I was falling."

"Ah, yes. Off a horse, perhaps? I heard about your little accident this afternoon, and naturally, I was worried." He sat on the side of her bed, patting her ice-cold hands, smiling at her. "You are not still in shock, are you? Were you hurt? I told that silly little maid of yours that she should have informed your parents at once. You should have been examined by a doctor." Still smiling, holding her hands tightly when she instinctively tried to draw them away, Ivan Sahrkanov leaned forward, kissing her deliberately on the mouth. And quite involuntarily, without thinking, Ginny felt herself shrink from his kiss.

He lifted his head and looked down at her reproachfully, his peculiar blue-green eyes like shining, opaque stones.

"My darling! What *is* this? I thought, after a separation of far too many days, that you would be glad to see me. Or perhaps your coldness is due to—the shock you must have had this afternoon. You're still so pale, I find myself growing more and more concerned!"

"Ivan—please! I'm—I'm all right, I tell you. It was an accident, and I wasn't hurt, just shaken up."

"Too shaken up to kiss your husband properly? You're shaking like a leaf, my love. Perhaps I should ask our charming host to send for a doctor for you."

"No!" Ginny exclaimed, far too quickly and sharply. And then, "That's not necessary, really Ivan."

"Of course. I'm sure you did not want to worry anyone, eh? But I must admit that when I saw *this,* I became most worried!" Suddenly, from behind his back, Ivan had produced her torn and crumpled riding habit; holding it up critically for a moment, he tossed it away. "All those tears and rips—and the stains from grass and water. Can you blame a husband for being concerned? You must have some bruises. Have they been seen to?"

"Ivan . . ." her voice sounded strained, and her thoughts

tumbled over each other. He was playing with her, like a great cat; his eyes narrowed slightly, watching her carefully, even while he continued to smile. What should she tell him? What could she say? Ginny swallowed dryly. "I—well, I was just lucky, I suppose! I fell on the grass, so—I wasn't really hurt, just stunned for a little while. Honestly, I'm fine now."

"No doubt your gown was torn on the bushes then. *Ma pauvre petite!* What a frightening experience for you. Is your pretty white skin all scratched? That would be too bad—let me see, my love."

With a sudden, swift motion, he pulled down the shoulder of her thin lawn bedgown. Ginny tried to squirm away.

"But I'm your husband! Or have I been away from you so long that you had forgotten? What a relief—not a single scratch. How lucky you are!"

"Oh—please!"

His hands tightened over her shoulders, pushing her down onto the pillows.

"Perhaps I have neglected you." Bending his head he pressed his lips against her throat, her half-exposed breasts; each kiss was as painful as a blow. And then, his fingers digging into the soft skin of her face, he kissed her mouth, forcing it open, his teeth bruising her lips. And at last, lifting his head, he said,

"Is *that* what you have been missing my little Virginie? A man to make love to you? You do not answer me—surely there must be no secrets between a husband and wife? Or must I have a doctor examine you to find out exactly what happened to you this afternoon, eh? You can speak frankly to me, my little one—am I not the most understanding of husbands?"

He leaned over her, pinning her down with the weight of his body, smiling into her pale face.

"Are you sure you feel well? I stopped at Sir Eric's house on my way here, and I heard—how strong you can be when you're defending your honor. *My* honor as well. The poor man was most upset. But I heard, also, that the gentleman who rescued you was none other than the rich and powerful Mr. Sam Murdock. What a stroke of good fortune, eh? So you are now here, right in the lion's den—is that the correct English phrase? He's taken with you, they tell me; he's paid you very obvious attention. But surely—surely it was not Mr. Murdock's attentions that caused your so-unfortunate accident this afternoon? Mr. Murdock was entertaining his *other* guests, as I understand it. What made you decide to go out riding in the hot sun?"

"I *told* you! I wanted to go riding—I thought I would find the others. But I got lost, and. . . . My horse became startled."

He stroked her hair, making her shudder.

"My poor darling. How upset you have become! Perhaps you hurt your head. I really think I should have a doctor take a look at you. You seem unusually on edge."

Backed into a corner, Ginny's eyes became brilliant with unshed tears of fear and frustration, and her body became rigid.

"What are you trying to do to me? You wake me out of a sleep to—to accuse me of. . . . I don't know what you are accusing me of! I tell you, I went riding, and I had a fall. But if you insist on calling a doctor in, go ahead. I can't stop you."

When he saw that he had made her defiant, Ivan Sahrkanov's voice softened to the familiar purr she had learned to dread.

"How thoughtless I've been! But surely you understand my concern? Very well, Virginie, I shall let the matter drop for the moment—I understand Mr. Murdock is anxiously awaiting your appearance at dinner tonight, and there will be dancing afterwards. So—if you're sure you really feel well enough, perhaps we can talk more about this later. And I'll find out if there's a doctor nearby."

Although she managed to keep her eyes fixed stonily on his, Ginny knew that Ivan had not backed down. He was merely giving her a little time in which to worry, and let her apprehension grow. He would enjoy watching her squirm all evening, wondering what he would do or say next, while he asked his clever, subtle questions. And how much did he know already? How much did he guess?

"What are you going to wear this evening? Will you let me choose?" Ivan had gone over to the cedar-scented closet where row upon row of dresses, carefully unpacked

and pressed by Delia, were hanging closely pushed together.

"Ah, yes—*this* one, I think. White and gold. Gold
which is the symbol of California—and white, for purity. I
have not seen you wear this gown before. You will look
well in it, I think."

Walking down the stairs on her husband's arm, Ginny
felt like a frozen statue of a woman; she tried to keep her
mind as blank as her face. Blank—this afternoon had
never happened. The hard-faced, black-bearded stranger
who had ravished her body without a word, satisfying his
own lusts, and had later stood smiling contemptuously at
her with his arm around Concepción's waist, had not been
Steve. . . .

The evening passed like a bad dream. Sam Murdock
was smilingly polite, but distant. Senator Brandon, whom
she could not help but think of as her father, seemed preoccupied. And so, in fact, was Sonya, although she seemed
concerned for Ginny and asked if she felt well.

"I heard you went riding and took a fall. Oh, Ginny,
why didn't you tell us what had happened? Ivan was most
upset."

But Sonya was easier to convince than Ivan had been,
because Sonya was worried about something this evening,
and it showed in the nervous twisting of her fingers and the
way she kept watching her husband.

Ginny felt as if she were in a sick, miserable daze.
Tonight, even the headache powder she'd swallowed surreptitiously didn't help to shut out reality. And there had
been Ivan's smiling presence in her room, his frosty-cold
eyes watching her speculatively as she dressed, so that Delia became nervous, too; her fingers clumsy. The heavy,
twisted gold chain that he had insisted she must wear
tonight, to go with her dress, felt like a rope around her
throat, choking her. Involuntarily, Ginny's fingers kept
going up to touch it, tugging at it.

"I should have taken two powders tonight . . . oh, God,
when will this evening end?" she thought.

First the dinner—one course following far too soon after the other. And she had played with her food, hardly
able to force a few mouthfuls down. She felt sick. And
Ivan's solicitous whisper:

"My darling, I do believe you are *not* 'all right' as you insisted earlier. You're certainly not your usual vivacious self. I'm going to have to insist on a doctor to make sure that fall hasn't hurt you."

Why had Ivan suddenly begun to frighten her? There was nothing he could do to her, after all—not here. She must keep remembering that. And forget Concepción's snarling, contemptuous tone when she had said, ". . . adulteress! She'll lie with any man, if given half a chance. . . . Why do you bother with her, Esteban?" Her possessive, clutching fingers on Steve's arm. . . .

This evening Concepción had come down gowned in shimmering silk and brocade—old gold flecked with green. And Concepción had been smiling, tawny cat-eyes heavy-lidded and glittering. Her glance had barely touched Ginny, and then swept past her, but those same eyes had rested for some time on Prince Sahrkanov, jewelled decorations glittering on his chest.

Ginny's wide green eyes had a haunted expression in them as they searched the room. Without seeming to, without wanting to, she had looked for Steve all evening, but he was not among those somberly-clad men whom everyone knew were Sam Murdock's bodyguards. And he wasn't boldly mingling with the guests either. Had he left already for San Francisco?

It was hot, under the brilliant glare of the crystal chandeliers. Music played softly from the gallery, and Ivan made sure that Ginny's wine glass was kept filled. Dark thoughts, like the brush of bat wings on the fringes of her mind. Ivan, Prince Sahrkanov. Her husband. Why had she married him? Why had he married her? Why Tsar's daughter—oh, no, *that* part of it was still unbelievable. Like everything that had happened to her, ever since Ivan had decided to visit Mexico. To find her.

"Come, my love. We are going to dance."

Like a puppet, she rose, moving out onto the patio with Ivan's hand guiding her. Like a porcelain doll, with a painted smile on its mouth, she danced, hardly feeling the coolness of the night-scented breeze on her face.

"You are so stiff tonight, my Princess. That unfortunate fall, eh? And yet I understand that only last night you danced like a little gypsy. How can I forget the first time I saw you dance?" Light, teasing words, but with a hidden meaning lurking beneath. How had Ivan learned so much during the short time that he had been here? How long would he continue to play with her?

The bad dream continued, and Ginny's half-empty stomach began to knot with a feeling of sickness and apprehension. She had a premonition that something was going to happen. In spite of the gaiety and the laughter and the inconsequential chatter that surged all around her, she seemed to sense an intangible tension. Or was it only within herself?

She passed from one pair of arms to another. There was Ivan, dancing with Concepción of all people, his head bent to hers as they laughed over some joke. Ivan was clever—what might he persuade Concepción to tell him?

Ginny could not remember who her own partners had been, or what she had said to them. Her head had begun to ache unbearably, and even Ivan was startled by the pallor of her face, the enormous brightness of her eyes.

"Go upstairs and take some of your medicine, then. You have been like a little ghost all evening!" Standing with her in the shadows, his fingers tightened cruelly about her bare arm, forcing an involuntary whimper of pain through her pale lips. "You are not as clever as I once thought, are you? You had Sam Murdock eating out of your hand, and then you had to go and spoil it, for a rendezvous in the woods with one of his servants! Oh, yes!" His teeth glimmered whitely as his lips stretched in the travesty of a grin. "Did you think I would not find out? I have my ways—and my spies. You'd do well to remember that, Virginie, the next time you need a man to cool your hot blood! A servant! If we were in Russia—well, I have my own methods of dealing with such things. You know that already, don't you?"

"Oh!" She gasped and his fingers tightened, pulling her against him, so that it would seem, to anyone who noticed them, that he merely meant to kiss her goodnight.

"Let us settle this one question between us, my dear. Now, and finally. I have no objection to your taking lovers, if you are very discreet, but they will be men of *my* choosing. Do you understand that? *Your* taste is deplorable. Mexican soldiers, common thieves and murderers. . . ."

No, in the future I will make the choice for you. Men of some status. Men who are rich enough and influential enough to help us both. Do you take my meaning? Because if you do not. . . ."

Ginny tried to focus her mind on what he was saying, but the effort was almost too much for her. He clamped one arm around her waist, holding her wrist between their bodies, and bent his head until his lips brushed her exposed ears.

"If you do not heed what I say, my darling Princess, I will have to use other means to make you understand. You realize that I have every right to chastise you, as an unfaithful wife? Or—there are these headaches you've been having. Perhaps they are a sign of incipient brain fever? A short stay in a private sanitarium might benefit you, perhaps, with no powders, no strong tonics to hide your symptoms. I would hate to sign the papers, of course, and it *would,* alas, delay our visit to Russia, but—"

"Please—please!"

"Ah." He lifted his head and stood looking down at her white, averted face, with a look of satisfaction in his eyes. So he had broken her at last. Yes, when it came to women, it was something he could sense, could almost smell out. At last, he had made her afraid—and she would have time to become even more afraid. It was strange, how knowing that made him suddenly desire her. But that could wait. There'd be time—and that old fool Chernikoff had to be pacified first with excuses, and sent on his way. He'd take Ginny to Russia himself—later. When he was sure of her final capitulation.

"All right, my love. Now that we understand each other, why don't you go upstairs to bed? I might be late—I've been invited to join in a game of cards with our charming host and some of his friends. Who knows, perhaps I can persuade him that your little excursion into the woods *was* perfectly innocent after all—or that you were raped!" His smile was cruel. "It won't be the first time, will it? I've heard that there are some women who actually enjoy rape."

Chapter Twenty-one

ᕫ᙭ᕬ

Images, called up by Ivan's sneering words, chased themselves across Ginny's numbed brain as she groped her way up the stairway to her room, clinging to the rail for support. Her head throbbed until she thought it would burst; her feet felt so heavy she could hardly lift them. What was the matter with her? She had retained enough sense to wonder at herself and the peculiar weakness that seemed to have seized her with a stranglehold.

"Please—please!" Had it really been she who had pleaded so abjectly? Should she not have known, from past experience, that pleading with a man who felt himself in command of the situation and of her did no good at all? She felt stunned—almost incapable of coherent thought. What had happened? How had it happened? Somehow, Ivan seemed to have gained the upper hand, and a few moments ago he had terriorized her into groveling like a whipped bitch.

"A servant! Well, I have my own methods of dealing with such things. . . ."

Oh, no—she must push her thoughts away, into the back of her mind. But there were too many pictures, superimposed upon each other. Herself, hair loose, dancing. The knife sinking to its hilt in Tom Beal's throat. Michel—calling her back to sanity and to life with his kindness, his tenderness; Miguel; and, God, above all, Steve, his blue eyes blazing down into hers: lazily mocking, or crinkled at the corners, or hard and furious, like sapphires between narrowed lids, or open, with dancing lights of devilry in them.

"Who are you dancing for, green-eyes?" he had asked. And then, later, "Damn you, Ginny! I've never known a woman who could satisfy me and torment me like you

have ... for God's sake, woman, isn't that enough for
you?" He had loved her—yes, her woman's instinct had
told her that. And for a short time they had been close;
she had been sure of him. Now she was sure of nothing.

"Oh, ma'am!" Delia's eyes looked swollen and red-
rimmed, as if she had been crying. "Ma'am, I'm sorry,
truly I am! But he—Prince Sahrkanov—it was just like he
already *knew* something had happened. He asked me all
kinds of questions—asked to see the dress you'd been
wearing—and then he said.... He said he'd have me
beaten and sent away if I didn't tell the truth; he said he
knew you hadn't been out riding alone. I didn't know what
to do, and I was so scared. ..."

So now even Delia knew that the Princess Sahrkanov
was an unfaithful wife, the kind of woman who was even
capable of dalliance in the woods with—what had Ivan
said? "A servant. ..."

"It doesn't matter," Ginny said tonelessly. All she
craved at the moment was forgetfulness. Tomorrow there
would be time enough to think of everything, and decide
.... But what was there to decide? She was Ivan's wife.

The bottle that had been half-full of her precious, cherry-
colored tonic now contained only an inch or so of liquid.

"Delia!"

"Ma'am, I couldn't help it!" Delia had begun to sniffle
again. "He took it. And your headache powders. Said they
were bad for you, that in the future he'd give them to you
when you needed them. Oh, ma'am! What are we going to
do?"

"You can give me some of the tonic now. And—and I'll
think about the rest later. Do you understand, Delia? It's
not your fault, and you're not to blame yourself."

It took an effort on Ginny's part to keep her voice from
shaking. There was no mistaking Ivan's intentions now. He
meant to bring her to heel, to make her crawl to him for
the medicines she had come to depend on. But she must
not, would not think of that tonight.

Ginny was ashamed of the way her fingers trembled as
she almost snatched from Delia the tiny glass containing
her tonic and drained it quickly.

Delia, still sniffling, helped her to undress, slipping a

thin silk nightgown over her head. Lying back in her bed, deliberately willing her mind to blankness, Ginny gradually felt the delightful feeling of drowsiness she waited for creep over her, relaxing her tense muscles. She heard the soft closing of the door as Delia went away, and kept her eyes closed, waiting for sleep to take her, bringing pretty dreams that were full of whirling colors and always pleasant. Oh, but nothing mattered except the comforting feeling of warmth that seemed to spread through her veins. How good it was to let go of unpleasant reality—to feel herself drift away, leaving everything behind. . . .

And so, when Ginny felt herself shaken roughly by the shoulder, she didn't *want* to come back. It wasn't fair—she was entitled to her few moments of escape. She refused to wake up.

"No—no!" Her lips merely mouthed the words as she turned her face against the pillow, trying to avoid whoever it was that sought to call her away from her pleasant dreamlike state.

"Ginny! Damn it, what's the matter with you? What have you taken to make you sleep so soundly?"

"Leave me be!" she muttered sullenly, her words slurred, eyes still tightly shut. "Perhaps I'll never be able to sleep so soundly again. Go away!"

She made an attempt to wriggle her body more deeply under the covers. Why had her dreams suddenly become strange and unsettling instead of bringing her peace, as they usually did? She was still dreaming, of course. How often she had dreamed of flying, floating far above the earth where she could see everyone and everything at a great, safe distance. And how wonderful it felt to ride cushioned among great puffy billows of clouds.

But now she felt she was being swept along in the center of a thunderstorm. Why was Steve always so angry with her? *Steve!* Ginny tried, belatedly, to struggle; to open weighted eyelids. But his arms only tightened around her until she felt they had become like iron hands, cutting off her breath.

"Why did you come back? He's going to have you beaten or killed, you know—just like the others."

At first she thought he had become so angry that he had released her. With a gasp of terror, Ginny forced her eyes open, and the first thing she saw, wavering through a kind of haze, heightening her feeling of unreality, was herself. Her own body, lying limp and sprawled against white sheets. Except for her eyes, which shone like dull green stones under water, she might have been a corpse. Perhaps she *was* dead, and that was why she could watch herself so detachedly!

And then Steve's face, dark with anger, loomed over hers, cutting off everything else.

"What others? Are you awake yet, or still in a drunken stupor?" His eyes narrowed dangerously, and his voice had become the hard, sarcastic drawl she remembered and hated so well. "I guess it might have been damned convenient for a lot of people if your husband's hired killer had done his job right—but as it happens, sweetheart, I've had a lot of experience at dodging bullets. And I don't like being shot at!"

He was leaning over her, hands on her shoulders, and when he shook her for emphasis an answering resistance made her momentarily strong enough to flare back at him.

"I don't care! What are you accusing me of now? Where am I? Why have you carried me here?" She tried to sit up, and his hands pushed her down—it was like some scene out of the past when he had spoken to her and used her just so, and almost without thinking Ginny swung her hand up and across his face, relishing his involuntary grunt of pain.

"Why must you continue to torment me so? Why won't you leave me alone? You're so selfish, so unfair—and you've brought me nothing but misery and unhappiness, ever since ... ever since. . . ."

She broke off, panting, suddenly appalled at her actions—at the wild, angry words that had spilled out of her without conscious thought or volition.

For one moment she had thought Steve was going to strike her back, for the look on his face was pure fury. And then the next instant it was as if all emotion had been wiped from it, and his hands dropped from her shoulders.

Without a word, he walked away from her, and Ginny had time to realize where she was. She was in a room that had already become unpleasantly familiar to her—Sam Murdock's room, with the ornamented mirror set in the ceiling above the bed, reflecting back her own half-clad body and wide, staring green eyes. Why had Steve brought her *here*? What had made him so angry with her?

He was back, quite suddenly, holding a glass of something to her lips, forcing her to drink. Cold liquid—and yet it burned like frosty fire as it trickled down her throat.

His voice was dispassionate—how quickly he could change his moods!

"Do you feel slightly less hysterical now? I'm sorry I dragged you out of such a deep sleep and your nice warm bed, Ginny, but like it or not, we've got some talking to do." An ominous hardness crept into his tone again, making her shudder weakly. I want the answers to some questions, baby, and you can begin by telling me just how much your husband knows. Did you feel impelled to confess you'd been an unfaithful wife? Did you encourage him to send that clumsy assassin after me?" Without giving her a chance to answer, he put his arm under her shoulders, half-dragging her upright, and set the glass against her lips again. "Better drink some more of this before you begin. It might help clear your head. And you can spare me your usual recriminations, too." His eyes burned worse than the liquor he forced down her throat until she gasped and gagged, weakly trying to push him away.

Was it possible that this same man had once told her he loved her and would never let her escape him? Or that his voice, so cold and harsh now, had once been tender as he whispered soft Spanish love words to her?

She could read no mercy in his eyes as he let her drop back against the pillows again, and sat looking down at her as if she were some stranger he didn't much like.

"Well, Ginny?"

She tried to resist him, sheer desperation forcing anger into her voice.

"You have no right to—to treat me in his high-handed fashion! You have no rights over me at all! And I think you were insane to carry me here. They are all downstairs—my father—Ivan—"

"Ah, yes." His lips twisted in a too-familiar, hateful sneer. "Your injured husband, who is so quick to defend his honor—and whatever you have left of yours! I gather from your reference to 'the others,' that you must make a habit of taking lovers. Is it a game you're both fond of playing? Do you always make a full confession afterwards? Or only when you want to get rid of one who has begun to make things awkward for you?"

"Oh, stop it! You've always managed to be more hateful than anyone else I've known," Ginny whispered painfully, turning her head away from him. "Steve—let it be! Let *me* be! I didn't tell Ivan anything at all. Do you think I was proud of what happened this afternoon? But he—he always seems to know everything! He told me this evening that he was having me watched. He said—"

"How did you know I'd been shot at, Ginny? That was almost the first thing you said to me."

"Because he *said* he would—he said he had his own methods of taking care of such things! Do you think that he'd have stopped at sending one man if I'd told him *you* were the *servant* he accused me of—of lying with? My father's offered rewards for your capture—*you* know that! Ivan would have—I think he would have sent a whole army after you if he as much as guessed."

"All right. Suppose I accept that for the moment. What about the others? And Carl Hoskins? Someone tried to pin that particular killing on me—they said that after the fight we had I came back to finish the job. And it was a damn good thing I had an alibi to prove I was over three hundred miles away at the time!" His tone became sarcastic again. "I suppose you don't know about that either. My God— it's a good thing I'm not your husband any longer, or I'd be kept far too busy killing off your legion of lovers!"

Ginny's eyes, turned back to him at last, held the look of a trapped, desperate forest creature.

"What are you saying? What are you talking about now? *I* killed Carl! You seem to know so much, why do you pretend you don't know that, too? Is it only because you had to try and force a confession from me? I killed him. I smashed a bottle of wine over his head, after he— he—oh, God, why did you have to bring that up? Haven't you done enough to me already?"

Her voice had risen, and he cut across it remorselessly.

"Did you stab him in the neck before or after you hit him with the bottle? It seems to have become quite a habit with you, hasn't it—stabbing the men who have ravished you, but only after they've had you over and over again! You tried that on me once, remember? Is that how you get rid of the lovers you've tired of?"

This time she tried to claw at his face, humiliation and rage driving her to it. And as he had only been waiting for the excuse, he caught her wrists, holding them widely apart over her head while he dropped his body over hers to keep her still, lying between her flailing thighs as if he meant to violate her.

"Damn you, answer me!"

Her head moved wildly, back and forth against the pillow, while tears of frustration and pain filled her eyes.

"I hate you—I hate you! I'm sorry that Ivan didn't have you killed after all!"

"I remember how you always said that—only minutes before you spread your legs and yielded everything. I suppose it's become a habit with you by now! Is that what you told your Ivan, too, before you stopped resisting and gave in? You're nothing but a bitch at heart, Ginny, and I was a fool to try and close my eyes to that fact. But thank God, it's your husband who has to worry about it now!"

She might have known better than to exhaust her strength struggling against him. They knew each other too well, she and Steve, and hadn't he always vanquished her in *this* kind of battle before? He could hurt her, wound her, abuse her—even hate her as much as she hated him at this moment. And yet, as he had so brutally reminded her, he could make her want him even when she despised him most—her only tiny victory lying in the fact that *he* could not disguise his desire for her either.

She opened her mouth to scream and he stopped it with his. Hadn't she expected it? Wasn't that what she secretly, wantonly craved, in spite of everything?

When Steve kissed her, she was lost. It was like being caught in a whirlpool, and sucked down into its center—a maelstrom of desire that left her almost mindless, helpless to resist the inevitable.

His fingers released their hold on her wrists, sliding down her arms to find her breasts. And her hands, instead of striking him, pushing him away, went around his body, pulling him even closer.

For a few short moments their minds continued to battle silently, but their senses had already declared a truce.

No matter how he vilified and accused her, he wanted her.

In spite of the hate and contempt she declared for him, she wanted him.

The mirror above the bed reflected everything, adding a different, almost wickedly exciting dimension to their lovemaking. Imagine being able to watch and feel at the same time! Ginny's wide-open green eyes could not tear themselves away from the reflection of their joined, entwined bodies; the smooth, driving movement of Steve's muscles that before she had only been able to *feel* under her clutching hands.

As if he had sensed the emergence of something primal and darkly primitive inside her that responded to the sensuality of making love on a silk-sheeted bed, under a mirror that gave back every movement and every caress, Steve deliberately held back, forcing her into boldness, into returning every caress he gave her until she was capable of holding back nothing; her passion was as uninhibited and wildly untrammeled as his.

They lay side by side at last, the shining thickness of Ginny's hair caught beneath his shoulder.

"Steve—what are you thinking?" She whispered the words almost compulsively, to ward off the creeping invasion of reality, and the unpleasant thought that she was lying on Sam Murdock's crumpled bed, in Murdock's room, while downstairs Murdock himself was engaged in a poker game with her father and her husband and God knows how many other men. Or were they? Suppose the game was over already? What would Steve do if Ivan found them together—like this?

"I was trying not to think, to tell you the truth." His voice sounded bleak, and he didn't turn his head to look at her. Was he still watching her in the mirror? And then, taking her by surprise, he pulled her body over his, with an impatient, almost angry motion. "Damn you, Ginny! I guess I'll never understand you!" He was frowning again, his voice ill-humored. "And I'm sure as hell not going to try. You were right—I should have stayed away from you."

Ginny stiffened, half-closing her eyes against the probing, dagger-like look in his, wondering how he meant to hurt her *this* time. Even after he had made love to her—as if he meant to wipe out time and the past with his caresses and reaffirm his diabolical possession of her senses—he could still turn on her the next minute. Why hadn't she remembered all the times he had done just so before?

He went on, unpleasantly. "For God's sake! There's no need to put on such a martyred look! I'm not going to give you away to your husband, sweetheart, in case that's what's worrying you. But I'm still looking for some answers."

When she stirred, trying to escape him, his arms tightened to hold her still. But this time there was neither passion nor a resurgence of desire in his forcible embrace.

"Ginny!" he said warningly, and she bit her lip, feeling all the stubbornness oozing out of her, leaving dull wretchedness in its place.

What was the use? He would only keep her here until she told him everything he wanted to know, uncaring of the consequences to her. And she did not want to think of what could happen if Ivan found out. Damn Steve—and damn her own weakness that gave him such power over her!

Before he could prod her with more sarcastic, ugly taunts, Ginny let everything come spilling out. She told him about Carl Hoskins—why had Steve kept trying to trip her up by insisting Carl had died of a stab wound? She knew better—and this time he didn't interrupt her, but listened grimly. Her neck ached from trying to keep her head averted, and finally, with an angry exclamation, he wrapped his fingers in her hair, pushed her head down against his shoulder.

"Go on." Why, why did he want to know everything? And at last she told him the wild story that Count Chernikoff had related to her that fateful night in Cuernevaca, when everything had been set in motion—and about Ivan. Telling him about Ivan was harder than she thought, and Ginny stumbled over her words. Ivan, whom she had married in a kind of stupor—how could Steve ever understand *that,* when she didn't understand what had driven her into it herself?

Pride prevented her from explaining the part that Steve himself had played in determining her actions. She wouldn't let him know of her agony of grief at his callous rejection of her. Let him think, if he chose to, that she was just as fickle as he was. And that what had just taken place between them was an explosion of passion—no more. Let him think—let him think the worst of her, as he always had in any case!

When her unwilling recital had stumbled into silence, Ginny took some meager comfort from the fact that his arms still continued to hold her, although his touch now seemed as impersonal as his voice. "How much of this does your—does the Senator know?" Steve asked.

Ginny raised her head, meeting his shadowed, unreadable eyes.

"Nothing! What did you expect me to do? Tell him he was tricked into marrying my mother—that I'm not his daughter after all, but a bastard? And I don't even know if any of it is true, or—or if it is all some trick I cannot understand yet. And even if it was—it's too late now, isn't it? As you've reminded me, I'm Ivan Sahrkanov's wife now—and a whore and an adulteress into the bargain. Isn't that what you wanted to prove? Well it's true, then! You've succeeded in convincing me that I might as well accept what I am. So there's no more need for you to—to concern yourself about me any longer, or to feel any responsibility. . . . Oh, *please,* Steve!" Humiliatingly, her voice broke. "Let me go back to my room now! I—my head's begun to ache again, and if I can only find one of my headache powders—perhaps he didn't take them all away after all. . . ." She sounded feverish, and when she began to struggle wildly against him, he let her go.

Escape—that was all that was in her mind now, as she sprang off the bed and then swayed on her feet because her knees were suddenly weak. Escape from tension, from the unhappiness that had suddenly begun to wrap tightening bands around her head and chest. Above all, escape from Steve, who only wanted to hurt her, to use her like the whore he'd named her.

She would have run outside just as she was if Steve hadn't stopped her. He must have sensed that she had reached the limit of her endurance, for he carried her back to her room without further argument. Faint sounds of music drifted up to Ginny's ears, scratching the surface of her mind as she wondered dully why they were all up so late tonight. Or was it possible that the long, terrible confrontation with Steve had been partly a dream, with minutes passing like hours? Oh, God, she was too tired, too confused, too miserable to think—or even to want to try.

She was naked—her torn silk nightgown was lying discarded at the foot of Sam Murdock's bed. And Steve was naked, too—they were *both* insane, obviously!

He put her down on her bed with surprising gentleness, drawing the covers up over her cold, suddenly shivering body.

Chapter Twenty-two

Morning crept into the room. And with it, memory. Stirring in bed, feeling all her limbs ache, Ginny did not know what to think. Did she want to think just yet? What had awakened her? She had been dreaming that she lay wrapped closely in Steve's arms, that he still loved her, and now Delia was whispering to her that she had not wanted to wake her up, but her husband desired that she join him for breakfast. Oh, thank God that Ivan had been allotted a separate room! It was the fashion, at these sophisticated house parties, but Ginny had wondered, for a while, if Ivan would let his desire to crush her override convention.

"Brought you some nice hot coffee, ma'am." Delia's eyes looked worriedly into hers, still blinking from the heaviness of sleep. Automatically, Ginny took the cup from the girl. No more powders to arm herself with. She had found one last night, tucked away at the bottom of an em-

broidered reticule, but Steve had taken it away with him.
He had tasted it, grimacing.

"Ginny. . . ." Something, perhaps it had been the meeting of their eyes, hers wild and pleading, had stopped
whatever he had been about to say. Instead, his voice unusually taut, he had said:

"All right. I'll get you some more. But I've got to know
what's in them first. So I'll have to take this with me."

He'd even tasted her tonic before letting her have a tiny
dose, because she had to hoard carefully what was left in
the bottle.

What had made him change so suddenly? He'd been angry and cruel at first—and then, quite unexpectedly kind.
Perhaps he had begun to feel sorry for her—oh, but that
thought was quite unsupportable!

Ginny sipped her coffee, and her fingers shook, rattling
the cup against its saucer. Delia had gone to pull apart the
drapes, and sunlight, almost blinding her, cascaded into
the room, falling in a golden stream across the soft Au-
busson carpet. Steve was gone again, of course, and she
should be relieved—he'd said, his voice distant and preoccupied, that he had urgent business in San Francisco. But
he wanted her to stay here—why? She was sure, by now,
that she meant nothing to him. Just another woman, to
satisfy his passing desires. And he had only come to her,
last night, because he was angry.

The coffee went down, burning her mouth. Ginny
wanted more, but Delia, her face unusually pale and
scared-looking, was begging her to dress. Why did she feel
as if she was going to her own execution?

Mechanically, as she splashed water over her body, feeling cold and shaken, Ginny wondered why Ivan had sum-
moned her so imperiously. Before, he would have come to
her room—now he sent for her. How the tables had been
turned. And of all the unpredictable ironies—she was actually married to Ivan, and Steve had become her lover!

Yesterday—last night—it seemed like a dream. Already, there was that ominous throbbing in her temples,
and a cold sweat had broken out all over her body. She
felt so strange! Her eyes itched, and her hands shook so
that Delia had to do everything for her.

"Ah, there you are my love! You slept well, I trust?"

Ivan was shaved, his hair carefully brushed. She could detect the faint odor of the cologne he always wore as he kissed her hand, then drew her unresisting body close, brushing her cold lips with his.

Ginny caught a glimpse of her own reflection in the mirror. Her pale green gown seemed to accentuate her pallor, and a pulse throbbed under the green ribbon Delia had fastened around her throat.

"Yes," Ivan said softly, as if he had read her thoughts, "we make such a handsome couple, do you not think so?" He slipped an arm around her waist, turning her so that she faced the mirror fully. Standing beside her, smiling, it was as if he had posed them for a photograph.

"You haven't said a single word yet, Virginie. Are you hungry? Perhaps a good breakfast will do something for those shadows under your eyes. And I really think you need some fresh air and exercise. Look at me. I've been up for most of the night, and I feel prepared for anything—even the rather unpleasant duty I have to face after we've eaten. I should have said *we* . . . but you must eat first. Come along."

"What?" She turned her head dazedly towards him, and he continued to smile, fixing her with his pale eyes.

"My dear—I said you must eat first. I don't want to spoil your appetite. Here, sit down. You'll take some tea? I took the liberty of ordering for us both—and I have been neglecting you, haven't I? Would you mind pouring for us, chérie?"

Her hands had begun to shake so badly that he was forced to take the silver pot from her, shaking his head with mock concern.

"Please, Ivan!" Unable to stop herself, she began to plead with him. "Please—I have such a headache, honestly! I can't eat. Why did you take my powders away? You got them for me, remember? For my—my—"

"Yes, yes! Of course, I remember. For your headaches. And I could understand why you needed them at the beginning. But you should be quite well, quite recovered from that unfortunate experience by now! Yesterday, you felt well enough to embark on a little adventure of your own, did you not? So I really don't think you need to coddle yourself any longer. I'll let you have a powder occasionally, if I feel you really need it, of course, but you must start letting me make the decisions for you, my dearest. I don't like the way you've been looking or acting recently."

Ginny gazed at him almost uncomprehendingly, with a hunted expression in her eyes. Still smiling, Prince Sahrkanov poured tea; he leaned forward to give her a benevolent pat on the cheek.

"Eat, my darling. And drink your tea. You must start getting used to it, you're a Russian now!"

She couldn't eat, of course, although with Ivan urging her she managed to swallow down a slice of dry toast, to take a bite of ice-cold nectarine. She almost gagged over the tea, which was sickly sweet and thick, Russian style.

And all the time he kept talking, his voice a silken purr—alternately stern and cajoling.

"We can't have this! Come, you must eat. You're like a bad, spoiled little child, do you know that? Too used to having your own way. But I'm going to change that, and you'll be much happier for it."

"I—really, I don't feel well. I think I've caught a cold. Can't I go back to my room and lie down? For a little while, at least. Please! I don't want to go downstairs."

Could that really be her voice, begging? Her fingers felt stiff, from the way she knotted them together to stop their shameful trembling. Even her lips shook.

"I'm afraid those powders could not have been very good for you, after all. You'll feel better with some fresh air in your face. Come—no pulling back, or I'm going to be angry with you, and I've tried to be patient. That's better." He clasped her wrists with both hands, pulling her to her feet. "We don't want to keep Mr. Murdock waiting. I must tell you, my love, that I find him a very sensible and understanding man. He won't hold your little escapade yesterday afternoon against you, if that's what you're afraid of. Not since I had the opportunity to confide in him privately. After all, rape's a very serious crime—and that *is* what happened to you, isn't it?"

Later, Ginny tried to push most of what followed out of her mind. In fact, she hardly remembered how, or where, Ivan led her, his hold on her arm painful enough to keep her from falling. She remembered clinging to the thought that he had promised to let her have a powder to swallow afterwards—if she remembered what was expected of her; if she behaved.

Ginny tried to keep thinking of that, tried to keep her mind detached, while Ivan's arm, clamped around her waist, kept her upright.

They were in some kind of cellar, or icehouse, steps going down beneath ground level. But big wooden double doors, creaking on their hinges, had been pushed open to let in the sunshine. Yellow light fell across a tarpaulin-covered shape. Sam Murdock, alone except for one of his bodyguards, a stern-looking man with a red mustache, looked everywhere but at her.

Murdock's voice was angry.

"There was really no need for the Princess to have to come down here. The whole business is unpleasant and up-setting enough for me—and for you, of course. If you hadn't acted as you did, I'd have arranged for the man to be flogged, or hanged."

"But it's better this way. And although Virginie is still in a state of shock, I think it's best for her to see that justice has been done. Perhaps it will make her less fearful of riding alone again."

They were talking over her head—what were they talking about?

"I still think—"

"My wife has lived through a nasty little war in Mexico. She's seen dead men before—haven't you, my angel? And in this case, I don't think she'll be too squeamish—after all, the man attacked her. I think she would have killed him herself, if she'd had a weapon."

Still trying to keep from shivering, Ginny caught Sam Murdock's eyes on her. Grim, appraising. He looked at her steadily for a moment, and in spite of her confused state of mind she had the strangest impression that he was trying to warn her. But of what?

At last, sighing almost imperceptibly, he nodded his head shortly at the silent bodyguard, who bent and pulled aside the tarpaulin.

Ginny screamed. A soft, choking sound.

Congealed blood, and black hair. Dark clothing, soaked through the darker stains. A dead man—his face shot away. Not Steve . . . not Steve!

From a distance that seemed to recede further and further, she heard Sam Murdock's quiet, angry voice.

"It's no sight for a woman! And the man's been dead for some time—we'll have him buried quickly now, with no fuss. He was a drifter—I wouldn't have hired him, except he'd once worked for me before, on the ranch. If I'd known what kind of scoundrel he was. . . ."

No—of course it wasn't Steve! "Dead for sometime," Murdock had said pointedly. And Steve, last night, angry because he'd been shot at. But then, who was this dead man? God, she should care, but she didn't—sheer relief made Ginny sway dizzily.

"You'd better take her outside," she heard Sam Murdock say, and then she heard Ivan's soft voice, and felt his arm tightening around her waist.

"No, no—Virginie's stronger than she looks, aren't you, my love? Open your eyes, we don't want any mistake to be made. Is that the man?"

She forced her eyes open, then quickly averted them, hands going up over her mouth to stop herself from retching.

"He—he's dressed the same—oh, how do you expect me to look closely? I don't want to remember, I don't!"

"Of course you don't, my darling. I know how very shocking and unpleasant it's been for you. But you understand, don't you, why I wanted you to see how he ended up for yourself? You have nothing to be afraid of now— he'll never come back to hurt you." Soft, comforting words. And only *she* could understand the hidden significance of Ivan's little speech.

"Princess, I'm deeply sorry. If I had only known earlier I'd have taken steps myself. And I'm sorry you had to be subjected to this as well. Please try to forget it, if you can. And you have my assurance that no one else knows—no one *will* know."

Upstairs, in her room, Ginny burst into tears. She cried from weakness, from wretchedness, from relief, from reaction. She hadn't been able to cry for a long time, and now she couldn't stop the great wrenching sobs that shook her; the tears streamed unendingly down her face.

She was aware that Ivan paced the floor, watching her,

but she no longer cared. Not even when he started to speak in his usual velvety, sneering tones.

"Such a passion of grief for a rapist! My dear—keep it up, and I might start thinking you gave him some encouragement! Does your taste run to commoners, then? This man, a half-breed rascal, a—what do they call them in Spanish?—yes, a vaquero, smelling of cattle and horses! How could you lower yourself? I'd like to think that you are crying with shame. The Tsar's daughter and a groom—my God, that would have made a juicy little scandal, would it not? If I hadn't nipped it in the bud! You see, my lovely Princess, in spite of your common ways and your common tastes, I do prize you—I keep an eye on what belongs to me. I've always had you watched, and I always will, make no mistake about that. But you aren't going to make any mistakes in the future, are you?" He stood looking down at her as she sat huddled in a velvet-backed chair, and repeated, "Are you?" and Ginny shook her head blindly.

Ivan Sahrkanov gazed thoughtfully at her bent head, her heaving shoulders, and was satisfied. Yes, she was properly submissive at last. She'd do anything he told her to do in the future, and she'd crawl to him for those powders she craved and couldn't do without now. And with that old fool Cherniknoff out of the way, and Sam Murdock backing him—he'd have everything he wanted and had planned for.

He began to think, with a certain amount of enjoyment, of returning to San Francisco. Of a certain street, a certain room and the kind of pleasure his perverse nature craved. But first—first, unfortunately, there were a few other matters to be taken care of. He'd have to tell Creighton to hire another man to take care of any dirty work that needed to be done. Creighton had a good pair of eyes and a long nose for gossip, and he was trustworthy, as long as he was paid well enough. Brandon's own valet—and that was a laugh on the pompous Senator! Ivan himself had recommended the man on his last visit to San Francisco, and who was to know that Creighton had once been one of the notorious "Sydney Ducks" who had been driven out of the city by the Vigilance Committee? The man had actually been a gentleman's valet once, and knew

his job—and he had also kept in touch with the under-
world. He'd recommended the silent, pock-faced killer
who had performed his job so efficiently yesterday, and
was by now, no doubt, drinking away the money he had
earned for it in some Barbary Coast saloon. But hired killers were easy to find, if you had the right connections.
Just as women were easy to manage, if you used the right
methods. Virginie was learning that he was her master.
Soon enough, he'd teach her a few more lessons, and take
a certain amount of pleasure in doing so, too—but not until after she made herself useful by being nice to Sam
Murdock. Murdock wanted her, and he was the kind of
man who was used to paying well for anything he wanted.

Ginny's sobs were trailing away into choking gasps. Her
eyes were swollen from the fury of her weeping, her
cheeks flushed and tear-stained.

Recalling himself to the present with a frown of annoyance, Ivan Sahrkanov strode over to her and tilted her
face up to his roughly.

"That's enough! I've let you have your cry, and now it's
time you recovered yourself. Go and wash your face—and
I'll let you rest a while before you join the rest of us
downstairs. Yes—Mr. Murdock has planned an alfresco
luncheon in his beautiful courtyard, and perhaps he'll ask
you to go riding with him afterwards. If he does, you are
to go. Do you understand? No excuses, no headaches. I'll
let you have a powder if you need it, but I want to see
you looking rested and presentable first. Run along—or
must I come with you to make sure you do as you're
told?"

Back in her room, staring at her swollen, tear-stained
face in the mirror, Ginny wanted to start crying all over
again, but there were no more tears left in her. Was that
wild-eyed, half-demented creature with strands of hair escaping to straggle damply about her face and shoulders really her? What had she allowed herself to become, how
much lower than this could she sink?

"You used to resist—I guess that was one of the things
that intrigued me most about you in the past. . . ."

Steve's words. Putting her firmly in the past. But it was
true—all the fight had gone out of her, all the strength
that had once carried her through untold horrors, and

even worse degradation than this. What had happened to her?

"Oh, it's just too hard to try to think—my head hurts ... he said he'd have me locked away in a sanitarium, and he'd do it—what does anything matter?"

Her brain was enmeshed in a web of self-pity and self-hate, while her body functioned obediently and without conscious thought.

With fumbling fingers, Ginny undressed, and then washed her face, scrubbing at it with a washcloth as if she wanted to take off the skin. And then she lay down and closed her eyes, trying not to notice the frighteningly swift pounding of her heart and the tiny shivers that shook her from head to toe, passing like ripples over her until she thought she was drowning.

Part Three
THE PIRATE

Chapter Twenty-three
ৎNৎ

One by one the golden millionaires, followed by their carriages and their retinues of servants, had left to return to the city or their various country homes. "Goodbye . . . goodbye . . . such a pleasant visit . . . we'll see you in town of course. . . ." Ginny felt as if her face would crack from smiling. Had it really been only four days? She felt like a wooden doll, with wires for nerves—steel wires drawn so taut that they would snap at any moment. She could think of nothing but the powders that Ivan gave her twice a day—her reward for "behaving." There was one in the middle of the morning, to arm her for the afternoon, when she would go riding, usually with Sam Murdock beside her. And a second just before she had to go down for dinner. Between those times she "rested" in her room, feeling the perspiration pouring off her body, writhing against her sheets to stop the itching of her skin and the pain in her temples that seemed to eat into her brain tissues. She had stopped asking herself what she was turning into. All of her mind that was capable of thinking was concentrated only on one thing—the relief, the joyous, relaxing wonderful relief when she felt herself become human again.

Murdock was attentive, kind. But his manner, even when they happened to be alone, remained irreproachable.

Every morning, he sent her fresh flowers; in the evening, there was an exotic, waxy orchid from his greenhouses. And Ivan smiled, his manner growing almost benevolent. Ah, yes—Murdock was a clever man, or he could not have made himself as rich and powerful as he was. But even he was vulnerable—and in his subtle, careful way, he had shown he was attracted to Ginny.

"We'll see," Ivan Sahrkanov thought. He was growing impatient, however. Murdock was being almost too careful. And his so-called father-in-law, the Senator, had become inexplicably reserved of late. Brandon was worried about something. Shares in some of the biggest Comstock mines had been dropping steeply recently, and only the big men seemed unworried. And Brandon had been speculating in real estate in southern California—not too successfully, if rumor were correct. There was also that shipping line, where some of the smaller stockholders had surprisingly banded together and sold out to someone else—no one knew who, yet. Which left Brandon without the controlling interest he had counted on. . . . Yes, and there was also the money they had invested jointly, and those investments weren't paying off too well either. There were always the big men, who had their own secretive methods of doing things, and no scruples at all when it came to making more money. Murdock was one of them—the mystery man, they used to call him; but upon meeting him, he seemed as human as the rest.

Ivan Sahrkanov was drunk with the sense of his own power. So far, all his careful plans had materialized. He had even been lucky at the gaming tables, for a change. Lucky at everything—even his fortuitous marriage, in the nick of time. Tsar Alexander, even if he should learn of certain manipulations in the shares of the Russian-American Company, and monies that were inexplicably missing, would hardly move against his long-lost daughter's husband. This time, his every gamble had paid off. Golden success lay just beyond the horizon, ready to fall into his hands.

Plans had been made, without Ginny being aware of them. The Senator and his son-in-law would leave for San Francisco with the other guests, a day earlier than Ginny and Sonya. *They* would be escorted back to the city by

Mr. Murdock himself, who had some business to transact there before he traveled on to Virginia City.

"Make the most of your time, my love." Ivan had come into Ginny's bedroom very early in the morning, to tell her good-bye. "I'm sure you know exactly how to go about making a man your captive. And be nice to his ward, too—she'll be going with you to San Francisco, you know. Mr. Murdock is building a house there—a Grecian-style mansion, I understand. But until it's finished, the lovely Señorita Sanchez will need a place to stay in town. Your stepmother has kindly consented to act as her chaperone, and, of course, your fluent knowledge of Spanish will prove helpful. You understand?"

Yes, she understood. Only too well. Concepción—to have Concepción, of all people, foisted upon her; an honored guest in her father's house! She had seen them dancing together, smiling at each other. And Concepción's tawny cat-eyes had more than once touched hers, with an expression of contemptuous triumph. Concepción hated her, would never forgive her . . . . Just how far would the girl go to be revenged?

But she didn't dare let Ivan guess her thoughts. Ivan controlled her now, through those magical powders that he could give her or withhold from her at his pleasure. Feeling well again—that was all that counted any longer.

"I'll leave you two powders. If you are sensible, Virginie, you will see that they last until I see you again in San Francisco." His voice became as soft, yet as subtly tempered, as fine-honed steel under velvet. "And you will be sensible, will you not, my darling? I think you've learned. No more secret assignations with grooms. It's a different matter if your host should ask you to ride out alone with him, or to visit his suite. You take my meaning?"

As soon as Ivan left, Ginny thankfully sought the refuge of her room. He had woken her up early in the morning—just when it seemed she had finally fallen off to sleep. Her eyes felt heavy and swollen, filled with moisture, like unshed tears. But she had no more tears left to shed; she was so empty, so empty inside, and only the thought of the blessed release that one of her precious powders would give her when she finally took it helped her to perform the mechanical motions of undressing, stripping to her shift.

With her eyes tightly shut she threw herself across the bed.

There was a soft tapping at the door, and before she could answer, Sonya came in, crossing the room determinedly, to stand looking down at her.

"Ginny! No, don't pretend to be asleep. This time I won't be thwarted. We have to talk."

Without waiting for a reply, Sonya drew up a chair, placing it beside Ginny's bed. Her large china-blue eyes, with only the slightest trace of wrinkles at their corners, looked as young and naive as ever, but Sonya's mouth had a stubborn look to it, her full, soft lips tight.

"Ginny, what on earth is the matter with you? You've been avoiding me—it seems as though you avoid everyone! And with Ivan hovering over you every moment—something's wrong. I've sensed it, and your father has, too. We've been worried. And I *must* know—why have you been allowing Mr. Murdock to pay you such marked attentions?" Sonya leaned forward, looking into Ginny's swollen, half-open eyes; they gazed back at her with a strangely blank look. Had the girl even *heard* what she had said? She had been acting like a marionette, activated by strings. There was something very wrong, and she didn't understand any of it.

"Ginny!" Sonya repeated sharply. "Are you listening to me? What is wrong? We weren't always such strangers to each other, we used to be friends. I only stayed behind here with you to find the opportunity to speak to you alone, and this time you will not avoid me."

"What is there to talk about? I'm only doing what everyone wanted me to do. I married Ivan; I'm being the kind of wife he wants me to be. Why can't you all leave me alone?"

"Leave you alone! That's a part of what I've been trying to say. Why are you so anxious to be left alone? If there is something wrong, perhaps I can help you. It might make you feel better to talk. And you haven't been looking well, either. I think you should see a doctor when we get back to the city."

Ginny half sat up, and then fell back against the pillows.

"A doctor! I suppose, like Ivan, you think I belong in a sanitarium. A nice long rest cure—isn't that how it's phrased? I wish you'd all stop worrying about me—it's too late for that anyway, and now I—I. . . ."

She wished Sonya would go away and leave her in peace. What did they want of her, all of them? Why must Sonya pick this time, this moment, to torment her with questions?

"You're not happy, are you? Ivan seems so devoted to you, and yet—I'm a woman, too, and there are things I can sense. What's the matter? What's wrong? Or is it—forgive me for being blunt, but are you expecting a child? Is that the cause for your strange moods?"

"No! No, I'm not pregnant, and if you think my moods are strange—well, we don't really know each other very well, do we? Not any longer. Please, Sonya. I have a terrible headache, and I'm not in the mood for girlish confidences. There's nothing to confide, in any case. Why don't you speak to Ivan?"

Ginny heard Sonya sigh.

"Ivan is—oh, he's such a charming man on the surface, but he's difficult to talk to. He—I shouldn't even be saying this to you, but even your father is—well, perturbed. Why does he stay away so much? Where does he go? Ginny, surely you ask yourself the same thing—is that what is eating at you?"

"I wish that Ivan would stay away more! Do you think I care what he does? Oh—now I have horrified you, haven't I? But it's the truth. There, does that satisfy you?"

In spite of her outburst, Ginny was vaguely surprised that Sonya, instead of protesting, merely bent her blonde head.

"I—I thought it might be something like that. And there's the way he deliberately seems to throw you at—at other men. Ginny—I'm so terribly sorry! And I think that even your father has begun to regret. . . . Well, I want you to know that if—you can always turn to us! Your father doesn't say much, I know, but he does love you, and he regrets the fact that he never knew you better. Please—don't shut yourself away from us, Ginny."

Sonya had meant to say more—to confide some of *her* worries, but her stepdaughter's white, distraught face stopped her. She felt as if there were a glass wall between them now. They could see each other, and communicate in a fashion, but did Ginny really hear? The girl had grown far too withdrawn—even her admission that she and Ivan weren't getting along had to be positively wrung from her. And now, Sonya could tell that there was no point in trying to prolong a one-sided talk.

Regretfully, patting Ginny's averted face, she left the room, a small frown lingering between her fair brows. William would have to be told, of course, in spite of the fact that he had more than enough worries of his own— some of them stemming from his son-in-law's strange actions. William had become disenchanted with the Prince recently. There were too many rumors flying around—he was a gamester; a speculator—and they said he wasn't above forgetting scruples. If only William had not agreed to help Ivan invest that money! If only the shares hadn't dropped in value . . . if only, if only! And Ginny moved around like a wraith—you had the feeling, even when she smiled and joined in some discussion, that the girl wasn't really *there*. In a way—yes, in a way it was a pity that she'd rushed into marriage with Ivan, even though they had thought it all for the best at the beginning. And there was another problem, too—something that Sonya hardly dared even think of. Problem? It could well turn out to be a disaster!

"There must be a way!" Sonya kept telling herself, as she had done over and over again before. As she had said to her husband consolingly just as many times. Yes, there just had to be a safe, secret solution.

Sonya had no way of knowing, of course, that her problems were well on the way to being compounded. Nor had her husband, the Senator, travelling in rather strained silence with his urbane son-in-law, who alone seemed content and completely satisfied with life.

As for Ginny herself, after a while she gave up trying to rest. She was too keyed up—Sonya's attempts at forcing her confidence had unnerved her. Afraid of her own thoughts, she swallowed a powder, and buoyed by the thought of the feeling of well-being it would soon bring her, she went downstairs.

Sonya was out riding, with Concepción—Ginny wrinkled her nose with distaste. If Sonya only knew that she had once faced Concepción with a knife! The thought was somehow quite amusing to her now. A poker-faced house-boy informed her that Mr. Murdock was busy in his study, but there was a light luncheon ready for her—perhaps she would care to have it outdoors, in the smaller patio? Mr. Murdock would join her there soon.

So now she would find out what Mr. Murdock really wanted. Now Ivan was gone, he wasn't wasting any time. Strangely enough, in her mood of lightness and relief, the thought merely intrigued her. And outside, beside the place that had been laid for her under a large shade tree, there was a big package, her name scrawled across the lit-tle card that accompanied it, and the bold initials "S.M." under it.

She tore away the expensive wrappings and gold ribbons. The candy-striped cardboard box opened to reveal a flat velvet jewelry case, and in it a wide bracelet—no, there were two. One for each wrist. Diamonds and emeralds, sparkling against an antique gold setting. Ginny sucked in her breath, eyes widening. Oh, God! What did he mean by boldly presenting her with a small fortune in jewels? How was she going to explain it?

She was female enough, even as she thought this, to hold the bracelets up against the light, fascinated by the bright sparks that seemed to make each separate stone come alive. She couldn't possibly accept such a gift, of course. She would have to tell him so—but she longed to try them on, just once. "Better not," she thought, with a sigh, and then she noticed something else shining against the velvet. A small gold key, suspended on a thin chain of the same metal.

"The key will unlock the side door to a certain house, which is being built on the hill they are calling Nob Hill, in San Francisco. You will find, if you are ever so in-clined, that it will also unlock the outside door to my suite here—the one you see up there. As for the jewels, they are yours. If you don't like them you may give them away, or sell them." Sam Murdock had come silently out into the sunshine, and stood regarding her impassively. What a strange man he was! What could she say to him?

"Please don't look so startled, Princess!" His voice be-came rather dry as he walked towards her. "There are no—er—conditions attached to these gifts, and as I'm sure

you know, I can well afford to indulge my whims occasionally. Call this a gesture of apology, if you will." He sat
down opposite her, and Ginny felt literally incapable of
speech; she watched his square, strong face—it gave nothing away. "As for the key," Murdock was continuing, "I
hope you will do me the favor of helping to choose some
of the furniture and other interior decorations for my
town house. My ward, alas, has no idea of good taste
where that kind of thing is concerned, and the house needs
a woman's touch."

"But," she finally managed to stammer, "but why *me*? I
mean—oh, I know you have been kind, and very helpful
and understanding, but. . . ." She hesitated, and then let
the words come out in a rush before she lost her courage,
"But I hardly think you want to seduce me, which is what
I would have thought if any other man had presented me
with such a gift! And I think you know far too much
about me to want to. Is it only because my—because Ivan
has been throwing me at your head?" She added, bitterly
and recklessly, "Surely you've guessed why? You must be
used to that kind of thing—I'm surprised you were not
disgusted with me instead. I am supposed to be extra *nice*
to you, you know. And you've noticed how I've been following orders. You've been decent enough to pretend not
to notice, and you've been—oh, for heavens sake! Will
you just tell me *why*?"

He nodded at her, and Ginny thought, for just an instant, that she had seen a look of approval cross his face,
which otherwise remained quite bland.

"Well said! And since you've been honest with me, I
only wish that I could be just as frank with you. But I'm
afraid, my dear, that I have to ask you to be patient with
an old man's whims. Let's just say that I chose to make
you this gift because I like you—and I do. It's also true
that I would be proud if you would consider me your
friend—if you would promise to turn to me first, if ever
you need any help or advice. But for the rest of it—I
make it a habit never to break a confidence. I'm sure I
can leave you to draw your own conclusions."

Ginny toyed with a glass of cold white wine.

"Steve," she said suddenly. "It's something to do with
Steve, isn't it? You arranged for us to meet that night—

and then, the other day...." She swallowed, and then said, "That man—Steve killed him, didn't he? And you covered up for him. At least he trusted me enough to be sure that I wouldn't give him away! I think you two know each other better than either of you will admit, but what I cannot understand is why—for heavens sake, *why* did Steve come here? Was it really a coincidence? Why?"

"I think you had better ask him that." Sam Murdock's voice was noncommittal, and he gave a short sigh, as if she had made the moment awkward for them both. He hesitated, and then went on. "Perhaps you'll remember that Steve has a way of keeping things to himself. But I can tell you this much—I was a friend of his father's, long ago. And I've been a friend of Don Francisco Alvarado ever since we met as enemies in the war of forty-seven— long before your time of course." He added rather oblique- ly, "Steve's worked for me before."

"You're not going to tell me anything more, are you? No one will. And Steve—oh, you don't understand! He— he despises me. He—"

"I think," Sam Murdock said softly and firmly, "that you underestimate yourself, my dear. If you want some advice from an old hand at all kinds of games, I'd just stand pat and wait this one out." He gave her a long, con- sidering look. "But that depends, of course, on what you really want."

Chapter Twenty-four

What *did* she want? For the past few months, existing in a kind of trance, Ginny had not even thought to ask herself such a question. Once, she could not remember where or when, someone had shown her a fly embedded in a highly polished chunk of amber, and that described best the way she felt: Like a living fossil, trapped in the center

of some sticky substance that enabled her to look out at
the rest of the world without really being a part of it—
without, in fact, feeling very much. Even when Steve
turned up so suddenly, she had somehow managed not to
open up her mind or her heart too widely. More than ever
she was convinced that she must, she *must* put him out of
her life forever if she didn't want to start suffering again.
But why, after all the cutting things he had said to her,
was Steve suddenly being kind?

He had sent her a packet containing eleven headache
powders; they were the only thing that kept her going
now. Sam Murdock himself had handed her the brown
manila envelope, without comment. "So he remembered,
after all," Ginny thought—and she wondered, soon afterwards, if he would make any effort to see her again. She
wanted him to—and she didn't. She felt torn in two directions, and didn't quite understand her strange mixture of
emotions.

"My old friend Chernikoff's invited us to dinner," Ivan
announced a few days after she had returned to San Francisco. Ginny pretended not to notice that he was eyeing
her narrowly as he continued. "I think we ought to take
your friend, the charming and outspoken Señorita Sanchez
along, don't you, my love? It would be a nice gesture, and
I think she'd liven the evening up a little. You're turning
into such a quiet little mouse recently! And, please—don't
embarrass us both by begging him for more medicine for
your . . . nerves. *I'll* see to that. I want him to take a good
impression of our state of married bliss back to Russia
with him when he returns."

She had learned to give Ivan quiet, submissive answers,
hoarding the secret of her own hidden supply of powders.
They weren't as strong as those that Ivan still doled out to
her twice a day, but they helped to keep her calm, at least.

"He's returning to Russia? Already?"

"My goodness! I do believe you've taken quite a liking
to the Count after all—are you going to miss him, Virginie? Do you wish that we were going, too?" He walked
over to where she stood by the window and put his hands
on her shoulders, in a gesture that would have been affec-

tionate in any other man. But when Ivan touched her, it was all she could do not to shrink away.

"I thought you were anxious to take me to Russia to meet my—the Tsar," Ginny said in a deliberately colorless voice. "And the last time I talked to Count Chernikoff, he mentioned nothing about leaving so soon."

"Well—perhaps he's changed his mind! After all, there's no need for him to hang around here now that the Senate has finally ratified the Purchase." His fingers tightened on her shoulders. She could guess how annoyed Ivan really was that in spite of all his efforts, and Senator Brandon's as well, it had all gone through.

"No he's got no more business here; he's done his part," Ivan said slowly. "And I've told him that we'll be following soon. You'll look forward to that, won't you my love? Perhaps we can go by way of Alaska—I'd like to show you some of the country around Sitka. I used to own quite a large estate there—perhaps I still do; I must ask your father to look into the legal technicalities for me." He smiled. "Those Eskimos, once they have been made tame, will make good serfs."

And turning her head to look at him directly, Ginny saw something secretive and almost gloating in his smile that made her tremble inside—she didn't quite know why.

Seizing on something to say quickly before he could see her reaction, Ginny said sullenly:

"But to go back to this evening—what makes you think Concepción would want to come? She'd probably be bored, and perhaps she has an engagement already."

He laughed, sounding quite pleased.

"You sound as if you are jealous of her! Or is it of that fiercely mustached bodyguard Murdock has shadowing her everywhere? As a matter of fact, I already asked her, and she said she'd love to accompany us. You don't mind, dearest? Of course *you* must make the invitation formal— I'll expect you to do that when we go down to luncheon."

"Oh, but how kind of you to ask me. How kind you *all* are to me!" Concepción's manner, as usual, was sugary-sweet when she spoke to Ginny in front of the others, but her tawny eyes smiled significantly into Ivan Sahrkanov's, as if to make it clear that she knew whose idea the invitation had actually been.

Ginny ground her teeth together with suppressed rage; and then, to her surprise, Concepción asked her if she would please, please go with her this afternoon to see Sam Murdock's new house—the decorators would be laying the rugs, which had just arrived by sea, and she could hardly wait to see them.

"You don't mind?" she appealed prettily to Ivan. "Smith—the man I call 'Red Mustache' to myself—will escort us, of course, so we'll be quite safe." She gave a laugh, making a moue with her full red lips. "Did you know that *all* Sam's bodyguards are called Smith? It is so confusing sometimes—*he* says it is the simplest way, and, of course, he only hires the *best,* but me, I make up my own nicknames for them. They are 'Red Mustache' or 'Blackbeard'—ah, that one really does look like a pirate!—or 'Yellow Hair'. . . ."

Everyone laughed, even the Prince, and his voice sounded quite benevolent when he told Ginny that, of course, she must go along, and the outing in the fresh air would do her good.

"I'm going over to the Exchange, and I will probably be there for most of the day. But I haven't forgotten I am to escort two lovely ladies to dinner—you won't keep me waiting, will you?"

And again it was Concepción who, taking the initiative, laughingly promised that they would be back in plenty of time to dress and be waiting for *him.*

When they were alone together, however, sitting side by side in the light, open victoria, Concepción's face had become sullen and tight-lipped again, and she had not a word to say as they waited for Red Mustache.

"Real fine day for a ride," the red-faced groom ventured, looking impatiently over his shoulder at the stables. And then, Ginny felt her heart give a lurch that drove all the color from her face, before it started pounding heavily.

Instead of the man she had expected to see, the black-clad bodyguard who walked out to the carriage with a long, easy-muscled stride was Steve—still bearded, his blue eyes as dark as the bay on a cloudy day.

He touched his hat politely to both of them, and took the reins from the visibly relieved groom, who had been having a hard time holding two spirited thoroughbreds still.

"It's Red's day off. Mr. Murdock said I was to take over until he got back."

"Oh, yes—Smith. You are driving us?"

Concepción's words sounded as if they had been forced from her, and Ginny, still speechless with shock and apprehension, saw a corner of his mouth twitch amusedly as he took the reins, springing up easily onto the elevated driver's seat in front.

"My pleasure, ma'am. Princess?"

Why did his voice always have to take on that mocking intonation when he addressed her? He must be mad—oh, God, if Ivan had seen him, or Sonya. . . . Still, she retained enough sense to stay silent until the groom had moved away, and they had started off. And no sooner were they around the sweeping driveway and through the gate than Concepción began to mutter angrily in Spanish, casting dark looks at Ginny as she did.

"Crazy—ah, sí, have I not always said you were? What's the matter with you, Esteban? Or with me for that matter, that I should do your dirty work for you, after all this slut has done to *me*! And I've no doubt she'll betray you again—what do you see in her?"

"Stop screeching like a fishwife, 'Cepción," he said calmly over his shoulder. "You're supposed to be two *ladies* out for an afternoon drive, remember?"

"No! And why should I always have to be remembering that now, suddenly, I am a lady? It bores me, this business of being a lady, and all the stupid things I have to learn. Eddie likes me just the way I am—he said so. And as for *you*, Esteban, and *her*"—Concepción's scathing look flicked contemptuously across Ginny—"at least before she had some life in her. Now—you see! She lets me say what I please! I tell you, Princessa, I could get that silly Prince away from you if I snapped my fingers. I could get any man I really wanted from you."

"And you could also be spilled into the street, fine new gown and all, if you don't stop that tirade," Steve said harshly, the warning note in his voice making Concepción shrug angrily and relapse with a sulky look into her corner of the open carriage. She muttered under her breath to Ginny:

"Well, it's true, and you know it, don't you?"

"If you're talking about *him*, it's no longer a matter of taking, is it?" Ginny responded tightly. It took all the will-power she had left to sit still, and try to keep her face controlled. It wasn't fair, that he should still have the power to do this to her—to make her knees feel as weak as water, to start every pulse in her body throbbing as if she had a fever. And he was only playing with her, re-venging himself on her for what he thought was her infidelity. Why did he have to keep on tormenting her?

She almost forgot her own angry thoughts when she saw the house—it seemed set into the hillside, rising white-columned and cleanly beautiful against a back-ground of green shrubs and blue sky. One whole side of the mansion, built in the Greek classical style, overlooked the city and the bay itself.

A man, who seemed to be expecting them, opened a massive gate set into a thick stone wall. The graveled drive wound upward for a short distance, ending under the enormous porch. Two flights of stone steps led upward to the front door, which was flanked by twin gaslights.

Ginny caught her breath, impressed in spite of her mood of tension. Even Concepción gave a gasp of admira-tion. It was beautiful; it reminded Ginny of a French chateau she had visited once. No pointed, conical towers or gothic scrollwork—its pure clean lines were classic.

The door stood open, and several workmen were busy in the entrance hall. Taking charge, Steve led Ginny and Concepción past them with a nod. Like a guide conducting a tour, he kept his voice entirely expressionless.

"The dining room—Sam calls it the banqueting hall. And through here is the main ballroom. There's another one on the first floor upstairs, with a terrace that seems to hang over a natural rock garden below. You can see the servants' wing through this window here—just the end of it. And I'm afraid they're still working in the kitchens and the parlors. Would you like to go upstairs?"

It was Concepción who took his arm possessively, mind-less of the sidelong stares of some of the workmen.

"It's very beautiful, 'Steban, querido. I would like to see the bedrooms most of all. They are done?"

"Most of them." For the first time, Steve looked directly at Ginny, and she noticed, with a tiny, uncontrollable shiver, that he was unsmiling; and that there was a hardness to his eyes. Because she had hung back, he took her arm impatiently, almost angrily. "I want to talk to you, in case you hadn't guessed. That's why I persuaded Concepción to bring you here today."

"More deception—but then, you're a past master at that, aren't you? I think you enjoy intrigue for its own sake, Steve Morgan, but I would rather not become involved, if you don't mind." She tried to hang back, but his grip tightened and if she had not given in no doubt he would have dragged her up the stairs.

"Sorry, baby—especially since you feel so strongly about it. But you are involved. More than you think. And that's part of what we've got to talk about. *Now*, damn it—like it or not!"

When he used that harsh, implacable tone of voice, his black brows drawing together ominously, sheer habit made Ginny quail. She bit her lip sullenly, her eyes shooting angry sparks the next moment, when Concepción gave a burst of caustic laughter.

"Oh—I see you two are going to quarrel again! And in *that* case, I think I should be tactful and take myself off, eh? I can find my way around alone, don't worry—and if you ask *me*, Esteban, you should have got into the habit of beating her a long time ago! It's the only treatment some women understand."

"Well in that case," Ginny hissed, her green eyes narrowing catlike, "I do hope he beats *you* quite regularly. You certainly need civilizing, to say the least!"

"And you! For all the milksop manners you've adopted of late, it's been obvious to everyone that you are still a puta at heart! What about those jeweled bracelets that Sam gave you? Have you paid him back yet, or are you waiting until your husband goes away again?"

"They're a couple of bitches whose hackles rise at the sight of each other," Steve thought as he separated them forcibly, sending a spitting Concepción off with a sharp slap on her rounded thigh. But at least he understood Concepción and was able to cope with her temperamental rages. He had begun to realize that he didn't understand Ginny at all—and worse, he was no longer certain how he should treat her. The thought made him furious with himself, as well as with her. Damn her! She had caused him nothing but trouble, ever since he'd first set eyes on her. If he had any sense left, he should have counted himself well rid of her when she ran off with her prince.

And yet—he had taken her into the master bedroom, an enormous room with massive furniture that matched its size, and a wall of windows that seemed to draw in the magnificent view: mountains, marching down to the foam-flecked blue waters of the bay, dotted now with vessels of various sizes, and beyond the mountains, the wide sweep of the sky, streaked with feathers of clouds.

"Well," Steve heard himself say, "do you like it? The splendid isolation of the very rich, who can afford to buy anything, even the view."

He pushed open one of the windows as he spoke, forcing her ahead of him onto a wide terrace, really a balcony, that ran the length of the room.

"Steve," she started to say, and then Ginny found herself leaning against the wrought-iron railing that dug into her back.

"You're not afraid of heights, are you? Why don't you look down? Turn your head, Princess. You'll see the whole city lying at your feet."

Involuntarily, she had clutched at his shoulders as he leaned over her, but now her hands fell away.

"Do you want to kill me? Is that why you brought me out here? If you do, there's nothing to stop you, is there? We're alone, and you could always say it was an accident. Even Ivan says I am unbalanced."

At the sight of her face, completely drained of color, but defiant for all that, Steve and already begun to regret his harshness. He hadn't brought her here to terrify her, but to try to talk to her. Why did she always have the effect of making him lose his self-control?

She was staring at him through those wide green eyes. Forest pools—he remembered thinking that once. They could grow darker, when she was in the throes of love— but he didn't want to remember the small sounds she made

in her throat, or the way she threw her head back, her arms
tightening, her body writhing. . . . For how many men had
she done the same thing? And why did the thought still
have the power to make him ragingly jealous?

Abruptly, he moved away from her. Just as if he could
not bear to touch her any longer, Ginny thought.

"What makes you imagine I should desire to kill you,
madam? I beg your pardon. Maybe you're used to being
spoken to more formally! Your Highness—Princess
Sahrkanov. Since you're the Tsar's daughter—there's no
need to flinch—you ought to get used to the adulation of
commoners!"

"And you'd use anything I tell you to stab at me,
wouldn't you? You won't tell me why you suddenly decided to come back into my life. All you've done so far
is—is try to hurt me. Why do you bother? What more do
you think you can do to me? If you're squeamish, all of a
sudden, I could very easily throw myself over this rail—
that should put an end to your problems, shouldn't it?"

And at the moment she flung the words at him, she actually felt like doing so. Putting an end to everything. . . .

She leaned back against the rail, as if she wished it
would break, and Steve grabbed her into his arms. It was
a purely instinctive action, something he could not help.
And once she was there, he could not let her go.

She was shaking—holding her, he could smell the
fragrance of her hair, feel the peculiar suppleness of her
body as she leaned against him. Anger, mixed with frustration, made him cruel. He wrapped his fingers in her
hair, pulling her head back, and jammed his mouth down
over hers.

Afterwards, it seemed to Ginny as if she had been
sucked under the surface of a raging torrent. Surfacing,
she became aware only of little, inconsequential things at
first. The screeching of seagulls—the beating of her own
heart—the familiar feel of his body against hers.

The top buttons of her high-necked gown lay open, and
Steve had pulled free the thin gold chain that she had
quite inexplicably worn today.

"Are you going to use that key? Will you?"

"I don't understand, Steve."

"What don't you understand?" He was drawing her into the bedroom with him as he spoke, and the sudden transition from light to dimness blinded her, so that she stumbled. She felt him catch her.

"What don't you understand?" he repeated, and his voice had suddenly turned harsh and hateful. "I think you do—your kind of woman always knows when a man wants her. And damn your wanton little soul, I continue to want you! So. . . ."

She said, in a low, breathless voice: "So? What are you trying to tell me? That I'm a slut, but you want me—the way a man wants a slut? Why feel you ought to have scruples, then? If that's why you brought me here, why don't you get it over with? Do as you please, I've learned better than to try and fight you."

His hold on her loosened suddenly, and he gàve her a contemptuous shove that sent her floundering backwards against the bed.

Ginny had the vague feeling that all of this had happened before, even the look in his eyes as he gazed down at her.

"There's no reason to fight. As a matter of fact, I have a proposition for you." She noticed that he still had the habit of hooking his thumbs in his belt, standing slightly astride as he looked down at her. He had his back to the sunshine that streamed in through the open windows, and it was impossible for her to read the expression on his face.

"Will you become my mistress, Ginny?" She couldn't believe, at first, that he had actually said the words. "I'll give you time to think about it, if you need time. But I'm talking about a formal arrangement, of course. The terms are up to you."

Chapter Twenty-five

She kept telling herself that she was dreaming. Having a nightmare. She struggled upright on the bed, feeling the mattress give beneath her weight. Quite without her own volition, her fingers pressed against her temples.

"No! You are trying to—"

"I'm not trying to do anything, for God's sake. Except talk some sense. Your'e on the market, my sweet, and I'm willing to buy. What do you want? Jewels? A discreet little apartment of your own? A bank account? If I don't make the offer, I'm sure someone else will. And I'd prefer no go-between, like your husband, for instance. What do you say?"

Mistress! He wanted her to become his mistress, of all things! He was actually *asking* her, instead of making it a fact with the harsh encroachment of his body, as he had done in the past. But the idea was monstrous—and now pain laced through her temples, weakening her.

"You're quite mad. And I'm not for sale. If Ivan knew, even this much—"

"Would he take me for another Frank Julius, do you think? Or a calf-eyed, lovesick boy? What does it take, Ginny? Shall I do my bargaining with him instead?"

Disarming him, she suddenly lay back, closing her eyes.

"Oh—why should you bother? You can do as you please with me. After all, I'm a slut. Why bother to bargain for what you can take for nothing?"

She had defeated him again. What was the matter with her? He had promised himself that he would be patient and tactful; that he would wring some kind of response from her. And instead, she was lying back like a martyr who had every expectation of being raped, and was nobly resigned to the prospect. All it had taken was a reference to her husband.

Steve swore, disgustedly and profanely, and her eyes flew open, to regard him with a look of distant surprise.

"Why are you so angry? After all, what choice do I have? I agree."

"You agree!" He was so taken aback, so furious, that he all but shouted the words at her. "You agree to what? Did you understand what I just asked you?"

"How could I help it, the way you have been yelling at me? If you really want me as your mistress, Steve, I agree." She sighed. "I'm so tired of being tormented! Of being constantly set upon and torn to bits by your words and your accusations. If you really want me, you can have me. And you don't need to bribe me—just be kind, if you're still capable of that much consideration."

If she had continued to fight against him as she had in the past, he would have enjoyed tearing the clothes from her body and forcing from her the kind of response she always gave in the end—yes, even while she cried out that she hated him. But her limp, almost indifferent surrender vanquished him, and he stood staring down at her with a sense of frustration that made him want to throttle her. How dare she play the passive whore—and particularly with *him*! And to ask him in that colorless voice to be *kind*—what in hell did she mean?

"Jesus God!" Steve said between his teeth. And then, still in the same soft, ugly voice: "Get up! Christ, do you always give in this meekly to any man who wants to take you? Even a good whore bargains first."

He pulled her roughly and brutally to her feet and then let her go just as abruptly, as if he could hardly bear to touch her any longer. And for a moment then, Ginny was tempted to weakness—or, in another way of looking at it, to testing her own strength, by flinging herself against him, forcing him to kiss her again.

But instead she flung her head back, saying in a voice as hard as his:

"But why should I trouble myself with bargaining? I am sure the sense of responsibility you have spoken of, and your considerable experience with whores, will make you deal generously with me. You can afford to keep a mistress, I hope?"

His eyes glittered dangerously at her for an instant, and it was all Ginny could do not to wince at the fury in them. But instead of the explosion of rage she had expected, he surprised her by inclining his head, as if in acknowledgement of her sarcastic barbs.

"I expect I can manage," he drawled, with a hard, twisted smile that did not reach the sapphire-blue glitter of his eyes. His gaze traveled along her body, from her mouth to her thighs, outlined by the tightly draped material of her gown—a slow, deliberately insolent inspection that made angry color flame in her cheeks. "After all, I know what I'll be getting, and I have to admit you'd be worth beggaring myself for—especially if our bargain includes buying a certain show of fidelity as well. No more Eric Fotheringays, please!" Suddenly, startling her, he put his fingers under her chin, tilting her face up to his; his touch was almost a caress. "Tell me, love, would you like some small token of my—mad passion for you, to put the seal on our arrangement? What would you like to have?"

Why did he have to touch her? In spite of the calculated irony of his speech, Ginny could feel herself start to tremble. With a too-quick, abrupt motion she twisted away from him, walked to the ornately mirrored dresser and began to pat at her hair, quite blindly.

"Make it a surprise, do. I love surprises," she flung at him in the most casual voice she could contrive.

"I suppose the way you are fiddling with your hair right now means that you demand payment in advance?" How she wished Steve would stop using such a caustic tone of voice; his words seemed chosen deliberately to sting. And yet—he actually seemed serious about his infamous proposition! Why did he want her?

Ginny kept asking herself that puzzling question, and could find no answer that seemed either sane or logical. The one solution she dared not *let* herself think about was. . . . Oh, God, could it be possible, or was she clutching at straws because she would like to believe it was so? Perhaps Steve *did* love her after all, even if he did not want to admit it until he had punished her.

But then the logical part of Ginny's mind protested lucidly. He took her marriage so calmly! Steve used to be so terribly jealous—no, if he loved her he'd have carried her off by now.

And yet, contradictorily, there remained the fact that he wanted her—and had actually admitted as much.

It took no pretense on Ginny's part to act, later that evening, as if she was far away, and rather listless. Ivan had actually given her a headache powder to swallow before they left for Count Chernikoff's bachelor apartments—to bring some liveliness into her manner, he'd said sarcastically.

"One has only to compare you with the exotic and vivacious Señorita Sanchez to become aware of the contrast between you. Come, my darling, you don't want the Count to think you're unhappy? We haven't been married long enough for boredom to set in. And, in fact, I am not at all bored with you—you excite me, as you did at the very beginning!"

How she hated the exaggeratedly flowery manner he adopted at times. His pale, cold eyes studied her all the time he was speaking and gave lie to his words. And his steady, cold-blooded pursuit of her now proved only that his reasons for marrying her had nothing to do with passion.

"How strange that I should be unfaithful to Ivan with Steve, of all people," Ginny thought dreamily as the large, comfortably-sprung carriage drove them through the gaslit streets of San Francisco that evening. She felt the sense of heady warmth and well-being that taking one of her powders always brought her; and the prospect of dinner and polite conversation did not seem nearly as bad now, in spite of Concepción's presence and her sidelong, slightly malicious looks. She and Concepción could never like each other, but what did it matter? Steve wanted *her*—in spite of his cutting words, and the way he could so quickly fly into a rage with her. He was risking his life staying in San Francisco, where he might be recognized at any moment. He had driven them back to her father's house—actually going into the stables to see to the horses after he had handed her and Concepción out of the carriage.

Sonya had returned from her round of visits and shopping at just that time, and had remarked casually about it.

"Surely that wasn't the man you call Red Mustache? It looked as if he was dark-haired, when I caught a glimpse of him just now."

"Oh, that was Blackbeard the pirate—he's much fiercer and more dangerous than Red Mustache, who had the afternoon off." It was Concepción who had given an airy reply, her reticule swinging from her wrist. "He's the one who looks after the house."

"Oh—perhaps I've seen him before, then. There was something familiar about the way he walked."

To silence her stepmother, Ginny had begun babbling about Mr. Murdock's house, and how grand it was. By now her head ached terribly again, and she hardly knew what she was saying.

Perhaps Sonya noticed, for her lips pursed slightly.

"You look as if you need to rest, my love. Do go and lie down for a while! Your husband is not back yet, so you'll have time."

Deception—and fear. Steve—not touching her again; leaving her alone in the big room while he went to find Concepción, who came bursting in afterwards with her red lips moist and rather pouting, as if she'd just been very thoroughly kissed.

"There is no time to bother with your hair, gringa." When they were alone, Concepción always spoke this way. "Besides, the wind will only blow it about again. We have to hurry, Esteban is waiting." The girl's eyes had slid to the bed, and back to Ginny's face. She laughed triumphantly. "So—you did nothing but quarrel, after all! I could have told you—Esteban is not the forgiving kind. Better that you stick to your husband, if you know what is good for you."

How much did Concepción know, or suspect about the strange relationship that existed between Ginny and the Prince Sahrkanov?

This evening, Concepción seemed in an exceptionally good mood, alternately teasing and flirtatious. Even Count Chernikoff unbent somewhat, responding to her light chatter with a smile. Concepción made a point of entertaining the old man, while Ivan, seated on a divan beside Ginny, acted the devoted husband—playing with a lock of her hair; fingers brushing her bare shoulders.

"So—you will not come to Russia yet?"

Dinner was over, and at last the Count had begun to concentrate his attention on the quietest of his guests.

"But you mustn't blame Virginie," Ivan responded smoothly. "She's only recently been reunited with the Senator and his charming wife. And she finds San Francisco a brash and exciting city, do you not, my love? I do not wish to force her into anything she does not want to do."

"Oh!" Concepción widened big, innocent eyes. "But I thought you were longing to see Russia—and to return to Europe. Me, I can hardly wait to travel on a ship. Sam says he will take me soon, to visit Spain."

"I leave in two weeks time." Count Chernikoff turned a questioning look on Ginny, on Ivan, whose face had not changed expression in the least. "If you change your mind. . . ."

"Is it possible you've changed your mind, my dearest? All those invitations we've accepted for the next two months—you should have told me, for you know how much I am looking forward to showing you Russia."

They were all looking at her; Concepción with a spiteful look. Ginny managed to shrug lightly.

"Of course I look forward to seeing Russia. And there are times when I almost feel impatient to do so. But there are also so many things to do in San Francisco—I suppose I am a typical female, changing my mind from one day to the next!"

"She's lying," the Count thought. And he wondered why, even while his face remained impassive, and he changed the conversation.

And, as time passed, Ginny paid only token attention to the conversation. She was thinking, in spite of all her resolutions, not of Ivan, but of Steve. Would he attempt to meet her again? Had he really meant that outrageous suggestion of his? Perhaps he'd only been trying to humiliate her, to see how far she would go.

Already, it was time for them to leave.

Count Chernikoff bent over Ginny's cold hand, kissing it.

"Remember—if you should change your mind. . . ." And then he said, in a firm, direct voice, his eyes fixed on hers,

"I hope you will visit me again soon. Surely you can spare a little time for an old man? Ivan must persuade you."

Outside, the night was unusually clear and warm for San Francisco.

"Oh, but it's so *early* yet!" Concepción pouted. "Must we go back? It would be so nice to drive by the ocean."

For a change, Ivan Sahrkanov did not respond to her teasing with his usual smiling charm. In the light from a streetlamp, Ginny thought his face looked harder than usual, as if his thoughts engrossed him.

"Another night perhaps, although I hate to disappoint a lady as lovely as you are. I have an appointment to keep."

He handed them politely into the carriage. First Concepción, who pouted with disappointment, and did not bother to hide it. Then Ginny, who by now was feeling tired enough from the tension of the day to drop off to sleep right away.

Ivan turned to the driver, his hand on the door.

"We will return now."

At that moment, one of the horses snorted and reared, and it was that, Ginny supposed afterwards, which warned the Prince.

A man had detached himself from the shadows, a short distance down the street, and had started towards them with a peculiar, rather loping gait. When she heard Concepción's muffled cry, Ginny found herself staring—wondering why the man kept running, his long pigtail flapping from side to side. He seemed to be wearing a fixed grin—lips drawn tightly back from his teeth. And in the flickering gaslight, she could see that he wore the black, rather baggy garments of a typical Chinaman, like so many she had seen on the streets.

"Sir! Look out!" the coachman called out urgently, his hands busy sawing at the reins as he attempted to control the frightened horses. Why did the man not swerve away? He might be run over very easily. But instead, he had started to say something in a shrill, sing-song voice; it sounded as if he were repeating the same words over and over, and in Spanish Concepción had begun to mutter:

"Ah, Dios! I think he is either drunk or crazy. Oh, look!"

It must have all taken just a few seconds, although it

seemed to Ginny that everything had happened very slowly, like one of her dreams of running in sand.

She heard Ivan give a low, mirthless laugh. He stood quite coolly, the gaslight shining on his burnished hair, and one arm was extended. There was a sharp report, and then another, and the Chinaman, who had stumbled at the first shot, fell sprawling, an ungainly puppet out of whose body all the stuffing had run. Something fell clattering to the pavement at the same time—and when Ivan, walking over quite calmly, kicked the man's body contemptuously and picked it up, both women saw the gleam of metal.

A hatchet! Ivan was still completely, almost inhumanly unmoved, except for the hard, pale glitter of his eyes as he returned to the carriage.

"A favorite weapon of these heathens. You see it?"

"It was a good thing you carried that little gun," Concepción said, with a suppressed note of excitement in her voice, craning her head to see better. And then, softly, "I wonder what he wanted?"

"Robbery, no doubt. I think the man was out of his mind—too much opium, or perhaps he wanted money to buy some more. In any case, he's dead, so it isn't important. Let us go, Jameson."

"But—you aren't going to leave him there? Isn't it strange that no one came out to see what the commotion was about? Ivan, shouldn't we—"

"My dear, please calm yourself. I am going to have the good Jameson take you ladies home, and then I will go to the police station, where I will give them this little souvenir, and tell them what happened. After that, the rest will be up to them."

Ivan, sitting opposite the two young women, leaned forward and put his hand on Ginny's knee as the carriage started off with a clatter. It was meant to look like a comforting husbandly caress, but Ginny bit her lip to keep from wincing: his fingers bit into her through the thin folds of her silk gown.

She fell silent, and let Concepción keep up what conversation there was until they finally drove up to the door of the Senator's house.

"You are an excellent shot. You hit him both times, did

you not, and in such poor light, with such a tiny gun. How could you stand there so calmly and wait for him to attack you?"

Ivan answered politely, but abstractedly. Silly, chattering creature! At least he had managed to keep Virginie silent—she had not said another word. Ivan Sahrkanov's mind moved quickly, skimming over names, attaching faces to some of these. Who? Was the man a "Boo How Doy"—a bodyguard to some rich Mandarin—or was he sent by someone else who felt a grudge against him? Damn Chinese, they were not even citizens—they *had* no rights except to work, and make enough money to live on, and do as they were told. There were very few of them who were clever—certainly not the one who had sent the clumsy would-be assassin he had so quickly dispatched.

But—and Ivan frowned into the darkness—*who?* Who knew enough about his movements or his activities? He would have to find out, and take steps, quickly. There must be no weakness or indecision shown.

And so, when they had reached the house, Ivan accompanied his wife upstairs and into her bedroom, smiling at her puzzled and rather nervous look.

"What's the matter with you, my darling? If I didn't know better, I'd say you wore an almost guilty look. You don't have a lover who's trying to kill me off, do you?"

"If I had I am sure you would have dealt with him first," she retorted, surprising him with her sudden show of spirit. He would have to remind her—but not just now. Later, when he had time.

"Well, you're right about that," Ivan said smoothly. He deliberately caressed her bare shoulders, running his fingers down the curve of her breasts, to be rewarded by her startled, widening green eyes. "I wish I was able to show you tonight how much I prize you, you lovely thing. But, alas—I must go to the police, and I am about to take a little trip out of town. Some urgent business I just remembered—it should not take me long. You will miss me, won't you? And be good? I am going to leave you—let's see—six powders? You look eager. I don't want you to become too accustomed to taking them—anything in excess is bad for you. So let us say—four. And in return. . . ."

Slipping an arm around her stiff waist, Ivan drew her over to the triple-mirrored dresser.

"Come, darling, don't act so coldly. Are you angry that I am leaving you? Shall I take the time to prove to you, before I leave, how much I prize you?" He was watching her face, in that narrow-eyed, almost predatory way that made her want to shiver. "Not tonight," Ginny's mind screamed, and she had to force herself not to pull away from his stroking, caressing fingers, which were sliding down her hip now. Because she knew by now that he only waited for her to shrink away, she stood still, beginning to unfasten her necklace with fingers she hoped did not shake visibly.

"I'm your wife, Ivan. And since you did marry me, I suppose it was because you wanted me."

He gave a short laugh, and then, surprisingly enough, moved away from her, picking up the necklace she had just put down, and holding it up to the light thoughtfully.

"Of course I wanted you. I told you so at the very beginning, did I not? A little gypsy, that is what you reminded me of. So flushed and lovely and wild. I promised myself then that I would be the man to tame you. But have I succeeded yet? Eh?"

Suddenly he gave an exclamation, frowning.

"Why—the catch is quite loose. It might have come off at any moment, and you would have lost these lovely jewels, these emeralds that match your eyes, Let me take it with me, my love. I'll have it fixed for you by the time I return."

"That's what he wanted from the beginning," Ginny thought. "The emeralds. I wonder why?"

But she only said aloud, in a rather subdued voice, "Thank you, Ivan. I'd have hated to lose your gift to me."

Chapter Twenty-six

Concepción had gone out with her ardent and devoted admirer, the young Viscount Marwood; Red Mustache, the bodyguard, accompanied them.

"I don't know when we'll be back. Eddie says he will take me on one of those fancy riverboats." She smiled insincerely at Sonya, but just before she left, while she was adjusting her fashionable bonnet on her high-piled hair, she hissed to Ginny:

"I am so bored! And I am sick of pretending to be polite to you. Eddie says he is going to give me a present of a high-perch phaeton, just like the one he drives, and then I shall be able to go out whenever I please. Don't you wish you were as lucky?"

"I count myself lucky at not having to spend a morning forcing myself to be polite to *you*," Ginny retorted, walking away from the girl.

"You do not like her, do you?" Sonya whispered to Ginny afterwards. And added, surprisingly, "I must confess that I cannot blame you, love. There is something quite—well, *vulgar* about her! I'll be glad when Mr. Murdock's house is ready." She gave Ginny a puzzled, almost considering look. "I must say that you do look better since we've returned to San Francisco." She did not add what she was thinking: "And especially when your husband is gone on one of his mysterious business trips."

To tell the truth, Sonya herself was relieved. There was something about Ivan Sahrkanov that disturbed her, especially since William had hinted that the man was not above polite blackmail, and that some of the more important men in the city had begun to distrust him. Even Sam Murdock, it appeared. And Murdock was still a mystery. Why did he stay away in Virginia City for so long? There

was Ginny, to whom he had presented such fabulously expensive jewels—jewels that Sonya kept locked in her husband's safe, at Ginny's particular request. Under normal
circumstances, she would never have encouraged such deception. But in this case, even William had agreed it was
best the Prince should not know. William could be very
pragmatic at times.

"Murdock is one of the few men who can really help
me, and especially now. Let's see what happens," he had
said.

And so, late in the morning, when a uniformed messenger brought flowers and a long, flat package for Ginny,
Sonya herself rushed up to her stepdaughter's room, where
the girl had gone to rest.

"Ginny—only look! And the messenger is waiting, or I
would not have disturbed you."

The flowers were long stemmed roses, each one a nest
of crimson velvet. They were accompanied by a card, with
boldly scrawled initials across it. "S.M."

"Mr. Murdock! Oh, Ginny, do you think he's back?"

Still drowsy looking, her hair hanging down her back,
Ginny had begun to open the gift-wrapped package, her
movements almost listless.

She heard Sonya's gasp.

"Oh!"

Fire opals—leaping out at her from a bed of velvet.
Necklace, bracelets, and long, dangling earrings that
would brush her shoulders. And a ring—a single, enormous opal surrounded by pearls and diamonds. Opals for
bad luck. How could she forget the last time she had worn
opals? A folded note—the same scrawled initials at its
bottom: *"One o'clock. Smith will come for you. Don't forget your key."*

Not Murdock, but Steve—who had the same initials,
and was unscrupulous enough to make use of that fact.

"Oh, how dare he—how dare he?" she thought. And
then, one thought overlapping the other, "How can he
afford it? What makes him think that I will. . . ."

But even as she thought that, Ginny knew that she
would.

For once, Sonya did not place objections in her way,
nor remind her that she should not go out unchaperoned.

When the light carriage arrived she tactfully stayed upstairs, helping Ginny put the last touches to her toilette. Surprisingly, a woman had come—a respectable chaperone. A woman with an olive skin, her hair almost completely covered by a dark-colored bonnet, she said that her name was Mrs. Mary Pleasants.

"What a gentleman he is! But Ginny, you will be careful? If Ivan should find out—"

"Ivan approves of Mr. Murdock. I'm sure he'd have no objections."

"Well . . ." and then Sonya's doubtful voice softened. "You do look lovely. I wonder where he means to take you?"

Sonya had not read the folded note, of course. And just as well, Ginny thought cynically.

It was Steve himself who drove the brand new Victoria, still "disguised" as one of Sam Murdock's impersonal bodyguards. How could he take such risks? What kind of mysterious game was he playing this time?

Even his voice was impersonal, as he helped her in.

"You look exceptionally well, Princess."

It was left to Mrs. Pleasants to make trivial conversation until the carriage stopped before an ostentatious-looking townhouse on Washington Street.

"You'll visit me again? Both of you? Princess, it's been a real pleasure meeting you."

And then Mrs. Pleasants was gone, and she was alone in the carriage. In spite of the powder she had taken before setting out, Ginny felt her head reel. She didn't know how to react, nor what to say. So she remained silent, even when Steve turned the carriage, and instead of driving up the hill, drove towards the waterfront instead. Let *him* make the first move this time. Let him explain—but how seldom Steve had bothered with explanations for his unpredictable behavior!

Now, however, at the last moment, he said over his shoulder:

"We're going sailing. I hope you don't mind."

"Since when have you asked me if I object to doing something or not?"

"I should have continued that way." His blue eyes, so dark under the shade of the black hat that shaded his forehead, rested on her briefly. "You don't get seasick, do you?"

They drew up before Ginny had a chance to answer. A tall, well-built colored man stepped forward to grasp the reins, grinning.

"Thought maybe you mightn't show up. But now that you're here, you've got a beaut of a day. Just enough wind, and no fog. Enjoy yourselves."

Almost in spite of herself, as if she were actually watching a stranger, Ginny was forced to notice the way Steve moved. He had swung his long legs to the ground, and was lifting her out of the carriage. His closeness, the way his hands closed about her waist, undid her. She felt breathless, no longer capable of the scathing retort she had planned. Let anything happen! The afternoon sun was warm on her shoulders and the back of her neck, and she felt ridiculously light-hearted.

She continued to feel that way as the small, white-sailed yacht left the dock, heeling away into the bay with the water reflecting the sun in a myriad of tiny ripples.

"Christ—take your stupid hat off! Throw it overboard—I'll buy you a dozen more if you must wear them. But not out here."

Laughing, she did as he had ordered, and saw the way his eyes crinkled at the corners, their blue even brighter in the sunlight.

Immediately, her hair blew out in the breeze, coppery strands almost blinding her until she tore its mass all down and began to braid it, still watching the way Steve's eyes watched her; he stood with his legs braced apart, hatless himself now, dark jacket discarded, white shirt open down to the waist. A pirate. Yes, he did look like a pirate after all. Hadn't she always thought so?

"Is that better?" Her voice was deliberately provocative, and she saw the grooves on either side of his mouth deepen.

"Much better, you damned green-eyed siren. I ought to throw you overboard."

"Now? But I'd probably take you overboard with me."

"I've no doubt you would. Hang on, now."

She did, and a gust of wind caught the boat, heeling it over.

She heard Steve laugh, and the spray stung her face, drenching her. What did it matter? Even if he did mean to throw her overboard later, there was no mistaking the look in his eyes *now*.

The whole afternoon was dreamlike, when Ginny tried to remember details later—the sun, the salt spray, the feel of the breeze beating against her face. Steve sailed a boat with the casual ease he rode a horse. Did the boat belong to Sam Murdock, too? She gave up asking herself questions after a while. It was easier not to—even when the small yacht hove to in the shadow of a clipper ship that lay at anchor, sails furled, deck swarming with men busy with various tasks.

"Can you climb up a rope ladder, do you think, or shall I have you hauled up aloft like a prize of war?"

Clinging, her wet skirts flattened against her body, Ginny managed the former course, not daring to look either down or up. But she was all too aware that Steve was close behind her, his hands reaching out to hold her steady when she seemed to hesitate or fumble for her footing.

And at the top there were other strong hands to draw her onto the deck, and a man who wore a peaked cap and gold braid on his jacket. Did Steve mean to carry her off, pirate fashion? Did she care?

"Mr. Morgan. I was wondering if you'd changed your mind, perhaps. Madam...."

"It was good of you to wait for us, Captain. Ginny, this is Captain Benson."

How casual Steve's introductions were! Before she knew it, Ginny found herself carried off to a cabin, its luxury surprising her, even though she had vowed to herself that nothing could surprise her any longer on this particular afternoon.

The door slammed behind them, and she found herself strangely breathless.

Time rolled back as Steve leaned against the door, his eyes travelling over her.

"You're damp all over. You look half drowned. I think you ought to change before we go out again."

Ginny thought she felt the ship move beneath her. But perhaps it was the sudden unsteadiness of her knees as

Steve crossed the small space between them. She felt her gown rip from neck to waist.

"It's time for you to pay off, Princess. And, by God, I've waited long enough."

Somehow, she was lying across the bed. Impatient, his hands tore away what was left of her gown and underclothes, to slide warmly and, oh God, too familiarly over her flesh.

Thinking stopped. His hands took her—his lips—and finally, with her arms clasping him closely, his body. Harddriving, inevitable, the whole world seemed to rock and sway about her, and she cried out and cried out until his mouth stopped her cries.

Afterwards, it was difficult to be forced back to reality. Ginny would have liked to stay within the safe, happy confines of her dream world forever. She had half-hoped, half-expected that Steve meant to carry her off somewhere, and keep her with him—she didn't care under what conditions. At least he had continued to want her, in spite of everything he had said. That much had remained unchanged—their bodies' response to each other.

She felt drowsy and contented, not wanting to think; she was content to lie this way in his arms while time passed and was no longer important. If only she could continue to believe that nothing had happened to tear them apart— that everything was the same!

Only, it was not. She was forcibly and unpleasantly reminded of that fact when Steve moved away from her and began to dress. His callous and somehow unfeeling action banished the dreamily satisfied feeling that had possessed Ginny only a moment before.

Angrily, raising herself on her elbow she snapped:

"And what am *I* supposed to wear? I suppose you'll borrow some clothes from one of the sailors for me."

"We're no longer running through the wilds of Mexico, sweetheart. Before you lose your temper, why don't you look around? This cabin has been especially equipped for female guests, and I'm sure you'll find something suitable here."

Impatiently, he pulled aside a panel she had believed to be merely ornamental, revealing a surprisingly deep closet, filled with women's clothing.

"Oh!" Sheer surprise and rage rendered Ginny almost speechless, until she caught the amused tilt of his eyebrow.

"You're not going to start swearing at me, are you, love? It wouldn't suit your regal status. And besides, none of these gowns have been worn yet, and they've all been made to your size—as nearly as I could remember it. Does that make you feel better, or would you prefer to go on deck just the way you are? Not that I don't think you look exceptionally fetching."

"You are the most—the most callous and calculating—"

"But you always knew what a villain I was, didn't you? And I thought there was an agreement between us." Half dressed, his thumbs hooked in his belt, Steve's hard blue gaze made her flush in spite of herself. "Ginny, we don't have enough time for you to play coy, if that's what you had in mind. We're already halfway to Benicia, and when we arrive there, you'd better be dressed and ready to play the grand lady." Adding to her frustration, Ginny thought she saw the old devil lights flare briefly in his eyes. "I'm sorry I didn't think to have a lady's maid brought on board, but if you need any help, I'd be glad to oblige. I've had some experience in my time."

He had brought her here only to humiliate her, of course! Why had she been so blind and foolish as to come with him so trustingly?

Questions without answers whirled around in Ginny's brain; and then there was no time even for that. She felt, all over again, as if she were dreaming—an actress in a carefully managed stage play.

Dressed, finally, in a gown that Steve chose for her, she had to submit, with gritted teeth, to the further humiliation of having him fasten a necklace about her throat—an enormous emerald pendant, suspended from a thin gold chain to hang between her breasts.

"What are you doing, for God's sake? What kind of game are you playing now? Does Mr. Murdock know? How—"

"I'll answer some of your questions later, Ginny. But for the moment, why don't you calm yourself and come outside with me? From the commotion I hear outside, I think we've already made the port of Benicia—and in record time, too."

They were all talking about the time the new ship had made, sparing Ginny the difficulty of trying to make conversation. Captain Benson was smiling, and his first mate looked jubilant.

"I knew the iron plating on her hull wouldn't slow her down, Mr. Morgan! She's going to be the best and fastest ship of the Lady Line, you mark my words."

"And one of the safest," the mate put in. His eyes touched Ginny briefly, and then quickly slid away, as if he had committed some indiscretion. Too late, she had begun to wonder what they all thought, and it was all she could do to pretend indifference, to play at being calm, as if she were used to being carried on board a ship by a black-bearded pirate, being made love to, and then paraded before everyone afterwards as if she had been nothing more than—than. . . . And then the thought struck her with all the force of a blow that she was, in actuality, Steve's mistress. And he was treating her as such!

"What did I expect?" Ginny thought wretchedly. She listened to the men talk, watching Steve in spite of her anger at him. Apparently the cabin, really a stateroom meant for the use of the owner of this vessel, contained men's clothing as well. He had changed into a quite respectable-looking dark suit, its somberness relieved by a brocade vest, with sapphire buttons that matched his cuff links. He looked positively handsome, in a rakish, devilish way, and when his eyes touched hers, as they did once or twice, Ginny felt the weakness seep into her very bones.

"Not fair . . . it's not fair, and I hate him," she thought rebelliously. "Look what he's doing to me, what he's made me go through!"

And it appeared, very shortly, as if he were determined that she should endure even more.

Boats had begun to dot the Carquinez Straits, all apparently headed for the clipper, which lay moored some distance out from the curved shoreline. And Steve had come to her side, taking her arm.

"I'm afraid we won't have time to go ashore, since I have to return you to your parents' house at a reasonable hour. But we're going to have a small celebration on board, all the same. Do you still like champagne?"

For just a moment, his eyes seemed to grow warmer,

reminding her of shared intimacies—the time she had gotten really drunk on champagne in a small Mexican village, and had helped Steve break Paco Davis out of jail. Why, why did he have to make her remember *now*?

She said in a subdued voice, from which she tried to keep all traces of emotion:

"Celebration? What do you mean? For how much longer do you intend being so mysterious?"

His fingers tightened around her arm, although his tone was mocking.

"No mystery. I thought you were paying attention to our discussions just now. We're here to name the ship. She was to be called 'Lady Benicia,' but I've changed my mind, as I was just telling Captain Benson. She's to be named 'Green-Eyed Lady' instead, and you, my love, are going to christen her."

Chapter Twenty-seven

The rest of the afternoon and early evening passed like a whirling kaleidoscope of impressions, none lasting long enough to imprint a real picture in Ginny's mind. People—she met so many people that she could remember none of them in the end. And every time that Steve introduced her as the Princess Sahrkanov, it was all she could do not to cringe. Oh, God, when Ivan found out! When her father found out! What was Steve doing?

There were many Spanish-speaking people—even fashionably dressed women who had accompanied their husbands on board. And after she had stood in a small, bobbing boat, with Steve's hands on her waist, supporting her while she swung a magnum of champagne against the ship's side, hearing the cheers mingled with the screeching of inquisitive seagulls, Ginny tried, deliberately, to keep her mind a blank.

It was Steve who made it difficult for her. Staying by her side, sometimes slipping a casual arm about her waist as if to announce his possession of her, he made it impossible for her to ignore the curious, somewhat sly looks she occasionally intercepted—the speculative whispers she knew were being exchanged.

By the time it was all over and they had started back for San Francisco, all the sails unfurled so that the vessel seemed to skim the surface of the water, Ginny was almost numb with a mixture of anger and apprehension.

"Would you like to stay out here on deck, or go back to the cabin for some more champagne?" How could he sound so calm, so matter of fact? As if—as if. . . .

Ginny swung on him in a sudden fury, wishing her head hadn't started to ache so.

"Have you succeeded in whatever it was you set out to do? Have you absolutely no conscience? Champagne! I've had so much champagne my head feels as if it is about to split in two, and you still have not given me any explanations for your behavior today—the way you tricked me."

Steve's voice hardened, and he caught her wrists in a grasp that made her wince.

"If you've a mind to make a scene, Ginny, we'd better go back to the cabin. You'll have your explanations there—if you're sure that's all you want."

She would have struck at him if he hadn't continued to hold her wrists, dragging her along with him in a typically high-handed fashion. And Ginny had time to wonder, after he had all but flung her into a chair and started to pour out two glasses of champagne without a word to her, why her feelings for Steve always kept her in such a state of turmoil. She had loved him, hated him, and thought she loved him again. And now—now she wasn't certain of anything!

"Here, drink your champagne. One more glass won't hurt you, and it might wipe that sullen look off your face. I thought you enjoyed surprises, Ginny. Or so you told me yesterday."

"I *know* what I said yesterday! And what *you* said. But today—why, Steve? What are you trying to prove? How is it—"

"I thought that should be obvious. I've been trying to

convince you that I can afford to keep a mistress—even if she happens to be the Tsar of Russia's daughter." In the face of her stunned silence, he made her a mocking half-bow, toasting her with his glass of champagne before he drained it. "Come to think of it, the situation *is* rather ironic, isn't it? Is that what's bothering you, my sweet? Don't worry—we'll both get used to it. After all, it's not as if we were strangers to each other, and I know how adaptable you are. In fact, I recall an occasion when you told me it was your ambition to have as many rich lovers as you wished. Surely you're not going to tell me you've changed your mind?"

White-faced, Ginny pressed her fingers against her temples, as if to still their throbbing; and the gesture, almost automatic with her of late, made Steve almost regret the studied cruelty of his words. Damn her! And damn his own obsession for her! One moment she was all spitting anger, and the next she looked exactly like a trapped, wounded creature.

"He really does hate me," Ginny was thinking dully. "He wants me only because he wants to hurt me more than he has done already. To make me his mistress, with the implication that I'm nothing but a high-priced whore. . . . Oh, I can't stand it!"

But he would make her stand it—hadn't he already shown how unscrupulous he was? And did she need reminding of how weak *she* was? Just now, at this very moment—she dared not meet his eyes for fear he would read, all too easily, what was in her mind. If he as much as touched her—if, instead of standing across the room, legs astraddle, studying her with that cruel, and yet strangely curious look, he were to take her in his arms. . . . Oh, no! Steve despised weakness. She had intrigued him in the first place because she had never stopped fighting him, forcing him to see her as an individual in her own right. She mustn't give in now.

"Well?" she heard him say, and then, in a sardonic drawl, "I must say that it's hardly flattering to have you go off into a brown study when I've been trying to get things straight between us. Or were you thinking of what explanations you'd make to your husband when he gets back from Sacramento?"

At last she raised her head and looked at him a trifle wildly, her eyes shining with the brilliance of the emerald she wore against her breasts.

"Sacramento? But how did you know that? He didn't even tell me where he was going."

Steve's face suddenly seemed closed and cold, as if a wooden shutter had dropped over it. But his voice remained unchanged.

"How inconsiderate of him, to be sure! Does he ever tell you where he goes or how long he plans to stay away?"

She imagined that there was something watchful in his eyes, and anger shook her, making her forget even the aching of her head for a moment.

"Why do you ask me such questions? What concern is it of yours?"

"But honey, anything that concerns you also concerns me—naturally! What's the matter, does it upset you to discuss your husband with me? Can it be that you actually feel some pangs of guilt?" As if her sudden silence irritated him, Steve slammed his empty glass down on the table and walked away from her, turning at last to lean one shoulder against the panelled side of the cabin, to regard her as if she had become a stranger.

"You're the only woman I've know who can try my patience to this extent. And make me lose my temper to the point where I lose my common sense! Thank God we're no longer married—at least *this* way, as lovers, we can still salvage the best part of the past! You always were an exciting and quite uninhibited mistress, Ginny. When I'm in bed with you I can forget what a scheming, faithless little bitch you are. It's a relief that *that's* your husband's problem now."

"Oh, God! You haven't changed at all, have you? You're still as cruel—and as selfish and used to getting your own way, no matter who you have to trample in the process! Why did you bring me here? Was it to tell me all this? To get your revenge on me?"

"Revenge?" He raised an eyebrow, his voice becoming caustic. "Why should I want to be revenged on you? We've both had a lucky escape, you and I, for we'd probably have led a miserable cat-and-dog existence if we continued to be tied to one another. Believe me, I'm almost grateful to you for using your head, and seizing the main chance, when it came along. A princess deserves a prince—and you, my love, glow like a jewel in your proper setting." She shuddered at the exaggeratedly flowery compliment, and he laughed shortly. "Ginny, we know each other too well to pretend, don't we? And I'm sure you're practical enough to see the advantages of an arrangement such as the one I've offered you. This way we can both have our cake and eat it—no jealous scenes, no questions. And since your husband travels about such a lot, we'll have lots of time to renew our ... acquaintance. Why don't you stop sulking and admit the truth of what I've been saying? I haven't had to rape you recently, after all."

"Oh, stop!" Ginny sprang to her feet, for all the world like a hunted animal, her hands clenched into fists at her side. "How can you speak so—so cold-bloodedly? Why do you continue to torment me so? You don't understand! You've told me nothing, nothing, of why you decided to come here; of why you take such risks—both with your own life and with—with *my* reputation! Yes, you can smile. What do you care, after all? You don't know what Ivan is like, but you have one thing in common, you and he—you are both completely without conscience or scruples! He'll have you killed, and if he finds out who you are he—"

With a long pantherish stride, Steve crossed the small space that separated them, his fingers clamping down on Ginny's shoulders, shaking her slightly as if to show how much he despised her sudden hysteria.

"Do you think I'm afraid of him? Or his hired strong-arm men? Or are you afraid *for* him? I don't like losing what's mine, Ginny; and I hadn't had time to tire of your passionate little body when he spirited you away. I realize that no man will ever possess you completely, because it's not in your nature to be faithful, any more than it is in mine. I think that's why we've always gotten along so well together—at least in bed! Don't tell me you've turned hypocrite at this late stage."

Pulling her against him, he kissed her. But after her first, almost mindless yielding, Ginny began to struggle

against him. She didn't quite understand why—perhaps it
was because of his contemptuously cutting words, or perhaps because he was kissing her as if he hated her; it was
the kind of kiss a man would bestow upon a whore who
pretended rejection but would give in, in the end. He
might desire her, but he also despised her—he had made
that much clear.

"Don't—don't!" she whispered frantically, twisting her
head away. "Please, Steve! I don't feel well, my head
aches."

"Christ!" He released her so suddenly that she stumbled
backward, ending up against a chair. "Have you turned
into a hypochondriac, too? Is this why your husband stays
away from you so much? All right, Ginny, I won't force
myself on you if the thought appalls you so much it gives
you a headache."

She felt almost blinded with pain, with the tears she was
trying to hold back. Somehow, fumbling, getting no help
at all from him, she felt along the back of the chair to
steady herself and dropped into it, her fingers going up in
the familiar motion, pressing hard against her temples as
if to push the agony away. Her whole body had begun to
shake with chills, and Steve's voice, suddenly charged with
some measure of humanity, seemed to come from a distance away.

"Ginny! My God—what's wrong? Are you really sick?
Was it the champagne?"

"My—I have to take a headache powder—please,
please, I cannot stand the pain! In my—I had one in my
reticule."

Without argument, without another word except the
ones he might have used to a strange woman who had embarrassed him by suddenly being taken ill, he brought her
what she wanted. The powder—a glass of cold water—
and then, over her muffled, half-formed protests, he carried her to the bed.

"Lie still, for God's sake, I'm not going to attack you!
How long does it take to act?"

"I don't—I can't think. It's one of those that you sent
me. Ivan's are stronger, but he only left me four—until he
came back, he said. I don't know what happens to me!
But Count Chernikoff says its just nerves."

"Ginny. . . ." She thought—imagined—that he sighed. "Close your eyes. Stop thinking, if you can." And surely it was only her imagination that she thought she heard him add, "I'm sorry. I let my temper get the best of me again." Steve never apologized, so, of course, she had to have dreamed it.

Later, swimming back to reality, it almost seemed as if no time had passed. There was still the rocking, creaking motion of the ship beneath her, and she was lying down in a comfortable bed, her hair miraculously loose around her shoulders. But it had become dark, somehow, except for a single dim light. She had opened her eyes. Her first feeling was one of relief, because the intolerable pounding in her temples had disappeared, and she felt relaxed and much stronger.

Steve sat at the table, the bottle of champagne replaced by a crystal decanter that was half-full of some amber colored liquid. His eyes caught and held hers. Why had he been watching her in such an intent fashion? He was frowning, but his voice, when he came to his feet and walked over to her, was quietly impersonal.

"Do you feel better?"

"Yes. Thank you."

How ridiculously formal they both sounded!

"Do you feel well enough to answer some questions?"

Her eyes widened. It was the last thing she expected, and especially from Steve.

"Questions, again?" she said, wondering why he continued to stand, looking down at her; the dim light behind him made his face unreadable.

"Yes, questions!" His voice had taken on the familiar, half-sarcastic note she was all too familiar with, and it helped her arm herself against him. "Don't look that way, Ginny. I'm not going to turn sea monster and attack you. But before I take you back, I think there are a few things we ought to find out about each other. Once we get them out of the way perhaps it will make for a smoother and less complicated relationship between us. Who knows, we might even end up becoming friends."

"Like you and Concepción, I suppose?" She couldn't resist the barb and saw his lips tilt in a one-sided smile.

"Yes—something like that."

He sat beside her, pretending not to notice that she stiff-ened instinctively.

"I don't trust you," she said honestly. "How can I? Right from the beginning you've tricked me and lied to me. You've pretended—"

"Damn it! I'm trying not to lose my temper again. Don't you see that's what I'm trying to put an end to?" And then, abruptly, the question startling her with its unexpectedness, "Are you in love with this new husband of yours? Is that why you married him?"

Ginny answered without thinking.

"No! No—I don't even like him! I never did, not from the beginning. But he—I don't even remember how it hap-pened, now! There was Carl—and before that, the shock of what they told me. I don't quite know how I found my-self on board that ship—I don't really even remember how we came to be married! That happened when Count Chernikoff was giving me medication because he said I was still suffering from the effects of shock. . . ."

It was strange, to be telling all this to Steve. To feel, as he listened carefully but without emotion, prompting her only occasionally, that he was someone she hardly knew.

"Are you trying to tell me that you were tricked into marriage? Just like Hoskins 'tricked' you into his clutches? Prince Sahrkanov must have fallen quite madly in love with you in the short time you knew each other! First, your captain is found dead in a cellar, with his throat slit; and the next thing one hears of you, you are on your way back to America with a Russian prince. His wife. He must have been impatient to make you his, and I suppose that once you found what had happened you decided to make the best of it. Is that how it was?"

Ginny sat bolt upright, glaring at him.

"There you go again! At one moment you pretend to be so understanding, and the next. . . . What about you? You're no saint, you know. And you haven't deigned to tell me yet what you're up to. I've heard nothing from you for months—you said yourself that you were well rid of me. And then—"

"You underestimate your powers of seduction, my love. How can any man turn his back on you? And besides, I had to find out."

"You're not Sam Murdock's bodyguard at all, are you?" Ginny said suddenly. "He told me he'd known your father, and that he's a friend of your grandfather—how did you persuade him to help you in your nefarious schemes? How could *you* re-name this ship, just on a whim?"

"Oh, Ginny! What a devious little mind you have! If you'll remember, I told you before that part of the reason I'm here is because I was curious to find out how you'd ended up. And then I discovered that you'd lost none of your attraction for me. Come on—" his voice changed, becoming harder, impatient. "We'd better hurry before they send out search parties to look for you. If we stay here, I'm liable to rape you after all."

She was almost weeping with rage and frustration.

"Is that all you have to say? You had to find out everything you could about me—even about my father, and Ivan. And you tell me nothing!" Her fingers tried to pull the heavy jewel from about her neck. "How did you afford this? Did you steal it, or is it only borrowed for the occasion? And those opals. . . ."

"I couldn't afford to buy you expensive trinkets before, but I can now. You see, I've been—lucky at speculation. For the first time in my life, I find myself in the possession of quite righteously acquired wealth. Sam Murdock and I are partners, in a way. Does that satisfy your curiosity?"

She was far too confused, too upset, to be fobbed off by his casually flung out and quite implausible explanations. Speculation—what did he mean by that? Why all the questions? And having dragged her on board this ship, he was now hustling her off it in a hurry.

This time the ship had sailed right into the bay and was moored by one of the docks at the section that was known as the Embarcadero. Ginny had driven down here before, to see the ships, and smell the salty air that seemed mixed with all the spices that were brought here from the Orient. During the day everything had been a bustle of activity: the shouts of dock laborers and seamen, the creaking of tall timbers, and the rattling whine of winches as cargo was unloaded.

But at night—how quiet it was by contrast. And it had turned quite cold. Ginny was glad of the warm silk and velvet cloak that Steve had flung around her shoulders, producing it, too, from the capacious closet set into the bulkhead of the stateroom they had occupied only minutes earlier.

"I suppose I shouldn't have kept you out so late, but you fell asleep as if someone had hit you over the head. How long have you been taking those powders, Ginny? Do you have any idea what's in those little packets?"

"All I know is that they make me feel—they send away my headaches, and make me stronger. If I don't have them, I begin to feel so ill. I—why do you look at me like that?"

"You didn't get headaches before, except when you'd had too much to drink. And I remember when your skin was a peachy-gold color—all over. Don't you go out in the sun any more?"

She wanted to pull away from him and run; she didn't care where to. How dare he keep tormenting her with his questions and criticism? It seemed that he liked nothing about her, and yet he kept telling her he still desired her—and he had placed her in an impossible, inconceivable position.

It was as if he could sense her rebellious thoughts. She felt his grip on her arm tighten, and he gave a curt, rather harsh laugh.

"At least you haven't forgotten how to argue! Or to make excuses for your behavior. I hope you have some plausible story ready to tell your parents when you get home—or shall I come in with you and explain?"

"Explain. . . ." She went quite pale. What on earth was she to say? And if Ivan had returned, it would be even worse. Yes, how was she to account for her long absence—her change of clothes?

Steve was already bundling her into the carriage, which seemed to have appeared from nowhere, the horses led by the same man who had seen them off earlier.

"Did you have a nice sail, sir? I guess you'll be wanting me to drive now."

The cloak had a hood which Steve adjusted politely over her windblown hair.

He sat beside her, too closely; as if by habit, he slipped one arm around her waist as they started off.

Ginny turned to him, her face a white blur in the darkness.

"It's all very well for you to talk of explanations, but if you come in the house with me my father would—I think he'd shoot you himself! *You're* the one who's so clever at deception, why don't *you* think of something?"

She had the feeling that he wasn't really listening to her. That already he was thinking of something else. He sounded almost absent-minded.

"Tell them you were with Sam—wasn't that what you originally had in mind? And don't worry, your husband won't be back yet. I think his business is going to take a little longer than he anticipated."

Chapter Twenty-eight

It was all Ginny could do to evade the questions that Sonya asked her later. And *those* questions were all mixed up with the questions that still remained in her own mind—questions she had asked Steve. So many puzzling things. And how cleverly he had managed to avoid answering them! He had silenced her with kisses, until her lips felt bruised, and she was out of breath. And the last thing he had said to her, before he boldly walked her up to the front door, was that he would see her again tomorrow.

Sonya followed Ginny up to her room, her manner agitated.

"Why couldn't you have sent us word? I'm glad your father had an engagement at his club tonight—he would have been really angry; and with me as well. Ginny, what happened?"

She felt reckless, careless, and almost too tired to lie.

"I went sailing. And then I had to christen a ship—the newest addition to the Lady Line. And afterwards there

was quite a party on board. Since the gown I had gone out
in was quite unsuitable—well, I was provided with another. Do you think it suits me?"

"And that jewel you're wearing, that emerald—do you
have any idea what it must be worth? Why, he's given you
a large fortune in jewels already, but *this*. . . . Ginny, are
you sure—"

"Mr. Murdock has not made me his mistress, if that's
what you are worried about."

Delia, silent and big-eyed, was unhooking Ginny's gown;
although pretending not to listen, she drank in every word.
And it was the maid's presence that made Sonya decide to
leave Ginny alone until morning. In any case, when her
stepdaughter withdrew into one of her stubborn moods,
there was nothing to be obtained by being persistent. Perhaps William would know how to handle the matter.

But Sonya had more to worry about the next day. She
had stayed up late, waiting for the Senator to return, and
had found him curiously unhelpful, far too absorbed in his
own problems.

"Sonya, we must try and remember that Ginny is an
adult now, and a married woman. We can only advise her.
And to tell you the truth—" he was taking a turn around
the room, frown-lines etched in his forehead—"I can't afford to antagonize Sam Murdock. He's my only hope right
now, as a matter of fact! I might as well tell you—I've
lost quite a packet on the market, and part of it is money
that Ivan gave me to invest for him. But Murdock has
been helpful—just the mention of his name has helped. I'll
be able to pay my princely son-in-law off now, and I cannot pretend that it won't be a relief. I've heard some
pretty unsavory things about him recently, and just
tonight. . . ." Here the Senator's lips clamped together as if
he had said too much, and Sonya, recognizing the stubborn look on his face, gave a small sigh.

"I suppose you won't tell me any more. And I will not
press you. But William, there's Ginny—she's your daughter! What are we going to do about her? I mean—if Mr.
Murdock is really taken with her, and it's obvious she is
willing to accept his attentions and the gifts he keeps
showering upon her—surely there's something we can do?
I don't think her marriage is a happy one, and I. . . . Oh,

William, surely there's a way out. I've been so much on edge, so terrified that somehow something might leak out."

"We promised each other we would not discuss that subject!" the Senator said sharply. "Do you have any conception of what such a scandal would mean to me, to my career—especially *now*? We've discussed the matter before, and there's no other solution than to keep silent. Do you understand?"

Sonya understood, only too well, and she kept discreetly silent as they went upstairs to bed. But all the same, she could not help wondering if for once William might be wrong. There *had* to be an answer, and perhaps, if she could persuade Ginny to confide in her, they could find one together. Tomorrow, Sonya thought, as she brushed out her hair before the mirror, tomorrow she would speak to Ginny, and find out exactly how far things have gone. Perhaps, if Ginny found her sympathetic and willing to help, she would talk to her at last.

Sonya slept late the next morning. They all did, except for Ginny.

Going down to breakfast on her husband's arm, Sonya was smiling, until she entered the sunlit morning room and encountered Concepción's sullen look. Really, there were times when she positively disliked the girl! For all her flamboyant beauty and the attention men paid her, there was something quite common about her—a hint of a jungle animal, barely leashed under her surface good manners. But this morning it seemed that even the good manners were lacking.

"If you're looking for *her*," Concepción said, "she's gone out already. And she didn't tell me when she'd be back." She looked as if she would have liked to say more, but instead she bit her full lower lip and looked more sulky than ever.

It was left to Sonya to smooth over the awkward moment, with William frowning again, and her own face flushing with apprehension. She gave a significant look at the soft-footed houseboy and said brightly:

"Oh? Well then, I expect she had some shopping to do and wanted to get it done early. She did go to bed before nine last night, after all."

"It wasn't for shopping she went out. I was awake early, too. *He* came for her, and she went out—just like that. It's a good thing Prince Sahrkanov is not here, is it not?"

It appeared, by dint of tactful questioning, that Ginny had been awakened by a message, carried by one of Sam Murdock's bodyguards. And with the pretext that she wanted to disturb no one, the girl had left without a word. She was really going too far!

But Sonya kept her thoughts to herself, and eventually Concepción excused hersel fairily, anonuncing that she intended to go for a ride in her new carriage. In fact, she intended to drive herself.

"I am going to meet Eddie. At the Cliff House," she added defiantly. "You don't have to worry that Sam would mind, he lets me do as I please. And Red Mustache can ride behind me." As a parting shot, she said over her shoulder, as if she'd only just remembered, "Oh, by the way, there was a letter—a note from Sam for you, Senator. I think the servant took it into your study. He's just come back to town, and he would like to lunch with you at ... what is the name of the place? Yes, the Auction Lunch Saloon—it is such a funny name, I always think when I hear it!"

"I suppose she read the note!" Sonya burst out uncontrollably when the door had closed. "Really, William, I hate to sound uncharitable, but I *do* hope his house is finished soon, or that he has other plans for her. I just cannot like her!"

But the Senator was frowning abstractedly down at his plate.

"I wonder. ... Murdock has been in Virginia City, you know. Perhaps he's learned the truth behind some of those wild rumors we've been hearing recently. But I wonder why she said he's only just come back to town? Ginny was out with him yesterday afternoon, was she not?"

Ginny herself was completely unaware of all the undercurrents that were even then swirling about, threatening to trap her. Last night, she had tried not to lie to Sonya. And when, far too early in the morning, Delia had tiptoed into her room with a conspiratorial air to inform her that a gentleman was waiting, she had dressed and gone downstairs without giving herself time to think.

He was standing in the entrance hall, looking perfectly at ease. But as he watched her descend the staircase, she could see the dancing, reckless devil-lights in his dark blue eyes.

"Have you gone completely out of your mind?" She hissed the words at him in an angry whisper, guiltily turning her head to make sure no one else was about. "What are you doing here? You're just lucky that my father and Sonya are still asleep."

"And so are you. But it's high time you were awake. There are too few days like this in San Francisco to be wasted."

Distractedly, Ginny put her hands to her hair, carelessly tied at the nape of her neck with a wide green ribbon that matched her gown.

"You *are* crazy!"

"How would you like to breakfast on oysters and hot French bread?"

He caught her hands in his, pulling her close, and her indrawn breath betrayed her. Why did she have to grow so weak whenever Steve touched her?

"You're insufferable!"

He bent his head, suddenly kissing the hollow at the base of her throat, and then brushing his lips over hers.

"Shall we give the servants something to gossip about, or are you coming with me?"

Ginny told herself, as an excuse, that there were still too many questions Steve had left unanswered. She had had time to think, when she lay in bed last night, her mind a tumult of mixed emotions. And he probably meant what he said about giving the servants something to gossip about—she wouldn't put anything past him!

In the end, the morning passed in a kind of haze. He took her to a small cafe that was run by an immigrant Frenchman and his wife, and then they walked on the beach, holding hands like lovers.

Ginny's mood seesawed between despair and exhilaration. She had still no idea of what Steve's real purpose was, or why he had suddenly made his pursuit of her—if pursuit it was—so obvious. But did she really want to think too hard about it yet? It was such a beautiful day—too beautiful to be spoiled by dark thoughts and suspicions. The usual morning fog had long since been burned away, and the sweep of the bay looked the color of lapis laz-uli—varying shades of blue and green, its surface was dotted with fishing boats.

For a little while, at least, she was determined to be happy, and to try and forget the barrier that existed between them, and Steve seemed to feel the same way. He had teased her and paid her extravagant compliments, and for the moment the cynical and somewhat guarded look had left his face.

He was actually laughing at her for not being quick enough to avoid a cold wavelet that had soaked through her shoes and stockings and left the hem of her dress sodden.

"And *now* what are you going to do? Take off your shoes and stockings and walk about barefoot?" He bent his head and whispered, with a tremor of laughter still underlying his voice. "Don't look now, but I can see two obviously maiden ladies of pompous respectability eyeing you through their lorgnettes. I think they must mistake you for a *fille de joie*, recuperating after a long night's work!"

"Of course I am going to take off my shoes," she retorted, clinging to his arm in order to keep her balance. You cannot imagine how unpleasant it feels to have a shoe full of sand and water! And I think you're teasing me about those respectable ladies, for what would they be doing out here at this time in the morning?"

"You can't see them—they're behind you, seated on one of those benches the city has so thoughtfully provided. But I think you ought to give them a better look at you, you green-eyed sea waif!"

Before she could protest, or even begin to struggle, Steve had scooped her up in his arms, carrying her willy-nilly depositing her on a stone bench that was located right beside the one occupied by the two ladies he had spoken of.

Ginny could not help shooting a swift sideways glance in that direction; and then, with a small gasp, she quickly lowered her head and began to fumble with the buttons of her ruined kid boots.

Perhaps if she pretended she had not seen them—but of all the unfortunate coincidences! One of them was none other than the sister-in-law of the same Mrs. Baxter she had met in Vera Cruz, and the other was an inveterate gossip to whom she had been introduced recently at a reception.

"Here, let me do that. Your fingers are fumbling as if they're frozen."

Steve's voice was noncommittal, but when he had hunkered down on his heels before her, Ginny caught his frowning upward glance. He said quietly, "You've gone as pale as. . . . Do you know them?"

Clasping her icy-cold fingers together to stop their trembling, Ginny nodded.

Everything she had tried to put out of her mind this morning had come flooding back. Ivan, who was due back at any time—who had boasted he had her constantly watched. Her impossibly untenable position. She must be mad—*Steve* must be mad! She felt terrified. And Steve sensed it. She knew it from the rather rough way he jerked her stockings off, and even before she saw his face.

"Afraid of gossip, Princess?"

Ginny flushed uncomfortably at the sarcasm in his tone, but before she could frame a reply, a rather high and piercing voice said:

"Excuse the intrusion, but—it *is* the Princess Sahrkanov, is it not? I was just telling Mrs. Atherton that I pride myself on my memory for faces. And *how* is the dear Senator? We were down at Belmont last week, and I understand we just missed each other. . . ."

Ginny had no recourse but to acknowledge the ladies politely, her color still embarrassingly high. And—there was no help for it—to introduce Steve, who seemed maliciously determined to place her in a worse position than ever.

"Mrs. Terence Atherton, Miss Baxter, this is Mr. Smi—" Ginny's voice stumbled, she could not help it, even while she thought furiously to herself that the ladies would never, never believe her!

Surprisingly, it was Steve himself who "rescued" her, interrupting with a charming smile and a bow for the two women who stared at him with narrow-eyed, disapproving curiosity.

"Oh, there's no need to bother with *that* where these ladies are concerned. Mrs. Atherton, I've had the great pleasure of meeting your husband in New York, ma'am.

Miss Baxter, I've heard Sam Murdock speak of your fine work as a trustee for the Select Young Ladies' Academy many times."

Both women bridled; Miss Baxter leaned forward, her lorgnette held to her nose, while Ginny wanted to stamp her foot with rage.

"But surely—is it possible that we have met before?"

"I've forgotten my manners. I apologize. The name is Morgan. Steven Morgan. Sam Murdock and I are business associates. And the Princess Sahrkanov, of course," he added, taking Ginny's hand and holding it a shade too long, is a very old friend. . . ."

"A very old friend indeed! The way you said it! You might as well have come right out and announced that you'd been my lover once. And you never mentioned that you had been in New York, *or* that Mr. Murdock was thinking of appointing you a trustee in his place. *You*, of all people! I'd fear for the virtue of those poor young girls in the Academy if *that* should ever happen." Ginny was breathless with rage—her eyes seemed to shoot fiery sparks at her companion, who leaned back in the carriage with his arms negligently crossed and his black hat pulled down over his forehead. "Ooh! Damn you, Steve! Will you stop pretending to—to ignore me? How *dared* you tell them you were going to buy me a new pair of shoes to replace the ones that were ruined by the water? It will be all over town by now—I've no doubt that even Sonya will have heard by the time I return. Oh—oh *damn*!" she swore furiously, on the verge of tears by now. "Don't you care about *anything*, Steve Morgan? Do you know what you've done?"

At last he pushed his hat back on his head and sat up with an expression that mixed anger and disgust.

"You sound like a virago, for God's sake! Why don't you try to control yourself? Those two old gossips will hold their tongues, I think—for a short while, anyhow, while they relish the thought that they've been let in on a secret. I told them I was using the name of Smith because I was negotiating a very imptrtant business deal—didn't you see how flattered they looked? Sam contributes quite a bit of money to Miss Baxter's precious Academy, so she won't be in a hurry to talk. And Mrs. Atherton will con-

fide in her husband, who will tell her to keep it dark while
he tries to find out what stock I'm buying. So—"

"Is that *all* you have to say? And what about *me*?
They've done nothing but whisper about me from the beginning, and *now*—oh, they won't let such a particularly
juicy piece of gossip go untold! They might protect you—
you're a man after all—but they'll tell everyone that I was
walking on the beach with a man who was not my husband. They'll say—"

"Is *that* who you're afraid of? Your devoted Prince?
Does he beat you, Ginny?"

She burst into tears, shocking herself, and heard Steve
curse softly and explicitly beside her.

"Have you just developed another of your headaches?
Or—does he really beat you? Somehow, I can't imagine
you putting up with anything like that!" His voice turned
harsh, and he put his hand under her chin, forcing her
face around to his. "Damn it, stop crying. It's not going to
help. Does he hurt you? How long have you been afraid
of him?"

In the space of less than an hour, everything had changed
between them again. Through eyes swimming with tears,
Ginny saw the face of a hard, unsympathetic stranger, who
slashed at her nerves with his questions.

"He only asks them to hurt me. He does not really
care," a voice kept whispering at the back of her mind,
making her stubborn in spite of her tears of weakness and
frustration.

"Of course he doesn't beat me!" she flung back at him,
choking over her own sobs. "I—we do not get on very
well, at times, but what does that matter, after all? At
least we don't see too much of each other, and when I go
to Russia—"

"To Russia!" Steve's fingers dropped from under her
chin, and he leaned back with a harsh, ugly laugh. "So
you're actually planning to carry your schemes all the way
through, are you? I'm sure the Tsar will be charmed—
who can help but be?"

"But as long as I am *here* I—I cannot afford a scandal,
don't you see? If—Ivan finds out, he'll kill you! And he—
no doubt he'd find some way to punish me. The last time
he took away all my powders, and even the tonic Count
Chernikoff prescribed for me. Steve, please."

She shrank from the look in his eyes, her fingers, which had instinctively clutched at his sleeve, dropping away.

"So *that's* it. It's not jewels or expensive gowns that can buy your favors, but your precious powders. And I'm supposed to leave town, I suppose, to keep your husband from creating a scandal until he gets you safely to Russia—where, no doubt, you'll get rid of one husband in order to pick another." He spoke between his teeth, and the contempt in his voice made Ginny want to scream at him hysterically. He was twisting everything up!

"You're wrong! You—"

"Am I? Do you mean to tell me that you don't realize what you've become? You're an addict—it's an expression they use to describe people who let themselves become slaves to some drug. And in your case, my dear Princess Sahrkanov, it's opium. Didn't you ever ask yourself why you had become so dependent on your powders and your tonics? Or why your head aches and you feel as if you are getting chills when you don't have them?"

"No—no! That's not true, you're only saying all these things to—"

"You're damn right! You need to be frightened back into the possession of your wits. And as long as Sahrkanov controls you by his threats to withhold your sweet dreams, you're not going to be rid of him as easily as you think!"

"I don't want to hear any more. And I don't know why you've been wasting your time and your money on me, unless it was to do just *this,* to ruin my life—ruin everyone connected with me!"

"Christ, spare me the melodrama, Ginny. You certainly didn't ruin my life by running off the way you did—in fact, when I didn't have to worry about you any longer I found I could concentrate on other things, such as making money! I ought to be grateful to you, in a way. So why in hell should I want to ruin your life?"

"Well, then"—almost hysterical with rage and humiliation now, she almost shrieked the words at him—"why did you come back into my life? Why?"

His face seemed closed against her, suddenly wiped clear of emotion of any kind, even the anger and contempt she had discerned earlier. Producing a handkerchief from his pocket he handed it to her, saying only:

"Wipe your face, Ginny. And for God's sake, take one of your powders, if that's what it takes to calm you. Can't you see it's pointless for us to indulge in recriminations at this stage?"

"Recriminations! What do you suggest I do?" She wadded up the handkerchief, longing to throw it back at him. "My father has posted a reward on your head—what do you think he's going to do when he finds out? I've been lying to everyone, and you've encouraged me to do so."

His next statement, although delivered in the same expressionless voice he had used earlier, reverberated in her mind with all the force of a thunderclap.

"Since you've asked my advice, you'd better not tell anyone you've been with Sam this morning. He's lunching with the Senator today at the Auction Lunch Saloon."

Chapter Twenty-nine

For as long as she lived, Ginny would never forget the rest of that afternoon. She was painfully reminded of the time when she had been Steve's hostage—his captive whore, forced to do whatever he demanded, in spite of her own rebellious thoughts.

She had become no more than a pawn to him again—to be used in whatever devious game he was playing this time. And again, as in the past, she was completely helpless to withstand him.

"You want me to save your precious reputation? Then you'll do exactly as I tell you, Princess. And wipe your face, to begin with. Do you want to start everyone asking questions?"

He bought her shoes and stockings at an exclusive little French boutique where the salesladies seemed to know him. And, against her will, he bought her several dainty items of female underwear. And an expensive ball dress at yet another, even more exclusive store.

"The gown will be delivered early this evening. Wear it."

"You—you're mad!" Ginny exclaimed feebly, dragged along—she felt—in his arrogant wake.

Steve gave her a long, considering look. "Wear that emerald pendant with it. I'll give you the earrings that match it when we go up to the house. And one of the maids will dry and press your gown."

"I—I have a headache. Steve, I really do! And I don't believe what you said, that I'm an—"

"'There are worse names I could call you. And will call you, if you don't shut up, Ginny!"

He took her up to Sam Murdock's house—*his* house? Dragged her up the stairs past the gaping workmen and into the bedroom he had taken her into before. Tumbled her on the bed and raped her. There was no other word for it.

And the worst part of it was that she was powerless to resist him. Her body responded in spite of herself, even while she cried out that she hated him, despised him beyond measure.

"Get dressed, Ginny." Even the sound of *that* was famliar. The gown she had worn that morning looked as fresh as if it had been taken from her closet at that very moment.

"What are you doing? You are making everything much worse."

"I'm giving you ten minutes, Ginny. That should be sufficient. Shall I send the maid in to help you with your hair?"

Only a few minutes ago she had imagined that his breathing was as fast as hers. Now, he seemed perfectly calm and unmoved, as if it had meant nothing to him.

"If I had a knife, I would use it on him—and this time I would aim for his black heart!" Ginny thought furiously to herself. He had even dared, on the way here, to question her again about Carl Hoskins' death. Had hinted that she and Ivan between them had planned it all, hoping that the blame would be laid at *his* door.

"He was found in the cellar of an abandoned building by some of his friends, with a knife wound in his throat. Are you sure you only hit him with a bottle? The knife— that seems more your style."

Ginny felt as if she had been dragged through a wringer by the time he handed her, overly politely, into the waiting carriage. He had allowed her to take one of her powders—he almost reminded her of Ivan! Yes, he was completely pitiless; why hadn't she realized that before?

And of all places, he took her to the Cliff House. Of course he had known that Concepción would be there, with her devoted Englishman. The Viscount was puzzled, but amiable. Concepción was, as usual, herself. And Ginny, to her fury, found herself carrying on a stiltedly polite conversation with young Marwood, to a background of angrily muttered Spanish that she could not help but understand.

"You go too far, Esteban! Why should I be the one to rescue her? I have scores to settle with her, the bitch! And you—you should count yourself well rid of her. No, I tell you—I am going to marry Eddie, and he will take me away, why should I care?"

Steve's voice softened to a steely murmur, and Concepción began to shrug sulkily.

"Oh, very well! Just this once then—and don't you dare lay a hand on me, bastardo!"

The hissed invective was close enough to its English equivalent to make the Viscount cast a confused look in the direction of Concepción, who gave him a flashing smile, and laid her hand on his arm.

"You must forgive us please, Eddie. Esteban thinks he must act like my big brother, and I keep telling him it is not necessary, this. Sì?" An uncontrollable touch of malice made her voice far too sweet. "*I* tell him he had much better think of his own safety, and his *friend's* reputation first."

"Uh—well. . . . Really, I don't feel—"

"Concepción likes to tease, don't you niña?" Steve smiled, but something in his expression made Concepción lower her eyes and murmur sullenly that of course she was joking, surely they all understood that.

By this time Ginny was almost past caring. She had been pushed around, manipulated, used. But surely she ought to be accustomed to that? It seemed to her that whenever she had begun to feel truly happy, that happiness had been snatched away from her. Feeling a wave of cynical self-pity, she looked up and met Steve's

eyes for a moment. They seemed the dark, opaque blue
eyes of a stranger, weighing her, calculating how much
further use she might be to him. How many more shocks
would he deal her before he tired of his game?

Ginny felt that she had already put up with too much
for one day, and although her return to the house with a
dangerously tight-lipped Concepción and her tactful escort
went unremarked except by the servants, she went straight
to her room to swallow one of her headache powders.
What if they did contain a small quantity of opium? It
was used in other medicines too, for its soothing effects.
Steve had no right to tell her she had become a slave to
the habit, just like those poor Chinese she had read about
who spent all their days in opium dens. Surely the stuff
had to be smoked in order to be habit-forming. And there
was a certain amount of opium in all tonics—even in
cough medicines.

"It's not true," Ginny said to her white-faced reflection
in the mirror. Steve was not a doctor—he had only made
it up to frighten her. Just as he'd made up that improbable
story about Carl Hoskins. Shock or not, she could remember far too clearly the look of agony on Carl's face when
she had hit him—the way the bottle had splintered, with
the wine and blood running together. . . .Steve was deliberately trying to confuse her.

Sighing, Ginny turned away from the mirror and crossed
to her bed, wearing only her shift. She was filled with
a sense of uneasy apprehension, knowing that the absence
of both Sonya and her father meant only a temporary
reprieve. What did Sam Murdock have to discuss with the
Senator? Perhaps he was tired of lying for Steve, partner
or not. But that meant. . . .

I won't think about it until I have to, Ginny told herself
firmly. As she lay down, closing her eyes, she felt the slow,
gradual easing of her tension. She had taken the last of
the little packets of white powder that Ivan had left for
her, and they always worked much faster than the others.
Why had Steve bothered to get her some if he thought she
was becoming addicted? Nothing made sense, and thinking, just now, was too much trouble.

She might have slept. Or perhaps she had only begun to
drift into that dream world that dwelt on the threshold of
sleep itself. Over and over, her mind had been repeating,

"I'm not going to be hurt again—no one will ever be allowed to hurt me." She had visions of watching herself tear her heart out and setting a smooth, polished stone in its place. The stone turned into a diamond that flashed like fire through her skin, blinding everyone who came too close to her.

Then the dream disappeared, and Ginny found herself staring up into Concepción's tawny eyes.

"Wake up!" the young woman repeated. "You could not have fallen asleep so soon—unless you have been doing something that would tire you out." She laughed sneeringly as Ginny sat up with her hair tumbling over her shoulders, an angry frown on her face.

"What are you doing here?" They had both slipped, almost unconsciously, into the familiar Mexican dialect, and the memories that this brought made Ginny's heart beat faster. She pushed her hair back from her forehead with an arrogant gesture that made Concepción's eyes narrow.

"I thought it was high time we had a heart-to-heart talk, you and I. I was not meant to play the hypocrite, and I am getting very tired of being forced to tell lies to protect you!" The girl had begun to pace back and forth across the rug, between the window and Ginny's bed. Her hair, too, hung loose, and she looked more of a wild animal than ever. "You cannot know how often I've longed to be able to use my knife on you—you tricked me the last time we fought, by tripping me, but *this* time. . . .I think this civilization has made you soft, and frightened, even of what people might say. Hah!" Concepción tossed her head, hair flying. "You are not much of a woman any more. You should stick to the kind of man who likes your type."

"A real woman doesn't have to advertise the fact, as crudely as you seem to do!" Ginny retorted, swinging her feet off the bed. "What did you come here for? Was it to provoke me into a screaming match with you?"

Concepción's red lips curled back from her teeth.

"I came here to tell you a few things—to tell you the truth, unless you are afraid to hear it. Or did you really imagine that Esteban came here because he wanted you?"

"You sound like a jealous shrew," Ginny said contemptuously. Ignoring Concepción, she walked to her dresser and began to brush out her hair. "Is that all you had to say?" She saw in the mirror how the girl's fingers curled into claws.

"No, that is not all!" Concepción burst out. "And if you have any pride, you had better listen. You see, I've known Esteban for many, many years. We've been friends, and more than friends, as you very well know. We were together, he and I, the day that interfering Mr. Bishop came to the hacienda."

"Mr. Bishop?" Ginny's hand paused in mid-stroke, and suddenly, the other woman's sneering laugh grated along her nerve ends.

"Yes! Mr. Bishop! Why did you think Esteban came to San Francisco in the first place? He was going to travel to Europe, and take me with him—he had already forgotten you! And then this Mr. Bishop came."

Ginny put the brush down very slowly and turned around.

"Go on."

"So now, at last, you are listening? You are beginning to understand? Yes, why do you think Esteban asked you so many questions, and particularly about your Prince? Did you think he was jealous, eh? You stupid, prideless fool! When he gave you jewels and made love to you, do you think it meant anything? He's rich enough now that a few trinkets have the same significance as the giving of flowers would to another man. And as for the other—" Concepción's eyes moved with contemptuous insolence over Ginny's body, and her white teeth gleamed. "Do I have to say it? You are a female, and it's clear that you still nurture a passion for him, for why else would you be so eager to succumb? Besides, it would make it easier for him to learn what he came here to learn—all about the wretched, dirty traffic your Prince has been mixed up in."

It all fell into place, quite relentlessly and with unbearable logic, as Ginny continued to listen in spite of herself and the sudden pounding in her ears. How clearly she saw the truth now. Steve had been politely blackmailed by Bishop—but Steve also had his own axe to grind. He was angry at her father. It was not only Ivan he meant to ruin, but her father as well.

"Your prince—" why did Concepción keep using the term? "Did you know that he's been stealing money from the Russian-American Company and giving it to your father to invest for him? And then, when the value of the shares started to drop, he went into another line of business. Your father owns shares in the Lady Line. Before Steve bought out the other shareholders to gain the controlling interest, that was how your prince got into the business of bringing both opium and pretty female slaves from China. Don't pretend you didn't know!"

No—how could she have known? Lost in her own misery, she had not even wondered, had never once asked Ivan in what "business" dealings he was involved.

"Well, let me tell you that it's all over now. They know—the people Esteban has been working for. And the people your Prince was working with, *they* know, too, that he is finished—why do you think they sent a man to kill him? Better watch out for yourself, because if he comes to trial *you* will be forced to give evidence against him—unless you are involved yourself! What a pretty scandal, eh?"

"But I'm Ivan's wife. They cannot make me give evidence against him."

Knowing that she had the upper hand now, Concepción's throaty laugh rang with a mixture of triumph and spite.

"So you would like to continue being a Princess? It's too bad. If I were you I'd run away to Russia and find another prince there. For you see, idiota, you are not Ivan's wife—and because of this, if Esteban wanted to make the facts public, there will be much more disgrace and trouble for your family. This annulment they told you of—there was never one. Your papa was never told where your ill-fated marriage took place, nor on what date—so after he had tried a few times, he gave up. But because he wanted a Prince for his son-in-law, instead of an outlaw, he said there was no marriage. . . . You begin, now, to comprehend? Your are a bigamist, Princessa! And if you do not want it made public, you should be a good little girl, sí? And do as you are told. No doubt," Concepción added carelessly, "Esteban will divorce you as soon as he can. I am sure he will have no difficulty."

With an effort of sheer will, Ginny straightened her shoulders, her eyes refusing to drop from the narrow, tawny ones that confronted her maliciously, waiting for her to break. But she would not break, she would not!

"Now that you've unburdened yourself, perhaps you

wouldn't mind telling me why you have done so? Surely your revenge, and Steve's, would have been much more effective if you'd let all this come as a surprise, and at exactly the right time. Don't try to tell me your black little heart was stirred by some notion of compassion!"

"You bitch, you haven't lost the edge off your tongue yet, have you? But I think you will, in the end. The only reason I told you is because Esteban has developed some strange sense of honor since he and his grandfather have made up." Concepción's mouth twisted in a sulky grimace for a moment. "He might feel sorry for you, especially since Don Francisco took such a liking to you. I have warned you—so that you can go away, while there's time. That old Count seemed very anxious to take you off to Russia with him—why don't you go? I think you would be better off there."

"Of course"—and Ginny was surprised that her voice managed to sound so cold and dispassionate—"you could be lying, to get me out of the way. Or because you're afraid you're going to lose Steve to me permanently. Why should I believe anything you say?"

"What a stupid cow you are!" Concepción stamped her foot, and for a moment Ginny actually thought she was going to spit. "Do not believe me then! Find out for yourself! Yes, maybe it would be better that way—you deserve what you get, and it will all work out the same way in the end. Even if Esteban decides to stay married to you, he's not going to feel more than contempt or pity—he'll send you back to the country. You can go to the hacienda and look after the old man with a duena trailing at your heels. Me, I'd rather be his mistress than a wife!" The young woman almost ran to the door, and then, turning, snarled with barely suppressed violence: "Why don't you go downstairs and find out what your father and stepmother are talking about behind the locked doors of his study? Ah, really! You're blind because you don't *want* to see! *They* have no choice now, either. Sam has been telling your father some facts—and we are all going to the opera together and after that to a grand reception at the Palace Hotel. Perhaps Esteban will choose to make his announcement then?"

The slamming of the door kept reechoing in Ginny's ears; a diminishing thunderclap. She swayed on her feet, her fingers clutching just in time at the edge of her dressing table.

"No, no, no!" She hardly realized she had said the words aloud until her mind answered her back. Yes, yes! It was all true. Concepción had been too triumphant, too sure of her facts to have been bluffing. The pieces clicked together in her brain, fitting as neatly as a jigsaw puzzle to form the whole, unpleasant picture. She should have guessed—but like some spineless bitch in heat she had allowed herself to be used, blinded by Steve's expert, calculated lovemaking. He didn't love her. If he ever had loved her, it was all gone now, leaving nothing but bitterness. His every move had been carefully planned—he would exhibit her publicly as his mistress before he casually admitted that she was his wife, after all. What did he plan to do afterwards? Divorce her? Send her into seclusion while he continued to go his way?

She had fallen asleep swearing that she would never let herself be hurt again. She had dreamed of tearing her own heart out. For a moment Ginny found herself bent almost double with the sick pain of grief and anguish that twisted like a knife inside her. She wanted to weep, to have the excuse to cry out hysterically, but no tears came to ease her. Then she pushed herself erect, staring at the reflection of her glaring eyes, like green lamps amid the coppery tangle of her hair.

With an unplanned, vicious gesture, Ginny snatched up her brush and flung it at the mirror, laughing at the crashing noise it made, unmindful of the tiny, flying splinters that cut her face and hands.

Closing her eyes, she sucked in a deep breath. "No one will ever use me again. I swear it to myself. No one. And I won't let myself be hurt—never again."

From now on she would depend only on herself. She would trust nobody. Not even her so-called father, who had also attempted to use her in his way. Had the Senator, her "father" ever cared for her? He'd wanted her only as a useful asset—when she was old enough and pretty enough to be an asset. And now—let Steve do whatever he pleased. She didn't care any longer. Let them all suffer for a change!

She was breathing heavily, as if she had been running for a long time. Anger, humiliation, a painful sense of her

own degradation made her move like an automation, not
conscious of anything beyond the urge to keep moving, to
get away from everyone and everything—to be the one
who dealt out hurt for a change. "I hate him, I hate him,"
her mind screamed silently. "I hate them all—hypocrites,
exploiters!"

She was dressed—her oldest, ugliest bonnet pulled over
her carelessly pinned-up hair. She had no idea yet where
she was running to, or what she would do, but what did it
matter? Just get away, and let them wonder, let them look
for her while everything crashed down about their heads.
She could be an entertainer, dance in some saloon somewhere. Or become a whore—she'd had plenty of experience in *that* line too! She almost giggled, from sheer hysteria, and swallowed one powder—then, recklessly, another,
stuffing all she had left right at the bottom of her reticule.
Addict, was she? A slave? We'll see. It shouldn't be too
hard to find a man who would be willing to provide anything she wanted. And then, some sense filtering through
the mist of rage, she flung open the lid of her jewelery
box, pushing everything into her purse. Jewels never lost
their value, and these were worth a fortune anywhere.
Hadn't everyone told her so? She smiled to herself, a
wicked thinning of her lips. Let Steve think about *that*
later. His carelessly bestowed gifts would bring her freedom. They were like so many eyes glinting up at her.
Opals and diamonds and the single big emerald—the eye
of an enormous cat, winking back at her with a fire that
matched that in her own eyes. "What will you do when
you find you've bought yourself a shadow, Steve, darling?
I'd like to make you a laughingstock, just like you've made
me." A pity she no longer carried a knife—this time, her
blade wouldn't miss if she saw him again. But she
wouldn't—she didn't want to set eyes· on him again, never,
never!

The house was very quiet, but she went down the back
stairs in any case, wanting no one to see her.

"Jameson, would you bring out the small buggy, please?
No—I'm going to drive myself, and it's all right. I won't
be gone long, there's just something very important I have
to do." She improvised quickly, seeing the doubtful look
on the man's face. "I have to meet some one. It's Mr.
Murdock, if anyone asks you, or if I'm not back in time.'

"Mr. *Sam* Murdock, Princess?"

The dark face suddenly became expressionless, and Ginny knew that the servants had heard all the gossip. Of course they would have!

She smiled. Charmingly, a trifle conspiratorially.

"Yes, although it's supposed to be a surprise. But I can tell *you*, I'm sure, and know it won't go further. Please, would you hurry? I have to be back in time to dress for the opera and the reception tonight, and it's getting awfully late. There'll be a big tip for you, of course, you know how generous Mr. Murdock is!"

"Yes ma'am!" And then, with a trace of doubt still remaining in his voice, the man said, "But the Senator. . . ."

"That's part of the surprise. You will not let us down, will you?"

He went away quickly then, and Ginny tried to hide her impatience. They couldn't stop her, of course. No one could, even if she had to hire a carriage. And Sam Murdock's name worked its usual magic.

It would be some time before Delia went up to her room to help her dress, and found the note she had addressed to Sonya!

I have decided to run away from my husband, whom I detest, to my lover. Attempting to find me, as I am sure you will realize, will only mean an even bigger scandal than is already brewing. It would be best for all concerned if you let me go in peace, or I will make the scandal.

Sonya would understand. Or if she did not, then Steve would. And there was time, yet. There were the riverboats—and ships that would take her to any part of the world.

The further she went, the better. For the first time in her life, Ginny would depend on no one but herself and her own wits.

Jameson, looking dubious again, brought the buggy around at last, and Ginny gave him a brilliant smile, along with two gold eagles.

"I should be back within an hour, with no one any the wiser. Thank you, Jameson!"

There—that had done it. And she had escaped! How easy it had been! Why hadn't she done so before? "Then I would not have had to meet Steve again, and realize. . . ." she cut off the treacherous thought, trying to concentrate on driving the buggy through the crowded streets and avoid the glances thrown at her at the same time. A woman, driving herself. What was so strange about that? She had tried to dress as plainly as she could, and the unshapely bonnet covered her hair. What made these men stare?

They were staring because in spite of what she considered a disguise, she was still a beautiful woman. The buggy she drove was new and obviously expensive, the horse a thoroughbred. And in any case, it was unusual to see a woman driving herself. The men who gaped asked themselves if she was a high-class whore. Or perhaps a lady playing at being one. In San Francisco, it was difficult to tell. But all the same, she was the kind of woman men would stare at.

Chapter Thirty

Ginny had no idea where she was. She had never driven herself around the streets of the city before, and the bustle of traffic, those staring eyes and half-voiced comments, had unnerved her. Which way were the docks? She knew the names of the streets, but in which direction did they go? She had to give most of her concentration to driving. The horse was fresh and spirited, and it took all of her strength to hold him. She had begun to feel light-headed and a little nauseous as well. Oh, God—this was not the time for weakness. She wouldn't return. Nothing in the world would make her return! Teeth biting into her lower lip, feeling the sweat break out under her armpits, she kept on. She'd see a familiar landmark soon enough. She had to! Avoid the hills. Keep going downhill. Eventually, she would see the bay, find the Embarcadero.

It was quite by chance, in the end, that she finally turned into a street that was familiar. And there were memories of Concepción's contemptuous voice. "Why don't you go to Russia? That old Count, he seemed anxious to take you with him."

Count Chernikoff! And why not? It seemed the logical, reasonable thing. At least, of them all, he had been honest with her. He would help her, if it meant that she agreed to go to Russia with him. He'd hide her, if she asked him to.

She turned the buggy up the street, and saw the pile of baggage, the two wagons and the closed carriage. A man—she had seen him before, but did not quite remember when or where—seized the reins of her horse.

And there was the Count himself, a fur cap perched incongruously on his head.

"Princess! How did you guess? Or was it fate that brought you here to visit me at this very hour?"

"Does it matter?" She slipped tiredly from the high seat, looking up at the strongly featured old face. "If you still want me to go to Russia, I'm ready. But it has to be *now*, or—there are some people who would try to stop me."

No questions.

"Come. I was about to leave, and I think you have found out why. But you are safe with me—you knew that too, did you not?" Suddenly, Count Chernikoff's voice seemed to echo Ginny's own muddled thoughts. "You belong in Russia; I think it was always meant to be. Don't worry, you are safe now." It was such a relief to have things taken out of her hands, to have someone to lean against. The Count's strong arm encircled her waist. "No one will know. I'll make sure of that. You will go back to your own people, my little Princess, and be welcomed."

Yes, that was it. She'd be welcomed. A person in her own right at last, no longer a misused pawn in somebody else's schemes. Princess, they called her. And not because she was Ivan's wife—she was not Ivan's wife after all, but wife to Steve Morgan, San Francisco's latest golden millionaire, and a stranger to her now—a few hasty words muttered in a deserted chapel and too many hateful memories were all that held them together. Ridiculous. She belonged to no one but herself.

"Did you come here to warn me?" a voice asked unexpectedly.

A Russian sailor, who was not a Russian sailor at all but Ivan. Ivan, looking at her with his piercing blue-green eyes. Strangely, the sight of him no longer made her afraid.

Ginny looked up at the Count, who was helping her into the covered carriage. She hardly noticed that Ivan had climbed in with them.

"I'm not married to him. I refuse to be married to anyone unless—unless *I* choose to!"

"I think she's had one of those powders. Look at her eyes."

She forced her eyes open to squint angrily at Ivan, wondering all over again why he did not worry her any longer.

"*Are* they really mostly opium? I don't like the way you threaten me, but I'd rather see you saved than be trapped by *him*!"

"You're safe. No one is going to threaten you or trap you. I'll see to it myself that you are protected, in the name of the Tsar," said the Count.

Ivan, his eyes bright, pulled the sailor's cap off his fair head, and he was smiling.

"There's no need for that, my dear Uncle. I intend to court her all over again—you see, she came to me. She's made her choice of her own free will. Even *you* must admit that. My darling. . . ." He took Ginny's cold hands, meeting her glazed, emotionless look. "All's fair in love and war, is it not? Let's forget the past, and our little misunderstandings. You're my wife."

"No." The carriage was moving now, and the fresh air fanned Ginny's cheeks, reviving her slightly. She sat up, with the Count's arm still supporting her. "I'm still married to Steve Morgan—or hadn't you heard that part of it? My—the Senator neglected to tell you that the annulment he spoke of had never actually been accomplished. Oh, it's true enough! But I don't want to be married to him, any more than I want to be married to you. Understand me, Ivan. No one is going to frighten or browbeat me again. There'll be no more tricks. If you intend to take me in one piece to the Tsar, you'd better make sure I don't have anything to complain about."

"Well said! You're a true Romanov!" Count Chernikoff, sitting stiffly erect with his arm still supporting her, sounded proud. Surprisingly, Ivan Sahrkanov laughed.

"Oh, but I agree. Well said, indeed, my Princess. You are more like the woman I first saw and desired now.

You've rediscovered your capacity for anger, and your courage. I think I shall enjoy courting you all over again—and this time, we will meet as equals." He threw back his head suddenly, his laughter becoming almost soundless. "Would you like to make a small wager on that? Dimitri? Xenia? You see, you are no longer the little half-French Virginie. You are Russian, and we can be true adversaries—or lovers. Shall we wager?"

"Ivan, you forget yourself!" the Count muttered stiffly. "Don't forget you are supposed to be a common seaman. It was your fever for gambling and your overwhelming arrogance that led us to this hasty and surreptitious departure. Exercise some caution, for God's sake!"

"Do you really want a cautious lover?" Ivan whispered, and his hand touched Ginny's, fingers stroking. She looked at him, neither accepting or rejecting.

"We'll see, won't we?" she said coldly, and she hardly recognized her voice as her own. Her eyes met his incuriously. Her slight feeling of surprise that he no longer had the power to frighten her but seemed just another man, was coupled with the knowledge that she could almost feel some admiration for him—at the way he could laugh at his losses and everything he had gambled for, and still persist. In his way, Ivan was an honest loser!

Along with a slight, creeping drowsiness, Ginny experienced a feeling of well-being. She hardly needed the Count's soft assurance.

"We are almost there. A Russian vessel is waiting; we'll find a veil for you. In this kind of crowd, no one will suspect anything."

Had he but known it, the Count's words were, at that moment, being paraphrased and enlarged upon.

The Senator's house on Rincon Hill was in a state of turmoil, as it had been ever since Sonya Brandon, against her husband's express wishes, had decided to have a talk with her stepdaughter.

She found the room in a shambles—drawers open, their contents scattered all over the floor; the mirror smashed; Ginny's jewel box gaping emptily—and a white square of paper placed tidily atop all the debris.

Sonya, already more than upset by the startling disclosures her husband had made in confidence, went into a state of quiet, controlled hysterics.

"She's gone! Run back to *him*! Why couldn't we have guessed? William! For God's sake—how can you stand there staring at that ridiculous note and do nothing?"

It was very seldom that the Senator raised his voice to his wife, and especially before her maid. But he did so now, his words cutting across and silencing her.

"You've read this note, you say? Then I beg of you to think with your usual clearness, my dearest. She's running away from her husband to her lover, she says."

"Of course! Do you think I have not read it until those words repeat themselves over and over in my mind? She's running away from Ivan—"

"But Ivan is *not* her husband. Didn't we learn the unpleasant truth this afternoon about her *real* husband? Have you stopped to wonder if *Ginny* had not learned it too? By God—" he looked thunderstruck for a moment, and then began to stroke his jaw thoughtfully. "If she knows. . . . I wonder who this lover is? The Prince Sahrkanov himself? Or—"

"But we'll never find her now! Not in this city. She could be anywhere. She could have friends who would hide her. She could have *left* the city by now! William. . . !"

Thrusting the note into the pocket of his jacket, the Senator took command. He said briskly, "You must lie down. Have Tilly bathe your eyes—and leave this to me."

"But—but what will you do? In the light of everything that has happened—"

"As I explained to you, my love, *my* hands are tied! Since Ginny is a married woman, I believe her present whereabouts should be the concern of her husband. My first duty, I believe, is to inform *him*."

Sonya was lying across a sofa, a handkerchief soaked in cologne held against her face. Now she raised her head, her china-blue eyes going wide.

"Oh, *no*, William! You would not—you will not ask that man to this house?"

"*That man*," the Senator repeated, with a certain dry emphasis, "happens to be my partner in several ventures. Not Sam Murdock, who it appears was merely acting for him. And he has the controlling interest in others. To put it bluntly, my love, I have no choice but to accept my newly discovered millionaire son-in-law—or suffer some

very unpleasant consequences! As for the other—we
should count ourselves fortunate that he's obviously learned
the game is up and has obligingly disappeared. Dear
Lord!"—Sonya could not help wincing at the note that
came into her husband's voice—"I *still* hardly credit what
I have heard this afternoon! If it had been anyone else but
Sam Murdock who told me—and if Ralston, of all people,
had not appeared to back up the story. . . . Well—on top of
everything else, this seems to be the last straw. You may
count yourself fortunate that you are a female and entitled to go into hysterics!"

And with these ominous words the Senator strode out
of the room, a vein throbbing in his forehead as a contra-
diction to his studiedly calm tone of voice. Behind him,
Sonya burst into tears.

For Ginny, there would be no more tears. It was another vow she made to herself, leaning against the rail of
the Russian schooner that was even now beating its way
up the coast and to the north.

"You're safe now, my child," the old Count had said
when they left the Golden Gate lying behind them. And
now the afternoon had faded into evening and the evening
darkened, turning first blue and then violet—sky and ocean
merging into each other, with the stars hanging above like
tiny, distant lamps.

Ginny wrapped the heavy silk shawl, decorated with colored tassels, more closely about her head and shoulders.
Salt spray stung her face, making the tiny cuts from the
broken mirror glass feel as if a million needles were piercing her skin. She didn't care. She hadn't cared even when
Count Chernikoff had clucked disapprovingly, dabbing at
them with alcohol before he announced that she mustn't
worry about being scarred, the marks would soon fade
away. Pinpricks. Reminding her that she was still alive.

"Safe," Ginny repeated to herself, wondering why the
thought did nothing to lift her spirits or relieve the dead,
empty feeling inside. Yes, she felt hollow, like the broken
porcelain doll she remembered crying over as a child.
Drained of all emotion, she felt herself to be nothing more
than a brittle shell.

She didn't turn her head when soemone came to stand
beside her, although she knew who it was. Ivan. Was it
possible that he had once made her feel cowed and terri-

fied? All they had in common now was the fact that they were both losers.

He might have read her thoughts. She heard him release his breath in a sigh before he murmured almost absently:

"So, the game is over. And now we begin another. This time—"

"We?" Ginny interrupted sharply. "I am no gambler myself. And I am sick of games."

"You were the stakes, chérie. I won—remember? The Tsar's daughter."

"But you became greedy and flew too high, didn't you, Ivan? That is always the trouble with compulsive gamblers. They don't see that they cannot keep on winning forever."

"Perhaps there is another player in this game I spoke about who has realized that by now, yes? And as for me—like all gamesters, I never give up. Who knows, I may be lucky enough to recoup at least a portion of what I've lost."

Ginny, already regretting the fact that she'd entered into conversation with him, made an impatient movement of her shoulder.

"Why should I be interested? I refuse to look back at the past."

"And the future? Does that not interest you? Think about it, my Princess. It lies before you, golden and glittering, and at last you have realized what you almost let yourself miss. Don't you owe me at least gratitude for that? Surely you're not still angry at me?" From the corner of her eye, Ginny caught the glimpse of white teeth as Ivan smiled. She refused to answer, and he went on with a shrug, "Oh, come! In a way, I have been honest with you. And I will be honest with you now, since you seem to have become strong and self-sufficient again. You should not blame me for—bullying you at times. You asked for it, my dear! Admit it. Every time I took you in my arms, it was like embracing a block of ice. And the rest of the time you floated around in some kind of dream. I married a wild, earthy gypsy, and found she had turned into an ethereal being who almost floated off the ground. Ah, you asked for me to be cruel! You practically begged to be forced into trembling, cowering submission! And to tell you the truth, if things had gone along as they were, I think I would have derived a considerable amount of pleasure from beating you."

Ginny could not help making a smothered sound, and he laughed softly. His old, purring laugh.

"Ah, yes! And you would have let me, as you allowed me to punish you in so many other little ways. I'd begun to feel that subconsciously you longed to be dominated and ordered around. If you only knew what glorious fantasies I used to have—but I waited too long, alas! Or did I? Would you like to find out the exquisite sensations, the delicious torments of mixing pleasure and pain?"

"Would *you*?" When she turned her head at last to face him fully Ginny could see an expression of surprise cross his features for a moment. Pressing home her advantage she gave a hard, short laugh. "If you were to offer yourself as a victim, Prince Sahrkanov, I might be glad to oblige you sometime. But *I* have no desire to taste the perverse delights you were speaking of. And now, if you'll excuse me, I think I will join the Count."

He made no move to stop her as she swept away with unconscious grace and dignity. But she could feel his eyes, following her.

The Count's cabin seemed warm and wonderfully safe and comforting after the chilly air on deck, and the strange conversation she had had with Ivan. The Count had promised to protect her, and although he'd warned her solemnly against taking too many headache powders, he had also agreed to let her have them at regular intervals.

"Opium? Nonsense, my child. A very tiny amount, perhaps, for its soothing effect. But hardly enough to make you addicted. Of course, since you are so much stronger now, you must start trying to do without them. Any medication loses its efficacy when taken constantly."

Ginny believed him. Another lie to be added to the list of lies that Steve had told her. He would say anything, do anything that would help him gain his own ends. She had been foolish enough to love him once, but now at last her eyes had been opened, and it was all over. Nothing left but hate.

"What's the matter, child? You're shivering! You must avoid standing at the rail at this time of night; you could catch a chill." Count Chernikoff's voice was as kind and

calm as it always was, and Ginny gave him a grateful
smile. He knew how things stood between her and Ivan,
and how things had been. She had told him. And in return
he had admitted that he'd been worried at what he'd ob-
served and what he'd heard. But it was all over. She
would have nothing more to worry about.

Ginny stayed there for a while, sipping the glass of
brandy the old man insisted she must have. It was excellent brandy, from the cellars of the Tsar himself, he informed her proudly. And she listened, composing her features into an expression of interest, while he rambled on
about the Tsar, his family, his closest intimates—all people
she would no doubt be presented to in due course. In Russia the Tsar's wishes, his word, were absolute. France and
England had democratic monarchs, but in Russia the Tsar
was still a despot, with the power of life and death.

"And suppose he does not approve of me? I am not
very good at obeying without question, you know! And I
don't want a husband chosen for me."

"Child, child! Wait and see. The Tsar is also a man who
has lived long enough to have seen how people live in
other countries. He knows you were brought up in France
and America—and you are his Genevieve's daughter.
Don't worry. I myself will be with you, to help explain everything."

In any case, Ginny thought wryly, she had already committed herself. She was on her way to Russia, with all the
old ties severed behind her.

Chapter Thirty-one

Ginny was leaning against the rail, watching the last,
pearly traces of fog melt away under the sun. The fresh
wind filled the white sails above her, and whipped copper-
gold tendrils of hair across her face. The sloop seemed to
skim the green surface of the water, sending white foam

flying up on either side of the bow. She let her mind follow the wind, not really thinking, not wanting to.

"You passed a comfortable night? You slept well?"

"Oh, yes. Your tonic helped. I feel relaxed this morning." Count Chernikoff gave her one of his rare smiles. "Good, good! That is what we want, da?"

A sailor called out something, and Ginny's head turned with the others: the sails of a clipper appeared to leap out of the distant horizon astern of them. Ginny's heart gave a sudden, inexplicable lurch. How beautiful she looked, and for all her size, how fast she travelled, with every one of her sails catching the wind.

The Count echoed her thoughts.

"A fine, clean-lined vessel, is she not? One of your American clipper ships going all the way to China."

Why was there a sudden pain in her heart? There were many clipper ships that sailed this very route. This could not possibly be the "Green-Eyed Lady"; she was only just christened, and not ready to take on her cargo yet.

By now—by now they would all know. Consoled by Concepción, only angry because she had foiled his plans for revenge, Steve would have put her completely out of his mind. It would be such a relief to so many people.

Ivan strolled up, bracing his legs against the movement of the ship in a practiced manner. As usual, he was impeccably dressed, his eyes looking like pale green glass in the reflected light of the late morning sun.

"You are admiring our fellow traveller? She travels very fast, does she not? And although she has seen us, she has not altered her course. Do you think it is merely a lack of courtesy, or—something else, perhaps?"

Startled, Ginny turned back to watch the other ship, which was, indeed, bearing down upon them at an alarming speed. She remembered reading advertisements in the newspapers: *"A hundred days from New York to San Francisco. . . ."* The fastest vessels upon the ocean, they looked all sail, the ship itself riding low in the wave troughs.

"Nonsense! She has seen us. The captain will signal us politely, and they will veer away."

But would they—*would* they? Ginny didn't know why she thought so, but there was something inexorable and almost menacing in the way the other ship seemed to follow

in their course, never hesitating, and becoming larger by
the minute.

She heard Ivan laugh at her side, and caught the pale
gleam of his eyes.

"A pirate ship, perhaps? You Americans—so crude, so
far behind the rest of the civilized world. Would you like
to take a wager with me, my Princess? Everything I possess, against—what else but yourself? I have an instinct
about some things, and in this case. . . .Well, Uncle Dimitri? Why do you frown at me? I intend no disrespect; I
merely remember. What do you say?"

Ginny had gone pale. Now she watched the other ship
carefully, and saw the string of little flags that were suddenly run up on a line between the foremast and the bow.

"A glass, quickly!"

While Ginny and the Count watched, a sailor handed
Ivan a brassbound telescope. And when he lowered it, he
was laughing soundlessly.

"Predictable. Why were you afraid to take my wager?
You see, they have just demanded that we heave to. They
wish to converse."

What followed next was confusion. The second mate
came tumbling down from the bridge, his face red, a
string of Russian words spewing from his mouth.

Of them all, only Ivan appeared to be quite unconcerned, and not in the least agitated.

"I think—yes, I think we have underestimated this determined husband of yours, Princess. And perhaps that
was my mistake, from the beginning. I should have had
him eliminated."

"What are you talking about?" Ginny almost screamed
the words at him. "What do you mean? It's impossible,
they would not—"

"But I think they would! Piracy on the high seas—and
what a prize at stake!"

"I won't go! If it is who you say—they can't make me!
Oh, no—I refuse."

"She flies the American flag."

"Did you expect the skull and crossbones? Nevertheless,
I think she is a pirate."

"Impossible!" Count Chernikoff kept repeating. "This is
a Russian ship. We are Russian citizens—"

"All except one of us. And now perhaps you understand?"

The Count went below to get his papers, but in spite of his pleading, Ginny would not go with him.

"I'll stay on deck. And if it is—if it is him, I won't go! I'll make it clear that I'm on board this ship of my own accord—I. . . ."

"Let's forget our old enmity." Ivan drew her aside, out of the way of the sailors who ran everywhere. "Listen, you know you are safe from me now. But how safe will you be with him? A savage—a barbarian—and yet, he is a gambler too, no? A reckless individual, from all I've heard, and from what little you've told me. If you really want your freedom, I have a plan. . . ."

Impossible, impossible! This wasn't happening, not any of it! Ivan himself had given Ginny one of her headache powders, but now, as she stood flanked by him and Count Chernikoff, her mind refused to accept what was taking place, or the impossible "plan" that Ivan had suggested to her.

Both ships rocked gently, seeming almost motionless except when they headed out of the wave troughs. The sailors on the Russian vessel all carried guns—Prince Sahrkanov had given the orders, over Count Chernikoff's protests.

He put an arm around Ginny's shoulders, and for once she did not flinch away. "Let him see!" she thought defiantly. "Let him think the worst. . . . Oh, how dare he, after everything?"

He, Steve Morgan. Inconceivably and distastefully, her husband. She refused to accept the thought.

With her face as stiff as a mask, Ginny watched Steve come over the side of the ship—with no effort, no fumbling, his every movement as smooth and as sure as she remembered. He wore a gun, low-holstered. And he was even dressed like a pirate, in a white linen shirt, open at the neck, black breeches worn with high boots, a blue silk scarf knotted carelessly around his throat.

He was followed by the Senator, of all people, looking uncomfortable in a dark suit. And there was a tall paunchy man with a silver star pinned to his vest.

"The boarding party!" Ivan said sarcastically, his arms

tightening around Ginny's shoulders. "I wonder if these pirates have come to arrest me, or to find you, my dear?"

The Russian Captain was protesting vociferously, and at
the same time Count Chernikoff, in his stilted English, was
also expostulating.

Ginny had already noticed Steve's eyes flick over her—
hard, gleaming sapphire blue. But after that first dagger-
like glance, he ignored her, addressing himself to the
Count instead, as he explained evenly that the sloop was in
American territorial waters, and that accompanying him
were a United States Senator, and the Sheriff of San
Francisco County.

"But your reasons for this high-handed act of—I can
only call it a form of piracy: I must demand—"

"Count Chernikoff, if I may dispense with preambles.
I'm here, quite simply, to collect my wife. I'm willing to
forget the several charges against Prince Sahrkanov, as
unpleasant as they are—and the Sheriff here agrees. But
you don't deny my rights over my wife, I hope?

"*Over* me!" Unable to keep silent any longer, Ginny almost shouted the words. And now, at last, she had forced
him to look directly at her. "And what about my feelings,
my inclinations? I refuse to go with you—why in hell did
you have to come after me? I became your wife under
duress. I will not continue with such a—a parody of a
relationship, do you hear? Take me back by force and I'll
sue for a divorce. I'll make such a scandal that—that—
why should you want a wife who does not want you? I
have made my choice! If you wished to be convinced that
I was not brought here under duress, you can be sure of it
now. Let me alone—let me be!"

If there was any emotion in Steve's face, it showed in
the whitening of the skin around his eyes and mouth.

"Ginny!" the Senator said, and she swung on him next,
her eyes blazing green fire.

"And why are *you* here? Of all people, you should be
most anxious to avoid a scandal, such a disgrace! I tell
you, I won't leave this ship—you'll have to drag me off by
force, and face the trouble that I swear I'll cause to all of
you!"

Steve looked at her as if they were the only two persons
present, and she almost shrank back from the naked fury
in his look.

"If I have to take you off by force, then I'll do it. And if a divorce is what you want you'll get that too, by God! But first—first you'll come back to San Francisco, and you'll appear in public, and you'll pretend to be a lady until all the talk dies down. Do you understand, Ginny? Six months from now, maybe, you can do as you please—you want to go to Russia? I'll send you there. You hear me, Count? But for now—*right* now, damn it—you're getting off this ship and you're coming with me, and I've got every right in the world to make you do so."

There was a sudden silence as the watching sailors gaped and Count Chernikoff seemed to search for words.

Casually, Ivan Sahrkanov's arm dropped from around Ginny's shoulders, and he stood with his hands at his sides, his voice deliberately contemptuous.

"I have heard, and now I believe it, that you Americans have no pride! To drag home a runaway wife by force—if you don't kill me first, I think I could make you the laughingstock of all Europe! Come—isn't it possible for us to be civilized? The Princess had expressed her preference. She is not to be bought by all your money, nor frightened by your threats. And, speaking of threats—" his voice became a purr, low and smooth—"have you not noticed the weapons that menace you on all sides? Is your ship equipped with guns? I think, gentlemen, that we have come to— what we call a stalemate, in chess. Come here to me, Virginie!"

Taken by surprise, Ginny found herself suddenly seized around the waist; and then, forcing herself not to resist, she was leaning against Ivan, held slightly in front of him.

"You see? She comes. She has made her choice. And if there is any reckless gunfire on the part of *your* men. . . . Would you rather see her dead than follow her own dictates, eh?"

The Sheriff's hand dropped to his gun butt, and froze there. Silent, unmoving, Ginny heard the Senator start to exclaim and then clamp his jaws together with an effort. Only Steve, like the Prince, remained cool.

"As you just said, Sahrkanov. A stalemate. But if, as you've reminded us, *we* are powerless, then so are you. Your ship isn't going anywhere. Shall we wait it out?"

"Why don't you go back? Be sensible. Virginie has just told you what her feelings are. And in gambling there is a phrase—'cut your losses.' Is it not true that one must always learn when to do so?"

Steve shrugged, his smile a mere lifting of one corner of his mouth.

"One must also learn when to call a bluff. Your hand against mine, Sahrkanov. Or did you have an extra ace up your sleeve?"

Ginny felt the most imperceptible tightening of the Prince's muscles as she stood with her body held closely against his, and now she caught her breath, wondering at the sudden feeling of weakness that made her want to call out—to scream violently at Steve to go, before he fell into their trap.

"I was thinking of an honorable way out of this stalemate we have both admitted," Ivan Sahrkanov was saying smoothly. "A gentleman's agreement, perhaps? Me, I do not know too much about your American customs, but in Europe, in a situation like this, there would only be one solution."

"Ivan—what are you saying?" Count Chernikoff's voice sounded hoarse; Steve Morgan's eyes were a blazing blue against his dark, bearded face.

"Go ahead, let's have your gentlemen's solution," Steve invited softly, and Ginny had the strangest feeling that he knew exactly what was coming and had expected it from the first moment Ivan started talking. Even now, his face didn't move a muscle—God, why must she keep watching him, and why was she suddenly assailed by a creeping feeling of nausea?

"There *is* only one solution, surely?" Ivan Sahrkanov put a note of surprise, mixed with condescension, into his voice. "Here we have a woman who is wanted by two men—need I remind you that I still continue to look on Virginia as *my* wife? I think that for *her* sake, and to protect *her* name, she ought to be left with just one husband. Then there will be no more problem, yes?"

Steve laughed, and the sound of his laughter, breaking across the sudden silence that had seized every single person on the deck, sent cold chills chasing up Ginny's spine.

"Now, why didn't I think of that before?" Steve's eyes slashed across her, and in spite of her resolution, Ginny paled. "Which would you rather be, my sweet, widow or wife? Or need I ask?"

His voice, with that caustic, biting note in it taunted her; she wouldn't let it pass!

"Haven't I made my feelings in this matter obvious? Oh, for God's sake—now you've made your conventional gesture and retrieved your damned pride, why don't you go and leave me in peace? All of you! There'll be no need for any duels to be fought over *me*—I refuse to leave this ship!"

It was no use. Even as she spoke, flinging her words at him as if she wished they were knives, Ginny knew that it was no good. Too well, she recognized Steve's temper, his high-strung reckless mood that made him laugh before he got ready to kill. But in this case—oh, why did he keep looking at her as if he was reading her thoughts, grooves deepening on either side of his mouth as he gave her a sarcastic smile; one black eyebrow slightly quirked as if to warn her. . . .

"You see, the lady reiterates that she knows her mind." Ivan Sahrkanov's silky smooth tone insinuated itself across the slight pause. "I take it that you challenge my right to protect her?"

"I take it you wish to make the choice of weapons?" Steve's voice was dry.

"I wish to be fair—shall we let Virginie choose for us?"

A sudden shaft of sunlight fell across Ginny's face, almost blinding her, so that she blinked her eyes quickly. She heard her own disembodied voice, sounding very clear and sharp.

"Why not sabers? I have always wanted to see a duel fought with swords."

Someone sighed, the sound abnormally loud. Count Chernikoff cleared his throat, as if he meant to say something and the words choked him.

It was the Senator who regained the use of his voice first, as he shouted explosively: "I've never heard such a pack of damnfool nonsense in my life! A duel—preposterous! Gentlemen, this is the nineteenth century, and we are supposed to be civilized."

"But your western gunfights—I have witnessed a few myself, you know—are these not duels to the death? This business of drawing a gun from the hip and shooting bang-bang-bang—there is no art, no skill involved. Whereas the saber. . . . Perhaps, my fine piratical rival, you have never learned the use of such a weapon?" Prince Sahrkanov's mocking eyes went from the Senator to Steve, who shrugged negligently as if neither the question nor the manner in which it was phrased were of great consequence.

"They gave us a few general instructions on its use in the Cavalry. But I suppose you were thinking of the fencing weapon?"

"You agree then? Everything to be decided by the outcome of our meeting?"

"Now listen here," Senator Brandon exploded, "you're surely not serious about this ridiculous idea? Ginny's obviously too overwrought to think clearly. I don't think she realizes the gravity—"

"I think Ginny knows exactly what she's about," Steve said dispassionately. He looked at her, and during the split second that their eyes clung together Ginny felt a sense of whirling back in time as she saw in his eyes the same look she had seen in them soon after she had stabbed him, almost killing him.

But this time—this time she had killed him. Ivan was going to kill him—and he would be out of her life forever.

The whirling sensation increased, narrowed down to a pair of dark blue eyes she had loved and hated and would never see again.

She opened her mouth to scream "no!" but not even a whisper emerged, and they were all talking around her— the Senator and the hitherto silent Sheriff arguing heatedly about legality and murder and practical common sense, and Ivan calling to his valet to fetch the case of matched sabers.

Hardly knowing how it happened, Ginny found that she was huddled back against a bulkhead with Count Chernikoff's arm comfortingly around her, and a space had been cleared on the deck.

"It is understood? We are all agreed? Soon, a regrettable accident will be taking place, and when it is over, it is done. We go our separate—and I trust peaceful—ways."

"That Prince feller sure thinks up some fancy tricks and funny rules, don't he?" Sheriff Meeker muttered under his breath. He didn't like it. He sure enough didn't like any of it, and he had begun to wish quite fervently that he had not let himself be persuaded to join in this mad pursuit for a runaway wife. It just went to show that females, no matter what walk of life they came from, were all the same! Contrary—and judging from *this* one, with her wicked green eyes, lethal as well.

The Senator, his lips a thin line, the vein in his forehead throbbing, was thinking what an impossible, appalling situation it was. Either way, he could see nothing but scandal and disgrace ahead. He was going to lose a son-in-law and gain a son-in-law, and all with one lucky swipe from a saber. Good God! It must be the hot sun that had made everyone a little mad—himself included. How had they been coerced into letting this happen? A gunfight was one thing; it was usually over quickly. But a fight with swords—ugh! He hoped Ginny had a strong stomach. In fact—and his eyes took on a hard, puzzled look as he glanced towards her—he felt as if he were looking at a statue of a woman who bore only a faint resemblance to the daughter he'd once been so proud of.

William Brandon moved so that his back was to the steadily climbing sun, his attention, in spite of all his misgivings, now wholly riveted on the two men who stood facing each other across a space of a few feet. From the deck of the clipper, "Green-Eyed Lady," every available telescope and pair of fieldglasses were also turned on the same scene, which because of its very starkness and primitive quality seemed almost unreal.

Two men, of almost equal height and build, both stripped to shirts and breeches: Steve Morgan, mercenary, outlaw and guerrillero-turned-millionaire, looking more like a corsair than ever with a sword in his hand, feet braced slightly apart, body deceptively relaxed-looking; and Prince Ivan Sahrkanov, last of his noble line, a cynic and a gambler and, in his way, an adventurer, looking sure of himself and his weapon.

A slight smile touched Ivan's lips as he kissed the hilt of his sword. "To the victor—to the spoils. And to the death of the deserving!" he said tauntingly.

Over the Prince's shoulder, Steve caught Ginny's tortured, glazed green eyes and tossed her a rather mocking smile. She didn't look as if she was enjoying the prospect of two men fighting over her at all. She bit her lip, hard, and a tiny drop of red stood out against the pearly white of her small teeth. He ought to hate her—the wild, crazy, unpredictable little baggage! But instead, like the fool he seemed to have turned into, he was fighting for her. At least the hate was gone from her eyes. They looked haunted—and unhappy. How would they look later?

"You have no farewells to make? No salute?"

"I'll leave that to you," Steve said curtly, and quite by instinct his feet and body moved lightly into the "en garde" position; his narrowed blue eyes watched those of his adversary for the warning of a move.

It had begun.

Chapter Thirty-two

Afterwards, only flashes of memory, impressions rendered all the more vivid by her surroundings, would come back when Ginny tried to recall them.

There was the undulating rise and fall of the deck beneath her feet; the smell of the tobacco that Count Chernikoff fancied; the creaking noises of rigging and timbers; even the dull thudding of her own heart, sounding like separate hammer blows in her chest and temples. All formed a background, an accompaniment to the clashing metal sound of swords, the slitherings of booted feet across wood, and the harsh breathing of the two men who circled each other warily one moment and leaped forward the next, with the sunlight reflecting off slashing blades.

A dream—a nightmare! Without realizing it, Ginny had begun to shake as if she had a chill.

Count Chernikoff whispered, his voice hoarse:

"Ivan is one of the best swordsmen I have seen. You see—already he has the other on the defensive; he is playing with him!"

Her fingers, each one of them feeling as stiff and taut as steel, clutched at the old man's arms. "Oh God, my God!" Was she praying to herself? Who was she praying for? She didn't know. She had begun to notice, since the Count had spoken, that Ivan wore a strange, taut smile, and that Steve, retreating cautiously but nonetheless steadily, was fighting for his life.

Steve knew it, too. He could handle a saber adequately, but that was all. And Sahrkanov, to give him credit, was an expert. Steve could even feel a detached kind of admiration for the clever way in which the man had maneuvered him around until the sun was in his eyes, and the ship's rail at his back. A matter of time now, unless he could continue to keep just beyond the reach of that flickering blade.

Seeing that his adversary had begun to squint his eyes against the sun as he fought to defend himself, Ivan Sahrkanov decided it was time to draw first blood, and he did so with almost contemptuous ease.

The saber became like a living thing in his hand now, as the Prince gave a demonstration of his consummate skill. He wanted them to realize, all the people who watched, that he could have made an end to the whole affair within the first minute or so if he had wished to do so. But he preferred to let it drag out—he wanted everyone to see how clumsily this Steve Morgan was when it came to handling a sword, which was, after all a gentleman's weapon. Above all, he wanted Morgan himself to have time to become afraid—to begin to wait, with ghastly, growing apprehension for the final thrust that would end everything.

"Here it comes," Steve thought, seeing the pale eyes change. Sahrkanov's blade flickered like a viper's tongue, sliding easily under his guard, making it only too apparent that the playing was over now and the Prince was closing in for the kill. But not yet. . . .

"I am going to cut you to pieces, but slowly enough for you to suffer a little," the prince said with a smile.

There was no pain yet, only a sharp, burning sensation as the blade slashed across Steve's ribs, and the warm trickle of blood. He sucked in his breath, body shifting out of the way instinctively, and Sahrkanov moved too. The sabers clashed for an instant and then the Prince's blade slithered along Steve's, deflecting it, slipping under it in a kind of twisting thrust. The point caught Steve in the shoulder, jarring off his collarbone. If not for that, and his quick reflexes, it would have gone deeper, paralyzing his arm. As it was, he had to leap backwards, and his saber went clattering to the deck.

There was a concerted sigh from the semicircle of on-lookers as the Prince kicked the fallen sword out of the way.

They faced each other, Ivan Sahrkanov standing in the classic duelist's pose—one foot before the other, knees slightly bent, his sword arm bent at the elbow, saber held before him. All he had to do now was make one smooth motion, shifting his weight from his left to his right foot as his arm and body lunged together. . . . But he waited. And Steve waited, unmoving except for the rise and fall of his chest under the tattered, bloody white shirt.

"No—" Ginny's voice, thin with hysteria, rose in the still air. "Ivan—please, that's enough! You've *won*, no one can argue that point. Don't. . . !"

Count Chernikoff was staring at her with an expression of surprise. Even the Senator had turned his head to stare at her, his face wearing a pale, rather dazed expression.

"But this is not a case of winning or losing, chérie." The Prince Sahrkanov's eyes did not shift from Steve's face—he watched for signs of fear, for the breaking out of beads of sweat on his enemy's forehead, the tongue moistening dry lips as he started to plead. "You forget—this duel is to the death. And in just a moment, I am going to set you free." There were no signs of emotion, none of the reaction he had expected to read in the guarded blue eyes that looked back at him.

"Don't!" Ginny's voice choked on the word. She might have run forward with the mad idea of throwing herself between them if the Count had not held her back by clamping a surprisingly strong arm about her waist.

"She's right—this will be cold-blooded slaughter, if you think to go through with it! Really Sahrkanov, I must re-mind you. . . ."

Amazingly, it was Steve Morgan's dispassionate voice that cut short the Senator's almost apoplectic remon-strances.

"He's right, you know. 'To the death' was the agree-ment we made. But after all, it's not over yet."

Ginny was to remember, afterwards, the ugly sound of Ivan's laughter.

"No? You are right. I don't intend that you will die ei-

ther quickly or pleasantly. It will be something for everyone to remember."

His last words, delivered in the smoothly purring tone
she recalled only too well, were for her, of course. Ginny
knew that, and pressed her knuckles against her mouth to
prevent herself from screaming as the saber flashed in the
sunlight, forcing Steve to move backwards, and then back
again until his back was to the rail and there was blood
dripping everywhere from the shallow cuts on his upper
arms and torso and down his face—cuts that would have
gone deeper and done worse damage if he had not moved
quickly enough.

But now, Ivan was laughing.

"You have been running from me, but where will you
run to now? Will you attempt to leap into the ocean to
avoid further punishment?"

"Is that why Su Lei hanged herself? Or had it something to do with her brother?"

What was Steve saying? What was he trying to do?
Ivan's body looked as rigid as if he had suddenly been frozen to one spot.

Steve said mockingly, "The act of inflicting pain is what
you enjoy most, isn't it? That's why you'd like to drag this
out. Would you like me to keep on talking while you
make up your mind what to do next?"

"I am going to skewer you to that rail behind you with
my sword through your belly, and listen to your screams
of anguish!"

Ginny's mind screamed. She bit down on her knuckles,
and the pain kept her from fainting.

It was like a ballet, grotesque and terribly beautiful at
the same time. Ivan Sahrkanov poised himself for the kill,
feet and body falling into the same position as earlier.
And Steve—Steve just stood there, balanced on the balls
of his feet, seemingly relaxed. . . . Until Ivan lunged, his
sword arm straightening, body following it.

After that everything happened almost too fast for the
young woman's stunned mind to follow, except as a series
of pictures superimposed upon each other. It was like
watching the sudden and violently explosive eruption of a
sleeping volcano.

The sharp-edged blade whistled by, actually slicing
across his chest as Steve pivoted from the hips, his body

twisting to the left, knife-edge of his left hand jarring
Sahrkanov's arm just enough to deflect his aim as Steve
brought the knuckles of his right hand down on the sensitive inner wrist bone, grabbing the wrist and pushing it upward in almost the same motion, and Sahrkanov's sword
dropped from paralyzed fingers.

Steve Morgan's body, moving with calculated precision,
had turned lethal weapon, one smoothly vicious movement
blending into another.

Left foot sliding forward, Steve's left hand smashed a
back-knuckle blow into Ivan's unprotected groin, and as
the unfortunate Prince started to double with a scream of
agony, there was a back-knuckle blow with the right hand
to his breastbone, and another with the edge of the hand
to the back of his neck.

"Sweet Jesus Christ!" somebody exhaled. And almost
before he could inhale again it was over, except for the
mind picture that kept playing itself over and over again
in Ginny's tortured imagination.

She had never seen, never imagined anything so savage,
so brutal, in all her life.

As the Prince crumpled forward, as if he were folding in
two, Steve's left knee caught him in the face, straightening
him up again, and Ginny could actually hear the sound of
crushing bones. Following his own momentum, Steve's
right foot came down in the direction of the falling man
as he delivered a snap-kick with his left foot to the rib
cage, caving it inwards like papier mâché. Down on the
ball of the same foot, pivoting slightly, and still moving
with the grace and precision of a dancer, he delivered the
coup de grace, a last crushing blow with the heel of the
right foot, over the heart.

"My God—if I hadn't seen it. . . . Less than a minute—
and he's dead!"

"I timed it at five seconds." For all the pedantic sound of
his words, Senator Brandon's voice sounded hoarse. He
and the Sheriff had been the first to break the frozen
silence as Steve Morgan, without another glance at the
broken, bleeding thing that had once been a man, strode
towards him, his breathing seemingly unimpaired.

"Thank you for holding my gun for me, sir. I'll take it
back now."

Wordlessly, Brandon held the gunbelt out, and watched

the man who, unbelievably, was his son-in-law, buckle it around his waist, easing the weighted holster until it lay low enough along his thigh. Was this same polite stranger the outlaw he had sworn to hunt down and kill? The same man who, as he had exploded into sudden violence, had given a deep throated yell which sounded almost like a primitive Indian war cry—enough like one to send the hackles up on the back of every man here?

He had "won" Ginny back—God, what a strange thought! And when Sonya heard ... but what of Ginny herself?

She was being sick over the rail, the Count's arms supporting her. And as if *that* humiliation was not enough, she heard Steve's voice behind her, talking to the Count in that overly polite tone he could adopt when it suited him—discussing her over her head while her shoulders still heaved and she vomited helplessly—just as if she had been a piece of goods; bargained for and finally bought.

"I'm going to take Ginny back with me now. You understand, Count Chernikoff? This was the wrong time for her to have thought of running away."

"So you are the man she spoke of." The Count sighed. "We underestimated you. And especially poor Ivan. You learned this style of fighting in China?"

"From a Chinese friend who had studied it all his life. It's useful—for a man who has forgotten how to use a saber."

"Ah—and you speak French, as well. It is true that your marriage—"

"Was never annulled? Yes, it's true. But I didn't find out myself until quite recently. Count—" Steve's voice hardened, became slightly impatient. "You understand why I cannot stay to explain everything? If you'll have someone fetch my wife's things. . . ."

"A moment! The Prince Sahrkanov is dead—it was a duel, very well! And there was an agreement made beforehand; you need not fear that I mean to go back on it. But, if Ginny still wants to go to Russia? You can see how overwrought she is, how ill. Surely—"

"I've no intention of beating Ginny, or killing her—if that is what is worrying you, sir. And I know why you want to take her to Russia with you. But she has certain other obligations to fulfill here first."

"I won't go with you! After everything I've learned, after what I've just seen ... I wouldn't go anywhere with
you!" Her face pale, her body shaking with chills, Ginny
turned away from the rail, her green eyes looking abnormally large. "You've lied to me, tricked me—and you only
came after me because too many people had learned we
were ... no! I won't stay married to you! You want me
because you think I'm your—possession! Because your stupid, hypocritical pride demands it, that's all! I—"

"Ginny! Go down below and get your things. Bring
your jewels with you, because you're going to be wearing
them, when we go out in public. You want to argue, we'll
argue later."

Against the inflexible note in his voice she was helpless,
and knew it. Even Count Chernikoff, being a man, with a
man's peculiar sense of honor, would not help her. And
Ivan was dead—the manner of his dying still capable of
making her stomach knot with recurring nausea.

"I'll make you sorry!" Ginny said childishly, her voice
cracking. And then she whirled and ran for the cabin.

"You are bleeding still. If you will let me tend to those
cuts while we discuss certain matters. . . ?"

Almost absent-mindedly, Steve wiped the sleeve of his
tattered linen shirt across his face.

"I'll get them tended to when we get back on board my
ship. And I know what you are going to tell me, Count
Chernikoff. The same story you told Ginny."

"It is true! Would you stand in her way? I think you
care more for her than she realizes, my poor little Princess. And I believe she cares for you. But to take her back
by force at this moment, when she is so confused, so much
upset. . . ."

"Oh, hell!" Steve leaned his back against the rail, suddenly tired, suddenly hurting all over. "I'll tell you what,
Count. Ginny must come back with me now, to stop an
ugly scandal that could ruin her, the Senator, everyone
connected with her. But if she still feels the same way she
does now in say—a year, then I give you my word I'll
send her to Russia myself. With grounds for a divorce.
Just don't give me any more problems *now,* for Christ
sake!"

Ginny was like a frozen, unyielding statue afterwards,
refusing to speak to anyone. Escorted to the all too famil-

iar stateroom aboard the "Green-Eyed Lady", she locked
the door behind her, and flung herself face downwards on
the bed.

She wanted to think—and no coherent thoughts would
come to her rescue. She closed her eyes, and the same terrible pictures seemd imprinted on her eyelids, so that she
started up with an involuntary cry, and then bit her already swollen lip.

She could feel the movement of the ship beneath her,
already familiar. Where was it taking her, and why—
oh God, why?

Someone tried the door, and she refused to answer it.
Eventually, they went away. Ginny continued to lie across
the bed, trying to still her mind and her nerves into drowsiness. She would refuse to go ashore!

There was another knock at the door.

"Ginny! Ginny, don't you understand that we must
speak with each other?"

The Senator. Her "father". She answered only because
she thought they might break open the door if she did not.

"I don't want to talk to anyone! I want to be left in
peace!"

Muffled voices outside the door, and then silence again.

How long? She took a powder out of her reticule,
flinging to the floor the jewels Steve had demanded she
bring. There was water in a carafe, and it cooled her
parched throat. Now, perhaps, she could sleep again. And
eventually, as the powder took effect, she did sleep, falling
off quite suddenly, as if she had slipped down the side of a
deep pit.

Waking to reality was much worse than the frightening
dreams that had pursued her down the dark corridors of
her drugged sleep.

She had been prepared—*almost* prepared—to do battle
with Steve again. But his first words, when she opened her
eyes to find him looking down at her, cut the ground from
under her feet.

"You took one of those damned powders again, didn't
you?"

Ginny rolled over on her side, wide-awake, eyes spitting
hate at him.

"Yes I did! What did you expect? How did you get in
here?"

"I have a key." His voice was dry, hardening as he added, "There'll be no more. You're going to have to learn
to do without crutches, Ginny."

"Crutches? What do you mean?"

He had shaved off his beard, and the saber cut was livid
across one side of his face as he looked down at her, eyes
shadowed.

"No more powders, no more tonics to make you sleep.
You're not going to need them, from now on. You'll find
that out."

A tremor shook her, but she forced herself to retaliate,
pouring all the scorn she could muster into her voice.

"You sound as if you are threatening me! What do you
intend to do? Keep me here as a prisoner?"

"We're on our way to Monterey. You've never been to
the ranch, have you? Your father and I decided that you
might enjoy spending a few weeks there, to give your
friends in San Francisco the chance to get used to your—
recent widowhood.

"And—then?" Ginny's voice was almost a whisper; she
only wished he did not see how white her knuckles were
from grasping the arms of her chair.

"And then we're going to be married. In church, with
your father giving you away. And half of San Francisco
will be invited to the reception afterwards. They might
whisper, for a while, about how soon you became a bride
after you were widowed. And they'll say you were my
mistress before. But it's better than being called a bigamist, isn't it, sweetheart? And in time they'll stop whispering and accept. I gave your friend Count Chernikoff my
word I'd let you travel to Russia within a year. If you still
want to go, or take a European trip then, you'll be free to.
You can make up your mind about a divorce then."

"My—oh, but I cannot believe this! You're *all* insane.
Steve, I won't be bullied or coerced any longer! I
refuse. . . !

In the end it did not matter what she said, or how
much she protested, crying out against his high-handed-
ness, affirming her hate.

After the first storming of tears and invectives, subsid-
ing eventually into abject pleading, the moments seemed
to run together like raindrops spattered against a dark
window.

BOOK TWO

Steve

Part Four
THE OPERA SINGER

Chapter Thirty-three

Senator Brandon lowered himself rather gingerly into the chair an obsequious waiter held for him. His son-in-law, who had risen politely, lifted a wicked eyebrow, his grin flashing for an instant under his black mustache.

"Too much riding, sir? I heard about the fox hunt at the Commodore's country estate."

Brandon, a still-handsome and distinguished looking man, gave a snort of disgust, taking the drink the waiter set before him.

"Fox hunt! The English can keep their quaint customs, as far as I'm concerned. I told Commodore Vanderbilt that the next time he visited California I'd arrange a real hunt for him. The hills behind the ranch are full of cougars." Taking a long swallow of his bourbon, the Senator shot a rather quizzical glance at his companion. "And you? What game have you been hunting of late? Louis Van Rink told me he saw you at the opera with an extremely attractive brunette. *Not* di Paoli, surely? I thought the lady was no longer on speaking terms with you!"

"I'm afraid so, sir. As it happened, the lady was anxious to hear one of her rivals sing *Lucia,* and since she lacked an escort. . . ."

Steve Morgan's lazy smile touched his eyes this time, crinkling them slightly at the corners; he leaned back in his chair, surveying his father-in-law.

"Ah." Brandon frowned, very slightly, his one comment speaking volumes. He stared rather thoughtfully at his glass, turning it between his fingers while he went on carefully: "Well—a man cannot very well go about in New York without a companion, I suppose! And especially—" he paused before adding heavily and significantly, "especially when his wife does not seem to lack for escorts in Paris and London and St. Petersburg!"

Steve Morgan gave a slight shrug, his face as impassive as an Indian's. "Ginny went to Europe to have some fun, and to renew old friendships. We have an understanding, sir."

"And *I* cannot understand these so-called modern marriages," Brandon said testily. "My daughter needs a firm hand, as *you* should know. And she seems to have grown far too headstrong. What's this I hear about her posing for some sculptor fellow in Paris? A friend of mine had the effrontery to suggest that she actually. . . .Well, damn it, I understand that the young man specializes in—er—"

"He usually specializes in statues of nudes, but in this case I understand there were some billowing draperies rather tactfully and strategically arranged—or so Ginny told me, when she last wrote." Steve saw Brandon's face begin to redden and he hastily added, "He's named it 'Figurehead'. When he exhibits the sculpture it isn't likely that there'll be more than speculation as to who the model was. In fact," Steve said, stretching his long legs negligently before him, his blue eyes narrowing very slightly, "I might arrange to buy it myself!"

The Senator's glass slammed down on the table.

"By God, Steve! I'm surprised you can take Ginny's escapades so lightly! If she were *my* wife, I'd take a whip to her. Now listen here." Brandon leaned forward slightly, nodding his head impatiently at the waiter who refilled his glass. "What is going on between you two? Sonya writes—damn it, there's no need to lift that infernal eyebrow at me. I'm sure you've heard the rumors just as I have! She's been seeing far too much of that French count she was engaged to once, and it seems that *his* wife isn't too happy about it! The question is, what are you going to do about it? She won't listen to advice from anyone— when Sonya ventured to protest Ginny went off and rented her own apartments, just as if she were some. . . . You should order her back immediately, and cut off her allowance if she will not agree!"

"What, and have her learn of my own peccadilloes?" Steve drawled; but his dark piratical face, with its lean, reckless lines, seemed to close for an instant under his father-in-law's close regard—and then his smile flashed out again.

"I apologize for sounding flippant, sir. Naturally you'd be concerned. But Ginny—you see, I do understand her. She's suddenly found herself rich and completely independent for the first time in her life, and of course she *is* a born flirt! But I think all she's doing is having her fling—and thoroughly enjoying shocking as many people as she can while she's about it."

Brandon was shaking his head.

"I don't understand either of you! I might as well be blunt. You two made news with that marriage of yours, and during the year you were together, because you were more like a man and his mistress than a respectable married couple! But, by God, when you're apart—"

"As you reminded me some time ago, sir, there's nothing like keeping busy."

In spite of the blandness of Steve's voice, Brandon gave him a sharp look; and then, with a resigned shrug, he took the menu one of the waiters held out to him.

Of course, it wasn't any of his business any longer. Ginny was Steve Morgan's responsibility now, and he hoped for all their sakes that she would decide to forget her foolishness and return soon. Either Steve would eventually lose his patience and his temper and go after her, probably killing a few of her lovers in the process—and the Senator shuddered inwardly and blocked out a remembrance of the bloody scene on the deck of the Russian's ship—or. . . . Just how serious was his son-in-law's liaison with Francesca di Paoli?

Brandon had had time to grow used to—and even slightly envious of—the effect Steve Morgan had on women. Even some of them who were old enough to know better. When he walked into a room, their eyes became watchful and aware. Lingering almost hungrily. For in spite of the civilized veneer, there was still something of the savage in Steve Morgan, and women sensed it. Perhaps it was that light, cat-footed walk of his that made them imagine they were being stalked. Or something only barely veiled behind the bold regard of his blue eyes that made every woman aware she was a female.

The Senator, being a man, was only aware that women liked Steve—some of them making it far too obvious. He found their open pursuit of his son-in-law rather amusing, in a way, for Steve was not only easily bored, but completely ruthless about showing it, too. He was not the kind of man who enjoyed, or wasted his time upon, drawing room flirtations or stolen assignations with some married woman. In fact, until di Paoli, Brandon had not discerned anything beyond a polite attentiveness in Steve Morgan's manner towards any woman in public.

He could hardly pry—but after their luncheon was over and the two men had gone their separate ways, Brandon sat back in his town carriage, puffing with more than usual energy on his cigar, his brows knitted. The trouble was that Francesca di Paoli was not the kind of woman any man could dismiss easily; she did not fit into any particular category. An Italian Princess, last of an impoverished but undeniably noble and ancient line, she was also possessed of an exceptional coloratura soprano voice, a great deal of determination, and hardly any inhibitions.

She had been acclaimed the toast of Europe, had had duels fought over her, and had turned down an offer of marriage from a king. Now in the process of taking the New World by storm, Francesca had turned out to be anything but the traditional voluptuously built Italian opera singer. She was slim—her voluptuousness limited to curves in all the right places. And she was exceptionally beautiful, with a pale, madonna-like skin; her classically oval features were set off by large, flashing dark eyes and masses of dark-brown, glossy hair which she usually wore coiled at the back of her small head to set off her slender neck. And that neck was always encircled by expensive jewels—gifts from her admirers. No, certainly not an ordinary woman—any more than Steve Morgan was an ordinary man. Uncomfortably, the Senator sensed danger; and had he known of Signorina di Paoli's reactions to her latest admirer, he would have been even more uneasy. As it was, he thought with relief that Steve had talked of returning to California soon, to see to some business affairs there. When he did, it would all be over; in the meantime, perhaps he would write to Ginny himself, and remind her of her obligations and her marriage, while at the same time dropping a discreet hint or two. . . .

Francesca, Princess di Paoli, was a woman who had become used to having things her own way. If she had an affair with a man, it was for one of two reasons. He had money and could help her with her career, or he appealed to her, for a short while, as a male animal—something to sate her desires. Either way, *she* was the one who dominated any relationship she entered into. *She* did the manipulating. But this time, it was different—the tables were turned, and while she raged against the thought, she also found herself challenged and more than a little intrigued.

It was, as she confided in her dresser—who had been her nurse in childhood, now acted as her chaperone, and was her closest friend—a case of like attracting like.

"You have often told me I was like a wild animal, who will claw and bite to get what it wants. Well? Have you not, Costanza? And you see, he is the same! There is something fierce, and almost frightening about him, hidden just under the surface. A—yes, a primitive sensuality, that is it! Ah—it makes me so angry, so furious that he will not take me seriously! There are times when I would like to sink my teeth and my nails into his flesh, but I am afraid to. Can you imagine that? *Me*—I am afraid!"

She was the applauded darling of two continents—a woman whose rages and temperamental tantrums were feared by lovers and theater managers alike. And yet, of late, she had caught herself acting almost like a lovesick girl over a man who took her just as lightly and casually as she had taken other lovers.

"And suppose I agree to sing at the opera house in this San Francisco of yours? They have offered me much money, of course, but I do as I please. Would you come to hear me there?"

The diamonds he had presented her with as casually as if they had been flowers sparkled in her ears, emphasizing her dark beauty. And on this occasion, the diamond earrings were all that she wore.

"Of course I'd come, sweetheart. If I happened to be in San Francisco at the time."

"But"—she could not help the slightly petulant tone that

crept into her voice—"suppose, by then, that your wife has returned?"

His blue eyes, looking almost as dark as hers in the lamplight, glinted lazily at her.

"Then I'd present her to you, of course."

"But you would not be my escort at the grand party they would hold afterwards?" she persisted.

"I don't know, 'Cesca. And by then, you might have found other amusements. There are a lot of millionaires in San Francisco. And in Texas, too," he added wickedly, knowing that she had already committed herself to sing in San Antonio, following several appearances in New Orleans.

She narrowed her eyes at him, crying between gritted teeth:

"I wonder if you know how angry you make me? I tell you, Stefan, that I do not care for—for all *those!*" Her nose wrinkled with disgust, and then she demanded, in the next breath, "Why are you not in love with me? Don't you find me beautiful and attractive enough?"

His long, brown fingers traced the outline of her breasts lightly.

"You're very beautiful. And if I were foolish enough to fall in love with you, cara, you'd rip me to pieces with those long, lovely nails of yours."

She sighed pensively, arms tightening around him.

"Why are we so much alike? I could almost hate you for it!"

"Almost? I think I like the way you hate. . . ."

His lips touched hers, very lightly at first, until her hands moved caressingly over his bronzed skin, feeling the play of muscles underneath—moving deliberately, teasingly, until she felt his desire mount, and his kisses became almost cruelly demanding.

He demanded—she gave. She—Francesca di Paoli, over whom men had killed themselves. And all because one night she had been intolerably bored and this tall, blue-eyed adventurer from California had looked her over as insolently as if she'd been some streetwalker, his eyes narrowing very slightly as they seemed to strip away the elaborate gown she wore—making her suddenly feel almost dizzy with weakness before he had looked away, ignoring her for the remainder of the evening.

Chapter Thirty-four

Mr. Bertram Fields, financier turned entrepreneur, had reserved three entire floors of the Astoria Hotel for the soiree he gave following the fabulous di Paoli's American debut in *La Traviata*. And by this time, Francesca di Paoli was already the talk of New York society. Not only was she a real princess, but she was beautiful, and could not only sing, but act as well.

Women hated the female alley-cat they sensed under the cool and poised exterior of society's latest rage, even while they gushed over the clear perfection of her voice. Men—all the men were mad over her; there was not one of them who didn't visualize what it would be like to spend a night with her. Even the critics had no fault to find with her. She was a triumph, the newest "Incomparable."

Francesca held court in the glass-domed ballroom on the topmost floor of the hotel, where one could watch the stars while dancing. Up here, only the elite and the very rich were permitted to enter.

Standing by the marble balustrade at one end of the magnificent ballroom, Francesca stood between Mr. Fields and Luigi, her manager; gracefully, she acknowledged the compliments of the distinguished guests that streamed by as they were presented to her. Those men who were not accompanied by their wives begged for the honor of dancing with her. Even the very richest of them argued among themselves for the privilege of at least half a dance—a few minutes of a waltz.

"Perhaps," she told them, smiling. A small moue, a helpless shrug indicating the long line of people who still waited to be presented to her. Her poise never deserted her; her smile was gracious and dazzling at the same time. Only her manager sensed her boredom, and grew nervous. When she was between lovers or tiring of a current one, Francesca was always bored and hungry. And capable of showing it, if the temper took her.

She had been presented to the President of the United States and his wife. To a few chosen Senators and Congressmen. As well as to some of the millionaires who played with railroads and oil wells and gold mines. Men who owned hundreds of thousands of acres of land and still talked wistfully and admiringly of Europe. And some of these very rich men dreamed of dazzling her with their wealth—of buying her, even if it was only for a night, for a few hours. For it was well known by now that she refused to become the full-time mistress of any man, be he king or rich commoner. It was rumored that she had told one titled lover that she had still too much to learn. "About music, which is my life—about life itself. About making love. . . . I want many teachers each one teaching me something different. And everything else must take second place to my career."

"Francesca, my dear—may I present Mr. Gould? Mr. *Jay* Gould." As if there was any other Mr. Gould! She had heard of him—who had not? Francesca di Paoli extended her hand to the stocky, whispery-voiced man and flashed her brilliant smile. He had spoken with an exaggeratedly English accent, just like that other man they all called the Commodore. Why were these rich Americans such fakes?

How dull, how boring they all were! What a waste—all those books about America she had carefully studied before she came here. She had thought to find virile men who would match this enormous, half-tamed land; as strong as the land itself. And had discovered only a set of pretentious hypocrites; aping the French, aping the English; acting as if they were ashamed of their origins.

"Pah!" she hissed in an undertone to Luigi. "These are not men at all! Where are all the rugged adventurers you told me of when you were persuading me to come here? I have not seen anything but dressed-up puppets! I think that already I am beginning to despise these Americans!"

Her angry, restless eyes swept over the enormous room without seeming to, while she stood with her head half-bent, appearing to be engrossed in something Mr. Fields was telling her.

He was an ex-lover himself, but old enough and wise enough to accept his congé gracefully, and even philosophically, while retaining a certain fondness for his protégée. Now, he chuckled suddenly.

". . . And you have not heard a word I've been saying, have you? Shall I order you some champagne to cheer you up?"

"What? Bertram—" Suddenly her hand, fingers sparkling with rings, touched his arm with a kind of urgency, and he saw the sudden dark sheen of her eyes. "Who is he? Tell me, quickly!"

"He?" Fields' eyes followed the direction that hers had taken, and he gave a soft, amused laugh, deliberately choosing to misunderstand her.

"Why—that, Illustrissima, is United States Senator William S. Brandon. Sometime Virginian, now one of our distinguished Senators from California. A handsome man still, is he not? And if I'm not mistaken, the lady with him is the wife of his good friend Senator Hartman, who is unfortunately indisposed tonight."

Francesca's jetty eyes flashed dangerously.

"You know very well that I did not mean the *older* man! He *looks* like a Senator—I need not have asked. I meant the other—the man with him who is dressed like a gentleman but has the face of a Sicilian banditti; the tall blue-eyed one with the thin saber scar on his face."

"Oh." Fields' voice was carefully noncommittal, but his eyebrows had shot up, joining in the middle to give him a faunlike look. He glanced again towards the newcomers, who still stood close to the door, talking to some acquaintances and obviously in no hurry to come forward in order to be presented to the guest of honor.

A good six inches taller than the Senator himself, the dark-haired man who had entered with him had bent his head to listen to something the vapidly pretty blond girl he was escorting whispered to him. She clung rather helplessly to his arm with both hands; her wrists were encircled with bracelets of pearls and black sapphires.

" 'Oh.' Is that all you have to say? Well? Is he perhaps a gate-crasher—someone you do not know? Is that why you hesitate?"

Francesca's voice hissed at him in the gutter Italian she used when she was angry, and then switched to perfect, charming English to greet a guest.

"Thank you, signore! It was such a pleasure for me to perform before an audience as appreciative as the one tonight. . . ."

When the gentleman had kissed her hand lingeringly and moved on, Bertram Fields intercepted Francesca's ominous look and said in a casual voice:

"I suppose you must mean the Senator's companion? The one who looks like a pirate? His name is Steven Morgan, and he is our latest millionaire from California, as well as being the Senator's son-in-law."

"He has a *wife*? He does not look the type! I suppose she is that blonde child who clings so tightly to his arm as if she is afraid he will escape?"

"The blonde child you refer to happens to be Senator Hartman's daughter. Mr. Morgan's wife is vacationing in Europe with her stepmother, I understand."

"How interesting!" Francesca half-purred, her long lashes shadowing her eyes. "He does not have a married look, that one! And he does look like a bandit." And then her voice became deliberately scornful. "But I suppose he is just as brash and boastful as the rest of them. Did he make his money on the railroads or the gold mines? Or by being fortunate enough to marry a Senator's ugly daughter?"

This time, Fields chuckled out loud.

"Your claws are showing, Francesca! Actually, the Senator's daughter is far from being ugly. And Mr. Morgan, although he comes from one of the richest families in Mexico, made most of his money by his own efforts, as I understand, although there are some people who might agree with you about his being a—how did you put it?—a banditti; yes. But I really think—"

"And you can tell me what it is you think afterwards, sí, my good friend?" Francesca's voice had suddenly dropped, sounding deceptively silky. "Because I think that at last these late guests of yours have decided to greet us."

The Princess di Paoli reserved her most winning, brilliant smile for the Senator from California, her manner suddenly becoming almost cold when her eyes met the dark, startling blue of Steve Morgan's—caught his amused, half-mocking smile as he bowed over her hand. Such a detestably arrogant-seeming man! His eyes had flickered over her with deliberate insolence, as if she'd been some whore for sale!

Hoping to confuse him, Francesca spoke in Italian,

showing her pearly-white teeth in an obviously insincere smile. He deserved to be put in his place!

"And you, signore, let me guess, must be either a goldminer or a lumberjack—still clumsy in a drawing room, like so many of your boorish compatriots!"

Francesca could not help noticing that when he smiled the sun-wrinkles fanned out at the corners of his eyes, the thin scar on his pirate's face deepening into a crease as his teeth flashed against sun-browned skin.

"And your biting wit is matched only by your truly magnificent voice, signorina! And your beauty—especially when it is enhanced by such flashing black eyes."

"You flatter me, signore," she said artlessly in English, smiling her mock apology at the others. "You must forgive me, please—sometimes I have the regrettable habit of forgetting myself and speaking in my own language! What a surprise that you should speak Italian, signore. And so fluently, too!"

Francesca scribbled her name on the program Miss Hartman shyly held out to her, looking past the girl at Steve Morgan with a mixture of anger and challenge that he ignored with a bow and a polite disclaimer.

The predatory light she had recognized in his eyes only a minute ago had vanished, to be replaced by indifference.

Francesca caught sight of him across the crowded room a few more times after that; he was every inch the devoted and gallant escort, in spite of the blond Miss Hartman's clinging-vine fingers. He danced with no other woman except Sally Hartman's mother; and as if to add insult to indifference, they left early.

"What a barbarian! Why am I expected to endure these clumsy, mannerless Americans—I ask you, why?"

Working herself up into a fine rage, Francesca di Paoli paced about her suite afterwards, while her wooden-faced maid, used to her tantrums, continued to fold away her clothes in one corner of the room; and Bertam Fields stood leaning against the mantlepiece with his arms folded and his eyebrows raised. Her manager, Luigi Rizzo, against whom her tirade was directed, seemed to cower in his chair as if he expected her to throw something at him at any moment—a not unusual happening.

Pausing, the Princess placed her hands on her hips in the

fashion of a Sicilian washerwoman, eyes shooting sparks
at the luckless Rizzo.

"That man! Why was he invited to *my* reception? Did
you see the way he looked at me? So crude and insolent!
If I had been a man I would have—I would have struck
him for that look!"

"But Principessa—"

"Don't speak to me! There are no men about me! And
he, that black-browed banditti—he did not even ask me to
dance, so that I could refuse him. Tell me, what kind of
man is this? To look me over from head to foot as if I
were a common slut up for sale, and then act the hypocrite—was it because his father-in-law was there? Is he
afraid of his wife? Afraid of women? Perhaps that is why
he prefers to escort little, simpering girls!"

Two nights later, Francesca di Paoli's pleasure in the
thunderous ovation she received when stepping out on to
the stage was spoiled when she recognized her bête noir
sitting alone in a box with a dazzlingly beautiful blonde
woman.

And after the act, while her patient dresser raised her
hands with a gesture of resignation, Francesca swept every
vase and crystal bowl of flowers in her dressing room onto
the floor.

She returned to the stage for the second act, playing a
subdued and simple Violetta—leaving both her manager
and Mr. Fields shaking their heads with relief while the
stony-faced Constanza cleaned up the mess.

Afterwards, she exploded again.

"So! Now tell me! The banditti—he likes these cold
northern types who are no challenge to his manhood, sí? I
suppose this wife of his is like that. Pale hair, with no col-
or in it, and a frozen body like ice?"

Bertram Fields, recognizing all the signs in his temperamental ex-mistress, had taken the trouble to make
some inquiries about Steve Morgan.

"His wife, from all accounts, looks like a Hungarian
gypsy; and her first husband was a Russian prince who
died mysteriously at sea. And as for this Mr. Morgan, I'd
be careful if I were you, Principessa. I've heard whispers
that he's not far removed from the bandit you call him.
Before he suddenly emerged on the financial scene, he was
a soldier of fortune. Fought for Juarez in the bloody Mex-

ican Revolution that overthrew the Emperor Maximilian. And before that—I've actually heard rumors he was an outlaw, with a reward posted for his capture dead or alive. Forget him. There are other men—and you like yours tame and adoring, do you not?"

"Like *you* were?" she snapped cruelly, and he shrugged helplessly.

"The brief relationship that you and I once shared was over a long time ago, bellissima! And at the moment you represent a considerable investment to me. What's the matter, doesn't your career matter to you any longer?" His voice strengthened as he added, "You ought to stick to the kind of man who will be content to escort you here and there and sends you jewels and flowers daily while he waits patiently until you are finished with your performance. Forget this Steve Morgan. In any case, he will be leaving for California soon."

With one of the sudden, volatile changes of mood that were characteristic of her, Francesca had stopped picking sullenly at the food on her plate. She picked up the thin crystal goblet by her plate and lifted it, smiling secretly, with narrowed eyes.

"You think so? But I will meet him again, before that. And then, we will see!" Her eyes had a strange glitter in them that Bertram Fields recognized only too well. Still smiling, she tilted her head to toss off the last of her wine before she leaned across the table. "You know how I insist upon getting my own way, do you not, Bertram? And since I am such a profitable investment to you, you will do everything to make me happy . . . yes, I know that. You are such a kind man! So we will accept the invitation of this very rich Mr. Gould to spend the weekend at his estate in some unpronounceable place—and I think he will also invite Senator William Brandon of California. And his son-in-law, of course!"

Chapter Thirty-five

Mr. Jay Gould's weekend house party consisted of not more than a hundred or so persons. Bertram Fields had explained to Francesca that the guest list was very select, and she shrugged as if she did not particularly care.

"You'll meet some very rich men—and Mr. Gould's partners in the Erie Railroad, of course." Almost to himself, Fields added, "I suppose his theme for the weekend bears out some of the rumors I've been hearing. Cornelius Vanderbilt invites *his* guests to English style foxhunts— Mr. Gould cultivates the American West. Of course, that's where the railroads will be spreading their tentacles next."

Mr. Fields had a good head for business, and Francesca, for once, displayed some interest, arching a dark eyebrow.

"So? Tell me more about this western theme, as you call it. Will we have to wear costumes, then?"

Flashing a quizzical look at her, Fields elaborated.

Mr. Gould had actually erected a typical western town on the extensive grounds of his estate. A saloon and false-fronted guest hotel. Even a jail and a bank. Boardwalks lining dusty streets. The guests who were not westerners themselves would be provided with appropriate clothing, and there would be a rodeo, with exhibitions of horse breaking, trick riding, and even cattle branding. The guest list included the owners of some of the largest ranches in the West and Southwest. Men like "Shanghai" Pierce and Colonel Goodnight, who might ship their cattle to market on the railroads that were being built even now at break-neck speed. Mr. Gould already owned a large block of shares in the Union Pacific railroad, and was rumored to be buying more. And, of course, Senator Brandon's son-in-law was already one of the major stockholders in the Central Pacific. . . .

"How very interesting!" Francesca purred. "You must tell me more. After all, I don't want to appear ignorant!"

Francesca di Paoli planned her arrival on Friday evening. Just a trifle late, she was accompanied by her faithful Costanza, her manager, Luigi Rizzo, and Mr. Fields. She protested herself rather startled by armed guards at the gatehouse, with their strange clothes, big hats, and their armory of rifles, and holstered revolvers. Already dressed for her role as a dance-hall singer, she wore a deliberately bright and vulgar satin gown, low-cut enough to show a great deal of her breasts. The skirt was slit provocatively up the side to display black mesh stockings and a red rose garter. And in spite of Costanza's protests, she had reddened her cheeks and her lips and put a red satin rose in the coil of dark hair at her neck.

"You are too excited already!" Costanza had scolded while she helped her to dress. "You do not need so much color in the face—or on your mouth!"

Francesca had replied mischievously, ignoring her maid's pursed lips.

"But if I am to play the part of a demi-monde, then I must look it, sí? You nag too much, Costanza!"

Leaving the too-watchful Costanza behind in the room that had been allotted to her, Francesca was escorted to supper by Mr. Fields, but found herself seated between Senator Brandon and Mr. Shanghai Pierce—a surprisingly small, strutting man with roving hands and eyes, whom she detested on sight.

Supper, for a few exceptionally distinguished guests, was an alfresco affair in a glass-roofed courtyard that gave the impression of the open air. She might have enjoyed it more, except for the absence of one particular man, and the obnoxious presence of Mr. Pierce, who seemed the very epitome of all the boorish Americans she had so far met. She understood that he was very rich; all the same, his strange accent was so pronounced that she could hardly understand a word he said. Besides which, she was compelled several times to slap his hands with her folded-up fan—which only had the effect of making him chortle shrilly and remark, "But dang it! That's how the dance-hall gals back home expect to be treated!"

Francesca was relieved to find that the Senator, on the other hand, was the perfect gentleman. Deliberately turning one bare shoulder on the obstreperous Mr. Pierce, she devoted most of her attention to the Senator, although her eyes, veiled by dark lashes, continued to move around restlessly. Where *was* he? If he hadn't come, she would kill Bertram, she thought furiously all the time she flirted modestly and discreetly with the Senator.

Tonight, she allowed her accent to become more pronounced than usual.

"But I understand that you have a very beautiful wife, signore. How is it that I have not met her?"

"She's holidaying in France, with my daughter, I'm afraid. If not, I'm sure she would not have missed a single one of your performances!" His gallant response won him a smile and a flirtatious sparkle of dark eyes.

"Ah, but I am sure you have not been *too* lonely, eh?" Francesca di Paoli said teasingly. "Such a handsome man ... you don't mind that I am blunt? In Italy, we accept life as it is. Your wife and your little girl—you miss them very much?"

"You flatter me, signorina! My daughter can hardly be called a child, I'm afraid. She's a married woman—quite grown up and far too headstrong. As a matter of fact, she was brought up in Pàris—"

"But—this I do not understand! Your daughter? It's difficult to comprehend you have a daughter old enough to be married! But why does she leave her husband to go to Paris? Perhaps he has gone with her?"

While Francèsca cast out her line, very delicately, Shanghai Pierce turned to the supper partner at his right, a shrill-laughed woman with an exceptionally big bosom. He peered down her decolletage while he placed his hand on her knee, chortling to himself when she did nothing more than giggle nervously.

Italians! Foreigners! He could never understand their lingo anyhow. And this Mrs. What's-her-name *did* understand his rather primitive overtures. Hell with teasing Italian opera-singers anyhow!

"You *like* opera?" Francesca was saying. "Alas, most men only come to the opera house because their wives insist. And then they fall asleep."

"I doubt if any man could fall asleep when *you* are onstage!" Still gallant, Brandon responded predictably.

"How you flatter me! But you see, you do not even remember the very first time we met. Admit it!"

"How could I forget? Bertram Fields was kind enough to invite us—I came only to be presented to you."

Dark eyes smiled teasingly under fringed lashes.

"You are being polite. You did not ask me to dance—and you left very early. You see, *I* notice, when I am interested. And you had two beautiful ladies with you, also. Am I not right?"

"I was escorting the wife of a very close friend of mine on that occasion." Brandon chuckled reminiscently to himself. "And, as I recall, I had to persuade my scapegrace son-in-law to escort her daughter."

"Oh?" Francesca sounded studiedly disinterested. "Oh, yes—now that I think about it, I recall that there was another man with you. Someone who spoke Italian. Your son-in-law, you say?"

William Brandon, who was nobody's fool, gave an inward sigh. He should have guessed, of course. Steve.

Aloud, he said politely, "Yes, that's right. My daughter Virginia's husband. He's somewhere around tonight—probably in the saloon with some of the Texas cowboys."

"Texas—what about Texas, huh?" As if he had suddenly come to life, Shanghai Pierce leaned deliberately across her, taking care to brush her all-but-naked breasts with his elbow as he did so. "Listen—don't you let him fool you with all that smooth talk, pretty gal! Ain't nothin' wrong about Texas—and California's got more of its share of violence than Texas! Hey, Brandon? You just ask that ornery son-in-law of yours—he's *still* wanted in some parts of Texas, last I heard! Goddamn! That daughter of yours must be something, to hogtie a bad hombre like him." Mr. Pierce began to laugh. "How come he ain't here? Whooping it up with my cowboys, eh?"

Senator Brandon cut across his slightly slurred speech, his voice frosty.

"I am sure the lady does not wish to hear. . . !"

Diverted, Shanghai Pierce fixed his small, pale blue eyes on Francesca. "Yeah—yeah! When are you going to do your stuff, eh, pretty gal? Sing in American, I mean. You gonna do that?"

Disappointed that he had changed the subject so quickly, Francesca shuddered delicately.

"*Soon,* Mr. Pierce. When Mr. Gould is ready, and we have all finished with supper. And I assure you that I can sing in English."

Senator Brandon was Signorina di Paoli's escort when the diners finally made their leisurely way to the gaudily painted wooden building that proclaimed itself to be the Nugget Saloon.

An impassive looking female escort, who looked and dressed for all the world like a red-satin madam, led Francesca up the back stairway.

"Nothin' to worry about, honey," the woman said reassuringly in a husky voice. "You just walk down the stairs behind me. And you'll do your singin' on the stage—you'll see it when we get to the landing."

"Oh, I am not afraid!" Francesca said lightly. Her split skirt showed a provocative glimpse of her thigh as she walked down the stairs, deliberately swaying her hips slightly.

For the first time, she heard a wild rebel yell—a bone-chilling sound that almost made her change her mind about singing before such a noisy and ill-assorted crowd. There was a tinkling piano somewhere in the background, and the loud buzz of voices and laughter, underlaid by the clinking of bottles against glasses. So *this* was what the inside of a western saloon was like.

Mr. Gould's more important guests sat at tables that were scattered around the room. Several men were clustered around gaming tables, and did not even look up. A long bar, running the length of one entire mirrored wall, was manned by several tireless bartenders who seemed expert at sliding glasses down the length of the mahogany topped bar. And it was here that the Texas cowboys had gathered to "celebrate" in their own peculiar way—making as much noise as possible, banging with bottles or glasses on the bar and telling each other questionable stories.

Francesca was used to awed silence or polite applause when she made an appearance on stage, and she thought viciously to herself that these men were obviously not far removed from brute level. *Their* way of expressing approval was to whistle and stamp their feet and call out ribald remarks! Her black eyes flashed with anger, even while she continued to smile.

"Any little ole gal who shows that much leg and bosom

is purely askin' for it!" Shanghai declared loudly to Senator Brandon, who sat next to him. " You watch my foreman, Jed Langley—that tall hombre there in the checkered shirt. Jed's got a way with the ladies, and when he sees something he wants. . . . He's fast enough with those six-guns to scare off the competition, too."

A brownhaired man, handsome in a rugged way, had cleared a space directly in front of the stage, and turned his straight-backed chair around so that he sat straddling it, arms resting across its back; he stared with open lust at the woman on the stage, who had begun to sing with a charming accent.

"I think *that* may depend upon who the lady wants," Brandon said thoughtfully in his soft Virginia drawl. Like all the other men present he had been watching di Paoli, and he'd noticed that she seemed to be dividing her smiles and flirtatious glances between two men—Langley, and a man who stood at the end of the bar.

"Bet you a thousand to start with that Langley gets her!" Shanghai pulled a wad of banknotes out of his jacket pocket, tossing them challengingly onto the table. His voice was loud enough to draw the attention of some of the other gentlemen seated with them, and Jim Fisk, an inveterate gambler, gave his booming laugh as he leaned across to wink at the frowning Senator.

"You going to cover his bet, Brandon? I believe the *other* man the lady has been paying some attention to happens to be your son-in-law!"

Annoyed at being trapped into such a ridiculous situation, Brandon managed to keep his face expressionless as he drew out his wallet. He had no choice; it had turned into a matter of pride.

Even Jay Gould's whispery voice seemed charged with some inner amusement as he raised an eyebrow. "Texas versus California, eh? It makes for an interesting wager, and one I'd take myself if I believed in gambling."

Already, several of the other gentlemen who were seated at the same table had begun to make their private bets, but it was left to the flamboyant and uninhibited Mr. Fisk to slyly fan the flames. He suggested that perhaps a gunfight might prove more entertaining than the rodeo.

"And isn't that the way men settled their differences out West? From what I observe right now, I believe that there *is* going to be a slight—um—disagreement between two of the lady's admirers!"

Senator Brandon's dismayed eyes followed the jerk of Fisk's head. Francesca di Paoli had finished her song, to an accompaniment of stamping boots and loud whoops from the appreciative cowboys. Accepting Jed Langley's gallantly outstretched hand, with a flashing smile and a provocative lowering of her eyelashes, she shook her head teasingly at something he whispered and chose to walk by herself to the bar instead, deliberately leaning one elbow on it as she tilted her head to smile into slightly mocking, quizzical blue eyes.

"Are you going to buy me a drink—cowboy?"

"Are you sure you don't mean trouble, Signorina? Your ardent admirer is scowling this way with blood in his eye." Steve's voice was dry, but nevertheless his mouth twitched up at one corner with sardonic amusement.

Francesca's nostrils flared, showing her temper, but she pouted deliberately.

"How ungallant! Or perhaps you are . . . afraid?"

He smiled down at her openly this time, clefts deepening in his face.

"That depends what you have in mind, signorina. If I'm going to get in a fight, I like to know what I'm fighting for."

"For—me? Do you consider the stakes high enough to be worth the trouble, signore?"

She caught and held his eyes for a moment, letting the half-taunting, half-defiant challenge leap into the open between them.

And it was this look that Jed Langley intercepted as he pushed himself aggressively up to the bar, men falling back to make room for him, until all in a moment they were isolated in a small, cleared space—Langley, the woman, and Steve Morgan.

Except for the tinkling piano, a hush seemed to have fallen over the crowded, smoky room. Brandon found himself watching his son-in-law, noticing the way Steve had shifted his position very slightly, without seeming to, so that he faced Langley, his left shoulder to the bar, right arm loose and relaxed by his side where his holstered gun was snug against his thigh. Tonight, Steve wore a faded blue shirt under a black leather vest, and dark blue pants tucked into high-topped boots. There was very little to distinguish him from the men from Texas, except, perhaps, the coiled-spring tension that one could sense in him, even at a distance; it was the sign, for those who could recognize it, of a professional gunfighter.

Langley should have seen it, but Langley, by this time, was too angry to think straight. He wasn't looking for a gunman. He saw a tall man with very blue eyes who was *dressed* like one, and wore a gun in a tied-down holster— all of which was pure fakery, because this man was what he thought of contemptuously as "an Eastern dude"—one of the guests; but that didn't matter, because the boss was doing nothing to stop what was going to happen. In fact, Langley could hear old Shang chortling out loud somewhere behind him. Pierce didn't like dudes any more than *he* did, and Langley had a feeling that his boss wouldn't mind one bit if he taught one of these playboys a lesson. Like—if a man wore a gun, he'd better know how to use it. And then, overriding everything else, there was the woman. A foreign woman—an opera singer, he'd heard somebody say. But that meant nothing to Jed Langley. Any woman who sang on the stage for money, no matter in what language she sang or how much she was paid, was a woman who'd been around. Not the kind you'd exactly call a lady, but not a tramp either. Somewhere in between. He meant to find out—and she'd flirted with him while she sang that sentimental love song. He'd been sure of himself, until she'd dropped her hand from his arm with a murmured word of thanks and had walked up to the dude, hips swinging in a way she knew damn well was provocative, meant to lead a man on. Well—she'd find out, soon enough, who was the *real* man.

"I do hope your son-in-law knows something about the use of that gun he's wearing," Dan Drew murmured. Like all the other gentlemen who sat with Jay Gould at the largest table, his head was turned to watch what seemed almost a staged tableau at the far end of the bar.

Senator Brandon's tension showed only in the pulsing of a vein in his forehead. His voice was calm. "Oh, I believe he does, gentlemen. I'm not worried for him."

Pierce laughed shrilly. "I'll say this much—Morgan's a hellion, from what I've heard. Or was, some years back, unless easy living has softened him up! When I make a bet

I like the odds to be close. I wouldn't let a tenderfoot go up against Jed Langley. But when I hire a gunman, I hire the best, and I think you're going to find that out pretty soon."

Ginny would have recognized the dancing, dangerous light in Steve Morgan's eyes, but Francesca di Paoli wasn't Ginny. Suddenly, what had started out to be an amusing, challenging game, was no game at all, and she tried not to shrink too obviously against the bar as Jed Langley came up to lean against it, his sleeve brushing her bare arm. She noticed that although he spoke to her, his narrowed eyes did not leave Steve Morgan's face.

"This hombre refuse to buy you a drink, ma'am? I'd be glad to oblige, once the air in here starts to smell better." He was spoiling for a fight, and showed it. Francesca felt a thrill of fearful anticipation shoot through her, but almost shamefully she realized that there was excitement mixed with her apprehension. This Steven Morgan had intrigued her, unwillingly, from the very first time she had set eyes on him. Now, perhaps she would find out what kind of man he was. And it was for that reason that she had come here. . . .

Her thoughts flashed across the surface of her mind in less than a second, as brown eyes clashed with blue.

"Seems to *me*," Jed Langley said in a voice that was heavy with contempt, "that you need a real man to look after you, ma'am. Buy you drinks, an' keep off dudes that think wearin' a gun an' range clothes make them a real man."

This time, as he looked across her again, meeting the tenderfoot's cold eyes, there was no mistaking his meaning. But at the same time, some warning signal flashed in Langley's brain, belatedly making him cautious.

This particular Eastern dude didn't act nervous, as he expected him to be. And he showed no signs of backing down. He was either brave or foolish—or perhaps he thought this was all play-acting?

"Listen—" Langley began, speaking directly to Steve for the first time, and was cut off by the flat, slightly impatient voice.

"*You* listen, Langley. You want to put on a show for Mr. Gould and his friends, let's go outside. The lady's already promised to spend the rest of the evening with whoever comes out on top—haven't you cara?"

Before Langley could answer, Shanghai Pierce's raucous voice cut through the sudden stillness.

"You ain't going to shoot up the place, you dang fools! Outside, on the street—an' we're gonna show everybody here what a real western gunfight is like."

The little man, in his high-heeled boots and incongruously large Stetson hat, seemed to have taken charge as he swaggered over to the bar.

"Jed, you take the north end of the street. Morgan, you can come from the south. An' we ain't gonna have no fooling, mind! This is for real, and the pretty lady here is gonna be the winner's gal for the evening, ain't you, honey?"

Challenged, Francesca reacted with a short, defiant laugh that Mr. Fields, at least, recognized with an inward groan of despair.

There was nothing he could do—*she* had already done it all. He watched eager hands catch her about the waist, lifting her up onto the bar. And she was still laughing, enjoying every minute of the attention she was being paid.

"A bet is a bet. I will sing for the winner and dance with him all evening. And for the one who loses—perhaps I will cry a little bit?"

Chapter Thirty-six

The "street" outside, lighted by coal-oil lanterns suspended from tall poles, was already lined with eager spectators.

Francesca di Paoli stood with Mr. Gould and his partner, Jim Fisk, on her left—Senator Brandon and Shanghai Pierce on her right. Behind her, she could sense the disapproving presence of Bert Fields.

She had the impression that all this was a carefully

stage-managed production—the lanterns were the foot-
lights. . . . And yet, only minutes ago she had been reminded that, like the bullfight she had enjoyed watching on a
visit to Spain, this contest with guns would be very real.
And Shanghai Pierce seemed determined to remind everybody of the fact.

"Those six-guns carry real bullets, and Jed Langley's
mad enough to kill that son-in-law of yours, Brandon.
Hope *he* savvies that."

"My son-in-law hardly regards a gun as a plaything,"
the Senator responded drily. His face looked hollowed and
older in the orange glow of the lanterns, for all his confident tone. "I hope your foreman realizes he's not up
against a tenderfoot."

"Ain't a day that Langley don't practice with them guns
he wears." Pierce laughed confidently before he added,
"Tell you what, I'll make that bet we made bigger, just to
show you how sure I am. Got fifteen hundred or more
acres of land near Baroque I won in a poker game not too
long ago. Good bottom land, watered by the Red River—
got a house an' everything on it. Used to be a plantation
belonging to some Frenchman, only he let it go since the
war. Best damn ranch in the county. Got several thousand
head of cattle running wild. Bet you that—against that silver mine you just bought over in New Mexico Territory.
You on, or not? These gentlemen here can be witnesses."

Mr. Gould's whispery voice seemed to hold a suppressed
note of excitement. "If the Senator's as sure of his son-in-
law as you are of your man, the outcome of this—er—gunfight should prove very interesting, don't you think,
gentlemen? Naturally"—his voice hardened almost imperceptibly, sending a cold shiver up Francesca's spine—"if
there should be a death, it will be termed an unfortunate
hunting accident. I presume we're all agreed upon *that*?"

A murmur of assent went through the crowd; and Brandon said grimly, jaws clamping down on his cigar, "An accident, of course. And Pierce—your bet's taken!"

"Signore?" Francesca di Paoli sounded oddly hesitant as
she said softly, "Are you really as confident as you sound?
I would not like to think—"

"I'm not worried about Steve. He can take care of himself, whether it's with a gun or. . . ." Brandon's grim voice
cut itself off, and then he added in a different tone, "But I

hope to God that my daughter never finds out what part I've played in this affair!"

"But your daughter, she is not here—and I am."

There was a note in her voice that made Brandon swivel his head to look at her sharply in spite of the tension in him. The same kind of tension that held them all— stark reality imposed upon unreality. Jay Gould's manufactured Western town had suddenly come to life—with death at the end of the street.

"Remember, boys." Shanghai Pierce's raucous voice broke into the sudden hush that seemed to have seized guests and cowboys alike. "We all keep out of it and, by God, if the winner ain't a Texan, the bet I've just taken will sure as hell make him one!"

A ragged cheer went up; and the scene fell into stillness again. Francesca's breath caught in her throat. She had had duels fought over her before, in Europe, but she had never watched one. This—this was so different! It didn't seem real, and yet. . . . Was she going to watch a man die? Which one?

There was no pompous formality here—no seconds, not even a doctor in attendance, as far as she knew. Perhaps there would be no doctor needed. And the two men who had suddenly emerged into the lamplight from opposite ends of the street did not pause to take careful aim at each other. They kept walking, no emotion showing on shadowed faces. What would happen when they stopped? It was true—everything she had sensed about these Americans. They were still savages; untamed violence was barely hidden beneath the surface veneer of civilization they pretended to adopt. Too late, Francesca began to realize just what she had provoked so thoughtlessly.

The two men on the street watched only each other.

"You sure you know what to do with a gun, dude?" Jed Langley's voice was deliberately mocking, to cover the uneasy feeling that had suddenly come over him.

"You sure I'm a dude?" Steve Morgan hadn't raised his voice, and they were close enough now for Langley to notice everything he should have noticed before: the tied-down holster, the easy walk, and above all, the eyes— slightly narrowed, looking almost black in the flickering light.

What the hell had Pierce called out to him earlier?

"Don't take any chances, Langley. This here hombre you're supposed to meet is from California. . . !"

He had wondered, at the moment, his brain still clouded by anger, just what in hell that was supposed to mean. He'd thought that Shang was trying to make it seem to the others like this wasn't going to be a one-sided gun fight, so he could double his bets. But was it possible that the boss had been warning him?

His thinking suddenly razor-sharp, his walk becoming slower, Langley studied his opponent, mind casting back in the few seconds that remained. Morgan—he'd heard the name, damn it! Some time back. But who in hell would expect to find a Western gunfighter out *here*? He'd stopped thinking about the woman, watching the way Steve Morgan's hand stayed loose—close to the butt of his gun.

"We going to kill each other for the entertainment of these rich folk, or are we going to settle for first blood?"

"I don't aim to kill you, Langley." Steve Morgan's voice was flat, slightly tinged with impatience. He was watching Langley's eyes and his face, waiting for the tautening of muscles that meant the man was going to draw. Langley would be good, instinct told him that. But he was the kind of man who liked to talk, to draw his opponent's attention, before he made his play.

"Don't aim to kill you either," Langley said easily, and almost the same moment his hand slashed downward.

But Steve was already drawing, body swivelling sideways as he shot from the hip. Jed Langley felt a jarring pain shoot through his arm as the barely-drawn gun dropped from nerveless fingers. Blood started to drip down the sleeve of his checkered shirt, and the smell of burned powder seemed to mingle strangely with the feeling of dizziness in his brain.

"By criminy!" Shanghai Pierce whooped into the silence that had followed. "Gotta admit it was almost worth losin' my bet just to see that draw! Jee—sus! You ever need a job, Morgan, you just apply to me, hear?"

William Brandon expelled his breath, wondering why he suddenly needed a drink very badly.

After the stillness, there was movement and talk everywhere—voices sounding unusually loud. It seemed as if everyone wanted to drink.

Francesca di Paoli stood as if she had turned into a frozen statue, dark eyes like bruises in her white face.

On the street, a couple of Langley's friends were binding up his arm.

"Bullet went clean through. . . . Hey, mister, how come we never heard of you?"

An older man, soft-voiced, said, "You ever call yourself Whittaker? I remember when Bart Haines got himself killed in San Antonio, about three years back. . . ."

"I need a drink," Langley said a trifle groggily. "Winner pays—don't you think that's fair, boys?"

Finding herself ignored by the same men who had just fought over her, Francesca caught Jay Gould's strangely smiling look and straightened her shoulders. For once, she was glad of Bertram Fields' supportive hand on her arm. Even the polite Senator Brandon had followed the small knot of grinning, whooping men who had just disappeared through the swinging batwing doors of the saloon.

"I think it's time you paid up, Principessa," Fields said with an usually hard note in his voice. "Or are you going to run away?"

"I'm going to sing, of course!" She tossed her head back, eyes flashing, and felt Mr. Pierce take her other arm.

"Atta girl! Guess there's no harm in us losers consoling each other, huh?"

The piano kept playing, and the small orchestra joined in when Francesca sang again—a second, and then a third song. Afterwards, it kept on playing while the dancing continued.

Jed Langley, his face a trifle pale, his arm now in a sling and stinging with the salve Mr. Gould's own physician had applied, looked at the woman a trifle wistfully.

"Still think she's the purtiest dance-hall girl I ever did see."

"Why don't you ask her to dance, then?" Steve Morgan's voice sounded almost indifferent.

"But you won her."

"And she'll keep. You boys go right ahead and dance. I think my father-in-law would like to speak to me."

Francesca was like a smoldering flame as she swung from one man's arms to another's. She had never encountered such *energetic* dancers as these cowboys, and it seemed as if every one of them was determined to dance with her at least once. All except *him*—Steve Morgan, who had won her in a ridiculous contest, a wager she had been stupid enough to challenge him with. It was almost as if he were deliberately showing his contempt by ignoring her.

He did not approach her until the evening was almost over, and by then Francesca felt as if the bright, uncaring smile she wore was pasted to her face like a clown's make-up.

He took her by surprise, suddenly appearing out of nowhere to catch her by the wrist as he drew her onto the section of the floor that had been cleared for dancing. He hadn't even offered her the cursory politeness of asking if she would be his partner, and by the time he put his hand on her waist, Francesca was so furious that she actually trembled, her pulses thudding with frustration.

She let forth a torrent of vituperative Italian, pitched low. And then:

"How dare you treat me in such a fashion? I think you forget that I am not—not one of these women you think you can use so lightly! I am sorry that the other man did not kill you! You Americans are all savages, and you—you are a worse barbarian than any I have met. Your manners—"

He laughed softly, as if she had said something to amuse him.

"Manners? I think you're more than half barbarian yourself, Francesca. Where did you learn all the gutter words you just used on me?"

"You deserve—if *I* was a man I would treat you as you deserve!"

"But I'm glad you're not a man." He was suddenly holding her far too closely, bending his head to whisper teasingly in her ear. "Are you going to turn hypocrite and retire behind that indignant look, or can we dispense with the polite, lengthy preliminaries, now that we have recognized each other?"

She hated herself for sounding breathless.

"You take far too much for granted!"

"And you turn from dance-hall girl back to princess in the morning. Will you spend what remains of the night with me, or shall I take you back to Bert Fields?"

As it happened, she hardly saw Bertram again during the rest of that fateful, famous weekend that was whispered about later. Francesca di Paoli had never cared about gossip, or what people said about her, and in this instance she cared even less.

The fact that Steve Morgan was married mattered not at all—most of Francesca's lovers were married men in any case. What *did* matter, after a while, was the discovery she made that he could not be pinned down, like the others. He wanted her, and showed it, but he wasn't prepared to crawl for her favors. He gave her the impression that he could too easily do without her, and forget her as easily as he'd forgotten and discarded countless other females before her.

Oh, he did all the correct things—gave her presents of expensive jewelry, sent her flowers. But there were no sentimental notes attached to any of his gifts, only his casually scrawled initials. And she could not make a puppet of him, nor bend him to her will. He would escort her here and there on occasion—to Saratoga, to Newport, to the theater, and to dinner in New York itself. But only when it suited *him*, and she was just as likely not to hear from him for days on end in between. The first time she threw a tantrum, he stalked out of her hotel room—and she did not see him again for over two weeks. There were times when Francesca wasn't sure if she hated him or wanted him only because he treated her so casually—as a mistress, nothing else. She was used to devotion, to men who alternately threatened and pleaded, making themselves look ridiculous in the end.

Steve Morgan was like none of the other men she had met. Hadn't she sensed, right from the beginning, a ruthlessness in him that, in a way, matched her own? He not only matched her, but beat her at her own game, and there came a time when even Bert Fields, who thought he knew Francesca better than most men, became seriously concerned, although he was wise enough to keep his doubts to himself.

In spite of Costanza's dire mutterings and Luigi Rizzo's despair, he tried to tell himself that it wouldn't last. Francesca fell in and out of love as easily and ephemerally as the wind changed direction. And Steve Morgan, from all accounts, wasn't the kind of man to take any woman seriously. Not even his wife, it seemed.

Making inquiries, Fields had learned that Morgan had kept a strikingly beautiful Spanish woman as his mistress just before his marriage to Senator Brandon's recently widowed daughter had stunned San Francisco with its suddenness—conveniently, his mistress had been married off to an English viscount first. And there were rumors that his marriage was hardly the conventional kind. Both Steve and Virginia Morgan had been seen out in public with other partners, while together they had scandalized society when he'd taken her with him to certain places where a man might take his mistress, but never his wife. A dangerous, unpredictable man—coldly ruthless in his business dealings, so Fields had heard. When he learned that Morgan planned to return to California soon, the entrepreneur could not help breathing a sigh of relief. Perhaps it would all end then. And by the time Francesca herself went to San Francisco, they would both have other lovers. Perhaps it was just as well for Mr. Fields' peace of mind that he had no inkling of Francesca's own plans, or certain other circumstances that were to change everything.

It was Senator Brandon, just as worried at the turn of affairs, who brought matters to a head in the end.

He met his son-in-law for luncheon, as was their usual custom when Steve happened to be in town; and he had not failed to notice that Steve, who was not given to showing outward signs of preoccupation, had been frowning into space for several seconds at a time. It had been a whole month since they had first discussed Signorina di Paoli—since then, Brandon had held his peace, hoping the whole affair would blow over. But now, even the yellow press had started printing stories that did more than hint slyly at an extremely close and intimate relationship between a young millionaire from California and New York's latest darling. Some reporter had even got hold of the story of a gun battle that had taken place at Mr. Jay Gould's country estate—and Steve, with his usual disregard for convention, had squired di Paoli far too often and too publicly since then. They had been to the races together, to the theater—had been seen in fasionable Saratoga and Newport. . . .

The Senator said suddenly and bluntly, "Have you heard from Ginny recently?"

Steve's frown disappeared; his eyes narrowed slightly as they rested on his father-in-law.

"Not for some weeks. But I'm not very good at writing letters myself, so I can scarcely blame her." He sounded indifferent, but some instinct warned him that this time Brandon was not going to let the subject drop.

"I had a letter from Sonya this morning. She tells me that since Ginny returned from Russia she has hardly spent a week at a time in Paris. And now time she's gone to Madrid, as the guest of a Spanish gentleman who breeds bulls, as well as fighting them. Virginia has announced that she is going to learn flamenco dancing from the gypsies in Madrid." Brandon cleared his throat rather awkwardly. "Look here, you'd better know that certain—er—rumors about you have actually found their way into the newspapers over there. And, of course, Sonya's been receiving the New York papers as well. She wants to come back, but Ginny. . . ."

Ginny. What in hell was she up to this time? She hadn't stayed in Russia, but she'd certainly been cutting herself a wide swathe through the capitals of Europe. Steve, too, had been hearing rumors, and he found himself thinking violently that it was perhaps a good thing Ginny had decided to extend her stay in Europe. If she'd returned, he'd have been far to tempted to break her neck! He'd forgotten that he had meant to be patient—to give her a chance to make up her own mind. He should have known better than to let her go in the first place. Why was it that Ginny was the one woman who had been capable, from the very beginning, of making him lose all the detachment he'd ever possessed? He was through being patient, or understanding. Understanding—hell! He felt cold fury wash through him for just an instant. Ginny had damn well better make up her mind in a hurry, or he was going to push her into it.

Steve Morgan's face remained hard, although he gave his father-in-law a twisted half-smile.

"Ginny's free to make up her own mind about what she wants to do, of course. We placed no restrictions on each other before she left. As a matter of fact—" Steve leaned back in his chair, long legs stretched before him, and the

Senator could not read the expression in his face as he lifted his glass in a kind of half-mocking toast. "I plan to leave New York for Texas soon. On my way to California. I have some business to attend to, and Signorina di Paoli is to give a concert in Austin, so I've promised her I'd escort her there."

As matter of fact, Steve had decided upon journeying down to Texas on a short business trip only this morning—and he hadn't, at the time, planned on taking Francesca with him, or even telling her of his plans. But there was, after all, no reason why business could not be mixed with pleasure—for a short time, anyhow. It only meant postponing his own arrangements for a week, until Francesca's New York engagement was at an end; and they could travel down by sea. Afterwards, he could take her as far as Austin and go on from there to take care of his own affairs.

Steve smiled blandly at his glum looking father-in-law. "I thought I'd look over that property near Baroque that you gave me as long as I'll be down there, too, so I might be away for a couple of months. You might ask Mrs. Brandon to explain to Ginny when you write to her next that I'll probably be too busy for letter writing myself."

Brandon, who thought he understood at last what Steve was about, spent the rest of the afternoon composing a long letter to his wife, in which he expressed his disapproval of his daughter's recent behavior in the strongest possible terms, and actually defended his son-in-law.

"... You mention that certain rumors have reached you of Steven's liaison with an opera singer...." Pausing to puff fiercely on his cigar, Brandon frowned down at the sheet of paper. How far could he go? He had intercepted the sudden flash of black anger in Steve's eyes, and the tautening of the muscles in his jaw when he'd been told his wife's latest escapade—obviously, Steve was not quite as indifferent as he pretended to be; and although Brandon could neither understand nor approve their unconventional marriage, he had gained the impression that Ginny had not been entirely too happy at the prospect of leaving her husband. Perhaps, he thought grimly, it was as well that matters be brought to a head before it was too late.

He picked up his pen, and began to write again, hoping that Sonya would show his letter to Ginny without thinking to spare her feelings. The girl needed to be shocked out of her complacency.

"The newspaper cuttings that I have enclosed should prove enlightening—and if you find them a trifle shocking, my love, I must remind you that the stories I have heard of Ginny's shockingly unconventional behavior had already reached New York *before* Steven made the acquaintance of Signorina di Paoli, who is hardly the type of female one can dismiss as being a cheap flirt—or the kind of woman a man may amuse himself with temporarily while his wife is gallivanting all over the continent of Europe without a thought for either her husband and family or her good name. I have the feeling that if Ginny cares for nothing but frivolity and the admiration of certain gentlemen of far from savory reputation, she had best stay where she is—and contrive to find some means of supporting herself when her husband decides to divorce her. Steven will be leaving for Texas soon, and asks that I inform Virginia he will hardly have time to write while he is there. . . ."

The letter filled more than ten pages, and together with the newspapers that the Senator had thoughtfully enclosed, made a good-sized packet for mailing on the next mail steamer that was leaving in the morning for Le Havre.

Chapter Thirty-seven

"This is the second night in a row that you tell me you are going to leave early—and tonight you are going to play cards!" Francesca pouted. But she did not sound *too* angry, and she wriggled her body with a graceful, feline movement. She was propped up on one elbow, staring down at the man who lay beside her. "Why do men so much enjoy playing cards with each other? Do you gamble for very high stakes? That man—that old friend of yours

we met in the Park yesterday?—*he* did not look as if he
was rich enough to afford it!"

When Steve kept his eyes purposefully closed, she
leaned forward with a teasing laugh and touched his eyelashes lightly with her fingers, the enormous square-cut
emerald ring she wore gleaming in the gold light like the
eye of some pagan god.

"Such long lashes on a man—it is not fair, that! And it
is also not fair that you can pretend to sleep when you do
not want to answer my questions. Perhaps I can make you
wide awake again?"

"*You* know you can and *I* know you can, so there's no
need for you to prove your power over me, you wild Italian she-cat!"

With a movement too quick for her to anticipate, Steve
knocked the supporting elbow from under her and rolled
his weight over her squirming body, pinning her down
beneath him. His eyes, open now and slightly narrowed,
looked down into hers unsmilingly before he bent his head,
lips against her ear.

"I have to go, 'Cesca, and you damn well know it. All
your wiles aren't going to keep me here tonight."

"You would not be able to tear yourself away if I *really*
meant anything to you!"

"Are you going to start nagging?"

She felt a shiver run through her as his lips caressed her
ear, and then her temple, and she could *feel* that he
wanted her, in spite of his determination to go.

But—she had learned a few things since she had known
this man, and one of them was that he would not be
pushed. So she whispered:

"No! I am not going to nag at you—but only because
you would not listen anyhow. But you'll come back to
have breakfast with me? You have the key—and I do not
care what time it is. I will promise to let you sleep afterwards, if you are really very tired."

Her fingers, supple and strong in spite of their deceptive
slenderness, had begun to massage his shoulders and the
back of his neck, smoothing away some of the tension that
had been in him all day, and Steve was, for a moment,
tempted to stay with her and forget his appointment.
Francesca was a complicated and temperamental creature—part feline and part cold calculation. But in some

strange way he understood her, especially since he had encouraged her to talk to him—of herself, and the way she had been brought up; her determination to claw her way up to the top on her own. She was talented—there was no question of that; and she was intelligent, and an interesting, delightful companion with whom a man could not become easily bored. He was by no means in love with her—any more, he suspected, than she was with him. But for the moment, they were good for each other.

The fact was that in some odd indefinable way, Francesca reminded him of Ginny. They had the same resiliency, the same knack of conquering even while they surrendered. And it was the thought of Ginny, and the rising anger that this thought always brought with it, that pulled him away from Francesca's arms and her too-comfortable bed that could bring forgetfulness.

Lying on her back, in the deliberately spread-legged sprawl of a whore, Francesca watched him dress.

"So you're really going to play cards, hmm? But you'll be back for breakfast? And must you frown so blackly at me? You see, I am not trying to keep you."

"I see," he said drily. But his mind was on the appointment he was already late for, and he hardly heard Francesca's casual chatter as she stretched like a lazy cat, continuing to watch him.

"Since you will not tell me too much about yourself, you don't mind if I make guesses? Let me see. You have been in a prison—you told me that was how you got all the scars you carry on your back. Perhaps this old friend you go to meet again was in prison with you? *That* would account for the way he dressed—in black, so respectable! Perhaps you two are planning another—what *did* you do to put you in prison, Stefano? You were a banditti—I guessed that from the first time I saw you. Perhaps you have committed murder as well. Is *that* what you plan again? If you need a woman accomplice, I would help, you know! And then we would escape to Texas together—"

"You should write romances instead of reading them, cara." In front of the mirror, Steve was shrugging into his jacket.

Francesca gave a gurgle of laughter.

"Anything is possible, I think—and especially with *you*! Why do you always wear a gun, for instance? I shall never

forget how quickly you shot that poor cowboy—the one
you became so friendly with afterwards. And I remember,
too, that that nasty Mr. Pierce, whom I did not like, said
something about you—what was it? Yes! He said you
were a—a man who used to fight with guns for a living, in
Texas. It *was* Texas, wasn't it? And the good Senator,
your respectable father-in-law, he did not like being reminded of this! But I have an admirer in Texas who is a
judge—a very important man, *he* says. He writes me letters, and sends me little presents through the mail. Perhaps, if you are ever in trouble, I can persuade him to use
his influence."

Halfway across the room already, Steve's face grew
suddenly taut, and she thought he hesitated for an instant.
Was it possible that she had finally made him a little jealous? But knowing him, it wasn't possible.

Bending over, Steve brushed her lips with his.

"You must tell me more about this secret admirer of
yours, mi amore. But not now. I'm late as it is."

He hired a hansom cab to take him to the unremark-
able brownstone building where, no doubt, the inevitable
poker game was already in progress. The streets were
crowded at this time of night, giving him time to think.

Coincidence—or not coincidence? The way the scattered pieces had seemed to fall together, making a pattern.
Jim Bishop had seen it all from the beginning, of course.
Why in hell did Jim have to turn up in his life at all the
wrong moments? Like their meeting this afternoon, in the
park. How had Bishop known he had promised to take
Francesca riding? He doubted that it had been a guess—in
fact, his first impulse had been anger, held in check only
by Francesca's presence beside him and her amused, curious eyes.

The usual politenesses carefully gotten out of the way,
Bishop had invited Steve to visit him. "Just a few old
friends. You'll know most of them. I've been meaning to
call on you, in fact, but you're rather difficult to meet
these days. Still—I feel sure you won't feel the time wasted. . . ."

Did Bishop's carefully uninflected voice carry a threat—
or a warning? Had *he* become a target for the secret, un-
publicized organization that Bishop headed, or was it
something to do with his recent acquaintances? His busi-

ness deals? Trust Bishop to contact him when Francesca was present, making sure he could not ask too many questions.

Old habit had made Steve dress inconspicuously. The apartment they met in was in a block of similar apartments in a rather shabby neighborhood. The men were in their shirt-sleeves; the table was covered with oilcloth. Through the wall, they could hear a baby squall; the drunken voice of a man yelling at his wife. The host, a worried-looking man called Ron Draper, explained that his wife and children were visiting her mother that week, and apologized for the lack of food.

But once they were settled around the table, the cards dealt, the usual bottles of bourbon and wine produced, everything else was familiar. Bishop seemed to be the only man who could concentrate on his cards and talk business at the same time.

There were five men, besides Draper, whom Steve had not met before, and Bishop himself. He knew the other four—they were Westerners, too, away from their usual territory at this time. Only one familiar face was missing; and Steve, angry enough by now to dispense with the preliminaries, asked the question he felt they were waiting for him to ask.

"Where's Paco?"

Someone cleared his throat. Bishop answered without inflection.

"He's in the hospital. Got shot up, rather badly, but the doctor say's he'll be all right. Only—it's going to take time. I'd have sent someone else, of course, but it appears the good citizens of Baroque, particularly a widow named Lassiter, and her brother-in-law, Judge Nicholas Benoit, don't like strangers. Paco was lucky, at that. He didn't end up dead, like the others."

"Baroque?" Steve lit a cigar; his eyes met Bishop's cool grey gaze over the match flame.

"I thought the name would sound familiar. Shanghai Pierce just happened to win one of the largest ranches in the territory in a poker game. And a few weeks later, he lost it in a wager he took with your father-in-law. As I understand it, Senator Brandon deeded that land over to you, because he figured you had won it for him."

Steve flipped the dead match into an ashtray and leaned back, studying his poker hand.

"You're well-informed. To save you further trouble—I haven't seen the land yet, although I plan to soon, and all I know is what I've been told. It might be good railroad land, and I mean to investigate that possibility. Is there something illegal about the title? Is that what this is all about?"

"There's nothing wrong where that is concerned. The land is yours, by some coincidental quirk of fate. And *that* is why I've arranged this meeting tonight."

Bishop fanned his cards out, tossing one onto the table. His voice was even, as noncommittal as usual. "You remember Dave Madden?"

The blue of Steve Morgan's eyes darkened.

"I remember Dave. But he retired—a long time ago, after he married. Or don't you let anyone retire?"

Bishop sounded unmoved, although his wintry gaze clashed with Steve's for an instant.

"Dave *lived* in that part of the country. Had himself a small spread. And then the carpetbaggers moved in. And the soldiers. And he came up against the Benoit-Lassiter clan. Dave was a good man. He could recognize something crooked when he saw it. And in this case, he was fighting for his own existence. I suppose that is what made him hesitate before he got in touch with us." Fastidiously, Bishop brushed ash off his jacket, his grey eyes hardening as they met Steve Morgan's cautious, suddenly watchful look. He said flatly, "Dave Madden's in jail. For murder. He works on a chain gang. His ranch was taken for non-payment of taxes and sold by public auction. And his wife. . . . Perhaps you remember Renate? She was blond, of German extraction, very pretty. I think you and Dave met her at about the same time, when you took her off a riverboat." Seeing the slight hardening of Steve's eyes, their sudden opaque look, Bishop had time, while he paused to draw on his cigar, to wonder exactly how well Steve Morgan had known Renate before she chose to marry Dave.

"What's happened to Renate?"

"She's working in a whorehouse in Matamoras. It was Baroque, before then. And before that, Judge Nicholas Benoit's fine mansion in Baroque. Rumor has it that she went to him to try and save Dave's life. And when he'd tired of her. . . ."

"The cigar moved, fine ash dropping on the table, to be swiftly brushed away by the nervous and obviously house-trained Ron Draper.

Steve Morgan had put his cigar down carefully in the ashtray, and now he poured himself half a glass of warm bourbon.

"*Why?*"

"An interesting place, Baroque," Bishop answered equivocally. "Very fertile land. Strategic, you might say, if you were talking railroad jargon. Not far from the Louisiana border—swampland on one side; irrigated by the Red River. Some of the best cattle grazing land in the whole of Texas—if you were a cattleman. Farmers and homesteaders call it damn good bottom land, good for raising crops. Used to be owned by just a few families be-fore the war; but since then—you've seen it happen! The Homestead Act. The usual results of any war. The Texans are being punished for supporting the wrong side, and the carpetbaggers are getting rich. It's hard on the men who fought for what they believed in. But. . . ."

During the silence that had fallen, Bishop's cool grey eyes flickered over every face, coming to rest on Steve Morgan's carefully guarded countenance. He continued softly, "But if you were a woman, a widow, friendly to the Northern soldiers when they first arrived? And if you had a brother-in-law who happened to live up North when the war began—a man of some consequence, now ap-pointed a federal judge—perhaps that would make matters different, might even prove advantageous! The greed for power and wealth is the strongest and most dangerous hunger of all, gentlemen. I think we all know that. And greed is especially dangerous when it is sanctioned—or rather, when it is under the protection of all the law that remains in that part of the world.

"Quite suddenly, gentlemen, there has been an influx of settlers, under the provisions of the Homestead Act. Small ranchers—earlier settlers—have been ousted for non-pay-ment of taxes or various other reasons. A few of them have vanished, or taken their families away. It is amazing how quickly the country in this particular section of the State is being filed on, and settled on. Still, the former plantation owners and cattle barons continue to run their cattle over all this fertile land. . . . And, as I've already mentioned, any strangers who cannot prove that they have particular business in that part of the world somehow contrive to meet with unpleasant 'accidents'—you take my meaning?"

By this time, Steve had begun to understand what Bishop's devious talk had been leading up to, and he watched and listened, as silent and grim-faced as the other men present, while Bishop began to draw his inevitable maps on the oilcloth-covered table; his cold, even voice produced facts and explanations out of thin air.

"You understand now, of course, why I—um—invited you here tonight? Pierce's land—the land he won just in time, before an unfortunate accident killed off its former owner—has not been molested so far, because everyone knows Shanghai Pierce, and his reputation. Judge Benoit has learned, by now, of the change in ownership—as far as he and the Lassiter woman are concerned, you are merely another Eastern millionaire; curious to see what you have won, but not too interested. You have the perfect excuse for visiting Baroque, of course. And they will not dare try to touch you. You can make an excuse to spend a short time there. All we need is a few facts, to tie together with what we already have! A few answers to certain puzzling questions. And then, when I have placed everything before the President himself, we can move in."

"And what in hell have you done for Dave? Or do you plan to do anything at all? Renate. . . . Damn you for a cold-blooded bastard, Jim! I guess I was just lucky, all the time I was working for you, that I. . . ."

And then Steve remembered the feel of a bullwhip on his bare back, and after that the "prison" he had been sent to—a silver mine cutting deeply into the bowels of a mountain, where he had forgotten what the daylight looked like, and become an animal. He had known then, and had been warned—just as they all had—of the risks they took. The hell of it was that Dave had dropped out, because Renate wanted him to, but even so . . . did a man ever drop out of the particular profession he had once accepted? Was he ever allowed to? There was the time, not too long ago, when Bishop had visited him in Mexico; beginning, in his oblique way, everything that had happened since then. And leading up to his sitting here tonight, listening to what Bishop had to say.

Smoke rose and curled in an atmosphere already thick with it. Draper had left the windows closed, and it was far too stuffy.

Perhaps Jim Bishop had read the thoughts in Steve's mind, for he went on calmly and dispassionately, as if he had not been interrupted, taking it for granted that all that remained was to fill in a few more details, map out a strategy.

"They're smart people—and they have the local law, such as it is, in their pocket. There's a Colonel Vance—he's the officer in command of the fort. A career man, careful of his reputation so far; but money talks, especially when you're getting close to retirement age. Like most of the men there, he eats out of Antoinette Lassiter's little hand. She's young for a widow, and most attractive. And although Nick Benoit's the brains, we think she's the real power and the push behind all that's been going on. Benoit's her dead husband's half-brother. They say he's more than halfway in love with Toni, too. She's about his only weakness—except for one other. . . ."

The one small detail, left until the last, made the slight coincidence almost too much to believe. For Nicholas Benoit, the local bigwig, happened to be an opera buff. And in particular, a fan of a certain Signorina Francesca di Paoli. The man adored her. He bombarded his idol with letters and flowers and expensive gifts. By spending a vast sum, and using all of his not inconsiderable influence, he had been instrumental in inducing Mr. Fields to contract for his protégée to sing at the opera houses of Texas.

As Steve already knew, her Southern intinerary would earn her tremendous sums of money—Francesca's only inducement for allowing herself to be persuaded to sing in such outlandish places: San Antonio; Austin; Houston; New Orleans and Natchez; and then Texas again, before she left for California and the comparative civilization of San Francisco.

Looking up from his contemplation of a full house, Steve had met Bishop's eyes.

"I'll let you know," he said shortly, wondering why he didn't refuse at once.

Face bland, Bishop began to go into more detail. "Just

in case," he said. And for a man who did not know enough, he knew plenty. He presented the general layout of the town of Baroque, and the neighboring towns. And names—more names! And then more background.

"There are the Carters. Used to be Cartier, but the old man changed it after he married Benoit's sister. Small-time swamp-ranchers, if you can call them that. Oldest son, Matthew, is one of those unreconstructed rebels. An outlaw, since he came back from the fighting. But the fact is that he'd do almost anything for Toni Lassiter—Mrs. Antoinette Lassiter. She's Louisiana-born—no one knows just where or when. She just turned up; blonde, very beautiful, smiling—old John Lassiter brought her back with him from a trip he took just before the war. Then he went away to fight, and didn't last long. She took over the running of things as if she'd been born to it. She says her family owned a large plantation, and that she ran away from a convent they put her in—and the marriage they arranged for her."

"It seems to me you know enough about these people already!" To Steve's surprise, it was Greg Porter, known as Port to his friends, who made the objection, sandy brows drawn together impatiently. He remembered then, belatedly, that Port and Dave Madden had been sidekicks for a long time—just about as long as he and Paco. And Paco was in a hospital, shot full of holes.

"But we don't know enough about what they are up to now. We suspect, but we need proof."

"And in the meantime Dave rots away on a goddamned chain gang, and his wife—tell me, Jim, does he know what's happened to his wife?"

Put myself in Dave's place, Steve was thinking bitterly. And Ginny in Renate's. Only there was a revolution going on at that time, and maybe—just maybe Bishop didn't know. But damn his cold-blooded brain anyhow!

Putting himself in Bishop's position, though, Steve supposed he understood. Bishop couldn't get Dave out without having a lot of questions asked—warning people who might cover up whatever it was they were up to. And Renate was just another female who had bought herself the kind of trouble she was in. No doubt they'd have tabs on her, too.

"When will you be ready to leave?"

They were all looking at him suddenly, especially Port, with those narrowed green eyes of his. Port wanted to go himself, but Port was too involved, and if Paco—who was very careful—had been shot up, Port would be a sitting duck.

Steve stretched, pouring himself another drink, grimacing at its rotgut taste. Another thing he'd have to get used to all over again. What the hell!

"Next week," he told Bishop. "By sea. You'll hear about it. Just give me the names of the contacts—and you can skip the usual reminder that I'll be on my own." His voice softened, becoming almost negligent. "I'll keep that fact in mind—and I'll get you the facts you need. But *you* remember that I'm on my own too, Jim."

Chapter Thirty-eight

Reporters mingled with distinguished guests on board the sleek clipper ship that had just been renamed "Lady Francesca"—a magnum of champagne had been broken against her side by the Signorina di Paoli herself. The ceremony had marked the beginning of festivities that were to go on until dawn, when the last sleepy guests would be escorted ashore before the ship sailed with the first tide.

Di Paoli was sparkling tonight, her dark eyes as bright as the stars that seemed to hang over the lamplit deck, gleaming with the same secret fire as the enormous emerald that seemed to weigh down one slim finger.

Luigi Rizzo, Francesca's manager, looked like an unhappy walrus with his drooping mustache, and he nursed numerous glasses of wine. Bertram Fields, who was also sailing, maintained his usual imperturbable poise and offered no comments to the reporters who questioned him, but, for a change, di Paoli was gracious when the usual reporters mobbed her with their inquisitive personal questions.

"Signorina, that truly magnificent ring—it's not an engagement yet, is it?"

Francesca gave the man her mysterious Botticelli smile.

"Oh, no! That is—not . . . yet."

They pounced on that little, shy hesitation.

"Is it true the emerald was the gift of a gentleman who comes from California?"

"It was a present from a . . . friend."

"Will Mr. Morgan be traveling all the way to Austin with you, Signorina?"

Di Paoli's smile curved as her eyes shadowed themselves for an instant.

"Why don't you ask *him*?"

Steve Morgan, tall and relaxed-looking in his immaculately tailored dark suit, a rich brocade vest showing under his jacket, gave his usual rather cynical smile to the reporters.

"I'm going to Texas on business, gentlemen."

"Mr. Gould's business?" one reporter, bolder than the rest ventured to ask.

Steve raised an eyebrow.

"Gentlemen, Mr. Gould handles his own business affairs and I handle mine. And now, if you'll excuse me. . . ."

"When is your wife expected back in the States, sir?" The question came from a tousle-haired young man with a cheeky grin.

"When she gets ready to return."

Steve Morgan's face hadn't changed; his tone was slightly amused. With a polite inclination of his head, he moved away, leaving the reporters still clustered around the radiant prima donna who was the object of so much curiosity.

"Signorina di Paoli—forgive the question—" a rather shy woman reporter, seated close to the singer, lowered her voice. "You've been seen everywhere in public with Mr. Morgan—is it true you two are in love?"

Francesca flashed the woman a demure, half-sensual smile.

"We happen to enjoy each other's company."

"But is he—there are rumors that he intends to divorce

his wife," the woman persisted, remembering her editor's instructions.

"A *gentleman* lets his wife do the divorcing." The signorina's voice was gently reproving as she rose to her feet, dismissing them all gracefully.

Not only the reporters, but the scandal-mongers and gossips had their field day.

"Do you notice the possessive way she holds his arm?"

"Ah, but the way he *looks* at her! My dear, I vow those dark blue eyes of his in that bronzed face make me positively shivery. . . ."

"What a divinely handsome, divinely suited couple they make, to be sure!" a sentimental woman sighed, and her neighbor, less sentimental, whispered significantly:

"But have you noticed that his father-in-law—Senator Brandon; you've met him, of course—is not present tonight? Rather . . . odd, don't you think?"

Senator Brandon, who had said his farewells to Steve earlier on that same day, had stayed away from the bon voyage celebration quite deliberately. Not too many months ago he had hosted a similar party to see his wife and daughter off to Europe; and if his absence tonight created some speculation, his being there would have been tantamount to offering his blessing to the fact that his son-in-law was taking his mistress with him on a sea cruise. And quite frankly, he would have been almost afraid to face Sonya's anger if he had done so. As for Steve—he hoped to hell Steve knew what he was doing.

Both Francesca di Paoli and Steve Morgan were flamboyant personalities, and whenever they were seen together, wherever they went, they caused tongues to wag. And as if that were not enough, she was flaunting the jewels he gave her. That emerald ring alone must have cost a small fortune, and it was the kind of gift that a man presented to his fiancee or his wife. What was Ginny going to say?

"If Ginny expects me to act like a husband, then she had better start acting like a wife," was the rather ambiguous comment Steve had made, with an indifferent shrug. And feeling that he had done his duty by making a last, half-hearted protest, the Senator said no more at the time.

"La Francesca" had begun her voyage. The shipboard

party was still in progress when Brandon retired to his study, sipping at a glass of bourbon and composing yet another letter to his wife. Having studied the plan of the ship, he knew what the few select guests who were privileged enough to be taken on a tour of the ship had also noticed. The Signorina di Paoli's sumptuous stateroom, especially redecorated in her favorite colors, adjoined the owner's more austere quarters. . . . .

The swaying, gently rocking motion of the ship seemed to add a different dimension to their lovemaking as the vessel cleared the Sound and turned the clean sleek lines of her prow towards the open ocean.

Movement over movement, as their bodies came together, separated, and came back together again. Light from the open portholes fell across the bed, and Steve's fingers traced the outline of her face, very lightly, as if he were committing her to memory.

"You have the most perfectly beautiful face I have ever seen, mi amore. Like a Madonna, sculptured out of porcelain. And your hair is like silk. . . ."

He sounded as if he were discovering her for the first time—or saying good-bye—and Francesca felt a sudden pang of fear, mixed with resentment that even after they had been making love, he could detach himself from her so easily. Even his compliments sounded lazy—half-teasing. Could she ever make him love her? Here, on a ship in the middle of the ocean, Steve could not go away and leave her in a hurry. Daringly, she felt the desire to experiment with emotion—to find out how far it could take them both. The idea was both frightening and intriguing at the same time.

She let her eyes open, very slowly, to look into his.

"And you? I heard someone say you were a pirate—a corsair. Are you going to carry me off with you? I think I would like that—to go somewhere with you I have never been before—somewhere wild, and primitive, where no one knows who I am, or who you are. Why don't you take me to Mexico with you? You told me it was your home once. I would like to see what it is like—please, Stefano, please?" She began to kiss him, teasingly, pleadingly. "Tell me you will think about it—we have time, have we not? Just a little longer voyage. . . . Have I ever begged you for anything before?"

"And you're not going to talk me into anything by pulling those sneaky woman tricks on me either!" he said roughly, but she felt his fingers slide up her bare shoulders, to close in the thickness of her hair.

She moved her body against his, in a motion that was counterpoint to the rising and falling of the ocean that cradled them both, whispering, "Please?" before she kissed him.

He kissed her back almost harshly, smothering her protesting exclamation. And kissed her and kissed her until she could hardly breathe and it felt like drowning. And she clung to him, blindly, forgetting everything else but the way his body could make her feel when he took her. . . .

Senator Brandon despatched another letter to his wife, the clippings he enclosed about the bon voyage party making an even thicker package than the last. The "Lady Francesca" sailed down the coast in perfect weather, making record time.

Bertram Fields watched Francesca become more glowing every day, and inwardly he began to worry, although the most he permitted himself to say to Francesca was a murmured, "Be careful, Principessa. Your bandit doesn't go by the rules."

But Costanza dared to be frank with her "bambina":

"You are falling in love. No—this you cannot deny to *me*, who has been your nurse since you were *so* high! Do you think I have not watched you with the others and cannot see the difference? I have wished for a long time that you would meet a real man, who would make you want to be a woman at last. But this one . . . it's bad—a married man! You should be careful, cara mia."

"I am not a fool, Costanza!" Francesca's voice, which had begun by being sharp, suddenly softened almost imperceptibly. "But he is different from those others. They were all fools, so silly. . . . And my bad banditti, I have only just begun to understand the kind of man he is. He likes a woman to stand up tall and not cling nor try to bind him too closely, and I am that kind of woman! And he—he does not say to me like other men, 'I love you . . . I adore you, Francesca, I will die if I cannot have you. . . .' No—he says nothing like this, and yet he does not pretend that he does not want me, in order to intrigue

me. He is beginning to *like* me—we *talk* to each other,
Costanza! Of many things. He does not look at me as a
beautiful creature meant only for lovemaking—he respects
the fact that I have a mind and have made my way to
where I am. I think—"

"You are in love," the old woman said flatly, and
Francesca shook her head, clasping her hands about her
knees as she had done when she was a little girl and had
been scolded.

"No! No, I am not in love! That is ... we play a little
game right now, the two of us, and I think it is to find out
which one of us is stronger, and which one will give way
first. ... And I ask myself, Costanza, when that happens,
then what? You understand? There is my music, which has
been my life, which *is* my life! And he is a man who demands and must live his own kind of life—how would it
end, if it ever began for us? This loving that I am so
afraid of?"

Her hands went wide in a gesture of uncertainty.

"Ah, Costanza, do not scold me! It is enough, for
now, that we—enjoy each other; and perhaps it is even a
little more than that already. You see, I want him, too,
and I will not let him go—not yet!"

"And his wife, to whom he was married in the Church?
Have you forgotten that he belongs already to her, when
you talk of not letting go?"

The older woman's voice was uncompromising; fiercely
her black eyes looked into those of her charge, seeing the
tell-tale sparks of rage flare into them.

"His *wife*? Pah!" Francesca ground her teeth together.
"She does not deserve to have a husband she cannot keep!
Why did she go to France? Why is she still there? If Stefano had really wanted her he would have gone himself to
bring her back, instead of being here with me. And he is
that kind of a man, too."

"So now you are thinking of marriage, are you? If he
divorces his wife for you, what will you do? Do you think
he will marry you, foolish, stubborn little one? Are you
prepared to give everything up to get fat and have many
bambini?"

Francesca said wildly, "And who is talking of marriage?
I am thinking of now, *now*! For now, what we have found
in each other is enough!"

It became hot and humid in the Gulf of Mexico, and when the fast China clipper discharged her passengers just outside of Matamoros—for Francesca had, surprisingly, persuaded Steve to make a short detour to Mexico—Francesca felt as if even her clothes were wilted.

"I warned you, cara. From here it's an uncomfortable journey by land to my friend's hacienda near Monterey. Are you sure you wouldn't like to turn around and go back to New Orleans?"

"I am used to the heat. And so is Costanza. As long as you are sure we can hire enough carriages to carry all my boxes."

Mr. Fields had disembarked at New Orleans to make arrangements for her performances in that city, Francesca was glad of that, for she could too-easily imagine the way his eyebrows would have lifted, meeting in the middle, as he complained about the heat, about the accommodations in this wretched town. But she was determined to prove to Steve that she was the kind of woman who could face any discomfort or emergency. "Is this really our country, Stefano? Is all of Mexico like this?"

"Matamoros is too close to the border to be truly representative of Mexico, sweetheart. That's why I thought you might like to visit my friend's hacienda for a short while."

And suddenly she was sorry she had talked him into this change in their plans. When he dressed in rough western clothes and wore a gun at his hip, she felt as if he had deliberately made himself into a stranger. He had arranged for passable accommodations for them—the best that this rather squalid town provided—but he had seemed preoccupied ever since they had been stopped unexpectedly by a grinning capitan of the Rurales who Steve greeted like an old friend—and he had ignored her during the entire rapid-fire conversation she could not understand that followed.

Francesca was even more annoyed when she woke up the next morning, hot and perspiring, to find that Steve had already left, very early, with the same Capitan Altamonte.

"He was dressed like a banditti, with two guns instead of one," Costanza grumbled. "What a terrible place this is!"

"Oh, be quiet!" Francesca's own anger made her tone sharper than usual. "All of Mexico is not like this—and he will be back soon."

He did not return, however, until late in the afternoon, wearing the kind of black frown Francesca had learned to be wary of.

By then she was very angry herself, stopping her frenzied pacing about the room to fix him with her snapping dark eyes.

"I've been across the border, into Brownsville," he said, forestalling her furious questioning. "I'm sorry, 'Cesca. I met some people I used to know."

"You—*you* are sorry? Why, I—"

Cutting across her words he said flatly, "I'm sorry I brought you here, too. It was unforgivable of me not to have made inquiries first. There's typhus everywhere."

He looked sunburned and tired and his voice had suddenly sounded absently thoughtful, as if he'd been almost talking to himself.

Francesca forgot her anger, flinging herself against him, but he held her away impatiently, voice roughening.

"For God's sake! I was talking to a man today who had typhus, and he died—only, damn it, I didn't know what he'd died of until later. Stay away from me until I've bathed and cleaned up, will you?"

She retreated unwillingly to the opposite end of the room, watching hungrily while he stripped the dusty clothes from his body, tossing them in an untidy pile on the floor, ignoring the giggling young woman who brought in hot water to fill the zinc bath.

"Let me help you—I can scrub your back for you. Stefano, this is all so silly! All these precautions, just because you talked to a man—"

"Who is dead—of typhus. Stay away from me until I'm clean, 'Cesca. I'm serious."

She stared at him, still unbelieving.

"But you—we are not *leaving*, are we? So soon after we arrived? We can go somewhere else."

"We sure as hell are leaving, as soon as your maid can get packed up again!" His voice had turned hard, inflexible. "You can argue with me all the way back to the ship, and until we reach New Orleans, if that's your pleasure. But we leave this town before sundown."

He stepped out of the tub, water dripping off his body, and Francesca tossed him a towel mechanically, her mind still trying to absorb the fact that he meant what he had said.

Annoyingly, she found herself wondering how his *wife* would have reacted.

Chapter Thirty-nine

Virginia Morgan returned from her impulsive, wildly impractical journey to Spain to find her stepmother in a coldly disapproving mood, just as she had expected.

Ginny looked pale and tired, and she had not troubled to take off her long velvet travelling cloak when she came in, but by this time, Sonya was too angry to notice.

"Well, so you are back at last? But where is your handsome matador? I had expected you to bring him back with you, trailing at the end of your bonnet strings!"

Sonya's tone was waspish, but for once her stepdaughter did not retort saucily. Instead, she removed her modish bonnet, tossing it carelessly onto a chair, and kept the cloak huddled around her as if the cold air outside had chilled her.

"He decided to stay in Madrid. And you don't have to look at me that way, Sonya! There was nothing wrong in his offering to escort me to Spain. In fact, he was a perfect gentleman, except for just once, and then I put him very quickly in his place!" Ginny's green eyes flew to the small desk by the window, where Sonya invariably sat to answer her correspondence. "Have there been any messages for me? Did the mail packet come in while I was away?"

"Your gentlemen friends have called almost daily, to inquire when you might be returning," Sonya said in a strangely tense, almost crackling voice. "The Compte D'Arlingen, of course—he professed himself worried! And that young English duke you used to go riding with every day—do you remember him? And, of course, there was a letter from your husband. It arrived the day after you had left. It is right on top of the other letters on the desk. Why don't you sit down while you are reading it?"

Recovering some of her former composure, Ginny raised an eyebrow as she crossed to the desk, deliberately trying to mask her eagerness. Sonya was being a bitch! And why was Steve's letter so thin? Damn Steve—and damn Sonya too, with her prissy, self-righteous airs!

Aloud, as she seated herself, Ginny said lightly, "Since when have you begun referring to Steve as my husband and in that tone? Honestly, Sonya, you are almost as aggravating as he is. Only one page—not even that. . . ." Her tone changed as she drew the letter out of its envelope, and forgetting that Sonya watched her, Ginny bit her lip with aggravation. "He might just as well not have taken the trouble to write at all!"

"Perhaps he was too busy to write." The irony in Sonya's tone escaped Ginny as she stared down at Steve's usual untidy scrawl, a frown knitting her brows.

He said nothing at all, except that New York was beginning to bore him, and he was thinking of returning to California soon. He said nothing about missing her—about wanting her to return. In fact, he had actually added the polite hope that she was enjoying herself, and would not hesitate to call upon the bank if she needed more money.

Why did his letters always sound so terse and uncommunicative? Was it possible that he did not miss her at all, and was relieved to have her out of his way? There had been months when she had let her imagination run riot. When she had actually expected—hoped—that he would come after her, to drag her back with him almost by force. She had missed him, actually cried foolish tears. The thought of him had spoiled everything for her, all the while she had pretended to enjoy herself with a frantic gaiety. Even in Russia. . . . And then, there were only the short, infrequent letters, telling her nothing. And money. Was it all designed to keep her away?

"Well? What does he have to say—or is it a secret?"

Ginny looked up, blinking her eyes to focus them, for they had become blurred while she stared at the page of writing.

Why did Sonya sound so—so strange? Amost smug.

"Of course there's no secret—in fact, there's nothing here that one of the servants could not read! Steve says only that he will be returning to California soon."

"Oh?" And now there was no mistaking the venom in Sonya's usually soft and placid voice. "But I suppose he might have changed his mind since he wrote to you. I have had several letters from your father, dated later, and according to him your husband must be well on his way to Texas by now."

"Texas?" Ginny repeated the word, not knowing why she did, unless it was to give herself time. There was something in Sonya's narrowed regard, a certain hardness in her voice that warned her, holding her stiff and speechless while Sonya went on grimly. "I think you had better read your father's letters to me. You'll find he is not nearly as reticent as Steven appears to have been. I have arranged them in order, along with certain newspaper cuttings. And for heaven's sake, take off that cloak! I vow you make me feel quite overheated!"

"I'd rather keep it on, thank you. Paris is chilly, after Spain."

But Ginny responded mechanically, already reaching her hand for the pile of letters and folded newspapers.

"In that case, I will ring for some hot tea—unless you would rather have sherry? Pray don't stop reading on account of me; I won't interrupt."

The fact was that once she had started reading, Ginny forgot Sonya's presence. She could feel herself growing colder, and there were times when words and letters seemed to blur into each other, so that she had to blink her eyes in order to go on reading.

Even her father's writing seemed angry—and he had not attempted to mince words. How could he have believed everything the scandal sheets printed about her? And gossip spread by nasty-minded old dowagers...?

Once, Ginny looked up angrily to say as much, and Sonya lifted one eyebrow. "Gossip? What do you expect people to infer when you spend a weekend alone in the country with an old flame? Or a whole week in London, without another woman to chaperone you? But if that is what you feel about *gossip*, then I'm sure that the publi-

city your husband seems to have courted recently won't upset you in the least!"

With an angry movement, Ginny put aside her father's
stern letter, and began to leaf through some of the newspaper cuttings.

An eulogistic account of the New York debut of an
Italian opera singer who called herself a princess. . . . A
long list of distinguished guests who had attended a reception given by Bertram Fields, millionaire entrepreneur.

And then, the headlines caught her eyes, even while she
wrinkled her nose with distate at the name of the newspaper: *Western weekend at Jay Gould's country home begins with a genuine gunfight.*

It was all a great exaggeration, of course! Steve's natural recklessness, breaking its bounds.

But there were other clippings—even a rather blurred
photograph or two:

*Di Paoli, with her constant escort, at the races; As
usual, California's latest millionaire, Steven Morgan, escorted the lovely Signorina di Paoli to the Vanderbilt's
ball; Which rich new admirer continues to shower the
Princess of the Opera with jewels befitting her radiant
beauty?; Signorina di Paoli has forsaken the fleshpots of
our fair city in favor of intimate candlelit suppers in the
company of a certain Mr. S. M. Could this be love at last?*

"It's vile, filthy gossip—all of it!" Ginny flung aside the
newspaper cuttings so that they scattered, fluttering to the
floor. "I'm surprised that my father should've taken the
trouble to send such—such garbage in the mail! An Italian
opera singer—some fat old cow with a screeching voice!
Steve would not—"

"Perhaps you forgot to read the description of this opera singer you dismiss so casually! And do you dare call
your father a vile, filthy gossip as well" Sonya's voice
rose slightly, before she controlled it with an effort. "Better read his last two letters, Ginny. Perhaps they'll explain
why your husband is openly pursuing another woman . . .
why he named one of his ships after her—threw a party
on board to which *everyone* was invited, and gave her an
enormous emerald set in a ring she proudly displayed on
her engagement finger!"

Ginny sprang to her feet at last, fists clenched at her
side, green eyes shooting fire.

"Oh! I think I know why you are telling me all this—you think to frighten me, to . . . the bastard! He's trying to make me jealous, *that's* it!"

"Virginia! I wish you would watch your language in my presence. And if you think Steven is only trying to make you jealous, why should he go to such lengths as to—to practically elope with this Signorina di Paoli?" Sonya added with deliberate calculation, seeing Ginny's eyes blaze in her white face, "Perhaps he is hoping that you will divorce him? One of those reporters hinted as much—she quoted your rival as saying that a gentleman always allows his wife to do the divorcing "

The next minute Sonya wondered if she had not gone too far, for Ginny suddenly sank back into the chair she had just vacated, her nostrils flaring as if she had to struggle for breath.

"It's not true! He doesn't love her—Steve's not capable of loving any woman, don't you think I ought to know that?"

"I'm certainly not condoning his behaviour. Any of it! But William seems to think—"

"How ironic!" Ginny laughed bitterly. "To think that *now* my father is actually standing up for Steve, of all people! And he places all the blame on me, because I happened to have been born a female!"

"Your behavior has hardly been unexceptionable," Sonya said sharply. "And a woman's reputation—"

"Oh, God! At least spare me *that* much!"

"Very well. I am not going to say anything else." In spite of the coldness of her voice, Sonya could no longer hide either her anger or her agitation.

She lifted her teacup, and it rattled against the saucer as she did.

"*You* must do exactly as you please, of course—just as you have always done! But I, for one, have already booked my passage back to America. In fact, the only reason I am still here is that I have to talk to you first. I have not seen you for almost two months, and I was beginning to wonder if you had decided against returning to Paris at all."

Ginny stood up again, as if she could not bear to be still, and Sonya wondered, as the young woman leaned over the desk, fingers gripping its edge, whether she had heard a single word. Really, Ginny, had become impossible to either understand or talk to.

Ginny found that her eyes had become fixed on a long newspaper cutting, lying on top of her father's latest letter. It was a gushing account, by a female reporter, of the magnificent bon voyage party given in honor of the Signorina di Paoli on board the clipper "Lady Francesca." It was true! Feeling herself dealt a mortal blow—turned to stone where she stood—Ginny was unable to stop herself from reading, eyes skimming over the closely-printed, smudged words. "It's true—it's true," her mind kept reading dully, even while her imagination conjured up pictures to torment her even more.

Steve—standing with his arm around this woman's waist, smiling down at her. "*A gentleman allows his wife to do the divorcing. . . .*" And the emerald ring winking like a great eye as the Italian put her hand on his sleeve later. Her touch would be possessive—was she already so sure of him, this di Paoli, or whatever her name was? And *he*—to place a whole ship at her disposal as casually as if it had been merely a yacht; to sail with her all the way to Texas; to make such an open show of his tawdry affair with her—but was it only an affair? Was it possible that Steve could love another woman?

"Ginny!" There was a note of annoyance in Sonya's voice. "Haven't you been listening to a word I've said? I asked you what your plans are."

Ginny swung around so quickly that her cloak caught on the edge of the table, making a small tear in the soft material. And in that moment, when the young woman's figure was outlined against the light from the window. . . .

Sonya broke off with an exclamation of mingled shock and horror, and quite unconsciously Ginny lifted her chin defiantly—this time making no move to pull the enveloping folds of the cloak about her.

"Yes! There is no need to ask the obvious question I see trembling on your lips. And no more need for me to hide the fact that I am, unfortunately, pregnant."

Sonya had gone quite pale—her mouth opened, but no words escaped her.

"Oh, for heaven's sake! Do you think *I* wasn't shocked when I found out?" In spite of her defiant attitude, Ginny had begun to twist her fingers together as she talked. "All these years. . . . Did you know how many specialists I've seen to find out if I was—if I had become barren or not? And then it has to happen—at the wrong time!"

"Oh, Ginny!" Sonya said faintly, and in spite of her obvious state of nerves the girl shot her a bitter, angry look from those slanted green eyes that gave her the look of a gypsy.

"Oh, Ginny—is that *really* all? I had half-expected you to launch into a tirade about retribution always catching up with sinners in the end! You might never have found out if I'd been—if I'd been brave enough! I didn't spend all that time in Spain after all—I went to Switzerland, because I've heard there was a famous doctor there who. . . . But I couldn't do it! It—it had begun to move by then, in spite of everything I tried: the tight corsets, the wild horseback rides—even the dancing you objected to! Nothing helped, as you can see. And I'm past the stage where I can disguise it—I'm going to become as big as a house before. . . . And now *this*! What am I going to do?"

"If you had only told me! Only hinted! Oh, heavens!" Sonya sprang to her feet, utterly distracted, torn between her first impulse to rush to Ginny and take the girl in her arms, and the practical common sense that warned her to try and remain calm.

"Why do you think I moved into my own apartments? I didn't want you to guess! I was never sick, I only thought that perhaps I was eating too much—until after I visited Russia. And then Count Chernikoff told me what was . . . wrong with me."

"What are we going to do?" Now it was Sonya's turn to ask the question, her brow furrowed, her china-blue eyes mirroring a welter of different emotions. Seeing that Ginny only stared back at her, as if she had relapsed into some kind of a trance after her wild outburst, Sonya tried again.

"Ginny, don't misunderstand! But there must be *something*—if no one knows. . . . Have you—" she bit her lip, but there was no way to phrase the next question delicately, so she rushed on—"have you told the father of the child you are carrying? Perhaps he—if you are going to divorce your husband in any case, perhaps. . . ."

At that, Ginny broke into hysterical laughter that changed suddenly into a torrent of tears. She clung again to the edge of the desk, and her words, mixed with sobbing, were so choked and indistinct that Sonya could barely manage to make sense out of them.

"The—the father! Did you really believe that I—oh, my God! You, too! If *you* think it, too, do you imagine that *Steve* will ever believe that it is *his*? And by now, perhaps he does not even care!"

Ginny despised herself bitterly for going into hysterics, but she could not help herself. First there had been the long, wasted journey, with doubts and regrets tormenting her like all the furies for every step of the way. And before that the months of trying to hide her condition, pretending to be happy and completely carefree while she hoped with all her heart she would have an "accident" that would relieve her of all anxiety. And then—and then she had planned to return, if Steve hadn't ordered her back before then.

But nothing had happened the way she had hoped, and here she was, trapped—not only that, but an unwanted wife, as well.

After a while her bitter sobs died away from sheer lack of breath, and Sonya, who had first made a point of locking the door, came to her side and patted her shoulders ineffectually while murmuring that it was useless upsetting herself, they would think of *something*!

"If only I had not written to your father that I intended to return within the month! And I have given up the lease here, but I suppose—"

"There is no need for you to go into seclusion just because I—I've put myself in a sorry position," Ginny said with a flare of her old spirit. "And besides, think how people will begin to whisper, and make guesses. You've just reminded me how they're already talking about me! As a matter of fact, I had already thought of making some arrangement of my own." She took a sip of the glass of sherry Sonya had thoughtfully handed to her, grimacing as it burned her sore throat. "I've told Pierre—no, it's useless looking at me like that; I had to tell someone, and Pierre ... we have always been very close; he understands, in his masculine way! I'm to go away on a holiday with him, and my Tante Celine will chaperone us. They have a small chateau in the country, far away from Paris, and in far too remote an area for friends to want to drop in. I'll have the child there, and—and decide afterwards what I must do."

Was it possible that, after such a storm of tears and sobbing, Ginny could actually sound so—so cold-bloodedly calculating! She would never understand the girl, Sonya thought in despair. And she wondered what she ought to tell William—if she should tell him anything at all!

Ginny was looking at her, green eyes like hard stones, for all that they were still shiny with tears.

"But—but afterwards. You are still a married woman *now*, and your child will have a name, but—what will you tell Steven? *Are* you going to tell him? Or will you divorce him after all?"

"Divorce him?" Ginny's voice went high, and then her eyes narrowed, making her look like an angry cat. "Oh, no—why should I make things easy and convenient for Mr. Steve Morgan? I'll be damned if I'll divorce him—I'll be damned before I let that woman have him! The baby I'm carrying is *his*, and he has a responsibility. Why should I let him get off lightly?"

Now that her first feelings of shock and humiliation were wearing off, Ginny seized on anger to make her resolute. To think that all this time she had been worrying herself into a positive frenzy, until she almost hated her own child because her pregnancy might come between her and Steve! And at the same time he had been carrying on quite openly with another woman!

At first, she had been deliberately trying to make him jealous, knowing he would hear how much she was enjoying herself, and how many different escorts she had. When she had posed, almost nude, for that young sculptor—even *then* she had been thinking of Steve, and his reactions. Oh—why had she wasted her time in silly pretense?

"I should have taken as many lovers as I've been accused of!" Ginny thought feverishly. "Perhaps I still may do so!" But she was almost eight months pregnant, and, when she undressed and stood before her mirror, woefully distended and ugly—yes, ugly!

"Ginny, dear—" Sonya's voice was surprisingly gentle. "I—I'm sorry if I have seemed quite unsympathetic! But don't you see how foolish you have been? If you had told someone, as soon as you discovered your condition—you should have written to Steven at once!"

"You don't understand," Ginny said, with a note of wretchedness creeping into her voice. "I did not really *want* to come to Europe. It was something I said long ago when I was angry with him that made him promise to send me. And then. . . . I don't know how it happened, but we had become like—like polite strangers to each other! If Steve had told me just once that he did not want me to leave him—but what is the point of thinking back *now*?"

"You *do* love him after all!" Sonya said, and there was a wondering note in her voice.

"Of course I love him! When the things he does or says do not make me hate him! And I won't let her have him, that Italian bitch!"

Sonya, by this time, was far too worried and upset to mention any of the doubts that sprang into her mind when she saw how determined and angry Ginny had become. Better anger than despair, and especially in her stepdaughter's present condition. But she could not help wondering, with an inward shudder, what the outcome would be.

It would be hard enough trying to explain to William. . . . What would Steve's reaction be? If only Ginny had not been so stubborn—so very foolish! And here she was in France, eight months pregnant, while her husband was gallivanting through Texas with an Italian Princess!

Chapter Forty

"So you will not even accompany me as far as New Orleans!" Francesca di Paoli's voice had turned husky from the force of her anger, and the bitter string of vituperations she had flung at him, couched in gutter Italian. "Tell me, Stefano, who is the woman you are in such a hurry to meet? And do not say again that it is business! I do not believe this *business* that suddenly makes you treat me as if I was a stranger—a common slut you picked up and used for your pleasure, only to discard at a moment's notice!" Her fingers curled into claws at her sides, and she let her voice rise. "Who is she? Did you meet her in that filthy town you went to? There isn't any thypus, is there? You—you whoreson! Barbarian *Americain*! Do you think you can treat me, *me* like the common females you are used to dealing with?"

She had already smashed every ornament in the room, and now her hand reached for the silver-backed brush that lay on the dresser behind her, while the other went up to claw at his face, but Steve forestalled her, his face a hard mask; catching her wrists, he twisted them until she could not help giving vent to a scream of pain and frustration.

"That's enough. Keep on acting like a bitch and I'm going to have to treat you like one. And I've reached the end of my patience right now—do you understand me? You don't own me, 'Cesca, any more than I own you. We made each other no promises, remember? I'm leaving in a few hours, and if you don't want to go to New Orleans you can do as you damn well please. Only, I won't be around to put up with your tantrums, or your fishwife screeching."

"Screeching. . . ! You dare say—"

"You screech like a guttersnipe, Francesca. You should save it for the stage, and the roles you play."

His words cut coldly across her rising hysteria, reducing her to temporary speechlessness.

Steve Morgan looked down into her frustrated, tear-contorted face and felt only impatience. And it showed in his narrowed, somehow contemptuous blue eyes, for suddenly, forgetting her rage, frightened in spite of her pride and her fury, Francesca gave a small sob. She stopped straining against his inflexible, hurtful grasp and let herself go limp, so that he was forced to catch her against him.

"Stefano! Don't talk to me so! Don't look at me as if I meant nothing to you—surely you understand why I am so angry? First, you will not touch me because of the typhus. And then, suddenly, it is business—business so urgent that you cannot accompany me to New Orleans. And you said you would! You told me we would be together for a while—you cannot deny this! And me—it is not in me to beg anything of any man, but you had begun to talk to

me, to treat me as if.... Oh, damn you! Why can't you
be honest with me, at least?"

Long after he had left her, and had already boarded the
flatboat that would take him up the Sabine River as far as
Brown's Bluff, and indeed, even after he had managed to
put both Francesca and her warm, sinuous body out of his
mind, Steve remembered her words.

He had too much time, staring down into the murky
green water, to think of Ginny. Ginny, crying out the very
same words at him, white teeth caught in her botom lip,
eyes shiny with tears. And why was it that where Ginny
was concerned, he always managed to react like a stupid,
lovesick calf? Once he had been honest with her, but then
pride had come between them both; and stubbornness, as
each waited for the other to be the first to give in. So he
had let Ginny go away, and had found Francesca, who
was too much like Ginny in too many ways, and yet
wasn't Ginny—could never be Ginny, who understood too
much about him and was the only woman who had somehow, insidiously and treacherously, managed to worm her
way under his skin, and into his mind, so that he could not
get rid of the thought of her, of too many memories. And
in his effort not to let her discover his weakness, he had
driven her away from him. . . .

As usual, thinking of Ginny had the power to make
Steve angry. Damn Ginny, anyhow! No doubt she was
thoroughly enjoying herself gallivanting around Europe,
enjoying the attention paid her. He had even heard rumors
that it was whispered in the highest circles that she was
the Tsar's latest little protégée—his mistress. And yet, she
had left Russia after a short visit. What had she found in
France and Spain that attracted her so?

It was high time he started concentrating on the job he
was here to do—and perhaps this was what he needed:
the challenge and excitement of danger to assuage the
reckless, restless devil in his blood. Why not admit it? He
had started to become bored, of late, with civilized games.

Steve deliberately pushed the thought of Ginny from his
mind and began to combine the information he had so
unexpectedly come across with the facts that Bishop had
given him. Bishop wouldn't approve of his sudden change
in plans, but what the hell did that matter as long as the
end results were what Bishop wanted? So he wasn't going

to ride into Baroque as an Eastern dude millionaire, with the lovely Signorina di Paoli accompanying him as bait to throw this Judge Nicholas Benoit off-guard. He could use that particular ploy later, if he needed to; but his unexpected meeting with Capitan Altamonte, an old friend from his Juarista days, had provided him with an opportunity to infiltrate the enemy camp, so to speak—and if it meant taking risks, why not? He was used to living with danger, and the chance was too good to pass up. Trouble was— Steve smiled ironically to himself—he had gotten out of the habit of taking orders, and had learned to take the initiative on his own. But in this case, at least, all he was risking was his own life; and the way he had it figured, even that risk wasn't too great.

He was going to make contact with a man called Refugio Orta, nicknamed Chucho—an ex-Comanchero, who had been working for Dave Madden.

Steve went over in his mind the few facts he had learned. Refugio was married, to a woman he called Teresita. The widow of a Comanche warrior, she was half Caddoan, and after Dave had been arrested and his small ranch seized for non-payment of taxes, Chucho, together with his wife, had taken refuge in the swamps that bordered Lake Caddo—a hiding place used by escaped slaves before the Civil War, and now for outlaws and "unreconstructed rebels." It was Chucho's brother Capitan Altamonte had taken Steve to see, and who had told him how to make contact before he had died of the typhus while Steve was in the room.

But Matamoros lay two and a half week's journeying behind him, and Steve had almost forgotten about the typhus and his exposure to it, until late on an unusually warm afternoon, the first chill shook him.

The small boat, travelling faster and more secretively than bigger ones, was close enough to Brown's Bluff to make Steve's sudden decision to be put ashore go unremarked. The boatman, a taciturn Cajun called Gaston, with a lined, young-old face, merely shrugged disinterestedly. He had been paid already, in gold, and he had already guessed that his passenger was a man who was running from the law—the kind of man who kept his plans to himself, and needed to hide. Here, or Brown's Bluff—it made no difference. Obviously, this blue-eyed, stubble

bearded man—who wore a gun as if it was a part of him,
and spoke excellent French into the bargain—knew where
he was going. Gaston didn't want to know anything about
it. He liked to say that he was a peaceful man who did
what he had to do for money. Whether it was smuggling
Mexican peons or wary outlaws up river, if he was ever
questioned, he knew nothing. He had a family to support—he was a poor man who kept himself alive by using
his little boat to carry supplies up and down river. Sometimes, if he was paid well enough, he also carried human
cargo. And why not? He believed in minding his own business, and letting others mind theirs.

Shrugging, he poled the boat to a stop under a gnarled
old cypress that hung its twisted shape over the water,
watching disinterestedly as his erstwhile passenger went
over the side, landing in mud that reached almost to his
boot tops. An unusually silent man, this one; and dangerous looking, for all his quietness. The kind of man who
followed trouble, if it did not find him first, and who
travelled light, as if he expected to be moving fast. . . .
Well, it wasn't any of his business! The small boat disappeared silently around a bend in the winding river as Steve
Morgan, with a muttered expletive, pulled his boots out of
the sucking, squishing mud and gained the shelter of the
trees that lined the waterway.

It was still hot—a humid, sultry afternoon that had persuaded Gaston to take his shirt off. But Steve wore his
jacket, and he had to keep his teeth clamped together to
prevent them from chattering. Long shudders wracked his
body; and several times, as he stumbled through the
closely growing trees, he had to stop and lean against one
until the spasm of coldness passed. The chills first, and
then the onset of fever. A detached part of his mind went
over the symptoms he had stopped watching for. How
long would it take before the fever made him mindless?
He had forgotten. Right now, while he was still able to
think lucidly, he had to try and remember the direction in
which he was headed—where he was going.

Stubbornly, he kept moving forward, even though it did
not take him long to realize that he was hopelessly lost.
Never mind. When it was night, if it was a clear night, the
position of the stars would help to steer him. *If* he were
still capable of coherent thought by then. The onset of

typhus came very suddenly—he had tried to learn all he could about it when he knew he had been exposed. But what good would all the knowledge he had gleaned do him now?

Mentally, between the chills that shook his body, Steve went over the few possessions he carried with him. His gun in its holster, and a spare one stuck in his belt. A knife. Some money—not too much. Nothing that would identify him—the old training held good.

His head had begun to ache. Every shaft of late afternoon sunlight, filtered through the trees, seemed to bounce off his eyeballs, sending a shaft of pain through his skull.

How far had he come since he left the main river? How far would he be able to go? It was very still—a mysterious, dark-green world, its silence broken only by his own stumbling footfalls and the small sounds of running water and tiny animals plopping into it as he passed. He forced himself to keep moving. Once, he almost staggered into a miniature stream, crawling snakelike through more lush greenery. He was well into a land that consisted mainly of swamps and bayous, with occasional, surprising islands rearing out of thick, muddy-green water. He tried to skirt the water carefully. Anything that looked like a harmless log might be an alligator. And apart from mud flats that could suck a man underneath the surface in a matter of minutes, there were water snakes—not to mention the human predators that also roamed these swamps. All things he would have been prepared to face and cope with under normal circumstances; but with all the dull pounding in his temples and the shivering fits that rendered him helpless. . . .

Steve heard himself swearing, but his own voice sounded like an unintelligible mumble. He continued to walk forward—fell—staggered upright, and then, after a while, stumbled and fell again.

"The onset of typhus is sudden. . . ." He had read that somewhere, or heard it from someone. But it was one thing to know what was happening to him, and another to try and make his body, already weakening, obey his mind's commands. The pain in his head had started to send tentacles down his neck, reaching down his spine. From being icy cold, he had suddenly started to feel hot; like a man in a desert, trapped without water, he had begun to pant. *"The*

onset of typhus is. . . ." Very sudden. Too quick. . . . He knew when his mind began to wander, and could do nothing to prevent it. Sometime, when he could no longer walk, he began to crawl forward; some deep-seated instinct told him he had to keep moving, even when he couldn't remember why, or where he was going. Somewhere along the way he had ripped off his jacket, throwing it aside. By now, with the fever climbing steadily, Steve Morgan was only barely conscious, incapable of lucid thought. He could hear running water somewhere, and his flesh felt as if it was consumed by heat; his throat was so dry he could hardly even groan. Every bone in his body ached, especially when he moved. Why was he moving, where was he going? He had been crawling, belly down, but now, suddenly, he lacked the strength to crawl further. Lying there, with his face pressed against cool, damp moss, Steve felt his head pounding, pounding . . . expanding with each hammer blow of his heart until it exploded into nothingness at last.

Part Five
THE SWAMP WOMEN

Chapter Forty-one

"Missie!" Her brother Matt's voice made her jump and almost drop pa's old pair of field glasses, which she carried with her everywhere. "Missie Carter—you up in that old tree dreaming half the day away as usual?"

"Matt, you go *away,* hear? And stop bothering me, sneaking up on me like an Indian and scaring me half to death! You *know* I'm here, so why do you keep teasing me?"

"You should be doing the chores instead of letting Teresita take care of them," he said.

But she wouldn't stir from her perch for him, and after a while, grumbling under his breath, her brother shrugged his big shoulders and moved away, his warning that she'd better not be late for supper again ignored by the girl who stayed hidden in the branches of the gnarled old tree that hung its head over the water.

When Matt had gone, as quietly as he'd come looking for her, his moccasins making hardly any sound at all in the damp, soft earth, Missie sighed. She put the field glasses down, resting them on her stomach as she shifted her position slightly to get more comfortable. Why did Matt think he had to keep checking on her? He had a way of making her mad, for all that she knew he loved her, and was worried for her in his own way. But why did he have to keep making fun of her daydreams?

Missie closed her eyes, ignoring the humming of the gnats and mosquitos around her, and determinedly continued with her daydreams. Most of them—her favorite ones—were about herself, and going back to live on the big plantation where her mother had been born, as its mistress. And why shouldn't that dream come true? Her mother had been born a true Lassiter, and Missie was her daughter, and old Tom Lassiter's granddaughter. *She* had much more right to the plantation than that nasty Toni, who was only a Lassiter because she'd trapped Uncle John into marriage when he was nearing middle age. Uncle Nick said her head was stuffed full of romantic notions and not much else; but he'd laughed indulgently when he'd said that, even if he *had* been angry because she refused to go to that school he wanted to send her to. But Uncle Nick, even if he, too, played along with Toni, had loved his little half-sister, even after her father had cast her off when she ran away from Pa. Maybe—maybe some day. And why shouldn't all her dreams come true, Missie told herself fiercely; and she remembered again the old story she never tired of hearing repeated.

Once, long ago, old Tom Lassiter had seen the land here; deep, fecund and wild, he had decided to settle here. He had been a mountain man—and a squaw man, too, folks whispered, to explain why the Caddo Indians had let him stay. But by the time he'd had his children, he'd had two white wives: an English woman, fresh off a ship, who had been John Lassiter's mother; and then, when she died young, he'd married again—a widow from Quebec, in Canada, who had a son of her own, Nick Benoit. Before she died of swamp fever, Tom Lassiter's second wife had given him a girl child they named Melissa Louise; and that Melissa had been Missie's own mother.

By then, of course, old Tom had built his big house of white stone, two stories high, with the remittance money his family sent him every month from England. He'd planted sugar cane, and he had slaves to work the plantation he'd clawed out of the bare earth.

Melissa Louise had been his favorite child, until she ran off with Joseph Cartier, a Louisiana Cajun, who had settled on a small strip of land bordering the swamps.

There were other settlers in the territory that Old Tom Lassiter had looked on as all his own by then. Farmers, small ranchers. From the time Texas became a state they had started to pour in, and there was nothing Tom could do about it.

But when his only daughter ran off with a dirt-poor Cajun, Old Tom had tried to have him killed—and *this* was the part that always made Missie angry.

Pa was a good man, and her grandfather, too, had begun with nothing. How could he have acted as if his daughter didn't exist for him, just because she'd fallen in love with a man he didn't approve of? If the swamp Indians hadn't been friendly, and if Joe Cartier hadn't known the swamps and bayous like the back of his hand, Missie, and her three brothers, might never have been born. As it was, her grandfather had acted as if he'd never had a daughter at all—leaving the plantation to his son John, and settling enough money on his stepson to pay for his education back east.

Melissa Cartier had been born with everything, but she had only two decent gowns to her back when she'd died—but in spite of that she'd been happy, and Missie could still remember the way Mama's face had lit up whenever Pa entered their little house. Mama was dead now, but while she lived she'd taught Missie to read and to write; and had told her stories from the books she'd brought with her when she ran away, and the books she'd remembered reading as a girl. And Missie, like her mother, had the red hair and green eyes of the Lassiters, while her brothers, Matt and Henry and Joe Junior, had their pa's dark coloring.

It was the books, and the romantic stories Mama used to tell her that made Missie such a little dreamer, her brothers would say, shaking their heads. But then, if Pa ever heard them tease her he'd tell them to let her alone, and he'd put his arms around her shoulders and squeeze, to show her how much he loved her.

Missie found herself thinking, all over again, "If only Toni hadn't come!" Toni, who was silver-blonde and beautiful, and evil and hard as nails underneath. Only, men didn't seem to see what she really was. She'd spoiled everything—taking over the running of the plantation and turning it into a ranch as if it had always been hers. Making even Uncle Nick, who was nobody's fool, into her

friend and ally. And not only Uncle Nick, who was old
enough to know better, but her own brother Matt as well.

As usual, thinking about Toni Lassiter made Missie
frown. Even if Pa didn't like her to swear, she could say it
to herself, couldn't she? Toni was a—a *bitch*! She pretended, on the surface; but she used people. And if they were
men, they let themselves be used. It was Toni who had
called Missie a wild creature from the swamps, and tried
to persuade Uncle Nick to send her away to a convent
school. Toni didn't like her, although she hid it under a
pretence of sweet concern when there were other people
about. Yes—Toni hated her all the more because she knew
Uncle Nick loved Missie, and wouldn't let her be harmed.

And there had been one other person who had seen
through Toni, too. Missie's frown deepened, and the unhappy, sick feeling she always got when she thought about
Renate Madden was like a knot tightening in her chest.
Renate had been her friend, and her husband, Dave, had
been a good man. Quiet, minding his own business. Until
they talked about the fight he'd gotten into in Baroque, and
the men he'd killed—one of them a Northern soldier. Dave
had been sent to prison; and soon afterwards, Renate had
vanished. And now Toni ran her cattle on the Madden place
as well. Just as she'd always planned to, Missie thought angrily. Why was it that Toni always got her own way in the
end? Half of their friends had left—gone broke, or dead,
or, like Missie's own father and brothers, forced to give up
their lands because they had fought for the South. Only
Toni survived and prospered—and Uncle Nick. . . . But
Missie didn't like to think that Uncle Nick had anything to
do with all the ugly happenings. He had been in Boston
when the Civil War began; and he, like the rest of them,
was blinded by Toni's beauty and her innocent act.

Poor Dave—chained by the leg like an animal. And poor
Renate—what had happened to her? Why had she gone
away so suddenly? Once, Missie had overheard Matt telling Hank something about Renate being seen in Baroque;
but when she'd burst out with questions, they'd all stopped
talking—faces going blank. Why did they all insist upon
treating her like a child, never telling her anything, when
she would be seventeen next week—the same age Mama
had been when she ran away with Pa? And if Hank had
seen Renate, why didn't he want to speak about it?

Renate had been Missie's friend, teaching her how to cook, and to sew with tiny neat stitches—and even teaching her a few words of German.

Painfully, Missie remembered the warm, good smell of baking bread that always seemed to fill the small house that Renate kept scrubbed and spotlessly clean and neat; the taste of spicy cookies and small, sweet cakes. And the sound of Renate's slow, calm voice with its German accent as she'd talk to Missie about her family and their small farm—how they'd all been killed by renegades wearing blue uniforms, except for Renate herself. And when the outlaws left, they set fire to her home so it would burn to the ground, and they had taken her off with them.

"It must have been so sad and so terrible for you!" Green eyes large with horror, Missie had caught her breath. "But then Dave rescued you, didn't he? *That's* the good part. Dave and his friend saved your life; just the two of them fighting against all those wicked men! How exciting it must have been to watch! Tell me again, Renate. How they boarded the boat, just like—like pirates."

The look of sadness that always came into Renate's eyes when she spoke of her family was smoothed away, and a half-smile curved her lips, as she sighed reminiscently. "Oh, *Ja*! Just like pirates. It was Dave's friend I saw first, coming over the side of the boat so silently, with a knife between his teeth. I thought it was the ghost of Jean Lafitte himself, and I was so frightened I could not even scream."

"It is just like one of the stories my mama used to read to me. You must have felt like a captive princess, rescued by two daring adventurers. Fancy—and then Dave fell in love with you and married you. . . . But what happened to his friend, the one you said looked like a real pirate? Didn't *he* fall in love with you, too? What was his name? Did you ever see him again?"

A slight shadow seemed to pass over Renate's smooth face. "Dave used to call him Whit, but I am sure that was not his real name. And he—he was an adventurer all right, but a little too much like an outlaw himself for me to like him too well. He was a restless man—the kind of man who would enjoy risking his life, because he thought it a kind of game, the taking of risks. I do not think he liked it when I persuaded Dave to settle down to safety, and leave the business they were in."

"But what were they? How did they come to rescue you?"

Missie had been full of questions, but at this point in her story, Renate would always purse her lips and refuse to say more. Dave's friend had gone his way, and Renate had not seen him again. Once, she said unwillingly, "I think he was killed by the French in Mexico, when they were having the revolution. He was the type to go looking for danger, in the guise of excitement. Dave and I, we do not have much, but at least we are happy, and make enough to pay the taxes and not go hungry. Dave says that soon our cattle will be worth almost fourteen or fifteen dollars a head at the stockyards in Forth Worth and Abilene."

Renate had been happy, and full of hope for the future she would share with Dave and the children they planned to have. Why did bad things have to happen to those who least deserved it? Dave in prison for life—Renate vanished or dead by now—and Missie's own family forced to grub for a living in the swamps, like outlaws, while Toni Lassiter, who was not a real Lassiter at all, took everything. There was talk that cattle were selling for premium prices in Kansas; and there were unbranded cattle running wild in the swamps. But whoever wanted to make the long drive to the nearest stockyards or a railhead would have to cross over lands recently homesteaded by ignorant Mexicans smuggled here up-river, or ex-slaves—all of them living in awe of Toni Lassiter and letting her run *her* cattle over most of their land, while they acted grateful at being allowed to cultivate four or five acres of it in order to keep themselves and their families alive. It made Missie mad whenever she thought of the injustice of it all, but what could *she* do? Pa only shook his head and chewed on his pipe, and it hurt her to see the sad, frustrated look come to his face. Hank and Joe Junior only scowled and told her that things were going to change pretty soon, she should just wait and see. She had given up protesting to her Uncle Nick—what was the point? Uncle Nick only smiled indulgently or started to talk pointedly about her needing a proper education. And Matt—when he wasn't gone on some mysterious errand, he'd talk darkly of States

Rights, and of a time when the northern soldiers and the dirty carpetbaggers would leave, and they'd all be rich.

It seemed to Missie that that time was a long way off—if it would ever come. She didn't believe Toni would ever let them have their old place back; and whenever Pa talked of getting together a big enough herd of swamp cattle to make the long drive to the stockyards at Abilene, Toni would always send them some kind of warning through Matt—telling them the soldiers wouldn't let them through, or that they should wait until she was ready to send *her* herd up, and that way, with *her* brand on all the cattle, it would be safe and she'd see they got a fair cut.

Toni—always Toni! She wanted to run all their lives, just like she ran the lives of those poor, ignorant homesteaders she'd brought in here. "Wish she'd get trapped in the swamp and drown!" Missie thought fiercely to herself; and then, wriggling on her perch to get more comfortable, she went back to her daydreams while she waited for Gaston's boat to come up river, wondering why he was so late this time. One reason Matt didn't grumble *too* much about her watching the river was because of Gaston, and the tobacco and the Mexican liquor he brought from his trips down to the gulf. If there wasn't anyone here to call out to him, showing him that it was safe to stop, Gaston would just keep going up river, for he was a cautious man.

This time, she almost missed him, for the light was just beginning to fade, and Missie's empty stomach was beginning to grumble as she thought about the supper that Teresita would have waiting. She had to be back home before it was dark—it was a promise she had made to Pa.

With a sigh, Missie had slipped off the tree, sliding down its branches, stretching her limbs one by one. And then she heard the faint sounds of a boat slipping through the water, the soft, tuneless whistle that Gaston always made when he passed this particular place.

She ran out onto the edge of the water, where he could see her clearly, and he poled the boat to a stop, scowling fiercely in a manner that made his face look more seamed than ever.

"Gaston! I thought you were never coming. You are late, do you know that? Did you bring—"

Gaston's already sour face looked sourer than ever.

"Did I bring—did I bring! Yes, I brought the aguardi-

ente for that thirsty brother of yours. But you can tell him
from me that if he went down to Mexico himself he could
have all he wanted, eh? I had to pay a lot for it—you can
tell him that, too! Prices are going up everywhere, and I
am only a poor man."

"Did you have no passengers this time?" Missie's curious green eyes travelled past him as he swung the heavy
jug onto the bank with an exaggerated groan of effort.
Gaston's frown deepened.

"Hey—what is this? Why do you always ask me such
questions? You know the kind of passengers who want to
travel on *my* boat always mean trouble in one form or another—like that Billy-Boy. Is he still bothering Teresita?"
Abruptly, before Missie could snap out an answer, Gaston
chuckled. "Hah! You were very angry with me for that
one, weren't you? But how was I to know what he was
coming up here for? You know I never ask questions—it's
bad for business. I didn't know he was a gunfighter going
to work for her. And *you*, little one, should keep your nose
out of bad business, and you can tell your papa I said so,
too. Your aunt wouldn't like it one bit if she knew how
many questions you keep asking—oui, and she'd probably
have my tongue cut out if she guessed I talk to you this
way."

"She's not my aunt! Don't you dare call Toni Lassiter
that! She—she's an evil, conniving . . . *witch*, that's what
she is, and I don't care if you tell her so! And if you only
want to *tease* me, when I've told you how worried I am,
I'll—I'll go away, and I'll never meet your boat again, nor
speak another word to you either, Gaston Labouche!"

Seeing that Missie, her eyes shooting sparks, was about
to make off like the half-shy, half-wild swamp child she
was, the man's voice turned cunning.

"Oho! She's in a temper now, is she? And with her own
godfather, too, ungrateful chit! Very well—run away then,
and you won't hear anything more from *me*, and that's a
fact."

Poised on bare feet, already turning to run, the sly,
somehow triumphant note in his voice made Missie hesitate, and then turn back slowly.

"Hear what? I'll bet you've got nothing to tell me at all,
old man! If you were a proper godfather, you'd be trying
to help me, instead of—of playing these silly games with

me, when you *know* I've stayed here all day, watching for you, and with not even a bite to eat, either."

"You'd better learn to talk to me with some respect, chit!" he scolded, and then, in a softer tone, "Don't you want the pretty silk ribbon I brought you, eh? It'll do to tie back your hair with, or to trim a pretty dress that would make a lady of you. Well?"

"Is it green?"

"Is it green, you ask. What else, to match your eyes? I got paid passably well this trip, you see. You can tell Joe I'll be by in a couple of days to share a bottle of wine with him." The ribbon fluttered in a ruffle of breeze, and Missie snatched at it, her eyes shining.

"Oh, oh! Thank you, Gaston, it's beautiful! The prettiest ribbon in all the world. And I'll think of you every time I wear it."

"Sure—sure! You'll forget about your poor old godfather the minute this boat is out of sight and be back to your dreaming again, won't you? Why don't you tell me who you're watching for?"

"I'm watching for...." She almost told him—almost told him that, ever since Dave's arrest, she had been waiting for his friend to come. But, of course, Gaston would not understand. Missie sighed, and because Gaston was watching her curiously with those sharp, squirrel eyes of his, she said cryptically:

"I don't suppose he's coming at all. Perhaps he's dead—or perhaps he doesn't care about his old friends any longer. If he did—don't you suppose he'd have come by now? It's only—" she looked back at Gaston and her voice strengthened, becoming stubborn. "I had a *feeling*. In here." Her hands touched the faded cotton of her dress, straining across young, growing breasts. "Teresita says it never does to discount feelings, or dreams—and you know that the Indians call her a witch-woman, and *they* believe in everything she tells them about their dreams."

"What? What are you gabbling about? You're a little young to start dreaming about strange men you've never met, aren't you? What is this, eh? *You* turning into a witch-woman too?"

"I'm not—I'm not! And I knew you wouldn't understand."

"Maybe I don't! I tell you, Missie—whoever you're

looking for isn't likely to be asking a ride up river in *my* boat, so you'd better stop pestering me with your fool questions. You know the kind of cargo I carry as well as I do—Mex peons running off from their haciendas looking for a piece of dirt land to grub a living off. Outlaws. Gunmen like Billy-Boy Dozier. And men on the run who don't want any questions asked, and ain't about to talk about themselves either. Like that dangerous-looking roughneck with the tied-down gun who rode all the way up river with me with hardly a word exchanged between us in two weeks, except to ask questions. Questions—hah! When he found out I was too smart to say anything he clammed up too. And *that's* the kind of passenger I carry! A real wolf, for all that he understood too well what I was saying when I started to talk at him in French. Was headed for Brown's Bluff, he said—and then, all of a sudden, he changes his mind. Wants to get right off. And just as well—I was beginning to think he was another of Miz Lassiter's hired guns, come to stir things up some more. . . . Hey, foolish girl! Watch out—do you want to fall in the water?"

Fortunately, it was Teresita, and not Matt, who came looking for Missie, and listened silently and expressionlessly to the girl's gasped out, almost incoherent explanations.

"It is he—I *know* it is he! Very tall, Gaston said, with black hair and dark blue eyes. And he carries a knife as well as a gun—Gaston saw it! We have to find him, don't you see? He'll be going straight to the Madden house—perhaps he doesn't know that Toni lets Billy-Boy live there now. He must be warned!"

Reed slim and straight-backed, her smooth, light-copper face impassive, the Indian woman did not, as Matt would have done, tell the girl to have done with her foolishness.

Instead she said practically:

"Be careful with that jug. If you spill any of the liquor or let it fall and break, your brother will be very angry with you. He is angry as it is because you stayed out so late."

Missie stamped a bare foot with impatience.

"I don't care what Matt thinks, or how angry he is! Gaston say's he dropped him off only about three miles down river, and he did not have a horse. If I take the secret way across the stream near Wildcat Bayou, then perhaps I will find him before he—"

"And if you find this man and he is a stranger? A bad man like the others? There are many men with black hair and blue eyes. Perhaps this one had business elsewhere. Perhaps, like so many others, he plans to use the swamps as a hiding place. And since you have not seen him, and cannot be certain—"

"But I am! Who else would know your husband's name? I am sorry, Teresita, to mention it, because I know it makes you sad to remember, but he asked Gaston if he knew a man called Refugio Orta—he said he was a friend of his brother in Mexico. Gaston didn't tell him anything, of course—you know how close-mouthed that old man can be. But he did admit this man might have been a Comanchero himself. Please—please, Teresita! Don't you see now why I am so sure? The feeling I had—everything! You must listen to me—I was coming to look for you in any case, and here you are."

Teresita's face remained unmoved, but her black eyes had begun to glitter.

"The friends of my dead husband did not call him by his given name, they called him Chucho. And he had many enemies. Last night, I had a strange dream, although its true meaning has not been shown to me yet. But I think—yes, I think it means very bad luck. Or death. But for whom? My feelings tell me that the coming of a stranger at this time is not good."

"You mustn't tell Pa or Matt that! And it isn't right. You said yourself you hadn't yet found the real meaning of your dream! And if you're not going to help me, or even try to understand, then I'll go find him myself. Because *I'm* sure!"

Teresita's voice sharpened almost imperceptibly.

"You are sure that this man the boatman spoke of so casually is the same man the German woman spoke of? A man you have never seen? A man who might even be dead by now? I do not like to say this to you, Missie Carter, but I think you are trying too hard to turn your daydreams into fact. And dreams are not to be captured in the hand—they are given us as signs. Please listen to me and be sensible! This man who mentioned my husband's name means trouble. Refugio knew some very bad men. . . ."

But, of course, Missie wasn't listening. The girl looked
as if she were in a trance—a small, secret smile on her lips
made her pointed little face look mysterious and bewitched.
She didn't care what anyone thought. She *knew*!

Chapter Forty-two

He knew, somehow, without being told, that he had
been very sick. He felt very weak, and his instincts told
him he wasn't used to weakness. He was lying in a brush
shelter of some sort, feeling very cold. When he tried
to think, pain lanced through his temples, dulling everything. And yet, with a detached part of his mind, he was
becoming aware. There were faces that bent over him. A
woman spoke to him, and he heard his voice, sounding
strange in his ears, replying. A woman. . . . But after a
while there were two women, each speaking a different
tongue; and yet he understood what both said. Understood, and knew what he was saying—but nothing else,
not who he was, or what he was doing in this place, or
even why he felt so weak. After a while, he gave up—finding it easier to escape from the pain in his head when he
slept.

When he was able to accept reality, what seemed like
an eternity later, he remembered nothing. Not his name, or
where he came from, nor even what he looked like.

He lived with Indians—and for some time afterwards
he thought he was one of them himself. He was married
to an Indian woman whose Comanche name meant Running Water, but she was known to everyone else as Teresita.

"You had a bad fever." Teresita's voice was low, and
sounded slightly husky from the force of her emotion.
"My first husband, your brother, had it once, but fortunately we were in Mexico then, and there was a doctor.
So I knew what to do."

"I kept having dreams of being in a prison somewhere."
He was frowning, black brows drawn together.

"And you were. During the revolution in Mexico. Do
you remember nothing else?"

Teresita's voice was calm and matter of fact, in spite of
the sudden thudding of her heart.

"Why in hell don't I remember anything at all? Except
for the dreams. . . . and even those I'm starting to forget."

"Then don't think about them. It's better, perhaps. You
were in some kind of trouble on your way here, but you
are safe now. The high fever took your memory away, but
it will come back, sooner or later."

He muttered, half under his breath, "For better or for
the worse, huh?" But when Teresita looked at him uncomprehendingly he felt a kind of tenderness for her, and
reached up to touch her smooth face with his fingers.

"Never mind. I guess you're right, and it'll all come
back. But I wish I remembered some things at least."

She had been kneeling beside him, bent over him, and
now suddenly his arm tightened, drawing her against him.
What kind of a man was he? Teresita wondered. How
could she have allowed Missie to persuade her, against her
own misgivings, to go searching the swamp for him that
evening?

"I think you remember far too much. And besides, you
are not strong enough yet. Please—you must not!"

"Why? If you're my woman, what's wrong with your
lying beside me? I'm clear-headed today, thank God, and I
cannot imagine how I could have forgotten how soft and
supple your body feels."

She felt his fingers against her flesh, and his lips against
her face and her throat. He made no rough move to push
her legs apart in order to mount her, but seemed content
to hold her close while he caressed her; and while she did
not understand, at first, Teresita could not help remembering that not even Chucho had behaved in this way with
her. She had been brought up to know what men wanted,
to be submissive, to perform the duties that were expected
of a wife. She had neither wanted nor expected anything
else. But this man—what did he want of her?

Her flesh shrank and quivered under his seeking hands
and lips, and then grew warm and warmer still until it was
she who burned as if she had a fever, and grew helpless.

The single garment she wore seemed to slip off her body, and he, under the coarsely woven blanket, wore nothing. The blanket, too, fell aside as he continued to seek her out, as if he was charting new territory. Touching, exploring, lingering over taut hillocks, discovering valleys and hollows.

And Teresita, for the first time in her life, was finding out how it felt to be made love to as opposed to being taken—although she could not have put these newly awakened feelings into words.

"Teresita," she heard him whisper, and it was like hearing her name for the first time, newly given to her, like the feelings he evoked in her body.

Teresita's upbringing had instilled in her that a woman was meant only to serve a man's needs and her experience of men had been limited to her two husbands. Neither had beaten her, or been overtly cruel, but they had the same standards, and would no more have dreamed of wasting time in preliminaries when they felt the need for her body than she would have expected them to. But this man—this stranger they had picked up, more dead than alive, half out of his mind with fever—had proved unexpected from the start.

Teresita had gone along with Missie because the girl was determined to go looking for Gaston's mysterious passenger. She had not expected them to find him; and when they did, Teresita recognized what kind of fever he had, and she had been of a mind to go away and leave him to die. But Missie had been determined, and the only way Teresita could keep Missie from coming too close and becoming infected herself was to promise the girl that she, who had already had the bad fever, would take him to her hut and look after him. Even then, Teresita had hoped that he would die. Her feelings told her that he had brought trouble with him in addition to typhus. She did not believe that he had been a friend to her husband's brother. Jesus-Maria had been a quiet, self-effacing man, content to farm for the meager crops that were barely sufficient to feed his rapidly growing family. What could he have had in common with the kind of man this half-conscious stranger seemed to be? But then, in his delirium, the stranger had spoken not only in Spanish, but in the Comanche tongue as well. He had seemed to have mo-

ments of lucidity, in the beginning, when he knew her
name, although she knew nothing of him. Perhaps he had
been a Comanchero himself? But why hadn't he come before, in that case? *Why* had he come here now?

Teresita had time to wonder, and to admit her own curiosity to herself, while for Missie's sake she nursed him.
In the months since Chucho had died, she had stayed
alone in her small brush hut, allowing no man to lie with
her. They had left her alone—the Indians as well as the
white men—because of her medicine dreams and her
skill with healing herbs. Now, the fact that she had taken
a man into her dwelling needed some explanation, and she
gave one, regretting the necessity to lie. She said he was her
late husband's brother—and that he had come to marry her,
in the manner of the Comanches. After he was well, and
left, she could say he had gotten lost in the swamps. . . .

And then he took her by surprise, that afternoon when
his maleness asserted itself, taking her off guard in the beginning, and then, soon afterwards, to surrender. How
could she have known that such feelings existed? Or that
there was such a thing as passion? He made her want him,
in a way she had not believed possible. He told her she
was beautiful, and undressed her completely so that he
could caress every inch of her body—bringing her such
pleasure that she thought she might faint from it. She had
not dreamed that it could be such a shattering, glorious
thing to be taken by a man; and it made her almost
afraid, so that at first she would hold back, wanting to belong to herself again, until he'd look at her with a slight
frown of surprise.

"Why do you grow so stiff? Haven't I told you before
how lovely you are? Haven't we made love this way before?"

"This way" was many ways, when she had only known
one before. And over her whispered half-protests, he made
her forget about right or wrong.

By this time, Teresita had realized that he had no memory of the past, and that he had accepted the story she
had told the others. That he was her man—the brother of
her dead husband.

As soon as he was strong enough, Teresita led him
deeper into the swamplands, along undefined trails known
only to the Caddo Indians who had lived here for longer

than even they could remember. There were islands here, where wild cattle and horses ran free, never knowing the feeling of rope or bridle. Game abounded, too, and they never went hungry, for the man she had named Manolo—from a name he had muttered in his delirium—knew how to hunt with a bow and arrows he made himself.

For almost a month they lived an isolated, completely primitive existence, seeing no other human beings but each other. Now Teresita was sure that Manolo, whom she had already begun to think of as her man, had lived with the Comanche Indians at one time—as she, herself, had. And at some other time, he had been in a prison. She shuddered at the marks that the lash had left on his back, and the strangely-shaped brand that had been burned into his flesh; he told her the brand was the symbol of a country far across the ocean. He had frowned when he said this, and she knew it was because it made him angry to know he remembered so many things, knew so many things, and had no idea of how or when he had learned them. But he was starting to accept his lack of a previous memory; and for herself, Teresita was guiltily aware that she hoped he would never remember, and find out that she had lied to him about who he was—making up plausible stories in response to his frequent, puzzled questions. It wasn't possible that he was the same adventurer that Missie had watched for and spoken of. She refused to think that he might be. For the first time in her life, Teresita felt her bones turned to water by the touch of a man—learned that it was possible to make love and laugh together at the same time; that making love could be an exchange of touch and kisses and caresses as well as emotion. And that they could make love whenever and wherever the notion took them—out in the open under the sun, or in the water, or at night, under the tiny shelter of their brush and hide tepee.

Teresita did not want to leave the secret, undisturbed place they had found. But in spite of the pleasure that her man seemed to take in her, she was wise enough to detect the restlessness in him, and to make no demur when he announced suddenly one day that it was time they returned to the others. Hardly realizing it, she had told him as much as she could of the swamp people, and the others who battened off the rich, fertile lands that adjoined the swamps. The trouble that had started up soon after the Civil War had ended—but not the injustice.

"Why doesn't somebody do something? Why do they let the Lassiter woman get away with whatever she pleases to do? There are cattle running wild right here in the swamps, and if she's selling hers to the markets up North, what's to prevent others from doing the same?"

She retorted, fear making her voice sharp, "It was that same question, asked by those others, that led them to their death or ruin. Those who remain alive are alive only because they do not ask such questions. Do not interfere. I beg of you. Let things be!"

But he was not the kind of a man who would let things be, as Teresita herself should have recognized at the beginning. He was the kind who made things happen. In spite of her fears and her foreboding, his voice was thoughtful when he said slowly:

"It seems to me, from all you've told me, that there's no reason anyone should not grow rich by branding enough of these wild cattle, and driving them up to a meat-starved market. There's enough profit to be made for everyone to share in, and if there are those who are selfish as well as greedy ... perhaps it is time they were brought to realize that one life is as cheap as another."

His casual words terrified her, and yet habit and instinct held her silent. Yes—it was time that they returned. Perhaps if he spoke to the others—men like Missie Carter's father and brothers, who had lived here all their lives— this reckless man of hers would realize what could and could not be dared. Perhaps Missie herself would be of some help. . . .

Teresita felt slightly guilty whenever she thought of Missie, but she brushed these feelings aside. Missie was still a child; and obviously, this man had come here to find *her*, Teresita. He had known her name. And that of her husband. But she was careful, not wanting to tempt fate, to tell him that it was Missie who had heard of his coming from Gaston, the boatman. When they got back, she would talk to Missie herself, and explain.

"Why does everyone keep treating me as if I was still a *child*?" Missie cried, stamping her foot with a mixture of rage and inconsolable grief. "There's no need for explaining anything to me, Pa—why does Teresita think she has to? She saved his life, I guess—and I know what the Indians believe: When you save someone's life it belongs to you. But—" her green eyes looked large and shiny, as if they were ready to spill over with tears, and Joe Carter could do nothing but shrug helplessly and wish that his Melissa hadn't died so young. "But Pa!" Missie burst out, letting some of her mixed up feelings show—"I *know* he's the same one Renate used to talk about! Maybe he did know Chucho—and why not? Chucho came here because *he* knew Dave . . . I mean, it stands to reason, doesn't it? But now—now he's forgotten *everything*! Even his name, or where he came from, or why! And it's not fair that Teresita should tell everyone he's Chucho's brother. Its not right, the way they went off into the deep swamp and stayed gone so long, coming back together just as if . . . as if—"

"Now, Missie! You heard Teresita say that this man—this Manolo—speaks Comanche and Spanish, too. I'll bet he's a Comanchero. At any rate, daughter, he's right at home living with the Indians."

"He seems right at home living anywhere—with anyone!" Joe Junior gave a sudden hoot of laughter, and her face flushing crimson, Missie ran; she hardly cared where she went, or if she tripped over roots or fell in the water. She hated them all! No one understood, not even Pa!

Without really thinking, Missie ended up in her favorite hiding place—the old tree by the water. She sat there, up in the branches, scowling across the torpid, dark green stream that seemed to run exceptionally sluggishly today; and through the old field glasses, she saw Billy-Boy Dozier mount his horse and take off like a bat out of hell. . . . Maybe he'd heard that Teresita was back from the wild country, with a man of her own. He'd been giving her the eye for a long time, in spite of the fact that he was Toni Lassiter's blue-eyed boy of the moment. Or maybe Billy-Boy had heard the rumors that some of the swamp ranchers were planning to drive a herd to Abilene. News carried fast around these parts. And in spite of feeling upset, Missie was still glad that Toni wasn't here, but already half-way to Abilene herself. With *her* gone, even Matt was different. Less irritable. More the big brother Missie could

remember from the old days, before the darned old war
came and spoiled everything.

Missie had to admit that she couldn't *really* remember
how things had been before the war—only what people
told her. She'd done most of her growing up in the
swamps and bayous though, and knew them almost as well
as the Indians did. If she wanted to, she could disappear
and find a place of her own, where no one would ever discover her ... and it would serve that nasty-minded Joe
Junior right if she did. If not for Pa. ...

Thinking of Pa made Missie feel guilty, and with a
cross little sigh she slid down the great, rough trunk of
"her" tree, landing agilely on her bare feet—only to stand
as if she, too, had taken roots; the color ebbing and rising
again in her face, she felt the strangest trembling inside
herself, from the pulse beat in her throat right down to
the curling of her bare toes.

He had the brightest, darkest blue eyes she had ever
seen—they seemed to leap right out at her from a sun-
brown face. And he was so tall she had to tilt her head
back to look up at him.

She found that he was studying her just as openly and
warily as she studied him; his eyes narrowed slightly as a
kind of puzzled frown drew his black brows together. And
then, as if he had suddenly sensed the nervousness in her,
she saw one corner of his mouth quirk in an unwilling grin
that made the thin scar running down one side of his face
kind of melt into the deep groove that appeared when he
smiled.

"Hi, green eyes."

Missie had the strangest feeling that the words had just
slipped out, as if he hadn't known himself he was going to
greet her that way. She felt just exactly as if she was
caught up for real in one of her dreams—and he was, too;
for there was no mistaking the warm, faintly caressing
note in his voice when he'd called her "green eyes," as if
he'd known her before.

But all this happened in the barest instant, and the next,
his face had taken on a closed look as he added, in a ridiculously formal fashion, that he hoped he had not startled
her.

"Were you looking for me?" Sheer nervous reaction

made Missie blunt—it surprised her when he was equally
plain-spoken.

"Yes. Your father told me I might find you in this partic-
cular spot. Do you mind?"

She shook her head, suddenly shy. What did he want
with her?

"They told me you thought I might be a friend of the
people who used to live across the river." He said it
abruptly, jerking his head in the direction of the Madden
place; and the careless way he referred to Dave and
Renate as merely "the people who used to live across the
river" made angry color flame in Missie's cheeks.

Because his callousness suddenly made her angry, she
answered him in the stilted patois French her Pa tried to
teach her.

"If you had really been their friend, monsieur, I think
you would have come a long time ago, when they needed
help. Now—it is too late!"

"Was that supposed to be some kind of a test?" he
asked her quietly. Switching to French that was far more
correct and idiomatic than hers, he went on thoughtfully,
"Yes, I speak French. I must thank you for helping me
rediscover the fact that I do. However, did—did these
friends of yours call *their* friend by a name?"

Strange, dancing lights seemed to have appeared in the
depths of his eyes as he watched her face, very carefully.

Missie answered unwillingly, her face still hot with anger and embarrassment.

"Renate told me once that Dave's friend was called
Whit. But she said she did not think it was his real name.
She . . . the description she gave fits you, though!" she said
quickly, before she lost her courage. "And you speak
French—you also speak Spanish, don't you? Don't you remember anything at *all*? What else would you be doing
here if you weren't—"

"But as you've just said, if I was really this friend
they—*your* friends were expecting, wouldn't I have come
before? Perhaps I'm from Louisiana and it grew too hot
for me over there. Maybe I drifted up this way to hire my
gun out for pay—I understand there's a market for gun-
slingers in this particular neck of the woods." His voice
had grown hard, and almost self-contemptuous. "I've been
practicing drawing that gun I was wearing." His eyes

touched Missie's, but she had the scary feeling he wasn't seeing her at all. "I guess I'm fast enough to give a fair account of myself. . . . This Whit character. What else do you know about him?"

Missie had her back to the tree now—mesmerized by him; but, oddly enough, she felt more excited than scared.

"Why do you ask if you don't think you're him? Renate said he killed three men that day—the day she was rescued off the boat. She said he was laughing, as if it was all an exciting game."

He frowned impatiently.

"Is that all? Look, I don't exactly enjoy being a stranger to myself. And before I ride on, I'd like to find out if there are any Wanted dodgers posted on me. Either I'm an ex-Comanchero or some kind of adventurer—was there a reward out for this Renate's rescue?"

Again, Missie felt stung into retorting by the deliberately calculated way he talked about riding on—imputing motives of nothing but money to what had always seemed to Missie to be a daring and gallant rescue of a maiden in distress.

"Dave Madden *married* Renate! And perhaps she'd heard right, after all, when she said you—that Dave's friend—had been mixed up in the revolution in Mexico, and was probably *dead!*"

Sheer disappointment and unhappiness made Missie's voice crack, and she thought she discovered a sudden softening in the blue eyes that had seemed to regard her so impersonally up to now.

"Are you really sorry because a man you never even knew might be dead?" His voice seemed to mock both her and himself, as if he despised his own sudden weakness. "Better learn to keep your feelings guarded, little green eyes. It's the soft ones in this world who always end up getting hurt."

"I can see now how wrong I was about you! You—you're the kind of man who doesn't care about anything or anyone, aren't you? So why should you care if I end up getting hurt or not? And why do you keep calling me green eyes, as if you've known me before from some place?"

Her sudden spurt of fury seemed to have no effect on

him at all, except to make him thoughtful. He raised one quizzical eyebrow at her.

"Maybe I remember your little pointy face, and those eyes, bending over me when I had the fever. Did you really risk getting typhus yourself, just because you thought I might be this mysterious 'friend'?"

She made as if to rush past him, and he trapped her with his hand on her arm, making her feel all weak and breathless.

"Stop making fun of me! I hate you!"

"I'm sorry, Missie Carter. Miss Melissa." The way he said her full name, like a caress, made Missie's breath catch in her throat. "I probably wouldn't be standing here upsetting you if not for you—and your feelings. And that's what I really came here to do. To thank you. And as for your green eyes"—he gave a laugh that sounded more like a short, angry sound in his throat—"I kept wondering why I was haunted by green eyes, in all the dreams I kept having. One time, I dreamed I was surrounded by wolverines, all with the same eyes, shining like lamps, waiting to tear me to bits. . . . There's an old saying that a man should never put his trust in a green-eyed woman!"

He was talking more to himself than to her, by now—perhaps because the particular green-eyed girl was no more than a child, with a freckled face and untidily braided hair. She was a long way from discovering she was a woman yet, and perhaps it was just as well.

The man who was called Manolo and knew that his name was not that but something different had begun to discover that he was a cynic—or, at least, that he was not easily given to trusting. But there were certain things that even *he* accepted—perhaps from instinct or from habit. There was the woman Teresita, who was his woman, her body giving him warmth and enjoyment once the first constraint had worn away. And now there was this green-eyed child-woman, to whom he owed his life—and the thought annoyed him, in some strange way, even while her very innocence and the direct simplicity of her look made him almost ashamed of his harshness. She had saved his life, as much or more so than Teresita had done. And since he had regained consciousness, with a mind wiped clean of memory, he found that the habits he had acquired were more Indian than white. In some measure, he owed Missie

Carter something. Honesty to match her own? Was there something he could give her to wipe away the wary, unhappy look he had put in her eyes?

Distant memory tugged at the corners of his mind, reminding him of the same look in another pair of green eyes—and then the memory disappeared.

Chapter Forty-three

Less than three weeks later, Manolo, with Missie's father and brothers and some of the other swamp ranchers, as they called themselves, took a herd of cattle up to Abilene.

He discovered, on the long drive North, that he must have done this same thing before. Perhaps he'd traveled the very same trail before, or perhaps he acted purely by instinct. But whether it was just that or not, he found himself their leader after less than ten days on the trail.

In Abilene, wearing his hair long by now, like that of the three half-breed Caddoes who had come along with them, Manolo stayed out of the bars, and he left the negotiating for the sale price of the cattle they'd brought to Joe Carter and to Matt.

Beef was fetching top prices, and they got eighteen dollars a head—and the first night old Joe Carter got himself drunk and had to be carried back to the hotel where they were staying. Matt and Hank and Joe Junior celebrated in style, too—they bought themselves clothes and some fancy women, and left it to the others to buy the supplies they needed and to put some money in the bank, like they'd agreed on before they started out.

It was Manolo—knowing, without knowing how—who told the boys to look for Texas Street for their pleasure.

"Seems like all these new cow towns have a Texas Street—and each one trying to build up a worse reputation than the last." He was frowning when he said it, though; and Matt, who had a chip on his shoulder since Toni Lassiter had up and taken *her* cattle on the long drive with not a word to him first, had said:

"Seems like you remember a helluva lot without rememberin' anything *really* important, amigo! You checked yet to find out if there's a reward poster on you in the marshal's office?"

"Thought I'd leave that to you—amigo."

There were times when Matt wasn't certain if he cared too much for Manolo—or whatever his name was. Especially his manner. But something about the way the man wore his gun, and the unafraid, almost mocking look in those damn blue eyes always made Matt hold his peace.

He did the same thing on this occasion, too; he merely shrugged his big shoulders as he moved off.

"Maybe I'll check on it for you, huh? Might be a useful thing to know."

Matt and the newcomer had acted like strange dogs around each other right from the start, anyhow. Circling . . . giving each other grudging respect . . . keeping their distance. Matt hadn't been too eager to make this drive in the beginning; he had let himself be persuaded only after his pride was pricked when his brothers began hinting slyly at his being hogtied and blinkered by Toni Lassiter. All the way here, he'd been watchful and surly—only to find that Manolo, even if he acted only by instinct, seemed to know what he was doing, and where they should be headed.

But now that they had reached Abilene and Matt had some money for the first time in years, he began to think about the other big herds they'd drive up here.

They'd adopt a brand of their own—the Circle Star—and put it on their horses—and on all the unbranded stuff that was running wild in the swamps and the islands that dotted the bayous. It wasn't stealing—although he didn't like to think of how Toni would react when she heard. But, hell! A man had to look out for his own.

Without quite knowing it, in the morning—when he was more or less sober from the excesses of the night before—Matt set out to find Toni. He left Texas Street and the cheap hotel and the bars that looked shabby and tawdry in the daylight, ignoring the calls of the early-rising girls who leaned out of their windows to whistle at him and call him a handsome dude. Let them look. He'd seen a couple of horses wearing the Lassiter LBQ brand; and his new clothes, still smelling of starch and proudly creased, were part of his plan to impress Toni.

They were the first new clothes he'd had since the war, and it was sheer luck that the big gent who had ordered this particular suit all the way from the East had died of lead poisoning before he could pay for it. As Mr. Bledsoe told Matt, sighing, there were very few men who were big enough in the shoulder and tall enough to carry off the smart plaid weave and close fit—the latest style. He didn't look like a country hick now, Matt thought, ignoring the squeak his new boots made with every step he took. He was on his way to the right side of the tracks this time, with enough honestly earned money to buy him a good breakfast at the finest restaurant in town. And then he was going to the bank, to draw out a few more dollars— and he'd make inquiries about a beautiful silver-blonde woman who just might be in town.

Mrs. Antoinette Lassiter exited the bank, furious underneath her cool, unruffled surface, although nobody but old Ben, the Negro man who drove her rig, would have guessed it. How dare they sell a herd of *her* cattle! And, that unctuous Mr. Daviot, the new manager of the bank— he had actually congratulated her on the grit and initiative of the Texans in her part of the state!

"That's what this country needs right now, of course! Rebuilding. People forgetting old differences, working to make something of themselves—to build something. Cattle, Mrs. Lassiter. You've got the beef on the hoof in Texas, and that's what they need in the North. Progress, ma'am. And good old American initative. Must be mighty good cattle country around Baroque!"

She had smiled, and continued smiling, inclining her head graciously while Mr. Daviot—who was utterly bemused by her—continued talking.

"And now, about your money. Are you sure you want to carry so much cash? Forgive me if I sound presumptuous, Mrs. Lassiter, but with the preponderance of crime since the war—"

"I pay my men top wages, Mr. Daviot. And I've been promised a Cavalry escort. Colonel Vance, who is a friend

of mine, has been visiting Fort Worth recently. I assure
you that I will go home extremely well protected. But
thank you for your concern, all the same."

Mrs. Antoinette Lassiter had brought her own rig with
her. The polished harnesses jingled, and the matched pal-
omino geldings—which were her trademark—tossed their
heads skittishly as if they were used to having everyone
turn to stare at them and the women they waited for, who
rode behind them in the English-style carriage, usually
with a dainty lace handkerchief that had miraculously
ver-blonde hair.

Old Ben, her driver, had come with Toni from
Louisiana when she married, and he sat with his back as
stiff as a ramrod, wearing the fancy uniform and silk top
hat Toni liked for him to wear. Just seeing Ben alone,
dressed so fancy, was enough to make folks stare, because
seeing him reminded some of the old days in the South,
when those who could afford it lived in style. And Toni
Lassiter was the kind of woman who would make any
man stop and take a second look. She was beautiful,
with a fine-boned, arrogant face and pale topaz eyes
that went with her fine, silky blond hair. Her mouth
was full and pouting, lips the palest shade of pink. When
she lowered her voice, it could sound husky and sensuous—enough to send shivers up any man's spine. And
while her waist was tiny, her hips and breasts were lush
and promising. Toni was used to turning men's heads,
and took it as her due. Ever since she was a child, and
had learned how easy it was to twist her father around her
little finger, merely by pouting or by crying, she had neither hesitated nor scrupled to use the power that her
beauty had given her over men. Even while she despised
them all. . . .

If Toni Lassiter was well aware of her own charms, and
their devastating effect on the male species, she also had
her own particular weaknesses—although she refused to
think of them as such.

She had loved her weak, handsome father—and had despised him at the same time. She had always enjoyed
watching cockfights, and battles between bare-fisted men
in the ring. And street fights, and duels—particularly when
they were being fought over her. In the old days, before
the war had come to upset everything, before her father

had lost the plantation with his gambling, Toni had enjoyed going with him to the slave auctions—just as much as she'd liked watching the overseer punish recalcitrant slaves.

Last night, with a night-black shawl covering her hair and half her face, and a black dress that disguised her figure, Toni had gone to a small ranch house a few miles out of town. She had gone to watch some of the things that took place there—and she did not mind paying for this privilege, for it amused her to observe the weaknesses of others; it gave her a heady, excited feeling that was mixed with contempt.

Big Sadie catered to rich customers, men or women— Sadie didn't care, as long as they paid what she referred to as their "dues"—who wanted the extra-special and un- usual. Sadie liked to say she catered to the connoisseurs, being originally from New Orleans herself.

She gave circuses, and her girls were pretty and catered to every taste. She was well known for her "talent-hunts"; she was constantly on the lookout for new studs—men who would keep her girls in line, beat them for the ed- ification of certain customers, and satisfy the customers themselves, if they were called upon to do so.

One didn't just *go* to Sadie's place. Only a few, select people knew where to find it and how to get in. You had to be introduced—and once in, if you didn't have enough money to afford the fancy prices, you had to have talent to pay in kind.

Toni Lassiter had the money, and she had experience if she felt like showing how much she knew without anyone being any the wiser as to her identify. Moreover, she had known Sadie when the woman had called herself by an- other name, and they had both lived in Louisiana. So Toni was a frequent visitor at Big Sadie's, sometimes showing herself—a mysterious, black-clad woman—and sometimes preferring to watch first and take her own brand of plea- sure privately afterwards. . . .

The dusty, bawdy brightness of the sunshine outside the bank made her tilt her silk parasol forward to shade her eyes. Toni Lassiter's rage at Matt Carter—who had dared to act without waiting for her say-so—and his stupid oaf of a father and even stupider brothers was tinged with anger from her experience at Sadie's the night before.

Sadie's was becoming low-class. She would never go there again!

Ben jumped off his perch and helped her into the carriage, and all the time Toni kept thinking of last night.

Everything had started out just fine. The wine Sadie kept for her special customers was as excellent as it always was. And the entertainment proved exciting, too—especially when Sadie turned her circus into an impromptu talent show, calling for volunteers from the "audience."

Afterwards, still sipping her wine, Toni had stripped to a gauzy wrapper, thoughtfully provided by Sadie herself, while keeping her face partially covered by her lace shawl.

"Honey, I sure as hell wish you were working for me! You and I together could make us a fortune!" Sadie had shaken her head, and Toni had laughed. She felt keyed-up, felt the pounding in her pulses and the flush in her face that always presaged what she called her wild times. God, yes. She felt wild tonight. Wilder than a wolf-bitch, and just as free. That was the most intoxicating thought of all. That she belonged to no one but herself tonight, and could pick and choose as she pleased—play whore or cruel mistress, either one.

At Sadie's place, anyting could happen, and her customers were used to voyeurs wandering into a room to stand watching for a while, and then wandering out again. There were peepholes, for those watchers who did not care to be seen themselves, and all of Sadie's customers knew this; just as they knew this was no ordinary whorehouse for the unadventurous.

Carrying a bottle of chilled champagne, Toni went hunting, after a while. She also carried a small, braided riding quirt, hugged close to her side. She was looking for a man. Any man, if it came down to it. A particular man, if she could find him—and she hoped he was one of Sadie's studs, because she wanted to grind him down and make him crawl before she used him. He'd called her Messalina, just before he turned his back on her to walk contemptuously away. A tall, rough-looking man with black hair that was shaggy and far too long. Blue eyes. She remembered *that* much. And the fact that he hadn't been much interested in the circus—nor in the hand that Toni had laid on his thigh. In fact, he hadn't looked real closely at a single one of the girls, prompting Toni to whisper maliciously that perahps he'd come here looking for a nice upstanding young man. And he'd only grinned at her and said with a slight shrug, "Maybe we've both come looking for the same brand of something, Messalina," and he'd gone on his way, leaving her wondering how a man like that would know anything about the old Romans.

She had not found him when she went looking; but she'd found what she had gone to Sadie's looking for, and by rights—if she hadn't heard about the Carters bringing a herd of those unbranded swamp cattle she'd always looked on as *hers* up here to Abilene—Toni should have been in a good mood.

She had even worn a new gown this morning—a pale shade of blue that made her blondness seem almost ethereal. But it had been wasted on that stupid oaf of a bank manager.

"Back to the hotel, Ben!" Toni snapped in a voice that was far from matching her appearance.

And then—by one of those coincidences that shouldn't have happened and had never in fact happened to Toni Lassiter before—a young man, who had followed her out of the bank, put his hand over her little gloved one that was clenching the side of her open landau.

"I knew it was you. From last night . . . over at Sadie's. Remember me now? I couldn't mistake the way you walk. The way you swing your—Aah!"

Snatching up the riding crop she always carried, Toni struck him across the face, her eyes blazing like gold dust against the paleness of her skin.

"How dare you address me? Ben, drive on!"

The young man, unfortunately, was Billy Jennings, the spoiled son of a rich rancher, who fancied himself a fast gun as well as a ladies' man. He *knew* he recognized the blond woman from the previous night, and all the excesses he had paid for—in fact, he wasn't even quite sure he hadn't paid for *her*. To be struck across the face, for all the world to see, by a whore masquerading as a lady was too much!

With an inarticulate growl of rage, the young man grabbed for the reins just as the snooty-looking black man who was driving the blond woman's carriage was about to get her away.

"Just a minute, uncle! And you—you. . . ."

It was this scene that Matt Carter, striding purposefully toward the bank, happened to come upon. And the same scene, with several added elements, that the man they all called Manolo sized up calmly before he decided to interfere.

Matt Carter, not stopping to argue, had knocked down the man who had insulted Toni Lassiter. And the lady, who had drawn a serviceable looking two-shot derringer from her reticule, was demanding coldly why she should not shoot Matt down like the thieving, conniving outlaw dog he was.

"But he—but darn it, Toni! That dirty son was bothering you, wasn't he? I thought—"

"And who gave you permission to call me by my first name? You're nothing but a low-down cattle thief, Matt Carter, and if you weren't a distant relative of my poor dead husband I'd. . . ."

Toni's eyes had filled with tears as she dabbed at them with a dainty lace handkerchief that had miraculously replaced the gun. She was well aware of her effect on men, and there was quite a crowd of them beginning to gather round. She hoped viciously that the town marshal would show up soon, so she could have Matt arrested, along with his father and brothers.

"Dirty cattle rustlers! Stealing me blind, just because I'm a widow, and then having the gall to parade yourself here, before my very eyes. . . . Aren't there any *men* left in these parts since the war?"

Matt Carter's jaw had dropped with stupefied disbelief as his face reddened. The poor fool didn't even realize yet what kind of a mess he'd just gotten himself into! And behind him, Billy Jennings, the man he'd knocked down with a powerful blow to the jaw, had started to stir, started to pull his gun and then stopped, slowly and carefully putting his hands above his head.

A low, threatening mutter went up from the rapidly gathering crowd, and Toni's pink lips parted again, only to close abruptly when a tall man, shaggy haired and roughly dressed, a drawn gun in his hand, appeared from nowhere to tell her worried-looking servant to drive on.

"You!" Toni's mouth formed the word; but no sound emerged except for the hissing of her breath.

A corner of his mouth lifted in a mirthless grin that was somehow taunting.

"This is no place for a lady. There's trouble brewing. Besides, there might be some others who were Sadie's guests last night helping to swell this crowd . . . ma'am."

There was something wolfish about the way he stood with one thumb hooked carelessly in his belt; a thin smile stretched his lips slightly without reaching those very cold blue eyes that had already stripped her and dismissed her contemptuously.

Toni's mouth tightened and her back stiffened, but she knew when she was licked. For the moment, anyhow. Because she wasn't through with him yet, and he'd be very, very sorry before she was.

"Let's go, Ben."

She ignored him. And that stupid Matt Carter, too. But as soon as they were out of earshot she told Ben to take her straight to the marshal's office.

Chapter Forty-four

Toni Lassiter was still burning with rage two days later, when she finally left Abilene with her escort of blue-clad soldiers.

She was angry because she had had to wait for that old fool, Colonel Philip Vance, who was late in arriving, as usual, and with some silly, pompous tale about chasing Indians to account for his delay. And she was furious because the thick-headed marshal had made her repeat her sobbed-out story several times before he decided he might as well "investigate"—and by then it was all over any way! The Carters had left town, with what Toni thought of as their ill-gotten gains; and the blue-eyed animal who had taunted her and called her Messalina had gone with them. It was *this* discovery that made Toni angrier than ever—furious enough to send several telegraph messages of her own in addition to the ones sent by Colonel Vance and the lethargic marshal.

"Don't worry—our boys will find those cattle-stealing rebs and put an end to their thievery and troublemaking before they can find their way back to those swamps they hide out in," Colonel Vance said consolingly. And the marshal, who was a gunman of some repute, kept shaking his head as he leafed through the Wanted dodgers trying to find one with a description that matched the particular man who'd outdrawn Billy Jennings.

"Not only got the drop on Billy—an' he's almost as fast as I am—but that New Mexico gunman they call Ace swore he knew him from someplace. It was he who advised Billy's friends to keep out of it."

"Of course he's an outlaw! Why else would he hide out in the swamps and bayous? Who else would get mixed up with those Carters in stealing my cattle? The man insulted me—he . . . why, he *threatened* me, Marshal! I'm going to be so afraid from now on. . . ."

She swore out a complaint, of course; and the marshal promised to pass the word along, but somehow Toni had the feeling of impending trouble. She wished now, sulkily, that she hadn't left Billy-Boy behind to look after things. Billy-boy Dozier was one of the fastest gunmen still alive, and if he hadn't begun to act so possessive he might have been along, and *then* she'd have had no more trouble from that half-breed Indian or Mexican or whatever the man was.

Where had he come from? Who was he? She'd have to tell Billy-Boy he was slipping—and Nick, too. How could a stranger have slipped past them all? And he'd brought dissension with him. Why else would the Carters, who had stayed hidden in the swamps since the war and minded their own business, suddenly have developed the gumption to drive a herd of cattle all the way to Abilene? And Matt, who had always been devoted and easily manageable . . . no, she wouldn't forgive Matt for turning against her this way. She was sorry she hadn't managed to get him lynched while he stood there on the street gaping stupidly at her, expecting her to be grateful because he'd punched that loud-mouthed young man.

Under her demure, softly smiling, subtly promising exterior, that had made fools of most of the men she'd ever met, Toni Lassiter hid her thoughts and made her own plans, even while she let Colonel Vance think that she trusted implicitly in his blustering promises.

When she got back, she would do what she should have done a long time ago. She would insist to Nick that something must be done about the Carters, whose unmolested presence in the swamps only encouraged other, lawless elements to come in. And at this point, trouble was the last thing they needed. When Nick heard how boldly Matt Carter had showed himself in Abilene, he'd have to agree with her at last. After all, dear Nicky had a stake in the same game, and just as much to lose if things went wrong.

Toni Lassiter's journey back to Baroque took her less time than it had going the other way, to Abilene. This time, with her escort of bluecoats, the way was smoothed for her—even the time of their setting out each day and stopping to rest for the night was arranged for her especial convenience. Toni took all this as her right, but she was anxious to return all the same, and she sensed that Phil Vance had his own reasons for wanting to get back to Baroque quickly.

It took the Carters well over a month—almost six weeks, in fact; they'd had to avoid as many towns as they could and cross the river into Louisiana, making their slow, careful way back by way of Lake Caddo and the myriad tiny streams and bayous that laced like capillaries across that part of the land. The Indians who were with them knew the way—and before they reached the lake, and after that the river, it had already become clear to them all that Manolo was a man used to running and hiding, doing both almost by instinct.

"He's a killer, I tell you that, Pa," Matt Carter said. "An' he's known. A gunman in Abilene knew him. Don't believe he's a Mex at all."

"Better make up your mind, Matthew. And remember, while you're about it, that he backed you up and got you out of a real tight spot."

"I don't care who he is or what he's done." Hank, who was the quietest one of the three Carter brothers, spoke up suddenly. "Since he's come he's made things happen. Made us all into feelin' like real men again."

"You know what? Mebbe he *is* that friend of Dave

Madden's that Sis is always talkin' about. I'll bet Dave used to be a sidewinder in the old days, for all his quiet ways. Women! Always have a real bad influence on a guy."

Matt scowled across the fire at Joe Junior, who grinned back at him impudently. But just then Manolo came back with an armload of wood, and the conversation just naturally turned to other things—like what they were going to do with the money they were taking back with them.

"No damn use thinking of putting any of it in the Baroque bank. They'd shoot us on sight if any of us showed our faces near the bank—say we was fixin' to rob it, most likely!"

"Well, there's plenty of places to spend money in Louisiana—like Shreveport or even New Orleans!"

"An' in San Antone or Dallas, where nobody knows us from some real rich ranchers like Colonel King, or Shanghai Pierce."

"Talking of Pierce, wonder whatever happened 'bout the old Desmoulins place? They say Shanghai won it in a poker game, night before that drunken fool Raoul shot his own fool head off."

"Heard Mr. Pierce lost the spread in some kind of bet himself. To some rich Eastern railroad man." Matt Carter's voice was carefully noncommittal, as it always was when he quoted Toni. Toni had been madder than a hornet when she'd heard the news—calming down only when she realized that the Easterner didn't know and wouldn't care about the land he'd won. The Desmoulins spread was prime land, strategically situated between all the other spreads in the area and the town—not to mention the trails that led eventually to the railheads. Old Amos Fenster, who'd run the place while Raoul Desmoulins, last of his line, was drinking and gambling himself to ruin, still gave the orders—theoretically, that was. Amos was real old now, and preferred to spend most of his time indoors, with a sheepskin jacket thrown over his shoulders to keep off the damp air from the swamps. He remembered Tom Lassiter, and John—and Toni had taken the trouble to make friends with him when she first arrived as a bride. Amos purely didn't give a damn any longer, letting Toni do as she pleased with the Desmoulins acres and even the unbranded stuff that ran wild and free on Desmoulins

land. Miz Lassiter was a stubborn-spirited proud little
Southern gal, wasn't she? Struggling to make ends meet—
and her a widow, and all. Amos didn't hold with absentee
landlords, and especially with Northerners who didn't give
a durn about Texas or State's Rights, and who couldn't be
gentlemen in the first place.

Manolo had all this explained to him—not purposefully,
but over tiny campfires and on cold nights when they
didn't dare light a campfire at all, and someone had to
keep awake. And by the time they got back "home" to the
swamps, the man who'd been a stranger some two or
three months before knew almost as much as anyone else
did about the County. But that didn't mean that anyone
knew anything more about *him*—apart from what they
could see or guess, that was. He'd lived with Comanche
Indians—or perhaps his knowledge of their language and
customs had come from his being a Comanchero, like Teresita's husband. He'd been in jail; on a chain gang. And he
was plenty fast and accurate with a gun as well as a knife.
All the same, that was mighty little to know about a man,
when you added up the sum total and thought about it.
And their homecoming, such as it was, went to show that
no one could really know what lay underneath the surface
a man showed to others. It shocked even Matt, who
hadn't quite liked or trusted Manolo from the beginning—
and Matt was the one, after Abilene, who had begun to
think that for sure Manolo wasn't a breed, like they'd
thought he was at the start.

They came home to weeping and anger and fear. Missie, her eyes swollen from days of crying, met them on the
path, running out of the brush and hide lodge of the old
Indian man who had been a chief once when he was
young.

"They burned our house! Everything—even Mama's
books. And when Uncle Nick came afterwards, pretending
he was all upset and worried, *I* pretended I didn't hear
him calling. It was—it was that Billy-Boy Dozier. And the
only way he got Teresita to go out and see what he
wanted was by saying—by saying you were dead! He said
you'd been shot down trying to get here . . . and we already knew the soldiers had been searching everywhere—
and the sheriff's men, those dirty carpetbagger hirelings,

with their big old bloodhounds. . . . I thought—we all thought they'd got you! Oh Pa—Matt—we thought. . . ."

She'd run at Manolo first, though. Throwing herself against his suddenly stiff body unthinkingly, like a child looking for comfort. Or, her father thought with a sudden pain in his heart, like a woman relieved to see her man safe. . . .

The soldiers had tried to fire up everything, to smoke out whatever or whoever they could out of the swamps. But they hadn't succeeded, of course. They got the small house the Carters had built themselves on an island, but that was about all. The rest of the swamp people had just withdrawn themselves even further, and there was a point past which even the bluebelly soldiers, with their guns and their sheriff's bloodhounds, wouldn't attempt to go.

Joe Carter, guessing already what had happened, drew Missie away with him, his arm holding her shaking shoulders real tight, just as he had done when she was a little girl and upset about something.

They left Manolo with the old man, the Caddoan Indian with a face that looked like old, wrinkled brown parchment; he had been Teresita's mother's brother.

"The young man who used to look at my niece with hot eyes came to the edge of the water, with a blanket-wrapped body. He laughed when he asked why she had chosen so foolishly for a third time, when she could have been *his* woman. He named this distant town where you all had gone, taking the cattle—and he said that the soldiers had killed you as you tried to get back here. She believed him."

The old man's face suddenly stiffened so that it looked like a piece of granite, worn in places where water had flowed over it.

"Do I have to tell more when my heart is bleeding as if a knife has thrust into it in many places? Your woman was the youngest child of my favorite sister. Only a few days before she had come to me, happy because she was carying your child beneath her heart. When the white man violated her, beating her first, when she fought against his strength. . . . She fell on her own knife rather than face you with the shame of what had been done to her."

The old man spoke in his own language, as he would

have spoken to one of his tribe, and the man he spoke to understood. For all that his eyes were blue instead of brown, the lights of anger and the desire for revenge were there to see like live fires in the semi-darkness of the old man's lodge.

"My woman will be avenged. And the hair of the white man who shamed her will decorate your lodgepole. I swear it."

Neither Missie nor her father nor her brothers knew any of this until afterwards. The Indians mourned their dead in their own way—and the man called Manolo was suddenly one of them, all Indian, in the days that followed.

He waited two days, until the prescribed period of mourning was over. And then, preparing himself very carefully, as a Comanche warrior would, he left the safety of the deep swamp at night, and on foot.

He had tied his hair, now grown to almost shoulder length, back from his face with a strip of rawhide. And he wore paint on his face and body; and apart from that, only a breechclout and moccasins.

The Lassiter woman's men were everywhere, of course. There was even a small band of soldiers, drinking heavily as they sat outside what had been the old Madden house. But a Comanche warrior, on foot, could slip by them like a ghost—so could an expert horse thief, which was what all Comanches were trained to be, from childhood.

Billy-Boy Dozier was not in the house he had been given to stay in. But in the big house, Toni Lassiter's window had a light in it, a rosy light that grew dimmer after a while and finally went out. The moon had started to show its face from behind black clouds.

There was a small, ornamental balcony just outside Toni Lassiter's window, and the old vines that climbed up the walls made it easy for the man to get up there. He stayed where he was for a while, listening to the sound of soft talking, and Toni Lassiter's brittle, mocking laughter.

It happened that Toni was in an unusually vile mood, even for her, and almost before Billy-Boy had stopped panting over her, she had begun to taunt him; her voice was softly vicious.

"You're a fool—and if there's anything I can't abide, it's a fool! So stupid! What did you think to gain by forcing

yourself on that Indian bitch anyhow? I could see it if you
were doing it to trap him—that man of hers. But now, if
he gets back here, he's going to track you down and kill
you. And all because you think you're some kind of stud,
and want every woman you lay eyes on. Why couldn't you
leave that damn squaw alone? Or at least wait until you
got your orders from me?"

"Shut up, damn it!" Billy-Boy's voice sounded sullen,
thick with suppressed resentment. "What in hell do you
expect a man to do when he's tired of picking needles out
from under his skin? You wouldn't let me go up to
Abilene with you, because you had to impress that fat
Yankee Colonel. And when you sent that telegraph message—hell, I thought anything would go! How was I to
know the silly bitch would go kill herself just because she
got fucked by a real man for a change, huh?"

"A *man* . . . is that what you're calling yourself now?
Why, even that old husband of mine—even that fat
Yankee Colonel—they're more *men* than you are, Billy-
Boy, with your swagger and your boasting and your puffing and panting before it's all over, quicker than a jack-
rabbit! Even Nicky, with all his peculiarities—" Toni's
high-pitched, mocking giggle gave way to a muffled shriek
as a dark shadow fell over her face for an instant, block-
ing out the moonlight. She could hardly believe that she
saw what she saw—a man had swung himself through the
open window in a kind of silent pounce, faint light glinting
off the weapon he held. But what *was* it—a gun or a
knife?

"Do not make any sound. Either of you." The voice
was softly conversational, but the coldness of steel underlay it.

Toni laughed suddenly.

"I *told* you, didn't I? You always were a fool, Billy-Boy
Dozier! Let's see what you're going to do now!"

As if he sensed which one of them was the strongest, it
was to Toni the man spoke again.

"I want *him*. But it's all one to me if I get you, too."

"Goddamn!" Billy-Boy sat bolt upright, eyes squinting in
the darkness as he tried to remember where he'd dropped
his gunbelt. There was one wild moment when he wondered if maybe *she* hadn't arranged for this to happen.
"Toni—"

"Don't look at *me*, darling! I've got nothing to do with this. And you heard what the man said—it's *you* he wants. Isn't that right?"

"Now, look . . ." Billy-Boy started, the full realization of his position—naked as a jaybird, not knowing where his clothes or his guns were—beginning to press in on him and fill him with blind panic.

He was still in bed with Toni, although he'd sat up real fast; but even in the dark of the room his quick, furtive movement to swing his feet off the bed must have been seen. Billy-Boy gasped, feeling the coldness of steel against his neck; he became very still.

"Stay," Manolo said softly, as contemptuously as he might have spoken to a dog. Billy-Boy stayed, still half poised over Toni's palely glimmering nude body. His flesh still touched her flesh, so that he could almost feel its quivering. He could see the rise and fall of her white, pink-budded breasts as she giggled.

"What are you going to do to him? If you're going to fight, I won't interfere—I promise you that. Are you going to cut his throat?" Almost in the same breath, her voice not changing its tone in the slightest, she went on in French, "And if you want to fight back, there is a knife under my pillow—only you will have to reach for it yourself, I do not want to be cut up."

Manolo laughed, white teeth gleaming for an instant against the darkness of his face. But the sound he made was short and ugly, not real laughter at all; and it made the hair rise on the back of Billy-Boy's neck.

"Good, why don't you reach for her knife? You heard her say you can expect no protection from *her*. But first—I think you'd better tie her hands behind her back. Use that night shift *she* didn't."

"So you speak French? An Indian who speaks a civilized language. Or are you a half-breed? Perhaps your father was a squaw man—is that why you're so angry with Billy-Boy for wanting your woman? He said she didn't fight him too hard . . . tell him what you told me, Billy-Boy. Maybe he'll change his mind about cutting your throat and content himself with cutting off your—"

"Shut up," Manolo said without any expression in his voice at all. "Shut up and turn on your side. And don't try reaching under your pillow, unless you want your pretty face slashed." He spoke in the French patois that Billy-Boy had spoken since childhood, voice like a knife: "Tie her hands—and then you can stand up, if your legs have not turned to water."

"Does that mean you're going to give him a chance to defend himself? Or are you scared to face him man to man? If you're good with that knife you're carrying, why should you be afraid? If it's a fair fight, and you kill him, I'll see you go free."

"I'm free now." The words were like a slap, but they made Toni giggle, high and breathless. And the way she twisted her body was an invitation in itself.

"So you are . . . and Billy-Boy's hands are shaking so hard he can't tie me up like you told him. Are you sure you wouldn't rather do it yourself?"

"Bitch! You . . . you bitch!" Billy-Boy's voice rose, then-cut itself off when he felt the cold kiss of a knifeblade at his groin. He groaned, almost sick with fear. "Oh, God! Listen—she'd been leading me on! I didn't—they tell you I didn't kill her? She was just ashamed because she knew what she'd been doing—letting me think she liked me, until *you* came along. . . . Toni, for God's sake!"

"Stop crying to me, Billy-Boy. Why don't you stand up like Comanche here just told you and give some account of yourself?"

Billy-Boy had thought for sure that the Indian would kill him *now*. He couldn't understand, for a moment, why the man had moved back from the bed, his back still to the window. Until he heard Toni laugh again.

"I think this is going to be—very exciting. And admit it—you would have killed poor Billy before, if you'd really wanted to. Isn't it better this way, in battle? Wouldn't the Indian part of you enjoy that, too, Comanche?"

The faint light glimmered along the short barrel of the silver-encrusted Derringer that had suddenly appeared in Toni's hand as she sat up. And Billy-Boy, purely by instinct, caught the knife she flung at him.

"You'll fight with no holds barred—and you'll fight silent. I'll shoot the first one of you that tries to run—or calls for help!"

Toni's high-pitched, obscenely excited laugh jarred Billy-Boy Dozier's already exacerbated nerves, and he had time to wonder—as he moved silently and with his knife held low, towards the unmoving tall shadow of the Indian—how he had ever gotten involved with Toni Lassiter. And then Billy-Boy stopped thinking of anything but survival—knowing, fatalistically, within the first few seconds after their knives clashed for the first time, that he was going to die.

He knew, within those same few seconds, that Toni wasn't going to save him by shooting. But then, he ought to have known better. Didn't he know a few things about Toni Lassiter? She was one reason he'd looked at the Indian woman, and wanted her. She had been the direct opposite of Toni. A woman brought up to give to a man. To make him feel like a man. A warm, golden skinned woman ... why in hell had she proved so unexpectedly stubborn?

And then, Billy-Boy had no more time in which to think. He had always considered himself an expert with a knife, but the Indian, this other man whose face he hadn't even seen—would probably never see—his knife moved so fast it was like the live, flickering tongue of a water snake.

"Damn you, Indian breed—damn you!" Billy-Boy's breathing sounded like sobs; and behind him, even when she must have realized he was going to die—was dying—Toni Lassiter kept giggling.

That was when the Indian tired of the game and came in for the kill. Billy-Boy's knife was contemptuously parried aside with a blow on the wrist that paralyzed his whole arm. And then there was a final, ripping knife-thrust in his belly—the heel of a hand, as hard and inexorable as the knife itself, choking off Billy-Boy's last scream of agony before it ever left his throat.

Without a word, without looking at Toni, Manolo took the dead man's scalp.

"Oh, God! I never saw anything like—you were magnificent—so savage—you're an animal—and a man—a primitive male creature—what are you waiting for? Do you think I'll use this silly little gun on you?" The small gun dropped on the carpet beside the bed. Toni stretched, languorously, and her voice sounded husky, almost drugged. "There! You see—I'm at your mercy. You can do anything you want with me—*he* took your woman, didn't he? An eye for an eye. That's why you came, isn't it, Comanche? Billy-Boy was my lover—now you can have me. Take me—rape me—isn't this part of the revenge you came looking for?"

He was silent, considering her. And now that the killing-lust in him was gone, the sight of her body—the faint light reflecting off the silver-blonde triangle in the vee of her thighs—replaced that lust with another.

"How many more hidden weapons?"

"Only *this*, lover." She arched her body and opened her legs, "You man enough for this kind of combat too?"

"You're a bitch right out of hell, Messalina."

"Yes. . . . And you want to fuck me as much as I want you. *Now*. Oh, God, yes, right now!"

She received him like the kind of bitch he'd named her. Like an animal, too hungry to wait—fastening her arms and legs around him, long nails tearing into the already scarred flesh of his back until he slapped her savagely into a whimpering but joyous kind of submission. Whimpers turned into whispers as she gasped soft obscenities at him, bit into the hand he held against her soft, pouting mouth; her body thrashing under his all the while.

"You've probably given me blood poisoning!" he grumbled afterwards, rubbing his hand, still sticky with his own blood, across her face.

"Then let me suck the poison out. . . ."

She seized his hand in both of hers and sucked until he used his other hand to back-hand her into the pillows.

"Now we're of the same blood—I'm your blood-sister, your *incestuous* sister, isn't that so? Isn't that so, Comanche?" she whispered insistently.

"Shut up—you're crazy!"

She laughed.

"Maybe! But so are you. That's why you're here, in my bed . . . and you know now what fun we could have had in Abilene, don't you? Were you afraid then?"

"There's a dead man with no hair bleeding all over your fine Persian rug, Messalina. Better start thinking what you're going to tell them about how he died. Shall I tie you up to make it look good?"

"But you're not going away yet, are you? The night's still young—and if you're not afraid, I can just pull at this cord, and Ben will bring wine upstairs. He won't come in the room, unless I tell him to. He'll leave it by the door.

Would you like that? Or ... do you appreciate wine at
all?"

She clung to him, running her fingers insistently down
his bare back.

"Comanche. ... How much Comanche *is* there in you?
All these scars—is that what they did to you in prison?
Did you break when they whipped you?"

"Sorry I can't stay to give you details," he said. "I'll let
you make them up for yourself."

"Don't go yet, Comanche! Listen to me. You don't trust
me, but after I've gotten rid of *him*—of what you've left
of Billy-Boy, with no one any the wiser then you'll re
member what I'm saying now, won't you? I want you to
work for me—to help me. I need a man who's strong.
Billy-Boy was fast with a gun, but he wasn't strong at
all—you saw how he crawled. *You* wouldn't crawl, would
you, Comanche? You're a brute, a devil, and I think you
have less conscience than even I have—and many fewer
scruples. Don't you understand?"

"Bitch!" he exclaimed harshly, when, on the heel of her
whispered speech, she bit his lip, drawing blood. She was a
bitch, all right. A blood-crazy she-wolf—and he should
have taken *her* hair, too ... or have slit her arched white
throat, stilling forever the chuckle that came from it now,
husky and triumphant and knowing, all at once.

"Yes, of course, Oh—Jesus! I like it when you do that.
Even when I feel as if you're going to rip me open. Hurt
me if you want to—make me—only make me *feel*!"

Chapter Forty-five

"Every time this Mr. Bishop 'just happens to drop by'
something happens. It strikes me that he is the kind of
man who invariably causes upheavals in our otherwise
quiet lives." Don Francisco's voice sounded dry and purposely expressionless. "Are you sure you wish to speak

with him, Genia?" He added, more to himself than to the young woman whose face had suddenly gone quite pale, "I wonder how he discovered you were here! Perhaps I should have Renaldo speak with him first, to find out just what he is up to this time."

In spite of the fact that he appeared to make idle conversation, the old man had not failed to notice the signs of agitation in his granddaughter-in-law. The listless, lethargic air she had seemed to carry like a burden since she had arrived at the hacienda three months before suddenly dropped away, and her green eyes seemed to brighten, flaring with hope.

"You didn't send him away? He's actually *here*? He has news of Steve—oh, I know it! Where is he?" And then, remembering herself, "I'm sorry, Don Francisco. But if Mr. Bishop's here, it must be for a reason. And *you've* been worried too, haven't you?"

Bushy white brows drew together frowningly over blue eyes that reminded Ginny all too forcibly of Steve.

"That rascally grandson of mine! When will he ever settle down? He had me convinced he had changed—and then this disappearing without a word to anyone. . . . So you think this Mr. Bishop might have some idea of his whereabouts, do you? And I can see quite plainly that you're in an almighty hurry to be gone—very well then, I won't keep you. I had Jaime show him into my study. You can talk to the man there, in privacy. But mind you, I give you only fifteen minutes alone with him! And you'll let me know what his real errand here is—I'll have no more mysteries and secrets, is that clear?"

For all his gruffness and assumed anger, Ginny had come to understand Don Francisco sufficiently well to know how upset he was at Steve's unexplained absence. Steve—what kind of wicked, hurtful game was he playing at this time? Where was he hiding himself, and why? She had thought, at first, that he was only trying to avoid *her;* but even Sam Murdock denied any knowledge of Steve's whereabouts or his plans. And now, out of nowhere, Jim Bishop had coincidentally turned up. Or *was* it a coincidence?

Already on her feet, her heart thudding quite sickeningly, Ginny's first impulse had been to run from the small patio where she had been resting—pretending to read a book while she stared unseeingly at the pages. Now, with Don Francisco's sharp blue eyes studying her from beneath hooded lids, she made a deliberate attempt to compose herself. It would not do to let Jim Bishop know exactly how miserable and confused she had been since she had arrived in Mexico with the twins—not knowing what she was coming to, nor what the future held for her. Ever since her father had written that Steve had suddenly dropped out of sight after he had taken the Princess di Paoli on the ocean voyage, she had not known what to think.

The arguments of her Tante Celine and Pierre—who had wanted her to remain in France—had had no effect on Ginny's determination. She sailed from France to Vera Cruz, and had taken refuge at the little hacienda—where she had first been reunited with Steve after the agonizing months when she had thought him dead—despite pleading letters from Sonya and her father to return home.

But she remembered Mexico—at least *this* part of Mexico—with affection, and, as she wrote Sonya:

"I won't have my babies exposed to gossip—all that filthy stuff they print in the newspapers, and old dowagers counting on their fingers. No, I don't *care* if people wonder why I decided to come to Mexico. I'm sorry, Sonya. But I've become far too used to doing just as I please!"

The children both reminded her, in their miniature way, of Steve. Her son had dark brown hair—shot through with copper, so that it almost looked bronze—and her eyes. And her daughter, Laura Louise, had Steve's coloring, both eyes and hair. Would Steve see that?

Whenever she thought about Steve, and the ambiguous state of affairs that had existed between them when she had sailed for France, compounded now by all the misunderstandings that had arisen since, Ginny could not help the sick, helpless feeling that knotted in the pit of her stomach—just as if a huge stone rested there; a heaviness that seemed to weigh her down.

She had moved to Don Franciso's large estancia at his insistence, the message being brought by her friend Renaldo Ortega, and, if she had not had the babies to remind her, she might almost have felt that time had turned back and stopped. She had the same suite of rooms she had occupied before, the rooms that had belonged to Steve's

mother. The second bedroom was occupied now by her
children and their nurse, instead of a duenna. She recognized the servants who had been working in the house
before, and just as she had been before, she was, in a way,
waiting for Steve to return.

It was in vain that she tried to tell herself that there
were the children to consider now—the twin babies that
she *still* could not quite believe she had produced, as
enormously distended as she had become during the last
two months of her miserable pregnancy.

"One of each, madame! How lucky!" the midwife had
said when Ginny opened her eyes, wondering why the
agonizing pain hadn't killed her. "Their father will be very
proud."

Steve. Would he be proud? Would he even believe the
children were his?

At least Don Francisco had no questions about who had
fathered the children! He had given her a miniature of his
own daughter, Steve's mother, painted when she was still a
baby, and it could have been her Laura Louise, even to
the dark blue eyes.

She would show it to Steve when he returned. But
would Steve return? Where had he gone when he left his
paramour? The questions that kept tormenting her and
making her feel drained of all the will and energy that had
first brought her to the hacienda might be answered this
very afternoon! There could be no other reason for Mr.
Bishop's unexpected visit.

"I refuse to think that it might be bad news," Ginny
told herself firmly as she forced herself to walk slowly to
the study. "He knows something—why else would he take
the trouble to come all the way here himself? I mustn't let
him see how upset I am. . . ."

Jim Bishop, in his usual conservatively cut jacket,
looked slightly ill at ease in the dark study, in spite of the
glass of wine that Jaime Perez had thoughtfully placed at
his elbow. He sat stiffly in an ornately carved chair, and
Ginny thought she could almost detect a look of relief
cross his usually controlled features as he rose to his feet
when she entered.

"So I'm to be allowed to speak with her alone," Bishop
was thinking, as he bowed politely over the hand she extended to him. He noticed how cold her fingers were and

guessed at the inner perturbation the young woman was obviously trying to conceal beneath her calm manner. Surprising even himself, Bishop caught himself thinking objectively that she was one of the few women who seemed to have grown even more beautiful after motherhood. Her figure had lost none of its slimness. He wondered if she were still as willful and headstrong as he remembered. Certainly she seemed unchanged, except for a certain maturity in her manner when she greeted him. She came straight to the point.

"Mr. Bishop! You have news of my husband?"

Bishop's voice was carefully noncommittal.

"You've never been the kind of woman with whom anyone has needed to beat around the bush, have you? But perhaps you'd prefer to sit down before I start to explain why I am here. It's a long story, I'm afraid, and of course, I don't need to remind you that what passes here between us *must* remain strictly confidential. It's best that not even Don Francisco should know too much. You'll understand why when I tell you."

It was a long speech for Mr. Bishop, and Ginny, who hardly knew the man, sensed it. She felt her knees grow weak, so that it was a relief to sink into the chair he offered politely. Oh, God! What was he going to tell her? There was something about the carefully guarded, expressionless look on his face that alarmed her even more than his opening words had done.

Forgetting all her earlier resolutions, Ginny leaned forward, her eyes looking unusually brilliant in the dimly-lit room.

"It's not—not bad news?"

Looking more at ease, Bishop leaned back, his cool grey eyes studying her face.

"He's alive. There's no need for concern on *that* score at least. But—" he paused deliberately, a slight frown touching his forehead for an instant. "If I may request that you hear me out without interruption until I have finished? Madam, let me admit that I am finding it unusually difficult to know where to begin! And this is not a confession I normally make to anyone."

"Mr. Bishop!"

Bishop gazed at her speculatively, taking in, quite objectively, the pale copper sheen of her hair, the soft swell of

her breasts under the plain cotton gown she had not bothered to change out of, and the unwittingly sensual curve
of her mouth. She had the face and the figure of a wanton
and the manners of a lady—until she chose to forget
them. And she was stronger-willed than she looked—resilient enough to overcome trials and circumstances that
most other woman could not have survived. For all her
delicate looks, she was a woman who had learned to take
care of herself. Bishop, a man who stored away every tiny
bit of information he learned, in case it might come in
useful later, had not forgotten certain things that Paco
Davis had told him. Yes, Ginny Morgan was the rare type
of female who could fend for herself in an emergency. He
could even permit himself a secret smile when he wondered how she would react to meeting Toni Lassiter. Yes,
he was right to come here. And now, if he could persuade
her. . . .

"A moment, madam. You see, what makes it—um—rather awkward for me is that your husband, when he set
out for Texas, had in fact—er—consented to make certain
inquiries for me. He was going to Baroque, as you perhaps
know. To inspect some property your father won in a
poker game and deeded to Steve. He was expected there
many months ago, but when we heard nothing, and not
even—well, not even your father, or his partner Mr. Sam
Murdock had heard anything from him we—ah. . . . Naturally, I became a trifle concerned."

Ginny opened her mouth to interrupt and then pressed
her lips tightly together again when Mr. Bishop lifted his
hand. A man who was usually not at a loss for words, he
was having some difficulty in finding the most tactful way
to tell her what he had come here to say. But, thank God,
at least she was the kind of woman who would *listen,* and
not in the least the hysterical type, as he ought to remember!

There were times, though, during Mr. Bishop's blunt
and purposely uninflected narrative that followed, when
Ginny felt as if she could very easily have pitched a fit.
How dare Mr. Bishop presume to act as if Steve had been
still working for him? And Steve himself—what devil
drove him into the constant taking of risks? Not that there
was supposed to be any risk involved, but, as Mr. Bishop
reminded her grimly, Steve had a bad habit of "improvis-

ing" when he was supposed to be carrying out orders to the letter. And Bishop admitted that he, himself, did not need reminding that Steve Morgan had always enjoyed the challenge of danger.

Ginny's mood veered from anger to fear, to despair and back to anger again as she continued to listen, her teeth worrying her lower lip, eyes beginning to sparkle dangerously. Now that her first utter relief at hearing that Steve was, after all, alive and apparently physically unhurt had begun to wear off, she didn't know which one of them she ought to be more angry with—Bishop, for starting it all, or Steve, who had accepted the assignment.

It was all too incredible. If it had been anyone but Jim Bishop telling her such an impossible tale—his colorless voice dropping one fact after another in her lap like miniature bombshells—she would have refused to believe any of it.

"I found it hard to believe myself," Bishop was saying, just as if he had read Ginny's thoughts. "But there is no other explanation for your husband's peculiar actions of late. That is, ever since he suddenly turned up, calling himself Manolo, stirring up more trouble than they had in Baroque to begin with! It was only after we had this Colonel Vance transferred to another command, and Colonel Belmont, who happens to be an old acquaintance of mine took over as military commander in that area, that I learned the facts behind it all. And just to make sure, I have also spoken with several very learned doctors—one of them a famous alienist from Vienna, who is lecturing in this country and is an expert in the field of mental disorders. Not that I'm implying Steve is deranged in any way!" he added hastily, seeing the expression on Ginny's face. "It's possible he contracted typhus. Captain Almonte of the Rurales mentioned that he had been exposed to it in Matamoras. An extremely high fever—even a blow on the head—any of these things could cause a temporary loss of memory. Or so the good doctor told me. We know, too, from Colonel Vance himself, that this Manolo hasn't tried to hide the fact he remembers nothing of his past, not even his real name. Which made it difficult for certain—um—interested parties to find out whether he was wanted by the law or not! The Indian woman I've told you about claimed he was her dead husband's brother, but it was Captain Almonte himself who told Steve to contact this Chucho—Refugio Orta was his real name. Do you begin to understand?"

An unbelievable as it had all seemed when Mr. Bishop began talking, Ginny had to admit that it all fell into place too neatly *not* to be true. The man Mr. Bishop had heard described *had* to be Steve. Steve—with no memory of the past; no memory of *her;* thinking himself half-Indian, acting like one. Steve, working for some ruthless, money-grabbing female—turned vicious killer for pay. But then Steve had always had a cold, ruthless streak underneath; hadn't she long-since discovered that for herself?

And what did Bishop expect of *her*? Why had he, surprisingly, told her so much about his operation?

"He's got to be stopped before they start fighting another civil war over there!" Mr. Bishop said now with unwonted grimness. "Before the whole darned country erupts in a monumental range war that will cost more lives—and not only that, it might set Texas back in its battle to be reaccepted as a state of the Union. If it starts in Baroque, it could spread everywhere—like a brushfire, or a series of explosions. You take my meaning? And, by God, if it isn't stopped soon, my own job will be at stake, too. The President is already becoming uneasy—there have been too many complaints. And I was the man who sent your husband there in the first place to stop a possible range war and look into some rather unusual happenings. And instead he's being instrumental in firing it off—he and that Lassiter woman. Even her brother-in-law, Judge Benoit, is becoming anxious. He's a cautious man, even though we have reason to think he's been in it up to his neck all this time. It was at *his* urging that a U.S. deputy marshal was sent down to Baroque, not too long ago. Undercover man—wish *I'd* been informed of it before they sent him. Anyhow—he was shot and killed." Bishop's voice hardened, and Ginny waited sickly for him to finish. "Steve did it, of course. They got in an argument in one of the saloons, and in *that* town there never are any witnesses to any of the killings that take place! But in this case the only thing that saved him from a hanging—or at least being posted as a wanted murderer—was the fact that Marshal Purdue hadn't let anyone know who he was, or what he was. And *that,* I'm afraid, isn't the only killing that's taken place recently. There have been other murders—there's no other word to describe them. Anyone who opposes the Lassiter faction. I've already told you how her other foreman disappeared so coincidentally just before your husband, madam, started to draw his wages from Toni Lassiter."

"Are you trying to tell me—" Ginny's voice emerged as a whisper and she had to swallow before she could speak clearly—"are you saying that Steve is ... that he's an *outlaw*? That he's joined up with this woman to—but how can you be *sure*? Mr. Bishop ... maybe Steve's playing some kind of game, pretending to join their side so that he can learn more. That *is* the way he used to operate before, isn't it? You never had any scruples about his methods before this—and you can't pretend you didn't set him to steal my father's gold either! Or that you reprimanded him when he kidnapped *me*! Or, for that matter, for any of the other horrible things he's done! Steve's been *trained* as a killer, hasn't he? Only, when he's killing for *your* side I suppose you call it execution!"

So she had quite a lot of the old fire and spirit left in her after all. Jim Bishop permitted himself a fractional lift of his eyebrows as he studied the flushed face of the young woman who now leaned forward in her chair, her eyes shooting sparks at him.

He never *had* been quite certain about just how strongly Steve Morgan felt about the woman he'd married, because Steve was just as clever about hiding his real feelings—if he had any, Bishop reflected cynically—as Bishop was himself. But Virginia Morgan's emotions were plainly readable—both from the changing play of expressions that crossed her face and from the heated way she'd defended her husband just now. Without reacting to her anger, Bishop said calmly:

"If I'd thought Steve had gone over to the other side, *or* that he was flagrantly disobeying my orders in order to promote some devious scheme of his own, I would not be here talking to you so frankly, madam. As you've just stated, the men in my particular department are quite ruthless. They are trained to be and they have to be. And they all know both the risks and the rules. If I thought that Steve was deliberately breaking the rules I would have sent a federal marshal, or one of my own men after him. It was perhaps fortunate, for us all, that Dave Madden escaped from the chain gang they'd put him on to serve out his sentence. And that he crossed the border, looking for his wife."

"Dave Madden?" Ginny felt more dazed than ever.

"I forgot. You wouldn't know him. He's a man who used to work for me. Retired when he married. But he and Steve knew each other well. The interesting thing is that it was Steve who got Dave free—and who knows why? Because Dave swore that Steve didn't know him."

Chapter Forty-six

It was Missie's begging, Missie's constant reproaches that had made him do it; and yet, once he had embarked on the crazy scheme of setting five men free, chained by the leg like beasts and laboring under the rifles of two guards, it had turned into a kind of adventure.

The men were working on one of the county roads that had been partially washed away by the sporadic floods that overflowed the levees, and on the first occasion Manolo had noticed them he had wondered at the strangely uneasy feeling that made him rein his horse around abruptly, to take a longer route than usual to the Carter place. Maybe it had something to do with the deeply-cut scars on his own wrists and ankles. He knew how it felt, to be chained like an animal and feel the bite of the whip as it cut into bare, shrinking flesh—and yet that memory, too, hovered on the edges of his mind like a blur, never becoming quite clear. When? And for what reason? And how had he escaped? As usual, not being able to remember made him angry and frustrated, and it didn't help when Missie started right off by asking him, with tears in her eyes, if he'd seen those poor men.

"Dave's one of them. Didn't you *see* him? He's the one

with the brown beard, and his hair has blond streaks in it. Don't you even care any longer? How would *you* like to be chained up like that, and forced to work in the hot sun, and the rain. . . ."

"Now, Missie!" Her father's warning voice made her stop, biting her lip, in the instant before she whirled around and ran from the room, the door banging shut behind her.

"Missie's at the age when everything upsets her," Joe Carter sighed, rubbing his hand against his whiskers. "She's too sensitive, like her mother was. And she took an inordinate liking for Renate Madden. I let her be, because Renate mothered her, and Missie always did need a lot of mothering."

Joe kept talking in his quiet voice because he had seen how tense and angry Manolo had become—the frown lines in his forehead matched the white tension lines alongside his hard mouth. Manolo was a hard man, a man who liked violence and fighting—they had all learned that. But he seemed to have developed a kind of fondness for Missie. Or maybe it was because he was part Indian and felt an obligation towards her for being instrumental in saving his life. Joe Cartier, as he had called himself before his sons had adopted the Anglicized version of their name, was a simple man in spite of his wildness as a youth. He recognized, in this stranger who had come so suddenly into their lives, a similar wildness, combined with a kind of violence that was barely under the surface, waiting to spill over. But he accepted Manolo, just as he had learned to accept everything that had happened since the war— even his wife's death. Some instinct, as deeply primitive as that which had driven Manolo to go looking for Billy-Boy Dozier after Teresita had killed herself, told him that Missie would meet with no harm from this man. And so, when after a few moments of strained politeness, Manolo left too, after Missie no doubt, Joe Carter held his son Matt back with a lifting of his hand.

"He's Toni Lassiter's latest lover. Pa, you gone crazy or something? To let him be alone with Missie—"

"He won't harm Missie. And you had better remember, my son, that it's because of *him* that we had enough money to pay the back taxes on our old ranch. Don't let

your jealousy blind you. For all your pursuit of that Lassiter woman, do you think she and Judge Benoit would
have allowed us to reclaim the ranch if he had not talked
her into it? You leave your sister alone. And be grateful
for what we've gained."

Manolo had guessed some of the conversation that
would have gone on between Joe Carter and Matt. But in
any case, he wasn't afraid of Matt; he treated him with a
kind of indifferent contempt, in spite of Matt's attempts to
prove himself a man as fierce as he was big—a sometime
lover of Toni's. At this moment, annoyingly, his mind was
on Missie. "That swamp brat," Toni called her. Young,
naive, a child in too many ways in spite of her seventeen
years. But for all that she was a little green-eyed witch,
another aggravating quirk of memory telling him she reminded him of something or someone . . . but, for Christ's
sake, who? He knew enough about himself by now to recognize that he wasn't a soft man, and yet he actually felt
protective towards Missie. Perhaps because there was no
pretense about her. And discreet or no, she always blurted
out the truth; her feelings were always on the surface, to
be clearly discerned. And because that was so, she was too
easily hurt—too sensitive, Joe had said, with a heavy sigh.

He thought, "Damn Missie anyhow!" and was of half a
mind to ride off again, back to Toni, whose moods at least
were familiar, and as easy to understand as they were to
control. Toni was a type—the kind of woman he sensed as
being familiar. Perhaps because she was part grasping animal, just as he was, and with as few or less scruples. But
Missie—perhaps it was her very innocence and her lack of
guile that brought him here, on the visits that both Toni
and Matt Carter resented. Maybe he just liked the idea of
pushing Matt, to see just how far he could be pushed. . . .

He knew where to find Missie—she would be half-way
to her favorite tree, for all that it meant crossing the
swamp. Barefoot, she travelled fast and as lightly as some
shy forest creature.

"You didn't have to come after me! Why should you
care about anyone else's feelings? You're like the rest of
them, hanging after *her*, jumping when she snaps her fingers. Sometimes I think you don't really *want* to find out
who you really are. You don't want to know who your

friends were before, and that's why you won't do anything about—about—"

"Your pa should have turned you over his knee a few times, and spanked the sharpness from your tongue! Fact is, I've a good mind to do just that myself. Two things that a man won't tolerate in a woman are a sharp tongue and a vicious temper, and you'd better remember that if you ever hope to catch yourself a husband."

"And how would *you* know? I'll bet you wouldn't let yourself get caught by any female—not unless she was as sneaky and wicked as that Toni!" Missie stamped her foot, making a squelching sound in the mud. "Oh, how *could* you? When I told you about her, and the way she is, I thought you'd see through her. But you're as bad as Uncle Nick. As Matt is. You don't care for anybody else, do you?"

"Goddamn!" He almost snarled the words at her, his blue eyes looking even darker when he was angry. "What in hell do you expect me to do? Bust that Madden guy I'm supposed to know and don't remember out of that nice, healthy open-air jail they got him in? Get those bluecoats after me? I must be crazy, following after you, just to listen to more of your nagging."

Her voice shook, but she stood her ground, looking up at him bravely with the tears still sparkling in her eyes.

"Why'd you come after me then? You don't care about what *I* think either, and I hear enough lectures from the others about how silly I am. Why don't you just leave me alone and go back to *her*?"

His voice changed so suddenly from anger to quietness that it took Missie's own rage away, making her feel empty and slightly ashamed of her outburst.

"Is it really that important to you, little green eyes? You want this Dave Madden set loose?"

And now, suddenly, her whole mood changed, making her afraid for him; scared enough to clutch at his arm.

"Not because of *me*—can't you understand? Because of Dave, and Renate, and because—because I want you to remember, to remember truly! Don't you see that?"

But all the same, even after he had calmed Missie down, he stayed in a thoughtful almost sullen mood, and the second time he saw those convicts, he was riding with Toni herself, because they were working on her land now.

She stopped to speak with one of the guards, and this morning there were two blue-coated soldiers from the Army post standing guard too, their tunics unbuttoned because of the heat. They were lounging comfortably in the shade, slopping water from their canteens like hogs, while the five miserable felons toiled in the sun, chests heaving. Toni stopped—she *would* stop; he knew her well enough to have guessed that by now. And he knew, without looking, that her eyes were gleaming with that particular glowing, shiny look they always took on when she was excited.

"So you're fixing this old road at last. I *must* remember to tell that kind Colonel Belmont how grateful I am! And now I can invite company to come visit me without having to apologize for that washed out bridge. Have they been giving you any trouble? Do you have to use that great big old whip often?"

Without wanting to, Manolo found himself glancing towards the convicts, in their prison-striped trousers. They looked more like scarecrows than like men with their shirts off, ribs standing out under sunburnt flesh. Which one of them was he supposed to recognize? Light eyes looked into his for a moment, before a blond-streaked thatch of hair was lowered. Dave Madden? Missie's friend, who was supposed to be his friend, too?

He told himself later, to explain away his own stupidity, that it was the gloating note in Toni Lassiter's high, breathless voice when she spoke to the guards that pushed him into doing what he did. Whether it was animals or humans in torment, Toni enjoyed watching the spectacle. And besides that, there was Missie, with her reproachful looks.

Even more—and he admitted this to himself later with a wry kind of inner amusement—he actually enjoyed the risks he had taken; even the killing of the fat guard he had taken care of himself, coming up behind the man as he sat cross-legged at the edge of the fire's light to slit his throat. And when he'd done that, watching the man slump forward without a sound, he had the strangest feeling that he'd done this kind of thing before, and all too often. In any case, the guard deserved to die—earlier, in Toni's presence, he had deliberately clubbed one of the wretched prisoners into insensibility because the man had dared to stare too hard.

No—he didn't regret it. Not even the fact that the killing of two soldiers would be blamed on the "unreconstructed Rebs hiding out in the swamps" and would bring more soldiers buzzing about like a horde of angry bees. There would be no positive way of proving that one of the convicts hadn't engineered the whole thing himself, and while the soldiers were kept busy attempting to search the swamps, it would take their minds off that herd of cattle that had just been rounded up on the old Desmoulins place. An absentee owner who was a millionaire didn't need the money those cattle would bring on the market.

The only thing that was faintly disturbing to Manolo was that Dave Madden had acted like he wanted to say something to him, soon after it was all over—but there hadn't been time to stay and talk, or listen to thanks, even if the half-dazed men had been capable of that much.

Manolo, and the two Indian men who had volunteered to come with him to test their manhood on a raid, had all but shoved the five men they had rescued into the tiny boat that would take them down river and to safety, if they didn't get lost.

Dave Madden, his eyes puzzled, had taken charge almost automatically when Manolo told them harshly to get moving.

"I know these bayous pretty well. We'll manage. But for God's sake, man, how did you—"

"You got no time for talk if you want to stay as you are—alive, and free. Now get going!" Manolo's voice was pitched low, but there was a hardness, even a kind of menace underlying it that was unmistakable, particularly when he added, "And remember, if they get you, you're on your own—all of you. Because I'd slit the throat of any man that talks—that clear?"

He pushed the boat away from the bank himself, giving it a shove so hard that the tiny skiff almost overturned.

"Christ!" one of the men muttered in a gasping undertone, "for a while there I wondered if he was goin' to kill us too, and laugh while he was doin' it! Don't mind sayin' he scares me worse than them guards did. . . ."

Throwing all his strength into rowing, trying to remember exactly where they were so he could get his bearings, Dave Madden had time only to throw one last frowning, perplexed glance at the bank before the overhanging trees hid them from sight. But Manolo was already headed back to Toni's house, and the big bed where Toni herself would be waiting—angry by now, no doubt, her nails curved and ready to rake at his eyes. But he had learned that there were ways of keeping Toni tame. . . .

She was still in a good enough mood, two days later, to smile a trifle maliciously at her brother-in-law's rage.

"But Nicky darling, what on earth are you so angry about? I've told you and *told* you that Comanche was right here with me all night long—and anyhow, why should he want to risk his neck rescuing those chained animals? I'll just bet that Madden man had something to do with it—the one whose little German frau you stole for a while. Are you afraid he'll come back and cut your throat, Nicky?"

Nicholas Benoit's voice, raised in anger a few moments before, suddenly became soft and deadly.

"Don't begin to make the mistake of underestimating me, Toni my pet. And don't forget that we agreed, long ago, on honesty between ourselves. Do you think you can really lie to me? That I don't know you and the way your devious, predatory little mind works? You're going to tire of that half-breed gigolo of yours just as quickly as you managed to forget the unfortunate Dozier, and my advice to you, dear sister-in-law, is to start getting used to the idea that he's—shall we say, the type of man who's fated to meet with a violent end?" Before Toni, who had begun to pout angrily, could burst out with a retort of her own, Benoit went on harshly: "Listen to me, Toni! He's nothing more than a mad dog killer, don't you see that? I think he's drunk on violence—he's liable to go berserk at any time, and wreck everything we've worked for all these years! That trick he pulled the other night, turning those damn convicts loose and setting loose half of Colonel Belmont's regiment, so that they're nosing everywhere now—what kind of a move do you call that? Why did he do it?"

"He didn't! I keep *telling* you that, darling, but you won't listen. And in any case—" Toni pulled sulkily at a loose thread on the arm of the brocade sofa—"whoever *did* do it was rather clever, don't you think? After all, it created a diversion—and whoever rustled over a thousand

head of cattle from the Desmoulins ranch is going to end
up becoming quite *rich,* isn't that so?"

Judge Benoit's voice grew deceptively mild.

"*Is* that so? You must tell me more about this hypothet-
ical genius some time *very* soon, so that I can guess what
might have happened to the *profits* from such a magnificently planned operation! But in the meantime, I really
came over to give you another piece of interesting information—and a warning, for old times' sake!" What was
almost a snarl replaced his former silky tones, making
Toni's amber eyes narrow.

"Nicky, now you're being nasty and spiteful! You know
I don't like—"

"And the hell with what you don't like, if you'll pardon
my bluntness, of course! It was a damnfool thing to do—
rustling that big a herd of cattle at this particular time!
Had you forgotten who *owns* the Desmoulins place now?
An Eastern millionaire called Steve Morgan—quite a
wheeler-dealer, from all accounts, and a hard, tough adversary. He also just happens to be the son-in-law of a
United States Senator, no less. Do you know what that
can mean? Federal marshals—government men nosing
around! To make matters worse, there was a telegraph
message only this morning from the Senator's daughter,
Mrs. Morgan. It appears she's on her way here herself, on
a holiday, can you imagine that? Her husband's travelling
abroad somewhere, and she's decided to visit his latest
property acquisition. Do you have any idea what a hor-
nets' nest the woman could stir up, and especially when
she is informed that most of her cattle have been stolen?"

"I do wish you'd stop worrying and *fussing* so, Nicky!
You're suddenly turning into quite an old maid, do you
know?" Toni had jumped to her feet, her voice studiedly
careless. "Oh, for heaven's sake!" she added quickly,
seeing the expression that came to her brother-in-law's
face. "Why don't you stop acting so darned *scared,* just
because some silly old cow of a Senator's daughter takes a
notion that it might be a delightful notion to visit the wilds
of Texas?" She giggled suddenly. "Why, I don't think she'll
like it at all here! I think she'll want to turn right around
and go back East, where it's safe and civilized. And
maybe she'll decide to sell the Desmoulins place. To
me. And you, Nicky my sweet, *you* must use your charm.

You can be so charming when you want to be. Why don't you just stop worrying, and leave the rest to me? Haven't I always managed to wriggle us out of tight corners before?"

Toni's offhand reception of his warning and the implicit threat in her parting words did nothing to improve Judge Benoit's mood as he rode back to town. Little Toni was far too greedy, and she was growing too sure of herself as well—he didn't like it. And he especially did not like or trust the man he referred to contemptuously as her "blue-eyed Indian." Who was the man? Where had he come from, and what had brought him here? It was strange that none of his careful inquiries had brought any results. No man was without a past—and a man who was as fast as this Comanche was with a gun and so entirely lacking in scruples had to have left some tracks somewhere. But the question was—*where*?

"I'll have to get in touch with the Pinkerton Agency, I suppose," Benoit thought glumly. "In fact, I should have done so before." He frowned thoughtfully to himself, thinking about the prison scars that Toni had mentioned casually once. The man had no prison record in this country—not that he had been able to ascertain. But he did speak Spanish fluently, and there had been rumors earlier that he'd been a Comanchero. Mexico, then? Yes. He would have them start their inquiries in Mexico this time; work forward from there. . . .

And then, when his manservant handed him the letter that had arrived on the last mail coach, Nicholas Benoit forgot everything that had been worrying him. He gazed down at the small, square vellum envelope that still carried a faint trace of some exquisite, expensive perfume.

Francesca! The incomparable di Paoli, object of his veneration for so long. She had actually written to him at last—her letter arriving all the way from San Francisco, where he'd ordered the most expensive flowers in season to be delivered to her after every performance.

The envelope held a thick sheet of notepaper, embossed with the ancient seal of the di Paoli's.

"I will be singing in your town of Dallas in about two month's time, and hope you will be able to join me for supper. . ." At last! At long last!

Sighing, Benoit settled himself in the velvet covered

wing chair that was his favorite, the letter that had transformed his whole life still in his hand.

Already, Judge Benoit began to make plans for the journey to Dallas. Suddenly Toni and her scheming mind—even her Indian lover and the reckless actions he had somehow persuaded her to condone—no longer seemed as important as they had some hours ago. Two months, she had said. He began to plan what he would say in reply—going over every word carefully in his mind. And he would have to persuade Toni, either with threats or with promises, to part with some of the money the sale of those stolen cattle must have brought her. Di Paoli must be wined and dined in a style that would surprise her and melt her mind towards him. She was used to European royalty and Eastern millionaires. Well, he would make her notice him—not only because of his long devotion but because of his generosity as well. And he happened to know, from careful study of the newspapers, that she was between lovers at the moment.

Because he was alone, the door of his study carefully locked behind him, Benoit permitted himself to laugh aloud. It was a coincidence he had not troubled to point out to Toni—that di Paoli's *last* lover had been the selfsame millionaire who now owned the old Desmoulin's plantation, and all its acres. Such irony! But of course Toni would not have appreciated it in any case.

This Steve Morgan had been sent packing by the princess, of course—she was bound to have tired of him in spite of his vaunted and too openly displayed generosity in the matter of jewels and other costly trinkets. So he had taken his broken heart off of Europe, while his wife sought seclusion! Perhaps, later, when they had grown to know and understand each other, he and Francesca could share the humor of the situation. Somehow, he had the feeling that with or without dear, unscrupulous little Toni's machination, Mrs. Morgan would not care to remain too long in her latest home.

Part Six
THE LONG JOURNEY BACK

Chapter Forty-seven

It was at Don Francisco's insistence that Ginny traveled so heavily chaperoned. She had, indeed, almost forgotten how autocratic the old man could be.

"So! If you must travel to some barbarous part of Texas to inspect some derelict plantation that even Esteban did not think important enough to remember, you will at least journey respectably, as a married woman of your position should."

Over his high-bridged nose, his blue eyes had gleamed fiercely at her, as if daring her to contradict his final, grudgingly given permission.

"Renaldo will go with you," he stated, startling her half-formed protests into silence. "And the Señora Armijo, who proved herself such an ineffectual duena before. Yes, I think the poor woman has been longing to prove her worth ever since the sudden occasion of your ill-starred marriage to Esteban, that precipitate function that gave rise to so much unhappiness and misfortune to so many— if you'll forgive an old man for saying so!"

"I will forgive you, Don Francisco, but I am capable of travelling by myself, and Mr. Bishop has very kindly promised an escort."

"Ah, yes—this mysterious Mr. Bishop, who is sometimes an ordinary cattle buyer, and at other times a gentleman of leisure who seems to do far too much travel-

445

ling on our side of the border! I am forced to wonder
what our Presidente thinks of his comings and goings—or
do you think he is aware of this gentleman's fondness for
travel? No, my dear Virginia, I am forced to insist, as I'm
sure your own father would, that if you must travel, you
shall do so in safety and respectability!" In a less forceful
voice he went on, "Rosa and that Frenchwoman you
brought with you will, of course, remain here to look after
the children. You did not think to take *them* with you, I
hope?"

All of which led her to wonder wryly afterwards just
how much Don Francisco knew of her conversation with
Mr. Bishop, and the startling disclosures he had made.

In spite of the slight limp and downward droop of one
side of his mouth that remained as evidence of the stroke
he had suffered, Don Francisco Alvarado was still very
much *el patron*, the head of his family. Ginny had no
doubt that he would have forcibly prevented her from
leaving the hacienda if she had not agreed to comply with
his edicts, and so, even while she wondered what Mr.
Bishop would have to say when she met him in San Antonio, she had agreed—with a false meekness that she suspected did not deceive Don Francisco in the least.

And, in the end, she found it comforting to have Renaldo's company. Even Tia Alfonsa's constant twittering
served to keep her mind off what would have, eventually,
to be faced when they arrived in Baroque. Dear Renaldo—
still the quiet scholar and her friend. The first real friend
she had made in Mexico, in that time, only a few years
before, that now seemed so remote and long ago. Steve's
second cousin, and *his* friend too. She found it a relief to
be able to confide in Renaldo, during the journey, to think
about segments of her strange and stunning conversation
with Jim Bishop, on that afternoon when he had arrived
to turn her world topsy-turvy again—his blunt, and even
stranger proposition.

"But why have you come all this way to tell me this?"
she had cried out at last. "Why aren't you *doing* something about it? This Colonel Belmont you appointed to
command the army post there—why doesn't someone give
him the authority to *act*, and put a stop to—to this powder keg you are talking about?"

Bishop had given his thin-lipped smile that was not a real smile at all.

"But I thought I had already made myself clear. Act, you say, madam? But on what grounds, and on what evidence? If Belmont arrests anyone, it would have to be your irresponsible husband. And since it has become apparant that he has no recollection of the past, or of his real identity, then we are left exactly where we started, are we not?" He had scrutinized Ginny's flushed face and her fever bright eyes with a contemplative look that gave nothing away. "I happen to respect you, Mrs. Morgan. For your intelligence, your spirit, and of course, your determination. And in this particular case, since we are dealing with an arch-villain who happens to be a woman ... you take my meaning?"

It was quite ironic, Ginny thought, her journey irrevocably begun, that she should now be working for Mr. Bishop, in a way. Of course the man was infernally cunning—he had even taken the trouble to warn her, after he'd led her on with his hints and his barely-veiled threats, that she might be running some slight risks.

"He said this Judge Benoit is a clever and cunning man—it wouldn't do to underestimate him," Ginny said now to Renaldo. "But Toni Lassiter is the key to the whole business. She has the morals of an alley cat, and far fewer scruples than the jungle variety. They know her for what she is, and Mr. Bishop believes there are quite a few who hate her, in addition to the people who fear her. But when it comes to outsiders horning in—she's one of *them*. A Lassiter, even if it's only by marriage, and a Southern lady. Of course, *part* of his warning about what I might have to cope with when we arrive there is because of the fact that—that Steve is obviously her lover."

Ginny tried to make her voice hard and emotionless for Renaldo's benefit, but the slight hesitation in her speech gave her away. And Renaldo, who knew Steve like a brother, could find nothing to say in reply, except to give a helpless shrug. Was there to be no end to the complications that continued to keep these two apart? He remembered, unwillingly, his Uncle's grim parting shot before they had left the hacienda.

"You are to see that Steve comes back to his senses, even if you have to shoot him in order to do so! I'm an

old man, by God, and now that he's a father, it's high
time my grandson gives up his irresponsible ways and set-
tles down! And if he cannot, then Virginia must have the
chance to make a new and more secure life for herself
and the children."

But was Ginny herself ready for such an existence yet?
Ruefully, Renaldo Ortega reflected that she had changed a
great deal from the frightened, but still spirited girl he first
remembered when Steve had brought her to his estancia—carried in his arms, wrapped in nothing but a blanket. Another one of his cousin's women, he had thought
grimly then, until he had found out who she was and how
she had happened to become Steve's virtual prisoner and
his mistress. That was all past now, and Steve and Ginny
were married—had been married twice, if one stuck to
facts. What had happened to drive them away from each
other again?

The last part of their journey, after they had left San
Antonio, was accomplished in virtual silence, for both
Renaldo and Ginny were lost in their own thoughts, and
the usually voluble Señora Armijo had closed her eyes in
order to ward off an incipient headache, caused by the
sun's monotonous glare.

Renaldo was wondering uneasily exactly what kind of
trouble might lie ahead of them once they arrived in
Baroque to play their various parts, and Ginny found her
mind going back to the meeting Mr. Bishop had arranged
for her with Renate Madden, in an anonymous hotel
room.

San Antonio, for her, had been filled with memories in
any case. The first time she had seen Steve—the first time
she had been seized in his arms to be kissed brutally, savagely, sealing her even then, without her knowing it, as his
possession. And then there was Renate—face all hollows,
eyes calm. In those days, she had smiled often, too. And
who reminded Ginny of herself at another time in her life,
when she had been Tom Beal's whore.

Renate Madden's face bore the same dull, trapped look
that Ginny's had worn once. She had once been a pretty
woman, her blonde hair always clean and shiny, her blue
eyes calm. In those days, she had smiled often too. And
now it was as if she did not care about her appearance

any longer—like a pale ghost she shrank when anyone spoke to her.

"She refuses to see her husband, or even to write to him," Bishop told Ginny, with an unusually baffled expression showing for an instant in his cold grey eyes. "In fact, she's been threatening to kill herself rather than shame him, or face his eyes. Those are *her* words. Quite frankly, Mrs. Morgan, I'm at a loss as to what to do with her. Perhaps I should have left her with Captain Altamonte's family, but I felt she might have some useful information for you—be able to fill you in on the background of these people you are going to meet."

"You have absolutely no pity and no conscience at all, have you, Mr. Bishop?" Ginny's voice had been angry. "That poor woman—after all she's been through, all you can think of is that she might, after all, prove *useful*!"

It was only after Ginny had told Renate, quite bluntly, of certain experiences *she* had been through that the other woman began to talk to her.

Nicholas Benoit—it was to him Toni Lassiter's men had brought Renate on the same night that Dave had been taken away to prison.

Terrified, fighting them every inch of the way until one of them hit her, she had angrily refused Judge Benoit's smiling offer of protection.

"But believe me, little girl, you are safer here. You don't know what that sister-in-law of mine is capable of, do you? I mean you no harm—I've always admired you, in fact. A lovely woman such as you are should glow in the proper surroundings, like a jewel. . . ."

In spite of her tears, her protests, he kept her in his house—surrounding her with luxury she had never known before, not touching her yet, but treating her instead like a pampered pet. She had silken wrappers to wear—fine silk stockings, perfumed baths and satin gowns she was forced to wear because he had left her with nothing of her own.

And every night she sat down to a sumptuous dinner, with Judge Nicholas himself impeccably dressed as a gentleman does in the evening.

This continued for a whole week, during which time he made no demands of her, merely kissing her hand when it was time for her to retire—a charming continental cus-

tom. He actually acted, Renate told Ginny, her voice
shaking, as if the only interest he had in her was a fa-
therly one. He had even told her once that he had always
wanted a pretty blond daughter, just like her.

And then there came the night when he must have put
something in her wine, for her head began to reel, and she
remembered nothing until she woke up beside him in the
morning. From then on he was no longer charming and
kind, but brutal.

He used her in ways she had not dreamed of. He made
her a boy—and she was a plaything for his friends as well,
like that fat Colonel Vance. And then at last, when he was
tired of her, he sent her away with a swarthy-faced man
who came to the house very late at night; and the man
turned out to be a pimp, who beat her and terrified her
even more than Judge Benoit had done. The man dragged
her from border town to border town, finally selling her to
a madam in Matamoras who specialized in blond gringas.
And it was there, Ginny found out from Bishop, that
Steve had sent Altamonte with an extremely large sum of
money to buy Renate's freedom.

"*Steve* did that?"

"Against my orders, of course," Bishop said grimly. He
did not tell her that even Dave Madden's premature release had been similarly against orders.

Still, he was forced to admit, if only to himself, that
things might have turned out for the best after all—except
for Steve's inconvenient memory loss, that was.

Renate Madden, who had hardly spoken two words to
him, seemed to have made a confidante of Ginny, telling
her as much as she could remember of people and places.
And naturally, it was Toni Lassiter, whom she already disliked, that Ginny was most interested in.

Ginny might have been surprised to know that Mrs. An-
toinnette Lassiter was interested in Mrs. Steven Morgan,
too, but in an impatient, half-contemptuous way.

"She's probably a horse-faced creature and a priggish
bore if even her own husband can't stand to be around
her," she snapped to Manolo, who merely lifted a sarcastic
black eyebrow as he continued to eat.

Messalina was in a bad mood this evening, and he knew
why, even while the fact left him unmoved. Judge Benoit
had called, early in the afternoon, to announce with a

malicious note of triumph in his voice that Mrs. Morgan and her entourage had arrived at last, and was being escorted to her new home by Colonel Belmont and his wife.

"Well? And why should it matter to *me*? She won't be staying long in any case!" Unable to resist her own curiosity, however, Toni had asked casually what the woman looked like, a sly expression coming into her eyes when Nicky had been forced to admit that he couldn't be certain of anything except the fact that Mrs. Morgan's hair appeared to be red. She had worn a travelling bonnet, with a veil to keep the dust from irritating her eyes, and in any case he had caught only a glimpse of the carriage as it rolled past.

"But I've been invited to dinner at the Belmont's tomorrow night, and she'll be there with this Spanish gentleman who accompanied her here. A distant cousin, I believe. You really should keep on better terms with the Colonel's wife, Toni dear! And it's a pity your pet Indian is such an uncouth, impetuous kind of bastard. You know our latest military commander is not a skirt-hungry fool like Vance was—he's as much as hinted to me he suspects your new foreman of being behind that prison break, not to mention the rash of cattle rustling we've been having recently! Didn't I warn you to keep him on a leash? One of these days, if you don't watch out, you'll find that he's doing the leading . . . although I must say I can't quite see you as a *tame* bitch, Toni love!"

So Toni was sullen and ill-tempered that evening; but because she was just the slightest bit afraid of Comanche, of the way he could erupt into violence when she pushed him too far, she contented herself for the moment with venting her spleen on her new neighbor.

"Well? Why in hell do you have to act like a deaf-mute sometimes? The least you can do when a lady invites you to dinner is make some conversation! What do you think we ought to do about that Eastern bitch? I told Nicky I'd scare her off, and we will, won't we?"

"*We*? Thought the Judge told you he didn't want any more trouble that might bring in the Federal marshals for a while. Meaning that he wants *me* to lay low." He gave Toni a mocking grin that only infuriated her more. "What do you want me to do with her, Messalina? Cut her throat some dark night? See that she meets with an unfortunate 'accident' in the swamps, if she's the kind of woman who likes to go riding? Maybe we should just kidnap her and hold her for ransom—even if she's ugly her father or her husband might just be willing to pay for her release, and if she's passable, there's always the prospect of raping her as well. That ought to amuse your twisted little mind!"

Pushing his plate away, he leaned back in his chair with his arms crossed—looking for all the world like a cross between an Indian and a pirate, Toni thought crossly, until the significance of his sarcastically uttered words began to seep in.

"Oh, God—Comanche, darling! How is it you're so damned clever? Yes—yes, of course! We'll give her a little time, of course, and if she doesn't look as if she's leaving. . . . And Nicky mustn't know! He mustn't suspect a single thing—*you* can take a herd up north. Or pretend to. And that'll give you an alibi. And we won't have to share the money with Nicky this time—do you know that the wretched, despicable man practically *forced* me to give him ten thousand dollars out of the money we got for the last herd we sent up? And after we had all the trouble with changing the brands; not to mention taking all of the risks! Sometimes I think I hate Nicky, only he's useful just now. But afterwards. . . ."

He knew better than to try and stop Toni when she got excited about some wild plan. And he regretted the casually thrown out words that he had meant to be satirical.

He shrugged, listening to her, watching the lamplight shining on her silvery blond hair, the avaricious gleam in her almond-shaped amber eyes, the pale pink lips, always looking as if they had just been moistened. When she leaned forward over the table, her breasts almost fell out of the high-waisted silk and lace negligee she wore—perfect globes, alabaster white, with tiny blue veins that stood out more markedly when she was excited. Which was most times. . . . Toni was one of those women who was always hungry, never completely sated. She would have made the perfect whore, and he had told her so once, hearing her gurgling, excited chuckle in return.

"But darling, I want to do my own choosing! I wish someone would set up whorehouses for women to frequent, with a whole array of handsome studs to choose from! Oh, I think I could go through them all in one evening! That's why I like visiting Sadie's, of course—it's the closest I've seen yet. You were really nasty to me that first evening, weren't you? Aren't you sorry, now that you know what you were missing?"

"Like you just said—I happen to like doing my own choosing, too," he had drawled, already prepared for her attempt to claw at his groin, catching her wrists easily and twisting them until she moaned and whimpered with pain.

That was another thing he'd discovered about Toni Lassiter. Not only did inflicting hurt, or even hearing of it excite her sexually, but the infliction of a certain amount of pain on her had the same effect. He knew, without having to make an effort to remember, that he had never met a woman quite like Toni Lassiter before—a woman who excited him against his will because of her complete amorality, even while her snakelike nature repelled him.

Tonight, even while Toni continued to talk, her body flirting with him at the same time, Manolo's thoughts went unwillingly from Toni to Missie Carter. Damn it—he was going to have to watch himself there. For if Toni was one end of the spectrum of women, Missie stood at the other. Wild, shy, pretty without being conscious of it yet, and with an innocent purity that belonged to nature itself. The strange thing was that he didn't *want* Missie—not in the way he desired other women. And yet, in spite of her quick, spitfire temper and a tongue that ran away with her, he enjoyed being around her—just talking to her, watching the different expressions that constantly came and went in her face, making all her feelings transparent.

Once, he had surprised himself thinking that if he lived long enough to have a daughter he'd want her to be like Missie. The thing was, he had gradually become uncomfortably aware that Missie herself didn't look on him as another father, nor as a surrogate big brother. If Matt Carter hadn't begun glowering whenever he saw them together, and if Toni hadn't started to throw her sharp, sarcastic barbs, he would have guessed in any case that Missie was developing a crush on him. She had begun to take more trouble with her appearance, combing her hair free of its usual snarls and tangles and washing it every day. And then there was the way she would color whenever he looked at her—the sometimes breathless note in her voice when he touched her or their shoulders brushed. What in hell was he going to do about Missie?

"Comanche! Have you been listening? What do you think of my plans?" Toni said.

To cover his own anger at himself he said harshly:

"Only plan I can think of right now is what we both had in mind when you asked me to supper. Take the goddamned robe off."

Chapter Forty-eight

It happened that Judge Benoit was the first citizen of Baroque to be introduced to the new owner of the Desmoulins place. "The locals," the Northern soldiers called the residents of the county, but the Judge, who had been educated in the East, held a unique position, and even the carpetbaggers were forced to respect him and the decisions he handed down in his court.

There was nothing unusual about the fact that Nicholas Benoit should have been asked to dine with the Belmonts. In fact, he had often entertained them, together with some of the other senior officers and their wives, in his magnificently furnished house. But, as he had pointed out maliciously to Toni, this was a very special occasion; and the Belmonts, by singling him out, were paying him an open compliment. Benoit resolved that if an opportunity offered itself he would repay the Colonel's hospitality by dropping a few hints—very discreet ones, to be sure; but perhaps Colonel Belmont, a tough, hard-bitten West Pointer, would save him the trouble and expense of hiring the Pinkertons after all.

"Ah, there you are, Judge! Good to have you." Colonel Belmont's greeting was expansive, friendly. "You know everyone here, I'm sure? Except for the Señor Ortega—cousin of Mrs. Morgan's."

A tall, fair-skinned man, his brown hair parted in the

middle, brought his heels together and bowed gravely as he acknowledged the introduction in flawless English. "There are rumors that Señor Ortega might be the next Mexican ambassador to Washington—eh?" Colonel Belmont unbent so far as to give Nick Benoit a discreet wink, while Renaldo Ortega made a deprecating motion of his long-fingered, well-kept hands.

"You are most flattering, Colonel. But indeed—I am here only to absorb some of your culture and customs, and to act as escort to Mrs. Morgan."

"I'm sure you're anxious to meet our guest of honor, Judge. I've already mentioned that you might be a great help if you can spare the time, that is. Your advice has always been invaluable to me, just as it was to my predecessor! She'll be down presently. Went upstairs with my wife and some of the other ladies, to freshen up after the ride over here."

Afterwards, Nicholas Benoit could not quite remember how he had pictured Virginia Morgan. He recalled his vague comment to Toni that she appeared to have red hair, and could have winced at his own lack of observation, for he was a man who prided himself on noticing details that other people were apt to miss—besides being a connoisseur of women in particular. Perhaps Toni herself had thrown him off with her sneering comments that a woman whose husband ignored her must be plain and frumpish.

Red hair, indeed! How could he have been so mistaken? Her hair was the color of pale-sheened, new minted copper, and it was fashionably styled—exposing tiny ears in whose lobes emeralds glittered—to fall in thick, shining ringlets that cascaded to her shoulders and down her back. He guessed that when her hair was brushed loose it would hang thick and heavy, all the way to her tiny waist. Used to beautiful women, Nicholas could not, nevertheless, prevent himself from an indrawn breath when he saw her come downstairs, one gloved hand touching the bannister very lightly, her face slightly turned as she laughed at something Mrs. Belmont had said.

He noticed her eyes later, when they were being introduced. Slightly tilted at the corners, they matched her emeralds exactly, and were just as brilliant. And was he

mistaken again, or did her voice carry the slightest trace
of an accent?

My God, but she was lovely! And that passionate, sensual mouth—he wondered if Ortega was her lover. As he
bowed over the hand she extended to him, Nicholas
Benoit felt, for the first time, a little more than an idle curiosity about this woman's husband, whose name had been
linked with that of the Princess di Paoli. Was he much
older, in addition to being so rich that he could afford two
beautiful women? And then he wondered what Toni would
think when she saw her, and the thought brought him a
feeling of malicious satisfaction.

Present at the Belmont's exclusive dinner party were
Army officers and their wives, and a sprinkling of the influential carpetbaggers who now controlled most political
offices in the state. But it was Judge Benoit who had the
honor of being seated next to Virginia Morgan at dinner.

She sparkled—there was no other word for it. And he
discovered, to his surprise, that she had more than her
beauty to commend her. She was an intelligent woman
and a witty one—obviously well read and well versed in
political affairs. She confided that her father had been a
Virginian before he settled in California, and actually displayed a sympathy for the conquered Southern states. But
what had brought her here, of all places? Benoit gathered
that she was only recently back from Europe—indeed, her
fashionable brocade gown of green and gold had been designed especially for her by the famous designer, Worth.
Why did she choose to hide her beauty and her elegance in
this remote part of Texas?

His carefully veiled questions brought a small sigh in response, and a darkening of her green eyes.

"But have you never felt the desire for seclusion? To be
alone, in order to *think*, and to make decisions? I have
had too much of large cities and polite society, Mr.
Benoit." She gave him a rather wistful smile. "And I think
you understand, or I would not be talking to you so
frankly!"

Ginny had deliberately set herself out to dazzle Nick
Benoit, although she disliked the man even before she had
met him. It was an effort, but she smiled, and flattered
him without seeming to. He was so pompous!

He dressed overly elegantly, and his hair, worn full and

slightly curly, with a short, carefully trimmed beard, shone with Macassar oil. He was the kind of man who fancied himself as a lady killer—and she had not missed the way he looked at her, shiny brown eyes lingering especially long on her mouth. But Mr. Bishop had warned her on no account to underestimate this Judge Benoit, and so she was careful not to flirt with him, but to be wistful and demure in turn, while showing him at the same time that she wasn't a brainless ninny.

It had been arranged beforehand, through the offices of the ubiquitous Mr. Bishop, that Ginny and Colonel Belmont's wife, Persis, were supposed to have known each other before, from the time when the Colonel had been stationed at the Presidio, in San Francisco. And Nick Benoit believed this, seeing how friendly the two women seemed to be.

Later, after the dinner was over, and the last guests had left, Persis Belmont asked laughingly:

"Well—what did you think of him?"

"The local Machiavelli? He looks the part!" Ginny retorted, turning away from the mirror. She caught Mrs. Belmont's humorously raised eyebrow and could not help smiling. "You don't like him very well either, do you?"

"But *you* charmed him! Just be careful, please do! Rodney will never be promoted to General if anything were to happen to you!"

"Oh, but nothing will. I'll continue to be charming, even if it hurts me. I've been warned by Mr. Bishop, too, you see."

It was, fortunately, easy for the two women to like each other. Persis Belmont was the daughter of a college professor, and she had married late in life, after her father died. She had wit, and a dry sense of humor that she tried to keep subdued for her husband's sake; and because she was also an intelligent woman, the Colonel was able to confide in her completely, trusting in her discretion. Persis did not like Antoinette Lassiter, and here again she and Ginny found themselves on common ground.

"She's the kind of female that other women cannot help but dislike!" Mrs. Belmont said vehemently. "And she has no time for women—it's the men she concentrates her charm upon. Of course she's quite lovely—but she makes capital of it. And even when she smiles, her eyes stay cold.

Rodney says I should make a point of cultivating her, but I—I just *cannot*! Perhaps it's because I've seen the way she looks at *him*; and she had Colonel Vance wrapped around her finger, from all accounts!"

Persis Belmont was starved for conversation with a woman of her own background and breeding, and moreover, she had not been told everything.

So Ginny was able to say, quite casually: "But is this Mrs. Lassiter the only personable female among the local people? Surely—"

"Oh, there *are* other women, of course. But most of them quiet, and dowdy, and frightened. And not very friendly either. I'm afraid they look on us almost as invaders. There *is* the little Carter girl, though. Her mother was a Lassiter, but the old man cut her off when she eloped. The biggest scandal going is that Toni Lassiter's latest foreman has taken quite an interest in Missie Carter, for all that she's barely seventeen, and still a child in too many ways. He even persuaded Toni to persuade Judge Benoit to let the Carters re-settle on their old ranch. Somehow they paid up all the back taxes they owed, and there were certain people who were not too happy about it! But we're only here to keep the peace. Rodney says we must not interfere in the affairs of these people, except to keep the peace. Although I must say—" Persis Belmont chewed on her lower lip for a moment—"this foreman, a man they call Manolo, is quite a troublemaker. He's vicious—far too fast with a gun, too. And I've heard them say that he's half Comanche Indian. He even looks—well, frightening! And Rodney says he belongs behind bars, like any dangerous animal. Just the kind of man who would appeal to Toni Lassiter, I suppose. But I'm surprised that Joseph Carter allows him near his daughter."

Later that night, when she was back in her rather gloomy looking bedroom, Ginny found it difficult to get to sleep. She had not been able to bring herself to tell even Renaldo of Persis Belmont's impulsive outburst, and she didn't want to cope with its implications herself—not yet.

They went riding the next day, the Colonel's lady and her new friend, leaving the conscientious Renaldo behind to go over the books of the Desmoulin's estate with the elderly and taciturn foreman who had been hired by Shanghai Pierce. Ginny rode sidesaddle, wearing a biscuit-colored velour riding habit trimmed with bronze ribbon that made Persis exclaim with envy.

Escorted by ten soldiers, even Colonel Belmont had decided they would be safe enough, even if they did ride along the borders of the river and its winding, secret bayous where lost and lawless men still hid out.

It was the impressionable Joe Junior, riding guard on the few head of cattle they had gleaned from the swamp islands, who first saw them; and when his first quick resentment at seeing the blue-coated soldiers, riding so much at ease on *their* land, had subsided, he found himself struck almost dumb by the loveliness of the young woman who rode beside Mrs. Belmont.

"I'm sorry—are we trespassing?" she called out before he could find any words at all. "We were only looking for a short-cut to the river—I'm sorry it doesn't run on *my* land." And then, smiling at him in a way that made the sweat pop out from every pore in his face, she added apologetically: "I'm Virginia Morgan. I've come to live for a while on what used to be Mr. Pierce's ranch. And before that the Desmoulins' plantation. I think we must be neighbors—do you think you can forgive us, and accept this as a formal call?"

So *she* was the one! The mysterious millionaire's wife whose coming Manolo had warned them about. Joe pulled off his hat, his face reddening. Tongue-tied, still searching for words, he found himself thinking confusedly: "But she's *young*! And so pretty it doesn't seem possible she's married at all—and she's a lady too, not at all the way we thought she would be."

Finally, with Mrs. Belmont smiling and the Yankee soldiers looking as if they'd bitten on something sour, Joe recollected himself enough to ask them down to the house. He didn't know what else to do, as he explained to Pa and Matt later. Not that Pa had too much to say; and even Matt, though he grumbled under his breath, couldn't hide the fact that he was impressed. It was Missie who seemed most excited, the freckles standing out on her face in spite of all the cucumber and buttermilk concoctions she'd been using on it of late. And it was Missie, not waiting for Pa's permission, who offered to escort the ladies to the river—just so Mrs. Morgan could see what it looked like.

Missie knew enough not to take them any further—and

in any case, Missie had been all keyed up, her green eyes
looking more than ever like a cat's since Manolo had
given her that funny ring he wore on his finger. It hung on
a ribbon around her neck, and she played with it nervously while she spoke to the ladies.

"Why, it's so beautiful and peaceful here!" Mrs. Morgan
said when she first saw the river slipping dark green and
silent between the moss-festooned cypresses that seemed to
crouch on either side of the water.

Mrs. Belmont was quiet, saying little, although she
smiled in a friendly fashion when she caught Missie's eyes.
But it was the other lady, who was so young and beautiful, that Missie found herself liking almost instantly. She
was friendly, and not at all stuck-up and grand; and she
told Missie, smiling, that she had such pretty hair, making
her blush with pleasure.

"Do you really think it looks peaceful and pretty?" Persis Belmont said with a small shudder. "I must confess
that I prefer even the wild mountain rivers of Colorado
and California. These gnarled, grotesque looking trees—
they are almost frightening, I think. And there are dangerous swamps back there."

Forgetting her manners, Missie said quickly, "But the
swamps aren't frightening at all, not if you know where to
step!" And then she reddened again, and her fingers tugged
nervously at the ribbon around her neck and the ring
he had given her, just as if she had truly been his
sweetheart.

And it wasn't all her imagination, she told herself
fiercely. Ever since the night he'd set Dave Madden and
those other poor men free, and she'd flung herself against
him, kissing his beard-stubbled face because she was so
happy to see him back safe, and because she couldn't find
the right words to tell him how happy she felt—he had
looked at her differently. He *had*! The subtle change in his
manner had puzzled and confused Missie at first, until one
day, when they were talking, it suddenly burst upon her
like a joyous explosion that Manolo had stopped treating
her like an aggravating, wayward child.

He brought her books—some of them, from the old
Lassiter place, had belonged to her mother.

"Toni'll never miss them," he said, shrugging; and then,

his blue eyes going kind of opaque and hard, "she doesn't bother with reading anyhow."

Missie read the books avidly—at first only because Manolo had brought them to her, and later because she found that she actually liked reading. And he—Manolo— he was the one who would help her with big words and phrases she couldn't understand. He had even started to teach her *real* French—so different from the Louisiana patois that Pa and her brothers spoke. He would lean with his back against her favorite tree, or against the corral fence, his eyes crinkling at the corners when she would pronounce something wrong.

It was at times like this, when he smiled at her—the smile reaching his eyes instead of being just a sardonic twist of his lips—that Missie forgot everything they said about him, about his being an outlaw and a killer without a conscience, and even the fact that he was Toni's lover. She knew she was falling in love with him, even if she didn't know him at all; and the thought scared her, even while it gave her a breathless, shaky kind of feeling.

He'd been wearing the ring she now had on his finger when they found him, she and Teresita. The Indian woman had told her afterwards that it was a symbol of the Comanche—the Snake People. It was fashioned of a strange, reddish gold that almost looked like copper, made in the shape of a snake, with two tiny green stones for eyes that Manolo told her later were emeralds. She was fascinated by the ring, and on that particular day when he'd come down to her favorite spot by the river with two new books for her, she hadn't been able to resist reaching out to touch it—wondering at the same time why the brushing of her fingers against Manolo's long brown ones sent a sudden shiver up her spine. To cover her confusion she said quickly:

"It looks like a real snake, doesn't it? Right down to the tiny, carved scales."

And he said teasingly that it reminded him more of a red-haired, green-eyed woman.

Missie gave him a round-eyed look.

"You mean like *me*? You called me green eyes, you know. The first time you ever saw me. But I don't know if I like being compared to that old snake or not!"

He grinned at her. "Oh, I don't know! You've got the

same pointy, triangular shaped face, of course—but I must admit you're prettier!"

And then, before she had been able to think of a retort, he'd surprised her by pulling the ring off his finger and tossing it casually at her as if it didn't mean anything to him at all. It was still warm from his flesh.

"Here, little bayou mermaid. You keep it. I've noticed it keeps getting in my way and snagging my shirts."

Later, when Missie carefully threaded the ring on the green ribbon that Gaston had brought her, she thought excitedly that it had to be some kind of an omen. And she'd keep it forever—maybe until the day when. . . . But she was afraid to think any further, although all night long the secret thought kept tugging at her mind that maybe, just maybe, Manolo had meant something more than just kindness. The next time she saw him he didn't say a word about it though—didn't even ask if she still had the ring or what she'd done with it.

Missie had developed the habit of pulling at the ribbon around her neck when she was nervous—just touching the ring every now and then to make sure it was still there. She did it again now, becoming embarrassingly aware that she'd gone into another one of her daydreams, and right in the middle of something Colonel Belmont's wife had been saying, too! What would they think of her?

Her face flushing a bright red, Missie looked from one to the other of the two smiling faces that watched her.

"I—I'm sorry, but I guess I wasn't paying attention," and each word she stuttered, she realized miserably, only made it worse! Oh, if only the ground would open up and swallow her, right this minute!

"There's nothing wrong with lapsing into a daydream, you know," Mrs. Morgan said softly. "I remember when I used to do the same thing. In fact, there was a favorite apple tree in the back garden of my Uncle's house where I used to hide and dream to my heart's content—until everyone learned where to look for me!"

Missie looked gratefully at the smiling young woman, who couldn't be more than a few years older than Missie herself, for all that she was married.

"There's a big old tree that's my secret place, too. But my brothers are always coming out after me—" Missie gave a dismayed gasp as the knot she'd tied in the ribbon came loose. Unmindful of what the ladies might think, she clutched at the ring with a sigh of relief.

"Here," Mrs. Morgan said, stretching her small gloved hand out to help as she leaned forward in the saddle. "It's only the knot—let me tie it back up for you."

Persis Belmont's eyes rested curiously on the ring that Missie was holding so carefully.

"Why, what a beautiful piece of workmanship!" she said suddenly. "It's an antique, isn't it?"

Missie didn't know why she felt forced to stammer out an explanation, her face flushing again.

"I—It's—a friend gave it to me. It's the nicest present I ever had—I couldn't bear it if I lost it!"

"Ginny, I do believe she's secretly engaged!" Mrs. Belmont laughed teasingly, but kindly too; her eyes twinkling. "Don't worry—I promise I won't tell a soul. I believe that every girl should be secretly engaged at least once in her life."

"Oh! Oh, yes—it *is* beautiful; and quite unusual in design." But Missie was too relieved, as she slipped the ring back into her blouse, to notice how still Virginia Morgan had suddenly become, and how curiously stilted her voice had sounded.

If Persis Belmont wondered why Ginny had suddenly grown so quiet, and seemed anxious to cut short their ride, she tactfully asked no questions. If she hadn't been the kind of woman who knew when to remain silent and had insisted upon chattering all the way back, Ginny probably would not have heard her, for her thoughts—some bitter, some frightened and some filled with a strange depression—had taken possession of her, blinding her to everything else for the moment.

Ever since she had seen that ring. . . .

Emerald chips set in red gold from the Black Hills. An unusual ring, meant to be worn on a man's little finger. And it was on the sheerest, mischievous impulse that she had bought it for Steve, even though she knew he despised rings. When had he begun to wear it? And what impulse had led him to give it to Missie Carter, of all people?

"She's just a child!" Ginny found herself thinking angrily. "Even *he* ought to have a few scruples," and then she remembered that he'd used none at all where *she* was concerned; and when he'd taken her for the first time, she'd only been two years older than Missie was now. She remembered, too, what Persis had told her last night. It had been one of the reasons why she had wanted to see Missie Carter for herself. Missie—who might have been herself when she was seventeen and still naive and child-like, her head filled with romantic dreams. Until time, and Steve himself, had turned her into the woman she now was.

For the first time, Ginny faced squarely the thought that when Steve saw her again he might not even know her. And if he ever did remember—would he still want her?

Chapter Forty-nine

It was the Señora Armijo, her lips thinning disapprovingly, who unwittingly provided Ginny with a solution for the questions that had been plaguing her ever since she had seen the ring that Missie Carter wore on the green silk ribbon around her neck.

They were sitting in what the Señora insisted upon calling the sala, and Ginny's fingers drummed absent-mindedly on the arm of her chair, while her eyes, slightly swollen from lack of sleep, gazed unseeingly out of the window.

"Really! I cannot say—forgive me, Genia—that I understand the customs of this barbarous place! In Mexico, as you know, people are much more friendly. There would be a fiesta given for a new arrival—I remember that when my late husband and I moved into our new home, everyone called upon us to wish us well. And I gave a later dinner party for all our neighbors. It was the first time I had entertained, of course, and I can still recall how nervous I felt!"

With an effort, Ginny dragged her attention back to the older woman. "Mrs. Belmont has already been kind enough to have a dinner for us. And I don't know that I feel inclined—"

"Ginny!" It was unlike Renaldo to interrupt, and her eyes widened at the sudden urgency in his tone. "Don't you see? It would be the perfect solution. After all, what would be more natural than for you to wish to become acquainted with your neighbors? You could send out invitations to an evening party. Announce that there will be dancing after supper. I think—" he gave her a thoughtful, almost stern look, and his voice became firm. "I think it's high time matters were brought to a head. There's no point in your moping about, worrying yourself sick about various possibilities that might not even exist." And then, more gently, "You've never been one to avoid a confrontation, have you? I think it's one of the qualities I've admired most in you. Why postpone the inevitable?"

Unconsciously, her chin lifted defiantly.

"Yes—you're right, of course, as you usually are. Why not, indeed? I *must* see Steve—this is all so ridiculous, this peculiar kind of limbo we have found ourselves in since we arrived. Yes, I'd rather face whatever has to be faced as quickly as possible!"

Her feelings were still confused, and her mood wavered between confidence, hope, and utter despair. But at least, since she had made a decision, there was plenty to do that would keep her busy during the long days that followed.

It was Renaldo, as conscientious as ever, who saw to business, spending long hours with their foreman and listening to his complaints—trying to bring some order to the erratically kept books.

"This place has possibilities—and with cattle fetching such high prices right now, you should be making a profit. But," and Renaldo had shrugged helplessly, "I have never seen such inefficiency! The fences have fallen down—all of the buildings need repair. Even this house—it must have been a fine place, when people lived in it. But now, as you have seen, it needs so much to be done to it. I'm afraid, Ginny, that you will need to go to the bank to draw out some money. And you'll have to hire workmen, and more cowboys." He gave her a half-humorous look. "You really cannot afford to have more of your cattle stolen!"

She didn't know, for a moment, whether she should laugh or cry. "Oh, Renaldo! Do you really think it was

Steve who was responsible for that whole herd being rustled? Colonel Belmont seems to think so."

"I've no doubt it was he," Renaldo said a trifle grimly. "He's very good at that kind of thing, if you'll recall! Ginny. . . ."

But her face had changed already, that strange, withdrawn expression that had become all too familiar of late coming over it.

Did she recall? She remembered far too much, it seemed, while Steve remembered nothing. Or did he? Was it all part of some cruel game he was playing? It was that thought which tortured her most. And the knowledge that Steve was somewhere within a few miles of her, and she hadn't seen him yet—didn't know how he would react to seeing her. She felt as if they had become complete strangers to each other again; as if he was a man she didn't know, and had never known. Thank God for Renaldo's comforting, sane presence! If he had not been here, she didn't know what she might have done, in spite of her brave resolutions earlier.

She went to the bank—the small one in Baroque. And she discussed guest lists with Persis Belmont, who threw herself into the whole scheme with enthusiasm. And there was Judge Benoit as well—belatedly and unwillingly remembering the advice that Jim Bishop had given her, Ginny made a point of discussing her plans with him as well, prettily confessing that she needed his advice, since she wanted everything to be just right.

"I want everyone to come. *Everyone.* Not just the important people, and the officers from the post, but the cowboys and the farmers and the enlisted men as well. As many as can be spared. You don't think I'm being foolish and whimsical, do you? I just want everyone to know me, and I want to know *them*. And I just knew you would understand!"

Nicholas Benoit paid another visit to his sister-in-law, catching her in an exceptionally bad mood.

"So she's passably pretty. And not a complete simpleton. Must I crawl behind her as everyone else seems to be doing? I won't do it, Nicky! Why should I let myself be patronized? And I thought you were just as anxious as I to be rid of her!"

"One thing you've never learned is patience, my dear

Toni! She's really not the kind of woman who'll be content to live here, shut away from everything she's been used to, for very long. I give her—oh, a month or so, before she becomes bored to distraction. And in the meantime, while this—*cousin* of hers is seeing to business matters, I do hope you'll keep your Indian on a leash. We can't afford any trouble while she's here."

"*She*! And what in hell is she, this—this paragon of all the virtues? A bitch, I've no doubt. Maybe she has some reason for wanting to hide out here—I'll bet you anything that's it! The man you talked about—he's her lover. They want to carry on their fornicating in private, I suppose. And then she puts on all these airs and graces—giving a party indeed! What does she think she's playing at, Lady Bountiful? Well, I'm not going. You hear that, Nicky? You can just go back and tell her I'm not coming."

Nick Benoit smiled, fastidiously dusting off his hat as he rose to his feet.

"Do you think Mrs. Morgan will miss you? You will probably miss a very interesting gathering, my sweet; but since you are afraid to face another woman who might prove competition for your charms—then there's nothing more to be said, is there?"

It didn't help Toni Lassiter's temper to find out that even her taciturn foreman planned to attend the party Mrs. Morgan had termed "a kind of fiesta." And when she learned that he was to escort Missie Carter, she flew at him—nails raking for his eyes. Blue eyes hard, feet astride, he seemed only to put his arm up, to ward her off, but Toni found herself sprawling on her back against the stair treads.

"Maybe you could pull that kind of stuff on Billy-Boy Dozier. But try it on me and I'll beat you before I ride out of here for good."

She was gasping with shock and rage, but the look in his eyes, coupled with the thinning of his lips as he gazed down at her, made Toni bite back the flood of vituperations that sprang to her lips.

She lay where she had fallen, the long skirt of her robe twisted halfway up her thighs, and began to whimper.

"Why are you always so cruel to me, Comanche? Don't you understand that it may all be a trap? Colonel Belmont will be there, with most of his soldiers, I'll bet. And you know he doesn't like you. What are you—stupid? And to go with that little swamp brat. . . !"

"Her Pa and her brothers will be along, too. And besides—it won't do for you to mingle publicly with your hired help, would it? If you had any sense, you'd go yourself—or with your brother-in-law. No telling what kind of useful information you might pick up."

"You bastard! And what's *your* reason for going?"

He grinned at her mirthlessly.

"Information. Finding out about the other side. And meeting Colonel Belmont face to face, maybe. Unofficially, he's made me target practice for his soldiers. Maybe he ought to see his quarry close up."

"You're a fool! I don't trust that woman—or that stuffy Colonel Belmont, either. I think it's a trap of some kind!"

"In that case, why not find out?"

She saw the devil-may-care lights dance in his eyes for an instant, before almost unnaturally long lashes hid them.

And this, Toni thought strangely, was one of the reasons for the peculiar affinity between them. They were both utterly reckless; completely unscrupulous. And because he was as hard and as cruel as she was, she wanted him.

Her mood suddenly changing, she twisted her body wantonly, so that her robe rode even higher.

"Well, don't turn to me for help if something goes wrong. I'll say I knew nothing—that I hired you because I needed a man in Billy-Boy's place. But he wasn't a real man—his gun was the only weapon he used passably well. Comanche. . . ." Her eyes became shiny, like the pink lips she moistened constantly, pointed tongue darting out to wet them. Soft lawn ripped, under her own tearing fingers, and she was all pink and white and silver. Her hips arched, and on her suddenly naked body each tiny silver-blonde hair seemed to catch the reflection of the oil lamp—lit earlier by her discreet servants.

She was a wanton bitch, crying out to be mounted. And because she was there, pointing it at him, he took her, wondering with a detached, somehow sickened part of his mind why he continued to have visions of green, cat-slanted eyes, and hair that felt soft and silky under his hands, even when it was all tangled.

There must have been a woman—somewhere, some time,

who had been important to him, to hover so frustratingly on the very edge of his memory. There were times, when he was relaxed and not consciously thinking of anything, when tiny things, like the sun on Missie's hair turning its fiery color into a paler copper-gold, would jolt him. And even Missie, as naive as she was, would begin to blush at moments like that, when his eyes narrowed at her, looking darker.

Was it possible that there had been a woman, once, whom he had not been able to detach himself from? It was this quality about the man she called Comanche that Toni Lassiter resented most, even while it made her want him even more. She was accustomed to men who crawled to her, begging for her favors. Men she could manipulate and use as she chose. But Comanche, whoever he was, was different. It was a change to feel used, as if she was nothing more than a cheap whore—in some perverse way, this feeling only made him even more exciting. As did the knowledge that he was a dangerous man, and more than half savage—for all that he surprised her by speaking like an educated man on occasion.

No, Toni thought, when she stretched like a cat afterwards; she wasn't through with him yet! And Nicky, with his dire warning and sour face, could go to hell! She'd find a way to get rid of Comanche when she was tired of him—or found someone else who appealed to her more.

Judge Benoit merely grunted sardonically when he received his sister-in-law's note the next morning. So she'd decided to accept Mrs. Morgan's invitation, after all, just as he'd guessed she woudl in the end. Trust little Toni's curiosity, and her scheming mind! It was only when he heard, from Matt Carter, that his niece was to be escorted by Toni's lover, that he began to frown. What was that old fool Joe thinking of? An innocent child like Missie, with no chance to meet decent young men closer to her own age—Joe should have let him send her to that Young Ladies Seminary as he'd wanted to. That's what Missie needed, the chance to learn to be a young lady. He'd have to ride out and talk to Joe again.

But in the end it was Ginny Morgan who forestalled his intentions. She had come to meet the stage in Baroque, she told him when she appeared in his office, sun-flushed and smiling and a trifle breathless because, she said, she'd

ridden all the way to the Carter place and back that same
morning.

"Missie told me who her guest is going to be—and since
I thought you'd probably worry, I thought I'd come over
and talk to you for a few minutes. If you have the time?"

"I'm honored that you've taken the trouble to visit me!"
Nick Benoit's manners were exaggeratedly courtly as he
tried to hide his curiosity. Mrs. Morgan intrigued him—
and in more ways than one. He sensed an underlying
passion in her that was borne out by her mouth and the
way she moved; and yet, she was always escorted by her
forbidding Spanish duena, or this so-called cousin of hers,
or by soldiers provided by Colonel Belmont. What had really brought a woman of her class, used to mixing in cosmopolitan society, to Baroque?

Ginny could almost read his thoughts, but she kept her
expression half questioning and half demure, as she accepted the chair he gallantly offered her.

"I don't know how to say this—after all, you're Missie's
uncle. But you see, I remember how it felt to be as young
as she is, and I feel it would be the very worst thing to try
and forbid her to bring along this—this fierce and mysterious man I've heard about as her guest. And I *did* tell her
she could ask whoever she pleased! You understand?" She
went on quickly, as if she was afraid of his reactions,
"And I did mean it when I said I wanted to meet everyone here. Both Renaldo and I are—well, frankly, curious
about this man who Colonel Belmont thinks is responsible
for stealing my cattle, as well as a great many other
things! I've asked Missie to come early—I like her, you
know, for she reminds me very much of myself when I
was her age. And I shall find a gown for her to wear. Perhaps, if she sees this man against a civilized background
she will realize how mistaken she is in her loyalty."

Even Judge Benoit, who prided himself upon his subtle
mind, could see how clever the plan was. Of course!
Hadn't he been telling himself earlier that his niece needed
to meet some decent young men, of the proper background and breeding? There were several unattached
young officers on Colonel Belmont's staff, and he had recognized, long ago, that Missie looked enough like her
mother to grow into a beauty some day.

Virginia Morgan, he decided, was an exceptionally astute and understanding young woman, besides being quite lovely herself. Her French background and upbringing no doubt. He found himself quite looking forward to the party she was giving, and not only because he knew he'd enjoy watching Toni's face when she first met the woman she had contemptuously labelled as being both horse-faced and puritanical.

"Ugh! He's such a slimy and hypocritical man!" Ginny said later to Renaldo. "He pretends that he is a gentleman, and a dandy, and yet I had the feeling, all the time I was talking to him, that his eyes were undressing me. And he's inquisitive, too—he tried to make his questions so casual and offhand, but I knew he was wondering about me. It's all I can manage to be nice to him."

She wondered, at the time, why a slight frown continued to knit Renaldo's forehead.

"And this Señorita Melissa—this young, innocent child. I hope, Genia, that you are thinking of her, too. What will happen to her when all this—this masquerade is over? What will her future be? I agree with this Judge Benoit, whom I do not like either, on one point at least. She deserves more than this! And I am also afraid that Steve, if he has no memory of the past—"

"You're afraid that he might have seduced her already?"

Ginny tried to keep her voice light, but it shook slightly, before she continued in a more confident tone. "Well, he hasn't done so. And you must not think that I have cultivated Missie merely to find out more about Steve. No—I really do like her. She's sweet, and she's honest, and I—oh, God! I almost wish that I was still as naive and full of romantic dreams as she is. I truly do not wish her to be hurt and disillusioned—you must believe that, Renaldo!"

He said heavily, with a bluntness that was unusual in him, "But you're as afraid as I am that Steve might not think the same way, aren't you?" And this time, she had no quick reply for him.

When Ginny had left to go upstairs to her room, pleading tiredness, Renaldo found himself restless—his nerves on edge.

Why must they tread so carefully, and so slowly? Such a ridiculous, unbelievable situation—and it was this Mr. Bishop, whose orders they were now committed to follow, who had created it in the first place.

Renaldo found himself concerned—not only for Ginny, and for Esteban, whom he had known and defended from childhood, but for this little Missie Carter as well. Little—and yet, by the standards he had been brought up with, she was a grown woman. Ready for marriage. But without the benefit of duennas, or a family who thought to protect her, she had obviously grown up to be innocent, and—yes, the word still applied—pure. Like the princess in the age-old folk-tale, Missie Carter was a sleeping beauty, waiting for the right man to awaken her to life and love. And his cousin was most definitely not the right man—look what he had done with Ginny herself! He had found himself on the verge of falling in love with Ginny once—he had even had vague dreams of "rescuing" her. But she hadn't wanted to be rescued, because in spite of everything, she was in love with Steve. And now, reminding him far too much of Ginny as she must have been once, there was Missie—how could they have transformed her lovely given name into such a diminutive? Melissa—it sounded almost Spanish, and it suited her.

Renaldo had met her, of course, and talked with her—and she had such potential, for all that she was shy and talked like the rest of her family. He had begun to teach her, half-jokingly, a few words of Spanish; and it had amazed him how eager she was to learn, and how quickly she learned—even the correct accent.

Renaldo, who had long preferred books to stupid, simpering women, had always maintained an old-fashioned, if somewhat cynical attitude towards the fairer sex. His first meeting with Ginny had altered his thinking somewhat, when he had learned that a woman could be intelligent, worldly-wise in some ways, and still remain a lady. Melissa Carter had proved to be something quite outside his experience, and now he actually found himself worrying about her.

Chapter Fifty

Missie was so excited by the time the morning of what she privately thought of as "the grand ball" arrived, that she was almost sick to her stomach—partly from anticipation and partly because she was scared. But the nice Mr. Ortega, and the prune-faced Spanish lady, drove over in one of Mrs. Morgan's smart buggies to get her; and by the time they had reached the Desmoulin's house, almost unrecognizable now that the workmen had finished painting and restoring its crumbling exterior, she was still wan-faced, but feeling less afraid.

Mr. Ortega—she *must* remember to call him "señor"—treated her just as if she was a grand lady, and when he made conversation he made no attempt to talk down to her, but waited seriously for Missie to express her views. And even the Spanish lady unbent enough to smile when she led her upstairs, murmuring that Genia had such excellent taste, and the gown she had chosen for Missie to wear was perfectly lovely, and entirely suitable for a young woman.

Missie, hearing herself called a woman for the first time, could only widen her eyes and blush. Mrs. Morgan had been so kind! And being here was all like a dream. Not even Matt's glum forebodings had been able to spoil her feeling of being like a Cinderella, about to be transformed into a beautiful princess. And of course Pa had been dear and wonderful, telling her firmly that she must remember who she was, and not let anything spoil her fairy tale evening for her.

The feeling Missie had of being part of some story she was imagining in her head grew even stronger when she first saw herself in the gown she was to wear.

"Do you mind that it's one of mine? I haven't worn it—I loved the design and the material, but once I tried it on it seemed a little too young for me. Do you believe in fate? Perhaps I only kept it because it was, in a way, meant to be worn by you."

Without giving Missie the chance to do anything more than gasp with wonder, Ginny turned her quickly around, removed the ring she wore on the ribbon, and clasped a string of lustrous pearls around her throat.

"Your ring will be safe, don't worry. My Tante Celine wouldn't let me wear anything but pearls to my first ball. And although I would have preferred emeralds, I discovered she was right. My cousin Pierre escorted me, I remember, and I had the most wonderful time of my whole life then."

More than ever, as she turned back to see her own reflection in the long triple mirror, Missie felt as if she were part of one of her own daydreams. She had been turned into a princess for the night—a beautiful fairy creature that even she could not recognize.

She had soaked for at least half an hour in a warm, perfumed tub, and after that there were large, fleecy towels to dry herself with. And the Spanish lady, whom Ginny called Tia Alfonsa, had helped arrange her hair—brushing it, after it was dry, until it shone like a dull flame, and then arranging it in a style that left curls cascading down to her shoulders.

Even her petticoats were silk, feeling strangely soft and slippery against her skin. And her gown was made of white brocade, with silver threads woven into the material, so that it shimmered each time she moved and the light caught it. It was cut lower in front than any dress Missie had ever possessed before—but not as low as Ginny Morgan's fire opal gown that set Tia Alfonsa sighing reminiscently.

"Ah—I remember such a dress! Esteban brought it for you from Mexico City, and you were married in it. Such a time you gave us that night! How can I ever forget? Poor Doña Maria was prostrated for days afterwards."

"But Missie doesn't want to hear about my dull past, I'm sure," Ginny said lightly, and Tia Alfonsa had pursed her lips together tightly as if she had said too much. Missie didn't really notice, because she was too busy staring at her own reflection in the glass.

The feeling of dreamlike unreality persisted, so that she

felt herself to be two separate persons; Missie-on-the-in-side, still the wide-eyed swamp brat; and Melissa-on-the-outside, who was a poised and lovely creature, not in the least little bit afraid.

"Will you help receive? I've still a few last-minute things to see to, and besides, I'm told the truly sophisti-cated hostess is *always* late to her own soirees!" Ginny Morgan's laugh told Missie that she was laughing at her-self—and then, seeing the way Mr. Ortega's eyes widened and lit up strangely while he watched her walk slowly and shyly down the stairs. . . . She felt she could face any-thing after that! For the very first time in her life, Missie had seen open admiration in a man's eyes—telling her she was beautiful; telling her she was a woman. How would Manolo see her when he came with her brothers? What would *his* look say?

And then, during the scary, exciting moments that fol-lowed, Missie forgot to wonder when her partner would arrive, and how he would be dressed, for she was far too busy.

With Renaldo Ortega's prompting, and his warm, reas-suring presence beside her, receiving the well-dressed guests was really not too difficult after all.

"I will introduce you as Ginny's houseguest. And then all you have to do is to stretch out your hand and smile as you tell them how pleased you are to meet them." He gave her hand, cold even through the white silk gloves, a small squeeze as he added in a low, rather hesitant voice, "I am sure that just as I am, all our guests will be struck dumb by your loveliness, Señorita Melissa."

She turned sparkling bright eyes up to his face, noticing, with a kind of surprise, that he was really quite a hand-some and distinguished looking man.

"Oh! But it is this lovely, lovely gown that changes me so much, of course! I could not recognize myself in the mirror, you know! Mrs. Morgan has been so kind—I only hope I will not disgrace her tonight!"

"I think you need not have any fear of that!" Renaldo said, more forcefully than he had intended. He found him-self thinking, as the first guests began to arrive, that he hoped Melissa would not be changed by all this—that she would not turn into a flirt, but retain her natural naivete and charm. "She's a little wood nymph!" he surprised him-

self thinking. "I must speak to Genia—Melissa must not
be spoiled or hurt in any way by this elegant masquerade.
And when I have the chance to speak to Esteban. . . ."

But would that chance ever come? Where was he? Unknowingly, Ginny echoed the thoughts of both Renaldo
and Missie, as she swept down the wide, curving staircase
some fifteen minutes later.

Now that the moment was near, she felt nervous—almost frightened, in spite of her brittle air of gaiety. If
seeing her did not jolt Steve into remembering—or if, for
some reason, he chose to pretend he did not—what then?
She had purposely ordered the gown she wore tonight—it
was an almost exact replica of the gown that Steve had
presented her with the night of their hurried, secret wedding. And she wore fire opals—glittering like multi-colored
flames in her ears, around her slender throat and wrists.

She must calm herself—be prepared for the very
worst—for anything! Her thoughts were feverish, even
while she smiled and smiled and murmured polite banalities.

When would he turn up? Would he come after all? She
clung to the thought that Missie's father and brothers had
not arrived yet either.

Toni Lassiter made a dramatically late entrance, on
Judge Benoit's arm. Her pale blond hair shone silvery under
the glittering chandeliers, her gown was of dull gold brocade, and brought out the color of her amber-gold eyes. Her
bared shoulders and arms gleamed with a pearly sheen,
and her pink lips, always shining moistly, curved upward
in a smile that was meant to be both mocking and challenging.

"I've heard so much about you from my dearest Nicky!
And goodness, what a marvelous job you've done on this
old, crumbling ruin of a house. Of course, it wasn't built
as strongly or designed as well as my late husband's home.
His father built it, you know, and when the river floods it
never reaches as far as the house. I do hope, for your
sake, that we don't have a disastrous flood like we did two
years ago. But then, you're not likely to *stay* here, are
you?"

"She's an un-subtle, overblown bitch!" Ginny thought
furiously. "How *could* Steve—even if he doesn't really
remember anything in the past!" She would dearly have

loved to tear out a handful of Toni Lassiter's silver blond hair, and to rip her gown, from its too-low décolletage, all the way to the waist; but instead she smiled sweetly, ignoring the Lassiter woman's provocative speech.

"And I'm so glad to meet you at last. You are exactly as I had imagined you would be, of course. And we must talk later. Judge Benoit, it's good to see you."

How could she do it? After what that nasty Toni said, how can she bear to be sweet to her? Missie wondered, and she was relieved that she was standing close to Renaldo Ortega. She could discern the unpleasant glitter in Toni's eyes, and the twist of her full lips, but she stiffened her back and inclined her head slightly as she had seen Ginny Morgan do.

"Why, Missie! I swear—I never would have recognized you without those grubby rags you seem to enjoy wearing! Are you playing at being Cinderella tonight, my love?"

Surprisingly, it was Nick Benoit who rescued Missie from Toni's venom.

"You look beautiful, Melissa. And just like your mother, at your age. You're going to turn the heads of all the young men here tonight, you know. Just be sure to save a dance for your uncle!" and he led Toni on, fingers tightening over her elbow, before she had a chance to make another catty remark. "Come. Let me get you a glass of punch, Toni darling. And do try to wipe that vicious look off your face; it doesn't quite match the role you were supposed to play this evening!"

It was, fortunately, a mild and balmy night, and already the three lighted courtyards were crowded with what Toni referred to contemptuously as "the hoi polloi." She had forbidden her cowboys to attend, but almost every other ranch in the vicinity had its representatives; not to mention the quiet Mexican homesteaders, who usually kept to themselves and referred to Toni Lassiter as their *patrona*.

It was another reason for Toni's barely-checked fury. "You see what I have been trying to tell you? She's far too nosy and interfering, that artificial bitch! She and that so-called cousin of hers have visited every single little adobe where those peons choose to live. Apparently, they speak the same language—can you imagine? And how does a Senator's daughter—her father a Virginian and her mother French—come to have a cousin who is Mexican? I

tell you, Nicky, you'd best look what's behind those expensive clothes she wears!" Toni gave a high-pitched angry
giggle. "Perhaps she was a whore when this husband of
hers picked her up! It wouldn't surprise me at all. And if
you're dazzled by her society airs, I am not! I won't have
her around here for much longer, I warn you!"

Surprisingly, Toni was not the only one worried about
the ranch hands and Mexicans. Persis Belmont stopped to
whisper to her hostess that her husband was all on edge—
afraid that some kind of fight might break out.

"There's not much love between our men and the locals,
you know! Some of these Texas cowboys have never forgotten the war. They don't like us, and they don't like
those poor, miserable Mexicans. Ginny, are you sure. . . ?"

"My men have been warned. And the Mexicans aren't
likely to start anything. I think everyone is too cautious to
make trouble—at least, not tonight. Please don't worry,
Persis. Nothing will happen!"

"Well, I'm sure I hope not . . . but I don't trust the
smirk on that Lassiter woman's face, if you want to know
the truth!" Persis Belmont hesitated, and then laid her
hand on Ginny's arm, lowering her voice slightly so that
Missie, standing close by with Señor Ortega, would not
hear. "And I hope that—that blue-eyed *Indian* decides to
stay away tonight, after all! I know the child will be disappointed, but she's far too sweet and ingenuous to be allowed to associate with a man like that. I do hate to keep
warning you of so many things, Ginny, but you must have
heard enough to know that he's a trouble-maker! Things
were comparatively peaceful around here until he turned
up, from nowhere—just as if he had been the devil himself, sent to stir everything up! I *do* hope . . . oh!"

Ginny had been listening to her friend's dire warnings
with a fixed, polite smile on her face, but now, following
the direction of Persis's eyes, she could not control the
sudden draining of color from her face.

He was here! And all at once, her heart was pounding
so loud she thought that Persis must surely hear it, and
she felt sucked back in time to all the nights when she had
waited for Steve to come to her—not knowing how he
would react, or what he might do to her. . . .

"But I can't very well go up to him and put a knife at
his throat in order to make him notice me," she thought

stupidly, and she felt angry and frightened and uncertain of herself, all at the same time—not sure whether she was ready for the moment when he would first look at her or not.

It was perhaps fortunate that Mrs. Belmont was far too taken aback herself to notice her friend's agitation.

Her eyebrows lifted, and she whispered in amazed tones:

"But I cannot believe it is the same man! Why, he's actually shaved and cut his hair—it was down to his shoulders, and he used to wear a headband, just like an Indian, only it was to shock us all, I think! And I've never seen him wearing anything but shabby, dirty buckskins before—I wonder what kind of mischief he's up to?"

It seemed as if a sudden, almost imperceptible hush had fallen when the five men walked into the large reception room whose doors had been left hospitably open: Joe Carter, looking uncomfortable and a trifle self-conscious in his store-bought clothes, was trailed by his three sons, and the tall, hard-faced man known as Manolo carried off the black and silver Mexican charro suit he wore with an almost insolent assurance. The short jacket and black pants, with silver thread ornamenting the sides, fit him closely; his white shirt was ruffled down the front.

Literally rooted to where she stood, Ginny heard the sudden, nervous burst of talk that arose too quickly after that first startled pause. And over it, Missie's glad cry.

"Oh! You came! You're here at last!" Missie cried, pointed face eager and suddenly lighted up—heedless of showing her feelings in front of the whole gathering present.

"So, she has not learned guile yet, or to cover her emotions up under an indifferent attitude or a smile," Renaldo thought, and wondered why there was suddenly a bitter taste in his throat.

A few minutes earlier, Missie had been approached by a group of eager, admiring young officers, each begging for the honor of a dance. But now, as she sped across the room, she noticed none of them—nor the shocked, disapproving looks that were sent in her direction.

She could only see how magnificent Manolo looked, like a Spanish Don—and all for her, because he wouldn't let her be shamed in front of all these people. And the dark-

ening blueness of his eyes as he narrowed them slowly at
her, one eyebrow slanting upward.

"Missie . . . you look like a princess tonight. Far too fine
for any of us commoners here."

Belatedly, she remembered to slow her steps down
slightly at the very last minute, but her voice sounded
breathless.

"Do you really think so? Do you like the way I look?
Pa—do you think I'm beautiful? Like Mama?"

"You're lovely, p'tite!" Joe Carter's voice was husky
with emotion, and her brothers gaped, although when
Matt started to scowl, Missie knew he was thinking angrily that she should not have let herself become obligated
to some strange, outsider woman. But tonight, she
wouldn't let herself worry about anything, and especially
when Manolo was looking at her as if she was a woman at
last, his mouth quirking at one corner in a smile that was
just for her.

"Your pa's right, princess. You're the prettiest young
lady in the room. Have you promised all your dances yet,
or did you remember to save one or two for me?"

"But I haven't promised a single one yet! That is, execpt
to Señor Ortega . . . and that was because I helped him receive, while Mrs. Morgan—she asked me to call her
Ginny!—while she was finishing getting dressed. He asked
me to open the dancing with him, and oh, he's been so
kind; he's her cousin, you know! Come meet her. She's
nice, she really is, and she's not—"

"Seem's like our little sister's let all these fancy clothes
and fancy talk she's been hearin' go to her head," Matt
growled, but he fell sullenly silent when his father gave
him a forbidding look.

"She has been kind to Missie, and we are her guests
tonight. You will remember that, my son."

"She's beautiful, and she's a real lady, too—she doesn't
smile with her lips and kill you with her eyes like Toni
does!"

Matt looked furious, but Manolo laughed, the thin scar
on his cheek melting into the deep groove that always appeared there when he smiled.

"You look like a little, spitting cat when you're mad,
and it doesn't go with that gown, and the pearls." And

now, seeing her dismayed look, he smiled a trifle crookedly. "Come. Why don't you introduce us to your new friends?"

Chapter Fifty-one

"So—it looks as if your Indian has managed to transform himself into a Spanish gentleman tonight," Nick Benoit said softly, although a puzzled note underlay his sarcastic words. "Perhaps I really should make more of an effort to find out who he is, and how he got here!"

"I thought you'd already been trying," Toni Lassiter snapped, her amber eyes as hard as polished stones. "And I told you he was an educated man—only you didn't want to listen, did you?"

"I suppose he's got himself up for my niece's benefit," Benoit murmured maliciously. "You must admit, my pet, that she is quite transformed this evening! I wonder why I hadn't realized before that little Missie is turning into quite a beauty. And it certainly seems as if she's managed to tame the beast, doesn't it?"

"Why don't you shut up?" Toni snarled viciously, although her pink lips continued to wear a fixed smile. "That dirty little swamp brat—that *child*! Do you think he bothered to dress for *her*? You'll see, Nicky darling— Comanche knows what he's doing. And your stupid little niece doesn't, for all her borrowed fine feathers!"

Joe Carter, his shoulders held unusually straight, and his sons, looking equally stiff and ill at ease, were following Missie and Manolo across the room to the receiving line. Only Missie, clinging proudly to the arm of her tall escort, and the man himself, seemed not to notice the sudden constraint that had seized everyone there.

Colonel Belmont inclined his head stiffly, catching Manolo's sardonic glance. "Colonel. . . ?" The slight nod of his head was an insult in itself, and the Colonel found himself holding back his fury with an effort. By God, this was almost too much to tolerate! Judge Benoit was right, and Persis was right. The man was insolent, and far too sure of himself, considering his rather ambiguous position here! Something had to be done about him. . . .

Ginny's confused thoughts pushed against each other, even while her spine stiffened. She was only vaguely aware that Renaldo had appeared from somewhere to stand beside her, and his presence strengthened her. Steve had still not looked directly at her!

In the end, the moment she had been both anticipating and dreading passed by so quickly and so casually that seconds later she could not quite believe it had happened at all.

Only Missie noticed the sudden tautness of Manolo's arm under her fingers, but she was too excited and too tense herself to wonder. They had walked past her Uncle Nick's tight, somehow questioning smile, and Toni's daggerlike look. And when she met Señor Ortega's steady eyes she suddenly felt more sure of herself. The beautiful white and silver gown, with its silk petticoats underneath, swished entrancingly every time she took a step, reminding her that tonight she was pretty—tonight she was a woman, and a lady. And hadn't even Manolo said she looked like a princess? Her daydream was real—it was all happening!

Mrs. Morgan saved her the trouble of stumbling over introductions. Missie thought she had never seen her new friend's eyes look so bright, nor her face so flushed, as she said lightly: "And this must be your guest, Missie. For shame, sir. Did you have to arrive so late?"

Their hands touched. Their eyes met. And—nothing! Only a slight narrowing of Steve's eyes, and the almost imperceptible tautening of the muscles in his face as Missie's breathless young voice, making the formal introduction, filled the sudden, small silence that dropped between them like a sharp pebble.

Had that really been her voice, sounding so insouciant? Why did he make her feel as if she were meeting a stranger for the first time? So much between them, so many memories of passion and violence and love. And now he was back to calling her "ma'am" again, in that drawling, half-sarcastic tone she had always detested!

"A pleasure meeting you, ma'am. And my thanks for the kind invitation."

How dared he?

She answered him in Spanish, deliberately challenging him.

"But the pleasure is mine, señor, for I have heard so much about you. My house is yours—for tonight."

"I wonder what you have heard, señora? I am surprised that a man as insignificant as I am should have come to your attention."

It was Renaldo, fearing some kind of explosion of wrath on Ginny's part, who interposed quickly.

"My cousin and I have been anxious to meet all our neighbors, of course. Ah, Mr. Carter—it is good to see you again. And your sons. You have arrived just in time for the dancing, but first—surely you must all be thirsty? We have set up a buffet for food and drink at the far corner of the room, and if you will forgive the informality."

And then they were walking away, with Missie still clinging ingenuously to Steve's arm. And, gritting her teeth, Ginny watched Steve stop to say something to Toni Lassiter, who, with her bitchy, insincere smile, actually had the gall to put her hand up to touch his clean-shaven face teasingly.

"Well—and what is your impression of our local bad man?"

It was fortunate that Persis Belmont's voice interrupted Ginny's thoughts just then. She had been on the verge of following Steve, bent on vengeance. But now, with an effort, she recollected herself, forcing a smile.

"It's too soon to form an impression, of course. But I think I don't like him!"

"Well, I'm not surprised. Did you notice the way that woman acted? She's such an obvious slut, and believe me, I do not usually use that word. Poor Judge Benoit, I could see how little he liked having to stand by while she. . . . He doesn't trust that man either. And he's worried about his little niece. He was telling Rodney, just yesterday. . . ."

Ginny made an effort to compose her face and to control her inner turmoil as she listened to what Persis had to say. It took every ounce of will power she possessed to stand there attentively when, across the room, Renaldo claimed Missie for a dance, and Toni Lassiter shamelessly and boldly left her own escort to walk up to Steve and put her hand on his shoulder. Shrugging, he put his glass down—and at that moment Ginny herself was claimed for a dance by Nicholas Benoit, his manner as suave as usual.

Soon, the space that had been cleared for dancing was crowded with whirling couples, as the hired musicians played vigorously.

Ginny couldn't remember afterwards how she managed to smile, and to answer Nicholas Benoit's compliments and half-veiled questions. One part of her mind was un-willingly occupied with Steve—dancing far too closely with Toni Lassiter, that same mocking, half-sarcastic smile she remembered all too well twisting his lips. And it was clear that Nick Benoit didn't care for the state of affairs any more than she did.

"I feel that I must apologize. Sometimes my sister-in-law delights in shocking people."

"And I'm sure *he* does too."

Ginny caught her partner's sudden, sharp look and gave a soft, deprecating laugh.

"Oh, it's only female intuition, I suppose. I should not have said that."

"But I'm glad you did. I hope that you will always feel free to say whatever you think with me." Ginny felt the slightest squeeze of Benoit's fingers over her own. He went on thoughtfully, "I'm glad you could see through him. I had been wondering, when I saw the startling transforma-tion in his usual appearance, exactly what his game is this time. It's almost as if he was playing some kind of joke on all of us here, and I must confess that I cannot trust his motives. A man who has nothing to lose but his life can be extremely dangerous!"

Ginny gave a slight, exaggerated shudder, green eyes widening.

"Oh, but I hope not! Why should he prove dangerous to me—to us? After all, neither my cousin nor I are mixed up in any local feuds, and I see no reason why we cannot all live together in peace."

"But I am afraid that there are some people who do not think that way," Benoit said grimly. "And although your intentions are laudable, I feel it is my duty to warn you to use caution."

Caution! It seemed to Ginny that for almost all of her

life people had been warning her not to be so impetuous—to be careful—to be cautious. And yet, here she was,
playing a silly part in an equally ridiculous drama. She
had learned to act, it was true, but she had never learned
to be circumspect.

She found her patience and her self-control sorely tried
while she was forced to watch her husband dance with
Toni—forced to pretend that he was a stranger to her.
And she wondered what Steve was thinking. . . .

Stormy green eyes, strangely slanted at the corners.
Pale copper hair, swept high on her head, to trail in
ringlets down her back. Her coloring was similar to Missie's, and yet, while the resemblance stopped there, there
remained a nagging, frustrating sense of familiarity. Steve
sensed, without knowing how, the way her hair would feel
to the touch—slipping as heavy as silk beneath his fingers.
And without having kissed her, or wanting to, he knew
how soft her lips would be as they parted under his—
yielding the sweetness of her mouth. Virginia Morgan—
Ginny. There was a tautening of his muscles when he repeated her name in his mind, remembering the defiant lift
of her chin.

As if she had sensed the withdrawal of his mind, Toni's
fingernails had dug into his shoulder.

"What did she say to you? That patronizing bitch—I
hate her! And I don't care how many people she has
fooled, including poor Nicky. I don't trust her. Comanche!
Are you listening to me? She's up to something—I can
sense it. Why else would she try so hard to ingratiate herself with everyone here? All the fuss she's made over Missie—why should she interest herself in the little swamp
brat? I think she wants something—and that's why she's
here. Look at the way she's been stirring things up—
asking those peons to a fiesta, just as if they were . . . as if
they were people who *counted.*"

Suddenly, he wanted to slap Toni's pouting, sensual
face, right across that full, pink-lipped mouth that knew
everything there was to know about arousing a man. He
made a disgusted exclamation, looking down at her with
one eyebrow slightly lifted.

"Messalina, you're just jealous—admit it!"

"Jealous of *her*? That pasty-faced, milk-mouthed sly
creature? Just because she's got enough money to buy her-

self clothes and jewels, she contrives to dazzle all those stupid fools—but you're not taken in by her, are you Comanche? Why, if I was as rich as she is I'd make myself the queen of this whole state! And I'll do it, yet, and you're going to help me, aren't you Comanche? You're the only man I've known who's hard enough and unscrupulous enough, and you do see now, don't you, that we have to get rid of her?"

"You're crazy," he said flatly, but his eyes were wary as they met her narrowed, excitement-sheened amber gaze.

"Oh, no I'm not! That woman is up to something—did you know that her father is very influential in Washington? Trust Nicky to know all that! Perhaps he sent her, for some reason of his own—you know how many government men we've had nosing around here? Maybe that's what she's come for. To find out as much as she can—to destroy everything I've been building up, ever since that silly war's been over. Why should she become so friendly with those dumb Mexican peasants? She even speaks their language—next thing, she'll be putting ideas in their heads about the land I let them file on; telling them of their *rights.* And look at her now—talking so softly to Colonel Belmont. What do you think they're talking about? You know the Colonel doesn't like you, Comanche. He'd have you arrested if he could. Maybe that's what they're planning at right this moment!"

Manolo frowned blackly. Toni loved to exaggerate, but in this case some of her furious diatribe made sense.

He heard Toni giggle softly. "You see? You do see it, too, don't you? Because you're like me, lover; you're as evil as I am and just as unscrupulous, and that's why we're together." She added slyly, "And aren't you worried about your little Missie-girl? Did you know how much she's been seeing of that cousin, that Señor Ortega? Why should that Morgan bitch dress Missie up like a doll? It's either information they want from her, or Renaldo Ortega will seduce her before you do, Comanche!"

"One of these days, Messalina, I'm going to take real pleasure in breaking your white neck between my hands." He made it a promise, but she only smiled up at the barely-concealed fury in his eyes.

"And one of these days maybe I'll get to you first. But

before then, we've both got uses for each other, don't we, my darling savage?"

Deliberately, without answering her, he guided her over to where Misssie stood, looking a trifle lost and wistful while she pretended to listen to something a young Army Lieutenant was telling her. Missie's whole face lighted up when she saw Manolo—as usual, she was incapable of hiding her feelings. That stupid little imbecile, Toni thought viciously, even while she smiled her sweetest smile at the young man, whose face promptly took on a stunned, bemused expression.

Before Manolo could suggest that they change partners, Toni herself suggested it, flashing him a malicious, upward look. Lieutenant Armitage could not believe his good fortune. Wait until his brother officers saw him, dancing with Mrs. Lassiter herself!

But as for Missie, even Toni's sneering look could not spoil the sheer ecstasy of the moment. Manolo was holding her in his arms, and she discovered without surprise that he danced with the same catlike grace with which he walked—leading her so cleverly that she found herself waltzing as if she had always done so.

"I've missed you, princess. Tired of dancing yet?"

Her voice was breathless. "Never! I'll never grow tired of dancing—I think I could dance all night!"

Dancing with Missie was like breathing clean air. He put Toni out of his mind with a mental shrug of distaste. And the copper-haired woman who had moved him so strangely and unwillingly. She reminded him of someone he must have known once. A not very pleasant memory, perhaps—that could account for the indefinable feeling of antagonism he had sensed when he had been presented to her. Nick Benoit had told Toni she was a clever woman—well, there was time enough to find out more about her later. Tonight was Missie's, and nothing must spoil it.

He said teasingly: "How many partners do you have lined up tonight? Maybe I shouldn't have stolen you from that handsome young lieutenant."

"But he was rather silly, you know! And so young! Besides, when he saw Toni he forgot all about me, and I'm just as glad—I was waiting for you."

"You're going to have to learn to hide your feelings, little girl."

She wondered why his voice suddenly sounded so harsh.

"But why should I? And I'm *not* a little girl! I'm seventeen, and my mama was already a married woman at my age. When will you stop treating me like a—a child? I'm a *woman*!"

She caught his lifted eyebrows and half-mocking smile, and sheer, frustrated rage made her suddenly melt her body against his, as she had seen Toni do. She'd make him notice her! She wasn't a child, and none of the other gentlemen here had treated her as if she was!

"Goddammit, Missie! Are you flirting with me?" Manolo's voice was grim, but he made no effort to hold her away, and Missie felt a rush of exultation sweep through her.

"Yes, I am!" she said defiantly. "Isn't that what a young woman is supposed to do? How do *you* act when a woman flirts with you?"

"Depends on the woman, and just what she's offering." His voice started out being hard, and then suddenly became light. "But if it's a pretty young thing like you, princess"—he bent his head then, and whispered in her ear— "I hold her closer, like this, and after a while I ask her if she'd care to go outside for a breath of fresh air."

"And then—if she does?" She sounded breathless—eyes like stars.

"Nice young women blush, and look away in embarrassment. And they whisper that they'd better not—people might think the wrong thing."

"But—but if it was *me*, and *you* wanted me to go outside, I wouldn't care what anyone thought! I don't think I like flirting, if it means pretending and saying a lot of things you don't mean. I want you to kiss me—to be the first one."

"My God, princess!" He was angry enough to want to shake her. What kind of ideas had this Morgan woman been putting into her head? And that cousin of hers, who'd claimed the first dance with Missie. One part of his mind thought wryly that he was beginning to understand how a father felt, and the other part—to cover his slowly growing dark rage he said sarcastically: "Do you have someone lined up for the second time? And the time after that? There are some men who think that a kiss promises them more—and that's why in Spain and Mexico curious little girls like you have a stern old duenna to look after them."

"Oh!" Tears of rage and frustration filled Missie's eyes. How dare he keep treating her like a baby—acting as if he was her father? She started to pull away from him, forgetting all the other dancing couples who kept eyeing them curiously. "But I'm *not* a little girl—do you hear me? And if you keep acting like I am, then I—I'll show you! And if Señor Ortega wants to kiss me, I'm going to let him, so there! He's much nicer than you are, and he doesn't flirt with every woman in sight either, and he—he treats me as if I was a grown lady, he doesn't just pretend and tease like you do!"

"Missie!" He spoke through gritted teeth, the harshness of his voice warning her, but she was too overwrought to care.

"Let me go! I don't think I want to dance with you any longer!" She was afraid that the tears might spill over, disgracing her. But suddenly Manolo's arm was like steel around her waist, and he squeezed her fingers so cruelly that she gave a little gasp of pain.

"Has anyone told you you're turning into a little spoiled brat? Now you quit struggling like a wildcat, and try to pretend you *are* a lady after all until I take you back to your Señor Ortega."

"I think I hate you!"

He rewarded her outburst with a hatefully sarcastic twist of his lips.

"Seems to me I've heard that said quite frequently before, you red-headed spitfire."

Missie, deposited without a word before a puzzled-looking Señor Ortega, felt sick inside as Manolo turned on his heel and stalked away. No doubt he was going after Toni, who was by no means an inexperienced little girl—what had he called her? A spoiled brat. . . . Oh, and now she'd lost him forever, because she had a temper and wasn't at all good at pretending.

There was a lump in her throat so big she felt she'd choke if she tried to swallow, and now, all she longed to do was to find Pa and tell him she wanted to go back home.

But instead, she found herself taken upstairs, with the Señora Armijo fussing over her, and Ginny, her new friend, telling her sternly that part of growing up to be a woman meant pretending—just a little bit, when it was necessary.

"Men are strange creatures, as you'll learn someday. They talk about honesty, but if a woman displays her feelings too openly, it makes them shy away. They say they hate pretense, but they expect a woman to blow hot and cold. It adds to the excitement of the chase, I suppose!"

In spite of her own misery, Missie wondered why Ginny's voice suddenly sounded so bitter. For the first time, she found herself thinking that perhaps her lovely, sophisticated friend, who seemed to have everything she wanted, wasn't really happy after all. Perhaps she missed her husband. . . .

Missie went back downstairs with the slightest touch of color glowing in her cheeks and lips—her head held high. No, she wouldn't run away, after all. That was what a child would do. She was going to dance, and flirt, and have fun—like a woman.

She had no lack of partners. Even Colonel Belmont begged for the honor of a dance, making her feel important. But most of all, when she wasn't wondering where Manolo had gone, and twisting her head to try to find him in the crowd, she enjoyed dancing with Renaldo Ortega, who neither talked down to her, nor murmured silly, meaningless compliments in her ear. He wasn't ashamed to admit he liked reading poetry, and had even written some himself. He'd travelled all over the world, and must have met all kinds of women, but yet he seemed to like *her*. Missie had the feeling that he was the kind of man who was honest and kind—and that there was no dark, violent side to his nature.

After a while she felt as if she had known him for a long time, and she relaxed enough to laugh and chatter with him while they danced, instead of concentrating on how she moved her feet.

"But why haven't you married?" she was bold enough to ask him, feeling the first glass of champagne she had ever drunk make her brave.

Instead of growing stiff and angry, he smiled at her a trifle pensively, and she was surprised to find how a smile made his whole face look younger and more carefree. He was really a very handsome man, Missie discovered, her eyes widening with the discovery. And he was tall, too. Almost as tall as Manolo.

"I suppose I should not have asked such a personal question," she said quickly and contritely, before he could answer her, but he shook his head, still smiling slightly.

"You can ask me anything you wish, Miss Melissa. I was merely wondering myself why I have not married—in spite of all my mother's efforts at match-making! I suppose it is because I am old-fashioned, and enough of a romantic, to wait for the right woman—one who is honest, and intelligent and spirited, and who will be a friend and companion, as well as a wife. Do you think I expect too much?"

Missie shook her head fiercely.

"Oh, no! I think it is wonderful that you are strong enough and patient enough to wait for just the right person. I always used to think that—" she hesitated, looking up at him, and then seeing that his face was serious and he listened attentively, as if he really cared what she had been about to say, she blurted out, "I suppose that is why my brothers and—and Manolo, keep telling me I am still a child. But I used to think that when the right man came, it would be—like lightning, striking us both. Like the pirate Renate used to tell me about. I'd know, and he'd know, and—but it isn't really like that, is it?" Her voice was desolate, and shook slightly, and for an instant Renaldo could almost have killed Steve. But he pushed that thought away as he looked steadily into Missie's eyes and gave her the truth.

"No—I don't think it is like that. Not for most people, anyhow. I have always thought that love is a strong, tall tree, that grows slowly. It begins with liking, and friendship, and finding things in common. Lightning is fierce and wild, and the thunder that follows it makes a loud, awesome noise. But it is gone as quickly as it comes—like a flash flood, that leaves destruction in its wake." He gave a deprecating shrug. "I suppose that is the hidden poet in me, always painting pictures! But I think that you have an understanding of what I mean."

Missie nodded, too full of feeling for words. How was it that he understood so well? She thought about Manolo,

and a tiny shiver went through her. He was like wild lightning, slashing across a storm-dark sky. Violent, savage,
bright enough to blind her to everything else. Even now,
didn't she secretly want to be caught up in the unfamiliar, frightening flood of her own emotions, and carried
away before she had time to think? But then—what would
be left of her afterwards? None of the books she had read
ever told what happened to the girl who was carried off
by the pirate chieftain who ravished her. Pirates were usually caught and hanged, or died as violently as they lived.
What came after the flash flood?

Chapter Fifty-two

The loud, gay music of Mexico assaulted her senses as
she stood at the door of the ballroom, feeling the cool
night air. The torches she had ordered lit and placed along
the walls cast their cheerful orange light and added sufficient warmth to prevent chill, as did the quantities of
tequila and pulque and red wine, for those with more dis-
cerning tastes. No subdued decorousness here. There was
laughter and noise and open enjoyment of a fiesta.
Tonight, even the sternest fathers smiled indulgently when
their pretty daughters danced with the Tejanos who had
wandered out here, attracted by the music. As long as the
young people stayed within the circle cast by the flickering
lights, what did it matter? A fiesta was a happy, festive
occasion, and the liquor and food were plentiful—not a
man but did not fill his plate several times, piling steaming
hot tortillas in stacks beside chili that burned the roof of
the mouth, just as it should, big chunks of good fresh meat
adding flavor to the beans.

A fire had been lit in the center of the brick courtyard.
And as if to add to the medieval atmosphere, a whole calf
turned slowly on an enormous spit, adding its delicious
odors to the night air.

"It's much more fun out here," Matt Carter said. "Seems more natural, somehow. Kept getting the feeling I was being smothered inside, with all those snooty people, and the women starin' like we was some kind of freaks who belonged out here in the first place." He added, with a sly, sidewise look, "How come you aint' in there with the rest? Missie find that Señor Ortega more to her likin' since she's started to mix with the fine folk?"

It was as if Manolo was oblivious to his barbs, although he'd been in an ugly temper when he first came out here; and even Matt had been a trifle dubious about approaching him in the beginning.

Manolo had a drink halfway to his mouth, and he drained it, before he drawled wickedly: "Talking of fine folk, there's one of them—and a mighty pretty, fancy piece too. Why don't you ask our hostess to dance, Matt? Seems to me, it would only be the polite thing to do—especially considering the interest she and her cousin have taken in your little sister."

Matt Carter squinted his eyes to look across the fire, and saw Ginny, her hair turned bronze by the leaping, flickering flame, her gown sparkling as each tiny, cunningly woven thread caught the light, turning it into a jewel to frame her.

He didn't know if he liked her or not—and from what Toni had said, she wasn't to be trusted. But damn, she was a lovely woman!

"You think she'll know how to dance a fandango? Or the Jarabe?"

"Maybe she came out here to learn. Maybe she'd like to be taught. Or do women of her kind scare you off?"

If Manolo was deliberately baiting him, Matt would get him for it later. But he was looking at the woman, and he kept thinking about what Toni had said, and the way Toni was acting recently, and he thought, "Why the hell not?" Besides, the way Manolo kept needling him, it had sounded like a kind of challenge.

Ginny stepped down the two shallow steps into the courtyard, lifting her skirts with one hand. She paused in the comparative darkness, glancing about her hesitantly. Her feelings, as well as she had managed to hide them, remained a mixed, stormy welter of varying emotions, with a growing frustration overriding everything else.

Where was he? And was she really ready to face him? What would she say. She felt confused and uncertain—as if she was preparing for a confrontation with an antagonistic stranger. And then, before she had time to think any further, a tall heavy-shouldered young man appeared in front of her. Missie's brother Matt.

"Care to try this dance with me, ma'am? The steps ain't too hard to follow."

The musicians were playing the traditional Jarabe Tapatio, and already, in spite of herself, Ginny's feet were tapping to the rhythm. Oh yes, Renaldo had been right. She should never have come out here, for the music made her forget herself, taking her too far back in time.

She put her arms up without hesitation, feeling Matt Carter's muscles harden under the light touch of her fingers.

"I have lived in Mexico. I do not think I have forgotten their dances."

And suddenly, fine gown and all, she was dancing with Matt, and they had joined the circle of dancers. She noted their surprised looks at first, but soon forgot everything but the dance itself.

And now the musicians played El Chinaco—the song of the Juarista guerrilleros, and after that, La Malaguena. Matt Carter, his face surprised, could not keep up with her, and she moved from one partner to another, in a widening circle of dancers who clapped and cried "ole," until suddenly she was dancing with a slim Mexican youth whose black eyes gleamed in the firelight, and whose body was as supple as hers.

He had forgotten who she was, and she had forgotten too, as she let the music move her. The rhythms changed from fast to slow and back again, and they danced face to face, alternately inviting and rejecting.

"Jesus Christ! She dances like one of them. And I was going to teach her the steps!" Matt Carter sounded as if he was still out of breath. "You see that? You got any more smart ideas?" he said to Manolo.

"Yes. I'm going to dance with her myself."

The musicians played tirelessly, as if they had been inspired, and it was somehow without surprise that Ginny suddenly found herself dancing with Steve. So he had been here all along! And what now, that she had found him?

The black-haired, black-eyed Mexican boy was dancing with a girl as young as himself now, but woman-like, Ginny was conscious of the hot fire of his eyes upon her. Was aware, without looking; for it was Steve's shadowed face that she consciously watched. And almost without volition, she did as she had done on their wedding night, when she had first danced to these fiery rhythms. Without smiling, not taking her eyes from his, she began taking the pins from her hair, letting them drop carelessly to the ground as she continued to dance.

In the firelight his blue eyes darkened until they looked almost black, and he was suddenly, vividly conscious of her, both of them knowing it. The last hairpin dropped, and she shook her hair free, sending it tumbling about her shoulders and down her back like a rivulet of copper. And the nagging familiarity ate into his temples, making him frown at her angrily.

She danced with the passionate abandon of a Mexican gypsy. With the half-smiling, taunting movements of a tease. And he wondered why he wanted to strangle her, even while he wanted her.

He said abruptly, deliberately choosing the Mexican dialect instead of the more formal Spanish: "Where did you learn to dance this way? You must forgive me if I find it rather unusual in a woman of your kind."

Her eyes began to sparkle angrily as she threw her head back, lifting the hair off the back of her neck in an age-old gesture of coquetry.

"And what is my kind of woman? How would you know? I learned to dance in Mexico—and where did you learn your manners, señor?"

"I guess I never learned any. Which makes my next question easier. What kind of little game are you playing?"

"You disappoint me. Why ask such a pointless question? I would have thought a man of your type would want to find out for himself."

"A man of my type finds that kind of statement an invitation. Is that what you meant it to be, Ginny?"

Her name came far too easily to his tongue, and when her face whitened, whether from anger or from shock, he couldn't be certain, his fingers closed over her wrist, tightening cruelly when she would have protested.

The music seemed to have become louder, closing the gap of their sudden disappearance. The Mexicans deliberately chose to look the other way, not wanting to cause embarrassment, nor to be involved in the trouble that might follow.

But Matt Carter, frowning with a mixture of malice and envy, saw how Manolo pushed the woman up against the far wall of the courtyard, where the light barely reached, crushing her dress while he kissed her as if she had been one of the Mexican girls—or a cheap whore. And he didn't notice that she fought what was happening either.

So that's the kind of woman she was—a bitch in heat, just like Toni had said. Matt grinned unpleasantly to himself. Maybe it would change the way Missie'd been acting recently to find out that her fine new friend wasn't as pure and prissy as she pretended to be. She had come out here among the common folk looking for something, hadn't she? He was sorry that he hadn't been the one. . . .

It took Ginny some time to realize that Steve wasn't kissing *her*—not knowingly. His mouth was a bruising punishment over hers—even the way he wrapped his fingers in her hair to keep her head still was brutal. He kissed her as he had the very first time, when he'd thought she was the prostitute he'd hired for the night—He kissed her like all the other times when his kisses had been meant only to silence her and force her into subjugation. He kissed her without knowing who she was, and it was only when that realization was forced upon her, taken together with the casual, almost insulting way one hand cupped her breast, that she began to struggle against him fiercely.

"Oh—no! Stop!"

His lips moved slowly down the side of her neck, pausing at the tiny indentation where neck and shoulder met. Oh, God! He was Steve, and not Steve—and yet, by pure instinct perhaps, he remembered all the devilishly subtle ways of exciting her to the point of mindlessness. Next, he would be kissing her breasts—tearing aside the expensive material of her gown if it got in his way, and then—no wonder Mr. Bishop, and even Renaldo had looked at her so dubiously from time to time. Because her biggest danger was from Steve himself, and the self-betrayal he might force her into.

If her voice shook treacherously, she hoped he would think it was with anger.

"Will you stop this minute? A stolen kiss is one thing, sir, but I have always found being—being *mauled* about in dark corners quite repulsive. I do hope this is not how you treat every woman you dance with!"

When he put his hand up, she thought he was going to strike her, and she flinched quite instinctively, hearing him laugh, softly and harshly. His finger traced the slight upward slant of her eyes; lightly and almost contemptuously.

"No, I don't drag every woman I dance with into a dark corner and—maul her. Only the ones who seem to be asking for it. Women with slanty green eyes who let their hair down while they dance and promise a lot of things with their bodies. But I suppose with you, ma'am, it's all promise and teasing. Why did you come out here? It become too tame for you inside?"

Ginny forced herself to look up at his dark, unreadable face, wondering if her heart would ever stop its pounding.

"Perhaps that was it," she said lightly. "And perhaps because there are times when I become homesick for the music and the dances of Mexico. Don't you?"

She sensed a strange stillness in him.

"Maybe that's it. Seems like I remember far too many thing I *don't* remember." And even while he was speaking he wondered with one part of his mind why he was standing here talking to this woman as if she was someone he had known a long time—and why she, instead of running away from him, all outraged dignity, also continued to stay, looking up into his face with those eyes that were at once challenging, provocative and—yes, damnably familiar! Even her name—mentioned only once by Missie— came far too easily to his tongue.

Caution, instilled in him a long time ago, warned him of danger. In her being here so close to him—in her being in this part of the country at all. A society woman, late of Paris and New York and San Francisco, who could dance the peasant Jarabe of Mexico and speak of that country as her home? A woman who would leave her important guests to mingle with peons and ordinary cowhands—unpinning her hair in public with as much unconcern as if she were in the privacy of her own bedroom? Not even Toni would have gone so far in flouting convention.

Ginny's mind, too, was saying, "Be careful—be careful!"
It would be far too easy to lean against him now, to put
her arms up and drag his head down to hers, touching
his hair where it curled at the nape of his neck. Perhaps
she could force him to remember her, at least with his
body, if nothing else. . . .

But he saved them both by moving away from her
abruptly, shrugging his shoulders.

"Maybe you'd better go back to the house now. Won't
your cousin be wondering where you disappeared to?"

And there was this about Steve that had always infuriated her, and infuriated her even more now. His ability to
detach himself from her, simply by dropping a shield of
indifference between them. Now, before she could protest,
or say something cuttingly sarcastic as she had intended
to, he simply turned on his heel and left her, as if she had
ceased to exist for him any longer.

Matt Carter began to make some sly, grinning comment, but he saw the dark, dangerous look on Manolo's
face and decided to say nothing instead.

"Looks like that hombre's got eleven devils after him—
with *him* makin' the twelfth," one of Matt's friends growled
sourly. "Can't understand, though, why a fine female like
her would let him treat her that way."

"You ask me, I think *fancy* is more like it. . . ."

Several pairs of eyes, some sly, some appraising, others
carefully hooded, watched as Ginny Morgan, without a
glance in their direction, took the time to knot her hair at
the nape of her neck before she walked back into her house.
And more than anything else, Matt Carter found himself
resenting her air of careless hauteur—as if her wealth and
her position gave her the right to put herself above convention, as if she cared not a damn for the opinions of
any of them. And what made her any better? A married
woman—an unfaithful wife. . . . Matt's teeth drew back
from his lips in an unpleasant smile as he began to wonder, with some enjoyment, what Toni Lassister would say
when he began to hint slyly that perhaps her Indian was
stalking more rarified game.

Chapter Fifty-three

Such festivity had not been seen in the ballroom since Jean Desmouline had first thrown his magnificent new mansion open to the curious, envious stares of his friends and neighbors. The glittering chandeliers turned like millions of tiny stars.

Missie was drinking champagne. Her cheeks flushed pink from excitement, she wrinkled her nose when the myriad tiny bubbles almost made her sneeze.

Renaldo smiled at the sight. "You are having a good time, aren't you, Miss Melissa."

"Oh, but how could I not?" Her eyes sparkled up at him ingenuously, with no coy attempt at pretense or provacativeness, and Renaldo found, with a sense of shock, that his pulses had quickened in a most unusual way. Her hair was like a bright flame under the lights, and her small pointed face glowed. Why—the child was actually beautiful! How could anyone have failed to notice? He reminded himself heavily, and with an effort, that she *was* a child, after all. She was far too young; realizing nothing of life and the intrigue that swirled around her even now. Naive and inexperienced, and God, so honest! Wearing all her feelings on her face—the innocent were so easily hurt! He hated to think that she would ever be robbed of her illusions. He must speak to Ginny—where was she? Missie musn't be used, they had had no right to bring her here, transforming her into a brilliant little butterfly the young men couldn't resist. For she had no defense against corruption except her transparent innocence, and in this kind of atmosphere, how long could that last?

"This is the most magical night of my life," Missie whispered. "How can I ever thank you and—and Ginny enough?"

When Señor Ortega smiled, she noticed, his eyes crinkled in the nicest way.

"Please thank me by dancing this dance!" He took her champagne glass, and led her out to the dance floor.

Dancing the waltz was so easy—the music as heady as the champagne she had just had. Now Missie knew what it meant to feel as if her feet hardly touched the ground.

She was so happy! And then suddenly, while she was still wondering why Señor Ortega had suddenly stopped dancing, there *he* was, looking for all the world like a Mexican bandit with those long sideburns he'd left when he'd shaved his beard off; his blue eyes hard and challenging as he stared at Renaldo, who had gone very stiff.

"You don't mind if I claim my dance with this lovely young lady, señor? I think I've neglected her for too long."

But what on earth did he mean? She hadn't ... when he'd just strode off and left her, she'd thought for sure that he didn't even like her any more! Missie's eyes had grown wide and bewildered as she looked confusedly from one man to the other, and it was only the thought that at all costs Melissa's evening must not be spoiled that kept Renaldo from bringing matters to a head right then.

Damn his cousin! He'd upset the girl enough. What kind of devilry was he up to now? His first unthinking surge of anger faded as caution took its place, for Renaldo discovered that he remembered far too well that particularly ugly look in Esteban's eyes. He was spoiling for a fight, for some reason, and—Renaldo realized this with an unpleasant, peculiar feeling of shock—Esteban actually did not recognize him! He had never seen Steve look at him as if he was some stranger he'd gladly brush out of the way, and the impression was by no means pleasant.

"I think he'd actually enjoy killing me," he thought detachedly, even while he heard himself say, quietly and evenly:

"I think that is up to the lady, don't you señor? Miss Melissa?"

"Well, Missie?"

Why did his voice have to sound so harsh, even when he was asking her to dance? And why did he have to look at Señor Ortega in that particularly nasty way? Sometimes, she didn't understand Manolo at all, nor particularly like him either! But he wasn't leaving her with much choice, and when he took her into his arms, without waiting for her answer, Missie had the sensation that she was really being carried off by a pirate.

They danced once down the length of the whole big ballroom, and Missie had the strangest, funniest feeling that Manolo did so deliberately, as if to show her off as if she had been—yes, just as if she had been a prize of war he'd stolen from under the noses of everyone else. This time, he held her differently too. No longer at a respectable distance, but far too close, making her feel breathless and awkward. Even the way he smiled down at her made her feel slightly afraid, as if he'd turned into a stranger. And yet, all evening long, and even before that, this was what she had waited for, wasn't it? To have Manolo look at her differently, as if she was a woman. . . .

"What's the matter, Princess?" She had stumbled, missing a step, but the tightness of his arms held her steady, and she tried to concentrate on the music again, pretending to herself that his voice was really teasing and not underlaid with a strange note she hadn't heard in it before. "Has all the dancing actually tired you out?"

"N—no . . ." but her voice sounded uncertain, and he gave a short laugh, suddenly bending his head so that his lips almost brushed her earlobe as he whispered teasingly:

"I thought you were learning to flirt—or don't you want to experiment any longer? Did one of your admirers scare you off, little one?"

"I told you! I'm *not* a little girl! And I *have* been flirting—all evening, if you want to know!"

"Taken a walk outside yet?"

She said defiantly, "Are you asking me to?" and heard him laugh again.

"I think the prettiest girl in the room ought to see what the stars look like."

"Am I still supposed to say 'no' because of what people might think about me?"

"There are some men who'd carry you off into a dark corner whether you said no or not, Missie. Especially if you'd been flirting with them before."

His voice had turned serious, and the way his eyes—as dark as the late evening sky—looked into hers, made Missie feel all weak and shivery inside. She didn't understand it—a minute ago she had been happy dancing with Señor Ortega, and now, now she wanted Manolo to kiss her! How would it feel, to be kissed by a man? And what was she supposed to do? In the books she had read, it was supposed to be a romantic, shattering experience—one that always changed a girl into a woman. And now, in just a little while, she would find out for herself. . . .

"But I wasn't *really* flirting with you. Flirting is pretending, and you know I wasn't pretending when I said I—"

"Oh, *Christ,* Missie!" he said in a muffled, furious voice, and he danced her through a small doorway she hadn't noticed before—taking her through a small room that looked like a library, and through a pair of long, narrow French windows into a small, grassed courtyard where a miniature fountain played. It was dark here—only the light that filtered through draped or shuttered windows and the stars allowing her to see his shadowed face, not able to read his expression at all. Missie felt as if her teeth wanted to chatter, and she knew her hands were cold. She said quickly and crossly, to cover her confused, embarrassing feeling of strangeness:

"How did you know about this place? Who did you bring here before?"

She thought there was a tremor of laughter in his voice. "I looked around. Always like to know my way about a strange house, and how to get out quickly if I have to."

"But that's—"

She didn't have time to finish, for suddenly his arm was about her waist, impatiently pulling her close, while he tilted her chin with one hand, and she could feel her knees shaking as he looked down into her eyes for just a fraction of a minute—not long enough for her to protest or say another word.

"Missie. . . ."

She closed her eyes, very tightly, and felt his lips brush her half-open mouth while she thought dazedly that she must be dreaming, she must, and if she opened her eyes everything would dissolve away and there'd be just the river and the branches of the tree where she always made up her favorite daydreams, with the sunlight filtering through.

He kissed her very gently, at first, fingers still cupping her face, and then suddenly, frighteningly, the way he was kissing her changed, and instead of being gentle his mouth bruised hers, forcing a smothered cry from her.

Snatched back to reality, Missie put both her hands up, pushing them against his chest. Why did he have to hold her so closely that she could hardly breathe? And the way he was kissing her—it wasn't at all romantic, or tender, or any of the things she'd imagined a first kiss would be.

His body was hard and unyielding as she felt herself pressed along its length; his arms were suddenly cruel, holding her an unwilling prisoner.

Missie's head fell back as she tried to twist her face away. Struggling frantically now, she felt as unreasoningly terrified as a small animal caught in a trap.

And perhaps some impression of her blind panic communicated itself to him, for just as she started to sob despairingly and desperately, he released her, and she would have stumbled backward, falling in her instinctive, headlong flight, if he had not caught her hands.

"No! Let me go! I don't want—I didn't know . . ." she caught her breath and ended on an accusing sob, "is that how men really want to kiss?"

"Not all men, baby. Just the ones like me." His voice was taut and harsh with anger, but it was more at himself than her, although Missie could not have known that. For some moments, feeling her softly yielding body against his, and seeing the way her hair seemed to catch and hold the light, he had forgotten. . . .

His fingers, suddenly gentle, brushed her cheeks.

"Missie—you see what can happen if you run off with some man into the shadows?"

"But it was *you*! And I thought—"

"Thought what? That I had suddenly been changed into a gentleman who would be content with one kiss and some whispered lies in the starlight? You might have found that some of those young officers back there know all the rules when it comes to playing romantic games, little one, but I've got no time for romance, or for games. Kisses are only a prelude to what comes after, and a damned waste of time where I'm concerned."

"Oh," she gasped weakly, not really understanding, but instinctively afraid of the sudden brutality in his voice. She was afraid, too, that he might kiss her again—and what had he meant about kisses being only a beginning? And a waste of time?

Missie's eyes were wide and frightened—cat-green, he used to tease her, before she had decided to masquerade as a woman. But the varying expressions that chased each other across her small, pointed face were still those of a transparent girl. Poor little scared child-woman! Her fingers were cold, even through her borrowed silk gloves as she struggled to free them.

"Stop crying, for God's sake!" he said roughly, and then, deliberately softening his voice, "I'm not going to hurt you, Missie. I'm going to take you inside in a minute, after I've wiped those tears off your face. You want them all to know what happened? Want me to get in a fight with your big brother?"

She shook her head dolefully, and he was suddenly kind again, producing a handkerchief with which he dried her tears, quite impersonally now.

She had seen his dark side for the first time, and didn't know that even this small gesture of tenderness was foreign to him.

"You—you think I'm silly, don't you? You still think I'm a child!"

"Jesus God, Missie! You need to be paddled, or kissed again—I'm not sure which! But if you want to get seduced to prove you're a woman, you pick someone else. And then, maybe, I'll kill him for you."

"I could kill him! No—don't look at me like that, Renaldo. I've come close to doing so before, and this time, I swear it, I wouldn't have any qualms. And don't bother to remind me that he's apparently lost his memory—it doesn't matter! Less than fifteen minutes ago he was kissing *me,* and now, to take advantage of Missie, of all people—she adores him! And she's such a child!"

Ginny's face was flushed, and although she spoke in an undertone, between gritted teeth, Renaldo was inclined to forget his own uneasiness in order to try and calm her.

"You are not supposed to know him at all. And it wasn't in our plans that you should go outside. If your coming here is to solve anything, you must try to stay calm—and detached. Steve isn't going to harm Missie." He spoke severely, but all the time his own mind was occupied by those same fears he told Ginny to forget. He even regretted having suggested this party in the first place. What was his rash, conscienceless cousin doing outside with Missie? He hadn't liked the angry, dangerous look of him when he'd snatched her away in the first place, and it had been all he could do not to follow them.

"Sometimes, I feel as if I don't really know him," Ginny said in a cold, too-controlled voice that only made Renaldo even more apprehensive. "I even wonder what I am doing here. I should have remembered that Steve was always so—self-sufficient! He doesn't really *need* anyone, don't you understand that? Even if he doesn't know who he is, he remembers enough to survive, no matter what it might take. And if he had no conscience where I was concerned, why should he have with Missie?" She laughed suddenly, a harsh, broken sound that tightened Renaldo's nerves. "I'm not even sure if Steve ever really loved me. I must be insane, to have agreed to play along with Mr. Bishop's devious schemes. And I should have put my children first. I'm not much of a mother, am I? They're still so little, and so helpless, and they have a father who might never acknowledge them.... Renaldo, what *am* I doing here?"

He could only look down at her with dismay, not knowing how to answer her without feeling a hypocrite. What could he have said? He found it hard to imagine, each time he looked at Ginny, that she had gone through so much, and come through unscathed and unbowed. How could anyone forget such a woman? He had to admit to himself, ruefully, that secretly he had been certain Steve would recognize his own wife—a women he had apparently loved. But was Steve capable of loving any woman? Or had he grown too used to using them to fill his own passing needs? Above all, what could he say to Ginny that would be honest and truthful, without hurting her any more than she had been hurt already?

He was saved that particular problem for the moment when suddenly Missie slipped into the room, her eyes suspiciously red-rimmed. And it was not for his cousin's sake that he gave a relieved murmur of reassurance and hurried to meet her.

"I think he's falling in love with Missie—and doesn't even know it!" Ginny thought, and she wondered why she suddenly felt so empty and drained of emotion. Missie was safe—and Renaldo, as honest and open in his own way as Missie was, had not been able to hide his relief. Detachedly, she thought that they would be good for each other, those two, if Missie would get over her girlish infatuation for Steve. Her husband. But tonight, no matter how often she repeated the words to herself, they seemed to have no meaning. Her husband. A stranger. Had he always been a stranger to her, without her being able to admit it?

And where had he disappeared to now? Determination stiffened Ginny's spine. She was sick and tired of pretense and uncertainty. Mr. Bishop and his intricate, devious plots be damned! She was going to find Steve again, and face him with facts. She should have done so earlier!

"Mrs. Morgan—I have been looking for you, you know! You promised me a dance, or am I being presumptuous?" Nick Benoit gave a short, deprecating laugh, fingers going up to stroke his mustache. "You looked so lost in thought I almost did not dare to disturb you. Surely you cannot be troubled about anything? Such a successful evening—and of course I cannot thank you enough for the transformation in my little niece. You've turned her into a lady overnight."

Mechanically, smiling stiffly, Ginny accepted his outstretched hand. What else could she do? And, at least, it postponed the inevitable confrontation with Steve, with all its violent and conceivably unpleasant results. She was a coward, after all. Nick Benoit couldn't hurt her, but Steve could—and far too easily, at that.

Still, she suddenly remembered Bishop's warning—

"Nicholas Benoit ... Judge Benoit. He's a self-important little man, who fancies himself a lady-killer. Don't underestimate him."—and in the back of her mind, was the memory of Renate Madden's broken, dead voice as she related what had happened to her at Benoit's hands. But so far, all she had seen was the dandy—and the flatterer; even his compliments were veiled with respect. Tonight, with her mind occupied by too many other things, Ginny hardly noticed the subtle change in his manner towards her.

His compliments were bolder, but she parried those easily enough, from habit. And if he held her a trifle more closely than convention decreed while they waltzed, she could put that, too, down to the lateness of the hour, and the freely flowing drinks they had all imbibed. Her fault—but then, what had she really expected as an outcome? That Steve would recognize her at once, and everything would fall into place? She was as naive as Missie, dancing now with Renaldo, her small face actually breaking into a smile at something he had said.

Almost automatically, Ginny's eyes had been searching the crowd of dancers for a glimpse of Steve. Perhaps he had decided to stay outside where both the music and the dancers were less formal? But she couldn't see Tom Lassiter either—and there was Matt Carter, Missie's brother, who had wandered in with a glass of wine in his hand; he stood leaning against the wall, staring at her in the most peculiar fashion.

"I have to leave tomorrow, for Dallas. But I shall look forward to meeting you again when I return. I hope you've decided to remain with us for a while?"

What was he talking about? Almost as if he had read her mind, Nick Benoit said softly: "I am an afficionado of the opera, if that is the correct expression. And a lady I have particularly admired for a long time will be honoring Dallas with her presence next week. Francesca di Paoli—the Princess di Paoli. She is—incomparable!"

Quite without volition, Ginny could feel herself grow stiff. That woman! The opera singer whose name all the newspapers had linked with Steve's. What was she doing back in Texas? Why return here? And how much of the gossip had Nick Benoit heard? Oh God, was there to be no end to her humiliation?

And Nick Benoit, who had been squeezing her hand a moment earlier, seemed to have adopted an almost rapt manner as he talked of his idol.

"Such a voice—so clear, so perfect, even in the highest notes. And since you are a lovely woman yourself, I'm sure you will not misunderstand when I talk of her beauty. But then, perhaps you have watched her on the stage."

"I have heard much of this latest opera singer, of course. But I'm afraid I've been denied the privilege of watching one of her performances."

Ginny knew she sounded stilted and rather arrogant, but her partner did not seem to notice.

"Then you should come to Dallas, too. Believe me, it will be worth the journey."

"Why, the nasty little man!" she thought. He had heard the rumors, and was testing her reactions! Suddenly alert, Ginny forced a brilliant smile.

"Perhaps I will be fortunate enough to see the Signorina di Paoli in New York, when I return there. Or in Europe—for I haven't made up my mind whether I prefer the new world to the old." She added abruptly, not caring what he might think, "But why are we talking of such a dull subject as the opera? I must confess that I prefer the ballet—and Strauss waltzes. And now you will think me a complete Philistine!"

He made a polite disclaimer, and Ginny rushed on: "What do you think of the musicians I hired? Do you think everybody is enjoying themselves? Your sister-in-law—"

"Ah, yes—but you haven't lived among us long enough to realize that Toni is a creature of moods. If she's appeared rude, it's because you have rather put her nose out of joint, you know! Toni's been used to queening it over us all. And if I may say so, without appearing too bold, I am glad you decided to visit Baroque."

He was back to flattering her again, but she could cope with that easily enough, Ginny thought. But why did he make a point of mentioning, a few seconds later, that he hoped she would forgive Toni for leaving so abruptly, and without formal thanks?

"She'll be quite safe, of course. Her foreman is escorting her home. The kind of man I certainly hope you won't judge the rest of us by! But then, ever since John died, I'm afraid Toni has developed some peculiar traits. She's been lonely, and he's taken advantage of that fact. I'm sure I do not need to say more. As you know, I've been worried for my niece—the way her father lets her run wild—but I really think you were right. Missie adapted herself to what should be her true environment quite well, don't you think?"

The man kept talking, apparently inconsequentially—moving from one subject to another. And yet, all through his virtual monologue, Ginny began to have the uneasy feeling that he was studying her secretly, and storing away her reactions to everything he said for future use. Ridiculous or not, she was glad when the dance ended and she was able to excuse herself.

The keyed-up feeling she had had when the evening began had disappeared, leaving in its place a dull, hopeless lassitude. It seemed inconceivable now that she had been so sure of herself—arrogant enough to think that she could cope with any eventuality, face anything. He hadn't recognized her—and worse, she knew that she wanted him to have loved her. Hadn't he loved her? Or had she believed it all this time only because she had wanted to believe it?

"He treats women as if they were — were merely objects to be used, when *he* is in the mood! That opera singer, and the way he flaunted his affair with her so publicly, as if he deliberately intended to humiliate me! The newspapers went so far as to hint that he contemplated a divorce in order to marry her! And Judge Benoit knows—he brought her name up several times, watching me slyly all the while. And then there is this Lassiter creature, who reminds me of Concepción, because she is just as greedy and grasping! Perhaps that is the kind of woman he should confine his attentions to—women of *his* type. But he gave Missie Carter a ring, and the poor child's head over heels in love with him—you saw how unhappy he made her tonight. Doesn't he have any scruples at all? I suppose that if the fancy takes him he may very well seduce her, just as he did me—Renaldo, why do you just sit there watching me rave? Why don't you tell me what a fool I am? Tonight I deliberately flirted with him, and let him kiss me in the shadows as if I was just some cheap trollop he'd picked up in a—a barroom! And that's how he treated me—I must have been crazy, to allow Mr. Bishop to talk me into this. I should never have come here, for now everything is worse than it ever was before."

Ginny stopped her angry pacing about the room to look accusingly at Renaldo. The last of the guests had departed a half hour ago, and Missie, who was to spend the night, had already gone up to the room alloted her, feet dragging with a tiredness she would not admit. The Señora Armijo had followed her, trying to stifle her yawns as she reminded Ginny sternly that she too needed her sleep, and she hoped Ginny meant to retire shortly. But Ginny was too overwrought to be sleepy.

"Why don't you say something?" she demanded now, green, tilted eyes dangerously bright. She wanted to burst into a storm of weeping—but whether from sheer rage or unhappiness even she could not be certain.

Renaldo stretched in his chair and sighed. He too had had a sorely trying evening, and his mind was full of thoughts that he had to try and sort out.

"Shall we go back home?" he said quietly, watching Ginny's face. "I am beginning to agree with you that coming here was a mistake. And you have the children to think of now. Tell your Mr. Bishop whatever you have learned, and let him handle matters from now on." His mouth lifted in a wry grimace. "Well, as you know, Steve has always managed to take care of himself. Sooner or later—"

"You mean that I should run away? And show the world, and Steve, too, what a coward I am? He took that Lassiter woman home tonight—and his opera singer is returning to Texas. Must I admit publicly that I'm not capable of holding my own husband? Oh, no!" Ginny's chin had tilted in the determined fashion that Renaldo recognized only too well, and her voice had become husky. "Before I leave here I'm going to settle matters in my own way—and there are more than a few scores with Steve himself! I can be just as hard and as unscrupulous as he is, if I must!"

It would be useless to try and reason with her. Not tonight, and not when she was in such a stubborn and contradictory mood. But tomorrow, perhaps, she would be more inclined to listen to reason. It was best that they should leave—and even while he lifted his shoulders in a helpless shrug, Renaldo was thinking unhappily that he too had his reasons now for—running away, Ginny had named it contemptuously.

Once, long ago, Steve had looked at him curiously as he stood by the window, cleaning his gun, one eyebrow raised.

"Are you really content to exist this way, Renaldo? Jumping when my grandfather calls—being everybody's friend and advisor? Christ—aren't you ever tempted to go out there and live for yourself instead of finding a vicarious kind of existence between the pages of one of those books of yours? I'm surprised you gave up the priesthood, cousin."

At the time, Renaldo remembered, he had merely smiled and shaken his head. No—he had no desire to lead the kind of reckless existence his cousin seemed to crave. All his life, he had sought peace, and while he did not exactly despise women, he had been his mother's despair because he would not take a wife. His mother, who was intuitive enough, for all her surface inanity, had told him bluntly that he was a fool to have encouraged what she termed "that disastrous marriage" between Steve and Ginny, because, after all, it stuck out as clearly as the nose on her face that he had developed more than a passing fondness for the young woman himself.

He was still more than ordinarily fond of her, Renaldo thought, watching the way she chewed on her lower lip, stormily tapping one foot on the floor as if she could not bear to be still. She was a beautiful and cultured woman, and deserved better than the misery his cousin had put her through. But he had come to know her well enough to realize that in spite of her outcries to the contrary, she continued to nurture a passion for Steve—although, of course, the predicament they all found themselves in now was quite untenable.

Ginny was right—and politics be damned. For all their sakes, even Missie's—and Renaldo's lips tightened at the thought—someone had to talk to Steve.

Chapter Fifty-four

Steve wasn't in a talking mood. He woke up with the morning sun filtering through the thickly entwined branches that arched over him, forming a kind of green cave. Water trickled somewhere, reminding him that he was thirsty, and he reached for his canteen, wincing as he stretched cautiously. His head ached, and he had the vague recollection that he had been dreaming again of a green-eyed woman—the same, recurrent dream that stayed annoyingly on the very fringes of his consciousness.

Still, as soon as he opened his eyes, he was suddenly wide awake, very much like the kind of predatory animal he had more than once been likened to. He knew where he was and remembered how he had come here, to a place he had noticed before and stored away in his mind as a possible shelter. And as he let tepid water trickle down his throat, grimacing at its brackish taste, he chose not to try and remember what he had been dreaming or why, and thought of Toni instead—foul vituperations spilling from between her pale pink lips until he had put one hand over her mouth, ripping the clothes from her body with the other, finally extracting the kind of submission she seemed to crave. And then, knocking aside her still-clinging arms, he had left her, still screaming abuse after him.

"Comanche! Damn you! One of these days, you rotten bastard, you're going to push me too far, and then I'm going to cut your heart out, while you're still alive. Do you hear me? Goddamn you! Come back here—I'm still paying your wages, and I'm not through telling you what I think of you yet. You made a fool of me tonight, making up to that red-haired bitch!"

Ginny. He frowned, wondering why her name came so quickly and easily into his mind. Well, Toni was right about one thing—this Ginny woman spelled trouble.

"Why is she still here? Why is she taking such an interest in us? She wants to make friends with everyone—that's what she told Nicky, the lying, hypocritical bitch! And if he's enough of a fool to believe her, I'm not! She doesn't belong here, and I won't let her interfere! She doesn't intend to leave, you can see that now, can't you? We're going to have to get rid of her!"

"Is that why you climbed off your high horse to come looking for me? To tell me that?"

"We've got unfinished business to talk about, damn your black heart! And she's part of it. Well?"

He noted without interest how snugly Toni's velour riding habit fit, showing off her voluptuous curves. And she had left her jacket open deliberately, so that the hardening, pointed nipples were clearly visible under her thin silk blouse. She wanted to be pulled off her horse and raped; the slowly enlarging pupils of her amber eyes told him that as she continued to stare down at him, challenging, tapping her riding whip against the top of one polished boot. But he wasn't in the mood this morning, and he was growing mighty damned tired of Toni and her tricks and tantrums. For a moment, he was almost tempted to tell her so.

He gave her a mirthless smile that was a mere thinning and lifting of his lips, not reaching his eyes.

"I haven't had my breakfast yet. Never did care to talk business before that first cup of coffee in the morning. You going to join me or sit up there on your horse and sulk?"

"I don't know why in hell I put up with you, you know that, Comanche? In fact, I don't even like you!" She had decided to pout, instead of riding off in a rage, and he shrugged, turning back to the small fire he had built.

"The feeling's mutual," he said equably. "You want coffee or not?" His look warned her to silence, and she closed her lips over her half-uttered retort, dismounting sulkily by herself when he made no move to help her.

But damn him, damn him, he would help her in the end! He had too much to lose and too much to gain not to, and in the end she would make him see that.

"Nicky's leaving for Dallas this afternoon, chasing after that stupid cow of an Italian opera singer he's always been so crazy about. But he said he'd find out all he could about Mrs. Morgan while he was there. I think Nicky would like to have her himself—and he's not half as much in awe of her as he was before, especially not after what Matt told him. Did you enjoy kissing her, Comanche? Is she as good as I am?"

"I didn't get to kiss her long enough to judge. But I'll be sure and let you know when I get around to finding out."

Toni's moods could veer from one extreme to another with no warning at all, and now she giggled delightedly.

"Will you really? I think I'd like to watch—do you think you'll have to rape her? Oh God, that would be exciting too. First her, and then me—how's that for comparing notes? And then we'll give her to Nicky—that would be better than killing her right away, don't you think? And if we did decide to let her go afterwards, she's not likely to want to talk about what happened, is she? I think she'd want to run far away from all the nasty scandal, don't you?" Her obscene, excited laughter grated on his nerves. Any minute now she'd be putting her hands on him, begging him to do it to her now, right here, with her skirts hauled up. And he still wasn't in the mood.

"You've got a cute, nasty little mind, Messalina," he drawled, pouring what remained of the coffee onto the small, smokeless fire as he came quickly and easily to his feet. "But now that we've settled what we're going to do with Ginny Morgan, maybe you should start figuring how we're going to get her—and I'll be damned if I'm going to be the only one to stick my neck out, so you'd better start thinking real hard."

Her triumphant smile warned him that she had already done some thinking.

"But I've thought of everything, darling. And to begin with, *we're* going to Dallas, too—only Nicky isn't going to know. You see—" her amber eyes narrowed at him while her full lips continued to smile, "I'm not sure if I can really trust him or not, and we do have some joint investments, you know. Only dear Nicky could get carried away too easily where that Italian woman is concerned, and spend far too much of our money on her!"

"And? What's the reason for my going along with you this trip?"

"But Comanche, you know I always feel so much safer with you to escort me! And I do have my share of enemies. Besides, you have the same kind of mind I have, and that might just be helpful, once we get to Dallas—you see, there is some mutual business that Nick's supposed to take care of while he's there, and I'm afraid he might allow himself to become far too distracted, so. . . ."

Another thing they had in common, he reflected sardonically, was that neither one of them trusted the other. And he had learned that Toni was especially dangerous when she purred and preened herself like a satisfied cat. But what the hell. He shrugged as if her little intrigues were of no importance to him, turned away and began to saddle his horse, wondering impatiently why his head continued to ache.

"Nick should be arriving in Dallas sometime tomorrow. And I've already told everyone I'm going to visit some cousins in Shreveport. We can leave here separately and arrange to meet somewhere." Her voice rose, suddenly becoming shrill. "Where do you think you're going? We've got lots more to discuss, and I don't want to ride back to the ranch alone!"

One hand already on the saddle horn, he turned his head to look at her, and as furious as she was Toni almost shrank from the cold look in those hard blue eyes.

"You did just fine when you came out here looking for me, didn't you? For the moment, I've got a few little chores to attend to, but I'll see you back at the house before sun-up—boss-lady, ma'am!"

He tipped his hat to her before he left, horse and rider disappearing almost instantly among the closely-growing trees that seemed to lean grotesquely twisted trunks against each other, leaving barely enough room for a man or animal to pass through.

"I hope you drown in the swamps, damn you!" Toni shouted after him furiously, even though she knew he was probably out of earshot already.

She didn't get back to her house until early afternoon, having managed to get herself lost—an experience that was frightening, even for her. And to learn that she had missed a call from her new neighbors, who had just happened to be passing by on their way to the Carter place, did nothing to improve her temper.

"That nosy, interfering bitch! I wonder what she really wanted? I was right not to trust her, and Nicky's going to see that too. . . . !"

Toni stamped upstairs in a foul mood, which might have been even worse had she known that her foreman also had been on his way to visit the Carters.

It was really Missie he wanted to see. Last night—what in hell had got into him last night? A mental vision of Ginny Morgan, her coppery hair slipping in heavy curls down her back and shoulders as she slowly drew the pins from it, one by one, made him frown blackly. Damn her! He should have held her against the wall and taken her right there, which was what she had been asking for, and that would have made an end of it. The thought of her slanted green eyes, shining like emeralds in the firelight, and her mouth, soft lips parting under his, wouldn't keep coming back to haunt him now. This morning, the green-eyed woman who laughed and teased the fringes of his dreams had had a face. Hers. And the memory both of his dream and of last night made him angry. Both at her, for the obvious way in which she'd led him on with her supple, sensuous body, and at himself for holding back—and for then taking his frustration out on Missie, who had trusted him. Missie was too damn naive, and Joe should stop letting her run loose the way he did. Last night, she had actually looked like a woman—Cinderella, he had called her teasingly—but he wasn't the kind of prince Missie should be looking for. He had to talk to her, and explain that she mustn't let herself trust too easily. And—his frown deepened, making his face look hard and dangerous—he wanted to talk to Matt Carter, too. Matt had a goddamn big mouth sometimes, when he got too much liquor inside him!

Habit made Manolo stop to take out his field glasses when he got to Missie's favorite tree. No use running the risk of bumping into some of Belmont's soldier boys, who might feel inclined to shoot first and ask questions later.

Squinting against the sun, he found himself frowning again. Where in hell was everyone? It was almost too quiet, for an afternoon. And then, moving the glasses, he saw the fancy new buggy with matching grey horses that were tethered to the hitching rail right in front, and knew the Carters had visitors. Swearing under his breath, he settled down to wait, telling himself that it was only curiosity that held him there.

Inside the house, Ginny was wondering, with one part of her mind, why she had decided to stay on here—for a while longer. Stubbornness, as Renaldo had termed it despairingly, when they had argued again after breakfast this morning? Or a sense of leaving something unresolved and unfinished? Every time she met Matt Carter's slyly insolent stare, she was reminded of last night, and Steve. . . . Where had he disappeared to? Neither he nor Toni had been at the Lassiter house, and she had stopped there deliberately, over Renaldo's protests, just to make sure—but of what? An old, grizzled Negro, Toni Lassiter's manservant, had told her that Madame had gone riding. Naturally, he had said nothing about Madame's foreman, who also shared Madame's bed at times. It had been left to Missie, eyes wide and curious as she looked around the

big, imposing looking hallway of the house that her mama
had once lived in, to ask ingenuously and openly:

"Where is Manolo? Hasn't he been here then?"

Henri's black face had tightened disapprovingly.

"No, Miss. I can't say as I've seen him this morning."

And Missie had looked relieved, while Ginny wondered
if her own face had ever been so transparent, or if she had
ever been so honest and so trusting.

"Maybe he's at our house," Missie had burst out when
Renaldo had helped her into the buggy again. "Oh, but I
do wish you could meet him when he's not scowling nor
looking fierce and angry. He's been our friend, and you
won't judge him by what other people say, will you?"

Ginny had seen Renaldo's lips tighten as they exchanged
quick looks over Missie's head.

Missie, at least, deserved not to be hurt—and Steve had
a habit of hurting all the women he came in contact with,
mainly because he didn't care about other people's feelings. More than ever, Ginny was determined to meet him
face to face and have it out with him, but now she was
beginning to wonder if she would have the opportunity
again. From what she could gather, he came and went as
he felt like it, and had managed, so far, to avoid the soldiers that Colonel Belmont had patrolling the fringes of
the swamps.

Again, after they had escorted her home and Joe Carter
had asked them inside to sample some of his home-made
peach brandy, it was Missie who brought up his name.

"Have you seen Manolo? Has he been by yet, Pa?"

It was Matt who answered, with a sidelong glance at
Ginny.

"Ain't set eyes on him since last night, sis, when he took
Miz Lassiter home. Maybe he's back in the swamp, pow-
wowing with them Injun friends of his."

Joe Carter interposed hastily, "Oh, he'll be by sometime,
I reckon. You know how he is. Missie, why don't you
show Mr. Ortega some of those pictures you drew?"

Missie was always shy about showing her rough
sketches to anyone, but Señor Ortega was different, just
like his name. Renaldo. Even if it did sound foreign she
liked the sound of it. And some deep sense within her that
she hadn't even known she possessed told her he really
liked her—he wasn't just being kind when he paid her so

much attention. She liked hearing him talk, making
all the places and the countries he had been in come
alive for her. When she had first met him, she had
thought him rather reserved and austere, but when he
smiled at her, as he did now, he looked much younger
than she had first thought; and she liked the way small
lines deepened in his sun-tanned face, on either side of his
mouth. He smiled a little like the way Manolo smiled—
and she thought this with a small shock of surprise, because otherwise they were so different! And half the time,
Manolo's smile never reached his eyes, which remained
hard and rather mocking. But when Renaldo Ortega
smiled at her, even his eyes crinkled at the corners, and
she could tell he smiled because he liked her.

"Why Miss Melissa, these drawings are very good! You
have captured the mood of the swamps—I see that these
trees are almost alive, like ugly old men!"

Missie laughed delightedly. "You see that, too? I have
always thought that about some of those old trees. A lot
of old gnomes, putting their heads together!"

"Well, you have certainly conveyed that feeling."

Missie leaned over his shoulder while Renaldo leafed
through her sketchbook, trying not to become distracted.
The trouble was that she was too open, too natural. And
compared to Missie, he was a cynical old man. Why didn't
he feel that way when he was with her, then? Missie, and
his unfamiliar, growing feelings toward her were part of
the reason he had tried to persuade Ginny to leave Baroque.
He was running away from life, as usual, he had told
himself morosely that very morning. But where would all
this end—and how? Ginny, for all her stormy moods, preferred to meet any situation head-on; she was as reckless,
in her way, as Steve. Poor Genia—how much more would
she have to endure?

When they finally left the Carter house, Ginny confessed to being more than half-drunk on peach brandy.

"But I don't care—for this way I don't have to think,
even if I do develop a headache afterwards. Oh, Renaldo—why am I so persistent? Why don't I just give up?"

"Because you are yourself," he said sternly. "Ginny—"

"Did you see the way Matt Carter looked at me? Just
as if he knew everything there is to know about me. I
think he saw what happened last night, with Steve. And at

the time, do you know, I didn't care! I wanted so much for Steve to know me, to recognize me—and now Matt thinks I'm a slut. And I suppose I am, in a way! Look at all the things I've done! I don't think Steve has ever forgiven me—Renaldo, do *you* think I'm a slut? What does Don Francisco really think of me?"

"Lean your head against my shoulder if you must, and stop distracting me when I am trying to control the horses." Renaldo forced a harshness he did not feel into his voice. "They are still far too fresh, after that long rest. And do not concern yourself about Matt Carter. What he thinks is not important. When we get back, we are going to have to decide what you are going to do—whether you will stay here and face whatever comes up or do the sensible thing and leave."

"But I don't feel sensible! And I don't want to think—not yet, Renaldo. I would rather fall asleep first."

She slept against his shoulder all the way back, barely rousing herself enough to walk up the stairs unassisted, while Señora Armijo clucked in the background.

"Hush, Tia. She is merely overtired. All she needs is to be allowed to sleep in peace. And we will not wake her for dinner."

It was very seldom that Renaldo commanded, but the note in his voice reminded the Señora of Don Francisco, and she cut short her muttering to incline her head grudgingly. Sometimes, Renaldo wondered what his aunt-by-courtesy thought of the intrigue they were all caught up in—and then the enormity of the situation made him wince. At least, Tia Alfonsa was a born duenna—she kept her thoughts to herself and concentrated on the task alloted to her!

Ginny was barely conscious of her chaperone's soft scolding as she helped her to undress, slipping her arms into a loose robe.

"Liquor! And so early in the afternoon too! It's a good thing Don Francisco has no idea of what's going on, or he'd be here himself, to settle matters! I don't know what the younger generation is coming to!"

Ginny felt her soft bed come up and hit her, as she subsided with relief into it. Time enough to think later. For now, she felt too sleepy, so limp. . . .

Chapter Fifty-five

ᏰᏉ

"That cousin of hers—or whoever he is—seems like he's
taken quite a shine to Missie. He's coming by for her tomorrow, to go ridin', he said. And you know how Pa is—
too easygoing. But *she*, now, it seemed to me like she was
far too interested in where you might be. Saw the way she
was dancing last night, and it just occurred to me. . . ."

Manolo had ridden as far as the corral, meeting Matt,
who seemed only too anxious to talk about their recent visitors, while he slipped in his sly insinuations.

"You coming up to the house?" Matt questioned now.
"Pa's broken out a jug of that old brandy he's been
hoardin' for years, and Missie, she got so mad at the way
he keeps drinkin' it, she took to her room, sulking. But I
guess she'll perk up if you come on in. Told us they'd been
by my Ma's old place—Miz Lassiter's house—to inquire
after her, and found no one home."

"Sometimes, Matt, you talk too damn much," Manolo
said between his teeth, waiting for Matt to get mad, because, Missie's brother or not, that was the kind of mood
Manolo was in.

But Matt only grinned, which was surprising, for him.

"Just thought you might be interested to know there's
been so much interest taken in you—an' especially if the
person interested is a damn good looking female. Wouldn't
mind trying some of that myself, if the time and the place
was right."

He kept grinning when Manolo whirled his horse
around and took off. He never had liked the idea of a
man like that hanging after his kid sister anyhow, and
never mind all Pa's lectures. Mex or Indian, what was the
difference? Sis was too good for him, and when Toni tired
of him maybe she'd start looking around for a man of her

own kind to help her run things. A man who'd been around all the time. . . .

At her ranch Toni Lassiter ordered dinner, and waited—forcing herself to lie down in her big bed, the clean linen having been neatly turned down by her maid.

And at the Desmoulins estate, while Renaldo sat in the library with a cigar, staring unseeingly at a book he had pickel out at random, Ginny slept with her door closed and her window open. Not even dreams pursued her as afternoon slipped into evening. She slept heavily, not wanting to wake even when someone shook her roughly by the shoulder.

Still drowsy and heavy-lidded, she had opened her mouth to protest when he gagged her, deftly slipping a wadded-up handkerchief between her jaws before he used the scarf he had worn around his neck to finish the job, knotting it at the back of her neck in spite of her suddenly frenzied struggles.

"Sorry it isn't silk," he offered caustically in the face of her wild-eyed squirming. "But I've got no time to waste on little details."

Quite instinctively she clawed at him, and then cried out behind the gag as he caught her wrists, forcing them up over her head as the weight of his body held her pinned down.

Where had he come from? How? The *why* of his being here so unexpectedly was all too apparent, for now he was tying her wrists tightly and painfully to the bedposts.

"Never did like leaving unfinished business behind. And I heard you'd been wondering about me—thought I'd come over and visit, just so you wouldn't have to wonder any more."

He was as hateful as he had ever been! And he was preparing, quite coldbloodedly, to rape her, still without recognition of who she was or what they had been to each other. Why did he have to gag her?

Her eyes screamed hate and frustration at him, and he grinned, in spite of his own strange tension, no longer questioning his reasons for being here. *She* knew. He could tell from the way her eyes seemed to deepen in color when they met his, and her sudden immobility when he threw the constricting covers off her bed and pulled loose the wide ribbon-sash which was all that held her flimsy robe together. He had the oddest feeling that all this had happened before, looking down at her nude body and the small, perfectly formed breasts that rose and fell with her quickened breathing.

She had been struggling against him only a few moments before. What held her so still now?

He had meant to take her quickly and brutally before he left her just as she was. But now, without volition, he bent his head and put his mouth against the small, pulsing hollow at the base of her throat, feeling the stifled sound she made.

She had skin as smooth as silk, the same sweet perfume clinging to every inch of it that he had noticed when, not able to help himself, he had buried his face in the tumbled masses of her hair.

And so, instead of raping her, he was seducing her. All over again, Ginny thought dazedly, forgetting how he had treated her and what he had done under the wild, familiar feel of his hands and lips on her body.

As long as she lived, he would always have this power over her—oh, damn him, damn him! And then her thoughts became jumbled and incoherent as he lowered his body over hers at last, answering the fierce, familiar need he had awakened in her in spite of herself.

He regretted having to leave her. There was something about her softly yielding, sweetly passionate body that would have held him beside her all night, if he had had the time. What had been meant to be his revenge, and a warning, had turned out very differently, and afterwards he was to wonder at his own weakness. But then—there was Toni. White-faced, amber-eyed bitch with her too-soft body and avid, pouting mouth.

Toni, who waited, and wanted—and demanded a man's soul as well as his balls, if she could have it. And he had nothing to give her, especially not tonight, except a few minutes of his sullen company.

"What do you mean, you can't stay? You bastard, I told you—"

"You just tell me where to meet you, Messalina, and I'll be there. But you just might get a visit from some of Colonel Belmont's soldier boys, if Ginny Morgan's mad enough to talk about the visit I just paid her."

"You did *what?*" Toni's voice rose, cracked, and then,

seeing his hard, unsmiling look she began to giggle hysterically. "You really did! Oh God, you're marvelous! What was it like? Did she fight very hard? Did you have to hit her? I hope you left ugly marks all over her body, the bitch! Oh, but she won't be quite so high and mighty after this, will she? Do you think you scared her away, Comanche?"

He was suddenly very tired, and Toni filled him with revulsion. He was sorry he had told her. He didn't owe her any explanations—not a damn thing!

"I'll give you all the details when we meet in Dallas—give you something to look forward to. But for now, I'd better head back to the swamps, just in case."

"But I want to hear everything *now!* I can hide you from the soldiers if they come—in the cellars! Don't you trust me, Comanche?"

He knew about her cellars—especially the one under the icehouse, that old Lassiter had fixed up just like a dungeon in an English castle, for the taming of his recalcitrant slaves. And he didn't trust Toni, not one inch.

"Hell, no, I don't trust you!" he told her harshly and uncompromisingly. And he rode off, ignoring her shiny eyes and shinier lips that she always moistened with her tongue when she was excited—leaving her with a half-promise that he'd find her before she got to Shreveport, and accompany her on the rest of the trip.

So now he was headed for Dallas, of all places. Half against his will, because he kept thinking back to the copper-haired woman, and wondering what might have happened if he had gone back to her. He kept hearing the soft noises she had made behind the gag he had put on her—feeling the sudden, surprising surrender of her body to his, green eyes half closed, thighs parting for him sweetly and eagerly one moment, before her legs had wrapped themselves around his body as it slid upward over hers, still tasting her, still wanting her, and the response she had given him. It hadn't been rape—not by then. And against all the warnings of his mind, he had loosened the strips of hide he had used to tie her wrists to the bedpost, so she could get free without too much difficulty. How would she have reacted if he went back? He must be crazy, thinking it. By now, she would be in hysterics, probably, and trying to wipe out of her mind the fact that she had not only given in but actually responded to his invasion of her body. Women of her kind were only good at teasing, and promising what they never intended to give. But did he really know what kind of woman she was?

Going away made sense, even if it also meant putting up with Toni, and all the intrigues she was so fond of, among other things. He didn't remember Dallas, not exactly and clearly as a man with a normal memory might remember it, but he had the feelings he'd been there before. From being content to exist and react to events as they occurred, Manolo was becoming curious about himself—the man he must have been before he opened his eyes to Teresita's worried face, his mind wiped as clean of the past as if it had been a schoolboy's slate. He didn't believe, any longer, that he had been Teresita's brother-in-law. But a friend of her husband's? Perhaps? A Comanchero? That much made sense, too, because it fitted in with his knowledge of the Comanche tongue. A Comanchero who knew French as well as Spanish? Far too often, when he consciously tried to remember, he developed a headache, like a warning, pushing him one way, while his strange, half-remembered dreams pushed him another.

In the end, he headed straight for Dallas, on his own. Toni would find him—or he'd find her. And in the meantime, Judge Benoit's activities made him curious. If he found out what was happening before Toni arrived he'd have the advantage over her, because she wasn't about to make her visit public. And it was always advisable to keep one jump ahead of Toni—it made her easier to manage.

Dallas, he discovered wrathfully, was plastered with posters advertising the performances of an Italian opera singer at the local opera house—and reward posters that offered the almost unheard of sum of thirty-thousand dollars for his own capture and return to Baroque—alive, they specified—for questioning. For cattle-rustling, "and other crimes." A far-too detailed description followed. . . . He should have blindfolded her, in addition to gagging her!

He had misjudged the bitch, he thought furiously. She was obviously smarter than he gave her credit for. There was no mention of rape, of course, but who would question her if she swore that some of her cattle had been stolen? Or if she said she recognized who had done it? Clever—or had it been her "cousin" who had thought it up? It meant he had to lie low, and be damn cautious as long as he remained in Dallas. And what he *should* do was go back and teach Ginny Morgan a lesson—a harsher one this time.

Still, after he had registered at a fleabag hotel, stubble-bearded and as shabby-looking as he could manage, he could not help a grudging feeling of admiration for the way in which she'd contrived things. Damn her to hell! Because she had only made everything he had intended to do more difficult.

Fortunately, Dallas was big enough, and close enough to Fort Worth, for him to appear indistinguishable from the rest of the cowboys and cattlemen and rogues that frequented the town, and others like it. The cattle business was booming, and Dallas was booming with it, even though, for the moment, it was only a stopping-off place for the herds that were driven on to the big Kansas railheads. The citizens of Dallas talked of the day when the railroad would spread its tentacles further south, and Texans would not have to take their herds through Indian territory. In the meantime, Dallas was a growing town; an important one, well situated. All kinds of men came to Dallas, or passed through it, and for the most part the town marshal turned a blind eye to the rowdy element, unless they got completely out of hand. Dallas had the reputation for being a wide-open town—as long as you were cautious.

Steve was being cautious. Those reward posters would be on public display in almost every town of some size and importance, and no doubt every bounty hunter for miles around would be looking for him—not to mention Nick Benoit, who would be only too glad to have his hide anyway. And Toni—sweet, rapacious Antoinette Lassiter, whose greed for money and power outweighed even her sexual appetites. He frowned, thinking of *that* complication. And quite apart from the money, Toni and Benoit would begin to wonder how much of their plans he might give away if he was captured—especially since the posters specified he was to be taken alive.

The frown became a grimace as he began to strip off his dirty, travel stained clothes, wondering how much time he had left. Obviously, Ginny Morgan was out for blood, and she didn't want to miss the personal pleasure of seeing him hang. Women were strange, often more vicious than men, especially when they felt themselves humiliated or placed at a disadvantage.

So what in hell was he still doing here, in Dallas, when he should be hightailing it into Indian territory, where he could hide out? The face that looked back at him from the tiny, cracked, flyspotted mirror, gave him no answers; because, in a way, he was looking at a stranger, even to himself. Damn it, what kind of a man had he been? And even if he forgot a whole chunk of his past life, did a man's character really change? He had the impression that he actually enjoyed danger—the feelings of walking, tight-rope fashion, balanced on the sharp edge of a sword. Certainly, there were no traces of fear in the blue eyes that gave him back his own frowning stare—and searching his own feelings cautiously, he could feel no foreboding sense of apprehension. Rather, there was a barely tamped-down sense of reckless exhilaration, which he would have to control.

He had registered downstairs with a bored looking clerk who had barely glanced up from his newspaper, as Sam Whittaker, the name popping into his mind for no particular reason unless—unless it was one he had used before? But right now he didn't want to start trying to pry bits and pieces of the past out of his stubbornly blank mind, giving himself a headache in the process. He was damn tired, and needed some sleep, so he could wake up clearheaded and decide on a plan of action.

The room was tiny—no more than a small cubbyhole near the top of the stairs. But it had a window that led out onto the roof, just in case he needed to escape very quickly, and he had already wedged the single chair the room boasted under the door handle, a precaution that showed he was used to this kind of life—running and hiding.

He looked down at the bed with distaste. The one thin cotton sheet it boasted was torn, and stained with tobacco juice and tiny splotches of blood that showed its previous occupant had been successful at killing some of the bedbugs with which, no doubt, it was infested. And the blanket was so thin it was worn through in patches, especially at the bottom, where spurred boots had rested. He should have bedded down with his horse in the livery stable, and he needed a bath, but what the hell, he had no desire to use the dirty, lukewarm water some cowhand had used already. And he was broke, except for a couple of dollars and a pair of emerald earrings he had taken from Ginny Morgan's dressing table—more for devilment than anything else; he'd thought at the time that Toni might enjoy looking at them. But the clever little bitch had made mention of the theft of her earrings too, so that selling them was out of the question now. Later, when he went back, he'd really make her pay—and he was suddenly, angrily and vengefully determined that he would go back, if only to make sure that this time she really would have something to scream blue murder about.

He slept on the dirty floor, in the end, wrapped up in his saddle blankets, preferring the smell of his horse to the sour-sweet smell of the bed—slept in uneasy snatches, with every small sound in the corridor outside pulling him back to awareness. How much time did he have? He needed to find Benoit, discover who he was seeing. . . .

Nicholas Benoit had taken a room at the best hotel in town, unimaginatively named The Cattleman's; by a fortunate coincidence, it was situated on the same floor as the rooms occupied by the gentlemen he was supposed to meet and talk business with: Mr. McGregor, a Scot, and Lord Lindhaven, an Englishman who was diffident about the fact that he bore a title. Both represented monied interests in Britain, and were eager to invest in the cattle business in the United States. The day of the individual cattle kings was fast vanishing, to be replaced by vast, company-owned empires, like the Matador and XIT ranches of the Panhandle. Now, with the invention of barbed wire and the taking up of most of the grasslands in the panhandle, far-sighted men with money to invest were looking to the Southwest. The Prairie Cattle Company Ltd. had just paid the astounding sum of $350,000 for the comparatively small ranch of one Thomas Bugbee—money was no object, if there was land that could be bought. And Nick Benoit was definitely interested—not so much in their first tentative offers, but in their casually thrown out bits of information about Ginny Morgan.

Lord Lindhaven, a lanky, loose-jointed man with fair

hair and thick sideburns confessed to having been one of her admirers, while she was cutting a swath through Europe.

"Heard she had—um—more or less retired into seclusion in your part of Texas, Mr. Benoit. Can't understand it, unless it's got something to do with that elusive husband of hers. Heard quite a bit about his sharp business dealings when I was in New York. Surprising he isn't with her, isn't it? Lovely woman! Tsar Alexander of Russia was quite taken with her—made an open show of taking her everywhere, and gave her some magnificent pieces of jewelry. Surprised everyone when she decided to go back to France." Lindhaven pulled at his sideburns deprecatingly. "Must admit I was quite bowled over by her myself—met her a few times, y'know. Invited her over to my place in Surrey. But she always had so many other chaps chasing her—used to be a member of poor old Maximilian's court in Mexico, I've heard since, although I suppose that was before she married." Carried away by the influence of port and fine cigars, Lord Lindhaven had actually winked slyly. "Heard she was living quite openly as the Comte D'Arlingen's mistress, before she jilted him to live with some Mexican Colonel. Same one who turned the poor Archduke over to the wolves. And after that she was married to a Russian Prince—forget his name now, but he didn't last long. Married this man Morgan, who appeared from nowhere, with a lot of money. He used to be a close friend of di Paoli's too—I heard they would have married if he hadn't already had a wife he'd conveniently packed off to Europe! But I can't understand, old boy, why he'd do a damn fool thing like that! The lovely Virginia—toast of Europe, she was! Could pick and choose her escorts. Pity about her becoming a little mother so unexpectedly. Wonder what she's done with the children?"

Nick Benoit had been so interested in his new friend's disclosures that he had let his cigar go out, but now Mr. McGregor interrupted forcefully:

"I don't know about *you*, Algernon, but I'm here to talk business. I'm a married man myself—and happily so, I might add. My wife doesn't want to go gallivanting all over Europe, and I might add, she wasn't too happy at my little business trip over here either. Now, sir, you were saying about this—er—rangeland, d'you call it?"

"Yes. I have the definite feeling that Mrs. Morgan will want to sell her land," Benoit said smoothly. "As Lord Lindhaven has pointed out, she's hardly the type of lady who would want to bury herself forever. And as for the rest of it, some Mexicans have homesteaded, but *they* will be only too glad to sell out their interests and go back across the border. It's unfortunate, but in Texas, Mexicans aren't exactly made to feel wanted. Now, my sister-in-law has authorized me to speak for her, too—I have her power-of-attorney, of course. . . ."

Chapter Fifty-six

It was not unusual for Francesca di Paoli to be in a bad mood—she had the kind of temperament that veered from one exteme to the other, although only those close to her bore the brunt of her vicious temper, when it was aroused. But this particular evening she was worse than usual, as the broken crystal littering the carpet of her bedroom bore evidence.

Bert Fields had already beat a hasty retreat, and her frightened manager had soon followed suit, trying to calm the over-awed tenor who was to sing opposite her at the evening performance.

It was the patient Costanza who was left to calm her volatile bambina, who stormed from one end of the room to another, hair swinging in two thick braids.

"Does that pasty-faced pipsqueak think he can play Alfredo? Pah! Violetta would have taken one look at his face and turned to the Baron instead. Must I be forced to pretend I am in love with him? He is far too fat, and his voice quavers on the high notes. He makes me sick! And he is not the only one—that other one, the little Judge who is such an admirer of mine—*he* makes me sick too! I do not like waxed mustaches and little men who gaze at me with big sheep's eyes—I do not even like the flowers he keeps sending me, their scent is too sweet, like his pretty speeches! Can you tell me what I am doing here, having made a most uncomfortable journey to get here? This dirty, dusty little place, with wooden buildings and a hotel that is not fit to house a—a goat? I ask you this—"

"And you know the answer very well," Costanza answered dourly. "You wanted to come here. And you had me mail your letter to this Judge, your faithful admirer. And why? Because you are foolish, carissima! You hope to see this blue-eyed banditti again, and I tell you that you should forget him! He was no good for you, and I told you that too, from the very beginning, did I not? You saw the way he treated you."

"I don't want to hear the same old croaking! He said he had business to take care of, didn't he? So what happened to him? His wife is here, in this place they call Texas—but she is by herself, sì? And even her father, the Senator, is not sure where he is. I spoke with Senator Brandon in San Francisco, and he did not want to say very much because his wife was with him—that washed out blonde creature! But I watched her face while he was speaking of his daughter, and stuttering over his words—all is not well there. Do you think I could not sense it? And this cousin—Senator Brandon did not say anything about a cousin! Costanza!"

"You are far too tense, my little one. Have you forgotten you are to sing tonight? And there is that important Englishman, Lord Lindhaven, who has also sent you flowers, and will be watching you tonight. It's not like you to keep hankering after a man."

"I am not hankering after him! I tell you, I hate him! But it is for *me* to tell a man good-bye, do you understand? And that is why I will see him again—to tell him what I think of him!"

Costanza's voice became soothing.

"Yes, and you will. But now it is time to dress. Which gown will you wear? And a fine Violetta you will make with your hair hanging down your back like that! Sit down now, and try to keep calm. Shall I put flowers in your hair? We have plenty, thanks to your friend the Judge."

"Don't mention his name to me! Did I really promise to have dinner with him tonight? Oh!" Francesca swore in gutter Italian, making her maid frown with displeasure.

"What's the matter with you? If anyone was listening, they would think the worst of your origins, and you are a princess!"

Francesca flung herself down on the stool before the mirror, lips pouting, although her dark eyes had taken on a kind of sheen that Costanza was, unfortunately, all too familiar with.

"Princess—pah! What did the stupid title mean before it was discovered I had a voice? And now it doesn't matter what I do—if I swear or throw tantrums. I am a prima donna, or had you forgotten? My poor Bert Fields calls me that. And I am practicing for my new opera—the one I mean to try out on the poor, unsuspecting citizens of this Dallas. It will be the kind of piece they will appreciate, don't you think?" Francesca leaned forward, suddenly smiling as she regarded her reflection in the glass. "*Carmen*—I think I could fit into the part very well. I understand how a woman like that would feel, and think. Poor Bizet—after the disaster of his opera's first performance at the Opéra Comique, perhaps I could make it famous for him, eh?"

"I do not like it," Costanza said uncompromisingly, but Francesca, her mood suddenly changing, only laughed.

"And I do not care what you, or anyone else may think! I shall only do as I please, and be myself. At least, Stefano understood that about me, because *he* was the same way. And I shall see him again—I have the feeling."

Francesca, diamonds glittering in her dark hair, at her throat and ears and wrists, rode in a closed carriage to the opera house, ignoring the crowd of loafers that clustered about the stage door to see her alight. To most of them, she was like a creature from another world—a real princess, looking exactly as one was supposed to look in her sparkling white silk and brocade gown. She was escorted by two heavily-armed deputies, looking self-conscious in their stiff new clothes.

Francesca, turning her head to flash the crowd a brilliant smile, waved her hand once before she disappeared behind the stage door, and a couple of over-excited cowboys began to whoop as they discharged their guns into the air.

"Stay back! And anyone who fires a gun is under ar-

rest!" The deputies tried to look menacing in the face of
the laughter from the crowd of on-lookers.

The thick wooden door thudded shut before them, and
with muttered grumbles, the men who had gathered
around it began to disperse, to seek more familiar plea-
sures elsewhere.

Manolo, who now went by the name of Sam Whittaker,
moved with the crowd. He had seen Benoit's opera singer,
who proved surprisingly lovely. If he'd been able to afford
the price of a ticket, he'd have been tempted to go inside
and hear her sing, like Benoit and those two visiting foreign dudes who stayed at the same hotel. Two gentlemen
who called themselves British and were interested in the
cattle business—it hadn't been difficult to find out that
much. Nor to deduce why Nick Benoit spent so much time
in their company when he wasn't chasing behind
Francesca di Paoli. But was guessing good enough? They
were all at the opera tonight—maybe he'd find something
in their rooms that would tell him more. And before that,
he needed a drink.

The nearest saloon was the Red Dog, a crowded, pretentious place where the girls wore lots of sequins and the
drinks came higher than usual. But it was right across the
street from the opera house, and it seemed as if everyone
drifted in there. Bad luck—because after a while one of
the deputies who'd been assigned to watch over the opera
singer wandered in, red-faced, sullen looking, and obviously spoiling for a fight. He was greeted with a chorus of
good-natured gibes.

"Hey, will you look who's here? Danged if it isn't our
brand-new deputy."

"Red, what happened to that fancy woman you was
supposed to escort? She decide she preferred someone else
to take her home?"

"Shut up! Want me to put you whisky-mouths under arrest for disturbing the peace?"

Red Moriarty was as Irish as his name—an ex-railroad
foreman who was better than average with a gun. Moreover, the marshal was his brother-in-law, a fact he was determined to live down. And tonight he was mad because
Lew had treated him like he was a shotgun guard, riding
herd on that bejewelled foreign woman who acted like he
didn't even exist for her. Right now, Red was looking for

his favorite girl, and after that, for a head to bash in, just to make sure he was shown proper respect. He found both—and at the same time. But it was the wrong time, when he was already too mad to be cautious, like the marshal had warned him.

The girl, who had been leaning far too close up against a tall, shabby looking stranger who had chosen to nurse his drink at the far end of the bar, looked up with an annoyed cry when Red grabbed her by the arm.

"What's the matter with you? I was just trying to get him to buy me a drink, that's all."

"Too bad you had to pick on a saddle-tramp who looks like he can't afford the price of a drink, Lola-Mae. You paid for this one you got, mister?"

Moriarty met a pair of blue eyes that were unafraid, and even contemptuous, and too late, the first warning bell rang in his mind.

"That part of your job, lawman? Checking on whether the customers have paid for their drinks? Or did you have another kind of problem?"

"This place don't cater to saddle-bums—especially the kind that can't afford to buy a gal a drink. Your kind usually ends up spending the night in jail, sleeping it off. Shoulda stuck to the other side of town, mister."

Moriarty was blustering now—going from the hard, dark-blue eyes, his gaze had already taken in the tied down gun, holstered low. But most gunfighters he'd seen or heard of were natty dressers. This man couldn't be more than he looked—a drifter, masquerading as a gunman.

"Look, Marshal"—the expelled breath could have been a sigh of impatience, or fear—"I'm not looking for trouble. Just standing here, minding my own business. Why don't we just leave it that way, huh? If you're spoiling for a fight, go find it someplace else—I plan to leave here right after I finish my drink, in any case."

Moriarty thought he sensed a backing down, and the thought that for a few moments he had actually been afraid made his anger rise.

"Insolent bastard, ain't you? Got no proper respect for the law, but I bet I can teach you that, when I take you in. Drunk an' disorderly—an' while I've got you locked up

I'll be checkin' on all those Wanted dodgers the marshal's got."

Red Moriarty made the mistake, right then, of reaching for his gun; and it was the last one he made. He'd only meant to show everyone here that he was a fast draw—and the last thing he saw was a blur as the stranger's gun cleared leather.

The girl Lola-Mae screamed, breaking the sudden silence that followed the explosion of the gunshot that sent Deputy Moriarty spinning backward on his heels to land with another, smaller explosion of sound on the sawdust-scattered floor.

Lola-Mae kept screaming hysterically when everyone else fell quiet, watching the gun—powder smoke still curling from its muzzle—that covered them steadily while its owner backed towards the rear entrance.

He was half-inclined to shoot the screaming female who stood, her mouth open in a fixed grimace, in the center of the floor. And he shouldn't have shot that deputy—at least, not to kill; although when it came to shooting it seemed as if pure instinct governed him. Like it did now—until suddenly, shockingly, he felt the shotgun barrel jabbed into his back, bringing him up short.

"You just hold it right there, mister!" And then, voice almost querulous, the marshal said: "What in hell is going on here anyhow? Heard the screaming, and its louder than what's going on at the opera house." And then everybody began to speak at once.

He ended up in what must have been a cellar originally, but was now converted into a cell for convicted felons—a dark hole with three shallow steps leading down to it, under the jailhouse.

At least he was still alive, and he might not have been—since he'd killed the marshal's brother-in-law—if he hadn't deliberately taunted the man with the fact that there was a reward for his capture, *alive*. How long before Nick Benoit, or someone else, came for him?

It was cold down here, and he had company—a Mexican, waiting resignedly to hang for murder and robbery.

"And what are you here for? A killing, just like me, eh? I do not think they will leave us here long enough to be tried in a court—the vigilantes will come for us, with cloth over their faces, and . . . phhft! Comprende?"

There was not even a cot down here, and no blankets. Only a bucket in one corner, and the cold floor. The Mexican, whose name was Ruiz, grew quite friendly when he discovered his recent companion was a compadre.

"They treat us like animals—worse than they treat their dogs. And here, in this jail, it is no better than elsewhere. Now, if you had been a gringo, perhaps they would have thrown in a couple of blankets, eh?" He laughed, but his laughter had a frightened, hollow sound. "What does it matter—we are going to die in any case. I have heard how they go about it—the gringos who call themselves vigilantes and cover their faces so that no one will recognize them. I have been here a whole day and a half now, and I expected them before this. But perhaps they were waiting until I had company. It is not good that a man should die alone."

Ruiz began to cough, suddenly, and the manacles on his wrists made a clanking sound in the pitch blackness.

"Amigo—you do not say much. Are you afraid?"

Cold iron, cutting into his wrists where there were already scars. The prison he had been in before had been worse than this—how had he escaped?

"I am just as much afraid as you are. Is that enough to keep you quiet? If we're going to hang, why not get some rest before?"

"You must like the idea of rest—do you think you can really sleep in here? There are rats—and you will find yourself listening for every sound, wondering, 'Are they coming for me now? Will this be the time?' These gringos—they will not even give a man the last courtesy of a priest."

He closed his eyes determinedly, lying on his back on the cold earth floor, shutting out the voice of Ruiz, who seemed to talk compulsively. Hanging—how would it feel to have the breath choked out of his body? Would the marshal bother to check, or hand him over to the vigilantes anyway?

He decided that it didn't really matter, and surprisingly, he must have slept, like an animal snatching rest when the hunters were almost upon it. Slept—to come wide-awake just as quickly and easily.

"Ah, Dios!" Ruiz muttered, his voice a croak in the darkness as the bolts on the trap door above them were drawn open. "I am not ready to die yet—did I say so? I must have lied. How is it they come so soon? I have a wife—two little children. Who will look after them now?"

Orange lantern-light streamed through the opening that led down into the cell, outlining the figures of their visitors. Recognizing at least one of them, in spite of the hooded cloak she wore, Ruiz' companion sighed.

"Why don't you shut up? If they hang you, it will probably be because you talk too much. Besides, I think these ones have come for me—stay quiet and they might not notice you."

"I'm sorry, Comanche." Toni's voice was meant to hold regret, but he recognized the breathless, excited tone that underlay it and braced himself for trouble. "But you shouldn't have killed the nice marshal's brother-in-law— and you shouldn't have come here instead of meeting me on the way! I thought—oh, I really thought you had changed."

Her face was lifted up appealingly to the marshal, who held the lantern high, lighting up the grim faces of the men who had followed him down the steps—Judge Benoit leading them.

And while Toni was putting on her performance, Manolo caught the maliciously triumphant look in Benoit's side-slanted brown eyes, before he had composed his face into stern lines.

"I'm afraid this *is* the man, Marshal. My sister-in-law hired him against my advice—trusting in his word that he had turned over a new leaf. But you can see how far that went! He seems to make it a practice to rob and prey on helpless widows—women without a husband to protect them. You've seen the charges detailed on that reward poster in your office."

"So much money!" Toni said breathlessly, softly, her shiny eyes catching his. "She must want you very badly."

"Toni!" Benoit snapped, warning her. And then, "You see, Marshal, we had expected something like this. That he might come here, following Mrs. Lassiter, to make trouble because she discharged him. And there are several other charges he'll have to answer to in Baroque—the cold-blooded murder of Mrs. Lassiter's former foreman, for one."

"This a hanging party or a trial?" Manolo's voice was

deliberately insolent, making Toni's white teeth catch in her full lower lip. He looked at the marshal, and the men behind him; grim looking men, with murder in their eyes. "That reward poster says thirty thousand dollars for my capture *alive,* Marshal. You going to let them collect it instead of you?"

The marshal, suddenly remembering the money, began to bluster.

"Now see here, who said anything about hanging? You'll get a fair trial, according to the law—"

"Law, hell!" one of the grim-faced men blurted out. "You know damn well what we came here for, Tolbert! This bastard killed your brother-in-law in cold blood—and Red was a deputy! An' that ain't all he's guilty of either, from what we've just heard. Boys, we going to let scum like this live long enough to get tried, and try to smear this pretty lady with his dirty accusations?"

"Now see here—" the marshal began, but someone took his gun from him, pushing him aside contemptuously. And Manolo guessed, from the looks on their faces and the way they glanced towards Benoit as if for approval, that these were *his* men—hired killers, to make up a mob scene.

Someone held the lantern up high, and someone else laughed.

"You bastard—you're going to hang!"

And Toni, her voice suddenly high: "Make him tell about those jewels he stole—make him tell that first!"

Benoit gave a twisted smile, nodding. And because Benoit was closest, and there was not much Steve could do with his wrists manacled, he hit Benoit, driving his fists into the man's soft belly and enjoying the gasping, retching noises he made as he bent over—managing to get at least two more of the men before the roof caved in and he went under their pounding fists and boots.

He had time to wonder, groggily, if they were going to beat him to death instead of saving him for a hanging, and then everything dissolved in a red fog of agony, with the only thought left in his mind the instinctive writhing of his body as he tried to get away from the boots that kept pounding into his ribs and his head—and from somewhere far away he heard the sound of Toni's high, excited giggle. . . .

He was lying on the floor, with a rope around his neck, and it came to him with an involuntary feeling of shame that the moaning, gasping noises he kept hearing were torn from his own throat.

"He's coming back to life, seems like, Mr. Benoit. Do we finish him off now?"

"So soon?" Toni's full lips would be wet and pouting when she said that. "Nicky, he hasn't told about those jewels he stole yet! And you promised me—"

"You'll have your turn, Toni-sweet—yes, I promise you that. Because I've had time to think, while the boys here were having their fun, and I've come up with—" Benoit's laughter was soft and ugly, boding no good—"a rather clever scheme, whereby we can both have our cake and eat it, so to speak." And then, voice hardening, "But first, it's my turn to teach this half-breed animal a lesson. And the other grovelling killer who's hiding in that corner there. I want them both to have a taste of what hanging feels like."

There were hooks in the wall, set up high, that must have been used for hanging meat and long rows of dried chili peppers and onions. They were strong enough to take the weight of a man's twisting, jerking body.

Ruiz screamed once, and the scream was abruptly cut off as gurgling noises came from his throat.

"That's one of 'em. Now haul *him* up—not too fast, because I don't want his neck broken, not yet. I want him to choke, very slowly."

Hanging was feeling a rope tighten around your throat cutting off breath while you clawed at the rope like an animal fighting for its life and wondered why your fingers had no feeling in them. Hanging was gasping and choking and feeling the twitching of your limbs as your feet jerked in the air, looking for a foothold.

And then, at the very last minute, the floor came up and hit him in the face as the terrible pressure around his throat was eased slightly; and he was sick, retching weakly with no control over his body's betrayal, and Toni was still giggling.

It wasn't over yet—Nick Benoit said something and they dragged his sagging body upright so that Benoit, who considered himself an excellent amateur boxer, could go to work on his face. It was like having something happen to someone else—or maybe, by this time, his body had absorbed all the pain and shock it was capable of registering.

Benoit was careful to wear gloves, and the half-conscious man his men held for him felt his head rock with each calculatedly vicious blow. He felt his nose break, and he tasted blood in his mouth, and he couldn't see as the cuts and bruises began to swell. He passed out again before Benoit was through; voices brought him unwillingly back to pain-fogged reality.

"Do you hear me, you swine? Before I leave you to the tender mercies of the *lady* here I want you to know what's in store for you."

Another voice, shrill-pitched: "Give him a taste of the whip—*that* ought to wake him up! He used to hit me all the time, Nicky—only after the way he killed Billy-Boy, right in front of me, I was afraid. But not I want him to know what we've got planned for him!" Again that obscenely excited giggle, and he felt the familiar sting of the lash on his back and knew he was back in prison. He was beyond pain now—almost beyond thought—but he remembered vaguely that if he didn't groan the guards would keep the whip coming down, over and over. . . .

"There! I told you that would do it! He's conscious—tell him, Nicky!"

"It's all very simple, really." Who in hell did that drawling, affected voice belong to? The young doctor? But the doctor had had shiny boots, and. . . . The pounding in his head became louder, almost drowning out the sound of the voice that went on and on, sounding very pleased about something.

"We mean to collect that reward money by delivering you to Baroque alive. But only *barely* alive, you understand? Because you're going to walk there, at the end of a rope, like the animal you are. And if you're fed, it'll be on the kind of scraps and slop one would feed to dogs—or swine! And if you don't behave, you'll be beaten."

"Oh, but I think he ought to be beaten in any case—with a whip, like my father used to beat his slaves." Toni giggled again. "I always did want to have a slave of my very own, who'd do anything, anything at all I order him to do—a man, of course. Will you enjoy that, Comanche?"

"Toni, be quiet. *You,* down there—you crawling, grovelling bastard, you're going to learn to crawl and cringe whenever I give the word, do you hear? And by the time you get to Baroque, you'll *be* an animal. Without a mind. Do you understand now? Toni and I will be quite safe, because you won't be capable of talking, much less remembering anything. . . ."

Pain—stabbing into his brain from all directions. What was he doing lying on the cold floor with his hands manacled and immobilized, in a welter of his own blood and vomit, feeling as if every bone in his body had been broken? And the voices, going on and on—why wouldn't they stop and leave him alone?

He actually made the effort to say something, but it seemed as if his throat, like the rest of him, had become paralyzed by the torture it had undergone. Only an unrecognizable sound—a choked off groan instead of the words he had planned to use—emerged; and he heard the same high-pitched laughter that seemed to have been grating on his nerves forever.

"You see, Nicky? I think he understood."

"Good—I hope so! And remember—you're not to kill him! Control those urges I see shining in your yellow cat's eyes, my love, and remember that thirty thousand dollars!"

The voices were saying things that didn't make sense—cutting through the separate lances of agony that shot through Steve's head.

Nicholas Benoit dusted off his gloves fastidiously—he'd have to get a fresh pair before he went back to the theater; these were covered with blood—and looked warningly at his sister-in-law.

"I'm going back—I have an important dinner engagement, if you'll remember. And I hope this—unpleasantness goes unnoticed. I wouldn't want the princess to think I didn't enjoy her performance—she makes such a lovely, madonna-like Violetta!"

"Oh, but you make me *sick* sometimes, Nicky—you really do! Even if you *are* much cleverer than I gave you credit for. What are we going to do with them now?

"The marshal's gone," one of the grinning men offered, spitting a long stream of tobacco juice in the direction of their prisoner. "He's probably geting himself a drink someplace—pretending none of this is happening. And we only got *one* of them to worry about now—got carried away and left that Mex hanging for too long; he's done stopped kicking."

"Well, just be sure and keep *this* one alive or there won't be that reward money coming to pay your wages with. I'm leaving it up to you, Toni."

Benoit left, quickly, and his mind was already on Francesca.

Toni stood there sullenly, chewing on her lower lip. Damn Nicky! It was just like him, to leave the really dirty work up to her. And it was really a shame, in a way, that Comanche had decided to try and cross them—he had been such an exciting lover, the only man who had been capable of dominating her and making her crawl. But now it would be *his* turn, and the thought of the things she would make him do for her, before they were finished with him, made her eyes start shining all over again.

"This place stinks! Drag him up the steps—and make sure you pour enough water over him when we get outside to make him wake up. I want him to enjoy every minute of what's happening to him."

Chapter Fifty-seven

Francesca di Paoli gave an encore and took her last bow for the evening. Trailed by her ever-faithful Costanza and her excitedly-chattering manager she hurried down the narrow, badly lit corridor that led to her dressing room, shivering a little until Costanza, muttering dourly, flung a white silk shawl about her bare shoulders.

"This barbarous town! They want my bambina to catch a chill, I think. And you should not have worn this gown that shows far too much of what a lady usually keeps hidden!"

"And you ought to know by now that I am *not* a lady!" Francesca snapped over her shoulder. "But you are right about one thing, my old dragon, this is a barbarous town. Listen to those shots, and those fearful yells—why do they have to celebrate by shooting at each other? It's a wonder they did not start shooting off those great big pistols while I was singing, although it would have been a relief if someone had shot that poor imitation Alfredo! He croaked like a frog tonight, and his breath reeked of garlic—Luigi!"

Her poor manager, already mumbling apologies for the tenor, felt himself stiffen with apprehension. What now? Was she going to throw another tantrum?

"Luigi—go and find out what that noise is all about. I cannot stand it—you know how tense my nerves are after I have been singing! And keep everyone away from me. Yes, everyone! I don't want their flowers and their cheap, nasty champagne, do you understand? Tell Signor Fields to entertain them all tonight. I must have some time to myself, to be alone."

"But—but Francesca, you promised you would have dinner—"

"Dinner? Do you think I can eat, or think of eating with that little man staring across the table at me as if he would like to gobble me up instead of the caviar? Keep him away from me—let him wait, if he wants to, I don't care. Costanza. . . ."

"Go away and do as she says. You know what she's like when she gets in a mood like this. Go away—I'll calm her down. . . ."

Luigi Rizzo stumbled away, clutching at his hair in despair. Why, why had he ever thought he wanted to manage a prima donna? Always the dirty work—the vases and cut-glass bottles of perfume thrown at him—Dio!

"That silly, silly man! Why do I put up with him? Why do I put up with all of this? Travelling, always travelling, to give my music to—to a herd of swine! Oh, I tell you, I am so sick of it, so tired! Costanza—these corsets are cutting off my breath! Why did you have to lace them up so tightly? Loosen them, quickly, before I die. And give me a glass of wine—and my robe—ah, it's so warm in here, I feel stifled. . . ."

It was always like this, after a performance. Francesca became a spoiled, demanding child, needing her old nurse to pet her and pamper her and reassure her that everything had gone perfectly, that she had never sung so well.

"Now you just calm down—be calm—Costanza will help you." It was a kind of ritual with them. Francesca let herself relax, feeling the tightly constricting stays come loose as her magnificent gown slipped carelessly around her ankles, to be quickly gathered up by an alternately scolding and coaxing Costanza.

"Sit down, my little one—here, in this nice, comfortable chair by the fire. And drink your wine, it's nice and cold. I'll brush your hair for you presently, just as I always do, and no one will bother you, no one at all."

Oh God, why did she have to feel so tense? It was that new opera she was going to sing tomorrow—*Carmen*. She had loved the libretto, from the moment she read it, and the music was so wild, so exciting—but she must be insane, to offer brand-new opera to an audience in *this* town, They would never appreciate it. Yes, she must certainly have been crazy to conceive of such an idea in the first place—to have come here at all. . . .

And then—and then, when the door that Costanza had carelessly left unlocked burst open and the man staggered in, Francesca thought she was really going mad. She was too terrified to move, even to scream, although her mouth opened in a soundless gasp.

Oh—dear God! He was covered with blood, and dirt— the tattered remnants of what had once been a shirt hanging from his shoulders. And his face was so bruised and battered it was almost unrecognizable as being human.

" 'Cesca. . . ." The voice was a hoarse whisper that she had to strain her ears to hear. And she saw, thinking she must be having a terrible nightmare, the deep purple bruises around his throat, still oozing blood.

The Hanged Man—symbol from an old deck of Tarot cards. It flashed into her mind, even while her thoughts struggled to fit into a coherent pattern, wondering how he knew her name, and why the intonation of his voice— if not the voice itself—was so achingly familiar. And then, just before he collapsed onto the rug with a kind of groan, she caught a glimpse of his eyes—or what there was of them to be seen in that horribly broken and swollen face.

"Dio! This town of animals—of beasts! What have they done to you?"

She was on her feet like a whirlwind, brushing past a

frozen, immobile Costanza to bang the door shut, and lock it with shaking fingers. And then she went to him, dropping to her knees on the floor, swearing and crying at the same time in a mixture of Italian and English.

"Look at you! Dear God, what happened? It serves you right, for leaving me the way you did! I haven't forgiven you—if you weren't such a—a terrible mess I would break a bottle of wine over your head! Costanza, will you stop standing there gaping? Bring a doctor, quickly!"

"No, no doctor. . . ." His voice was the same, horribly strained whisper. And she had to bend her head closer to try and make out what he was muttering.

But you—you are—you look as if you are dying! Stefano—"

"No—doctor. . . . In . . . some kind of . . . trouble . . . hanging kind. . . ."

"Be quiet! Don't try to speak! Costanza! Why do you continue to stand there? Help me—*do* something. . . ."

"Much better to have let them take him," Costanza grumbled afterwards. "That man! Didn't I tell you from the beginning he was nothing but a banditti? A ruffian? You heard them say he killed a man—not one, but several! No doubt that's how he came by all that money he used to throw around so freely! And by lying to protect him, *you* are in much trouble, too!"

"Be quiet, you croaking old woman! Do you understand nothing? And you will keep your mouth closed, do you understand?"

Costanza shrugged sullenly—not really understanding, but not daring to argue further. At least, she was entitled to her thoughts. Why had that man, who had been so bad for her bambina from the very beginning, thrown himself back in their lives? And just as Francesca was starting to forget him, too. She could foresee nothing but trouble as long as he stayed here.

Bert Fields and Luigi Rizzo knew—but no one else. And Francesca had done a magnificent job of acting when the men had come knocking at her dressing room door, led by an apologetic Judge Benoit.

"What *is* this? Am I not to be allowed to change my clothes in peace? Or perhaps you hoped to catch me undressed—is that the truth of the matter, Signore? I tell you, I am not used to such barbarous, uncivilized manners."

"Princess—my humblest apologies! But it was only out of concern for your safety that I dared knock at your door. You see, a vicious criminal has escaped—a murderer. He was seen coming into the theater, in here, and of course my first thought—"

"In here, you say? Into my dressing room, through a locked door? Must I be subjected to such humiliation? Are your vicious criminals all devotees of the opera then? Or are you calling me a liar, Signore?"

The note of rising hysteria in her voice was real enough, and Nicholas Benoit flinched from it.

That he should have offended her—and especially now, when he had felt she was unbending toward him. . . . No, it was not possible that the man they were looking for would have been bold enough to walk into the theater, still crowded with people. Someone had helped him escape—the same mysterious man who had created a drunken diversion that enabled him to disappear from under the noses of Toni and eight of his own men.

"Your pardon, Princess," he said again, hastily. "But just in case he is still lurking around here somewhere, I'll send Mr. Fields to you—and ensure you have protection when you return to the hotel."

"You Americans! Why did I ever leave Europe? Savage—barbarous. . . ." She had switched to Italian, fortunately, for the men who accompanied him were listening with fascinated interest to her tirade.

Nicholas Benoit was furious, although he managed to hide it from his idol. Furious at himself, and at Toni, who had allowed such a thing to happen. How could a man who was already half-dead, and half-hanged, escape? And where had he disappeared to?

"He can't go far," Toni kept repeating. "Perhaps, like an animal, he crawled into some hole to die! And even if he did manage to get away, what could he do? We have other ways out, Nicky darling. You're so clever—surely you can see what I mean?"

He didn't want to see—not then. But his searching drew a blank, and Francesca di Paoli seemed deliberately to seclude herself—in the space of just a few weeks, everything he had planned seemed suddenly to come crashing about his ears.

His foreign contacts—Lord Lindhaven, who had appeared so friendly, and the dour Scotsman McGregor—seemed suddenly withdrawn and noncommittal. Cables from the "principals" in New York and London suddenly urged caution. It was "wait and see" now, instead of "proceed with the negotiations," and surely it couldn't be because he had bungled the matter of one escaped felon these gentlemen knew nothing about?

For the first time, in the business meetings, and in overheard conversations, Nicholas Benoit began to hear the name Steve Morgan. The mysterious financier-tycoon. Husband of the woman who chose to hide herself away in Baroque—and for what reason? From her husband?

"Morgan's as unscrupulous as Gould, or Vanderbilt. Always gets what he goes out to get—and too bad for the little man caught in the middle. And you watch out for one of his partners, a certain gentleman by the name of Sam Murdock. They used to call him the Silver King, before they found out Morgan was the brains and the money behind him. But don't make any mistakes—Murdock's as sharp as they come."

By the time Toni left, discreetly and quietly for Baroque, Nick felt dazed—what had gone wrong? He had had everything figured out—beginning with his gradual seduction of Francesca di Paoli, who treated him now as if he did not exist for her; she had had dinner, on several occasions that he knew of, with Lord Lindhaven.

Neither Benoit nor Toni knew anything of Francesca di Paoli's unexpected guest.

"But how did you find me? If you remembered nothing at first, how?"

That part was still blurred in his mind. He remembered the cellar, in flashes, and with the memory, pain—and a confusion in his mind. And then, crawling up some steps, each one seeming more than a mile high. And a voice—Toni Lassiter's—in the background.

"Go on—crawl! Up all the steps, Comanche. You'd better get used to crawling, you're going to be doing a lot of it from now on."

And after the steps, there had been more pain, and more darkness, until they had thrown water on him from a horse trough, soaking him—chilling him so that he'd started shivering. And then, with the rope still around his neck, they'd hooked his manacled wrists around Toni's saddle pommel, and he remembered that she'd looked down at him, smiling her moist, triumphant smile.

"You'd better have enough life left in you to run, Comanche. Because we're going to be travelling awful fast."

Dragged forward for a while, his dulling mind had barely registered the first shots. And then there was a drunken, slurred voice:

"Hey, what *is* this, a lynching? Always did enjoy a lynching—can't I join in?"

"Port," his mind had registered, hardly knowing how; and then there had been more shots, and he was falling free, struggling to his knees, with Port's urgent voice in his ears:

"Look, there's only me and I can't hold all of them off. Run, damn you! The theater—you can make it that far."

And there had been the crowd, pouring out of the theater, shouting, milling, questioning, while somehow he had managed to run, plunging through the first dark, unguarded doorway he came to. Finding Francesca. . . .

"There's a man to see you," she told him some time on the second—or was it the third?—day.

"So you made it all right. I thought you would. What in hell have you been up to, anyhow? Bishop's madder than I've ever seen him, and it was just by a stroke of luck that I happened to be here keeping tabs on Benoit. Christ's sake, Steve—don't you ever learn?"

"It comes hard, I guess," he said cautiously, his voice still a hoarse whisper, and he caught Port's disgusted look.

"Ah, shit! I keep forgetting this is all a kind of game to you now that you've become so rich. But what the hell—there was a time when I was ready to go after you myself—until I heard you'd turned Dave free. And his woman before that. But what kind of game have you been playing since then? I'm supposed to give Bishop a report, in case you'd forgotten."

"Do you think he'd believe I've just started to remember?"

Port gave him a cynical, disbelieving look. And it was the same kind of look he'd be getting from everybody who

didn't know the real truth, Steve Morgan realized with
suppressed fury. He's been so sure of himself—and had
made such a mess of everything. He could even see why
Bishop might be more than slightly annoyed. And what in
hell was *Ginny* doing in the middle of everything?

It was left to Francesca, who had picked up all the
latest gossip from Lord Lindhaven who continued to linger
in Dallas, and to Port, who didn't realize what he was
saying, to fill him in.

His enforced rest, in Francesca's big, soft bed, gave his
own mind a chance to fill in the gaps while his body was
healing. From somewhere, Bert Fields had produced a
doctor who was discreet enough to ask no questions and
forget to gossip—for the large price he was being paid.
And then there was Francesca herself—alternately demanding and tender, full of questions. He was honest with her,
for Francesca di Paoli, of all the women he had met and
wanted and taken, had come closest to being a friend as
well as a lover—and for all her displays of temperament,
she was also an intelligent woman. They understood each
other, he and Francesca; and not only in bed, but more
basically too, because they were both adventurers who had
made good—both cynics who had learned not to give too
much of themselves.

It was only Ginny, damn her, who remained like a burning question mark in his mind, hiding there stubbornly
even when he did not want to think about her. Hell, what
was there to think? He had to learn from a complete outsider that his wife had become a mother, making him legally, at least, the father of two—not one, but *two*; trust
Ginny never to do things by halves!—infants of indetermi-
nate age and sex, whose existence he had not been informed of. So her sojourn in Europe had had *some* results,
after all! What really amazed him was that she had returned, boldly bringing her children back with her, as cool
as she pleased—and then she had deserted them without a
qualm to find *him*. And for what? To find out just how far
she could go? To make sure he was in no danger of regaining his memory? Or merely to test the extent of his
damnable weakness where she was concerned?

More questions—and he kept thinking up new ones,
gritting his teeth with steadily mounting rage. What new
trick was she up to this time? If he'd had any sense, he

should have let her stay married to her damned Russian, and gone his own way. Which was what he ought to do now. Let *her* ask the questions for a change!

Chapter Fifty-eight

Ginny had done nothing but ask herself questions, ever since the afternoon when Steve himself had brought everything to a head. He had gagged her, made love to her without words, and then, after robbing her of her pride, he had taken her emerald earrings as well. Why? What had been the point of such a useless, wasted gesture unless—and her jaws clenched together with burning rage as the thought struck her—unless he had wanted to prove to someone that he'd been in her bedroom. That anger made her offer the reward for his capture—alive.

"I won't let him get away with what he did! And I do not care what you, or Mr. Bishop, or anyone else might say—I've had my fill of secrecy, and of waiting ... waiting ... and for what? For a casual, occasional little rape by my own husband? When he can tear himself away from that Lassiter bitch, that is! Oh no—no, Renaldo! It's time matters were brought to a head, and I want Steve to learn that I am not to be taken with such—such casual contempt!"

Yes, Ginny thought furiously, she'd teach him that *her* mind could be just as devious and cold-bloodedly calculating as his!

But the weeks passed, dragging by, and she heard nothing. Toni Lassiter had gone to Shreveport, to visit relatives there—with Steve, Ginny wondered? The thought twisted like a knife in her heart when it wasn't filled with hot, unreasoning fury against him. And Missie, hurt and upset that her new friend could be so vindictive, no longer confided in her, although her shy friendship with Renaldo continued to grow.

Ginny found herself left more and more alone, as Renaldo rode nearly every day to the Carter ranch—always polite enough to ask if she cared to come along. And always, she would shake her head a trifle sullenly.

"No, you go ahead. My presence would only serve to make everyone act awkwardly—you know that's so. They don't trust me any longer."

Even Renaldo could say nothing to refute that, but his brown eyes had begun to take on a worried look when they studied her, and off-handedly he had begun to hint that perhaps they should be making plans to go back to Mexico, or perhaps pay a visit to her father and Sonya in California.

"You could take the children with you—even my uncle cannot fail to understand that it is high time they became acquainted with their other grandparents."

"Oh!" Ginny gave a high, almost hysterical laugh. "Do you think Sonya would ever forgive me if I made all her friends aware that she is a step-grandmother? How funny that sounds!"

Renaldo gave her a frowning, brooding look before he said abruptly:

"How long do you intend to try and hide the fact that you're a mother? For God's sake, Ginny, those children are yours and Steve's. You have no right to hide them away as if—as if you are ashamed of them. And I'm sorry to be so blunt, but you do owe those two poor little mites something—if only a mother's care!"

She stared at him, stricken to silence, her eyes slowly widening.

"So you think I'm being selfish? But I do miss them, Renaldo—I do! There are times when all I can think of is seeing them again, of running away from this whole ugly mess! I don't know what to do any longer! But I have to find Steve—he has to know, no matter what he might decide to do afterwards. Don't you understand that? I cannot go on any longer, living with indecision, with fear!" She jumped to her feet, putting her hand on his sleeve. "Renaldo—surely you can see it? If I'm to be a proper mother to my children, then I must know where I stand—I must know something, *anything* to end this horrible nothingness. I'm not even sure if I still have a husband or not. . . ."

When she heard, a week later, that Toni Lassiter had returned to Baroque. Ginny gritted her teeth. Renaldo was now her only pipeline to what she had begun to think of, grimly, as "the other side."

Renaldo had it from Missie, who had heard it from her brother Matt, that Toni had returned alone—and not in a very good mood either, and Missie had been upset because Matt had actually spent a night in "that woman's" house.

"I don't like it," Renaldo said thoughtfully, wondering why his senses suddenly warned him of impending trouble. Even Missie had seemed white-faced and depressed—and how much of her depression was due to her worry about Steve, whom she still called Manolo?

Renaldo had his own problems to keep him preoccupied—not the least of them being that he now had to admit to himself, unwillingly, that he was falling in love with Missie.

Ridiculous! A man his age, and a child-woman who was barely seventeen—still unready, unsure of herself and her feelings—he must be mad! And, uneasily, he could not help wondering what Missie's reactions would be when she discovered that he had deceived her. She was so completely honest and so open—no doubt she'd turn away from him, disillusioned. Oh, God, why had he ever volunteered to accompany Ginny here on her hare-brained scheme? He could forsee nothing but disaster ahead, for them all.

It came as a shock to Ginny when Toni Lassiter came to visit on a hot afternoon only two days after her return to Baroque.

Toni—who disliked her as intensely as she, Ginny, hated her in return. Then—why? She wished that Renaldo was here, for she suddenly had the most unpleasant feeling that Toni had only come to tell her something disagreeable.

Toni, to begin with, was at her most affable.

"How beautiful everything is! You've done marvels with this old, crumbling house, although I for one would not care to shut myself away here forever, especially if I could travel wherever and whenever I pleased!"

Amber eyes, holding a peculiar, shiny glitter in their depths, met Ginny's, and then Toni gave a small laugh, moistening pink lips with her tongue.

"But you really seem to like it here, don't you? I do

hope everything remains as quiet and peaceful as it seems to be now—and that is why I really came to see you, although I do owe you a visit, do I not? Henri told me you had called, just before I left for Shreveport. *Such* a dull place!" She sighed, stretching catlike, but Ginny could still discern the glitter of those eyes behind the deliberately lowered fan of silvery lashes.

"Oh?" Ginny made her polite query sound deliberately unconcerned, and suddenly Toni was leaning a little forward in her chair, just like a wolverine ready to pounce, although her full lips continued to smile.

"I could not stand it—and so I decided to go to Dallas, to see for myself this opera singer my brother-in-law is so fond of. And what a disappointment! I suppose she has an adequate voice, and she's pretty enough—but in such an overblown way! The kind of woman who will soon grow fat. I cannot understand what any man could see in her, unless it is the fasion to have an opera singer as a mistress!" The first tiny jab of the knife—and when Ginny merely shrugged, Toni went on sweetly, "But men are so foolish! I suppose they consider her kind of woman cheap, and fair game. Princess or not, I think any woman who performs publicly is only advertising the fact that she's for sale—don't you?"

The knife went in a little deeper this time—how much did Toni Lassiter know, and why had she really come here?

"I see no reason why a woman who has talents that may be displayed publicly should waste them," Ginny said, her green eyes meeting and clashing with Toni's; and the veil of forced, over-done politeness between them dropped.

Toni lifted one white shoulder. "I suppose we think differently on the subject then. To me, it is all a matter of taste—of *good* taste. An opera singer or a flamenco dancer, what is the difference? To a man, that is."

"But you seem to know so *much* about men!" Ginny widened her eyes innocently, savagely pleased when she saw the expression that flashed across Toni's face for an instant. Pressing home the advantage she had momentarily gained, she went on in the most casual tone she could muster. "And speaking of men, I suppose I should apologize for swearing out that warrant for your foreman's arrest. I would have consulted with you first, if I could, for after all we *are* neighbors now, but both my cousin and Colonel Belmont advised me that any sign of weakness might be misconstrued as an excuse for further depredations."

"Well, but that is part of the reason why I came to see you—to apologize. What a terrible experience, for you! Of course, I was able to keep him in his place—and that is why I felt that you really ought to be warned. Nicky, my brother-in-law, would never forgive me if I did not, and he thinks so highly of you, too!"

"Warned?" It was all Ginny could do not to reach out and slap the other woman's smiling face. Had Steve actually told her what he'd done? What was she getting at this time?

"Yes—warned. For I'm afraid I have discovered what a dangerous, violent man he is! He had the effrontery to follow me to Dallas, you see—I don't know what he hoped to gain, unless it was to squeeze some money out of me. But he was reckless enough to kill a deputy marshal in some saloon brawl over a woman, and then. . . ."

It was all Ginny could do to keep her face stiff and un-revealing. Steve had actually followed this woman to Dallas? Steve—arrested, and then escaping. . . .

"I had to go and—and identify him. It was such an un-pleasant experience! All those very ugly threats he made—and especially towards *you!* For some reason, he had not expected you to press charges against him. But you *will* be very careful, won't you? I've already sent a message to Colonel Belmont, but I would blame myself forever if something were to happen to you, and so would Nick. I wouldn't go riding alone again, if I were you!"

But Steve wouldn't hurt her—couldn't hurt her, more than he had done already.

"And I'll be damned if I'll let that woman think her warnings frightened me," Ginny said angrily to Renaldo. "Oh, we were a couple of bitches—you would *not* have heard all her hints, her sly innuendoes. How could he been proud of me. But I hate her—she's the kind of woman I would enjoy using a knife on! You should have have—have *rutted* with a creature like that? Renaldo, where do you think he is now?"

Renaldo had no answers for her. So he reminded her

again that they could leave—that she was free, that even Mr. Bishop seemed to have forgotten her existence. . . .

Steve Morgan had not, in spite of himself. And surprisingly enough it was Francesca who insisted upon reminding him he had a wife.

He was fortunate. His body healed quickly, in spite of the broken ribs. His face would take longer to come close to being normal again, but what the hell did that matter, when he was alive? And Francesca did not seem to mind.

They were lying together in bed, having breakfasted very late, and the afternoon sun made thin streaks across the rug. Steve would have preferred to sleep again, but Francesca, in a playful mood, insisted upon tickling him with her hair, and then running her fingers lightly over the contours of his averted face.

"Do you know—I actually think I like you better this way? No—I am serious, Stefano, even if you will not be. You were handsome before—and you knew it, did you not? And you are still a good-looking man, but—how shall I put it? Now you are more rugged-looking. Even the broken nose suits you."

" 'Cesca, for God's sake! Maybe I should get myself beaten up every month, just so I'll suit you."

"Would you really do that for me? Stefano—how much would you do for me?"

He half-opened one eye, gazing at her suspiciously.

"And what in the hell does that mean?"

"Don't pretend to sleep—I will not let you. I mean, how long will you stay with me this time? How long before some silly, dangerous 'business' takes you away again?"

This time he opened both eyes, regarding her thoughtfully as he began to twist a dark curl around his finger.

"You have beautiful hair, 'Cesca. It feels like silk."

"And you are changing the subject! Why won't you talk to me seriously?"

"About what? You make it hard for a man to keep his mind on serious subjects when you act the way you're doing now." Her body stopped its twisting, sensual motions against his.

"Well—you know I want you. But you—what do *you* want, Stefano? What are you going to do about your wife? Will you go back to her?"

Without answering her, he began to run his fingers teasingly down the length of her spine, and back up again, and she sighed, feeling her flesh quiver.

"You are a devil, Stefano! The kind of bastard who would beat his woman—and be constantly unfaithful. Dio mio—what a miserable life we'd lead each other if—if we were to fall in love! What drives you to the crazy risks you take? You are rich enough to do as you please—you do not need to lead the life of a bandit!"

"Getting rich was almost too easy, I guess." His voice turned somber, momentarily. "And the need for excitement must be in my blood, even if I know that one of these days I might not get up and walk away in one piece."

"What a thought for a woman to have to live with! Have you no heart at all?"

"None. But I do have a weakness for dark-haired prima donnas. You're a kind of excitement in yourself, 'Cesca. And I think we understand each other so well because we're both takers—and we can be unscrupulous about getting what we want."

"But what do you want? Not me, not permanently, I know that, and I don't care; because, as you say, we are almost too much alike. But for yourself? For me, there is my music, and I know I will be great—the best opera singer in the whole world one day, with the whole world at my feet. I know there I am going, but you—where do *you* travel to?"

His fingers stopped their caressing motion, and he sounded almost surprised.

"Damned if I know! I hadn't thought about it. Damn you. 'Cesca—that's enough probing."

She threw at him, deliberately testing his reactions, "I will be leaving Dallas in a few days. First for San Antonio, and after that New Orleans, and then New York again. And after that I think I will go back to Europe, before they forget about me! You could come with me, if you had nothing else to do."

"And join your adoring entourage? No, baby. Not even if I do admit I find you completely fascinating. But like you, I'm just not used to ties."

And as he said it, he remembered, far too vividly, having said the same thing to Ginny. What a too-apt pupil of

his own philosophy she had proved to be! Far too eager to
learn, and to practice, what he had been the first man to
teach her.

He could not be jealous of Francesca who, in her own
way—like Concepción before her—was as amoral as he
was. But Ginny—damn her slanty green eyes and her too-
easily yielding body—she had always been the only
woman capable of making him fly into a jealous rage that
could blind him to everything else, even caution or reason.
He should have done what he had threatened to do far
too often and never carried out—beaten her a few times,
to show her he meant business. Patience—hell! There
were some women who mistook restraint for weakness on
a man's part, and Ginny was one of those. How dared she
cuckold him? It was an ugly, mocking word in any language, and every time he thought of her defiant, open indiscretions he wanted to strangle her with his bare hands.
That, too, was something he should have finished doing a
long time ago. . . .

Unreasonably—*knowing* he was being unreasonable—
Steve Morgan preferred to ignore his own indiscretions. If
he had to be so foolish as to get himself married, why
hadn't he picked on the kind of wife who would accept a
man's occasional, understandable straying, instead of acting as if what was sauce for the gander was sauce for the
goose as well? To make matters worse, she had had the
gall to use money he had supplied to her in order to offer
a reward for his capture, and even the fact that she had
specified he was to be taken alive didn't alter the facts.

Another fact he did not want to admit, until Francesca
reminded him of it, was that he couldn't get Ginny off his
mind. Was she still in Baroque? What was she waiting
for—his head on a platter? What he ought to do was divorce her, and get her out of his system once and for all.
But could he really do that? Even now?

"I think you are in love with your wife, and ashamed to
admit it," Francesca said with a magnificent disregard for
modesty or tact. "If you were not, I would have taken you
from her by now. And if you won't come with me—why
don't you go back and have it out with her?"

It was Francesca, too, who reminded him of Nicholas
Benoit, who had gone back to Baroque nursing a bruised
ego. And there was Toni, with her glittering amber eyes

and wet, greedy mouth. Quite suddenly, Steve remembered the ridiculous plan he'd thrown out so casually to Toni one evening—and Nick Benoit's reputation with woman.

"We'll give her to Nicky, Comanche. Don't you think he'd like that? Wouldn't you like a share in whatever she's got to give?"

And knowing Toni—especially *now*, when as Steve Morgan he had seen to it that Nick's grandiose plans had gone astray. . . .

When Francesca left for San Antonio, they said goodbye—with some regrets on both sides. Only Costanza had none at all—and Bert Fields heaved a sigh of relief. Thank God *that* affair was over! At any rate, he hoped fervently it was. Francesca had let herself become far too distracted of late. . . .

Steve Morgan, no longer bearing any resemblance to the shabby saddle-tramp who was still supposed to have been hanged by vigilantes, left Dallas a day after the Princess di Paoli did, having sent off several long and mysterious-sounding cables to various parts of the country signing them Steve Morgan.

And from Dallas, he went to Shreveport, where he made the announcement that he was on his way to New Orleans, on business—but instead, taking his time, he headed slowly for Baroque. After a while, the gossips reluctantly found something else to talk about, other than their speculations as to why that interesting, dangerous looking Mr. Morgan should prefer to spend his time inspecting sugar plantations in Louisiana, when his wife was less than three hundred mile away, in Texas, and his mistress had just taken San Antonio by storm with her fiery performance as *Carmen.*

Chapter Fifty-nine

It was inevitable that some of the rumors, at least, should be filtered back to Ginny.

It was bad enough that she should have been forced to receive Toni Lassiter, with her "warnings" and sly innuendos. Judge Benoit, on his return from Dallas, seemed also to have changed, in some indefinable way, his manner towards her growing at first insinuatingly familiar, and then far too bold. He covered it, at first, under an air of hurt reproach.

"I didn't know your husband had ideas about hanging onto this property here. Or that he had returned from Europe—or was it South America? He's a friend of Jay Gould's, did you say?"

She hadn't said—and it was all she could do to try and keep her manner composed when she felt her heart leap into her mouth at the mention of Steve's name.

"I see no reason to hide the fact, Mr. Benoit, that my husband and I go our separate ways. He enjoys travelling about, and I crave peace and seclusion."

But what had he meant? What *did* he mean?

"I understand, of course," Nick Benoit said soothingly, although she could feel his little pop-eyes taking in all the inner confusion she was attempting to hide. He was a clever man—hadn't Mr. Bishop warned her of the fact?

"I found the Princess di Paoli most 'distrait' when I had the privilege of meeting her in Dallas. And your husband, Mrs. Morgan—I mean no disrespect to you, of course— seems to have queered a business deal I was engaged in. I am not certain, but I happened to hear his name mentioned several times. And, of course, since I know he's connected with the railroad business, I wondered if, perhaps, Mr. Gould intends bringing one of his railroads this far south. Forgive me for mentioning it. I suppose it's a secret!"

"If it is, I know nothing about it!" Ginny caught herself saying, far too sharply. And then, trying to collect herself, "Steve is—a very unpredictable man, Mr. Benoit. Even I do not know what his plans are."

"I'm surprised he does not take a woman of your intelligence into his confidence," Benoit said smoothly, shrugging deprecatingly. "I'm only interested, of course, because Baroque is my home. If I can be of any help—you'll let me know, won't you? I have a great admiration for you, you know!"

And after Nick Benoit had taken his leave, all on the same day, Persis Belmont came to visit, with some gossip she professed herself unwilling to divulge—at first.

"I don't know if I should tell you or not, for the last thing I wish is to upset you. And Rodney said I should keep my mouth shut, but men are so obtuse sometimes, aren't they? But if Rodney was involved, I'd much rather know, at once!"

"If it's a woman Steve's involved with, believe me, it'll come as no shock!" Ginny said through stiff lips. "I suppose I should be used to it."

"Oh, you poor darling!" Persis Belmont's voice was at once shocked and angry, the militant Puritan in her coming to the fore at once. "How do you stand it? That opera-singing female who flaunts the jewels her admirers present her with. . . . There are times when I positively despise all men, for being so easily taken in!"

It all came out in the end. Francesca di Paoli's sudden desire for seclusion—Steve's appearance at the opera house during her last performance of the opera. And the inevitable rumors that they had left for San Antonio together. And again she was "Poor-Ginny"—the wronged wife. Oh God! She didn't think she could stand more. When had he regained his memory? And what had Toni meant with her hints and warnings?

The last straw was when Renaldo rode in from town, looking worried and flustered, bearing a curt telegraph message from Steve—despatched from Shreveport, Louisiana, and addressed to Renaldo instead of to her:

"Imperative you return to Mexico immediately. And

take Ginny with you. My representative will be arriving in Baroque soon, to take over."

"His representative, indeed! What does he mean? What kind of cruel game is he playing this time? Perhaps he means to bring that woman here, and wants me out of the way! Well, he shan't give *me* orders! I'm still his wife. I won't be pushed aside so casually!"

Unwillingly, the memory of that last afternoon forced itself into her mind. Steve—both himself and a stranger. Opening her loose robe down the front, his insidious, too-familiar caresses making her open herself for him, forgetting reserve, forgetting anger, forgetting everything but the hunger that he alone could evoke in her treacherous body. Lips on her throat, her breasts, moving lower to exact surrender in spite of the gag he'd put in her mouth and her bound, aching wrists. Why—why? What had he been trying to prove?

"I won't go!" she cried now, in the face of Renaldo's concerned headshaking. "Do you hear me? You can go back if you want to—but I won't. Steve is going to have to face me—I'll make him face me!"

Matt could hardly believe his luck. He was Toni's lover! And she wanted him—had always wanted him, she confided in a whisper. Only, he had been so *slow!* And so shy . . . hadn't he been able to tell? As for Manolo—he had frightened her. She hadn't yet got over the shock of seeing poor Billy-Boy killed before her very eyes—and his scalp taken.

"He told me he'd kill me, too—if I didn't give in. Oh, Matt! What was I to do? He took me by force, on this very bed, and I was too terrified to do anything about it. I felt as if I had no one to turn to—not even *you!* And you were so brave, the day you knocked down that cowboy who insulted me—I was only testing you, when I pretended to be angry. I thought you'd understand. . . ."

Well, he understood now. He understood that Toni was *his*—*his* woman, the one woman he'd always dreamed about. He loved her—he'd do anything for her, and she understood that at last. Why else would a woman like Toni, who could have any man she wanted, give herself to him so willingly? They would be married someday, and by then, even Pa would understand how it was with them.

Under the hardness she put on for everyone else, Toni was really soft, and helpless. She needed a real man to look after her. And for all her softness and her yielding, she was smart too—wanting a future for them, and for the children they'd have some day.

Missie smarted off at him, one morning, and he slapped her right across the mouth, sending her crying back into the house—to Pa, who wasn't ready to understand yet, and his brothers, who had no ambition at all. And after that, he stayed in the big Lassiter house with Toni, who said softly that, after all, it should be his by right, through his mother, since he was the eldest son of a woman born a Lassiter. And she hoped he didn't hate her for marrying Tom. But she had been so young, straight out of a convent, and her family had forced her into it. . . .

She fascinated him—and he was hungry for her, each minute of the day, for her white, beautiful body undulating under his, and her whispered words that almost drove him mad when he was loving her. Toni—Toni. . . ! He'd give his life for her, if she wanted it. Anything—as long as she kept wanting him.

So when Toni started talking about Ginny Morgan, and the kind of woman Nick Benoit had learned she was, when he was up in Dallas, Matt listened, frowning, and agreeing. She was a tramp, for all her husband's money and her fine clothes. Hadn't he seen that for himself, the night of the party when she had danced in front of those Mexicans, and for Manolo, who had known how to treat her? And then, after letting him kiss her—and sleep with her, Toni said—she had offered that reward, making up the charge of cattle-stealing. . . .

"Matt—she's bad! She doesn't care for any of us, for all that she's good at pretending—you saw the way she made up to Missie at first, and then dropped her."

"What are you trying to tell me, sweetheart?"

"I'm trying to say we don't need her sort here in Baroque. Surely you can see that? And that so-called cousin of hers who hangs around your own little sister. I don't trust him either. Nick says her husband is trying to buy up all the land he can around here, for the railroads—and you know what that would mean? People—outsiders—Northerners—coming here to take over and to run things.

We'd all be forced to sell out in the end. Oh, Matt! You won't let it happen?"

When she appealed to him like that, her voice breaking, he would have charged an army for her single-handed.

"Toni, baby! Look—I'm not going to let it happen. Not any of it. I'm going to look out for you. From now on, you're not to feel like you're alone. You just tell me what you want me to do, and I'll. . . ."

She told him—eyes wet and shiny looking, and Matt was stunned.

"*Kidnap* her? Carry her off into the swamps? But sweetheart—Jesus God, they'd have the whole army out looking for her!"

"You said you'd do anything for me! But if you don't love me deep enough, Matt Carter—"

"Toni, you know I love you! Goddamn, haven't I proved it? Haven't I waited long enough for you? It's only that—"

"You're afraid!" she accused, and he crushed her in his arms, making her cry out.

"Damn it, I ain't afraid! Not the way you think. But it would only stir everyone up, can't you see that? And—"

"Not if they thought it was Manolo who did it—for revenge! Don't you see? They'd all blame *him*, and go looking for *him*—and we'd send a ransom note, signed with his name, just to make sure. Asking for enough money to make us all rich, Matt! And warning her husband to stay out of Baroque. And even if he doesn't care two pins for her, he'd have to—even if it's only because of what people would say! Oh Matt, Matt darling—it's the only way to save us all! If you really love me—"

"Toni—dammit, of course I love you. More than anything and anyone in my whole life, even my family. Didn't I give them up for you?"

"But even they'll understand—afterwards. Don't you see how all the bad things started happening after *she* got here? She's evil, Matt! And she's lying and dangerous—pretending all along. Maybe her husband sent her here, just to feel things out. Matt—"

"I'll think about it," he said hastily to calm her down.

But by the time Toni gave him wine, and love—her own special brand—up in her bedroom, he had already

stopped thinking. He'd never let her escape him now—
he'd do anything to hold her.

Toni smiled her wet, satisfied smile into the darkness,
gauging his thoughts and his surrender to her will. Big,
stupid Matt Carter! How easily she had always been able
to twist him around her finger. But he had proved useful,
after all, and so easy to manipulate. She proceeded to do
just that, using her hands and her mouth, and she heard
him groan out loud. Yes—Matt would do whatever she
told him to. And afterwards, Nick would have no choice
either. *She* would be the one to call the shots, and she
wouldn't bungle any of them.

Unaware of Toni's scheming, and in spite of Ginny's
continued stubbornness, Renaldo went ahead with plans
for their impending departure—the hardest part of all
being trying to explain to Missie, who looked desolate.

"Oh! But I thought—I thought maybe you'd be staying.
For a while longer, anyhow. Are you going back to Mexico? What is it like there, where you have your home?"

Forgetting himself, Renaldo swore distractedly in Spanish. And when he saw the tears that welled up in Missie's
eyes, he forgot himself even further and took her in his
arms, holding her far too closely.

"Dios! What a clumsy ox I am! Melissa—Missie—it is
not that I *want* to go, you understand? But—perdición! I
am too old for you—and far too dull! I—"

"I think you are swearing," Missie said in a small voice.
"And that is rude, since I cannot properly understand the
words you use. And you are *not* old, and *not* dull at all—
and I shall be very very unhappy when you go away. . . . I
don't *want* you to go away!" She began to sob, pressing
her face against his shoulder, and Renaldo Ortega, whose
own mother had labeled him a woman-hater, lifted her
chin with clumsy, shaking fingers, and kissed her.

He kissed her gently, tenderly, as if she were a fragile
object that might break—and he kissed her with love.
Missie, not knowing and yet beginning to discover for
herself, found herself shaking, from her curled toes up.

How could she have been so stupid and so childish, not
to understand? Her first kiss had meant nothing—and
Manolo had tried, in his rough way, to tell her that. She
didn't want a pirate to carry her off and keep her a
prisoner—she wanted *this*! This was what she had been

waiting for, all her life, and she had almost not seen it. A kiss that was gentle, and loving, and tender, not a forceful attack on her mouth, forcing her lips open. A kiss that offered her everything, promised her everything, and waited—for *her!*

And Renaldo was shaking as hard as she was! Missie felt it, and started to become a woman as she sighed, closing her eyes and putting her arms around his strong, broad shoulders.

"Renaldo—Renaldo. . . ." she started to say his name in her mind. And Renaldo himself was hopelessly lost, irretrievably compromised.

He had to ask her father at once, being formally Spanish; and, as he confessed to her, old-fashioned. And Missie didn't mind at all—realizing a value put on herself, and liking it.

"Had a notion it might come to this," Joe Carter said gruffly to the man who stood so stiffly before him. "Would have done the same with *my* Melissa's Pa—only he wasn't the kind who would listen, and so, because we loved each other so strong, we had to run away across the border to get married. You do love my little girl, though, don't you? It ain't something passing?"

"No, it's not. I love her, and I want her for my wife. I can provide for her."

"I guess you can. There's no need for all that, if you're sure you love her. Don't want to lose her, but it's better than seeing her mope around, like she would have, if you'd gone without saying anything!"

"Oh, Pa!" Missie said, but she said it lovingly happily. Her whole face seemed to glow, freckles and all. And all Joe Carter had to do was to watch the way they looked at each other, to be sure.

Chapter Sixty

"I cannot believe it," Nicholas Benoit kept saying dazedly. "I cannot believe that he would dare—"

"We found her horse," Colonel Belmont said curtly, more upset then he cared to show. "And her hat. Apart from that—only this insolent note from Manolo! My God, man—" he said suddenly, "do you think I am not concerned? This could mean my whole career—if you know of any places where he might be hidden out, or where he might conceivably take her—"

"If I knew, do you think I would be standing here talking with you?"

The Judge was visibly agitated. Enough to make the Colonel pause to apologize for his show of temper.

"I understand," Benoit said swiftly, his face showing nothing but horror. "All right. How are you proceeding?"

"The sheriff is rounding up a posse to join the soldiers I've already sent out to search the swamps, wires have been sent, and I've dispatched messengers to all the nearby towns."

"Good," Benoit said. "And we'll all help look, of course. I know a few men, born and raised in the swamps, who know their way in there better than any outsider could. We'll find her."

"But what a good actor you are, Nicky darling," Toni said softly when they had started back. " 'We'll find her,' " her voice mimicked his, before she laughed tauntingly. "How gallant! I'm sure the Colonel was impressed. And I am, too. But would you really like to find her? What would you do with her if you did?"

"My God, Toni! Even you would not be so crazy as to—"

"I didn't, of course! Wasn't I with you all afternoon?

But Matt did—for me—and now, Nicky, we hold the trump card, don't we? Aren't you proud of me, for having the guts to do what you were afraid to do?"

"You're crazy," Nicholas Benoit repeated in a half-whisper. And Toni giggled, the sound running up his spine like the involuntary shiver of apprehension he could not help.

"Am I? Would you like to find out how far I can go, Nicky? Do you want her? The bitch—do you really think she's any better than any other, knowing what you know about her? You can have her, Nicky—and no one will know but us. You can do anything you want with her—doesn't that thought excite you? And—if she's difficult—I'll have her too. It might be fun to get her ready for you." Again that high-pitched giggle. "If we can get rid of Matt for a while, that is. He's so old-fashioned, and so stuffy! But I'll have to keep him, for a while—until he stops being useful to me."

"Toni, you're a fiend!"

"Of course I am, darling! And you'd like to be, wouldn't you? Well, you're going to have your chance. Tonight. We'll leave her alone today, and you can join the search party. She should be hungry and thirsty—and positively hysterical with fear by then," Toni said with satisfaction. "I'll send Matt out to keep an eye on the soldiers, so she's all yours, for a while. Doesn't that thought exicte you, or are you still too afraid to be a man?"

"Shut up, damn you! Shut up!"

But he *was* excited, in spite of himself, and in spite of all the old, careful instincts that warned him to caution. Toni saw things too simply—and Toni took far too many risks, counting on the fact that she was a woman. It had taken him years of careful thought and planning to get where he was now. But women had always been his undoing. Treacherous, deceitful bitches! Ungrateful—like Francesca, whom he had worshipped. His Princess—only she had chosen to soil her skirts by going back to her former lover. Steve Morgan. . . . The name tasted bitter on his tongue. Rich—and that was why Francesca preferred him. Rich and arrogant. But he had a wife—and a wife was any man's weak point. Ginny—just as arrogant in her own way as her husband must be. But not now, Nick was sure. Not now! As Toni had said, by now she would be shrinking with terror—crying in the dark. Like

Renate Madden, who was not so very different, after all. She would soon begin to beg, and to plead, and from then on. . . .

As if she had been able to read his mind, Toni whispered, "You'd like to see her naked and crawling, wouldn't you? I've let her keep her clothes on—just so you could take them off, Nicky. Wasn't that thoughtful of me?"

And clever Toni—instead of hiding her out in the swamp, where, with all the soldiers searching for her, she might be found, Toni had been smart enough to hide her prisoner in her "dungeon"—the cellar beneath a cellar, that no one knew about, or almost no one.

"There's a bed down there—and I chained her by the ankle," Toni said, her eyes becoming shiny. "That's the way the old man used to chain his female slaves—the ones he was breaking in. I'll bet even you didn't know that. I wonder how she feels, to find herself chained up like a slave!"

There was a thin blanket thrown over the cot, but Ginny Morgan disdained to use it. And she didn't seem afraid either. She sat calmly on the edge of the bed.

Nicholas Benoit noticed all this as Toni hung the lantern she was carrying on a hook in the wall.

"You're not shy, are you? Or maybe you're used to showing whatever you've got to the customers."

"Is *he* a customer? Have you charged him the usual fee?"

Nick Benoit's face flushed, in spite of all his resolves, and he heard Toni hiss with rage.

"You whore, you!"

"I suppose, being one yourself, it's easy for you to recognize one of your kind. And do *you* make it a custom to frequent whores, Judge Benoit?"

Ginny's contemptuous use of his title and her easy way with words stung him to anger.

"Perhaps you'll be glad to play the part for me, before I'm through with you," he sneered. "You were one of the Archduke Maximilian's whores, weren't you? And then you passed from hand to hand. A Frenchman, who called himself a Count. A Mexican Colonel—did you think I was taken in by your act?"

"I think you have been misinformed, Judge Benoit."

Her voice was cool. "And what an elaborate plot this is, to be sure. Was this kidnapping your idea? Or all hers?"

"Nicky—she's being impertinent. Teach her! Or shall I?"

Ginny Morgan's green eyes were narrowed—and surprisingly unafraid. They flicked contemptuously from one to the other of them, and Nick Benoit, wincing at first, was filled with a determination to see those eyes change—to hear her screaming to him for mercy.

"Beat her, Nicky," Toni Lassiter said breathlessly. "That's what she needs. I'll get you a whip. We can tie her to those iron rings in the wall."

"Do you really think that's necessary?" Ginny said coldly. "Or is Nicky not capable of persuading a woman to desire him?"

His breath became a thick fog in his throat. She was a temptress, as well as being a bitch! He moved forward, like a sleep-walking man, and reached for her, tearing the gown she wore off her shoulders, to bare her breasts. He felt her shudder, although she refused to give ground. He laughed, running his fingers over the rounded curves of her nakedness, thinking, "Good!" Because the harder she was to break, the more satisfying his eventual conquest of her spirit, as well as her body, would be.

"I don't think she likes you, Nicky! Look how cold she is! Perhaps we should find her another lover, to get her ready for you—what do you think? It's too bad Matt isn't here—he loves me madly, but I think he wouldn't mind trying her out. Or maybe we really should tie her up and beat her first. Do hurry up, Nicky! There she is, and I haven't seen her try to fight you off yet. After all—"

"After all what?"

It was Ginny who gasped first, her eyes widening. Toni Lassiter swung around, and Nick Benoit stood as still as if he had been stricken.

"Comanche!" Toni breathed the name.

"Don't let me stop you. It looked like there were at least two people having fun."

"Comanche," Toni said again, and then, "darling—I had a *feeling* you'd turn up. Just in time, too. I need a *real* man around me, for a change. Nicky thinks he is, but he's so slow! And this was all your idea in the beginning! Darling, you don't have any hard feelings, do you? After all—there was all that money offered, and you would have done the same things too, wouldn't you?"

"Maybe."

His thumbs were hooked lightly in his belt, but he wore both a gun and a knife. And his face, unshaven, looked different. Harder. . . . Had he been in a fight?

"You see, Nicky? Comanche doesn't bear us any grudges. And I think he deserves another turn at her."

"Hell," he said then, contemptuously, casually, "I've already had my turn. Why don't you keep right on with what you were doing, Benoit?"

"You rotten, lowdown bastard!"

It was at him, at Steve that Ginny swore, seeing him stand there just *looking*, those very blue eyes of his flickering rudely over her while he calmly invited Nicholas Benoit to keep pawing her.

Toni laughed, shrilly, and Benoit made a grab for Ginny, pushing her backwards onto the cot. He had thought, because Toni had chained her by the ankle, that she would be helpless. And she hadn't tried to fight him off, all this time. But now, with a sudden fury that took him by surprise, she brought her knee up into his groin, chopping viciously at his Adam's apple with the heel of her hand at the same time.

Nick Benoit gave a gurgling scream of agony, doubling over. Toni's high giggle rang in his ears.

"Poor Nicky!" She knows all of a whore's tricks, doesn't she? Is it your turn now, Comanche, or mine?"

"You take her, if you can. But get that damn chain off her ankle first. You shouldn't need that, Messalina."

Toni, her voice changing to a snarl, snapped: "Get on your back on that cot, bitch, if you want your ankle free. And don't try the same thing you did on poor Nick here, or I'll smash your face in."

Still breathing hard, but without another word, warned by the look in Steve's eyes, Ginny lowered herself onto the cot gingerly.

"Lie down! Think I trust you?"

Ginny bit her lip, forcing herself to lie back. Her ankle, aching and throbbing, was already swollen. Toni took a key from the pocket of her riding skirt and bent over. The key clicked in the clumsy padlock, and then Ginny was free—and Toni, at the same time, seemed to slump forward.

Steve could move as fast and as quietly as a striking puma when he chose, and even Ginny, who had been watching him, had hardly seen the blur of motion as his hand came down on the back of Toni's neck.

From the way he stood there looking at her, legs planted casually apart, fingers of one hand still hooked in his belt, he might not have moved at all.

Suddenly unsure of herself or any of the things she had planned to say when she met him again, Ginny looked back at him, searching for something, some spark of feeling or emotion in his eyes. But they were a cold, hard, sapphire blue—and completely unfathomable.

She opened her mouth to say something—anything at all to bridge the silence between them, and he said flatly, a kind of hateful derision edging his voice:

"You keep lying there on your back and I'm going to think you were looking forward to what they were planning to do with you. Sorry I don't have the time right now to oblige."

Ginny sat up quickly, as if she had been shot at, color flaming in her face.

"Why, you—."

"You swear at me just once more, and you'll get what she got—with a smack right across that dirty little mouth for good measure. Now get off that bed, unless you mean to stay there and wait for Matt Carter. And get that chain around *her* ankle. Move."

There was something so dangerous in his look and the harsh, biting tone of his voice that Ginny almost quailed. And the next moment, even while she took a vicious kind of pleasure in snapping the padlock that would hold the chain firmly around Toni Lassiter's ankle, she was angry again. Both at him and herself. Although—oh, thank God he had come when he did! Or—the sudden thought struck her, stiffening her spine—had his sudden, opportune arrival really been a coincidence? Was it possible that Steve could have planned her abduction with these people? What was it Toni Lassiter had said? And come to think of it, she never had seen the man who had dragged her off her horse, wrapping a malodorous piece of blanket around her face before his fist caught her hard and painfully on the temple. Steve?

She looked up to say something angry and accusing and saw that he had crossed over to where Nicholas Benoit still gasped sickly, clutching at his groin.

"No!" Benoit muttered now, forcing the word from between his stiff, cold lips. "For God's sake, Manolo—like Toni said, it was that money! But now . . . now we'll cut you in if you want, we'll—"

"I already did cut myself in. After all, I'm the one taking the blame for carrying her off. And I never did like taking the blame for something I didn't do."

His eyes flickered just once in Ginny's direction and she bit her lip angrily. What on earth was he about this time?

"Don't! No—please don't!" she heard Benoit croak suddenly, and he tried to cringe backward from the look that suddenly flared in those blue, merciless eyes.

"Thought I was the one that was supposed to do the crawling—Judge."

"It wasn't me—it was *Toni*, I tell you. Oh, God!"

"Didn't sound that way that night. It's true I was in no shape to remember too much, but I recall you were the one giving the orders." The cold, harsh voice suddenly cut like a whip, biting into the tattered shreds of Nick Benoit's nerves, shattering the last vestiges of his self-control. "Just to be fair, I think *you* ought to find out how it feels to hang."

Benoit screamed, and then the scream was choked off as he felt the bite of rope around his neck. He gasped and thrashed, his eyes rolling, feeling himself half-carried with contemptuous ease across the room. And then the rope loosened somewhat, and he was standing, tottering, trying desperately to keep his balance on the broken, rickety chair he had been hauled up onto. And his wrists were being tied behind him. . . . His knees were so weak they would hardly hold him up, and he tried to scream again as the rope bit into his flesh.

"Better try standing as still as you can, Judge. That chair doesn't look too strong, but it's the best Toni's dungeon has to offer, I'm afraid."

Through dilating, horror-stricken eyes, Ginny watched as Steve calmly finished fastening the other end of the rope to one of the hooks in the wall, testing the knot before he stepped back.

She found her voice at last, wondering why it emerged almost as a scream.

"You can't do it! You can't just leave him that way to—to choke to death! What kind of a—a beast have you turned into?"

His voice was steely-soft, his smile the travesty of a grin—a mere, sarcastic twisting of his lips.

"That, baby, is something you're going to have plenty of time to find out!"

"What—what do you mean?" And then, as Nicholas Benoit choked again, beginning to sob raspingly, a shudder ran through her. "Oh, God! How can you be so—so heartless?"

"I could kill him—but a knife in his fat gut isn't going to be half as slow and painful. And he has a chance to get lucky, this way. Matt Carter might come back."

She remembered then where she was and how she had come here—and when Steve reached out and caught her wrist, the way his eyes flicked over her made her suddenly conscious of her nakedness under the torn riding habit.

"Seems like you make a habit of getting the clothes ripped off your back, Ginny." And then, his voice hardening, "What the hell are you hanging back for? I've already wasted enough time coming down here to look for you."

Already, he was starting to drag her along with him, paying no attention to the gasp of pain she emitted when her sore ankle took her weight.

How had he known where to find her? How was it he was so familiar with Toni Lassiter's house? The amazing part was that no one tried to stop them. Toni's old butler, the man called Henri, scuttled out of the way, averting his eyes. And outside there were horses in a corral, but no one else to be seen.

Gasping, panting, her hair falling in her face to half-blind her, and her ankle throbbing sickeningly, Ginny began to wonder where his horse was. She couldn't walk another step—but she had the unpleasant feeling that if she couldn't walk, he would drag her along the ground, like a roped heifer. Where was he taking her? Why wouldn't he give a chance to catch her breath?

She stumbled—fell—and he only pulled her unfeelingly

and impatiently to her feet, continuing with their headlong pace which was easy on his long legs perhaps, but not on hers.

Tree branches flailed at her face and naked breasts, scratching her thighs painfully. Ginny screamed once, when one foot sank into slimy ooze and her boot came off—and still he wouldn't stop, even when she began to whimper as she actually felt the blisters come up on her bare foot. Each breath she took seemed to burn her lungs, and she couldn't—she couldn't possibly go on further, even if he left her where she fell.

"Stop—stop!" She beat at him wildly with her one free hand, lost her balance, and fell to her knees, sobbing wildly; the force of her fall made him pause for an instant. She wanted to lie there and die—at this point, she didn't care. Why didn't he just leave her? If he had taken the trouble to come and rescue her it was only to punish her for—but for what? None of this was her fault, it was all his—how dare he treat her this way?

"Let me be!" The breath rasped in her throat, making her cry of pain and frustration almost unintelligible. And then she felt as if her arm was being pulled from its socket as he hauled her roughly and unfeelingly back onto her aching feet.

"Not yet, Ginny. Colonel Belmont's soldier boys are everywhere, hunting for us both, and I'm in no mood to answer questions at gunpoint. Come on—keep moving—or I'll drag you on your pretty face, if I have to."

"Brute! Bastard!"

He slapped her, the shock of the blow clearing her head for an instant, so that she was able, somehow, to stumble along in his wake, tasting blood from her cut lip now, along with the bitter taste of rage and frustration.

"*You* ought to know about that, baby!"

It seemed as if they had come full circle, she and Steve; as if they were back at the beginning again. She remembred the way he would tighten the barrel of his rifle under her breasts to stop her from swearing at him, on that first nightmare ride into Mexico, and the brutal way he had treated her afterwards. What did he intend doing with her now? The mask of civilization had dropped away from him, as if it had never really existed and he had gone back to being what he really was—a savage—a beast, as she

had called him earlier, making him angry. It was only surprising that he hadn't yet resorted to dragging her along
by her hair, like some primitive caveman.

Chapter Sixty-one

They had stopped to rest at last—to rest *her*, just as if
she had been a horse, but of less importance, she thought
rebelliously, wondering if she would ever get her breath
back, so that she could tell him what she thought of him.

Almost imperceptibly, it had been getting dark—or was
it only the way the branches seemed to close over them,
shutting out light and sound, except for the unceasing
trickling of water?

"The back door to the swamps," he had said earlier, his
voice the same sarcastic drawl he had used on her before,
grating on her nerve ends. "The old Indian trail. . . ."

They were enclosed in a dark-green, miasmic cage—or
so it seemed when Ginny lifted her head.

When he finally let her go, she had fallen thankfully to
lie full-length on the ground, which seemed to be composed chiefly of moss, and mud; she was too exhausted
and breathless during the moments that followed to think
of anything but regaining her breath. She ached in every
bone and every muscle of her body—but for a few moments, as she lay there shaking with sobs and reaction, all
she could feel was relief. And then, unpleasantly, thoughts
began to push themselves back into her pain-dulled mind.
Why had he brought her here, instead of taking her back
home, to safety? She remembered Nick Benoit, standing
with a rope around his neck while he choked for breath
and cried for mercy, and icy shivers trembled all the way
up her spine. How could she have forgotten how coldly
merciless Steve could be, and how cruel? She had the feeling that he had turned into a frightening stranger, and she
didn't know him at all. He was like the man she had faced

one night in the little bedroom of the hacienda who had almost strangled her to death with his bare hands about her throat. Was that what he intended to do with her now, having dragged her into the middle of a wet wasteland where no one would ever find what was left of her?

Nick Benoit had cowered and screamed for mercy. But she would be damned if she would! Damn him! She was his *wife*!

Steve Morgan saw the blaze start up in Ginny's eyes, and the way her face, mud-and-tear-streaked as it was, became stiff and set with anger. In spite of her bedraggled, more than half-naked appearance, in spite of everything, she was still capable of defiance. And, also in spite of everything, he could still want her. Ginny. Green-eyed vixen. Dangerous siren. His fatal, damned passion, in spite of what she was and everything she'd done.

Ginny could read none of his thoughts behind the blazing, mocking blue eyes that surveyed her from head to foot.

"Nakedness suits you as well as your unusual silence does. With your clothes off, and your tongue cut out, you might come close to being the perfect woman."

Sheer fury chased out fear, and she came up on her hands and knees like a wild creature, swearing at him in French and the Mexican dialect she'd picked up as a soldadera, until his blow sent her sprawling.

"I can see you haven't learned a damn thing all those months you were chasing around Europe—or maybe you just didn't meet up with the kind of man who knew how to deal with the kind of woman you are."

"And you think *you* are?"

Her eyes flashed hate and defiance at him, and he grinned, hatefully.

"I haven't made up my mind if you're worth the effort, madam."

"Madam! Why—"

"There are other things I might call you, but you might not like the sound of them."

This time, she was cautious, as she climbed painfully to her knees again, glaring at him.

"I can see that we have nothing left to say to each other," she said coldly, mustering an effort at dignity.

"And when you have finished insulting me, perhaps you will take me back."

He lifted one eyebrow, still staring down at her with the new, coldly unfathomable look she was already learning to hate.

"Back where? After all, you're still my wife, whether either of us likes it or not, and it seems to me you went to a lot of trouble to find me. And do you know, madam, I find myself wondering why." There was suddenly a dangerous note in his voice that made her pale, quite involuntarily.

"Is it possible that you are still possessed of some remnants of a conscience? Or perhaps you only wished to make sure just how much or how little I remembered—before you pursued your own little schemes!"

"Schemes!" Ginny's voice rose. "You actually accuse me of scheming when you—"

"You'd do well to spare me your usual hysterical denials and recriminations, Ginny. And, while we are on the subject"—he paused deliberately, and then, steely-soft, each word dropping into the sudden void in her mind like a separate explosion—"how is it that you overlooked informing me, several months ago, that you were about to become a mother? Did you consider a fact that would make most women overjoyed too unimportant to be mentioned? I've heard that you—or should I say *we*, since they bear my name—are possessed of twins. Do they have names? And how is it that you have neglected your natural duties as a mother to meddle in political intrigues that should be no concern of yours?"

So he knew—he knew! And for how long had he known? Why was he tormenting her?

"It's unusual for you to be at a loss for words, madam. Well?"

Pure rage came to Ginny's rescue, although she was careful to keep her distance from him, recognizing too well the dangerous glint in his narrowed eyes.

"Why should I attempt to defend myself? Why should I try to explain anything to you when you have always chosen to think the worst of me? I left my children—deserted them if you will—because I was foolish enough to be anxious about *you*, and especially after I had received a visit from Mr. Bishop! But you were always unreasonable and unfair, and a—a heartless brute into the bargain! I ought to have known how you would react—throwing all the blame on *me*, as usual. I should have guessed that you would try to twist things about to avoid taking responsibility for anything. Oh, but you were always so good at that, Steve Morgan! I'm surprised that you were able to force yourself out of the arms of your opera singer long enough to come back here to find me—or was it Toni Lassiter you came looking for? You and she must have found much in common at one time! And—and—" Ginny drew in a deep, panting breath before she spat at him, "I only wish I had a knife on me now! *This* time I would not miss your black, conniving heart!"

"Do you know what has always been your greatest fault, and still is, apart from your aptitude for facile lies? You have never been taught what a woman's proper place is—nor, I'm afraid the duties of a wife and mother. It's a pity I didn't marry that pretty little Ana Dos Santos, if I had to be foolish enough to marry at all." His voice sneered at her. "At least, she was properly brought up, to know her place, whereas you, madam, seem to go about inviting either rape or seduction from every man you meet."

"Ohh!"

"In fact—I've come to the conclusion that you're the kind of woman who needs to be beaten regularly! My mistake was in allowing you far too much freedom."

"Allowing me!" Ginny gritted her teeth, resentment and rage almost choking her. That he should dare talk as if she was a piece of property he had unwillingly acquired. That, having shifted all the blame for everything onto her, he had dragged her here, oblivious to her pain and discomfort—had struck her and threatened her. . . .

He went on in the same sneering, sarcastic tone—just as if she had not spoken at all, "And it's only because I blame myself, to some extent, that I've decided to give you another chance. But only one, I warn you, for my patience has grown extremely thin!"

And this time, sheer fury at his effrontery was all that kept her silent—her mouth opening in a soundless gasp. She would have screamed, if she could, to bring the soldiers running. Yes, and Matt Carter too! She hoped that they would shoot him without asking questions—he was hateful, cruel, and she would show him how she would, and would not, be treated!

"She looks like a bedraggled little alley cat, with those spit-fire green eyes," Steve thought, wondering if he had pushed her far enough. And then, sensing her resolve, he made a grab for her wrist as she whirled about to run.

Caught, she fell against him, and there was one instant, as she seemed content to lie against his chest, still panting with the force of her rage and her exertions, when he thought he had her tamed.

"You're hurting me!" she whispered in a small, hurt whimper, and then, as his grip loosened involuntarily, she turned wildcat—spitting fury as her nails raked for his eyes.

"You bastard! I hope I've blinded you!"

And she might have, if he hadn't jerked his head aside, acting reflexively. As it was, her nails gouged vicious streaks down the side of his face and neck, drawing blood, while she made a grab for his knife at the same time.

He should have followed his own long-ago advice, never to underestimate her! But by now, he was as angry as she was. Little, vicious bitch!

Ginny felt the force of his vicious, chopping blow run all the way up her arm from wrist to shoulder, numbing it, and she screamed, striking at him again with her free hand, trying to bring her knee up so that she could—could maim him!

"I don't care if he kills me," she thought as he caught both her wrists with contemptuous ease, forcing them behind her with a cruel twist that made her scream again, as loudly as she could, struggling all the while.

Her scream sent some birds flapping wildly overhead, the beating of their heavy wings almost as loud as the pounding of her heart.

"As long as he has to hold me, he can't stop my screaming, damn him!" her mind prompted her slyly, and she kept screaming until he pulled her so closely against him she could hardly move—the force of his mouth coming down over hers as hard and hurtful as a slap.

Ginny continued to struggle, trying to kick at him, with the folds of her ripped skirt getting in her way, until she felt herself growing weaker; her head falling back, she heard a buzzing noise in her brain as she fought for breath twisting her head vainly from side to side.

She was half-fainting when he released her, with an angry shove that sent her falling, arms trying to save herself and not succeeding. Her lips were bruised and bleeding, and trying to breathe again was still an effort.

Somewhere in the distance, though, Ginny thought she heard a shout—and then a shot, far away but still distinct, its echoes fading in faint drumrolls across the water.

"Sounds like you've managed to rouse them, after all," she heard him mutter between gritted teeth, and she found herself yanked to her feet again, shaken with his fingers biting into her shoulders until her head flopped helplessly back and forth—flying tangled hair blinding her.

"What the hell did you think to gain? If they start shooting, it's likely that you could catch a stray bullet too, or had you thought of that? Damn you, Ginny—"

"Let me go—let me go!" she began to gasp wildly. "Why don't you leave me here? I'd rather take my chances with those flying bullets than with you!"

It seemed unbelievable, but had there actually been a tremor of laughter in his voice? Or was it only rage?

"My God! To think I had actually forgotten what a termagant you are!" And then, without another word, he began to drag her along again; pausing only to rip what remained of her riding habit off her back when she continued to struggle and pull back.

"The clothes you insist on wearing only serve to get in the way—and you'll travel faster, and maybe more willingly without them, sweetheart!"

Why hadn't she realized how helpless she was against his strength? Just as she had always been. . . . And after a while, as it became dark, and her angry, rebellious mood had sparked out into dull indifference, Ginny found that she had almost ceased to think of anything but continuing to put one foot in front of the other, as they continued to move deeper and deeper into the swamps—now shrouded over with long streamers of moss that brushed against her face and shrinking body; trees that were incredibly gnarled and old crouched over them, hiding the sky like ancient, leering witches. She had even forgotten to be afraid, or to ask herself where he was taking her. What did it matter? He was taking her. . . .

Finding his way almost by instinct, with Ginny clinging wearily to his belt by now, her feet dragging, he took her to the island in the swamps where Teresita had once taken him.

Steve was so unpredictable! After the cruel and heartless way he had treated her, he had given her his shirt to wear, slipping her stiff, aching arms into sleeves that were far too long, during one of their short stops. And now—now when they had finally reached a place where her feet did not sink ankle-deep into mud and slime, and there was actually some sort of crude brush shelter, he carried her inside, shaking out the blankets before he laid her on them.

Dazedly, Ginny thought how quiet it was out here—the blackness of night seeming to press all around her after he had left her. And then she began to hear all the noises of the swamp—the chirping of millions of crickets pitched shrill against the deeper croaking of bullfrogs; the hushing noise of silkily flowing water somewhere and the creaking of the bent trees that were everywhere. Night sounds of night creatures—scuttling noises and small squeaks and rustlings; from somewhere close, startling her, the predatory screech of an owl as it pounced on some tiny prey. The swamps were awake and alive—and as her eyes grew used to the inky blackness, Ginny could suddenly see the infinitesimal pinpoints of stars against an ebony velvet sky. So high—so far away and coldly impersonal. What had she read somewhere? That each one was a sun in its own right, wrapped in splendid, distant isolation—just as she was.

Her mind was wandering, from hunger and chill and sheer exhaustion. Nothing seemed quite real any longer, not even the fact of her being here. Ginny felt tiny, and insignificant and lost. No one would ever miss her—no one would find her. She was lost and lonely and too tired to be afraid; not even when Steve came back.

He gave her something to drink, and she let the burning, fiery liquid course down her throat obediently. Even if it had been a cup of poison she would have accepted it just then, without question or caring.

She had been cold, and now suddenly she was warm with the heat of his naked flesh against hers, as his arms took her and held her, all without words. Time dropped away, and all the barriers thrown up by months and words—too many words! What was it he had said one night that seemed years ago until just now?

"Body heat's the best thing for keeping warm on a night like this, baby. . . ." And then, too, as now, there had been a single thin blanket covering them both—a blanket that came off some time much later, during the night, when he made love to her; still part of the dream she had been lost in.

Part Seven
THE CONSUMING FLAME

Chapter Sixty-two

"There's hell to pay, if you must have the plain, unvarnished truth, Señor Ortega!"

It was not usual for Colonel Belmont to be so blunt. A West Pointer and a diplomat raised in the hard school of Army politics, he had learned to keep his thoughts to himself and say as little as possible. But in this case—hadn't he just left his usually pragmatic wife in semi-hysterics, demanding why he hadn't *done* something, anything to prevent himself *and* the men under his command from becoming a laughingstock?

"To think that one man could hold us all up to ridicule—to think that you haven't found her yet—why, none of us are safe here any longer! My poor Ginny . . . Rodney—*do* something!"

But what in God's name was he supposed to do? In some ways, his hands were tied, although he couldn't very well tell Persis *that*—she would never understand!

Renaldo Ortega, who might have expected to be the one most concerned and worried when his cousin disappeared, had instead stayed calm and rational—if a trifle thoughtful. Colonel Belmont hoped he would stay calm now, and perhaps be inclined to shed some light on a mysterious train of events that had started with a telegram from Jim Bishop in Washington. Bishop, head of some mysterious organization that was answerable directly to the President of the United States himself, had requested that he give every courtesy and consideration to Mrs. Morgan and her cousin, and to see that they were afforded the opportunity to meet all of the local people. Belmont had thought, at first, that the lady was a member of Mr. Bishop's organization herself, until his wife, an avid follower of the society pages and the Social Register had informed him excitedly that Virginia Morgan was the wife of a California millionaire—and the daughter of Senator William Brandon. What had she come here for? Where was her husband? Colonel Belmont had asked himself that question at the beginning, growing more puzzled as time went on. But he had kept his surmises to himself. His duties here were to follow orders, and to keep the peace. But ever since that—that damned *Indian* had showed up. . . .

And now he had the unpleasant task of informing Señor Ortega that Mrs. Morgan was in worse danger than they had thought—that Manolo had committed murder and rape in addition to his other crimes. How to tell him? But in this case, under Ortega's steady, questioning look, there was nothing to do but to tell him the truth.

"I'm afraid I don't really know how it happened. Mrs. Lassiter, quite understandably, was quite hysterical; and Matt Carter, who rode over to headquarters to inform me, was upset. Mrs. Lassiter was—is—rather soft-hearted when it comes to a certain type of man. Big, good-looking brutes. She hired this Manolo without knowing too much about him, because she said she needed a good foreman— a strong man to look after her interests. And this, mind you, was soon after her other foreman, this Billy-Boy Dozier, disappeared very suddenly. Got lost in the swamps, they said, but I never believed the story. Matt Carter all but blurted out that Manolo had killed him, in some kind of a quarrel. . . . But that's something we can't prove yet."

Renaldo found himself listening unbelievingly as Colonel Belmont went on with the story that Matt Carter, panting and pale-faced as he flung himself off his horse, had related.

"At first, I could hardly credit it! The man must be some kind of maniac, his mind deranged by hatred and blood-lust. He walked quite boldly into Mrs. Lassiter's house, finding her with her brother-in-law in an old cellar, which they had gone to inspect for dampness. As I understand it, he accused her of betraying him—not standing up for him. And he was even more vindictive towards the Judge, who threatened him sternly with hanging.

"You've met Judge Benoit—he was not a very large man, nor one used to violence. He was knocked out first, while this—this savage forced himself on Mrs. Lassiter, and then shackled her to a bed while he forced her to watch her brother-in-law slowly choke to death."

"*What?*"

Colonel Belmont's face hardened, settling in grim lines.

"I could hardly believe such barbarity myself, at first! He set the judge upon a chair, with a rope around his neck, tied in a hangman's noose, taunting him all the while. And then, when he was tired of his sport, he kicked the chair away. And Mrs. Lassiter, gagged, and almost swooning from her own ordeal, was forced to watch. You may well look shocked! I was myself, and I've seen some ugly things during my career. An Apache could not have done worse."

Renaldo tried to compose himself. To think rationally. Esteban? No—for all his wildness and his evil temper, his cousin was not capable of *this* kind of violence! And especially if he had finally regained his memory.

Renaldo had been worried when Ginny had turned up missing—his worry turning into downright anxiety until the ransom note had arrived. And then he had begun to think that it was another of Steve's macabre jokes. He had kidnapped his own wife—well, the relationship between Steve and Ginny had always been a volatile one, with both of them constantly trying to outdo the other. He had thought that perhaps this time, after the inevitable sparring, they might come to the realization that they loved each other. But *this*? What could Steve have been thinking of? What did he think to gain?

Colonel Belmont had talked to Toni Lassiter, lying prostrated in a darkened room, and in a small, halting voice she had confirmed what Matt Carter had said.

"Oh, I checked everything out. Redoubled the patrols I sent out into the swamps. And—I don't know how to tell you this—but one of them reports they heard a woman scream, several times, and then the screams seemed to be cut off. And of course, by the time they got to where they thought they heard the screams coming from, there was no one there. Nothing, except—" Colonel Belmont cleared his throat, and then (almost in the manner of a magician producing a rabbit from his hat, Renaldo thought bemusedly) his voice becoming gruffer, he tossed a clumsily wrapped package upon the table between then. "One of my men picked it up. Do you—hrrm—recognize it, Señor?"

"It's—or it *was*—Ginny's riding habit. The one she was wearing when. . . ." In spite of himself, Renaldo found his voice faltering. The implications were obvious, of course. But good God!

"You understand now why I am so concerned. The question is—what am I to do now? The local sheriff has formed a posse, and they intend to search the swamps. But the Indians won't help them, for they consider this man one of them. And I am afraid that if my men get too close, he might. . . . I have sent a telegraph message to Mr. Bishop, of course. But it might be some time before I hear from him. And during that time—well, you can see how I am in a quandary!"

And now Renaldo was in a quandary, too. How much could he tell Colonel Belmont, a sincere man who was only interested in performing his duty? And even if the Colonel were told at least part of the truth, wouldn't he be understandably annoyed? Above all, what could any of them do? Guiltily, Renaldo thought of Missie, who still didn't know the truth. And now, her own brother was leading a posse that was supposed to hunt Steve down. He didn't trust Matt, who was completely besotted by Toni Lassiter—nor Toni herself, for that matter. But how to tell Missie that, or the Colonel?

What neither Renaldo, nor the Colonel knew was that Toni herself had joined in the hunt; for her own reasons.

"We've got to find them, Matt! And stop them from talking. Matt! After what he did. . . ."

"Look here sweetheart, I'll cut his heart out for you myself, for that. But her—why do we have to kill her? She's a woman, and—and my sis is going to marry that cousin of hers. If there's some way—"

"But there isn't any other way—Matt, don't you see that? She can tell about us—about *you*! She knows it was you who took her—Nick told her that; he was boasting. And if she tells—surely you understand? We've got to find

them before anyone else does. You have to help me, Matt,
I—I trust you! And you know how much I need you."

"I'll find them," Matt vowed doggedly, closing his mind
to everything but Toni, and her saying that she needed
him, counted on him. He knew some Indian trails himself,
having hidden out on the swamps for too long. Pa—Missie—he wouldn't let himself think of them. Like the Bible
said, when a man took himself a woman, she came first,
over everybody else. And Toni was his woman. Good or
bad, he wanted her. Even if he knew, at the back of his
mind, that the wanton white body that could twist so maddeningly under his had moved just so for other men—even
then, he could not help loving her, wanting her. He'd do
anything to keep her.

Now there were three separate parties of searchers,
probing deeply into the swamps like groping, spread fingers. But the swamps and inlets stretched as far as the
Louisiana border, and even further. As Matt himself knew,
there was no better place for hiding out if you didn't want
to be found. But how far would Manolo run, and especially with the woman in tow?

"Have you gone insane? How long do you think it'll be
before they'll find you? And when they do, I hope—"

"That you'll be fortunate enough to find yourself a
widow? I wouldn't count on it, my love."

Ginny bit her lip, seeing the dancing devil lights come
up in Steve's blue eyes. Why did he have to insist on
playing dangerous games? Why was he playing with her?

He had kept her warm during the night; had even pretended tenderness. But only to lull her into a false sense of
security, Ginny thought now, angrily brushing a strand of
hair out of her eyes. When morning came, he had been
just as distant and as sarcastic as he'd been earlier. There
was no understanding him, or his motives, except for
one—he wanted to break her spirit; and she wouldn't let
him! The humiliation of his caustic, biting words from yesterday still remained with her, together with the memory
of the way in which he had treated her. No, she wouldn't
forgive him this time. She hated him. She said as much,
and he only laughed.

"My God—that sounds familiar! How many times have

you told me that, Ginny?" His eyes narrowed wickedly. "Are you challenging me to prove otherwise?"

"No!" She said it too sharply, betraying herself, and then added with an attempt at coolness, "Why should I want to challenge you? As long as you're still my husband you told me that, Ginny?" His eyes narrowed wickedly. my mind, and you'll never change me into a—a slave, or a puppet, dancing to your tune! Since I obviously don't live up to your expectations as a wife, why can't you be sensible and end this whole silly farce? What are you trying to prove?"

With a suddenness that took her by surprise he hunkered down on his heels beside her, taking from her unwilling fingers a cup of the coffee she had just made.

"Damned if I know! What made you go to the lengths you did, Ginny?"

"What do you mean?"

"Take it any way you please. What makes you do anything you do?"

She gave him a sullen, suspicious look. What kind of confession was he trying to force from her this time? Were there no lengths to which he would not go to exact submission from her?

The morning had been a continuation of the nightmare of the evening before, wiping out the night itself, with its strange mood of a suspension in time. He had been caustic, threatening and hateful in turn, taking pleasure in reminding her that she was completely at his mercy—to be used as his mistress while he decided if he would keep her as his wife. She didn't need reminding that he was stronger than she—he had proved it, and her body still ached. There was not a patch of her skin, she thought resentfully, that wasn't covered with scratches and bruises. Now, reversing his former tactics, he was trying to disarm her.

"She looks as wary as a cornered vixen," Steve thought wryly, and asked himself the same question she had a few moments earlier. What *was* he trying to prove? And when had they lost the capacity to communicate with each other?

Damn her! Why wouldn't she yield? Why not her mind, as easily as she could give her body? That was the trouble with Ginny. She could give without giving in. She was the only woman he could never be quite certain of, and it was precisely for that reason she made him lose his self-control. Hadn't she always.

Looking at her soot-smudged, scratched-up face with those cat-slanted emerald eyes that had haunted so many of his dreams and nightmares, it came to him with a shock of surprise that he still loved her. In spite of everything—in spite of the fact that he was all kinds of a fool. He had gone to all these lengths not for revenge, but because he continued to want her. And he had no intention of giving her up.

Ginny—dancing for those gaping faces in Vera Cruz, eyes widening when she recognized him. Ginny—holding a knife point at his throat, saying in a small, matter of fact voice: "You're my husband, Steve. And you owe me some rights. . . ." And the very first time he had taken her, as a virgin, lying trembling in his arms, whispering: "I don't know what it is I'm supposed to do—or feel. . . ." She had crept under his skin from the very first time he had kissed her, the little witch! And when he had deliberately hurt her, he had only been fighting himself. Why did he have to keep rediscovering that fact?

Almost indiscernibly, there was a change in the way he looked at her, blueness of his eyes darkening. "Oh God," Ginny thought wildly, "why does he have to do this to me?"

The coffee spilled, putting out the small fire she had built so painstakingly under his mocking supervision.

"Ginny. . . ."

There was a moment when he made a movement toward her and she waited, feeling as if they were both poised on the brink of some new discovery.

And then the moment was lost—shattered by the low, trilling bird call that sounded from somewhere to the left. His half-made movement stilled, Steve's body tensed.

"What is it?" Ginny's heart was still beating thickly and heavily, and her voice sounded breathless.

He was already on his feet—one swift, lithe movement—like a leopard, she thought irrelevantly, still staring at him.

"Think we've got company. But not too close yet." He looked down at her almost absent-mindedly, and she had the feeling he wasn't really seeing her at all. "This place is difficult to find, in any case. There's only one safe trail, and that's pretty narrow and hard to follow. Step off it, and. . . ."

He didn't have to complete his sentence. Ginny shuddered, thinking that he had led her over the same narrow trail, and at night, with only the faint starlight to guide him. She remembered the feeling of muddy ooze, sucking at her ankles when her foot had slipped on a few occasions, and her shudder became a shiver. What could be more horrible than to die that way, drowning in slime, feeling it block your throat and eyes and nostrils. But he had brought her here safely instead. Why?

Steve—stranger-lover in whose arms she had lain so many nights. Angry, tender; hurtful, gentle. What did he really want from her?

Their eyes met and locked, and then, as if he deliberately wanted to refute the surge of feeling between them he said harshly: "You're hardly dressed for visitors, my sweet. Better go inside and wait for me. And I'll give you a gun to keep. You haven't forgotten how to use one, have you?"

She ignored the sarcasm that had tinged his question.

"Where are you going?"

"Never did like being the hunted," he said shortly. "I'd rather do the hunting myself, if it comes to that."

"No!" She startled herself with the vehemence of the one word.

"Ginny—" a warning note had crept into his voice. "I'm not going to stand here arguing with you!"

"Then don't waste your time. I'm coming with you." She started to scramble to her feet, and automatically he reached out his hand to help her up. She clung to his fingers, not letting go, with all the tenacity that he remembered. "Steve—oh, don't you see? I'm tired of being left behind, waiting. You've been trying to make an Indian squaw of me—didn't the Comanche women follow their men, and fight beside them if they had to?"

"You crazy, irresponsible, unpredictable female!" But he said it softly, almost disbelievingly. "Can you tell me why in hell I should trust you, after all the tricks you've pulled on me already?"

She shook her head. "No, I can't. Unless—isn't there a point when we have to start trusting each other? Or—or just give up?"

There it was—the final challenge, the final question. And it was she, and not he who had dropped it between them, her chin tilted defiantly in the way he remembered far too well.

Without a word, he reached forward and began to button up the shirt she was still wearing, his fingers brushing her skin.

"Steve . . . !"

"Comanche squaws walk soft and don't speak until they're spoken to. And they don't run around half-naked. Try remembering that, you impossible woman!"

Chapter Sixty-three

It was difficult, at first, for Missie to understand. And even harder for Renaldo, who had to explain.

"Manolo is your *cousin*? And her—and Ginny's husband? But why—"

"There is such a long story behind it all! Are you sure you still want to listen? Melissa—"

"I like the way you say my name. Just like it was Spanish. And I like the way your name sounds, too. Renaldo. Why do you look so worried? If it was all a big secret, of course you couldn't tell it to me! But it sounds like—" she flushed guiltily, and then, when he caught her hand, gave a little laugh and went on—"it sounds like a romance! The kind I used to read all the time. Are you sure you want to tell it to me?"

"Oh, Dios!" He caught himself squeezing her hand apologetically. "Of course I want to tell you. I've wanted to from the very beginning, only I didn't know how."

She said, matter of factly, "I thought I was in love with him. But it was those stories Renate used to tell me—and the ones I read. They weren't real, any of them, and I know that now." She blushed. "I guess he helped me find that out. Are you mad?"

"How could I be angry with you? I kept thinking, all the

way here, that perhaps you would not want to have anything more to do with me!"

"You're not at all like him," Missie decided, and smiled.
"And you know what? I'm glad. He is like a whirlwind—
you watch it from a distance, and it's beautiful and wild,
but when it touches you. . . ."

He told her everything at last, and she listened, her
small, pointed face solemn for the most part.

And then, when he had finished, she said practically:
"But I don't see what else you can do! And I don't think
he killed poor Uncle Nick. I think Toni did. And she
doesn't want anyone else to know. Oh—Matt's so dumb!
Why did he have to take up with her? And she's *not* sick,
either—I saw her ride off with Matt, into the swamps, and
I was wondering what she was up to. She's got Matt all
twisted around her little fingers, you know. And it's him
I'm worried for, only I couldn't tell Pa, or Hank or Joe—
because I'm not supposed to sneak off with Pa's old field
glasses any more. I'm supposed to act like a lady, so that
you won't change your mind."

Renaldo, being only human, spent a few minutes convincing Missie that he wasn't about to change his mind
about her. How could he? He loved her to distraction.

It took both of them some time to come back to reality,
and the present. And then it was Renaldo who remembered that Matt had been supposed to lead the sheriff's
posse.

"That old Sheriff Arnett? He won't find anything in the
swamps, unless it's 'gators," Missie said scornfully. "And
the Indians won't help him or his silly old posse. They're
Manolo's friends. I mean—your—oh, it's all so puzzling! I
can't get used to his name not being Manolo! But they
wouldn't help anyway, they mind their own business, and
when there's trouble they just move deeper into the
swamps. Only Matt knows half of the secret trails they
use. In the old days, he used to—"

She broke off suddenly, eyes growing enormous as she
saw the look on Renaldo's face.

"I thought your brother was leading the sheriff's posse,"
he said tightly, and she shook her head at him.

"I *told* you—I saw him start out alone with Toni. She
was wearing a gun, just like a man. And Matt was carrying his hunting rifle. . . ."

Matt's hunting rifle seemed frozen to his hand at the moment, its long barrel pointed downward.

"I don't want to have to kill you, Matthew," the cold, soft voice said from somewhere behind them. Matt, recognizing it, froze involuntarily, his brain going numb with shock.

It was Toni, wearing leather breeches and an apricot-colored silk shirt, who whirled around.

"Comanche! Comanche, we were looking for you, to warn you."

"I'm sure you were. And don't touch the gun, Toni." His voice was level—toneless. Bare chested, wearing knee-high, Apache style moccasins, he looked more like an Indian than ever, except for the mocking, blazing blue eyes that looked out of his sun-browned pirate's face.

"But darling, why should I? You were *very* nasty yesterday, but I've forgiven you for that. I suppose you had to get even. And you took her as—as insurance didn't you? I always did think you were clever. And I tried to tell Nicky so, but he wouldn't listen. Poor Nicky!"

Toni sighed, but her wet, pink lips smiled provocatively, pouting slightly. It really was a mistake to kill him, Comanche. Even though you did have your reasons. Sheriff Arnett is out looking for you with a posse, as well as all of Colonel Belmont's bluecoats. Matt and I thought you ought to be warned—didn't we, Matt?"

"Matt, you drop that rifle before you turn around—and do it slow."

"If I don't get him, Toni will," Matt thought. He didn't like the way she had spoken to Manolo—that caressing note in her voice when she called him "Comanche" and "darling". She was playing a game—pretending, of course. And it was up to him to prove himself enough of a man to take care of her; to do what they had come out here to do.

"But why are you so untrusting, darling?" Toni purred, her words cut off suddenly as she gave a gasp of shock and anger.

Steve didn't turn his head, but he knew that Ginny had come up beside him; and no doubt her fingers were aching to claw at Toni Lassiter's eyes. He had told her to stay hidden—but then, Ginny had never been too good at following orders.

And it was precisely at that moment that Matt Carter chose to make his play, swinging round on his heels, with the rifle coming up. It shattered in his hands, numbing them. And while he stared disbelievingly, wondering why he was still alive, he heard Toni's shrill cry.

"Comanche! No—don't kill me! It was Matt! He was always jealous of you, because he wanted me. But you know I wanted you, because you're clever, and he's just— just a big dumb ox! You understand, don't you Comanche? We're alike, you and I. You would have done the same thing I did! Why don't you kill him? And kill *her*, too. Then we won't have anyone to worry about, and it'll be just us, just you and me. We'll make up some story to tell the Colonel, and in the end—in the end we'll own half of Texas! Nick bungled things with those Englishmen, but *I* can make it right again. I *need* you, darling! I've always needed a strong man, you know that!" Her voice grew shrill. "Comanche! What are you waiting for? Kill them! It's the only way!"

It seemed as if they were all waiting, frozen in their places. Matt Carter's face had turned a pasty grey color under his tan as he stared at Toni—his hands still held out before him, as if he continued to hold his broken, smoking rifle.

"Yes—what are you going to do, *darling?*" Ginny's voice dripped sarcasm as she stood with her feet planted apart, glaring at Toni. "I suppose you two do have a lot in common, as she's just reminded you. Are you going to kill me off? And poor, confused Matt Carter, too? I suppose it might prove convenient for you in the end. Did you plan all this with your opera singer? And does this bitch know she has a rival?"

"What's she talking about? Shut her up, Comanche, she's crazy! Kill her—I'd like to see that."

"How would you like your pasty white face carved up with a knife? Ramera—cheap puta!" Ginny swore, her green eyes narrowing.

"Ginny, be quiet. I thought you were going to act the part of a Comanche squaw."

"Ohh!" Her breath hissed between her teeth—and part of her anger was because Steve had not once taken his eyes off Toni, his gun still held almost carelessly at hip-level.

"Comanche! If you want me!"

"I don't want you, Toni; I never did, although I took what you were offering at the time because it was convenient." Toni's amber eyes widened unbelievingly, seeing his lip curl upward in a mocking, unpleasant grin, as he continued in a conversational, casual voice. "There's been only one woman who ever managed to get under my skin; and I'm married to her. Although I sometimes wonder why," he added between gritted teeth.

"Married? What are you talking about? Not to *her*—her husband is. . . ."

"Steve," Ginny said in a cold, clear voice, "why are we wasting our time explaining?" Clad only in his old shirt, a gunbelt sagging down over her left hip, she still contrived to sound haughty, even if she looked like hell! ·

Matt's eyes moved from one to the other of them, resting longest on the man he had known as Manolo.

It was Toni, her face contorting, who reacted first. "You dirty, rotten—you hear what they're up to Matt? Matt! You've still got a gun—do something!"

When he didn't answer, her voice rose into a half-demented screech, lips pulling back to show her small, pointed teeth. "You forgotten how to be a man, Matt? They planned all this between them, they—kill them, damn you, you big, stupid oaf, or I'll do it myself!"

"I'd be glad of an excuse to use this gun on you," Ginny snapped, watching Toni Lassiter's curved fingers, their long nails reminding her of talons, hovering close to her gun.

Contemptuously, Steve's eyes went beyond Toni, to Matt, who stood with a dazed, thunderstruck expression on his face.

"You want to fight me, Matt? Or do we go our separate ways?"

He blinked, as if the weak shaft of sunshine that had just pierced through the closely interwoven branches overhead had blinded him.

"You're not going to run! They've got to *die*, Matt—"

"Like you wanted him to kill *me* a minute ago?"

Toni had half-turned around, to gaze imploringly into Matt's face, and had begun to reach for him—or was it only for the belted gun he wore on his hip? Afterwards, Ginny thought it had all happened too quickly, too suddenly. She made an involuntary movement for her own gun and felt Steve's fingers close over her wrist. And at almost the same time, like a man driven by some dark dream, Matt Carter struck Toni violently across the face—the whole force of his heavy, hairy arm behind the blow.

The sound Toni made was not so much a scream but a high, mewling squeal. Her nose and her pink, pouting mouth seemed to crumble in a gush of blood as she reeled backward—like a broken puppet whose string had suddenly broken, Ginny thought sickly, trying to shut her mind to the sounds, the horrible animal sounds the woman made as she tried to scream again, choking on her own blood. And then she fell, the sound of her slow falling wet and heavy—her writhing, flailing body crushing the matted bed of water hyacinths and long grass.

"Steve—oh, God!"

Matt Carter turned his head, very slowly, and his eyes were bloodshot and still dazed looking.

"You leave her to me, hear? She's mine—bad or not, she's my woman!"

"But that's *swamp*! It isn't solid ground at all, and she. . . ."

Matt didn't look at Ginny. It was as if he could not bear the sight of another woman. And he didn't look at Toni either, nor seem to hear the sounds that came from her broken, bleeding face. He had the half-crazed look of a man who had seen a vision crumble, and still couldn't let loose of it.

"You leave what's mine to me!" he said again, his voice hoarse. "And I'll answer for what's mine. She killed Nick—you didn't know that, did you? Kicked the chair from under him while he was still crying and moaning, and stood there laughing while he—oh, Christ! Can't you see how it was! She—she was . . . she was going to let *you* take the rap for it. I already told the soldiers you done it. But she had to find you first, and the woman, to make sure. . . . She's real smart, for a woman! A brain, and all that beauty—oh God, she's so lovely, so—" His voice broke, and he said suddenly, in a kind of growl, "You go on now. Because I'm going to save her, see? I'm going to look after her—no one's going to take her from me."

"Matt!" came the horrible, rasping travesty of Toni Lassiter's voice. "Matt, help me! Matt. . . ."

"You see? She needs me. It was *me*, all the time, she told me so. She didn't mean any of those things she said when she was mad, it's me she wants. You take your woman and go now and let me see to mine."

Ginny felt as if she had been turned, literally, to stone—incapable of sound or motion. But when Steve moved, all without a word to her, or to Matt—who was already turning back to Toni as if they had both ceased to exist for him—Ginny began to struggle, only to find herself swept up helplessly into Steve's arms.

"No, Steve—no! You can't—"

"And when are you going to stop trying to tell me what I can or cannot do?" He was walking with long, angry strides, not seeming to look for his footing, and in spite of her horror and sick revulsion, Ginny started to tremble.

"Damn it, when are you going to stop interfering with other people's business and tend to your own? If I didn't need you to prove I didn't kill Benoit, I'd throw you into the swamp for the 'gators to find!"

"Alligators!" And now she was really sick, to the pit of her stomach. She became aware of the swamp, as she hadn't been last night, or even this morning when she had concentrated on stepping very carefully and quietly, following Steve.

It was so dark here, in spite of the sunlight somewhere above, filtered only faintly through thickly intertwined branches, festooned with grey lace curtains of moss. Brushing her face, even the moss seemed damp. And it was silent now, as if all sound had been cut off by the thick, miasmic growth of trees and vines, all dripping, dripping; minute droplets of water trickling like slow, everlasting tears.

"Steve?" Her voice emerged as a soft, hesitant whisper. "You don't think—he wouldn't just let her—"

"Like he said, she's his woman. Whatever happens is between just the two of them now. Don't you understand that?"

"I—I don't know. It was just so—so horrible!"

"There are a few other things you ought to be thinking about instead, Ginny."

How could he sound so dispassionate? How . . . ? And then he let her slip from his arms, leaning her up against a tree trunk to kiss her half-spoken question into silence, and his kisses on her mouth first, and then her throat and the curve of her breasts, were not dispassionate at all.

Her arms clung to him tightly, feeling the familiar play of the muscles under his skin and the warmth of his body leaning into hers. He seemed to have forgotten that there were soldiers as well as a sheriff's posse searching for them.

How far had they come? Where were they? The swamp seemed as endless as the way Steve was kissing her—as limitless as passion. Everything had passed from Ginny's mind but the way his touch—the lightest brush of his lips or fingers against her flesh—could make her feel. Dreamily, her eyes half-closed, she felt him undo the buttons he had done up so impatiently only a few hours ago.

"Steve, you're not being fair—"

"How am I not fair, you maddening, irresistible creature?"

Ginny's eyes flew open and she began to frown, trying vainly to twist from under his caressing hands.

"I don't understand you! One moment you can be an absolute devil, and I wonder if you are capable of any feelings at all. And the next you—you—ohh!" It was almost a wail. "What are you doing now? If someone should come up suddenly, one of those Indian friends of yours who whistle like birds and I've never seen, or—or—"

"Damn you, woman! I've been trying to make love to you, and all you can do is babble! Will nothing change you or turn you into a docile, submissive creature?"

Ginny shook her head stubbornly, lips parting in a soft, involuntarily gasp the next minute when he pulled her up hard against him, whispering against her hair: "I suppose I'm going to have to put up with you just the way you are, then, in spite of all your irritating faults such as running off and leaving me at the drop of a hat! And let me warn you, madam—since you seem to have a habit of getting into mischief whenever my back is turned—I'm seriously considering locking you up somewhere. Maybe I should keep you down in Toni's dungeon, with a chain around your ankle. I must say you looked very desirable when I walked in—your clothes torn and your eyes spitting fury. . . ." His tone changed suddenly, becoming harsh and almost violent as he turned his head; blue eyes blazed down into hers as he muttered, with his mouth grazing hers: "Did you know that I could easily have killed you at that minute? It was all I could do to keep my hands off you, you green-eyed witch!"

She put her hands behind his neck, clinging as if she was drowning. And loving a man like Steve was exactly like that, Ginny thought bemusedly. Like being sucked beneath the surface and carried along by a powerful, relentless current. She loved him—she realized it all over again—and knew she was helpless to fight the strong attraction that had brought them together in the first place, and still persisted, in spite of everything. But oh, God—in how many more ways would he hurt her? She was sure of nothing any longer, except herself, and the fact that she loved a man who was both her husband and a stranger—her lover and an antagonist.

"It doesn't matter . . . it doesn't matter!" her mind whispered, and Steve sensed her sudden surrender in the almost abandoned way she pressed herself against him. But was she really his? Her body yielded, as it always had. But what of her mind? What of *her*, the essence of all that was Ginny, his wife—his maddeningly resilient, unpredictable mistress? It was too easy to lose sight of all the questions when she was in his arms like this, her mouth opening under his, the curved contours of her body all giving. One moment a wildcat, out for his blood, and the next. . . . What in hell could a man do with a woman like her? What was there to do except kiss her into silence and then take both her and himself to forgetfulness?

Familiar—everything about this moment was familiar in some way, except for the setting; and Steve, in all the time she had known him, had never seemed to care where or when they made love. Whenever he had wanted her, he had taken her—disregarding any inhibitions that *she* might have. And most of the time, moments like this occurred after they had quarrelled violently—as if there was no other way they could come back together again, as if all the anger, all the frustration of too many words said and just as many unsaid could only be wiped out by the almost desperate fusing of their bodies and the suspension of thought.

Brave streaks of sunlight, escaping through the leaves, dappled the dark green silently sliding water, making it look faintly luminescent in patches. Every now and then the still, shiny looking surface was broken by a bubble, bursting into a slow, spreading ripple. Alligator? Or only a catfish? And the ancient cypresses brooded over everything—primeval tree-gods, their bony black "knees" protruding knobbily out of the water.

Ginny noticed all this as Steve made a bed for her, laying the shirt over damp moss. The wavery green light that was everywhere reminded her of being in a greenhouse—the one at the old Chateau where she had gone to have the twins. Looking up at the sky through the paned roof had always made her feel as if she were floating suspended at some distance under the surface of the sea, miraculously able to breathe. And now she felt the same strange suspended feeling, with moss trailing on either side of her like moth-eaten lace curtains on a four-poster bed.

God—oh, God! Her head moved, and she heard herself moan softly. Why think of anything but this present, with his lips and tongue tracing patterns over her too willing, too avid flesh; and his hands teasing her, preparing her, and finally his mouth, making her cry out; preceding his final, in-driving possession of her.

The artless, naturally seductive movements of her supple body under his excited him as they always did. Like the way she cried out softly, urging him, showing her need as all her stubborn reserve dropped away and she became his, all his—woman to his man, Eve to his Adam. And that was what made their lovemaking unique. The complete concentration on each other—the sensation of being, for the moment, the only two people in the world, wanting only each other, needing nothing else.

Chapter Sixty-four

Why did there always have to be an afterwards? A moment of return from the high plateau of shared passion and fulfillment?

Steve had half-turned onto his side, taking her with him, and his arms still held her with her head cradled against his shoulder.

Lying in Steve's arms, hearing the quickened cadence of his breathing become slower and more regular, Ginny let her eyes half-close, trying to fight the insidious serpent that uncoiled itself in her mind—questioning, weighing, doubting, fearing. What now? What next? How will it end his time?

A distant sound—she could not quite tell what it had been—made every muscle under Ginny's skin jump.

"What is it, restless one?" He had spoken to her in Spanish; a half-whisper—so perhaps he, too, had been remembering!

But no—she did not want to move from the safe, close circle of his arms; nor feel his flesh remove itself from hers.

"I thought—I thought I heard—"

"A gunshot? Shouting? It doesn't matter, *querida*, they're still a long way off." His voice gentled her stirring, as it had on the very first occasion when they had been together like this—under a canvas-sheeted wagon, with the danger of an Apache attack at dawn heightening their senses and their awareness of each other. He was suddenly, all over again, the sun-browned, blue-eyed scoundrel who had taken her from virgin to woman; all in one night.

"But Steve—"

"When will you ever learn to hush, woman?" His arms tightened around her, negating the sudden harshness of his tone. "A short time ago, you were talking about trusting. What are you afraid of now?"

From somewhere, she found the boldness to reply: "Of you! And *for* you too, because you're so—so reckless sometimes. And because. . . ." She tilted her head to look into his eyes, and they were hard now, like the darkly pitiless blue of the skies of Mexico.

"Because what, Ginny?"

She stared back at him, refusing to give ground.

"Because I love you, damn you! Why else? And because I know that's not enough; there has to be more, Steve— don't you see? We turn into strangers—even enemies—too easily, and that's because we haven't really had enough time in which to know each other and to understand each other. I've borne your children—and they *are* yours, Steve—but do you know, I almost didn't. . . . I almost—oh God, it doesn't bear thinking of, now. Because I was always afraid of what you would think, and how you would hurt me afterwards, just as I am now. . . ."

"Ginny!" His lips were within an inch of crushing hers, and he held back, caught in the trap of her desperate wrenched-out words, and his own guilt. He was too used to dealing with other women, but not with Ginny. It had been far too easy to condemn her in order to cover up his own sins, and yes, damn it, his own stupidity in not holding onto her when he should have. What he had failed to take into account was the plain, inescapable fact that he loved her. And had continued to love her, even during those dark days when he had doubted her, come close to hating her; and, even then, he kept wanting her. The past ought to have taught him something. He was here with her at this moment because he had no intention of turning loose of her.

He had to admit, returning her wide, green-eyed gaze, that he had meant to punish her a little bit first—for the trouble she had caused him. He had wanted her to suffer before he took her back on *his* terms. But as usual, she had contrived to turn the tables neatly, disarming him by her very lack of reserve and subterfuge. And her persistence, even now. . . .

"I don't want to go back to the way we were living before, Steve." His frowning, thoughtful silence prompted Ginny to speak, before she lost her courage completely. "Polite, civilized strangers occupying separate rooms in big, luxurious houses, surrounded by other strangers. I want *you*, and I want you to want *me*, not your—your opera singers and your gypsy dancers, and—"

He started to laugh, rolling his body over hers to keep her still.

"You crazy, insatiable creature! Is there no limit to your demands? What else must I give up to keep you happy?"

"Nothing." Her voice, with his lips pressed against her throat, emerged as a whisper. "Nothing, except that you might—you might tell me occasionally that you loved me. But only if you really mean it. Only if—"

"Damn you! Will you stop dictating terms? What do

you think I'm doing here with you, with a sheriff's posse and half the United States Army after me? Must you have a string of romantic words to convince you?"

"Oh! Oh, Steve—I'd forgotten!"

"I'm glad I was able to make you forget something." Ignoring her sudden, alarmed movements under him, he ran his fingers lightly over her flesh. "Motherhood agrees with you. Your body's just as firm and beautiful as ever. And the next time you make me a father, I'm going to make sure I'm around, to watch your little flat belly grow big. . . . Maybe I'll get to name the next one myself, you sly, untrusting haggage!"

She flushed guiltily.

"Steve, I—"

"Save it until later. Have you forgotten the sheriff and the soldiers? And probably my cousin as well, worrying his head off. It's all your fault, of course." With a return of his old impatience he was already on his feet, pulling her up with him.

"But they're looking for you. What are you going to do? If they start shooting first—"

"Why don't you leave a few things to me for a change? You've grown far too independent, Ginny, and I intend to remedy that."

Naked, feet planted apart, she began to tilt her chin defiantly at him, until he took her face between his hands, stilling her.

"Listen, green eyes, and stop arguing with me, or I'm liable to lose my temper again. As soon as you put that shirt back on, we're looking for them. I don't doubt I'll have a lot of explaining to do, but Renaldo will help. And after that. . . ."

All her resolute, half-planned arguments died into silence when he bent his head, mouth grazing hers. All she could do was repeat, breathlessly, questioningly, "And after that?"

"After that I'm going to carry you off with me again— what did you think, you infuriating little temptress? And spend a lot of time telling you just how much I love you, if you'll shut up long enough to listen."

Ginny's lips parted, and then closed firmly. But her green eyes sparkled like emeralds. Without a word, as if they were back in some elegant drawing room, she held her arms out to him, and just as solemnly, lips quirking, he slipped the moss-stained shirt over her shoulders.

The long swamp-grass shook in a sudden drift of breeze and the water hyacinths danced over a slow, undulating ripple. But where they walked, with Steve's fingers closed firmly over hers, the ground was firm, and the sunlight waited beyond the trees.